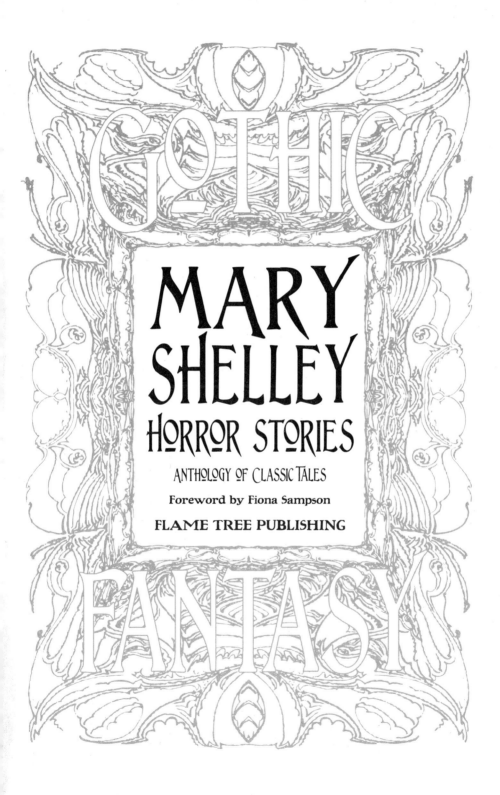

GOTHIC

MARY SHELLEY

HORROR STORIES

ANTHOLOGY OF CLASSIC TALES

Foreword by Fiona Sampson

FLAME TREE PUBLISHING

FANTASY

This is a FLAME TREE Book

Publisher & Creative Director: Nick Wells
Project Editor: Laura Bulbeck
Editorial Board: Gillian Whitaker, Josie Mitchell, Catherine Taylor

FLAME TREE PUBLISHING
6 Melbray Mews, Fulham,
London SW6 3NS, United Kingdom
www.flametreepublishing.com

First published 2018

22
5 7 9 10 8 6 4

ISBN: 978-1-78664-807-5

The cover image is created by Flame Tree Studio
based on artwork by Slava Gerj and Gabor Ruszkai.

A copy of the CIP data for this book is available from the British Library.

Printed and bound in China

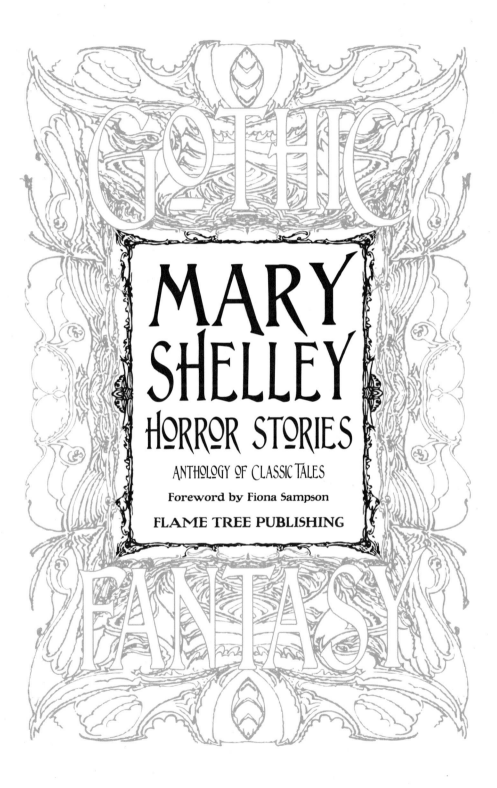

MARY SHELLEY
HORROR STORIES

ANTHOLOGY OF CLASSIC TALES

Foreword by Fiona Sampson

FLAME TREE PUBLISHING

Contents

Eerie Supernatural
Mary Shelley

Gothic Tales
Mary Shelley

The Horrors of Isolation
Mary Shelley

Foreword:
Mary Shelley Horror Stories

MARY SHELLEY'S *Frankenstein*, now over 200 years old, was the world's first science fiction novel. Its story about what happens when a mad scientist creates a terrifying near-human being is so famous it's not just become a cliché in our culture: it's even entered the language. We use 'Frankenstein' to mean something that has outgrown our control, whether in technology or science, AI or gene therapy. Actually, we use it to mean our *fears* about loss of control. This principle of fear is what makes Mary Shelley's best-known work not simply science fiction – a story about science – but horror, too.

And it's fear doubled. In the famous James Whale film of 1931, *Frankenstein* is a story about a scientist who creates a lumbering, mindless monster that must finally be destroyed by a lynch mob in order to allow the happy ending. At the film's close the scientist is released from his obsessional research to marry the fiancée he's neglected. In Shelley's novel, Frankenstein is a dropout from what today we'd call post-graduate research at university, who creates an emotional, intelligent, articulate being: someone who knows guilt and responsibility, loneliness – and much of Western Philosophy. Someone, in short, who's not dissimilar to ourselves, yet is kept horribly apart from us, trapped in his ill-made body until, driven mad by rejection and misunderstanding, he kills his maker.

This scenario, the horror of being trapped inside a 'wrong' body, is nowadays also familiar from Franz Kafka's short story *Metamorphosis*, about a young man who turns into a cockroach, and the 1958 and 1986 film versions of *The Fly*, about a scientist who accidentally turns himself into a giant bluebottle. It's also familiar from real-life accounts by sufferers from Locked-in Syndrome, like Jean-Dominique Bauby's *The Butterfly and the Diving Bell*, by survivors of anaesthetic blunders that leave patients paralysed and unable to call out, but feeling every cut of the surgeon's knife, and indeed by transgender people.

Mary Shelley brings this to life: her horror fiction compels us not because she was a pioneer – in any case, she wasn't first in *this* genre – but because of its vivid imagining. There's nothing primitive or experimental about *Frankenstein*, even though it was written when she was just a teenager and published on January 1st 1818, when the novel form was still in flux. Its precocious author was a fine storyteller who had a real eye for a scenario: eight years later, she also wrote the world's first dystopian science fiction novel. *The Last Man* (1826) imagines a future gone terrifyingly wrong when a pandemic sweeps the globe: the sole survivor roams the world alone, grappling like Frankenstein's creature with horrifying loneliness.

But Shelley didn't just write horror fiction, she also read it, and in this she was a woman of her time. In England, the Romantic era produced the Gothic novel, a mystery genre set in medieval times and often including an element of the supernatural. One of its most famous examples, Matthew Gregory Lewis's *The Monk* (1796), was praised by Lord Byron, a personal friend of Shelley's: though, oddly, while working on *Frankenstein* she declined his invitation to dine with Lewis.

At the same time, in Europe, the German *Schauerroman* or 'shudder fiction', usually involving ghosts or black magic, had become fashionable. A collection of these stories in French translation, the *Fantasmagoriana ou Receuil d'Histoires de Spectres, Revenants, Fantômes, etc.* (1812), triggered the competition to write 'a ghost story' that, one dark night in June 1816, Byron set his house-guests Mary and Percy Bysshe Shelley – and John William Polidori, who with *The Vampyre* invented the genre of vampire fiction in response. Though roused by their initial discussion of the possible scientific 'principles of life', neither poet persevered, but Byron himself produced the fragment of an 'oriental' mystery story included here.

The *Fantasmagoriana* stories also collected here are translated directly from the German originals, and are the ones Mary mentions in the Introduction to her 1831 edition of *Frankenstein*, where she talks about how her novel came to be written. The evenings with Byron on the slopes of Lake Geneva, in that 'Year without a Summer', were spent reading these horror stories and Samuel Taylor Coleridge's horror poem 'Christabel', which gave Percy Bysshe Shelley hallucinations. Like the committed writer she already was, though, Mary Shelley persuaded him to reread the poem with her: she was already researching supernatural ideas and fictional techniques. And in many ways this fascinating anthology *is* her research for *Frankenstein*. Her astonishing creature and his inventor stalk these pages.

Fiona Sampson

Publisher's Note

MARY SHELLEY is an iconic figure in the history of horror and science fiction, widely known to this day for her incredible novel *Frankenstein*. Encouraged to think for herself from an early age by her father William Godwin, and undoubtedly deeply affected by growing up without her mother, Mary Shelley became a powerful writer of incredible depth. We have brought together here a fantastic collection of her works with an emphasis on horror in its many forms. Upon working through Shelley's stories, some clear themes developed: from supernaturally chilling tales to those with a Gothic tone focused on love and loss, and science fiction driven stories which explore man's deep fear of isolation. Similar themes do of course abound throughout Shelley's works, and so we have grouped them in a way we hope proves both interesting and satisfying, but also offer two recommended reads at the end of each story to direct the reader to similar stories across the chapter boundaries.

As *Frankenstein* is such an important – and frankly excellent – story, we decided not only that it must be included, but that we should explore its origins. This also allowed us the great opportunity to include some wonderful works by some of Shelley's contemporaries, or those who influenced her. Therefore the first chapter of this book includes the contributions from Byron and Polidori to the ghost-writing competition that gave rise to *Frankenstein*; as well as some translations of ghost stories and Coleridge's poem 'Christabel' – all of which were known to have been read by the Villa Diodati group to 'set the mood'. With *Mary Shelley Horror Stories* we hope we have created a really special collection, and that we might even reintroduce some of Shelley's lesser-known tales to a new audience.

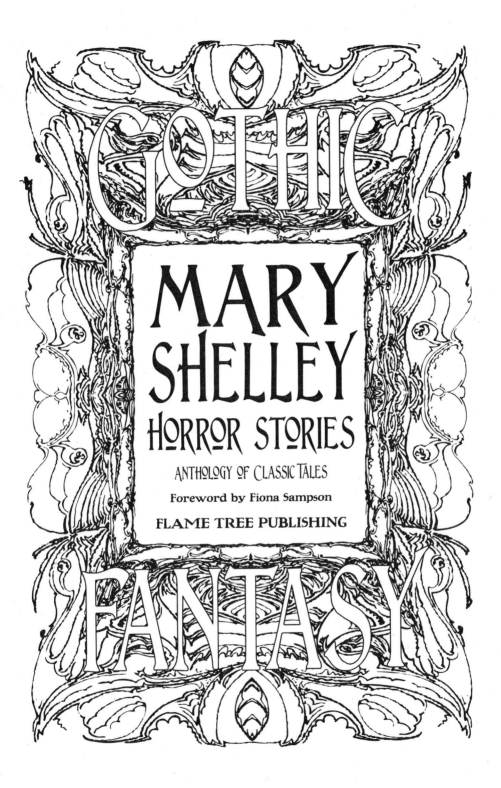

GOTHIC

MARY
SHELLEY
HORROR STORIES

ANTHOLOGY OF CLASSIC TALES

Foreword by Fiona Sampson

FLAME TREE PUBLISHING

FANTASY

The Birth of Frankenstein

Tales by Mary Shelley and her friends

Frankenstein
or, The Modern Prometheus
Mary Shelley

Introduction to the 1831 Edition

THE PUBLISHERS of the Standard Novels, in selecting *Frankenstein* for one of their series, expressed a wish that I should furnish them with some account of the origin of the story. I am the more willing to comply, because I shall thus give a general answer to the question, so very frequently asked me – "How I, when a young girl, came to think of, and to dilate upon, so very hideous an idea?" It is true that I am very averse to bringing myself forward in print; but as my account will only appear as an appendage to a former production, and as it will be confined to such topics as have connection with my authorship alone, I can scarcely accuse myself of a personal intrusion.

It is not singular that, as the daughter of two persons of distinguished literary celebrity, I should very early in life have thought of writing. As a child I scribbled; and my favourite pastime, during the hours given me for recreation, was to 'write stories.' Still I had a dearer pleasure than this, which was the formation of castles in the air – the indulging in waking dreams – the following up trains of thought, which had for their subject the formation of a succession of imaginary incidents. My dreams were at once more fantastic and agreeable than my writings. In the latter I was a close imitator – rather doing as others had done, than putting down the suggestions of my own mind. What I wrote was intended at least for one other eye – my childhood's companion and friend; but my dreams were all my own; I accounted for them to nobody; they were my refuge when annoyed – my dearest pleasure when free.

I lived principally in the country as a girl, and passed a considerable time in Scotland. I made occasional visits to the more picturesque parts; but my habitual residence was on the blank and dreary northern shores of the Tay, near Dundee. Blank and dreary on retrospection I call them; they were not so to me then. They were the eyry of freedom, and the pleasant region where unheeded I could commune with the creatures of my fancy. I wrote then – but in a most common-place style. It was beneath the trees of the grounds belonging to our house, or on the bleak sides of the woodless mountains near, that my true compositions, the airy flights of my imagination, were born and fostered. I did not make myself the heroine of my tales. Life appeared to me too common-place an affair as regarded myself. I could not figure to myself that romantic woes or wonderful events would ever be my lot; but I was not confined to my own identity, and I could people the hours with creations far more interesting to me at that age, than my own sensations.

After this my life became busier, and reality stood in place of fiction. My husband, however, was from the first, very anxious that I should prove myself worthy of my parentage, and enrol myself on the page of fame. He was forever inciting me to obtain literary reputation, which even on my own part I cared for then, though since I have become infinitely indifferent to it.

At this time he desired that I should write, not so much with the idea that I could produce anything worthy of notice, but that he might himself judge how far I possessed the promise of better things hereafter. Still I did nothing. Travelling, and the cares of a family, occupied my time; and study, in the way of reading, or improving my ideas in communication with his far more cultivated mind, was all of literary employment that engaged my attention.

In the summer of 1816, we visited Switzerland, and became the neighbours of Lord Byron. At first we spent our pleasant hours on the lake, or wandering on its shores; and Lord Byron, who was writing the third canto of Childe Harold, was the only one among us who put his thoughts upon paper. These, as he brought them successively to us, clothed in all the light and harmony of poetry, seemed to stamp as divine the glories of heaven and earth, whose influences we partook with him.

But it proved a wet, ungenial summer, and incessant rain often confined us for days to the house. Some volumes of ghost stories, translated from the German into French, fell into our hands. There was the History of the Inconstant Lover, who, when he thought to clasp the bride to whom he had pledged his vows, found himself in the arms of the pale ghost of her whom he had deserted. There was the tale of the sinful founder of his race, whose miserable doom it was to bestow the kiss of death on all the younger sons of his fated house, just when they reached the age of promise. His gigantic, shadowy form, clothed like the ghost in Hamlet, in complete armour, but with the beaver up, was seen at midnight, by the moon's fitful beams, to advance slowly along the gloomy avenue. The shape was lost beneath the shadow of the castle walls; but soon a gate swung back, a step was heard, the door of the chamber opened, and he advanced to the couch of the blooming youths, cradled in healthy sleep. Eternal sorrow sat upon his face as he bent down and kissed the forehead of the boys, who from that hour withered like flowers snapt upon the stalk. I have not seen these stories since then; but their incidents are as fresh in my mind as if I had read them yesterday.

"We will each write a ghost story," said Lord Byron; and his proposition was acceded to. There were four of us. The noble author began a tale, a fragment of which he printed at the end of his poem of 'Mazeppa'. Shelley, more apt to embody ideas and sentiments in the radiance of brilliant imagery, and in the music of the most melodious verse that adorns our language, than to invent the machinery of a story, commenced one founded on the experiences of his early life. Poor Polidori had some terrible idea about a skull-headed lady, who was so punished for peeping through a key-hole – what to see I forget – something very shocking and wrong of course; but when she was reduced to a worse condition than the renowned Tom of Coventry, he did not know what to do with her, and was obliged to despatch her to the tomb of the Capulets, the only place for which she was fitted. The illustrious poets also, annoyed by the platitude of prose, speedily relinquished their uncongenial task.

I busied myself *to think of a story,* – a story to rival those which had excited us to this task. One which would speak to the mysterious fears of our nature, and awaken thrilling horror – one to make the reader dread to look round, to curdle the blood, and quicken the beatings of the heart. If I did not accomplish these things, my ghost story would be unworthy of its name. I thought and pondered – vainly. I felt that blank incapability of invention which is the greatest misery of authorship, when dull Nothing replies to our anxious invocations. *Have you thought of a story?* I was asked each morning, and each morning I was forced to reply with a mortifying negative.

Everything must have a beginning, to speak in Sanchean phrase; and that beginning must be linked to something that went before. The Hindoos give the world an elephant to support it, but they make the elephant stand upon a tortoise. Invention, it must be humbly admitted, does not consist in creating out of void, but out of chaos; the materials must, in the first place, be afforded: it can give form to dark, shapeless substances, but cannot bring into being the substance itself. In all matters of discovery and invention, even of those that appertain to the imagination, we are continually reminded of the story of Columbus and his egg. Invention consists in the capacity of seizing on the capabilities of a subject, and in the power of moulding and fashioning ideas suggested to it.

Many and long were the conversations between Lord Byron and Shelley, to which I was a devout but nearly silent listener. During one of these, various philosophical doctrines were discussed, and among others the nature of the principle of life, and whether there was any probability of its ever being discovered and communicated. They talked of the experiments of Dr. Darwin, (I speak not of what the Doctor really did, or said that he did, but, as more to my purpose, of what was then spoken of as having been done by him,) who preserved a piece of vermicelli in a glass case, till by some extraordinary means it began to move with voluntary motion. Not thus, after all, would life be given. Perhaps a corpse would be re-animated; galvanism had given token of such things: perhaps the component parts of a creature might be manufactured, brought together, and endued with vital warmth.

Night waned upon this talk, and even the witching hour had gone by, before we retired to rest. When I placed my head on my pillow, I did not sleep, nor could I be said to think. My imagination, unbidden, possessed and guided me, gifting the successive images that arose in my mind with a vividness far beyond the usual bounds of reverie. I saw – with shut eyes, but acute mental vision, – I saw the pale student of unhallowed arts kneeling beside the thing he had put together. I saw the hideous phantasm of a man stretched out, and then, on the working of some powerful engine, show signs of life, and stir with an uneasy, half vital motion. Frightful must it be; for supremely frightful would be the effect of any human endeavour to mock the stupendous mechanism of the Creator of the world. His success would terrify the artist; he would rush away from his odious handywork, horror-stricken. He would hope that, left to itself, the slight spark of life which he had communicated would fade; that this thing, which had received such imperfect animation, would subside into dead matter; and he might sleep in the belief that the silence of the grave would quench forever the transient existence of the hideous corpse which he had looked upon as the cradle of life. He sleeps; but he is awakened; he opens his eyes; behold the horrid thing stands at his bedside, opening his curtains, and looking on him with yellow, watery, but speculative eyes.

I opened mine in terror. The idea so possessed my mind, that a thrill of fear ran through me, and I wished to exchange the ghastly image of my fancy for the realities around. I see them still; the very room, the dark *parquet*, the closed shutters, with the moonlight struggling through, and the sense I had that the glassy lake and white high Alps were beyond. I could not so easily get rid of my hideous phantom; still it haunted me. I must try to think of something else. I recurred to my ghost story – my tiresome unlucky ghost story! O! if I could only contrive one which would frighten my reader as I myself had been frightened that night!

Swift as light and as cheering was the idea that broke in upon me. "I have found it! What terrified me will terrify others; and I need only describe the spectre which had haunted my midnight pillow." On the morrow I announced that I had *thought of a story*. I began that day with the words, *It was on a dreary night of November*, making only a transcript of the grim terrors of my waking dream.

At first I thought but of a few pages – of a short tale; but Shelley urged me to develope the idea at greater length. I certainly did not owe the suggestion of one incident, nor scarcely of one train of feeling, to my husband, and yet but for his incitement, it would never have taken the form in which it was presented to the world. From this declaration I must except the preface. As far as I can recollect, it was entirely written by him.

And now, once again, I bid my hideous progeny go forth and prosper. I have an affection for it, for it was the offspring of happy days, when death and grief were but words, which found no true echo in my heart. Its several pages speak of many a walk, many a drive, and many a conversation, when I was not alone; and my companion was one who, in this world, I shall never see more. But this is for myself; my readers have nothing to do with these associations.

I will add but one word as to the alterations I have made. They are principally those of style. I have changed no portion of the story, nor introduced any new ideas or circumstances. I have mended the language where it was so bald as to interfere with the interest of the narrative; and these changes occur almost exclusively in the beginning of the first volume. Throughout they are entirely confined to such parts as are mere adjuncts to the story, leaving the core and substance of it untouched.

M.W.S.
London, October 15, 1831

Original Preface to the 1818 edition

THE EVENT on which this fiction is founded, has been supposed, by Dr. Darwin, and some of the physiological writers of Germany, as not of impossible occurrence. I shall not be supposed as according the remotest degree of serious faith to such an imagination; yet, in assuming it as the basis of a work of fancy, I have not considered myself as merely weaving a series of supernatural terrors. The event on which the interest of the story depends is exempt from the disadvantages of a mere tale of spectres or enchantment. It was recommended by the novelty of the situations which it develops; and, however impossible as a physical fact, affords a point of view to the imagination for the delineating of human passions more comprehensive and commanding than any which the ordinary relations of existing events can yield.

I have thus endeavoured to preserve the truth of the elementary principles of human nature, while I have not scrupled to innovate upon their combinations. The Iliad, the tragic poetry of Greece, – Shakspeare, in the *Tempest,* and *Midsummer Night's Dream* – and most especially Milton, in *Paradise Lost,* conform to this rule; and the most humble novelist, who seeks to confer or receive amusement from his labours, may, without presumption, apply to prose fiction a licence, or rather a rule, from the adoption of which so many exquisite combinations of human feeling have resulted in the highest specimens of poetry.

The circumstance on which my story rests was suggested in casual conversation. It was commenced partly as a source of amusement, and partly as an expedient for exercising any untried resources of mind. Other motives were mingled with these, as the work proceeded. I am by no means indifferent to the manner in which whatever moral tendencies exist in the sentiments or characters it contains shall affect the reader; yet my chief concern in this respect has been limited to the avoiding the enervating effects of the novels of the present day, and to the exhibition of the amiableness of domestic affection, and the excellence of universal virtue. The opinions which naturally spring from the character and situation of the hero are by no means to be conceived as existing always in my own conviction; nor is any inference justly to be drawn from the following pages as prejudicing any philosophical doctrine of whatever kind.

It is a subject also of additional interest to the author, that this story was begun in the majestic region where the scene is principally laid, and in society which cannot cease to be regretted. I passed the summer of 1816 in the environs of Geneva. The season was cold and rainy, and in the evenings we crowded around a blazing wood fire, and occasionally amused ourselves with some German stories of ghosts, which happened to fall into our hands. These tales excited in us a playful desire of imitation. Two other friends (a tale from the pen of one of whom would be far more acceptable to the public than any thing I can ever hope to produce) and myself agreed to write each a story, founded on some supernatural occurrence.

The weather, however, suddenly became serene; and my two friends left me on a journey among the Alps, and lost, in the magnificent scenes which they present, all memory of their ghostly visions. The following tale is the only one which has been completed.

Marlow, September, 1817

The Story

Letter 1

St. Petersburgh, Dec. 11th, 17–

To Mrs. Saville, England

You will rejoice to hear that no disaster has accompanied the commencement of an enterprise which you have regarded with such evil forebodings. I arrived here yesterday, and my first task is to assure my dear sister of my welfare and increasing confidence in the success of my undertaking.

I am already far north of London, and as I walk in the streets of Petersburgh, I feel a cold northern breeze play upon my cheeks, which braces my nerves and fills me with delight. Do you understand this feeling? This breeze, which has travelled from the regions towards which I am advancing, gives me a foretaste of those icy climes. Inspirited by this wind of promise, my daydreams become more fervent and vivid. I try in vain to be persuaded that the pole is the seat of frost and desolation; it ever presents itself to my imagination as the region of beauty and delight. There, Margaret, the sun is forever visible, its broad disk just skirting the horizon and diffusing a perpetual splendour. There – for with your leave, my sister, I will put some trust in preceding navigators – there snow and frost are banished; and, sailing over a calm sea, we may be wafted to a land surpassing in wonders and in beauty every region hitherto discovered on the habitable globe. Its productions and features may be without example, as the phenomena of the heavenly bodies undoubtedly are in those undiscovered solitudes. What may not be expected in a country of eternal light? I may there discover the wondrous power which attracts the needle and may regulate a thousand celestial observations that require only this voyage to render their seeming eccentricities consistent forever. I shall satiate my ardent curiosity with the sight of a part of the world never before visited, and may tread a land never before imprinted by the foot of man. These are my enticements, and they are sufficient to conquer all fear of danger or death and to induce me to commence this laborious voyage with the joy a child feels when he embarks in a little boat, with his holiday mates, on an expedition of discovery up his native river. But supposing all these conjectures to be false, you cannot contest the inestimable benefit which I shall confer on all mankind, to the last generation, by discovering a passage near the pole to those countries, to reach which at present so many months are requisite; or by ascertaining the secret of the magnet, which, if at all possible, can only be effected by an undertaking such as mine.

These reflections have dispelled the agitation with which I began my letter, and I feel my heart glow with an enthusiasm which elevates me to heaven, for nothing contributes so much to tranquillize the mind as a steady purpose – a point on which the soul may fix its intellectual eye. This expedition has been the favourite dream of my early years. I have read with ardour the accounts of the various voyages which have been made in the prospect of arriving at the North Pacific Ocean through the seas which surround the pole. You may remember that a history of all the voyages made for purposes of discovery composed the whole of our good Uncle Thomas' library. My education was neglected, yet I was passionately fond of reading. These volumes were my study day and night, and my familiarity with them increased that regret which I had felt, as a child, on learning that my father's dying injunction had forbidden my uncle to allow me to embark in a seafaring life.

These visions faded when I perused, for the first time, those poets whose effusions entranced my soul and lifted it to heaven. I also became a poet and for one year lived in a paradise of my own creation; I imagined that I also might obtain a niche in the temple where the names of Homer and Shakespeare are consecrated. You are well acquainted with my failure and how heavily I bore the disappointment. But just at that time I inherited the fortune of my cousin, and my thoughts were turned into the channel of their earlier bent.

Six years have passed since I resolved on my present undertaking. I can, even now, remember the hour from which I dedicated myself to this great enterprise. I commenced by inuring my body to hardship. I accompanied the whale-fishers on several expeditions to the North Sea; I voluntarily endured cold, famine, thirst, and want of sleep; I often worked harder than the common sailors during the day and devoted my nights to the study of mathematics, the theory of medicine, and those branches of physical science from which a naval adventurer might derive the greatest practical advantage. Twice I actually hired myself as an under-mate in a Greenland whaler, and acquitted myself to admiration. I must own I felt a little proud when my captain offered me the second dignity in the vessel and entreated me to remain with the greatest earnestness, so valuable did he consider my services. And now, dear Margaret, do I not deserve to accomplish some great purpose? My life might have been passed in ease and luxury, but I preferred glory to every enticement that wealth placed in my path. Oh, that some encouraging voice would answer in the affirmative! My courage and my resolution is firm; but my hopes fluctuate, and my spirits are often depressed. I am about to proceed on a long and difficult voyage, the emergencies of which will demand all my fortitude: I am required not only to raise the spirits of others, but sometimes to sustain my own, when theirs are failing.

This is the most favourable period for travelling in Russia. They fly quickly over the snow in their sledges; the motion is pleasant, and, in my opinion, far more agreeable than that of an English stagecoach. The cold is not excessive, if you are wrapped in furs – a dress which I have already adopted, for there is a great difference between walking the deck and remaining seated motionless for hours, when no exercise prevents the blood from actually freezing in your veins. I have no ambition to lose my life on the post-road between St. Petersburgh and Archangel. I shall depart for the latter town in a fortnight or three weeks; and my intention is to hire a ship there, which can easily be done by paying the insurance for the owner, and to engage as many sailors as I think necessary among those who are accustomed to the whale-fishing. I do not intend to sail until the month of June; and when shall I return? Ah, dear sister, how can I answer this question? If I succeed, many, many months, perhaps years, will pass before you and I may meet. If I fail, you will see me again soon, or never. Farewell, my dear, excellent Margaret. Heaven shower down blessings on you, and save me, that I may again and again testify my gratitude for all your love and kindness.

Your affectionate brother, R. Walton

Letter II

Archangel, 28th March, 17—

To Mrs. Saville, England

How slowly the time passes here, encompassed as I am by frost and snow! Yet a second step is taken towards my enterprise. I have hired a vessel and am occupied in collecting my sailors; those whom I have already engaged appear to be men on whom I can depend and are certainly possessed of dauntless courage.

But I have one want which I have never yet been able to satisfy, and the absence of the object of which I now feel as a most severe evil, I have no friend, Margaret: when I am glowing with the enthusiasm of success, there will be none to participate my joy; if I am assailed by disappointment, no one will endeavour to sustain me in dejection. I shall commit my thoughts to paper, it is true; but that is a poor medium for the communication of feeling. I desire the company of a man who could sympathize with me, whose eyes would reply to mine. You may deem me romantic, my dear sister, but I bitterly feel the want of a friend. I have no one near me, gentle yet courageous, possessed of a cultivated as well as of a capacious mind, whose tastes are like my own, to approve or amend my plans. How would such a friend repair the faults of your poor brother! I am too ardent in execution and too impatient of difficulties. But it is a still greater evil to me that I am self-educated: for the first fourteen years of my life I ran wild on a common and read nothing but our Uncle Thomas' books of voyages. At that age I became acquainted with the celebrated poets of our own country; but it was only when it had ceased to be in my power to derive its most important benefits from such a conviction that I perceived the necessity of becoming acquainted with more languages than that of my native country. Now I am twenty-eight and am in reality more illiterate than many schoolboys of fifteen. It is true that I have thought more and that my daydreams are more extended and magnificent, but they want (as the painters call it) KEEPING; and I greatly need a friend who would have sense enough not to despise me as romantic, and affection enough for me to endeavour to regulate my mind. Well, these are useless complaints; I shall certainly find no friend on the wide ocean, nor even here in Archangel, among merchants and seamen. Yet some feelings, unallied to the dross of human nature, beat even in these rugged bosoms. My lieutenant, for instance, is a man of wonderful courage and enterprise; he is madly desirous of glory, or rather, to word my phrase more characteristically, of advancement in his profession. He is an Englishman, and in the midst of national and professional prejudices, unsoftened by cultivation, retains some of the noblest endowments of humanity. I first became acquainted with him on board a whale vessel; finding that he was unemployed in this city, I easily engaged him to assist in my enterprise. The master is a person of an excellent disposition and is remarkable in the ship for his gentleness and the mildness of his discipline. This circumstance, added to his well-known integrity and dauntless courage, made me very desirous to engage him. A youth passed in solitude, my best years spent under your gentle and feminine fosterage, has so refined the groundwork of my character that I cannot overcome an intense distaste to the usual brutality exercised on board ship: I have never believed it to be necessary, and when I heard of a mariner equally noted for his kindliness of heart and the respect and obedience paid to him by his crew, I felt myself peculiarly fortunate in being able to secure his services. I heard of him first in rather a romantic manner, from a lady who owes to him the happiness of her life. This, briefly, is his story. Some years ago he loved a young Russian lady of moderate fortune, and having amassed a considerable sum in prize-money, the father of the girl consented to the match. He saw his mistress once before the destined ceremony; but she was bathed in tears, and throwing herself at his feet, entreated him to spare her, confessing at the same time that she loved another, but that he was poor, and that her father would never consent to the union. My generous friend reassured the suppliant, and on being informed of the name of her lover, instantly abandoned his pursuit. He had already bought a farm with his money, on which he had designed to pass the remainder of his life; but he bestowed the whole on his rival, together with the remains of his prize-money to purchase stock, and then himself solicited the young woman's father to consent to her marriage with her lover. But the old man decidedly refused, thinking himself bound in honour to my friend, who, when he found the father inexorable, quitted his country, nor returned until he heard that his former mistress was married according to her inclinations. "What a noble fellow!" you will exclaim. He is so; but then he is wholly uneducated: he is as silent as a Turk, and a kind of ignorant carelessness attends him, which, while it renders his conduct the more astonishing, detracts from the interest and sympathy which otherwise he would command.

Yet do not suppose, because I complain a little or because I can conceive a consolation for my toils which I may never know, that I am wavering in my resolutions. Those are as fixed as fate, and my voyage is only now delayed until the weather shall permit my embarkation. The winter has been dreadfully severe, but the spring promises well, and it is considered as a remarkably early season, so that perhaps I may sail sooner than I expected. I shall do nothing rashly: you know me sufficiently to confide in my prudence and considerateness whenever the safety of others is committed to my care.

I cannot describe to you my sensations on the near prospect of my undertaking. It is impossible to communicate to you a conception of the trembling sensation, half pleasurable and half fearful, with which I am preparing to depart. I am going to unexplored regions, to "the land of mist and snow," but I shall kill no albatross; therefore do not be alarmed for my safety or if I should come back to you as worn and woeful as the "Ancient

Mariner." You will smile at my allusion, but I will disclose a secret. I have often attributed my attachment to, my passionate enthusiasm for, the dangerous mysteries of ocean to that production of the most imaginative of modern poets. There is something at work in my soul which I do not understand. I am practically industrious – painstaking, a workman to execute with perseverance and labour – but besides this there is a love for the marvellous, a belief in the marvellous, intertwined in all my projects, which hurries me out of the common pathways of men, even to the wild sea and unvisited regions I am about to explore. But to return to dearer considerations. Shall I meet you again, after having traversed immense seas, and returned by the most southern cape of Africa or America? I dare not expect such success, yet I cannot bear to look on the reverse of the picture. Continue for the present to write to me by every opportunity: I may receive your letters on some occasions when I need them most to support my spirits. I love you very tenderly. Remember me with affection, should you never hear from me again.

Your affectionate brother, Robert Walton

Letter III

July 7th, 17–

To Mrs. Saville, England

My dear Sister,

I write a few lines in haste to say that I am safe – and well advanced on my voyage. This letter will reach England by a merchantman now on its homeward voyage from Archangel; more fortunate than I, who may not see my native land, perhaps, for many years. I am, however, in good spirits: my men are bold and apparently firm of purpose, nor do the floating sheets of ice that continually pass us, indicating the dangers of the region towards which we are advancing, appear to dismay them. We have already reached a very high latitude; but it is the height of summer, and although not so warm as in England, the southern gales, which blow us speedily towards those shores which I so ardently desire to attain, breathe a degree of renovating warmth which I had not expected.

No incidents have hitherto befallen us that would make a figure in a letter. One or two stiff gales and the springing of a leak are accidents which experienced navigators scarcely remember to record, and I shall be well content if nothing worse happen to us during our voyage.

Adieu, my dear Margaret. Be assured that for my own sake, as well as yours, I will not rashly encounter danger. I will be cool, persevering, and prudent.

But success SHALL crown my endeavours. Wherefore not? Thus far I have gone, tracing a secure way over the pathless seas, the very stars themselves being witnesses and testimonies of my triumph. Why not still proceed over the untamed yet obedient element? What can stop the determined heart and resolved will of man?

My swelling heart involuntarily pours itself out thus. But I must finish. Heaven bless my beloved sister!

R.W.

Letter IV

August 5th, 17–

To Mrs. Saville, England

So strange an accident has happened to us that I cannot forbear recording it, although it is very probable that you will see me before these papers can come into your possession.

Last Monday (July 31st) we were nearly surrounded by ice, which closed in the ship on all sides, scarcely leaving her the sea-room in which she floated. Our situation was somewhat dangerous, especially as we were compassed round by a very thick fog. We accordingly lay to, hoping that some change would take place in the atmosphere and weather.

About two o'clock the mist cleared away, and we beheld, stretched out in every direction, vast and irregular plains of ice, which seemed to have no end. Some of my comrades groaned, and my own mind began to grow watchful with anxious thoughts, when a strange sight suddenly attracted our attention and diverted our solicitude from our own situation. We perceived a low carriage, fixed on a sledge and drawn by dogs, pass on towards the north, at the distance of half a mile; a being which had the shape of a man, but apparently of gigantic stature, sat in the sledge and guided the dogs. We watched the rapid progress of the traveller with our telescopes until he was lost among the distant inequalities of the ice. This appearance excited our unqualified wonder. We were, as we believed, many hundred miles from any land; but this apparition seemed to denote that it was not, in reality, so distant as we had supposed. Shut in, however, by ice, it was impossible to follow his track, which we had observed with the greatest attention. About two hours after this occurrence we heard the ground sea, and before night the ice broke and freed our ship. We, however, lay to until the morning, fearing to encounter in the dark those large loose masses which float about after the breaking up of the ice. I profited of this time to rest for a few hours.

In the morning, however, as soon as it was light, I went upon deck and found all the sailors busy on one side of the vessel, apparently talking to someone in the sea. It was, in fact, a sledge, like that we had seen before, which had drifted towards us in the night on a large fragment of ice. Only one dog remained alive; but there was a human being within it whom the sailors were persuading to enter the vessel. He was not, as the other traveller seemed to be, a savage inhabitant of some undiscovered island, but a European. When I appeared on deck the master said, "Here is our captain, and he will not allow you to perish on the open sea."

On perceiving me, the stranger addressed me in English, although with a foreign accent. "Before I come on board your vessel," said he, "will you have the kindness to inform me whither you are bound?"

You may conceive my astonishment on hearing such a question addressed to me from a man on the brink of destruction and to whom I should have supposed that my vessel would have been a resource which he would not have exchanged for the most precious wealth the earth can afford. I replied, however, that we were on a voyage of discovery towards the northern pole.

Upon hearing this he appeared satisfied and consented to come on board. Good God! Margaret, if you had seen the man who thus capitulated for his safety, your surprise would have been boundless. His limbs were nearly frozen, and his body dreadfully emaciated by fatigue and suffering. I never saw a man in so wretched a condition. We attempted to carry him into the cabin, but as soon as he had quitted the fresh air he fainted. We accordingly brought him back to the deck and restored him to animation by rubbing him with brandy and forcing him to swallow a small quantity. As soon as he showed signs of life we wrapped him up in blankets and placed him near the chimney of the kitchen stove. By slow degrees he recovered and ate a little soup, which restored him wonderfully.

Two days passed in this manner before he was able to speak, and I often feared that his sufferings had deprived him of understanding. When he had in some measure recovered, I removed him to my own cabin and attended on him as much as my duty would permit. I never saw a more interesting creature: his eyes have generally an expression of wildness, and even madness, but there are moments when, if anyone performs an act of kindness towards him or does him the most trifling service, his whole countenance is lighted up, as it were, with a beam of benevolence and sweetness that I never saw equalled. But he is generally melancholy and despairing, and sometimes he gnashes his teeth, as if impatient of the weight of woes that oppresses him.

When my guest was a little recovered I had great trouble to keep off the men, who wished to ask him a thousand questions; but I would not allow him to be tormented by their idle curiosity, in a state of body and mind whose restoration evidently depended upon entire repose. Once, however, the lieutenant asked why he had come so far upon the ice in so strange a vehicle.

His countenance instantly assumed an aspect of the deepest gloom, and he replied, "To seek one who fled from me."

"And did the man whom you pursued travel in the same fashion?"

"Yes."

"Then I fancy we have seen him, for the day before we picked you up we saw some dogs drawing a sledge, with a man in it, across the ice."

This aroused the stranger's attention, and he asked a multitude of questions concerning the route which the demon, as he called him, had pursued. Soon after, when he was alone with me, he said, "I have, doubtless, excited your curiosity, as well as that of these good people; but you are too considerate to make inquiries."

"Certainly; it would indeed be very impertinent and inhuman in me to trouble you with any inquisitiveness of mine."

"And yet you rescued me from a strange and perilous situation; you have benevolently restored me to life."

Soon after this he inquired if I thought that the breaking up of the ice had destroyed the other sledge. I replied that I could not answer with any degree of certainty, for the ice had not broken until near midnight, and the traveller might have arrived at a place of safety before that time; but of this I could not judge. From this time a new spirit of life animated the decaying frame of the stranger. He manifested the greatest eagerness to be upon deck to watch for the sledge which had before appeared; but I have persuaded him to remain in the cabin, for he is far too weak to sustain the rawness of the atmosphere. I have promised that someone should watch for him and give him instant notice if any new object should appear in sight.

Such is my journal of what relates to this strange occurrence up to the present day. The stranger has gradually improved in health but is very silent and appears uneasy when anyone except myself enters his cabin. Yet his manners are so conciliating and gentle that the sailors are all interested in him, although they have had very little communication with him. For my own part, I begin to love him as a brother, and his constant and deep grief fills me with sympathy and compassion. He must have been a noble creature in his better days, being even now in wreck so attractive and amiable. I said in one of my letters, my dear Margaret, that I should find no friend on the wide ocean; yet I have found a man who, before his spirit had been broken by misery, I should have been happy to have possessed as the brother of my heart.

I shall continue my journal concerning the stranger at intervals, should I have any fresh incidents to record.

* * *

August 13th, 17–

My affection for my guest increases every day. He excites at once my admiration and my pity to an astonishing degree. How can I see so noble a creature destroyed by misery without feeling the most poignant grief? He is so gentle, yet so wise; his mind is so cultivated, and when he speaks, although his words are culled with the choicest art, yet they flow with rapidity and unparalleled eloquence. He is now much recovered from his illness and is continually on the deck, apparently watching for the sledge that preceded his own. Yet, although unhappy, he is not so utterly occupied by his own misery but that he interests himself deeply in the projects of others. He has frequently conversed with me on mine, which I have communicated to him without disguise. He entered attentively into all my arguments in favour of my eventual success and into every minute detail of the measures I had taken to secure it. I was easily led by the sympathy which he evinced to use the language of my heart, to give utterance to the burning ardour of my soul and to say, with all the fervour that warmed me, how gladly I would sacrifice my fortune, my existence, my every hope, to the furtherance of my enterprise. One man's life or death were but a small price to pay for the acquirement of the knowledge which I sought, for the dominion I should acquire and transmit over the elemental foes of our race. As I spoke, a dark gloom spread over my listener's countenance. At first I perceived that he tried to suppress his emotion; he placed his hands before his eyes, and my voice quivered and failed me as I beheld tears trickle fast from between his fingers; a groan burst from his heaving breast. I paused; at length he spoke, in broken accents: "Unhappy man! Do you share my madness? Have you drunk also of the intoxicating draught? Hear me; let me reveal my tale, and you will dash the cup from your lips!"

Such words, you may imagine, strongly excited my curiosity; but the paroxysm of grief that had seized the stranger overcame his weakened powers, *and many hours of repose and tranquil conversation were necessary to restore his composure. Having conquered the violence of his feelings, he appeared to despise himself for being the slave of passion; and quelling the dark tyranny of despair, he led me again to converse concerning myself personally. He asked me the history of my earlier years. The tale was quickly told, but it awakened various trains of reflection. I spoke of my desire of finding a friend, of my thirst for a more intimate sympathy with a fellow mind than had ever fallen to my lot, and expressed my conviction that a man could boast of little happiness who did not enjoy this blessing. "I agree with you," replied the stranger; "we are unfashioned creatures, but half made up, if one wiser, better, dearer than ourselves – such a friend ought to be – do not lend his aid to perfectionate our weak and faulty natures. I once had a friend, the most noble of human creatures, and am entitled, therefore, to judge respecting friendship. You have hope, and the world before you, and have no cause for despair. But I– I have lost everything and cannot begin life anew."*

As he said this his countenance became expressive of a calm, settled grief that touched me to the heart. But he was silent and presently retired to his cabin.

Even broken in spirit as he is, no one can feel more deeply than he does the beauties of nature. The starry sky, the sea, and every sight afforded by these wonderful regions seems still to have the power of elevating his soul from earth. Such a man has a double existence: he may suffer misery and be overwhelmed by disappointments, yet when he has retired into himself, he will be like a celestial spirit that has a halo around him, within whose circle no grief or folly ventures.

Will you smile at the enthusiasm I express concerning this divine wanderer? You would not if you saw him. You have been tutored and refined by books and retirement from the world, and you are therefore somewhat fastidious; but this only renders you the more fit to appreciate the extraordinary merits of this wonderful man. Sometimes I have endeavoured to discover what quality it is which he possesses that elevates him so immeasurably above any other person I ever knew. I believe it to be an intuitive discernment, a quick but never-failing power of judgment, a penetration into the causes of things, unequalled for clearness and precision; add to this a facility of expression and a voice whose varied intonations are soul-subduing music.

* * *

August 19, 17–

Yesterday the stranger said to me, "You may easily perceive, Captain Walton, that I have suffered great and unparalleled misfortunes. I had determined at one time that the memory of these evils should die with me, but you have won me to alter my determination. You seek for knowledge and wisdom, as I once did; and I ardently hope that the gratification of your wishes may not be a serpent to sting you, as mine has been. I do not know that the relation of my disasters will be useful to you; yet, when I reflect that you are pursuing the same course, exposing yourself to the same dangers which have rendered me what I am, I imagine that you may deduce an apt moral from my tale, one that may direct you if you succeed in your undertaking and console you in case of failure. Prepare to hear of occurrences which are usually deemed marvellous. Were we among the tamer scenes of nature I might fear to encounter your unbelief, perhaps your ridicule; but many things will appear possible in these wild and mysterious regions which would provoke the laughter of those unacquainted with the ever – varied powers of nature; nor can I doubt but that my tale conveys in its series internal evidence of the truth of the events of which it is composed."

You may easily imagine that I was much gratified by the offered communication, yet I could not endure that he should renew his grief by a recital of his misfortunes. I felt the greatest eagerness to hear the promised narrative, partly from curiosity and partly from a strong desire to ameliorate his fate if it were in my power. I expressed these feelings in my answer.

"I thank you," he replied, "for your sympathy, but it is useless; my fate is nearly fulfilled. I wait but for one event, and then I shall repose in peace. I understand your feeling," continued he, perceiving that I wished to interrupt him; "but you are mistaken, my friend, if thus you will allow me to name you; nothing can alter my destiny; listen to my history, and you will perceive how irrevocably it is determined."

He then told me that he would commence his narrative the next day when I should be at leisure. This promise drew from me the warmest thanks. I have resolved every night, when I am not imperatively occupied by my duties, to record, as nearly as possible in his own words, what he has related during the day. If I should be engaged, I will at least make notes. This manuscript will doubtless afford you the greatest pleasure; but to me, who know him, and who hear it from his own lips – with what interest and sympathy shall I read it in some future day! Even now, as I commence my task, his full – toned voice swells in my ears; his lustrous eyes dwell on me with all their melancholy sweetness; I see his thin hand raised in animation, while the lineaments of his face are irradiated by the soul within.

Strange and harrowing must be his story, frightful the storm which embraced the gallant vessel on its course and wrecked it – thus!

Chapter I

I AM BY BIRTH a Genevese, and my family is one of the most distinguished of that republic. My ancestors had been for many years counsellors and syndics, and my father had filled several public situations with honour and reputation. He was respected by all who knew him for his integrity and indefatigable attention to public business. He passed his younger days perpetually occupied by the affairs of his country; a variety of circumstances had prevented his marrying early, nor was it until the decline of life that he became a husband and the father of a family.

As the circumstances of his marriage illustrate his character, I cannot refrain from relating them. One of his most intimate friends was a merchant who, from a flourishing state, fell, through numerous mischances, into poverty. This man, whose name was Beaufort, was of a proud and unbending disposition and could not bear to live in poverty and oblivion in the same country where he had formerly been distinguished for his rank and magnificence. Having paid his debts, therefore, in the most honourable manner, he retreated with his daughter to the town of Lucerne, where he lived unknown and in wretchedness. My father loved Beaufort with the truest friendship and was deeply grieved by his retreat in these unfortunate circumstances. He bitterly deplored the false pride which led his friend to a conduct so little worthy of the affection that united them. He lost no time in endeavouring to seek him out, with the hope of persuading him to begin the world again through his credit and assistance. Beaufort had taken effectual measures to conceal himself, and it was ten months before my father discovered his abode. Overjoyed at this discovery, he hastened to the house, which was situated in a mean street near the Reuss. But when he entered, misery and despair alone welcomed him. Beaufort had saved but a very small sum of money from the wreck of his fortunes, but it was sufficient to provide him with sustenance for some months, and in the meantime he hoped to procure some respectable employment in a merchant's house. The interval was, consequently, spent in inaction; his grief only became more deep and rankling when he had leisure for reflection, and at length it took so fast hold of his mind that at the end of three months he lay on a bed of sickness, incapable of any exertion.

His daughter attended him with the greatest tenderness, but she saw with despair that their little fund was rapidly decreasing and that there was no other prospect of support. But Caroline Beaufort possessed a mind of an uncommon mould, and her courage rose to support her in her adversity. She procured plain work; she plaited straw and by various means contrived to earn a pittance scarcely sufficient to support life.

Several months passed in this manner. Her father grew worse; her time was more entirely occupied in attending him; her means of subsistence decreased; and in the tenth month her father died in her arms, leaving her an orphan and a beggar. This last blow overcame her, and she knelt by Beaufort's coffin weeping bitterly, when my father entered the chamber. He came like a protecting spirit to the poor girl, who committed herself to his care; and after the interment of his friend he conducted her to Geneva and placed her under the protection of a relation. Two years after this event Caroline became his wife.

There was a considerable difference between the ages of my parents, but this circumstance seemed to unite them only closer in bonds of devoted affection. There was a sense of justice in my father's upright mind which rendered it necessary that he should approve highly to love strongly. Perhaps during former years he had suffered from the late-discovered unworthiness of one beloved and so was disposed to set a greater value on tried worth. There was a show of gratitude and worship in his attachment to my mother, differing wholly from the doting fondness of age, for it was inspired by reverence for her virtues and a desire to be the means of, in some degree, recompensing her for the sorrows she had endured, but which gave inexpressible grace to his behaviour to her. Everything was made to yield to her wishes and her convenience. He strove to shelter her, as a fair exotic is sheltered by the gardener, from every rougher wind and to surround her with all that could tend to excite pleasurable emotion in her soft and benevolent mind. Her health, and even the tranquillity of her hitherto constant spirit, had been shaken by what she had gone through. During the two years that had elapsed previous to their marriage my father had gradually relinquished all his public functions; and immediately after their union they sought the pleasant climate of Italy, and the change of scene and interest attendant on a tour through that land of wonders, as a restorative for her weakened frame.

From Italy they visited Germany and France. I, their eldest child, was born at Naples, and as an infant accompanied them in their rambles. I remained for several years their only child. Much as they were attached to each other, they seemed to draw inexhaustible stores of affection from a very mine of love to bestow them upon me. My mother's tender caresses and my father's smile of benevolent pleasure while regarding me are my first recollections. I was their plaything and their idol, and something better – their child, the innocent and helpless creature bestowed on them by heaven, whom to bring up to good, and whose future lot it was in their hands to direct to happiness or misery, according as they fulfilled their duties towards me. With this deep consciousness of what they owed towards the being to which they had given life, added to the active spirit of tenderness that animated both, it may be imagined that while during every hour of my infant life I received a lesson of patience, of charity, and of self-control, I was so guided by a silken cord that all seemed but one train of enjoyment to me. For a long time I was their only care. My mother had much desired to have a daughter, but I continued their single offspring. When I was about five years old, while making an excursion beyond the frontiers of Italy, they passed a week on the shores of the Lake of Como. Their benevolent disposition often made them enter the cottages of the poor. This, to my mother, was more than a duty; it was a necessity, a passion – remembering what she had suffered, and how she had been relieved – for her to act in her turn the guardian angel to the afflicted. During one of their walks a poor cot in the foldings of a vale attracted their notice as being singularly disconsolate, while the number of half-clothed children gathered about it spoke of penury in its worst shape. One day, when my father had gone by himself to Milan, my mother, accompanied by me, visited this abode. She found a peasant and his wife, hard working, bent down by care and labour, distributing a scanty meal to five hungry babes. Among these there was one which attracted my mother far above all the rest. She appeared of a different stock. The four others were dark-eyed, hardy little vagrants; this child was thin and very fair. Her hair was the brightest living gold, and despite the poverty of her clothing, seemed to set a crown of distinction on her head. Her brow was clear and ample, her blue eyes cloudless, and her lips and the moulding of her face so expressive of sensibility and sweetness that none could behold her without looking on her as of a distinct species, a being heaven-sent, and bearing a celestial stamp in all her features. The peasant woman, perceiving that my mother fixed eyes of wonder and admiration on this lovely girl, eagerly communicated her history. She was not her child, but the daughter of a Milanese nobleman. Her mother was a German and had died on giving her birth. The infant had been placed with these good people to nurse: they were better off then. They had not been long married, and their eldest child was but just born. The father of their charge was one of those Italians nursed in the memory of the antique glory of Italy – one among the *schiavi ognor frementi*, who exerted himself to obtain the liberty of his country. He became the victim of its weakness. Whether he had died or still lingered in the dungeons of Austria was not known. His property was confiscated; his child became an orphan and a beggar. She continued with her foster parents and bloomed in their rude abode, fairer than a garden rose among dark-leaved brambles. When my father returned from Milan, he found playing with me in the hall of our villa a child fairer than pictured cherub – a creature who seemed to shed radiance from her looks and whose form and motions were lighter than the chamois of the hills. The apparition was soon explained. With his permission my mother prevailed on her rustic guardians to yield their charge to her. They were fond of the sweet orphan. Her presence had seemed a blessing to them, but it would be unfair to her to keep her in poverty and want when Providence afforded her such powerful protection. They consulted their village priest, and the result was that Elizabeth Lavenza became the inmate of my parents' house – my more than sister – the beautiful and adored companion of all my occupations and my pleasures.

Everyone loved Elizabeth. The passionate and almost reverential attachment with which all regarded her became, while I shared it, my pride and my delight. On the evening previous to her being brought to my home, my mother had said playfully, "I have a pretty present for my Victor – tomorrow he shall have it." And when, on the morrow, she presented Elizabeth to me as her promised gift, I, with childish seriousness, interpreted her words literally and looked upon Elizabeth as mine – mine to protect, love, and cherish. All praises bestowed on her I received as made to a possession of my own. We called each other familiarly by the name of cousin. No word, no expression could body forth the kind of relation in which she stood to me – my more than sister, since till death she was to be mine only.

Chapter II

WE WERE BROUGHT UP together; there was not quite a year difference in our ages. I need not say that we were strangers to any species of disunion or dispute. Harmony was the soul of our companionship, and the diversity and contrast that subsisted in our characters drew us nearer together. Elizabeth was of a calmer and more concentrated disposition; but, with all my ardour, I was capable of a more intense application and was more deeply smitten with the thirst for knowledge. She busied herself with following the aerial creations of the poets; and in the majestic and wondrous scenes which surrounded our Swiss home – the sublime shapes of the mountains, the changes of the seasons, tempest and calm, the silence of winter, and the life and turbulence of our Alpine summers – she found ample scope for admiration and delight. While my companion contemplated with a serious and satisfied spirit the magnificent appearances of things, I delighted in investigating their causes. The world was to me a secret which I desired to divine. Curiosity, earnest research to learn the hidden laws of nature, gladness akin to rapture, as they were unfolded to me, are among the earliest sensations I can remember.

On the birth of a second son, my junior by seven years, my parents gave up entirely their wandering life and fixed themselves in their native country. We possessed a house in Geneva, and a campagne on Belrive, the eastern shore of the lake, at the distance of rather more than a league from the city. We resided principally in the latter, and the lives of my parents were passed in considerable seclusion. It was my temper to avoid a crowd and to attach myself fervently to a few. I was indifferent, therefore, to my school-fellows in general; but I united myself in the bonds of the closest friendship to one among them. Henry Clerval was the son of a merchant of Geneva. He was a boy of singular talent and fancy. He loved enterprise, hardship, and even danger for its own sake. He was deeply read in books of chivalry and romance. He composed heroic songs and began to write many a tale of enchantment and knightly adventure. He tried to make us act plays and to enter into masquerades, in which the characters were drawn from the heroes of Roncesvalles, of the Round Table of King Arthur, and the chivalrous train who shed their blood to redeem the holy sepulchre from the hands of the infidels.

No human being could have passed a happier childhood than myself. My parents were possessed by the very spirit of kindness and indulgence. We felt that they were not the tyrants to rule our lot according to their caprice, but the agents and creators of all the many delights which we enjoyed. When I mingled with other families I distinctly discerned how peculiarly fortunate my lot was, and gratitude assisted the development of filial love.

My temper was sometimes violent, and my passions vehement; but by some law in my temperature they were turned not towards childish pursuits but to an eager desire to learn, and not to learn all things indiscriminately. I confess that neither the structure of languages, nor the code of governments, nor the politics of various states possessed attractions for me. It was the secrets of heaven and earth that I desired to learn; and whether it was the outward substance of things or the inner spirit of nature and the mysterious soul of man that occupied me, still my inquiries were directed to the metaphysical, or in it highest sense, the physical secrets of the world.

Meanwhile Clerval occupied himself, so to speak, with the moral relations of things. The busy stage of life, the virtues of heroes, and the actions of men were his theme; and his hope and his dream was to become one among those whose names are recorded in story as the gallant and adventurous benefactors of our species. The saintly soul of Elizabeth shone like a shrine-dedicated lamp in our peaceful home. Her sympathy was ours; her smile, her soft voice, the sweet glance of her celestial eyes, were ever there to bless and animate us. She was the living spirit of love to soften and attract; I might have become sullen in my study, through the ardour of my nature, but that she was there to subdue me to a semblance of her own gentleness. And Clerval – could aught ill entrench on the noble spirit of Clerval? Yet he might not have been so perfectly humane, so thoughtful in his generosity, so full of kindness and tenderness amidst his passion for adventurous exploit, had she not unfolded to him the real loveliness of beneficence and made the doing good the end and aim of his soaring ambition.

I feel exquisite pleasure in dwelling on the recollections of childhood, before misfortune had tainted my mind and changed its bright visions of extensive usefulness into gloomy and narrow reflections upon self. Besides, in drawing the picture of my early days, I also record those events which led, by insensible steps, to my after tale of misery, for when I would account to myself for the birth of that passion which afterwards ruled my destiny I find it arise, like a mountain river, from ignoble and almost forgotten sources; but, swelling as it proceeded, it became the torrent which, in its course, has swept away all my hopes and joys. Natural philosophy is the genius that has regulated my fate; I desire, therefore, in this narration, to state those facts which led to my predilection for that science. When I was thirteen years of age we all went on a party of pleasure to the baths near Thonon; the inclemency of the weather obliged us to remain a day confined to the inn. In this house I chanced to find a volume of the works of Cornelius Agrippa. I opened it with apathy; the theory which he attempts to demonstrate and the wonderful facts which he relates soon changed this feeling into enthusiasm. A new light seemed to dawn upon my mind, and bounding with joy, I communicated my discovery to my father. My father looked carelessly at the title page of my book and said, "Ah! Cornelius Agrippa! My dear Victor, do not waste your time upon this; it is sad trash."

If, instead of this remark, my father had taken the pains to explain to me that the principles of Agrippa had been entirely exploded and that a modern system of science had been introduced which possessed much greater powers than the ancient, because the powers of the latter were chimerical, while those of the former were real and practical, under such circumstances I should certainty have thrown Agrippa aside and have contented my imagination, warmed as it was, by returning with greater ardour to my former studies. It is even possible that the train of my ideas would never have received the fatal impulse that led to my ruin. But the cursory glance my father had taken of my volume by no means assured me that he was acquainted with its contents, and I continued to read with the greatest avidity. When I returned home my first care was to procure the whole works of this author, and afterwards of Paracelsus and Albertus Magnus. I read and studied the wild fancies of these writers with delight; they appeared to me treasures known to few besides myself. I have described myself as always having been imbued with a fervent longing to penetrate the secrets of nature. In spite of the intense labour and wonderful discoveries of modern philosophers, I always came from my studies discontented and unsatisfied. Sir Isaac Newton is said to have avowed that he felt like a child picking up shells beside the great and unexplored ocean of truth. Those of his successors in each branch of natural philosophy with whom I was acquainted appeared even to my boy's apprehensions as tyros engaged in the same pursuit.

The untaught peasant beheld the elements around him and was acquainted with their practical uses. The most learned philosopher knew little more. He had partially unveiled the face of Nature, but her immortal lineaments were still a wonder and a mystery. He might dissect, anatomize, and give names; but, not to speak of a final cause, causes in their secondary and tertiary grades were utterly unknown to him. I had gazed upon the fortifications and impediments that seemed to keep human beings from entering the citadel of nature, and rashly and ignorantly I had repined.

But here were books, and here were men who had penetrated deeper and knew more. I took their word for all that they averred, and I became their disciple. It may appear strange that such should arise in the eighteenth century; but while I followed the routine of education in the schools of Geneva, I was, to a great degree, self-taught with regard to my favourite studies. My father was not scientific, and I was left to struggle with a child's blindness, added to a student's thirst for knowledge. Under the guidance of my new preceptors I entered with the greatest diligence into the search of the philosopher's stone and the elixir of life; but the latter soon obtained my undivided attention. Wealth was an inferior object, but what glory would attend the discovery if I could banish disease from the human frame and render man invulnerable to any but a violent death! Nor were these my only visions. The raising of ghosts or devils was a promise liberally accorded by my favourite authors, the fulfillment of which I most eagerly sought; and if my incantations were always unsuccessful, I attributed the failure rather to my own inexperience and mistake than to a want of skill or fidelity in my instructors. And thus for a time I was occupied by exploded systems, mingling, like an unadept, a thousand contradictory theories and floundering desperately in a very slough of multifarious knowledge, guided by an ardent imagination and childish reasoning, till an accident again changed the current of my ideas. When I was about fifteen years old we had retired to our house near Belrive, when we witnessed a most violent and terrible thunderstorm. It advanced from behind the mountains of Jura, and the thunder burst at once with frightful loudness from various quarters of the heavens. I remained, while the storm lasted, watching its progress with curiosity and delight. As I stood at the door, on a sudden I beheld a stream of fire issue from an old and beautiful oak which stood about twenty yards from our house; and so soon as the dazzling light vanished, the oak had disappeared, and nothing remained but a blasted stump. When we visited it the next morning, we found the tree shattered in a singular manner. It was not splintered by the shock, but entirely reduced to thin ribbons of wood. I never beheld anything so utterly destroyed.

Before this I was not unacquainted with the more obvious laws of electricity. On this occasion a man of great research in natural philosophy was with us, and excited by this catastrophe, he entered on the explanation of a theory which he had formed on the subject of electricity and galvanism, which was at once new and astonishing to me. All that he said threw greatly into the shade Cornelius Agrippa, Albertus Magnus, and Paracelsus, the lords of my imagination; but by some fatality the overthrow of these men disinclined me to pursue my accustomed studies. It seemed to me as if nothing would or could ever be known. All that had so long engaged my attention suddenly grew despicable. By one of those caprices of the mind which we are perhaps most subject to in early youth, I at once gave up my former occupations, set down natural history and all its progeny as a deformed and abortive creation, and entertained the greatest disdain for a would-be science which could never even step within the threshold of real knowledge. In this mood of mind I betook myself to the mathematics and the branches of study appertaining to that science as being built upon secure foundations, and so worthy of my consideration.

Thus strangely are our souls constructed, and by such slight ligaments are we bound to prosperity or ruin. When I look back, it seems to me as if this almost miraculous change of inclination and will was the immediate suggestion of the guardian angel of my life – the last effort made by the spirit of preservation to avert the storm that was even then hanging in the stars and ready to envelop me. Her victory was announced by an unusual tranquillity and gladness of soul which followed the relinquishing of my ancient and latterly tormenting studies. It was thus that I was to be taught to associate evil with their prosecution, happiness with their disregard.

It was a strong effort of the spirit of good, but it was ineffectual. Destiny was too potent, and her immutable laws had decreed my utter and terrible destruction.

Chapter III

WHEN I HAD ATTAINED the age of seventeen my parents resolved that I should become a student at the university of Ingolstadt. I had hitherto attended the schools of Geneva, but my father thought it necessary for the completion of my education that I should be made acquainted with other customs than those of my native country. My departure was therefore fixed at an early date, but before the day resolved upon could arrive, the first misfortune of my life occurred – an omen, as it were, of my future misery. Elizabeth had caught the scarlet fever; her illness was severe, and she was in the greatest danger. During her illness many arguments had been urged to persuade my mother to refrain from attending upon her. She had at first yielded to our entreaties, but when she heard that the life of her favourite was menaced, she could no longer control her anxiety. She attended her sickbed; her watchful attentions triumphed over the malignity of the distemper – Elizabeth was saved, but the consequences of this imprudence were fatal to her preserver. On the third day my mother sickened; her fever was accompanied by the most alarming symptoms, and the looks of her medical attendants prognosticated the worst event. On her deathbed the fortitude and benignity of this best of women did not desert her. She joined the hands of Elizabeth and myself. "My children," she said, "my firmest hopes of future happiness were placed on the prospect of your union. This expectation will now be the consolation of your father. Elizabeth, my love, you must supply my place to my younger children. Alas! I regret that I am taken from you; and, happy and beloved as I have been, is it not hard to quit you all? But these are not thoughts befitting me; I will endeavour to resign myself cheerfully to death and will indulge a hope of meeting you in another world."

She died calmly, and her countenance expressed affection even in death. I need not describe the feelings of those whose dearest ties are rent by that most irreparable evil, the void that presents itself to the soul, and the despair that is exhibited on the countenance. It is so long before the mind can persuade itself that she whom we saw every day and whose very existence appeared a part of our own can have departed forever – that the brightness of a beloved eye can have been extinguished and the sound of a voice so familiar and dear to the ear can be hushed, never more to be heard. These are the reflections of the first days; but when the lapse of time proves the reality of the evil, then the actual bitterness of grief commences. Yet from whom has not that rude hand rent away some dear connection? And why should I describe a sorrow which all have felt, and must feel? The time at length arrives when grief is rather an indulgence than a necessity; and the smile that plays upon the lips, although it may be deemed a sacrilege, is not banished. My mother was dead, but we had still duties which we ought to perform; we must continue our course with the rest and learn to think ourselves fortunate whilst one remains whom the spoiler has not seized.

My departure for Ingolstadt, which had been deferred by these events, was now again determined upon. I obtained from my father a respite of some weeks. It appeared to me sacrilege so soon to leave the repose, akin to death, of the house of mourning and to rush into the thick of life. I was new to sorrow, but it did not the less alarm me. I was unwilling to quit the sight of those that remained to me, and above all, I desired to see my sweet Elizabeth in some degree consoled.

She indeed veiled her grief and strove to act the comforter to us all. She looked steadily on life and assumed its duties with courage and zeal. She devoted herself to those whom she had been taught to call her uncle and cousins. Never was she so enchanting as at this time, when she recalled the sunshine of her smiles and spent them upon us. She forgot even her own regret in her endeavours to make us forget.

The day of my departure at length arrived. Clerval spent the last evening with us. He had endeavoured to persuade his father to permit him to accompany me and to become my fellow student, but in vain. His father was a narrow-minded trader and saw idleness and ruin in the aspirations and ambition of his son. Henry deeply felt the misfortune of being debarred from a liberal education. He said little, but when he spoke I read in his kindling eye and in his animated glance a restrained but firm resolve not to be chained to the miserable details of commerce.

We sat late. We could not tear ourselves away from each other nor persuade ourselves to say the word "Farewell!" It was said, and we retired under the pretence of seeking repose, each fancying that the other was deceived; but when at morning's dawn I descended to the carriage which was to convey me away, they were all there – my father again to bless me, Clerval to press my hand once more, my Elizabeth to renew her entreaties that I would write often and to bestow the last feminine attentions on her playmate and friend.

I threw myself into the chaise that was to convey me away and indulged in the most melancholy reflections. I, who had ever been surrounded by amiable companions, continually engaged in endeavouring to bestow mutual pleasure – I was now alone. In the university whither I was going I must form my own friends and be my own protector. My life had hitherto been remarkably secluded and domestic, and this had given me invincible repugnance to new countenances. I loved my brothers, Elizabeth, and Clerval; these were 'old familiar faces,' but I believed myself totally unfitted for the company of strangers. Such were my reflections as I commenced my journey; but as I proceeded, my spirits and hopes rose. I ardently desired the acquisition of knowledge. I had often, when at home, thought it hard to remain during my youth cooped up in one place and had longed to enter the world and take my station among other human beings. Now my desires were complied with, and it would, indeed, have been folly to repent.

I had sufficient leisure for these and many other reflections during my journey to Ingolstadt, which was long and fatiguing. At length the high white steeple of the town met my eyes. I alighted and was conducted to my solitary apartment to spend the evening as I pleased.

The next morning I delivered my letters of introduction and paid a visit to some of the principal professors. Chance – or rather the evil influence, the Angel of Destruction, which asserted omnipotent sway over me from the moment I turned my reluctant steps from my father's door – led me first to M. Krempe, professor of natural philosophy. He was an uncouth man, but deeply imbued in the secrets of his science. He asked me several questions concerning my progress in the different branches of science appertaining to natural philosophy. I replied carelessly, and partly in contempt, mentioned the names of my alchemists as the principal authors I had studied. The professor stared. "Have you," he said, "really spent your time in studying such nonsense?"

I replied in the affirmative. "Every minute," continued M. Krempe with warmth, "every instant that you have wasted on those books is utterly and entirely lost. You have burdened your memory with exploded systems and useless names. Good God! In what desert land have you lived, where no one was kind enough to inform you that these fancies which you have so greedily imbibed are a thousand years old and as musty as they are ancient? I little expected, in this enlightened and scientific age, to find a disciple of Albertus Magnus and Paracelsus. My dear sir, you must begin your studies entirely anew."

So saying, he stepped aside and wrote down a list of several books treating of natural philosophy which he desired me to procure, and dismissed me after mentioning that in the beginning of the following week he intended to commence a course of lectures upon natural philosophy in its general relations, and that M. Waldman, a fellow professor, would lecture upon chemistry the alternate days that he omitted.

I returned home not disappointed, for I have said that I had long considered those authors useless whom the professor reprobated; but I returned not at all the more inclined to recur to these studies in any shape. M. Krempe was a little squat man with a gruff voice and a repulsive countenance; the teacher, therefore, did not prepossess me in favour of his pursuits. In rather a too philosophical and connected a strain, perhaps, I have given an account of the conclusions I had come to concerning them in my early years. As a child I had not been content with the results promised by the modern professors of natural science. With a confusion of ideas only to be accounted for by my extreme youth and my want of a guide on such matters, I had retrod the steps of knowledge along the paths of time and exchanged the discoveries of recent inquirers for the dreams of forgotten alchemists. Besides, I had a contempt for the uses of modern natural philosophy. It was very different when the masters of the science sought immortality and power; such views, although futile, were grand; but now the scene was changed. The ambition of the inquirer seemed to limit itself to the annihilation of those visions on which my interest in science was chiefly founded. I was required to exchange chimeras of boundless grandeur for realities of little worth.

Such were my reflections during the first two or three days of my residence at Ingolstadt, which were chiefly spent in becoming acquainted with the localities and the principal residents in my new abode. But as the ensuing week commenced, I thought of the information which M. Krempe had given me concerning the lectures. And although I could not consent to go and hear that little conceited fellow deliver sentences out of a pulpit, I recollected what he had said of M. Waldman, whom I had never seen, as he had hitherto been out of town.

Partly from curiosity and partly from idleness, I went into the lecturing room, which M. Waldman entered shortly after. This professor was very unlike his colleague. He appeared about fifty years of age, but with an aspect expressive of the greatest benevolence; a few grey hairs covered his temples, but those at the back of his head were nearly black. His person was short but remarkably erect and his voice the sweetest I had ever heard. He began his lecture by a recapitulation of the history of chemistry and the various improvements made by different men of learning, pronouncing with fervour the names of the most distinguished discoverers. He then took a cursory view of the present state of the science and explained many of its elementary terms. After having made a few preparatory experiments, he concluded with a panegyric upon modern chemistry, the terms of which I shall never forget: "The ancient teachers of this science," said he, "promised impossibilities and performed nothing. The modern masters promise very little; they know that metals cannot be transmuted and that the elixir of life is a chimera but these philosophers, whose hands seem only made to dabble in dirt, and their eyes to pore over the microscope or crucible, have indeed performed miracles. They penetrate into the recesses of nature and show how she works in her hiding-places. They ascend into the heavens; they have discovered how the blood circulates, and the nature of the air we breathe. They have acquired new and almost unlimited powers; they can command the thunders of heaven, mimic the earthquake, and even mock the invisible world with its own shadows."

Such were the professor's words – rather let me say such the words of the fate – enounced to destroy me. As he went on I felt as if my soul were grappling with a palpable enemy; one by one the various keys were touched which formed the mechanism of my being; chord after chord was sounded, and soon my mind was filled with one thought, one conception, one purpose. So much has been done, exclaimed the soul of Frankenstein – more, far more, will I achieve; treading in the steps already marked, I will pioneer a new way, explore unknown powers, and unfold to the world the deepest mysteries of creation.

I closed not my eyes that night. My internal being was in a state of insurrection and turmoil; I felt that order would thence arise, but I had no power to produce it. By degrees, after the morning's dawn, sleep came. I awoke, and my yesternight's thoughts were as a dream. There only remained a resolution to return to my ancient studies and to devote myself to a science for which I believed myself to possess a natural talent. On the same day I paid M. Waldman a visit. His manners in private were even more mild and attractive than in public, for there was a certain dignity in his mien during his lecture which in his own house was replaced by the greatest affability and kindness. I gave him pretty nearly the same account of my former pursuits as I had given to his fellow professor. He heard with attention the little narration concerning my studies and smiled at the names of Cornelius Agrippa and Paracelsus, but without the contempt that M. Krempe had exhibited. He said that "These were men to whose indefatigable zeal modern philosophers were indebted for most of the foundations of their knowledge. They had left to us, as an easier task, to give new names and arrange in connected classifications the facts which they in a great degree had been the instruments of bringing to light. The labours of men of genius, however erroneously directed, scarcely ever fail in ultimately turning to the solid advantage of mankind." I listened to his statement, which was delivered without any presumption or affectation, and then added that his lecture had removed my prejudices against modern chemists; I expressed myself in measured terms, with the modesty and deference due from a youth to his instructor, without letting escape (inexperience in life would have made me ashamed) any of the enthusiasm which stimulated my intended labours. I requested his advice concerning the books I ought to procure.

"I am happy," said M. Waldman, "to have gained a disciple; and if your application equals your ability, I have no doubt of your success. Chemistry is that branch of natural philosophy in which the greatest improvements have been and may be made; it is on that account that I have made it my peculiar study; but at the same time, I have not neglected the other branches of science. A man would make but a very sorry chemist if he attended to that department of human knowledge alone. If your wish is to become really a man of science and not merely a petty experimentalist, I should advise you to apply to every branch of natural philosophy, including mathematics." He then took me into his laboratory and explained to me the uses of his various machines, instructing me as to what I ought to procure and promising me the use of his own when I should have advanced far enough in the science not to derange their mechanism. He also gave me the list of books which I had requested, and I took my leave.

Thus ended a day memorable to me; it decided my future destiny.

Chapter IV

FROM THIS DAY natural philosophy, and particularly chemistry, in the most comprehensive sense of the term, became nearly my sole occupation. I read with ardour those works, so full of genius and discrimination, which modern inquirers have written on these subjects. I attended the lectures and cultivated the acquaintance of the men of science of the university, and I found even in M. Krempe a great deal of sound sense and real information, combined, it is true, with a repulsive physiognomy and manners, but not on that account the less valuable. In M. Waldman I found a true friend. His gentleness was never tinged by dogmatism, and his instructions were given with an air of frankness and good nature that banished every idea of pedantry. In a thousand ways he smoothed for me the path of knowledge and made the most abstruse inquiries clear and facile to my apprehension. My application was at first fluctuating and uncertain; it gained strength as I proceeded and soon became so ardent and eager that the stars often disappeared in the light of morning whilst I was yet engaged in my laboratory.

As I applied so closely, it may be easily conceived that my progress was rapid. My ardour was indeed the astonishment of the students, and my proficiency that of the masters. Professor Krempe often asked me, with a sly smile, how Cornelius Agrippa went on, whilst M. Waldman expressed the most heartfelt exultation in my progress. Two years passed in this manner, during which I paid no visit to Geneva, but was engaged, heart and soul, in the pursuit of some discoveries which I hoped to make. None but those who have experienced them can conceive of the enticements of science. In other studies you go as far as others have gone before you, and there is nothing more to know; but in a scientific pursuit there is continual food for discovery and wonder. A mind of moderate capacity which closely pursues one study must infallibly arrive at great proficiency in that study; and I, who continually sought the attainment of one object of pursuit and was solely wrapped up in this, improved so rapidly that at the end of two years I made some discoveries in the improvement of some chemical instruments, which procured me great esteem and admiration at the university. When I had arrived at this point and had become as well acquainted with the theory and practice of natural philosophy as depended on the lessons of any of the professors at Ingolstadt, my residence there being no longer conducive to my improvements, I thought of returning to my friends and my native town, when an incident happened that protracted my stay.

One of the phenomena which had peculiarly attracted my attention was the structure of the human frame, and, indeed, any animal endued with life. Whence, I often asked myself, did the principle of life proceed? It was a bold question, and one which has ever been considered as a mystery; yet with how many things are we upon the brink of becoming acquainted, if cowardice or carelessness did not restrain our inquiries. I revolved these circumstances in my mind and determined thenceforth to apply myself more particularly to those branches of natural philosophy which relate to physiology. Unless I had been animated by an almost supernatural enthusiasm, my application to this study would have been irksome and almost intolerable. To examine the causes of life, we must first have recourse to death. I became acquainted with the science of anatomy, but this was not sufficient; I must also observe the natural decay and corruption of the human body. In my education my father had taken the greatest precautions that my mind should be impressed with no supernatural horrors. I do not ever remember to have trembled at a tale of superstition or to have feared the apparition of a spirit. Darkness had no effect upon my fancy, and a churchyard was to me merely the receptacle of bodies deprived of life, which, from being the seat of beauty and strength, had become food for the worm. Now I was led to examine the cause and progress of this decay and forced to spend days and nights in vaults and charnel-houses. My attention was fixed upon every object the most insupportable to the delicacy of the human feelings. I saw how the fine form of man was degraded and wasted; I beheld the corruption of death succeed to the blooming cheek of life; I saw how the worm inherited the wonders of the eye and brain. I paused, examining and analysing all the minutiae of causation, as exemplified in the change from life to death, and death to life, until from the midst of this darkness a sudden light broke in upon me – a light so brilliant and wondrous, yet so simple, that while I became dizzy with the immensity of the prospect which it illustrated, I was surprised that among so many men of genius who had directed their inquiries towards the same science, that I alone should be reserved to discover so astonishing a secret.

Remember, I am not recording the vision of a madman. The sun does not more certainly shine in the heavens than that which I now affirm is true. Some miracle might have produced it, yet the stages of the discovery were distinct and probable. After days and nights of incredible labour and fatigue, I succeeded in discovering the cause of generation and life; nay, more, I became myself capable of bestowing animation upon lifeless matter.

The astonishment which I had at first experienced on this discovery soon gave place to delight and rapture. After so much time spent in painful labour, to arrive at once at the summit of my desires was the most gratifying consummation of my toils. But this discovery was so great and overwhelming that all the steps by which I had been progressively led to it were obliterated, and I beheld only the result. What had been the study and desire of the wisest men since the creation of the world was now within my grasp. Not that, like a magic scene, it all opened upon me at once: the information I had obtained was of a nature rather to direct my endeavours so soon as I should point them towards the object of my search than to exhibit that object already accomplished. I was like the Arabian who had been buried with the dead and found a passage to life, aided only by one glimmering and seemingly ineffectual light.

I see by your eagerness and the wonder and hope which your eyes express, my friend, that you expect to be informed of the secret with which I am acquainted; that cannot be; listen patiently until the end of my story, and you will easily perceive why I am reserved upon that subject. I will not lead you on, unguarded and ardent as I then was, to your destruction and infallible misery. Learn from me, if not by my precepts, at least by my example, how dangerous is the acquirement of knowledge and how much happier that man is who believes his native town to be the world, than he who aspires to become greater than his nature will allow.

When I found so astonishing a power placed within my hands, I hesitated a long time concerning the manner in which I should employ it. Although I possessed the capacity of bestowing animation, yet to prepare a frame for the reception of it, with all its intricacies of fibres, muscles, and veins, still remained a work of inconceivable difficulty and labour. I doubted at first whether I should attempt the creation of a being like myself, or one of simpler organization; but my imagination was too much exalted by my first success to permit me to doubt of my ability to give life to an animal as complete and wonderful as man. The materials at present within my command hardly appeared adequate to so arduous an undertaking, but I doubted not that I should ultimately succeed. I prepared myself for a multitude of reverses; my operations might be incessantly baffled, and at last my work be imperfect, yet when I considered the improvement which every day takes place in science and mechanics, I was encouraged to hope my present attempts would at least lay the foundations of future success. Nor could I consider the magnitude and complexity of my plan as any argument of its impracticability. It was with these feelings that I began the creation of a human being. As the minuteness of the parts formed a great hindrance to my speed, I resolved, contrary to my first intention, to make the being of a gigantic stature, that is to say, about eight feet in height, and proportionably large. After having formed this determination and having spent some months in successfully collecting and arranging my materials, I began.

No one can conceive the variety of feelings which bore me onwards, like a hurricane, in the first enthusiasm of success. Life and death appeared to me ideal bounds, which I should first break through, and pour a torrent of light into our dark world. A new species would bless me as its creator and source; many happy and excellent natures would owe their being to me. No father could claim the gratitude of his child so completely as I should deserve theirs. Pursuing these reflections, I thought that if I could bestow animation upon lifeless matter, I might in process of time (although I now found it impossible) renew life where death had apparently devoted the body to corruption.

These thoughts supported my spirits, while I pursued my undertaking with unremitting ardour. My cheek had grown pale with study, and my person had become emaciated with confinement. Sometimes, on the very brink of certainty, I failed; yet still I clung to the hope which the next day or the next hour might realize. One secret which I alone possessed was the hope to which I had dedicated myself; and the moon gazed on my midnight labours, while, with unrelaxed and breathless eagerness, I pursued nature to her hiding-places. Who shall conceive the horrors of my secret toil as I dabbled among the unhallowed damps of the grave or tortured the living animal to animate the lifeless clay? My limbs now tremble, and my eyes swim with the remembrance; but then a resistless and almost frantic impulse urged me forward; I seemed to have lost all soul or sensation but for this one pursuit. It was indeed but a passing trance, that only made me feel with renewed acuteness so soon as, the unnatural stimulus ceasing to operate, I had returned to my old habits. I collected bones from charnel – houses and disturbed, with profane fingers, the tremendous secrets of the human frame. In a solitary chamber, or rather cell, at the top of the house, and separated from all the other apartments by a gallery and staircase, I kept my workshop of filthy creation; my eyeballs were starting from their sockets in attending to the details of my employment. The dissecting room and the slaughter – house furnished many of my materials; and often did my human nature turn with loathing from my occupation, whilst, still urged on by an eagerness which perpetually increased, I brought my work near to a conclusion.

The summer months passed while I was thus engaged, heart and soul, in one pursuit. It was a most beautiful season; never did the fields bestow a more plentiful harvest or the vines yield a more luxuriant vintage, but my eyes were insensible to the charms of nature. And the same feelings which made me neglect the scenes around me caused me also to forget those friends who were so many miles absent, and whom I had not seen for so long a time. I knew my silence disquieted them, and I well remembered the words of my father: "I know that while you are pleased with yourself you will think of us with affection, and we shall hear regularly from you. You must pardon me if I regard any interruption in your correspondence as a proof that your other duties are equally neglected."

I knew well therefore what would be my father's feelings, but I could not tear my thoughts from my employment, loathsome in itself, but which had taken an irresistible hold of my imagination. I wished, as it were, to procrastinate all that related to my feelings of affection until the great object, which swallowed up every habit of my nature, should be completed.

I then thought that my father would be unjust if he ascribed my neglect to vice or faultiness on my part, but I am now convinced that he was justified in conceiving that I should not be altogether free from blame. A human being in perfection ought always to preserve a calm and peaceful mind and never to allow passion or a transitory desire to disturb his tranquillity. I do not think that the pursuit of knowledge is an exception to this rule. If the study to which you apply yourself has a tendency to weaken your affections and to destroy your taste for those simple pleasures in which no alloy can possibly mix, then that study is certainly unlawful, that is to say, not befitting the human mind. If this rule were always observed; if no man allowed any pursuit whatsoever to interfere with the tranquillity of his domestic affections, Greece had not been enslaved, Caesar would have spared his country, America would have been discovered more gradually, and the empires of Mexico and Peru had not been destroyed.

But I forget that I am moralizing in the most interesting part of my tale, and your looks remind me to proceed. My father made no reproach in his letters and only took notice of my science by inquiring into my occupations more particularly than before. Winter, spring, and summer passed away during my labours; but I did not watch the blossom or the expanding leaves – sights which before always yielded me supreme delight – so deeply was I engrossed in my occupation. The leaves of that year had withered before my work drew near to a close, and now every day showed me more plainly how well I had succeeded. But my enthusiasm was checked by my anxiety, and I appeared rather like one doomed by slavery to toil in the mines, or any other unwholesome trade than an artist occupied by his favourite employment. Every night I was oppressed by a slow fever, and I became nervous to a most painful degree; the fall of a leaf startled me, and I shunned my fellow creatures as if I had been guilty of a crime. Sometimes I grew alarmed at the wreck I perceived that I had become; the energy of my purpose alone sustained me: my labours would soon end, and I believed that exercise and amusement would then drive away incipient disease; and I promised myself both of these when my creation should be complete.

Chapter V

IT WAS ON A DREARY NIGHT of November that I beheld the accomplishment of my toils. With an anxiety that almost amounted to agony, I collected the instruments of life around me, that I might infuse a spark of being into the lifeless thing that lay at my feet. It was already one in the morning; the rain pattered dismally against the panes, and my candle was nearly burnt out, when, by the glimmer of the half-extinguished light, I saw the dull yellow eye of the creature open; it breathed hard, and a convulsive motion agitated its limbs.

How can I describe my emotions at this catastrophe, or how delineate the wretch whom with such infinite pains and care I had endeavoured to form? His limbs were in proportion, and I had selected his features as beautiful. Beautiful! Great God! His yellow skin scarcely covered the work of muscles and arteries beneath; his hair was of a lustrous black, and flowing; his teeth of a pearly whiteness; but these luxuriances only formed a more horrid contrast with his watery eyes, that seemed almost of the same colour as the dun-white sockets in which they were set, his shrivelled complexion and straight black lips.

The different accidents of life are not so changeable as the feelings of human nature. I had worked hard for nearly two years, for the sole purpose of infusing life into an inanimate body. For this I had deprived myself of rest and health. I had desired it with an ardour that far exceeded moderation; but now that I had finished, the beauty of the dream vanished, and breathless horror and disgust filled my heart. Unable to endure the aspect of the being I had created, I rushed out of the room and continued a long time traversing my bed-chamber, unable to compose my mind to sleep. At length lassitude succeeded to the tumult I had before endured, and I threw myself on the bed in my clothes, endeavouring to seek a few moments of forgetfulness. But it was in vain; I slept, indeed, but I was disturbed by the wildest dreams. I thought I saw Elizabeth, in the bloom of health, walking in the streets of Ingolstadt. Delighted and surprised, I embraced her, but as I imprinted the first kiss on her lips, they became livid with the hue of death; her features appeared to change, and I thought that I held the corpse of my dead mother in my arms; a shroud enveloped her form, and I saw the grave-worms crawling in the folds of the flannel. I started from my sleep with horror; a cold dew covered my forehead, my teeth chattered, and every limb became convulsed; when, by the dim and yellow light of the moon, as it forced its way through the window shutters, I beheld the wretch – the miserable monster whom I had created. He held up the curtain of the bed; and his eyes, if eyes they may be called, were fixed on me. His jaws opened, and he muttered some inarticulate sounds, while a grin wrinkled his cheeks. He might have spoken, but I did not hear; one hand was stretched out, seemingly to detain me, but I escaped and rushed downstairs. I took refuge in the courtyard belonging to the house which I inhabited, where I remained during the rest of the night, walking up and down in the greatest agitation, listening attentively, catching and fearing each sound as if it were to announce the approach of the demoniacal corpse to which I had so miserably given life.

Oh! No mortal could support the horror of that countenance. A mummy again endued with animation could not be so hideous as that wretch. I had gazed on him while unfinished; he was ugly then, but when those muscles and joints were rendered capable of motion, it became a thing such as even Dante could not have conceived.

I passed the night wretchedly. Sometimes my pulse beat so quickly and hardly that I felt the palpitation of every artery; at others, I nearly sank to the ground through languor and extreme weakness. Mingled with this horror, I felt the bitterness of disappointment; dreams that had been my food and pleasant rest for so long a space were now become a hell to me; and the change was so rapid, the overthrow so complete!

Morning, dismal and wet, at length dawned and discovered to my sleepless and aching eyes the church of Ingolstadt, its white steeple and clock, which indicated the sixth hour. The porter opened the gates of the court, which had that night been my asylum, and I issued into the streets, pacing them with quick steps, as if I sought to avoid the wretch whom I feared every turning of the street would present to my view. I did not dare return to the apartment which I inhabited, but felt impelled to hurry on, although drenched by the rain which poured from a black and comfortless sky.

I continued walking in this manner for some time, endeavouring by bodily exercise to ease the load that weighed upon my mind. I traversed the streets without any clear conception of where I was or what I was doing. My heart palpitated in the sickness of fear, and I hurried on with irregular steps, not daring to look about me:

> *Like one who, on a lonely road,*
> *Doth walk in fear and dread,*
> *And, having once turned round, walks on,*
> *And turns no more his head;*
> *Because he knows a frightful fiend*
> *Doth close behind him tread.*
> (Samuel Taylor Coleridge, 'The Rime of the Ancient Mariner')

Continuing thus, I came at length opposite to the inn at which the various diligences and carriages usually stopped. Here I paused, I knew not why; but I remained some minutes with my eyes fixed on a coach that was coming towards me from the other end of the street. As it drew nearer I observed that it was the Swiss diligence; it stopped just where I was standing, and on the door being opened, I perceived Henry Clerval, who, on seeing me, instantly sprung out. "My dear Frankenstein," exclaimed he, "how glad I am to see you! How fortunate that you should be here at the very moment of my alighting!"

Nothing could equal my delight on seeing Clerval; his presence brought back to my thoughts my father, Elizabeth, and all those scenes of home so dear to my recollection. I grasped his hand, and in a moment forgot my horror and misfortune; I felt suddenly, and for the first time during many months, calm and serene joy. I welcomed my friend, therefore, in the most cordial manner, and we walked towards my college. Clerval continued talking for some time about our mutual friends and his own good fortune in being permitted to come to Ingolstadt. "You may easily believe," said he, "how great was the difficulty to persuade my father that all necessary knowledge was not comprised in the noble art of bookkeeping; and, indeed, I believe I left him incredulous to the last, for his constant answer to my unwearied entreaties was the same as that of the Dutch schoolmaster in The Vicar of Wakefield: 'I have ten thousand florins a year without Greek, I eat heartily without Greek.' But his affection for me at length overcame his dislike of learning, and he has permitted me to undertake a voyage of discovery to the land of knowledge."

"It gives me the greatest delight to see you; but tell me how you left my father, brothers, and Elizabeth."

"Very well, and very happy, only a little uneasy that they hear from you so seldom. By the by, I mean to lecture you a little upon their account myself. But, my dear Frankenstein," continued he, stopping short and gazing full in my face, "I did not before remark how very ill you appear; so thin and pale; you look as if you had been watching for several nights."

"You have guessed right; I have lately been so deeply engaged in one occupation that I have not allowed myself sufficient rest, as you see; but I hope, I sincerely hope, that all these employments are now at an end and that I am at length free."

I trembled excessively; I could not endure to think of, and far less to allude to, the occurrences of the preceding night. I walked with a quick pace, and we soon arrived at my college. I then reflected, and the thought made me shiver, that the creature whom I had left in my apartment might still be there, alive and walking about. I dreaded to behold this monster, but I feared still more that Henry should see him. Entreating him, therefore, to remain a few minutes at the bottom of the stairs, I darted up towards my own room. My hand was already on the lock of the door before I recollected myself. I then paused, and a cold shivering came over me. I threw the door forcibly open, as children are accustomed to do when they expect a spectre to stand in waiting for them on the other side; but nothing appeared. I stepped fearfully in: the apartment was empty, and my bedroom was also freed from its hideous guest. I could hardly believe that so great a good fortune could have befallen me, but when I became assured that my enemy had indeed fled, I clapped my hands for joy and ran down to Clerval.

We ascended into my room, and the servant presently brought breakfast; but I was unable to contain myself. It was not joy only that possessed me; I felt my flesh tingle with excess of sensitiveness, and my pulse beat rapidly. I was unable to remain for a single instant in the same place; I jumped over the chairs, clapped my hands, and laughed aloud. Clerval at first attributed my unusual spirits to joy on his arrival, but when he observed me more attentively, he saw a wildness in my eyes for which he could not account, and my loud, unrestrained, heartless laughter frightened and astonished him.

"My dear Victor," cried he, "what, for God's sake, is the matter? Do not laugh in that manner. How ill you are! What is the cause of all this?"

"Do not ask me," cried I, putting my hands before my eyes, for I thought I saw the dreaded spectre glide into the room; "He can tell. Oh, save me! Save me!" I imagined that the monster seized me; I struggled furiously and fell down in a fit.

Poor Clerval! What must have been his feelings? A meeting, which he anticipated with such joy, so strangely turned to bitterness. But I was not the witness of his grief, for I was lifeless and did not recover my senses for a long, long time.

This was the commencement of a nervous fever which confined me for several months. During all that time Henry was my only nurse. I afterwards learned that, knowing my father's advanced age and unfitness for so long a journey, and how wretched my sickness would make Elizabeth, he spared them this grief by concealing the extent of my disorder. He knew that I could not have a more kind and attentive nurse than himself; and, firm in the hope he felt of my recovery, he did not doubt that, instead of doing harm, he performed the kindest action that he could towards them.

But I was in reality very ill, and surely nothing but the unbounded and unremitting attentions of my friend could have restored me to life. The form of the monster on whom

I had bestowed existence was forever before my eyes, and I raved incessantly concerning him. Doubtless my words surprised Henry; he at first believed them to be the wanderings of my disturbed imagination, but the pertinacity with which I continually recurred to the same subject persuaded him that my disorder indeed owed its origin to some uncommon and terrible event.

By very slow degrees, and with frequent relapses that alarmed and grieved my friend, I recovered. I remember the first time I became capable of observing outward objects with any kind of pleasure, I perceived that the fallen leaves had disappeared and that the young buds were shooting forth from the trees that shaded my window. It was a divine spring, and the season contributed greatly to my convalescence. I felt also sentiments of joy and affection revive in my bosom; my gloom disappeared, and in a short time I became as cheerful as before I was attacked by the fatal passion.

"Dearest Clerval," exclaimed I, "how kind, how very good you are to me. This whole winter, instead of being spent in study, as you promised yourself, has been consumed in my sick room. How shall I ever repay you? I feel the greatest remorse for the disappointment of which I have been the occasion, but you will forgive me."

"You will repay me entirely if you do not discompose yourself, but get well as fast as you can; and since you appear in such good spirits, I may speak to you on one subject, may I not?"

I trembled. One subject! What could it be? Could he allude to an object on whom I dared not even think? "Compose yourself," said Clerval, who observed my change of colour, "I will not mention it if it agitates you; but your father and cousin would be very happy if they received a letter from you in your own handwriting. They hardly know how ill you have been and are uneasy at your long silence."

"Is that all, my dear Henry? How could you suppose that my first thought would not fly towards those dear, dear friends whom I love and who are so deserving of my love?"

"If this is your present temper, my friend, you will perhaps be glad to see a letter that has been lying here some days for you; it is from your cousin, I believe."

Chapter VI

CLERVAL THEN PUT the following letter into my hands. It was from my own Elizabeth:

> *My dearest Cousin,*
> *You have been ill, very ill, and even the constant letters of dear kind Henry are not sufficient to reassure me on your account. You are forbidden to write – to hold a pen; yet one word from you, dear Victor, is necessary to calm our apprehensions. For a long time I have thought that each post would bring this line, and my persuasions have restrained my uncle from undertaking a journey to Ingolstadt. I have prevented his encountering the inconveniences and perhaps dangers of so long a journey, yet how often have I regretted not being able to perform it myself! I figure to myself that the task of attending on your sickbed has devolved on some mercenary old nurse, who could never guess your wishes nor minister to them with the care and affection of your poor cousin. Yet that is over now: Clerval writes that indeed you are getting better. I eagerly hope that you will confirm this intelligence soon in your own handwriting.*

"Get well – and return to us. You will find a happy, cheerful home and friends who love you dearly. Your father's health is vigorous, and he asks but to see you, but to be assured that you are well; and not a care will ever cloud his benevolent countenance. How pleased you would be to remark the improvement of our Ernest! He is now sixteen and full of activity and spirit. He is desirous to be a true Swiss and to enter into foreign service, but we cannot part with him, at least until his elder brother returns to us. My uncle is not pleased with the idea of a military career in a distant country, but Ernest never had your powers of application. He looks upon study as an odious fetter; his time is spent in the open air, climbing the hills or rowing on the lake. I fear that he will become an idler unless we yield the point and permit him to enter on the profession which he has selected.

Little alteration, except the growth of our dear children, has taken place since you left us. The blue lake and snow-clad mountains – they never change; and I think our placid home and our contented hearts are regulated by the same immutable laws. My trifling occupations take up my time and amuse me, and I am rewarded for any exertions by seeing none but happy, kind faces around me. Since you left us, but one change has taken place in our little household. Do you remember on what occasion Justine Moritz entered our family? Probably you do not; I will relate her history, therefore in a few words. Madame Moritz, her mother, was a widow with four children, of whom Justine was the third. This girl had always been the favourite of her father, but through a strange perversity, her mother could not endure her, and after the death of M. Moritz, treated her very ill. My aunt observed this, and when Justine was twelve years of age, prevailed on her mother to allow her to live at our house. The republican institutions of our country have produced simpler and happier manners than those which prevail in the great monarchies that surround it. Hence there is less distinction between the several classes of its inhabitants; and the lower orders, being neither so poor nor so despised, their manners are more refined and moral. A servant in Geneva does not mean the same thing as a servant in France and England. Justine, thus received in our family, learned the duties of a servant, a condition which, in our fortunate country, does not include the idea of ignorance and a sacrifice of the dignity of a human being.

Justine, you may remember, was a great favourite of yours; and I recollect you once remarked that if you were in an ill humour, one glance from Justine could dissipate it, for the same reason that Ariosto gives concerning the beauty of Angelica – she looked so frank-hearted and happy. My aunt conceived a great attachment for her, by which she was induced to give her an education superior to that which she had at first intended. This benefit was fully repaid; Justine was the most grateful little creature in the world: I do not mean that she made any professions I never heard one pass her lips, but you could see by her eyes that she almost adored her protectress. Although her disposition was gay and in many respects inconsiderate, yet she paid the greatest attention to every gesture of my aunt. She thought her the model of all excellence and endeavoured to imitate her phraseology and manners, so that even now she often reminds me of her.

When my dearest aunt died everyone was too much occupied in their own grief to notice poor Justine, who had attended her during her illness with the most anxious affection. Poor Justine was very ill; but other trials were reserved for her.

One by one, her brothers and sister died; and her mother, with the exception of her neglected daughter, was left childless. The conscience of the woman was troubled; she began to think that the deaths of her favourites was a judgement from heaven to chastise her partiality. She was a Roman Catholic; and I believe her confessor confirmed the idea which she had conceived. Accordingly, a few months after your departure for Ingolstadt, Justine was called home by her repentant mother. Poor girl! She wept when she quitted our house; she was much altered since the death of my aunt; grief had given softness and a winning mildness to her manners, which had before been remarkable for vivacity. Nor was her residence at her mother's house of a nature to restore her gaiety. The poor woman was very vacillating in her repentance. She sometimes begged Justine to forgive her unkindness, but much oftener accused her of having caused the deaths of her brothers and sister. Perpetual fretting at length threw Madame Moritz into a decline, which at first increased her irritability, but she is now at peace forever. She died on the first approach of cold weather, at the beginning of this last winter. Justine has just returned to us; and I assure you I love her tenderly. She is very clever and gentle, and extremely pretty; as I mentioned before, her mein and her expression continually remind me of my dear aunt.

I must say also a few words to you, my dear cousin, of little darling William. I wish you could see him; he is very tall of his age, with sweet laughing blue eyes, dark eyelashes, and curling hair. When he smiles, two little dimples appear on each cheek, which are rosy with health. He has already had one or two little WIVES, but Louisa Biron is his favourite, a pretty little girl of five years of age.

Now, dear Victor, I dare say you wish to be indulged in a little gossip concerning the good people of Geneva. The pretty Miss Mansfield has already received the congratulatory visits on her approaching marriage with a young Englishman, John Melbourne, Esq. Her ugly sister, Manon, married M. Duvillard, the rich banker, last autumn. Your favourite schoolfellow, Louis Manoir, has suffered several misfortunes since the departure of Clerval from Geneva. But he has already recovered his spirits, and is reported to be on the point of marrying a lively pretty Frenchwoman, Madame Tavernier. She is a widow, and much older than Manoir; but she is very much admired, and a favourite with everybody.

I have written myself into better spirits, dear cousin; but my anxiety returns upon me as I conclude. Write, dearest Victor – one line – one word will be a blessing to us. Ten thousand thanks to Henry for his kindness, his affection, and his many letters; we are sincerely grateful. Adieu! my cousin; take care of your self; and, I entreat you, write!

Elizabeth Lavenza.

Geneva, March 18, 17—

"Dear, dear Elizabeth!" I exclaimed, when I had read her letter: "I will write instantly and relieve them from the anxiety they must feel." I wrote, and this exertion greatly fatigued me; but my convalescence had commenced, and proceeded regularly. In another fortnight I was able to leave my chamber.

One of my first duties on my recovery was to introduce Clerval to the several professors of the university. In doing this, I underwent a kind of rough usage, ill befitting the wounds that my mind had sustained. Ever since the fatal night, the end of my labours, and the beginning of my misfortunes, I had conceived a violent antipathy even to the name of natural philosophy. When I was otherwise quite restored to health, the sight of a chemical instrument would renew all the agony of my nervous symptoms. Henry saw this, and had removed all my apparatus from my view. He had also changed my apartment; for he perceived that I had acquired a dislike for the room which had previously been my laboratory. But these cares of Clerval were made of no avail when I visited the professors. M. Waldman inflicted torture when he praised, with kindness and warmth, the astonishing progress I had made in the sciences. He soon perceived that I disliked the subject; but not guessing the real cause, he attributed my feelings to modesty, and changed the subject from my improvement, to the science itself, with a desire, as I evidently saw, of drawing me out. What could I do? He meant to please, and he tormented me. I felt as if he had placed carefully, one by one, in my five * those instruments which were to be afterwards used in putting me to a slow and cruel death. I writhed under his words, yet dared not exhibit the pain I felt. Clerval, whose eyes and feelings were always quick in discerning the sensations of others, declined the subject, alleging, in excuse, his total ignorance; and the conversation took a more general turn. I thanked my friend from my heart, but I did not speak. I saw plainly that he was surprised, but he never attempted to draw my secret from me; and although I loved him with a mixture of affection and reverence that knew no bounds, yet I could never persuade myself to confide in him that event which was so often present to my recollection, but which I feared the detail to another would only impress more deeply.

M. Krempe was not equally docile; and in my condition at that time, of almost insupportable sensitiveness, his harsh blunt encomiums gave me even more pain than the benevolent approbation of M. Waldman. "D—n the fellow!" cried he; "Why, M. Clerval, I assure you he has outstript us all. Ay, stare if you please; but it is nevertheless true. A youngster who, but a few years ago, believed in Cornelius Agrippa as firmly as in the gospel, has now set himself at the head of the university; and if he is not soon pulled down, we shall all be out of countenance. – Ay, ay," continued he, observing my face expressive of suffering, "M. Frankenstein is modest; an excellent quality in a young man. Young men should be diffident of themselves, you know, M. Clerval: I was myself when young; but that wears out in a very short time."

M. Krempe had now commenced an eulogy on himself, which happily turned the conversation from a subject that was so annoying to me.

Clerval had never sympathized in my tastes for natural science; and his literary pursuits differed wholly from those which had occupied me. He came to the university with the design of making himself complete master of the oriental languages, and thus he should open a field for the plan of life he had marked out for himself. Resolved to pursue no inglorious career, he turned his eyes toward the East, as affording scope for his spirit of enterprise. The Persian, Arabic, and Sanscrit languages engaged his attention, and I was easily induced to enter on the same studies. Idleness had ever been irksome to me, and now that I wished to fly from reflection, and hated my former studies, I felt great relief in being the fellow-pupil with my friend, and found not only instruction but consolation in the works of the orientalists. I did not, like him, attempt a critical knowledge of their dialects, for I did not contemplate making any other use of them than temporary amusement. I read merely to understand their meaning, and they well repaid my labours. Their melancholy is soothing, and their joy elevating, to a degree I never experienced in studying the authors of any other country. When you read their writings, life appears to consist in a warm sun and a garden of roses – in the smiles and frowns of a fair enemy, and the fire that consumes your own heart. How different from the manly and heroical poetry of Greece and Rome!

Summer passed away in these occupations, and my return to Geneva was fixed for the latter end of autumn; but being delayed by several accidents, winter and snow arrived, the roads were deemed impassable, and my journey was retarded until the ensuing spring. I felt this delay very bitterly; for I longed to see my native town and my beloved friends. My return had only been delayed so long, from an unwillingness to leave Clerval in a strange place, before he had become acquainted with any of its inhabitants. The winter, however, was spent cheerfully; and although the spring was uncommonly late, when it came its beauty compensated for its dilatoriness.

The month of May had already commenced, and I expected the letter daily which was to fix the date of my departure, when Henry proposed a pedestrian tour in the environs of Ingolstadt, that I might bid a personal farewell to the country I had so long inhabited. I acceded with pleasure to this proposition: I was fond of exercise, and Clerval had always been my favourite companion in the ramble of this nature that I had taken among the scenes of my native country.

We passed a fortnight in these perambulations: my health and spirits had long been restored, and they gained additional strength from the salubrious air I breathed, the natural incidents of our progress, and the conversation of my friend. Study had before secluded me from the intercourse of my fellow – creatures, and rendered me unsocial; but Clerval called forth the better feelings of my heart; he again taught me to love the aspect of nature, and the cheerful faces of children. Excellent friend! how sincerely you did love me, and endeavour to elevate my mind until it was on a level with your own. A selfish pursuit had cramped and narrowed me, until your gentleness and affection warmed and opened my senses; I became the same happy creature who, a few years ago, loved and beloved by all, had no sorrow or care. When happy, inanimate nature had the power of bestowing on me the most delightful sensations. A serene sky and verdant fields filled me with ecstasy. The present season was indeed divine; the flowers of spring bloomed in the hedges, while those of summer were already in bud. I was undisturbed by thoughts which during the preceding year had pressed upon me, notwithstanding my endeavours to throw them off, with an invincible burden.

Henry rejoiced in my gaiety, and sincerely sympathised in my feelings: he exerted himself to amuse me, while he expressed the sensations that filled his soul. The resources of his mind on this occasion were truly astonishing: his conversation was full of imagination; and very often, in imitation of the Persian and Arabic writers, he invented tales of wonderful fancy and passion. At other times he repeated my favourite poems, or drew me out into arguments, which he supported with great ingenuity. We returned to our college on a Sunday afternoon: the peasants were dancing, and everyone we met appeared gay and happy. My own spirits were high, and I bounded along with feelings of unbridled joy and hilarity.

Chapter VII

ON MY RETURN, I found the following letter from my father:

My dear Victor,

You have probably waited impatiently for a letter to fix the date of your return to us; and I was at first tempted to write only a few lines, merely mentioning the day on which I should expect you. But that would be a cruel kindness, and I dare not do it. What would be your surprise, my son, when you expected a happy and glad welcome, to behold, on the contrary, tears and wretchedness? And how, Victor, can I relate our misfortune? Absence cannot have rendered you callous to our joys and griefs; and how shall I inflict pain on my long absent son? I wish to prepare you for the woeful news, but I know it is impossible; even now your eye skims over the page to seek the words which are to convey to you the horrible tidings.

William is dead! – that sweet child, whose smiles delighted and warmed my heart, who was so gentle, yet so gay! Victor, he is murdered!

I will not attempt to console you; but will simply relate the circumstances of the transaction.

Last Thursday (May 7th), I, my niece, and your two brothers, went to walk in Plainpalais. The evening was warm and serene, and we prolonged our walk farther than usual. It was already dusk before we thought of returning; and then we discovered that William and Ernest, who had gone on before, were not to be found. We accordingly rested on a seat until they should return. Presently Ernest came, and enquired if we had seen his brother; he said, that he had been playing with him, that William had run away to hide himself, and that he vainly sought for him, and afterwards waited for a long time, but that he did not return.

This account rather alarmed us, and we continued to search for him until night fell, when Elizabeth conjectured that he might have returned to the house. He was not there. We returned again, with torches; for I could not rest, when I thought that my sweet boy had lost himself, and was exposed to all the damps and dews of night; Elizabeth also suffered extreme anguish. About five in the morning I discovered my lovely boy, whom the night before I had seen blooming and active in health, stretched on the grass livid and motionless; the print of the murder's finger was on his neck.

He was conveyed home, and the anguish that was visible in my countenance betrayed the secret to Elizabeth. She was very earnest to see the corpse. At first I attempted to prevent her but she persisted, and entering the room where it lay, hastily examined the neck of the victim, and clasping her hands exclaimed, "O God! I have murdered my darling child!"

She fainted, and was restored with extreme difficulty. When she again lived, it was only to weep and sigh. She told me, that that same evening William had teased her to let him wear a very valuable miniature that she possessed of your mother. This picture is gone, and was doubtless the temptation which urged the murderer to the deed. We have no trace of him at present, although our exertions to discover him are unremitted; but they will not restore my beloved William!

Come, dearest Victor; you alone can console Elizabeth. She weeps continually, and accuses herself unjustly as the cause of his death; her words pierce my heart. We are all unhappy; but will not that be an additional motive for you, my son, to return and be our comforter? Your dear mother! Alas, Victor! I now say, Thank God she did not live to witness the cruel, miserable death of her youngest darling!

Come, Victor; not brooding thoughts of vengeance against the assassin, but with feelings of peace and gentleness, that will heal, instead of festering, the wounds of our minds. Enter the house of mourning, my friend, but with kindness and affection for those who love you, and not with hatred for your enemies.

Your affectionate and afflicted father,
Alphonse Frankenstein.
Geneva, May 12th, 17—

Clerval, who had watched my countenance as I read this letter, was surprised to observe the despair that succeeded the joy I at first expressed on receiving new from my friends. I threw the letter on the table, and covered my face with my hands.

"My dear Frankenstein," exclaimed Henry, when he perceived me weep with bitterness, "are you always to be unhappy? My dear friend, what has happened?"

I motioned him to take up the letter, while I walked up and down the room in the extremest agitation. Tears also gushed from the eyes of Clerval, as he read the account of my misfortune.

"I can offer you no consolation, my friend," said he; "your disaster is irreparable. What do you intend to do?"

"To go instantly to Geneva: come with me, Henry, to order the horses."

During our walk, Clerval endeavoured to say a few words of consolation; he could only express his heartfelt sympathy. "Poor William!" said he, dear lovely child, he now sleeps with his angel mother! Who that had seen him bright and joyous in his young beauty, but must weep over his untimely loss! To die so miserably; to feel the murderer's grasp! How much more a murderer that could destroy such radiant innocence! Poor little fellow! one only consolation have we; his friends mourn and weep, but he is at rest. The pang is over, his sufferings are at an end forever. A sod covers his gentle form, and he knows no pain. He can no longer be a subject for pity; we must reserve that for his miserable survivors."

Clerval spoke thus as we hurried through the streets; the words impressed themselves on my mind and I remembered them afterwards in solitude. But now, as soon as the horses arrived, I hurried into a cabriolet, and bade farewell to my friend.

My journey was very melancholy. At first I wished to hurry on, for I longed to console and sympathise with my loved and sorrowing friends; but when I drew near my native town, I slackened my progress. I could hardly sustain the multitude of feelings that crowded into my mind. I passed through scenes familiar to my youth, but which I had not seen for nearly six years. How altered everything might be during that time! One sudden and desolating change had taken place; but a thousand little circumstances might have by degrees worked other alterations, which, although they were done more tranquilly, might not be the less decisive. Fear overcame me; I dared no advance, dreading a thousand nameless evils that made me tremble, although I was unable to define them. I remained two days at Lausanne, in this painful state of mind. I contemplated the lake: the waters were placid; all around was calm; and the snowy mountains, 'the palaces of nature,' were not changed. By degrees the calm and heavenly scene restored me, and I continued my journey towards Geneva.

The road ran by the side of the lake, which became narrower as I approached my native town. I discovered more distinctly the black sides of Jura, and the bright summit of Mont Blanc. I wept like a child. "Dear mountains! My own beautiful lake! How do you welcome your wanderer? Your summits are clear; the sky and lake are blue and placid. Is this to prognosticate peace, or to mock at my unhappiness?"

I fear, my friend, that I shall render myself tedious by dwelling on these preliminary circumstances; but they were days of comparative happiness, and I think of them with pleasure. My country, my beloved country! who but a native can tell the delight I took in again beholding thy streams, thy mountains, and, more than all, thy lovely lake!

Yet, as I drew nearer home, grief and fear again overcame me. Night also closed around; and when I could hardly see the dark mountains, I felt still more gloomily. The picture appeared a vast and dim scene of evil, and I foresaw obscurely that I was destined to become the most wretched of human beings. Alas! I prophesied truly, and failed only in one single circumstance, that in all the misery I imagined and dreaded, I did not conceive the hundredth part of the anguish I was destined to endure. It was completely dark when I arrived in the environs of Geneva; the gates of the town were already shut; and I was obliged to pass the night at Secheron, a village at the distance of half a league from the city. The sky was serene; and, as I was unable to rest, I resolved to visit the spot where my poor William had been murdered. As I could not pass through the town, I was obliged to cross the lake in a boat to arrive at Plainpalais. During this short voyage I saw the lightning playing on the summit of Mont Blanc in the most beautiful figures. The storm appeared to approach rapidly, and, on landing, I ascended a low hill, that I might observe its progress. It advanced; the heavens were clouded, and I soon felt the rain coming slowly in large drops, but its violence quickly increased.

I quitted my seat, and walked on, although the darkness and storm increased every minute, and the thunder burst with a terrific crash over my head. It was echoed from Saleve, the Juras, and the Alps of Savoy; vivid flashes of lightning dazzled my eyes, illuminating the lake, making it appear like a vast sheet of fire; then for an instant everything seemed of a pitchy darkness, until the eye recovered itself from the preceding flash. The storm, as is often the case in Switzerland, appeared at once in various parts of the heavens. The most violent storm hung exactly north of the town, over the part of the lake which lies between the promontory of Belrive and the village of Copet. Another storm enlightened Jura with faint flashes; and another darkened and sometimes disclosed the Mole, a peaked mountain to the east of the lake.

While I watched the tempest, so beautiful yet terrific, I wandered on with a hasty step. This noble war in the sky elevated my spirits; I clasped my hands, and exclaimed aloud, "William, dear angel! This is thy funeral, this thy dirge!" As I said these words, I perceived in the gloom a figure which stole from behind a clump of trees near me; I stood fixed, gazing intently: I could not be mistaken. A flash of lightning illuminated the object, and discovered its shape plainly to me; its gigantic stature, and the deformity of its aspect more hideous than belongs to humanity, instantly informed me that it was the wretch, the filthy daemon, to whom I had given life. What did he there? Could he be (I shuddered at the conception) the murderer of my brother? No sooner did that idea cross my imagination, than I became convinced of its truth; my teeth chattered, and I was forced to lean against a tree for support. The figure passed me quickly, and I lost it in the gloom.

Nothing in human shape could have destroyed the fair child. He was the murderer! I could not doubt it. The mere presence of the idea was an irresistible proof of the fact. I thought of pursuing the devil; but it would have been in vain, for another flash discovered him to me hanging among the rocks of the nearly perpendicular ascent of Mont Saleve, a hill that bounds Plainpalais on the south. He soon reached the summit, and disappeared.

I remained motionless. The thunder ceased; but the rain still continued, and the scene was enveloped in an impenetrable darkness. I revolved in my mind the events which I had until now sought to forget: the whole train of my progress toward the creation; the appearance of the works of my own hands at my bedside; its departure. Two years had now nearly elapsed since the night on which he first received life; and was this his first crime? Alas! I had turned loose into the world a depraved wretch, whose delight was in carnage and misery; had he not murdered my brother?

No one can conceive the anguish I suffered during the remainder of the night, which I spent, cold and wet, in the open air. But I did not feel the inconvenience of the weather; my imagination was busy in scenes of evil and despair. I considered the being whom I had cast among mankind, and endowed with the will and power to effect purposes of horror, such as the deed which he had now done, nearly in the light of my own vampire, my own spirit let loose from the grave, and forced to destroy all that was dear to me.

Day dawned; and I directed my steps towards the town. The gates were open, and I hastened to my father's house. My first thought was to discover what I knew of the murderer, and cause instant pursuit to be made. But I paused when I reflected on the story that I had to tell. A being whom I myself had formed, and endued with life, had met me at midnight among the precipices of an inaccessible mountain. I remembered also the nervous fever with which I had been seized just at the time that I dated my creation, and which would give an air of delirium to a tale otherwise so utterly improbable. I well knew that if any other had communicated such a relation to me, I should have looked upon it as the ravings of insanity. Besides, the strange nature of the animal would elude all pursuit, even if I were so far credited as to persuade my relatives to commence it. And then of what use would be pursuit? Who could arrest a creature capable of scaling the overhanging sides of Mont Saleve? These reflections determined me, and I resolved to remain silent.

It was about five in the morning when I entered my father's house. I told the servants not to disturb the family, and went into the library to attend their usual hour of rising.

Six years had elapsed, passed in a dream but for one indelible trace, and I stood in the same place where I had last embraced my father before my departure for Ingolstadt. Beloved and venerable parent! He still remained to me. I gazed on the picture of my mother, which stood over the mantel-piece. It was an historical subject, painted at my father's desire, and represented Caroline Beaufort in an agony of despair, kneeling by the coffin of her dead father. Her garb was rustic, and her cheek pale; but there was an air of dignity and beauty, that hardly permitted the sentiment of pity. Below this picture was a miniature of William; and my tears flowed when I looked upon it. While I was thus engaged, Ernest entered: he had heard me arrive, and hastened to welcome me: "Welcome, my dearest Victor," said he. "Ah! I wish you had come three months ago, and then you would have found us all joyous and delighted. You come to us now to share a misery which nothing can alleviate; yet you presence will, I hope, revive our father, who seems sinking under his misfortune; and your persuasions will induce poor Elizabeth to cease her vain and tormenting self-accusations. Poor William! He was our darling and our pride!"

Tears, unrestrained, fell from my brother's eyes; a sense of mortal agony crept over my frame. Before, I had only imagined the wretchedness of my desolated home; the reality came on me as a new, and a not less terrible, disaster. I tried to calm Ernest; I enquired more minutely concerning my father, and her I named my cousin.

"She most of all," said Ernest, "requires consolation; she accused herself of having caused the death of my brother, and that made her very wretched. But since the murderer has been discovered –"

"The murderer discovered! Good God! How can that be? Who could attempt to pursue him? It is impossible; one might as well try to overtake the winds, or confine a mountain-stream with a straw. I saw him too; he was free last night!"

"I do not know what you mean," replied my brother, in accents of wonder, "but to us the discovery we have made completes our misery. No one would believe it at first; and even now Elizabeth will not be convinced, notwithstanding all the evidence. Indeed, who would credit that Justine Moritz, who was so amiable, and fond of all the family, could suddenly become so capable of so frightful, so appalling a crime?"

"Justine Moritz! Poor, poor girl, is she the accused? But it is wrongfully; everyone knows that; no one believes it, surely, Ernest?"

"No one did at first; but several circumstances came out, that have almost forced conviction upon us; and her own behaviour has been so confused, as to add to the evidence of facts a weight that, I fear, leaves no hope for doubt. But she will be tried today, and you will then hear all."

He then related that, the morning on which the murder of poor William had been discovered, Justine had been taken ill, and confined to her bed for several days. During this interval, one of the servants, happening to examine the apparel she had worn on the night of the murder, had discovered in her pocket the picture of my mother, which had been judged to be the temptation of the murderer. The servant instantly showed it to one of the others, who, without saying a word to any of the family, went to a magistrate; and, upon their deposition, Justine was apprehended. On being charged with the fact, the poor girl confirmed the suspicion in a great measure by her extreme confusion of manner.

This was a strange tale, but it did not shake my faith; and I replied earnestly, "You are all mistaken; I know the murderer. Justine, poor, good Justine, is innocent."

At that instant my father entered. I saw unhappiness deeply impressed on his countenance, but he endeavoured to welcome me cheerfully; and, after we had exchanged our mournful greeting, would have introduced some other topic than that of our disaster, had not Ernest exclaimed, "Good God, papa! Victor says that he knows who was the murderer of poor William."

"We do also, unfortunately," replied my father, "for indeed I had rather have been forever ignorant than have discovered so much depravity and ungratitude in one I valued so highly."

"My dear father, you are mistaken; Justine is innocent."

"If she is, God forbid that she should suffer as guilty. She is to be tried today, and I hope, I sincerely hope, that she will be acquitted."

This speech calmed me. I was firmly convinced in my own mind that Justine, and indeed every human being, was guiltless of this murder. I had no fear, therefore, that any circumstantial evidence could be brought forward strong enough to convict her. My tale was not one to announce publicly; its astounding horror would be looked upon as madness by the vulgar. Did anyone indeed exist, except I, the creator, who would believe, unless his senses convinced him, in the existence of the living monument of presumption and rash ignorance which I had let loose upon the world?

We were soon joined by Elizabeth. Time had altered her since I last beheld her; it had endowed her with loveliness surpassing the beauty of her childish years. There was the same candour, the same vivacity, but it was allied to an expression more full of sensibility and intellect. She welcomed me with the greatest affection. "Your arrival, my dear cousin," said she, "fills me with hope. You perhaps will find some means to justify my poor guiltless Justine. Alas! Who is safe, if she be convicted of crime? I rely on her innocence as certainly as I do upon my own. Our misfortune is doubly hard to us; we have not only lost that lovely darling boy, but this poor girl, whom I sincerely love, is to be torn away by even a worse fate. If she is condemned, I never shall know joy more. But she will not, I am sure she will not; and then I shall be happy again, even after the sad death of my little William."

"She is innocent, my Elizabeth," said I, "and that shall be proved; fear nothing, but let your spirits be cheered by the assurance of her acquittal."

"How kind and generous you are! everyone else believes in her guilt, and that made me wretched, for I knew that it was impossible: and to see everyone else prejudiced in so deadly a manner rendered me hopeless and despairing." She wept.

"Dearest niece," said my father, "dry your tears. If she is, as you believe, innocent, rely on the justice of our laws, and the activity with which I shall prevent the slightest shadow of partiality."

Chapter VIII

WE PASSED a few sad hours until eleven o'clock, when the trial was to commence. My father and the rest of the family being obliged to attend as witnesses, I accompanied them to the court. During the whole of this wretched mockery of justice I suffered living torture. It was to be decided whether the result of my curiosity and lawless devices would cause the death of two of my fellow beings: one a smiling babe full of innocence and joy, the other far more dreadfully murdered, with every aggravation of infamy that could make the murder memorable in horror. Justine also was a girl of merit and possessed qualities which promised to render her life happy; now all was to be obliterated in an ignominious grave, and I the cause! A thousand times rather would I have confessed myself guilty of the crime ascribed to Justine, but I was absent when it was committed, and such a declaration would have been considered as the ravings of a madman and would not have exculpated her who suffered through me.

The appearance of Justine was calm. She was dressed in mourning, and her countenance, always engaging, was rendered, by the solemnity of her feelings, exquisitely beautiful. Yet she appeared confident in innocence and did not tremble, although gazed on and execrated by thousands, for all the kindness which her beauty might otherwise have excited was obliterated in the minds of the spectators by the imagination of the enormity she was supposed to have committed. She was tranquil, yet her tranquillity was evidently constrained; and as her confusion had before been adduced as a proof of her guilt, she worked up her mind to an appearance of courage. When she entered the court she threw her eyes round it and quickly discovered where we were seated. A tear seemed to dim her eye when she saw us, but she quickly recovered herself, and a look of sorrowful affection seemed to attest her utter guiltlessness.

The trial began, and after the advocate against her had stated the charge, several witnesses were called. Several strange facts combined against her, which might have staggered anyone who had not such proof of her innocence as I had. She had been out the whole of the night on which the murder had been committed and towards morning had been perceived by a market-woman not far from the spot where the body of the murdered child had been afterwards found. The woman asked her what she did there, but she looked very strangely and only returned a confused and unintelligible answer. She returned to the house about eight o'clock, and when one inquired where she had passed the night, she replied that she had been looking for the child and demanded earnestly if anything had been heard concerning him. When shown the body, she fell into violent hysterics and kept her bed for several days. The picture was then produced which the servant had found in her pocket; and when Elizabeth, in a faltering voice, proved that it was the same which, an hour before the child had been missed, she had placed round his neck, a murmur of horror and indignation filled the court.

Justine was called on for her defence. As the trial had proceeded, her countenance had altered. Surprise, horror, and misery were strongly expressed. Sometimes she struggled with her tears, but when she was desired to plead, she collected her powers and spoke in an audible although variable voice.

"God knows," she said, "how entirely I am innocent. But I do not pretend that my protestations should acquit me; I rest my innocence on a plain and simple explanation of the facts which have been adduced against me, and I hope the character I have always borne will incline my judges to a favourable interpretation where any circumstance appears doubtful or suspicious."

She then related that, by the permission of Elizabeth, she had passed the evening of the night on which the murder had been committed at the house of an aunt at Chene, a village situated at about a league from Geneva. On her return, at about nine o'clock, she met a man who asked her if she had seen anything of the child who was lost. She was alarmed by this account and passed several hours in looking for him, when the gates of Geneva were shut, and she was forced to remain several hours of the night in a barn belonging to a cottage, being unwilling to call up the inhabitants, to whom she was well known. Most of the night she spent here watching; towards morning she believed that she slept for a few minutes; some steps disturbed her, and she awoke. It was dawn, and she quitted her asylum, that she might again endeavour to find my brother. If she had gone near the spot where his body lay, it was without her knowledge. That she had been bewildered when questioned by the market-woman was not surprising, since she had passed a sleepless night and the fate of poor William was yet uncertain. Concerning the picture she could give no account.

"I know," continued the unhappy victim, "how heavily and fatally this one circumstance weighs against me, but I have no power of explaining it; and when I have expressed my utter ignorance, I am only left to conjecture concerning the probabilities by which it might have been placed in my pocket. But here also I am checked. I believe that I have no enemy on earth, and none surely would have been so wicked as to destroy me wantonly. Did the murderer place it there? I know of no opportunity afforded him for so doing; or, if I had, why should he have stolen the jewel, to part with it again so soon?

"I commit my cause to the justice of my judges, yet I see no room for hope. I beg permission to have a few witnesses examined concerning my character, and if their testimony shall not overweigh my supposed guilt, I must be condemned, although I would pledge my salvation on my innocence."

Several witnesses were called who had known her for many years, and they spoke well of her; but fear and hatred of the crime of which they supposed her guilty rendered them timorous and unwilling to come forward. Elizabeth saw even this last resource, her excellent dispositions and irreproachable conduct, about to fail the accused, when, although violently agitated, she desired permission to address the court.

"I am," said she, "the cousin of the unhappy child who was murdered, or rather his sister, for I was educated by and have lived with his parents ever since and even long before his birth. It may therefore be judged indecent in me to come forward on this occasion, but when I see a fellow creature about to perish through the cowardice of her pretended friends, I wish to be allowed to speak, that I may say what I know of her character. I am well acquainted with the accused. I have lived in the same house with her, at one time for five and at another for nearly two years. During all that period she appeared to me the most amiable and benevolent of human creatures. She nursed Madame Frankenstein, my aunt, in her last illness, with the greatest affection and care and afterwards attended her own mother during a tedious illness, in a manner that excited the admiration of all who knew her, after which she again lived in my uncle's house, where she was beloved by all the family. She was warmly attached to the child who is now dead and acted towards him like a most affectionate mother. For my own part, I do not hesitate to say that, notwithstanding all the evidence produced against her, I believe and rely on her perfect innocence. She had no temptation for such an action; as to the bauble on which the chief proof rests, if she had earnestly desired it, I should have willingly given it to her, so much do I esteem and value her."

A murmur of approbation followed Elizabeth's simple and powerful appeal, but it was excited by her generous interference, and not in favour of poor Justine, on whom the public indignation was turned with renewed violence, charging her with the blackest ingratitude. She herself wept as Elizabeth spoke, but she did not answer. My own agitation and anguish was extreme during the whole trial. I believed in her innocence; I knew it. Could the demon who had (I did not for a minute doubt) murdered my brother also in his hellish sport have betrayed the innocent to death and ignominy? I could not sustain the horror of my situation, and when I perceived that the popular voice and the countenances of the judges had already condemned my unhappy victim, I rushed out of the court in agony. The tortures of the accused did not equal mine; she was sustained by innocence, but the fangs of remorse tore my bosom and would not forgo their hold.

I passed a night of unmingled wretchedness. In the morning I went to the court; my lips and throat were parched. I dared not ask the fatal question, but I was known, and the officer guessed the cause of my visit. The ballots had been thrown; they were all black, and Justine was condemned.

I cannot pretend to describe what I then felt. I had before experienced sensations of horror, and I have endeavoured to bestow upon them adequate expressions, but words cannot convey an idea of the heart-sickening despair that I then endured. The person to whom I addressed myself added that Justine had already confessed her guilt. "That evidence," he observed, "was hardly required in so glaring a case, but I am glad of it, and, indeed, none of our judges like to condemn a criminal upon circumstantial evidence, be it ever so decisive."

This was strange and unexpected intelligence; what could it mean? Had my eyes deceived me? And was I really as mad as the whole world would believe me to be if I disclosed the object of my suspicions? I hastened to return home, and Elizabeth eagerly demanded the result.

"My cousin," replied I, "it is decided as you may have expected; all judges had rather that ten innocent should suffer than that one guilty should escape. But she has confessed."

This was a dire blow to poor Elizabeth, who had relied with firmness upon Justine's innocence. "Alas!" said she. "How shall I ever again believe in human goodness? Justine, whom I loved and esteemed as my sister, how could she put on those smiles of innocence only to betray? Her mild eyes seemed incapable of any severity or guile, and yet she has committed a murder."

Soon after we heard that the poor victim had expressed a desire to see my cousin. My father wished her not to go but said that he left it to her own judgment and feelings to decide. "Yes," said Elizabeth, "I will go, although she is guilty; and you, Victor, shall accompany me; I cannot go alone." The idea of this visit was torture to me, yet I could not refuse. We entered the gloomy prison chamber and beheld Justine sitting on some straw at the farther end; her hands were manacled, and her head rested on her knees. She rose on seeing us enter, and when we were left alone with her, she threw herself at the feet of Elizabeth, weeping bitterly. My cousin wept also.

"Oh, Justine!" said she. "Why did you rob me of my last consolation? I relied on your innocence, and although I was then very wretched, I was not so miserable as I am now."

"And do you also believe that I am so very, very wicked? Do you also join with my enemies to crush me, to condemn me as a murderer?" Her voice was suffocated with sobs.

"Rise, my poor girl," said Elizabeth; "why do you kneel, if you are innocent? I am not one of your enemies, I believed you guiltless, notwithstanding every evidence, until I heard that you had yourself declared your guilt. That report, you say, is false; and be assured, dear Justine, that nothing can shake my confidence in you for a moment, but your own confession."

"I did confess, but I confessed a lie. I confessed, that I might obtain absolution; but now that falsehood lies heavier at my heart than all my other sins. The God of heaven forgive me! Ever since I was condemned, my confessor has besieged me; he threatened and menaced, until I almost began to think that I was the monster that he said I was. He threatened excommunication and hell fire in my last moments if I continued obdurate.

Dear lady, I had none to support me; all looked on me as a wretch doomed to ignominy and perdition. What could I do? In an evil hour I subscribed to a lie; and now only am I truly miserable."

She paused, weeping, and then continued, "I thought with horror, my sweet lady, that you should believe your Justine, whom your blessed aunt had so highly honoured, and whom you loved, was a creature capable of a crime which none but the devil himself could have perpetrated. Dear William! Dearest blessed child! I soon shall see you again in heaven, where we shall all be happy; and that consoles me, going as I am to suffer ignominy and death."

"Oh, Justine! Forgive me for having for one moment distrusted you. Why did you confess? But do not mourn, dear girl. Do not fear. I will proclaim, I will prove your innocence. I will melt the stony hearts of your enemies by my tears and prayers. You shall not die! You, my playfellow, my companion, my sister, perish on the scaffold! No! No! I never could survive so horrible a misfortune."

Justine shook her head mournfully. "I do not fear to die," she said; "that pang is past. God raises my weakness and gives me courage to endure the worst. I leave a sad and bitter world; and if you remember me and think of me as of one unjustly condemned, I am resigned to the fate awaiting me. Learn from me, dear lady, to submit in patience to the will of heaven!"

During this conversation I had retired to a corner of the prison room, where I could conceal the horrid anguish that possessed me. Despair! Who dared talk of that? The poor victim, who on the morrow was to pass the awful boundary between life and death, felt not, as I did, such deep and bitter agony. I gnashed my teeth and ground them together, uttering a groan that came from my inmost soul. Justine started. When she saw who it was, she approached me and said, "Dear sir, you are very kind to visit me; you, I hope, do not believe that I am guilty?"

I could not answer. "No, Justine," said Elizabeth; "he is more convinced of your innocence than I was, for even when he heard that you had confessed, he did not credit it."

"I truly thank him. In these last moments I feel the sincerest gratitude towards those who think of me with kindness. How sweet is the affection of others to such a wretch as I am! It removes more than half my misfortune, and I feel as if I could die in peace now that my innocence is acknowledged by you, dear lady, and your cousin."

Thus the poor sufferer tried to comfort others and herself. She indeed gained the resignation she desired. But I, the true murderer, felt the never-dying worm alive in my bosom, which allowed of no hope or consolation. Elizabeth also wept and was unhappy, but hers also was the misery of innocence, which, like a cloud that passes over the fair moon, for a while hides but cannot tarnish its brightness. Anguish and despair had penetrated into the core of my heart; I bore a hell within me which nothing could extinguish. We stayed several hours with Justine, and it was with great difficulty that Elizabeth could tear herself away. "I wish," cried she, "that I were to die with you; I cannot live in this world of misery."

Justine assumed an air of cheerfulness, while she with difficulty repressed her bitter tears. She embraced Elizabeth and said in a voice of half-suppressed emotion, "Farewell, sweet lady, dearest Elizabeth, my beloved and only friend; may heaven, in its bounty, bless and preserve you; may this be the last misfortune that you will ever suffer! Live, and be happy, and make others so."

And on the morrow Justine died. Elizabeth's heart-rending eloquence failed to move the judges from their settled conviction in the criminality of the saintly sufferer. My passionate and indignant appeals were lost upon them. And when I received their cold answers and heard the harsh, unfeeling reasoning of these men, my purposed avowal died away on my lips. Thus I might proclaim myself a madman, but not revoke the sentence passed upon my wretched victim. She perished on the scaffold as a murderess!

From the tortures of my own heart, I turned to contemplate the deep and voiceless grief of my Elizabeth. This also was my doing! And my father's woe, and the desolation of that late so smiling home all was the work of my thrice-accursed hands! Ye weep, unhappy ones, but these are not your last tears! Again shall you raise the funeral wail, and the sound of your lamentations shall again and again be heard! Frankenstein, your son, your kinsman, your early, much-loved friend; he who would spend each vital drop of blood for your sakes, who has no thought nor sense of joy except as it is mirrored also in your dear countenances, who would fill the air with blessings and spend his life in serving you – he bids you weep, to shed countless tears; happy beyond his hopes, if thus inexorable fate be satisfied, and if the destruction pause before the peace of the grave have succeeded to your sad torments!

Thus spoke my prophetic soul, as, torn by remorse, horror, and despair, I beheld those I loved spend vain sorrow upon the graves of William and Justine, the first hapless victims to my unhallowed arts.

Chapter IX

NOTHING IS MORE PAINFUL to the human mind than, after the feelings have been worked up by a quick succession of events, the dead calmness of inaction and certainty which follows and deprives the soul both of hope and fear. Justine died, she rested, and I was alive. The blood flowed freely in my veins, but a weight of despair and remorse pressed on my heart which nothing could remove. Sleep fled from my eyes; I wandered like an evil spirit, for I had committed deeds of mischief beyond description horrible, and more, much more (I persuaded myself) was yet behind. Yet my heart overflowed with kindness and the love of virtue. I had begun life with benevolent intentions and thirsted for the moment when I should put them in practice and make myself useful to my fellow beings. Now all was blasted; instead of that serenity of conscience which allowed me to look back upon the past with self-satisfaction, and from thence to gather promise of new hopes, I was seized by remorse and the sense of guilt, which hurried me away to a hell of intense tortures such as no language can describe.

This state of mind preyed upon my health, which had perhaps never entirely recovered from the first shock it had sustained. I shunned the face of man; all sound of joy or complacency was torture to me; solitude was my only consolation – deep, dark, deathlike solitude.

My father observed with pain the alteration perceptible in my disposition and habits and endeavoured by arguments deduced from the feelings of his serene conscience and guiltless life to inspire me with fortitude and awaken in me the courage to dispel the dark cloud which brooded over me. "Do you think, Victor," said he, "that I do not suffer also? No one could love a child more than I loved your brother" – tears came into his eyes as he spoke – "but is it not a duty to the survivors that we should refrain from augmenting their unhappiness by an appearance of immoderate grief? It is also a duty owed to yourself, for excessive sorrow prevents improvement or enjoyment, or even the discharge of daily usefulness, without which no man is fit for society."

This advice, although good, was totally inapplicable to my case; I should have been the first to hide my grief and console my friends if remorse had not mingled its bitterness, and terror its alarm, with my other sensations. Now I could only answer my father with a look of despair and endeavour to hide myself from his view.

About this time we retired to our house at Belrive. This change was particularly agreeable to me. The shutting of the gates regularly at ten o'clock and the impossibility of remaining on the lake after that hour had rendered our residence within the walls of Geneva very irksome to me. I was now free. Often, after the rest of the family had retired for the night, I took the boat and passed many hours upon the water. Sometimes, with my sails set, I was carried by the wind; and sometimes, after rowing into the middle of the lake, I left the boat to pursue its own course and gave way to my own miserable reflections. I was often tempted, when all was at peace around me, and I the only unquiet thing that wandered restless in a scene so beautiful and heavenly – if I except some bat, or the frogs, whose harsh and interrupted croaking was heard only when I approached the shore – often, I say, I was tempted to plunge into the silent lake, that the waters might close over me and my calamities forever. But I was restrained, when I thought of the heroic and suffering Elizabeth, whom I tenderly loved, and whose existence was bound up in mine. I thought also of my father and surviving brother; should I by my base desertion leave them exposed and unprotected to the malice of the fiend whom I had let loose among them?

At these moments I wept bitterly and wished that peace would revisit my mind only that I might afford them consolation and happiness. But that could not be. Remorse extinguished every hope. I had been the author of unalterable evils, and I lived in daily fear lest the monster whom I had created should perpetrate some new wickedness. I had an obscure feeling that all was not over and that he would still commit some signal crime, which by its enormity should almost efface the recollection of the past. There was always scope for fear so long as anything I loved remained behind. My abhorrence of this fiend cannot be conceived. When I thought of him I gnashed my teeth, my eyes became inflamed, and I ardently wished to extinguish that life which I had so thoughtlessly bestowed. When I reflected on his crimes and malice, my hatred and revenge burst all bounds of moderation. I would have made a pilgrimage to the highest peak of the Andes, could I when there have precipitated him to their base. I wished to see him again, that I might wreak the utmost extent of abhorrence on his head and avenge the deaths of William and Justine. Our house was the house of mourning. My father's health was deeply shaken by the horror of the recent events. Elizabeth was sad and desponding; she no longer took delight in her ordinary occupations; all pleasure seemed to her sacrilege toward the dead; eternal woe and tears she then thought was the just tribute she should pay to innocence so blasted and destroyed. She was no longer that happy creature who in earlier youth wandered with me on the banks of the lake and talked with ecstasy of our future prospects. The first of those sorrows which are sent to wean us from the earth had visited her, and its dimming influence quenched her dearest smiles.

"When I reflect, my dear cousin," said she, "on the miserable death of Justine Moritz, I no longer see the world and its works as they before appeared to me. Before,

I looked upon the accounts of vice and injustice that I read in books or heard from others as tales of ancient days or imaginary evils; at least they were remote and more familiar to reason than to the imagination; but now misery has come home, and men appear to me as monsters thirsting for each other's blood. Yet I am certainly unjust. Everybody believed that poor girl to be guilty; and if she could have committed the crime for which she suffered, assuredly she would have been the most depraved of human creatures. For the sake of a few jewels, to have murdered the son of her benefactor and friend, a child whom she had nursed from its birth, and appeared to love as if it had been her own! I could not consent to the death of any human being, but certainly I should have thought such a creature unfit to remain in the society of men. But she was innocent. I know, I feel she was innocent; you are of the same opinion, and that confirms me. Alas! Victor, when falsehood can look so like the truth, who can assure themselves of certain happiness? I feel as if I were walking on the edge of a precipice, towards which thousands are crowding and endeavouring to plunge me into the abyss. William and Justine were assassinated, and the murderer escapes; he walks about the world free, and perhaps respected. But even if I were condemned to suffer on the scaffold for the same crimes, I would not change places with such a wretch."

I listened to this discourse with the extremest agony. I, not in deed, but in effect, was the true murderer. Elizabeth read my anguish in my countenance, and kindly taking my hand, said, "My dearest friend, you must calm yourself. These events have affected me, God knows how deeply; but I am not so wretched as you are. There is an expression of despair, and sometimes of revenge, in your countenance that makes me tremble. Dear Victor, banish these dark passions. Remember the friends around you, who centre all their hopes in you. Have we lost the power of rendering you happy? Ah! While we love, while we are true to each other, here in this land of peace and beauty, your native country, we may reap every tranquil blessing – what can disturb our peace?"

And could not such words from her whom I fondly prized before every other gift of fortune suffice to chase away the fiend that lurked in my heart? Even as she spoke I drew near to her, as if in terror, lest at that very moment the destroyer had been near to rob me of her.

Thus not the tenderness of friendship, nor the beauty of earth, nor of heaven, could redeem my soul from woe; the very accents of love were ineffectual. I was encompassed by a cloud which no beneficial influence could penetrate. The wounded deer dragging its fainting limbs to some untrodden brake, there to gaze upon the arrow which had pierced it, and to die, was but a type of me.

Sometimes I could cope with the sullen despair that overwhelmed me, but sometimes the whirlwind passions of my soul drove me to seek, by bodily exercise and by change of place, some relief from my intolerable sensations. It was during an access of this kind that I suddenly left my home, and bending my steps towards the near Alpine valleys, sought in the magnificence, the eternity of such scenes, to forget myself and my ephemeral, because human, sorrows. My wanderings were directed towards the valley of Chamounix. I had visited it frequently during my boyhood. Six years had passed since then: I was a wreck, but nought had changed in those savage and enduring scenes.

I performed the first part of my journey on horseback. I afterwards hired a mule, as the more sure-footed and least liable to receive injury on these rugged roads. The weather was fine; it was about the middle of the month of August, nearly two months after the death of Justine, that miserable epoch from which I dated all my woe. The weight upon my spirit was sensibly lightened as I plunged yet deeper in the ravine of Arve. The immense mountains and precipices that overhung me on every side, the sound of the river raging among the rocks, and the dashing of the waterfalls around spoke of a power mighty as Omnipotence – and I ceased to fear or to bend before any being less almighty than that which had created and ruled the elements, here displayed in their most terrific guise. Still, as I ascended higher, the valley assumed a more magnificent and astonishing character. Ruined castles hanging on the precipices of piny mountains, the impetuous Arve, and cottages every here and there peeping forth from among the trees formed a scene of singular beauty. But it was augmented and rendered sublime by the mighty Alps, whose white and shining pyramids and domes towered above all, as belonging to another earth, the habitations of another race of beings.

I passed the bridge of Pelissier, where the ravine, which the river forms, opened before me, and I began to ascend the mountain that overhangs it. Soon after, I entered the valley of Chamounix. This valley is more wonderful and sublime, but not so beautiful and picturesque as that of Servox, through which I had just passed. The high and snowy mountains were its immediate boundaries, but I saw no more ruined castles and fertile fields. Immense glaciers approached the road; I heard the rumbling thunder of the falling avalanche and marked the smoke of its passage. Mont Blanc, the supreme and magnificent Mont Blanc, raised itself from the surrounding aiguilles, and its tremendous dome overlooked the valley.

A tingling long-lost sense of pleasure often came across me during this journey. Some turn in the road, some new object suddenly perceived and recognized, reminded me of days gone by, and were associated with the lighthearted gaiety of boyhood. The very winds whispered in soothing accents, and maternal Nature bade me weep no more. Then again the kindly influence ceased to act – I found myself fettered again to grief and indulging in all the misery of reflection. Then I spurred on my animal, striving so to forget the world, my fears, and more than all, myself – or, in a more desperate fashion, I alighted and threw myself on the grass, weighed down by horror and despair.

At length I arrived at the village of Chamounix. Exhaustion succeeded to the extreme fatigue both of body and of mind which I had endured. For a short space of time I remained at the window watching the pallid lightnings that played above Mont Blanc and listening to the rushing of the Arve, which pursued its noisy way beneath. The same lulling sounds acted as a lullaby to my too keen sensations; when I placed my head upon my pillow, sleep crept over me; I felt it as it came and blessed the giver of oblivion.

Chapter X

I SPENT the following day roaming through the valley. I stood beside the sources of the Arveiron, which take their rise in a glacier, that with slow pace is advancing down from the summit of the hills to barricade the valley. The abrupt sides of vast mountains were before me; the icy wall of the glacier overhung me; a few shattered pines were scattered around; and the solemn silence of this glorious presence-chamber of imperial nature was broken only by the brawling waves or the fall of some vast fragment, the thunder sound of the avalanche or the cracking, reverberated along the mountains, of the accumulated ice, which, through the silent working of immutable laws, was ever and anon rent and torn, as if it had been but a plaything in their hands. These sublime and magnificent scenes afforded me the greatest consolation that I was capable of receiving. They elevated me from all littleness of feeling, and although they did not remove my grief, they subdued and tranquillized it. In some degree, also, they diverted my mind from the thoughts over which it had brooded for the last month. I retired to rest at night; my slumbers, as it were, waited on and ministered to by the assemblance of grand shapes which I had contemplated during the day. They congregated round me; the unstained snowy mountaintop, the glittering pinnacle, the pine woods, and ragged bare ravine, the eagle, soaring amidst the clouds – they all gathered round me and bade me be at peace.

Where had they fled when the next morning I awoke? All of soul-inspiriting fled with sleep, and dark melancholy clouded every thought. The rain was pouring in torrents, and thick mists hid the summits of the mountains, so that I even saw not the faces of those mighty friends. Still I would penetrate their misty veil and seek them in their cloudy retreats. What were rain and storm to me? My mule was brought to the door, and I resolved to ascend to the summit of Montanvert. I remembered the effect that the view of the tremendous and ever-moving glacier had produced upon my mind when I first saw it. It had then filled me with a sublime ecstasy that gave wings to the soul and allowed it to soar from the obscure world to light and joy. The sight of the awful and majestic in nature had indeed always the effect of solemnizing my mind and causing me to forget the passing cares of life. I determined to go without a guide, for I was well acquainted with the path, and the presence of another would destroy the solitary grandeur of the scene.

The ascent is precipitous, but the path is cut into continual and short windings, which enable you to surmount the perpendicularity of the mountain. It is a scene terrifically desolate. In a thousand spots the traces of the winter avalanche may be perceived, where trees lie broken and strewed on the ground, some entirely destroyed, others bent, leaning upon the jutting rocks of the mountain or transversely upon other trees. The path, as you ascend higher, is intersected by ravines of snow, down which stones continually roll from above; one of them is particularly dangerous, as the slightest sound, such as even speaking in a loud voice, produces a concussion of air sufficient to draw destruction upon the head of the speaker. The pines are not tall or luxuriant, but they are sombre and add an air of severity to the scene. I looked on the valley beneath; vast mists were rising from the rivers which ran through it and curling in thick wreaths around the opposite mountains, whose summits were hid in the uniform clouds, while rain poured from the dark sky and added to the melancholy impression I received from the objects around me. Alas! Why does man boast of sensibilities superior to those apparent in the brute; it only renders them more necessary beings. If our impulses were confined to hunger, thirst, and desire, we might be nearly free; but now we are moved by every wind that blows and a chance word or scene that that word may convey to us.

> We rest; a dream has power to poison sleep.
> We rise; one wand'ring thought pollutes the day.
> We feel, conceive, or reason; laugh or weep,
> Embrace fond woe, or cast our cares away;
> It is the same: for, be it joy or sorrow,
> The path of its departure still is free.
> Man's yesterday may ne'er be like his morrow;
> Nought may endure but mutability!
> Percy Bysshe Shelley, 'Mutability'

It was nearly noon when I arrived at the top of the ascent. For some time I sat upon the rock that overlooks the sea of ice. A mist covered both that and the surrounding mountains. Presently a breeze dissipated the cloud, and I descended upon the glacier. The surface is very uneven, rising like the waves of a troubled sea, descending low, and interspersed by rifts that sink deep. The field of ice is almost a league in width, but I spent nearly two hours in crossing it. The opposite mountain is a bare perpendicular rock. From the side where I now stood Montanvert was exactly opposite, at the distance of a league; and above it rose Mont Blanc, in awful majesty. I remained in a recess of the rock, gazing on this wonderful and stupendous scene. The sea, or rather the vast river of ice, wound among its dependent mountains, whose aerial summits hung over its recesses. Their icy and glittering peaks shone in the sunlight over the clouds. My heart, which was before sorrowful, now swelled with something like joy; I exclaimed, "Wandering spirits, if indeed ye wander, and do not rest in your narrow beds, allow me this faint happiness, or take me, as your companion, away from the joys of life."

As I said this I suddenly beheld the figure of a man, at some distance, advancing towards me with superhuman speed. He bounded over the crevices in the ice, among which I had walked with caution; his stature, also, as he approached, seemed to exceed that of man. I was troubled; a mist came over my eyes, and I felt a faintness seize me, but I was quickly restored by the cold gale of the mountains. I perceived, as the shape came nearer (sight tremendous and abhorred!) that it was the wretch whom I had created. I trembled with rage and horror, resolving to wait his approach and then close with him in mortal combat. He approached; his countenance bespoke bitter anguish, combined with disdain and malignity, while its unearthly ugliness rendered it almost too horrible for human eyes. But I scarcely observed this; rage and hatred had at first deprived me of utterance, and I recovered only to overwhelm him with words expressive of furious detestation and contempt.

"Devil," I exclaimed, "do you dare approach me? And do not you fear the fierce vengeance of my arm wreaked on your miserable head? Begone, vile insect! Or rather, stay, that I may trample you to dust! And, oh! That I could, with the extinction of your miserable existence, restore those victims whom you have so diabolically murdered!"

"I expected this reception," said the daemon. "All men hate the wretched; how, then, must I be hated, who am miserable beyond all living things! Yet you, my creator, detest and spurn me, thy creature, to whom thou art bound by ties only dissoluble by the annihilation of one of us. You purpose to kill me. How dare you sport thus with life? Do your duty towards me, and I will do mine towards you and the rest of mankind. If you will comply with my conditions, I will leave them and you at peace; but if you refuse, I will glut the maw of death, until it be satiated with the blood of your remaining friends."

"Abhorred monster! Fiend that thou art! The tortures of hell are too mild a vengeance for thy crimes. Wretched devil! You reproach me with your creation, come on, then, that I may extinguish the spark which I so negligently bestowed."

My rage was without bounds; I sprang on him, impelled by all the feelings which can arm one being against the existence of another.

He easily eluded me and said:

"Be calm! I entreat you to hear me before you give vent to your hatred on my devoted head. Have I not suffered enough, that you seek to increase my misery? Life, although it may only be an accumulation of anguish, is dear to me, and I will defend it. Remember, thou hast made me more powerful than thyself; my height is superior to thine, my joints more supple. But I will not be tempted to set myself in opposition to thee. I am thy creature, and I will be even mild and docile to my natural lord and king if thou wilt also perform thy part, the which thou owest me. Oh, Frankenstein, be not equitable to every other and trample upon me alone, to whom thy justice, and even thy clemency and affection, is most due. Remember that I am thy creature; I ought to be thy Adam, but I am rather the fallen angel, whom thou drivest from joy for no misdeed. Everywhere I see bliss, from which I alone am irrevocably excluded. I was benevolent and good; misery made me a fiend. Make me happy, and I shall again be virtuous."

"Begone! I will not hear you. There can be no community between you and me; we are enemies. Begone, or let us try our strength in a fight, in which one must fall."

"How can I move thee? Will no entreaties cause thee to turn a favourable eye upon thy creature, who implores thy goodness and compassion? Believe me, Frankenstein, I was benevolent; my soul glowed with love and humanity; but am I not alone, miserably alone? You, my creator, abhor me; what hope can I gather from your fellow creatures, who owe me nothing? They spurn and hate me. The desert mountains and dreary glaciers are my refuge. I have wandered here many days; the caves of ice, which I only do not fear, are a dwelling to me, and the only one which man does not grudge. These bleak skies I hail, for they are kinder to me than your fellow beings. If the multitude of mankind knew of my existence, they would do as you do, and arm themselves for my destruction. Shall I not then hate them who abhor me? I will keep no terms with my enemies. I am miserable, and they shall share my wretchedness. Yet it is in your power to recompense me, and deliver them from an evil which it only remains for you to make so great, that not only you and your family, but thousands of others, shall be swallowed up in the whirlwinds of its rage. Let your compassion be moved, and do not disdain me. Listen to my tale; when you have heard that, abandon or commiserate me, as you shall judge that I deserve. But hear me. The guilty are allowed, by human laws, bloody as they are, to speak in their own defence before they are condemned. Listen to me, Frankenstein. You accuse me of murder, and yet you would, with a satisfied conscience, destroy your own creature. Oh, praise the eternal justice of man! Yet I ask you not to spare me; listen to me, and then, if you can, and if you will, destroy the work of your hands."

"Why do you call to my remembrance," I rejoined, "circumstances of which I shudder to reflect, that I have been the miserable origin and author? Cursed be the day, abhorred devil, in which you first saw light! Cursed (although I curse myself) be the hands that formed you! You have made me wretched beyond expression. You have left me no power to consider whether I am just to you or not. Begone! Relieve me from the sight of your detested form."

"Thus I relieve thee, my creator," he said, and placed his hated hands before my eyes, which I flung from me with violence; "thus I take from thee a sight which you abhor. Still thou canst listen to me and grant me thy compassion. By the virtues that I once possessed, I demand this from you. Hear my tale; it is long and strange, and the temperature of this place is not fitting to your fine sensations; come to the hut upon the mountain. The sun is yet high in the heavens; before it descends to hide itself behind your snowy precipices and illuminate another world, you will have heard my story and can decide. On you it rests, whether I quit forever the neighbourhood of man and lead a harmless life, or become the scourge of your fellow creatures and the author of your own speedy ruin."

As he said this he led the way across the ice; I followed. My heart was full, and I did not answer him, but as I proceeded, I weighed the various arguments that he had used and determined at least to listen to his tale. I was partly urged by curiosity, and compassion confirmed my resolution. I had hitherto supposed him to be the murderer of my brother, and I eagerly sought a confirmation or denial of this opinion. For the first time, also, I felt what the duties of a creator towards his creature were, and that I ought to render him happy before I complained of his wickedness. These motives urged me to comply with his demand. We crossed the ice, therefore, and ascended the opposite rock. The air was cold, and the rain again began to descend; we entered the hut, the fiend with an air of exultation, I with a heavy heart and depressed spirits. But I consented to listen, and seating myself by the fire which my odious companion had lighted, he thus began his tale.

Chapter XI

"IT IS WITH considerable difficulty that I remember the original era of my being; all the events of that period appear confused and indistinct. A strange multiplicity of sensations seized me, and I saw, felt, heard, and smelt at the same time; and it was, indeed, a long time before I learned to distinguish between the operations of my various senses. By degrees, I remember, a stronger light pressed upon my nerves, so that I was obliged to shut my eyes. Darkness then came over me and troubled me, but hardly had I felt this when, by opening my eyes, as I now suppose, the light poured in upon me again. I walked and, I believe, descended, but I presently found a great alteration in my sensations. Before, dark and opaque bodies had surrounded me, impervious to my touch or sight; but I now found that I could wander on at liberty, with no obstacles which I could not either surmount or avoid. The light became more and more oppressive to me, and the heat wearying me as I walked, I sought a place where I could receive shade. This was the forest near Ingolstadt; and here I lay by the side of a brook resting from my fatigue, until I felt tormented by hunger and thirst. This roused me from my nearly dormant state, and I ate some berries which I found hanging on the trees or lying on the ground. I slaked my thirst at the brook, and then lying down, was overcome by sleep.

"It was dark when I awoke; I felt cold also, and half frightened, as it were, instinctively, finding myself so desolate. Before I had quitted your apartment, on a sensation of cold, I had covered myself with some clothes, but these were insufficient to secure me from the dews of night. I was a poor, helpless, miserable wretch; I knew, and could distinguish, nothing; but feeling pain invade me on all sides, I sat down and wept.

"Soon a gentle light stole over the heavens and gave me a sensation of pleasure. I started up and beheld a radiant form [the moon] rise from among the trees. I gazed with a kind of wonder. It moved slowly, but it enlightened my path, and I again went out in search of berries. I was still cold when under one of the trees I found a huge cloak, with which I covered myself, and sat down upon the ground. No distinct ideas occupied my mind; all was confused. I felt light, and hunger, and thirst, and darkness; innumerable sounds rang in my ears, and on all sides various scents saluted me; the only object that I could distinguish was the bright moon, and I fixed my eyes on that with pleasure.

"Several changes of day and night passed, and the orb of night had greatly lessened, when I began to distinguish my sensations from each other. I gradually saw plainly the clear stream that supplied me with drink and the trees that shaded me with their foliage. I was delighted when I first discovered that a pleasant sound, which often saluted my ears, proceeded from the throats of the little winged animals who had often intercepted the light from my eyes. I began also to observe, with greater accuracy, the forms that surrounded me and to perceive the boundaries of the radiant roof of light which canopied me. Sometimes I tried to imitate the pleasant songs of the birds but was unable. Sometimes I wished to express my sensations in my own mode, but the uncouth and inarticulate sounds which broke from me frightened me into silence again.

"The moon had disappeared from the night, and again, with a lessened form, showed itself, while I still remained in the forest. My sensations had by this time become distinct, and my mind received every day additional ideas. My eyes became accustomed to the light and to perceive objects in their right forms; I distinguished the insect from the herb, and by degrees, one herb from another. I found that the sparrow uttered none but harsh notes, whilst those of the blackbird and thrush were sweet and enticing.

"One day, when I was oppressed by cold, I found a fire which had been left by some wandering beggars, and was overcome with delight at the warmth I experienced from it. In my joy I thrust my hand into the live embers, but quickly drew it out again with a cry of pain. How strange, I thought, that the same cause should produce such opposite effects! I examined the materials of the fire, and to my joy found it to be composed of wood. I quickly collected some branches, but they were wet and would not burn. I was pained at this and sat still watching the operation of the fire. The wet wood which I had placed near the heat dried and itself became inflamed. I reflected on this, and by touching the various branches, I discovered the cause and busied myself in collecting a great quantity of wood, that I might dry it and have a plentiful supply of fire. When night came on and brought sleep with it, I was in the greatest fear lest my fire should be extinguished. I covered it carefully with dry wood and leaves and placed wet branches upon it; and then, spreading my cloak, I lay on the ground and sank into sleep.

"It was morning when I awoke, and my first care was to visit the fire. I uncovered it, and a gentle breeze quickly fanned it into a flame. I observed this also and contrived a fan of branches, which roused the embers when they were nearly extinguished. When night came again I found, with pleasure, that the fire gave light as well as heat and that the discovery of this element was useful to me in my food, for I found some of the offals that the travellers had left had been roasted, and tasted much more savoury than the berries I gathered from the trees. I tried, therefore, to dress my food in the same manner, placing it on the live embers. I found that the berries were spoiled by this operation, and the nuts and roots much improved.

"Food, however, became scarce, and I often spent the whole day searching in vain for a few acorns to assuage the pangs of hunger. When I found this, I resolved to quit the place that I had hitherto inhabited, to seek for one where the few wants I experienced would be more easily satisfied. In this emigration I exceedingly lamented the loss of the fire which I had obtained through accident and knew not how to reproduce it. I gave several hours to the serious consideration of this difficulty, but

I was obliged to relinquish all attempt to supply it, and wrapping myself up in my cloak, I struck across the wood towards the setting sun. I passed three days in these rambles and at length discovered the open country. A great fall of snow had taken place the night before, and the fields were of one uniform white; the appearance was disconsolate, and I found my feet chilled by the cold damp substance that covered the ground.

"It was about seven in the morning, and I longed to obtain food and shelter; at length I perceived a small hut, on a rising ground, which had doubtless been built for the convenience of some shepherd. This was a new sight to me, and I examined the structure with great curiosity. Finding the door open, I entered. An old man sat in it, near a fire, over which he was preparing his breakfast. He turned on hearing a noise, and perceiving me, shrieked loudly, and quitting the hut, ran across the fields with a speed of which his debilitated form hardly appeared capable. His appearance, different from any I had ever before seen, and his flight somewhat surprised me. But I was enchanted by the appearance of the hut; here the snow and rain could not penetrate; the ground was dry; and it presented to me then as exquisite and divine a retreat as Pandemonium appeared to the demons of hell after their sufferings in the lake of fire. I greedily devoured the remnants of the shepherd's breakfast, which consisted of bread, cheese, milk, and wine; the latter, however, I did not like. Then, overcome by fatigue, I lay down among some straw and fell asleep.

"It was noon when I awoke, and allured by the warmth of the sun, which shone brightly on the white ground, I determined to recommence my travels; and, depositing the remains of the peasant's breakfast in a wallet I found, I proceeded across the fields for several hours, until at sunset I arrived at a village. How miraculous did this appear! The huts, the neater cottages, and stately houses engaged my admiration by turns. The vegetables in the gardens, the milk and cheese that I saw placed at the windows of some of the cottages, allured my appetite. One of the best of these I entered, but I had hardly placed my foot within the door before the children shrieked, and one of the women fainted. The whole village was roused; some fled, some attacked me, until, grievously bruised by stones and many other kinds of missile weapons, I escaped to the open country and fearfully took refuge in a low hovel, quite bare, and making a wretched appearance after the palaces I had beheld in the village. This hovel however, joined a cottage of a neat and pleasant appearance, but after my late dearly bought experience, I dared not enter it. My place of refuge was constructed of wood, but so low that I could with difficulty sit upright in it. No wood, however, was placed on the earth, which formed the floor, but it was dry; and although the wind entered it by innumerable chinks, I found it an agreeable asylum from the snow and rain.

"Here, then, I retreated and lay down happy to have found a shelter, however miserable, from the inclemency of the season, and still more from the barbarity of man. As soon as morning dawned I crept from my kennel, that I might view the adjacent cottage and discover if I could remain in the habitation I had found. It was situated against the back of the cottage and surrounded on the sides which were exposed by a pig sty and a clear pool of water. One part was open, and by that I had crept in; but now I covered every crevice by which I might be perceived with stones and wood, yet in such a manner that I might move them on occasion to pass out; all the light I enjoyed came through the sty, and that was sufficient for me.

"Having thus arranged my dwelling and carpeted it with clean straw, I retired, for I saw the figure of a man at a distance, and I remembered too well my treatment the night before to trust myself in his power. I had first, however, provided for my sustenance for that day by a loaf of coarse bread, which I purloined, and a cup with which I could drink more conveniently than from my hand of the pure water which flowed by my retreat. The floor was a little raised, so that it was kept perfectly dry, and by its vicinity to the chimney of the cottage it was tolerably warm.

"Being thus provided, I resolved to reside in this hovel until something should occur which might alter my determination. It was indeed a paradise compared to the bleak forest, my former residence, the rain-dropping branches, and dank earth. I ate my breakfast with pleasure and was about to remove a plank to procure myself a little water when I heard a step, and looking through a small chink, I beheld a young creature, with a pail on her head, passing before my hovel. The girl was young and of gentle demeanour, unlike what I have since found cottagers and farmhouse servants to be. Yet she was meanly dressed, a coarse blue petticoat and a linen jacket being her only garb; her fair hair was plaited but not adorned: she looked patient yet sad. I lost sight of her, and in about a quarter of an hour she returned bearing the pail, which was now partly filled with milk. As she walked along, seemingly incommoded by the burden, a young man met her, whose countenance expressed a deeper despondence. Uttering a few sounds with an air of melancholy, he took the pail from her head and bore it to the cottage himself. She followed, and they disappeared. Presently I saw the young man again, with some tools in his hand, cross the field behind the cottage; and the girl was also busied, sometimes in the house and sometimes in the yard. "On examining my dwelling, I found that one of the windows of the cottage had formerly occupied a part of it, but the panes had been filled up with wood. In one of these was a small and almost imperceptible chink through which the eye could just penetrate. Through this crevice a small room was visible, whitewashed and clean but very bare of furniture. In one corner, near a small fire, sat an old man, leaning his head on his hands in a disconsolate attitude. The young girl was occupied in arranging the cottage; but presently she took something out of a drawer, which employed her hands, and she sat down beside the old man, who, taking up an instrument, began to play and to produce sounds sweeter than the voice of the thrush or the nightingale. It was a lovely sight, even to me, poor wretch who had never beheld aught beautiful before. The silver hair and benevolent countenance of the aged cottager won my reverence, while the gentle manners of the girl enticed my love. He played a sweet mournful air which I perceived drew tears from the eyes of his amiable companion, of which the old man took no notice, until she sobbed audibly; he then pronounced a few sounds, and the fair creature, leaving her work, knelt at his feet. He raised her and smiled with such kindness and affection that I felt sensations of a peculiar and overpowering nature; they were a mixture of pain and pleasure, such as I had never before experienced, either from hunger or cold, warmth or food; and I withdrew from the window, unable to bear these emotions.

"Soon after this the young man returned, bearing on his shoulders a load of wood. The girl met him at the door, helped to relieve him of his burden, and taking some of the fuel into the cottage, placed it on the fire; then she and the youth went apart into a nook of the cottage, and he showed her a large loaf and a piece of cheese. She seemed pleased and went into the garden for some roots and plants, which she placed in water, and then upon the fire. She afterwards continued her work, whilst the young man went into the garden and appeared busily employed in digging and pulling up roots. After he had been employed thus about an hour, the young woman joined him and they entered the cottage together.

"The old man had, in the meantime, been pensive, but on the appearance of his companions he assumed a more cheerful air, and they sat down to eat. The meal was quickly dispatched. The young woman was again occupied in arranging the cottage, the old man walked before the cottage in the sun for a few minutes, leaning on the arm of the youth. Nothing could exceed in beauty the contrast between these two excellent creatures. One was old, with silver hairs and a countenance beaming with benevolence and love; the younger was slight and graceful in his figure, and his features were moulded with the finest symmetry, yet his eyes and attitude expressed the utmost sadness and despondency. The old man returned to the cottage, and the youth, with tools different from those he had used in the morning, directed his steps across the fields.

"Night quickly shut in, but to my extreme wonder, I found that the cottagers had a means of prolonging light by the use of tapers, and was delighted to find that the setting of the sun did not put an end to the pleasure I experienced in watching my human neighbours. In the evening the young girl and her companion were employed in various occupations which I did not understand; and the old man again took up the instrument which produced the divine sounds that had enchanted me in the morning. So soon as he had finished, the youth began, not to play, but to utter sounds that were monotonous, and neither resembling the harmony of the old man's instrument nor the songs of the birds; I since found that he read aloud, but at that time I knew nothing of the science of words or letters.

"The family, after having been thus occupied for a short time, extinguished their lights and retired, as I conjectured, to rest."

Chapter XII

"I LAY ON MY STRAW, but I could not sleep. I thought of the occurrences of the day. What chiefly struck me was the gentle manners of these people, and I longed to join them, but dared not. I remembered too well the treatment I had suffered the night before from the barbarous villagers, and resolved, whatever course of conduct I might hereafter think it right to pursue, that for the present I would remain quietly in my hovel, watching and endeavouring to discover the motives which influenced their actions.

"The cottagers arose the next morning before the sun. The young woman arranged the cottage and prepared the food, and the youth departed after the first meal.

"This day was passed in the same routine as that which preceded it. The young man was constantly employed out of doors, and the girl in various laborious occupations within. The old man, whom I soon perceived to be blind, employed his leisure hours on his instrument or in contemplation. Nothing could exceed the love and respect which the younger cottagers exhibited towards their venerable companion. They performed towards him every little office of affection and duty with gentleness, and he rewarded them by his benevolent smiles.

"They were not entirely happy. The young man and his companion often went apart and appeared to weep. I saw no cause for their unhappiness, but I was deeply affected by it. If such lovely creatures were miserable, it was less strange that I, an imperfect and solitary being, should be wretched. Yet why were these gentle beings unhappy? They possessed a delightful house (for such it was in my eyes) and every luxury; they had a fire to warm them when chill and delicious viands when hungry; they were dressed in excellent clothes; and, still more, they enjoyed one another's company and speech, interchanging each day looks of affection and kindness. What did their tears imply? Did they really express pain? I was at first unable to solve these questions, but perpetual attention and time explained to me many appearances which were at first enigmatic.

"A considerable period elapsed before I discovered one of the causes of the uneasiness of this amiable family: it was poverty, and they suffered that evil in a very distressing degree. Their nourishment consisted entirely of the vegetables of their garden and the milk of one cow, which gave very little during the winter, when its masters could scarcely procure food to support it. They often, I believe, suffered the pangs of hunger very poignantly, especially the two younger cottagers, for several times they placed food before the old man when they reserved none for themselves.

"This trait of kindness moved me sensibly. I had been accustomed, during the night, to steal a part of their store for my own consumption, but when I found that in doing this I inflicted pain on the cottagers, I abstained and satisfied myself with berries, nuts, and roots which I gathered from a neighbouring wood.

"I discovered also another means through which I was enabled to assist their labours. I found that the youth spent a great part of each day in collecting wood for the family fire, and during the night I often took his tools, the use of which I quickly discovered, and brought home firing sufficient for the consumption of several days.

"I remember, the first time that I did this, the young woman, when she opened the door in the morning, appeared greatly astonished on seeing a great pile of wood on the outside. She uttered some words in a loud voice, and the youth joined her, who also expressed surprise. I observed, with pleasure, that he did not go to the forest that day, but spent it in repairing the cottage and cultivating the garden.

"By degrees I made a discovery of still greater moment. I found that these people possessed a method of communicating their experience and feelings to one another by articulate sounds. I perceived that the words they spoke sometimes produced pleasure or pain, smiles or sadness, in the minds and countenances of the hearers. This was indeed a godlike science, and I ardently desired to become acquainted with it. But I was baffled in every attempt I made for this purpose. Their pronunciation was quick, and the words they uttered, not having any apparent connection with visible objects, I was unable to discover any clue by which I could unravel the mystery of their reference. By great application, however, and after having remained during the space of several revolutions of the moon in my hovel, I discovered the names that were given to some of the most familiar objects of discourse; I learned and applied the words, 'fire,' 'milk,' 'bread,' and 'wood.' I learned also the names of the cottagers themselves. The youth and his companion had each of them several names, but the old man had only one, which was 'father.' The girl was called 'sister' or 'Agatha,' and the youth 'Felix,' 'brother,' or 'son.' I cannot describe the delight I felt when I learned the ideas appropriated to each of these sounds and was able to pronounce them. I distinguished several other words without being able as yet to understand or apply them, such as 'good,' 'dearest,' 'unhappy.'

"I spent the winter in this manner. The gentle manners and beauty of the cottagers greatly endeared them to me; when they were unhappy, I felt depressed; when they rejoiced, I sympathized in their joys. I saw few human beings besides them, and if any other happened to enter the cottage, their harsh manners and rude gait only enhanced to me the superior accomplishments of my friends. The old man, I could perceive, often endeavoured to encourage his children, as sometimes I found that he called them, to cast off their melancholy. He would talk in a cheerful accent, with an expression of goodness that bestowed pleasure even upon me. Agatha listened with respect, her eyes sometimes filled with tears, which she endeavoured to wipe away unperceived; but I generally found that her countenance and tone were more cheerful after having listened to the exhortations of her father. It was not thus with Felix. He was always the saddest of the group, and even to my unpractised senses, he appeared to have suffered more deeply than his friends. But if his countenance was more sorrowful, his voice was more cheerful than that of his sister, especially when he addressed the old man.

"I could mention innumerable instances which, although slight, marked the dispositions of these amiable cottagers. In the midst of poverty and want, Felix carried with pleasure to his sister the first little white flower that peeped out from beneath the snowy ground. Early in the morning, before she had risen, he cleared away the snow that obstructed her path to the milk-house, drew water from the well, and brought the wood from the outhouse, where, to his perpetual astonishment, he found his store always replenished by an invisible hand. In the day, I believe, he worked sometimes for a neighbouring farmer, because he often went forth and did not return until dinner, yet brought no wood with him. At other times he worked in the garden, but as there was little to do in the frosty season, he read to the old man and Agatha.

"This reading had puzzled me extremely at first, but by degrees I discovered that he uttered many of the same sounds when he read as when he talked. I conjectured, therefore, that he found on the paper signs for speech which he understood, and I ardently longed to comprehend these also; but how was that possible when I did not even understand the sounds for which they stood as signs? I improved, however, sensibly in this science, but not sufficiently to follow up any kind of conversation, although I applied my whole mind to the endeavour, for I easily perceived that, although I eagerly longed to discover myself to the cottagers, I ought not to make the attempt until I had first become master of their language, which knowledge might enable me to make them overlook the deformity of my figure, for with this also the contrast perpetually presented to my eyes had made me acquainted.

"I had admired the perfect forms of my cottagers – their grace, beauty, and delicate complexions; but how was I terrified when I viewed myself in a transparent pool! At first I started back, unable to believe that it was indeed I who was reflected in the mirror; and when I became fully convinced that I was in reality the monster that I am, I was filled with the bitterest sensations of despondence and mortification. Alas! I did not yet entirely know the fatal effects of this miserable deformity.

"As the sun became warmer and the light of day longer, the snow vanished, and I beheld the bare trees and the black earth. From this time Felix was more employed, and the heart-moving indications of impending famine disappeared. Their food, as I afterwards found, was coarse, but it was wholesome; and they procured a sufficiency of it. Several new kinds of plants sprang up in the garden, which they dressed; and these signs of comfort increased daily as the season advanced.

"The old man, leaning on his son, walked each day at noon, when it did not rain, as I found it was called when the heavens poured forth its waters. This frequently took place, but a high wind quickly dried the earth, and the season became far more pleasant than it had been.

"My mode of life in my hovel was uniform. During the morning I attended the motions of the cottagers, and when they were dispersed in various occupations, I slept; the remainder of the day was spent in observing my friends. When they had retired to rest, if there was any moon or the night was star-light, I went into the woods and collected my own food and fuel for the cottage. When I returned, as often as it was necessary, I cleared their path from the snow and performed those offices that I had seen done by Felix. I afterwards found that these labours, performed by an invisible hand, greatly astonished them; and once or twice I heard them, on these occasions, utter the words 'good spirit,' 'wonderful'; but I did not then understand the signification of these terms.

"My thoughts now became more active, and I longed to discover the motives and feelings of these lovely creatures; I was inquisitive to know why Felix appeared so miserable and Agatha so sad. I thought (foolish wretch!) that it might be in my power to restore happiness to these deserving people. When I slept or was absent, the forms of the venerable blind father, the gentle Agatha, and the excellent Felix flitted before me. I looked upon them as superior beings who would be the arbiters of my future destiny. I formed in my imagination a thousand pictures of presenting myself to them, and their reception of me. I imagined that they would be disgusted, until, by my gentle demeanour and conciliating words, I should first win their favour and afterwards their love.

"These thoughts exhilarated me and led me to apply with fresh ardour to the acquiring the art of language. My organs were indeed harsh, but supple; and although my voice was very unlike the soft music of their tones, yet I pronounced such words as I understood with tolerable ease. It was as the ass and the lap-dog; yet surely the gentle ass whose intentions were affectionate, although his manners were rude, deserved better treatment than blows and execration.

"The pleasant showers and genial warmth of spring greatly altered the aspect of the earth. Men who before this change seemed to have been hid in caves dispersed themselves and were employed in various arts of cultivation. The birds sang in more cheerful notes, and the leaves began to bud forth on the trees. Happy, happy earth! Fit habitation for gods, which, so short a time before, was bleak, damp, and unwholesome. My spirits were elevated by the enchanting appearance of nature; the past was blotted from my memory, the present was tranquil, and the future gilded by bright rays of hope and anticipations of joy."

Chapter XIII

"I NOW HASTEN to the more moving part of my story. I shall relate events that impressed me with feelings which, from what I had been, have made me what I am.

"Spring advanced rapidly; the weather became fine and the skies cloudless. It surprised me that what before was desert and gloomy should now bloom with the most beautiful flowers and verdure. My senses were gratified and refreshed by a thousand scents of delight and a thousand sights of beauty.

"It was on one of these days, when my cottagers periodically rested from labour – the old man played on his guitar, and the children listened to him – that I observed the countenance of Felix was melancholy beyond expression; he sighed frequently, and once his father paused in his music, and I conjectured by his manner that he inquired the cause of his son's sorrow. Felix replied in a cheerful accent, and the old man was recommencing his music when someone tapped at the door.

"It was a lady on horseback, accompanied by a country-man as a guide. The lady was dressed in a dark suit and covered with a thick black veil. Agatha asked a question, to which the stranger only replied by pronouncing, in a sweet accent, the name of Felix. Her voice was musical but unlike that of either of my friends. On hearing this word, Felix came up hastily to the lady, who, when she saw him, threw up her veil, and I beheld a countenance of angelic beauty and expression. Her hair of a shining raven black, and curiously braided; her eyes were dark, but gentle, although animated; her features of a regular proportion, and her complexion wondrously fair, each cheek tinged with a lovely pink.

"Felix seemed ravished with delight when he saw her, every trait of sorrow vanished from his face, and it instantly expressed a degree of ecstatic joy, of which I could hardly have believed it capable; his eyes sparkled, as his cheek flushed with pleasure; and at that moment I thought him as beautiful as the stranger. She appeared affected by different feelings; wiping a few tears from her lovely eyes, she held out her hand to Felix, who kissed it rapturously and called her, as well as I could distinguish, his sweet Arabian. She did not appear to understand him, but smiled. He assisted her to dismount, and dismissing her guide, conducted her into the cottage. Some conversation took place between him and his father, and the young stranger knelt at the old man's feet and would have kissed his hand, but he raised her and embraced her affectionately.

"I soon perceived that although the stranger uttered articulate sounds and appeared to have a language of her own, she was neither understood by nor herself understood the cottagers. They made many signs which I did not comprehend, but I saw that her presence diffused gladness through the cottage, dispelling their sorrow as the sun dissipates the morning mists. Felix seemed peculiarly happy and with smiles of delight welcomed his Arabian. Agatha, the ever-gentle Agatha, kissed the hands of the lovely stranger, and pointing to her brother, made signs which appeared to me to mean that he had been sorrowful until she came. Some hours passed thus, while they, by their countenances, expressed joy, the cause of which I did not comprehend. Presently I found, by the frequent recurrence of some sound which the stranger repeated after them, that she was endeavouring to learn their language; and the idea instantly occurred to me that I should make use of the same instructions to the same end. The stranger learned about twenty words at the first lesson; most of them, indeed, were those which I had before understood, but I profited by the others.

"As night came on, Agatha and the Arabian retired early. When they separated Felix kissed the hand of the stranger and said, 'Good night sweet Safie.' He sat up much longer, conversing with his father, and by the frequent repetition of her name I conjectured that their lovely guest was the subject of their conversation. I ardently desired to understand them, and bent every faculty towards that purpose, but found it utterly impossible.

"The next morning Felix went out to his work, and after the usual occupations of Agatha were finished, the Arabian sat at the feet of the old man, and taking his guitar, played some airs so entrancingly beautiful that they at once drew tears of sorrow and delight from my eyes. She sang, and her voice flowed in a rich cadence, swelling or dying away like a nightingale of the woods.

"When she had finished, she gave the guitar to Agatha, who at first declined it. She played a simple air, and her voice accompanied it in sweet accents, but unlike the wondrous strain of the stranger. The old man appeared enraptured and said some words which Agatha endeavoured to explain to Safie, and by which he appeared to wish to express that she bestowed on him the greatest delight by her music.

"The days now passed as peaceably as before, with the sole alteration that joy had taken place of sadness in the countenances of my friends. Safie was always gay and happy; she and I improved rapidly in the knowledge of language, so that in two months I began to comprehend most of the words uttered by my protectors.

"In the meanwhile also the black ground was covered with herbage, and the green banks interspersed with innumerable flowers, sweet to the scent and the eyes, stars of pale radiance among the moonlight woods; the sun became warmer, the nights clear and balmy; and my nocturnal rambles were an extreme pleasure to me, although they were considerably shortened by the late setting and early rising of the sun, for I never ventured abroad during daylight, fearful of meeting with the same treatment I had formerly endured in the first village which I entered.

"My days were spent in close attention, that I might more speedily master the language; and I may boast that I improved more rapidly than the Arabian, who understood very little and conversed in broken accents, whilst I comprehended and could imitate almost every word that was spoken.

"While I improved in speech, I also learned the science of letters as it was taught to the stranger, and this opened before me a wide field for wonder and delight.

"The book from which Felix instructed Safie was Volney's Ruins of Empires. I should not have understood the purport of this book had not Felix, in reading it, given very minute explanations. He had chosen this work, he said, because the declamatory style was framed in imitation of the Eastern authors. Through this work I obtained a cursory knowledge of history and a view of the several empires at present existing in the world; it gave me an insight into the manners, governments, and religions of the different nations of the earth. I heard of the slothful Asiatics, of the stupendous genius and mental activity of the Grecians, of the wars and wonderful virtue of the early Romans – of their subsequent degenerating – of the decline of that mighty empire, of chivalry, Christianity, and kings. I heard of the discovery of the American hemisphere and wept with Safie over the hapless fate of its original inhabitants.

"These wonderful narrations inspired me with strange feelings. Was man, indeed, at once so powerful, so virtuous and magnificent, yet so vicious and base? He appeared at one time a mere scion of the evil principle and at another as all that can be conceived of noble and godlike. To be a great and virtuous man appeared the highest honour that can befall a sensitive being; to be base and vicious, as many on record have been, appeared the lowest degradation, a condition more abject than that of the blind mole or harmless worm. For a long time I could not conceive how one man could go forth to murder his fellow, or even why there were laws and governments; but when I heard details of vice and bloodshed, my wonder ceased and I turned away with disgust and loathing.

"Every conversation of the cottagers now opened new wonders to me. While I listened to the instructions which Felix bestowed upon the Arabian, the strange system of human society was explained to me. I heard of the division of property, of immense wealth and squalid poverty, of rank, descent, and noble blood.

"The words induced me to turn towards myself. I learned that the possessions most esteemed by your fellow creatures were high and unsullied descent united with riches.

A man might be respected with only one of these advantages, but without either he was considered, except in very rare instances, as a vagabond and a slave, doomed to waste his powers for the profits of the chosen few! And what was I? Of my creation and creator I was absolutely ignorant, but I knew that I possessed no money, no friends, no kind of property. I was, besides, endued with a figure hideously deformed and loathsome; I was not even of the same nature as man. I was more agile than they and could subsist upon coarser diet; I bore the extremes of heat and cold with less injury to my frame; my stature far exceeded theirs. When I looked around I saw and heard of none like me. Was I, then, a monster, a blot upon the earth, from which all men fled and whom all men disowned?

"I cannot describe to you the agony that these reflections inflicted upon me; I tried to dispel them, but sorrow only increased with knowledge. Oh, that I had forever remained in my native wood, nor known nor felt beyond the sensations of hunger, thirst, and heat!

"Of what a strange nature is knowledge! It clings to the mind when it has once seized on it like a lichen on the rock. I wished sometimes to shake off all thought and feeling, but I learned that there was but one means to overcome the sensation of pain, and that was death – a state which I feared yet did not understand. I admired virtue and good feelings and loved the gentle manners and amiable qualities of my cottagers, but I was shut out from intercourse with them, except through means which I obtained by stealth, when I was unseen and unknown, and which rather increased than satisfied the desire I had of becoming one among my fellows. The gentle words of Agatha and the animated smiles of the charming Arabian were not for me. The mild exhortations of the old man and the lively conversation of the loved Felix were not for me. Miserable, unhappy wretch!

"Other lessons were impressed upon me even more deeply. I heard of the difference of sexes, and the birth and growth of children, how the father doted on the smiles of the infant, and the lively sallies of the older child, how all the life and cares of the mother were wrapped up in the precious charge, how the mind of youth expanded and gained knowledge, of brother, sister, and all the various relationships which bind one human being to another in mutual bonds.

"But where were my friends and relations? No father had watched my infant days, no mother had blessed me with smiles and caresses; or if they had, all my past life was now a blot, a blind vacancy in which I distinguished nothing. From my earliest remembrance I had been as I then was in height and proportion. I had never yet seen a being resembling me or who claimed any intercourse with me. What was I? The question again recurred, to be answered only with groans.

"I will soon explain to what these feelings tended, but allow me now to return to the cottagers, whose story excited in me such various feelings of indignation, delight, and wonder, but which all terminated in additional love and reverence for my protectors (for so I loved, in an innocent, half-painful self-deceit, to call them)."

Chapter XIV

"SOME TIME ELAPSED before I learned the history of my friends. It was one which could not fail to impress itself deeply on my mind, unfolding as it did a number of circumstances, each interesting and wonderful to one so utterly inexperienced as I was.

"The name of the old man was De Lacey. He was descended from a good family in France, where he had lived for many years in affluence, respected by his superiors and beloved by his equals. His son was bred in the service of his country, and Agatha had ranked with ladies of the highest distinction. A few months before my arrival they had lived in a large and luxurious city called Paris, surrounded by friends and possessed of every enjoyment which virtue, refinement of intellect, or taste, accompanied by a moderate fortune, could afford.

"The father of Safie had been the cause of their ruin. He was a Turkish merchant and had inhabited Paris for many years, when, for some reason which I could not learn, he became obnoxious to the government. He was seized and cast into prison the very day that Safie arrived from Constantinople to join him. He was tried and condemned to death. The injustice of his sentence was very flagrant; all Paris was indignant; and it was judged that his religion and wealth rather than the crime alleged against him had been the cause of his condemnation.

"Felix had accidentally been present at the trial; his horror and indignation were uncontrollable when he heard the decision of the court. He made, at that moment, a solemn vow to deliver him and then looked around for the means. After many fruitless attempts to gain admittance to the prison, he found a strongly grated window in an unguarded part of the building, which lighted the dungeon of the unfortunate Muhammadan, who, loaded with chains, waited in despair the execution of the barbarous sentence. Felix visited the grate at night and made known to the prisoner his intentions in his favour. The Turk, amazed and delighted, endeavoured to kindle the zeal of his deliverer by promises of reward and wealth. Felix rejected his offers with contempt, yet when he saw the lovely Safie, who was allowed to visit her father and who by her gestures expressed her lively gratitude, the youth could not help owning to his own mind that the captive possessed a treasure which would fully reward his toil and hazard.

"The Turk quickly perceived the impression that his daughter had made on the heart of Felix and endeavoured to secure him more entirely in his interests by the promise of her hand in marriage so soon as he should be conveyed to a place of safety. Felix was too delicate to accept this offer, yet he looked forward to the probability of the event as to the consummation of his happiness.

"During the ensuing days, while the preparations were going forward for the escape of the merchant, the zeal of Felix was warmed by several letters that he received from this lovely girl, who found means to express her thoughts in the language of her lover by the aid of an old man, a servant of her father who understood French. She thanked him in the most ardent terms for his intended services towards her parent, and at the same time she gently deplored her own fate.

"I have copies of these letters, for I found means, during my residence in the hovel, to procure the implements of writing; and the letters were often in the hands of Felix or Agatha. Before I depart I will give them to you; they will prove the truth of my tale; but at present, as the sun is already far declined, I shall only have time to repeat the substance of them to you.

"Safie related that her mother was a Christian Arab, seized and made a slave by the Turks; recommended by her beauty, she had won the heart of the father of Safie, who married her. The young girl spoke in high and enthusiastic terms of her mother, who, born in freedom, spurned the bondage to which she was now reduced. She instructed her daughter in the tenets of her religion and taught her to aspire to higher powers of intellect and an independence of spirit forbidden to the female followers of Muhammad. This lady died, but her lessons were indelibly impressed on the mind of Safie, who sickened at the prospect of again returning to Asia and being immured within the walls of a harem, allowed only to occupy herself with infantile amusements, ill-suited to the temper of her soul, now accustomed to grand ideas and a noble emulation for virtue. The prospect of marrying a Christian and remaining in a country where women were allowed to take a rank in society was enchanting to her.

"The day for the execution of the Turk was fixed, but on the night previous to it he quitted his prison and before morning was distant many leagues from Paris. Felix had procured passports in the name of his father, sister, and himself. He had previously communicated his plan to the former, who aided the deceit by quitting his house, under the pretence of a journey and concealed himself, with his daughter, in an obscure part of Paris.

"Felix conducted the fugitives through France to Lyons and across Mont Cenis to Leghorn, where the merchant had decided to wait a favourable opportunity of passing into some part of the Turkish dominions.

"Safie resolved to remain with her father until the moment of his departure, before which time the Turk renewed his promise that she should be united to his deliverer; and Felix remained with them in expectation of that event; and in the meantime he enjoyed the society of the Arabian, who exhibited towards him the simplest and tenderest affection. They conversed with one another through the means of an interpreter, and sometimes with the interpretation of looks; and Safie sang to him the divine airs of her native country.

"The Turk allowed this intimacy to take place and encouraged the hopes of the youthful lovers, while in his heart he had formed far other plans. He loathed the idea that his daughter should be united to a Christian, but he feared the resentment of Felix if he should appear lukewarm, for he knew that he was still in the power of his deliverer if he should choose to betray him to the Italian state which they inhabited. He revolved a thousand plans by which he should be enabled to prolong the deceit until it might be no longer necessary, and secretly to take his daughter with him when he departed. His plans were facilitated by the news which arrived from Paris.

"The government of France were greatly enraged at the escape of their victim and spared no pains to detect and punish his deliverer. The plot of Felix was quickly discovered, and De Lacey and Agatha were thrown into prison. The news reached Felix and roused him from his dream of pleasure. His blind and aged father and his gentle sister lay in a noisome dungeon while he enjoyed the free air and the society of her whom he loved. This idea was torture to him. He quickly arranged with the Turk that if the latter should find a favourable opportunity for escape before Felix could return to Italy, Safie should remain as a boarder at a convent at Leghorn; and then, quitting the lovely Arabian, he hastened to Paris and delivered himself up to the vengeance of the law, hoping to free De Lacey and Agatha by this proceeding. "He did not succeed. They remained confined for five months before the trial took place, the result of which deprived them of their fortune and condemned them to a perpetual exile from their native country.

"They found a miserable asylum in the cottage in Germany, where I discovered them. Felix soon learned that the treacherous Turk, for whom he and his family endured such unheard-of oppression, on discovering that his deliverer was thus reduced to poverty and ruin, became a traitor to good feeling and honour and had quitted Italy with his daughter, insultingly sending Felix a pittance of money to aid him, as he said, in some plan of future maintenance.

"Such were the events that preyed on the heart of Felix and rendered him, when I first saw him, the most miserable of his family. He could have endured poverty, and while this distress had been the meed of his virtue, he gloried in it; but the ingratitude of the Turk and the loss of his beloved Safie were misfortunes more bitter and irreparable. The arrival of the Arabian now infused new life into his soul.

"When the news reached Leghorn that Felix was deprived of his wealth and rank, the merchant commanded his daughter to think no more of her lover, but to prepare to return to her native country. The generous nature of Safie was outraged by this command; she attempted to expostulate with her father, but he left her angrily, reiterating his tyrannical mandate.

"A few days after, the Turk entered his daughter's apartment and told her hastily that he had reason to believe that his residence at Leghorn had been divulged and that he should speedily be delivered up to the French government; he had consequently hired a vessel to convey him to Constantinople, for which city he should sail in a few hours. He intended to leave his daughter under the care of a confidential servant, to follow at her leisure with the greater part of his property, which had not yet arrived at Leghorn.

"When alone, Safie resolved in her own mind the plan of conduct that it would become her to pursue in this emergency. A residence in Turkey was abhorrent to her; her religion and her feelings were alike averse to it. By some papers of her father which fell into her hands she heard of the exile of her lover and learnt the name of the spot where he then resided. She hesitated some time, but at length she formed her determination. Taking with her some jewels that belonged to her and a sum of money, she quitted Italy with an attendant, a native of Leghorn, but who understood the common language of Turkey, and departed for Germany.

"She arrived in safety at a town about twenty leagues from the cottage of De Lacey, when her attendant fell dangerously ill. Safie nursed her with the most devoted affection, but the poor girl died, and the Arabian was left alone, unacquainted with the language of the country and utterly ignorant of the customs of the world. She fell, however, into good hands. The Italian had mentioned the name of the spot for which they were bound, and after her death the woman of the house in which they had lived took care that Safie should arrive in safety at the cottage of her lover."

Chapter XV

"SUCH WAS the history of my beloved cottagers. It impressed me deeply. I learned, from the views of social life which it developed, to admire their virtues and to deprecate the vices of mankind.

"As yet I looked upon crime as a distant evil, benevolence and generosity were ever present before me, inciting within me a desire to become an actor in the busy scene where so many admirable qualities were called forth and displayed. But in giving an account of the progress of my intellect, I must not omit a circumstance which occurred in the beginning of the month of August of the same year.

"One night during my accustomed visit to the neighbouring wood where I collected my own food and brought home firing for my protectors, I found on the ground a leathern portmanteau containing several articles of dress and some books. I eagerly seized the prize and returned with it to my hovel. Fortunately the books were written in the language, the elements of which I had acquired at the cottage; they consisted of Paradise Lost, a volume of Plutarch's Lives, and the Sorrows of Werter. The possession of these treasures gave me extreme delight; I now continually studied and exercised my mind upon these histories, whilst my friends were employed in their ordinary occupations.

"I can hardly describe to you the effect of these books. They produced in me an infinity of new images and feelings, that sometimes raised me to ecstasy, but more frequently sunk me into the lowest dejection. In the Sorrows of Werter, besides the interest of its simple and affecting story, so many opinions are canvassed and so many lights thrown upon what had hitherto been to me obscure subjects that I found in it a never-ending source of speculation and astonishment. The gentle and domestic manners it described, combined with lofty sentiments and feelings, which had for their object something out of self, accorded well with my experience among my protectors and with the wants which were forever alive in my own bosom. But I thought Werter himself a more divine being than I had ever beheld or imagined; his character contained no pretension, but it sank deep. The disquisitions upon death and suicide were calculated to fill me with wonder. I did not pretend to enter into the merits of the case, yet I inclined towards the opinions of the hero, whose extinction I wept, without precisely understanding it.

"As I read, however, I applied much personally to my own feelings and condition. I found myself similar yet at the same time strangely unlike to the beings concerning whom I read and to whose conversation I was a listener. I sympathized with and partly understood them, but I was unformed in mind; I was dependent on none and related to none. "The path of my departure was free," and there was none to lament my annihilation. My person was hideous and my stature gigantic. What did this mean? Who was I? What was I? Whence did I come? What was my destination? These questions continually recurred, but I was unable to solve them.

"The volume of Plutarch's Lives which I possessed contained the histories of the first founders of the ancient republics. This book had a far different effect upon me from the Sorrows of Werter. I learned from Werter's imaginations despondency and gloom, but Plutarch taught me high thoughts; he elevated me above the wretched sphere of my own reflections, to admire and love the heroes of past ages. Manythings I read surpassed my understanding and experience. I had a very confused knowledge of kingdoms, wide extents of country, mighty rivers, and boundless seas. But I was perfectly unacquainted with towns and large assemblages of men. The cottage of my protectors had been the only school in which I had studied human nature, but this book developed new and mightier scenes of action. I read of men concerned in public affairs, governing or massacring their species. I felt the greatest ardour for virtue rise within me, and abhorrence for vice, as far as I understood the signification of those terms, relative as they were, as I applied them, to pleasure and pain alone. Induced by these feelings, I was of course led to admire peaceable lawgivers, Numa, Solon, and Lycurgus, in preference to Romulus and Theseus. The patriarchal lives of my protectors caused these impressions to take a firm hold on my mind; perhaps, if my first introduction to humanity had been made by a young soldier, burning for glory and slaughter, I should have been imbued with different sensations.

"But Paradise Lost excited different and far deeper emotions. I read it, as I had read the other volumes which had fallen into my hands, as a true history. It moved every feeling of wonder and awe that the picture of an omnipotent God warring with his creatures was capable of exciting. I often referred the several situations, as their similarity struck me, to my own. Like Adam, I was apparently united by no link to any other being in existence; but his state was far different from mine in every other respect. He had come forth from the hands of God a perfect creature, happy and prosperous, guarded by the especial care of his Creator; he was allowed to converse with and acquire knowledge from beings of a superior nature, but I was wretched, helpless, and alone. Many times I considered Satan as the fitter emblem of my condition, for often, like him, when I viewed the bliss of my protectors, the bitter gall of envy rose within me.

"Another circumstance strengthened and confirmed these feelings. Soon after my arrival in the hovel I discovered some papers in the pocket of the dress which I had taken from your laboratory. At first I had neglected them, but now that I was able to decipher the characters in which they were written, I began to study them with diligence. It was your journal of the four months that preceded my creation. You minutely described in these papers every step you took in the progress of your work; this history was mingled with accounts of domestic occurrences. You doubtless recollect these papers. Here they are. Everything is related in them which bears reference to my accursed origin; the whole detail of that series of disgusting circumstances which produced it is set in view; the minutest description of my odious and loathsome person is given, in language which painted your own horrors and rendered mine indelible. I sickened as I read. 'Hateful day when I received life!' I exclaimed in agony. 'Accursed creator! Why did you form a monster so hideous that even you turned from me in disgust? God, in pity, made man beautiful and alluring, after his own image; but my form is a filthy type of yours, more horrid even from the very resemblance. Satan had his companions, fellow devils, to admire and encourage him, but I am solitary and abhorred.'

"These were the reflections of my hours of despondency and solitude; but when I contemplated the virtues of the cottagers, their amiable and benevolent dispositions, I persuaded myself that when they should become acquainted with my admiration of their virtues they would compassionate me and overlook my personal deformity. Could they turn from their door one, however monstrous, who solicited their compassion and friendship? I resolved, at least, not to despair, but in every way to fit myself for an interview with them which would decide my fate. I postponed this attempt for some months longer, for the importance attached to its success inspired me with a dread lest I should fail. Besides, I found that my understanding improved so much with every day's experience that I was unwilling to commence this undertaking until a few more months should have added to my sagacity.

"Several changes, in the meantime, took place in the cottage. The presence of Safie diffused happiness among its inhabitants, and I also found that a greater degree of plenty reigned there. Felix and Agatha spent more time in amusement and conversation, and were assisted in their labours by servants. They did not appear rich, but they were contented and happy; their feelings were serene and peaceful, while mine became every day more tumultuous. Increase of knowledge only discovered to me more clearly what a wretched outcast I was. I cherished hope, it is true, but it vanished when I beheld my person reflected in water or my shadow in the moonshine, even as that frail image and that inconstant shade.

"I endeavoured to crush these fears and to fortify myself for the trial which in a few months I resolved to undergo; and sometimes I allowed my thoughts, unchecked by reason, to ramble in the fields of Paradise, and dared to fancy amiable and lovely creatures sympathizing with my feelings and cheering my gloom; their angelic countenances breathed smiles of consolation. But it was all a dream; no Eve soothed my sorrows nor shared my thoughts; I was alone. I remembered Adam's supplication to his Creator. But where was mine? He had abandoned me, and in the bitterness of my heart I cursed him.

"Autumn passed thus. I saw, with surprise and grief, the leaves decay and fall, and nature again assume the barren and bleak appearance it had worn when I first beheld the woods and the lovely moon. Yet I did not heed the bleakness of the weather; I was better fitted by my conformation for the endurance of cold than heat. But my chief delights were the sight of the flowers, the birds, and all the gay apparel of summer; when those deserted me, I turned with more attention towards the cottagers. Their happiness was not decreased by the absence of summer. They loved and sympathized with one another; and their joys, depending on each other, were not interrupted by the casualties that took place around them. The more I saw of them, the greater became my desire to claim their protection and kindness; my heart yearned to be known and loved by these amiable creatures; to see their sweet looks directed towards me with affection was the utmost limit of my ambition. I dared not think that they would turn them from me with disdain and horror. The poor that stopped at their door were never driven away. I asked, it is true, for greater treasures than a little food or rest: I required kindness and sympathy; but I did not believe myself utterly unworthy of it.

"The winter advanced, and an entire revolution of the seasons had taken place since I awoke into life. My attention at this time was solely directed towards my plan of introducing myself into the cottage of my protectors. I revolved many projects, but that on which I finally fixed was to enter the dwelling when the blind old man should be alone. I had sagacity enough to discover that the unnatural hideousness of my person was the chief object of horror with those who had formerly beheld me. My voice, although harsh, had nothing terrible in it; I thought, therefore, that if in the absence of his children I could gain the good will and mediation of the old De Lacey, I might by his means be tolerated by my younger protectors.

"One day, when the sun shone on the red leaves that strewed the ground and diffused cheerfulness, although it denied warmth, Safie, Agatha, and Felix departed on a long country walk, and the old man, at his own desire, was left alone in the cottage. When his children had departed, he took up his guitar and played several mournful but sweet airs, more sweet and mournful than I had ever heard him play before. At first his countenance was illuminated with pleasure, but as he continued, thoughtfulness and sadness succeeded; at length, laying aside the instrument, he sat absorbed in reflection.

"My heart beat quick; this was the hour and moment of trial, which would decide my hopes or realize my fears. The servants were gone to a neighbouring fair. All was silent in and around the cottage; it was an excellent opportunity; yet, when I proceeded to execute my plan, my limbs failed me and I sank to the ground. Again I rose, and exerting all the firmness of which I was master, removed the planks which I had placed before my hovel to conceal my retreat. The fresh air revived me, and with renewed determination I approached the door of their cottage.

"I knocked. 'Who is there?' said the old man. 'Come in.'

"I entered. 'Pardon this intrusion,' said I; 'I am a traveller in want of a little rest; you would greatly oblige me if you would allow me to remain a few minutes before the fire.'

"'Enter,' said De Lacey, 'and I will try in what manner I can to relieve your wants; but, unfortunately, my children are from home, and as I am blind, I am afraid I shall find it difficult to procure food for you.'

"'Do not trouble yourself, my kind host; I have food; it is warmth and rest only that I need.'

"I sat down, and a silence ensued. I knew that every minute was precious to me, yet I remained irresolute in what manner to commence the interview, when the old man addressed me. 'By your language, stranger, I suppose you are my countryman; are you French?'

"'No; but I was educated by a French family and understand that language only. I am now going to claim the protection of some friends, whom I sincerely love, and of whose favour I have some hopes.'

"'Are they Germans?'

"'No, they are French. But let us change the subject. I am an unfortunate and deserted creature, I look around and I have no relation or friend upon earth. These amiable people to whom I go have never seen me and know little of me. I am full of fears, for if I fail there, I am an outcast in the world forever.'

"'Do not despair. To be friendless is indeed to be unfortunate, but the hearts of men, when unprejudiced by any obvious self-interest, are full of brotherly love and charity. Rely, therefore, on your hopes; and if these friends are good and amiable, do not despair.'

"'They are kind – they are the most excellent creatures in the world; but, unfortunately, they are prejudiced against me. I have good dispositions; my life has been hitherto harmless and in some degree beneficial; but a fatal prejudice clouds their eyes, and where they ought to see a feeling and kind friend, they behold only a detestable monster.'

"'That is indeed unfortunate; but if you are really blameless, cannot you undeceive them?'

"'I am about to undertake that task; and it is on that account that I feel so many overwhelming terrors. I tenderly love these friends; I have, unknown to them, been for many months in the habits of daily kindness towards them; but they believe that I wish to injure them, and it is that prejudice which I wish to overcome.'

"'Where do these friends reside?'

"'Near this spot.'

"The old man paused and then continued, 'If you will unreservedly confide to me the particulars of your tale, I perhaps may be of use in undeceiving them. I am blind and cannot judge of your countenance, but there is something in your words which persuades me that you are sincere. I am poor and an exile, but it will afford me true pleasure to be in any way serviceable to a human creature.'

"'Excellent man! I thank you and accept your generous offer. You raise me from the dust by this kindness; and I trust that, by your aid, I shall not be driven from the society and sympathy of your fellow creatures.'

"'Heaven forbid! Even if you were really criminal, for that can only drive you to desperation, and not instigate you to virtue. I also am unfortunate; I and my family have been condemned, although innocent; judge, therefore, if I do not feel for your misfortunes.'

"'How can I thank you, my best and only benefactor? From your lips first have I heard the voice of kindness directed towards me; I shall be forever grateful; and your present humanity assures me of success with those friends whom I am on the point of meeting.'

"'May I know the names and residence of those friends?' "I paused. This, I thought, was the moment of decision, which was to rob me of or bestow happiness on me forever. I struggled vainly for firmness sufficient to answer him, but the effort destroyed all my remaining strength; I sank on the chair and sobbed aloud. At that moment I heard the steps of my younger protectors. I had not a moment to lose, but seizing the hand of the old man, I cried, 'Now is the time! Save and protect me! You and your family are the friends whom I seek. Do not you desert me in the hour of trial!'

"'Great God!' exclaimed the old man. 'Who are you?'

"At that instant the cottage door was opened, and Felix, Safie, and Agatha entered. Who can describe their horror and consternation on beholding me? Agatha fainted, and Safie, unable to attend to her friend, rushed out of the cottage. Felix darted forward, and with supernatural force tore me from his father, to whose knees I clung, in a transport of fury, he dashed me to the ground and struck me violently with a stick. I could have torn him limb from limb, as the lion rends the antelope. But my heart sank within me as with bitter sickness, and I refrained. I saw him on the point of repeating his blow, when, overcome by pain and anguish, I quitted the cottage, and in the general tumult escaped unperceived to my hovel."

Chapter XVI

"**CURSED, CURSED CREATOR**! Why did I live? Why, in that instant, did I not extinguish the spark of existence which you had so wantonly bestowed? I know not; despair had not yet taken possession of me; my feelings were those of rage and revenge. I could with pleasure have destroyed the cottage and its inhabitants and have glutted myself with their shrieks and misery.

"When night came I quitted my retreat and wandered in the wood; and now, no longer restrained by the fear of discovery, I gave vent to my anguish in fearful howlings. I was like a wild beast that had broken the toils, destroying the objects that obstructed me and ranging through the wood with a staglike swiftness. Oh! What a miserable night I passed! The cold stars shone in mockery, and the bare trees waved their branches above me; now and then the sweet voice of a bird burst forth amidst the universal stillness. All, save I, were at rest or in enjoyment; I, like the arch-fiend, bore a hell within me, and finding myself unsympathized with, wished to tear up the trees, spread havoc and destruction around me, and then to have sat down and enjoyed the ruin.

"But this was a luxury of sensation that could not endure; I became fatigued with excess of bodily exertion and sank on the damp grass in the sick impotence of despair. There was none among the myriads of men that existed who would pity or assist me; and should I feel kindness towards my enemies? No; from that moment I declared everlasting war against the species, and more than all, against him who had formed me and sent me forth to this insupportable misery.

"The sun rose; I heard the voices of men and knew that it was impossible to return to my retreat during that day. Accordingly I hid myself in some thick underwood, determining to devote the ensuing hours to reflection on my situation.

"The pleasant sunshine and the pure air of day restored me to some degree of tranquillity; and when I considered what had passed at the cottage, I could not help believing that I had been too hasty in my conclusions. I had certainly acted imprudently. It was apparent that my conversation had interested the father in my behalf, and I was a fool in having exposed my person to the horror of his children. I ought to have familiarized the old De Lacey to me, and by degrees to have discovered myself to the rest of his family, when they should have been prepared for my approach. But I did not believe my errors to be irretrievable, and after much consideration I resolved to return to the cottage, seek the old man, and by my representations win him to my party.

"These thoughts calmed me, and in the afternoon I sank into a profound sleep; but the fever of my blood did not allow me to be visited by peaceful dreams. The horrible scene of the preceding day was forever acting before my eyes; the females were flying and the enraged Felix tearing me from his father's feet. I awoke exhausted, and finding that it was already night, I crept forth from my hiding-place, and went in search of food.

"When my hunger was appeased, I directed my steps towards the well-known path that conducted to the cottage. All there was at peace. I crept into my hovel and remained in silent expectation of the accustomed hour when the family arose. That hour passed, the sun mounted high in the heavens, but the cottagers did not appear. I trembled violently, apprehending some dreadful misfortune. The inside of the cottage was dark, and I heard no motion; I cannot describe the agony of this suspense.

"Presently two countrymen passed by, but pausing near the cottage, they entered into conversation, using violent gesticulations; but I did not understand what they said, as they spoke the language of the country, which differed from that of my protectors. Soon after, however, Felix approached with another man; I was surprised, as I knew that he had not quitted the cottage that morning, and waited anxiously to discover from his discourse the meaning of these unusual appearances.

"'Do you consider,' said his companion to him, 'that you will be obliged to pay three months' rent and to lose the produce of your garden? I do not wish to take any unfair advantage, and I beg therefore that you will take some days to consider of your determination.'

"'It is utterly useless,' replied Felix; 'we can never again inhabit your cottage. The life of my father is in the greatest danger, owing to the dreadful circumstance that I have related. My wife and my sister will never recover from their horror. I entreat you not to reason with me anymore. Take possession of your tenement and let me fly from this place.'

"Felix trembled violently as he said this. He and his companion entered the cottage, in which they remained for a few minutes, and then departed. I never saw any of the family of De Lacey more.

"I continued for the remainder of the day in my hovel in a state of utter and stupid despair. My protectors had departed and had broken the only link that held me to the world. For the first time the feelings of revenge and hatred filled my bosom, and I did not strive to control them, but allowing myself to be borne away by the stream, I bent my mind towards injury and death. When I thought of my friends, of the mild voice of De Lacey, the gentle eyes of Agatha, and the exquisite beauty of the Arabian, these thoughts vanished and a gush of tears somewhat soothed me. But again when I reflected that they had spurned and deserted me, anger returned, a rage of anger, and unable to injure anything human, I turned my fury towards inanimate objects. As night advanced I placed a variety of combustibles around the cottage, and after having destroyed every vestige of cultivation in the garden, I waited with forced impatience until the moon had sunk to commence my operations.

"As the night advanced, a fierce wind arose from the woods and quickly dispersed the clouds that had loitered in the heavens; the blast tore along like a mighty avalanche and produced a kind of insanity in my spirits that burst all bounds of reason and reflection. I lighted the dry branch of a tree and danced with fury around the devoted cottage, my eyes still fixed on the western horizon, the edge of which the moon nearly touched. A part of its orb was at length hid, and I waved my brand; it sank, and with a loud scream I fired the straw, and heath, and bushes, which I had collected. The wind fanned the fire, and the cottage was quickly enveloped by the flames, which clung to it and licked it with their forked and destroying tongues.

"As soon as I was convinced that no assistance could save any part of the habitation, I quitted the scene and sought for refuge in the woods.

"And now, with the world before me, whither should I bend my steps? I resolved to fly far from the scene of my misfortunes; but to me, hated and despised, every country must be equally horrible. At length the thought of you crossed my mind. I learned from your papers that you were my father, my creator; and to whom could I apply with more fitness than to him who had given me life? Among the lessons that Felix had bestowed upon Safie, geography had not been omitted; I had learned from these the relative situations of the different countries of the earth. You had mentioned Geneva as the name of your native town, and towards this place I resolved to proceed.

"But how was I to direct myself? I knew that I must travel in a southwesterly direction to reach my destination, but the sun was my only guide. I did not know the names of the towns that I was to pass through, nor could I ask information from a single human being; but I did not despair. From you only could I hope for succour, although towards you I felt no sentiment but that of hatred. Unfeeling, heartless creator! You had endowed me with perceptions and passions and then cast me abroad an object for the scorn and horror of mankind. But on you only had I any claim for pity and redress, and from you I determined to seek that justice which I vainly attempted to gain from any other being that wore the human form.

"My travels were long and the sufferings I endured intense. It was late in autumn when I quitted the district where I had so long resided. I travelled only at night, fearful of encountering the visage of a human being. Nature decayed around me, and the sun became heatless; rain and snow poured around me; mighty rivers were frozen; the surface of the earth was hard and chill, and bare, and I found no shelter. Oh, earth! How often did I imprecate curses on the cause of my being! The mildness of my nature had fled, and all within me was turned to gall and bitterness. The nearer I approached to your habitation, the more deeply did I feel the spirit of revenge enkindled in my heart. Snow fell, and the waters were hardened, but I rested not. A few incidents now and then directed me, and I possessed a map of the country; but I often wandered wide from my path. The agony of my feelings allowed me no respite; no incident occurred from which my rage and misery could not extract its food; but a circumstance that happened when I arrived on the confines of Switzerland, when the sun had recovered its warmth and the earth again began to look green, confirmed in an especial manner the bitterness and horror of my feelings.

"I generally rested during the day and travelled only when I was secured by night from the view of man. One morning, however, finding that my path lay through a deep wood, I ventured to continue my journey after the sun had risen; the day, which was one of the first of spring, cheered even me by the loveliness of its sunshine and the balminess of the air. I felt emotions of gentleness and pleasure, that had long appeared dead, revive within me. Half surprised by the novelty of these sensations, I allowed myself to be borne away by them, and forgetting my solitude and deformity, dared to be happy. Soft tears again bedewed my cheeks, and I even raised my humid eyes with thankfulness towards the blessed sun, which bestowed such joy upon me.

"I continued to wind among the paths of the wood, until I came to its boundary, which was skirted by a deep and rapid river, into which many of the trees bent their branches, now budding with the fresh spring. Here I paused, not exactly knowing what path to pursue, when I heard the sound of voices, that induced me to conceal myself under the shade of a cypress. I was scarcely hid when a young girl came running towards the spot where I was concealed, laughing, as if she ran from someone in sport. She continued her course along the precipitous sides of the river, when suddenly her foot slipped, and she fell into the rapid stream. I rushed from my hiding-place and with extreme labour, from the force of the current, saved her and dragged her to shore. She was senseless, and I endeavoured by every means in my power to restore animation, when I was suddenly interrupted by the approach of a rustic, who was probably the person from whom she had playfully fled. On seeing me, he darted towards me, and tearing the girl from my arms, hastened towards the deeper parts of the wood. I followed speedily, I hardly knew why; but when the man saw me draw near, he aimed a gun, which he carried, at my body and fired. I sank to the ground, and my injurer, with increased swiftness, escaped into the wood.

"This was then the reward of my benevolence! I had saved a human being from destruction, and as a recompense I now writhed under the miserable pain of a wound which shattered the flesh and bone. The feelings of kindness and gentleness which I had entertained but a few moments before gave place to hellish rage and gnashing of teeth. Inflamed by pain, I vowed eternal hatred and vengeance to all mankind. But the agony of my wound overcame me; my pulses paused, and I fainted.

"For some weeks I led a miserable life in the woods, endeavouring to cure the wound which I had received. The ball had entered my shoulder, and I knew not whether it had remained there or passed through; at any rate I had no means of extracting it. My sufferings were augmented also by the oppressive sense of the injustice and ingratitude of their infliction. My daily vows rose for revenge – a deep and deadly revenge, such as would alone compensate for the outrages and anguish I had endured.

"After some weeks my wound healed, and I continued my journey. The labours I endured were no longer to be alleviated by the bright sun or gentle breezes of spring; all joy was but a mockery which insulted my desolate state and made me feel more painfully that I was not made for the enjoyment of pleasure.

"But my toils now drew near a close, and in two months from this time I reached the environs of Geneva.

"It was evening when I arrived, and I retired to a hiding-place among the fields that surround it to meditate in what manner I should apply to you. I was oppressed by fatigue and hunger and far too unhappy to enjoy the gentle breezes of evening or the prospect of the sun setting behind the stupendous mountains of Jura.

"At this time a slight sleep relieved me from the pain of reflection, which was disturbed by the approach of a beautiful child, who came running into the recess I had chosen, with all the sportiveness of infancy. Suddenly, as I gazed on him, an idea seized me that this little creature was unprejudiced and had lived too short a time to have imbibed a horror of deformity. If, therefore, I could seize him and educate him as my companion and friend, I should not be so desolate in this peopled earth.

"Urged by this impulse, I seized on the boy as he passed and drew him towards me. As soon as he beheld my form, he placed his hands before his eyes and uttered a shrill scream; I drew his hand forcibly from his face and said, 'Child, what is the meaning of this? I do not intend to hurt you; listen to me.'

"He struggled violently. 'Let me go,' he cried; 'monster! Ugly wretch! You wish to eat me and tear me to pieces. You are an ogre. Let me go, or I will tell my papa.'

"'Boy, you will never see your father again; you must come with me.'

"'Hideous monster! Let me go. My papa is a syndic – he is M. Frankenstein – he will punish you. You dare not keep me.'

"'Frankenstein! you belong then to my enemy – to him towards whom I have sworn eternal revenge; you shall be my first victim.'

"The child still struggled and loaded me with epithets which carried despair to my heart; I grasped his throat to silence him, and in a moment he lay dead at my feet.

"I gazed on my victim, and my heart swelled with exultation and hellish triumph; clapping my hands, I exclaimed, 'I too can create desolation; my enemy is not invulnerable; this death will carry despair to him, and a thousand other miseries shall torment and destroy him.'

"As I fixed my eyes on the child, I saw something glittering on his breast. I took it; it was a portrait of a most lovely woman. In spite of my malignity, it softened and attracted me. For a few moments I gazed with delight on her dark eyes, fringed by deep lashes, and her lovely lips; but presently my rage returned; I remembered that I was forever deprived of the delights that such beautiful creatures could bestow and that she whose resemblance I contemplated would, in regarding me, have changed that air of divine benignity to one expressive of disgust and affright.

"Can you wonder that such thoughts transported me with rage? I only wonder that at that moment, instead of venting my sensations in exclamations and agony, I did not rush among mankind and perish in the attempt to destroy them.

"While I was overcome by these feelings, I left the spot where I had committed the murder, and seeking a more secluded hiding-place, I entered a barn which had appeared to me to be empty. A woman was sleeping on some straw; she was young, not indeed so beautiful as her whose portrait I held, but of an agreeable aspect and blooming in the loveliness of youth and health. Here, I thought, is one of those whose joy-imparting smiles are bestowed on all but me. And then I bent over her and whispered, 'Awake, fairest, thy lover is near – he who would give his life but to obtain one look of affection from thine eyes; my beloved, awake!'

"The sleeper stirred; a thrill of terror ran through me. Should she indeed awake, and see me, and curse me, and denounce the murderer? Thus would she assuredly act if her darkened eyes opened and she beheld me. The thought was madness; it stirred the fiend within me – not I, but she, shall suffer; the murder I have committed because I am forever robbed of all that she could give me, she shall atone. The crime had its source in her; be hers the punishment! Thanks to the lessons of Felix and the sanguinary laws of man, I had learned now to work mischief. I bent over her and placed the portrait securely in one of the folds of her dress. She moved again, and I fled.

"For some days I haunted the spot where these scenes had taken place, sometimes wishing to see you, sometimes resolved to quit the world and its miseries forever. At length

I wandered towards these mountains, and have ranged through their immense recesses, consumed by a burning passion which you alone can gratify. We may not part until you have promised to comply with my requisition. I am alone and miserable; man will not associate with me; but one as deformed and horrible as myself would not deny herself to me. My companion must be of the same species and have the same defects. This being you must create."

Chapter XVII

THE BEING finished speaking and fixed his looks upon me in the expectation of a reply. But I was bewildered, perplexed, and unable to arrange my ideas sufficiently to understand the full extent of his proposition. He continued:

"You must create a female for me with whom I can live in the interchange of those sympathies necessary for my being. This you alone can do, and I demand it of you as a right which you must not refuse to concede."

The latter part of his tale had kindled anew in me the anger that had died away while he narrated his peaceful life among the cottagers, and as he said this I could no longer suppress the rage that burned within me.

"I do refuse it," I replied; "and no torture shall ever extort a consent from me. You may render me the most miserable of men, but you shall never make me base in my own eyes. Shall I create another like yourself, whose joint wickedness might desolate the world. Begone! I have answered you; you may torture me, but I will never consent."

"You are in the wrong," replied the fiend; "and instead of threatening, I am content to reason with you. I am malicious because I am miserable. Am I not shunned and hated by all mankind? You, my creator, would tear me to pieces and triumph; remember that, and tell me why I should pity man more than he pities me? You would not call it murder if you could precipitate me into one of those ice-rifts and destroy my frame, the work of your own hands. Shall I respect man when he condemns me? Let him live with me in the interchange of kindness, and instead of injury I would bestow every benefit upon him with tears of gratitude at his acceptance. But that cannot be; the human senses are insurmountable barriers to our union. Yet mine shall not be the submission of abject slavery. I will revenge my injuries; if I cannot inspire love, I will cause fear, and chiefly towards you my archenemy, because my creator, do I swear inextinguishable hatred. Have a care; I will work at your destruction, nor finish until I desolate your heart, so that you shall curse the hour of your birth."

A fiendish rage animated him as he said this; his face was wrinkled into contortions too horrible for human eyes to behold; but presently he calmed himself and proceeded –

"I intended to reason. This passion is detrimental to me, for you do not reflect that YOU are the cause of its excess. If any being felt emotions of benevolence towards me, I should return them a hundred and a hundredfold; for that one creature's sake I would make peace with the whole kind! But I now indulge in dreams of bliss that cannot be realized. What I ask of you is reasonable and moderate; I demand a creature of another sex, but as hideous as myself; the gratification is small, but it is all that I can receive, and it shall content me. It is true, we shall be monsters, cut off from all the world; but on that account we shall be more attached to one another. Our lives will not be happy, but they will be harmless and free from the misery I now feel. Oh! My creator, make me happy; let me feel gratitude towards you for one benefit! Let me see that I excite the sympathy of some existing thing; do not deny me my request!"

I was moved. I shuddered when I thought of the possible consequences of my consent, but I felt that there was some justice in his argument. His tale and the feelings he now expressed proved him to be a creature of fine sensations, and did I not as his maker owe him all the portion of happiness that it was in my power to bestow? He saw my change of feeling and continued:

"If you consent, neither you nor any other human being shall ever see us again; I will go to the vast wilds of South America. My food is not that of man; I do not destroy the lamb and the kid to glut my appetite; acorns and berries afford me sufficient nourishment. My companion will be of the same nature as myself and will be content with the same fare. We shall make our bed of dried leaves; the sun will shine on us as on man and will ripen our food. The picture I present to you is peaceful and human, and you must feel that you could deny it only in the wantonness of power and cruelty. Pitiless as you have been towards me, I now see compassion in your eyes; let me seize the favourable moment and persuade you to promise what I so ardently desire."

"You propose," replied I, "to fly from the habitations of man, to dwell in those wilds where the beasts of the field will be your only companions. How can you, who long for the love and sympathy of man, persevere in this exile? You will return and again seek their kindness, and you will meet with their detestation; your evil passions will be renewed, and you will then have a companion to aid you in the task of destruction. This may not be; cease to argue the point, for I cannot consent."

"How inconstant are your feelings! But a moment ago you were moved by my representations, and why do you again harden yourself to my complaints? I swear to you, by the earth which I inhabit, and by you that made me, that with the companion you bestow I will quit the neighbourhood of man and dwell, as it may chance, in the most savage of places. My evil passions will have fled, for I shall meet with sympathy! My life will flow quietly away, and in my dying moments I shall not curse my maker."

His words had a strange effect upon me. I compassionated him and sometimes felt a wish to console him, but when I looked upon him, when I saw the filthy mass that moved and talked, my heart sickened and my feelings were altered to those of horror and hatred. I tried to stifle these sensations; I thought that as I could not sympathize with him, I had no right to withhold from him the small portion of happiness which was yet in my power to bestow.

"You swear," I said, "to be harmless; but have you not already shown a degree of malice that should reasonably make me distrust you? May not even this be a feint that will increase your triumph by affording a wider scope for your revenge?"

"How is this? I must not be trifled with, and I demand an answer. If I have no ties and no affections, hatred and vice must be my portion; the love of another will destroy the cause of my crimes, and I shall become a thing of whose existence everyone will be ignorant. My vices are the children of a forced solitude that I abhor, and my virtues will necessarily arise when I live in communion with an equal. I shall feel the affections of a sensitive being and became linked to the chain of existence and events from which I am now excluded."

I paused some time to reflect on all he had related and the various arguments which he had employed. I thought of the promise of virtues which he had displayed on the opening of his existence and the subsequent blight of all kindly feeling by the loathing and scorn which his protectors had manifested towards him. His power and threats were not omitted in my calculations; a creature who could exist in the ice caves of the glaciers and hide himself from pursuit among the ridges of inaccessible precipices was a being possessing faculties it would be vain to cope with. After a long pause of reflection I concluded that the justice due both to him and my fellow creatures demanded of me that I should comply with his request. Turning to him, therefore, I said:

"I consent to your demand, on your solemn oath to quit Europe forever, and every other place in the neighbourhood of man, as soon as I shall deliver into your hands a female who will accompany you in your exile."

"I swear," he cried, "by the sun, and by the blue sky of heaven, and by the fire of love that burns my heart, that if you grant my prayer, while they exist you shall never behold me again. Depart to your home and commence your labours; I shall watch their progress with unutterable anxiety; and fear not but that when you are ready I shall appear."

Saying this, he suddenly quitted me, fearful, perhaps, of any change in my sentiments. I saw him descend the mountain with greater speed than the flight of an eagle, and quickly lost among the undulations of the sea of ice.

His tale had occupied the whole day, and the sun was upon the verge of the horizon when he departed. I knew that I ought to hasten my descent towards the valley, as I should soon be encompassed in darkness; but my heart was heavy, and my steps slow. The labour of winding among the little paths of the mountain and fixing my feet firmly as I advanced perplexed me, occupied as I was by the emotions which the occurrences of the day had produced. Night was far advanced when I came to the halfway resting-place and seated myself beside the fountain. The stars shone at intervals as the clouds passed from over them; the dark pines rose before me, and every here and there a broken tree lay on the ground; it was a scene of wonderful solemnity and stirred strange thoughts within me. I wept bitterly, and clasping my hands in agony, I exclaimed, "Oh! Stars and clouds and winds, ye are all about to mock me; if ye really pity me, crush sensation and memory; let me become as nought; but if not, depart, depart, and leave me in darkness."

These were wild and miserable thoughts, but I cannot describe to you how the eternal twinkling of the stars weighed upon me and how I listened to every blast of wind as if it were a dull ugly siroc on its way to consume me.

Morning dawned before I arrived at the village of Chamounix; I took no rest, but returned immediately to Geneva. Even in my own heart I could give no expression to my sensations – they weighed on me with a mountain's weight and their excess destroyed my agony beneath them. Thus I returned home, and entering the house, presented myself to the family. My haggard and wild appearance awoke intense alarm, but I answered no question, scarcely did I speak. I felt as if I were placed under a ban – as if I had no right to claim their sympathies – as if never more might I enjoy companionship with them. Yet even thus I loved them to adoration; and to save them, I resolved to dedicate myself to my most abhorred task. The prospect of such an occupation made every other circumstance of existence pass before me like a dream, and that thought only had to me the reality of life.

Chapter XVIII

DAY AFTER DAY, week after week, passed away on my return to Geneva; and I could not collect the courage to recommence my work. I feared the vengeance of the disappointed fiend, yet I was unable to overcome my repugnance to the task which was enjoined me. I found that I could not compose a female without again devoting several months to profound study and laborious disquisition. I had heard of some discoveries having been made by an English philosopher, the knowledge of which was material to my success, and I sometimes thought of obtaining my father's consent to visit England for this purpose; but I clung to every pretence of delay and shrank from taking the first step in an undertaking whose immediate necessity began to appear less absolute to me. A change indeed had taken place in me; my health, which had hitherto declined, was now much restored; and my spirits, when unchecked by the memory of my unhappy promise, rose proportionably. My father saw this change with pleasure, and he turned his thoughts towards the best method of eradicating the remains of my melancholy, which every now and then would return by fits, and with a devouring blackness overcast the approaching sunshine. At these moments I took refuge in the most perfect solitude. I passed whole days on the lake alone in a little boat, watching the clouds and listening to the rippling of the waves, silent and listless. But the fresh air and bright sun seldom failed to restore me to some degree of composure, and on my return I met the salutations of my friends with a readier smile and a more cheerful heart.

It was after my return from one of these rambles that my father, calling me aside, thus addressed me:

"I am happy to remark, my dear son, that you have resumed your former pleasures and seem to be returning to yourself. And yet you are still unhappy and still avoid our society. For some time I was lost in conjecture as to the cause of this, but yesterday an idea struck me, and if it is well founded, I conjure you to avow it. Reserve on such a point would be not only useless, but draw down treble misery on us all."

I trembled violently at his exordium, and my father continued – "I confess, my son, that I have always looked forward to your marriage with our dear Elizabeth as the tie of our domestic comfort and the stay of my declining years. You were attached to each other from your earliest infancy; you studied together, and appeared, in dispositions and tastes, entirely suited to one another. But so blind is the experience of man that what I conceived to be the best assistants to my plan may have entirely destroyed it. You, perhaps, regard her as your sister, without any wish that she might become your wife. Nay, you may have met with another whom you may love; and considering yourself as bound in honour to Elizabeth, this struggle may occasion the poignant misery which you appear to feel."

"My dear father, reassure yourself. I love my cousin tenderly and sincerely. I never saw any woman who excited, as Elizabeth does, my warmest admiration and affection. My future hopes and prospects are entirely bound up in the expectation of our union."

"The expression of your sentiments of this subject, my dear Victor, gives me more pleasure than I have for some time experienced. If you feel thus, we shall assuredly be happy, however present events may cast a gloom over us. But it is this gloom which appears to have taken so strong a hold of your mind that I wish to dissipate. Tell me, therefore, whether you object to an immediate solemnization of the marriage. We have been unfortunate, and recent events have drawn us from that everyday tranquillity befitting my years and infirmities. You are younger; yet I do not suppose, possessed as you are of a competent fortune, that an early marriage would at all interfere with any future plans of honour and utility that you may have formed. Do not suppose, however, that I wish to dictate happiness to you or that a delay on your part would cause me any serious uneasiness. Interpret my words with candour and answer me, I conjure you, with confidence and sincerity."

I listened to my father in silence and remained for some time incapable of offering any reply. I revolved rapidly in my mind a multitude of thoughts and endeavoured to arrive at some conclusion. Alas! To me the idea of an immediate union with my Elizabeth was one of horror and dismay. I was bound by a solemn promise which I had not yet fulfilled and dared not break, or if I did, what manifold miseries might not impend over me and my devoted family! Could I enter into a festival with this deadly weight yet hanging round my neck and bowing me to the ground? I must perform my engagement and let the monster depart with his mate before I allowed myself to enjoy the delight of a union from which I expected peace.

I remembered also the necessity imposed upon me of either journeying to England or entering into a long correspondence with those philosophers of that country whose knowledge and discoveries were of indispensable use to me in my present undertaking. The latter method of obtaining the desired intelligence was dilatory and unsatisfactory; besides, I had an insurmountable aversion to the idea of engaging myself in my loathsome task in my father's house while in habits of familiar intercourse with those I loved. I knew that a thousand fearful accidents might occur, the slightest of which would disclose a tale to thrill all connected with me with horror. I was aware also that I should often lose all self-command, all capacity of hiding the harrowing sensations that would possess me during the progress of my unearthly occupation. I must absent myself from all I loved while thus employed. Once commenced, it would quickly be achieved, and I might be restored to my family in peace and happiness. My promise fulfilled, the monster would depart forever. Or (so my fond fancy imaged) some accident might meanwhile occur to destroy him and put an end to my slavery forever.

These feelings dictated my answer to my father. I expressed a wish to visit England, but concealing the true reasons of this request, I clothed my desires under a guise which excited no suspicion, while I urged my desire with an earnestness that easily induced my father to comply. After so long a period of an absorbing melancholy that resembled madness in its intensity and effects, he was glad to find that I was capable of taking pleasure in the idea of such a journey, and he hoped that change of scene and varied amusement would, before my return, have restored me entirely to myself.

The duration of my absence was left to my own choice; a few months, or at most a year, was the period contemplated. One paternal kind precaution he had taken to ensure my having a companion. Without previously communicating with me, he had, in concert with Elizabeth, arranged that Clerval should join me at Strasbourg. This interfered with the solitude I coveted for the prosecution of my task; yet at the commencement of my journey the presence of my friend could in no way be an impediment, and truly I rejoiced that thus I should be saved many hours of lonely, maddening reflection. Nay, Henry might stand between me and the intrusion of my foe. If I were alone, would he not at times force his abhorred presence on me to remind me of my task or to contemplate its progress?

To England, therefore, I was bound, and it was understood that my union with Elizabeth should take place immediately on my return. My father's age rendered him extremely averse to delay. For myself, there was one reward I promised myself from my detested toils – one consolation for my unparalleled sufferings; it was the prospect of that day when, enfranchised from my miserable slavery, I might claim Elizabeth and forget the past in my union with her.

I now made arrangements for my journey, but one feeling haunted me which filled me with fear and agitation. During my absence I should leave my friends unconscious of the existence of their enemy and unprotected from his attacks, exasperated as he might be by my departure. But he had promised to follow me wherever I might go, and would he not accompany me to England? This imagination was dreadful in itself, but soothing inasmuch as it supposed the safety of my friends. I was agonized with the idea of the possibility that the reverse of this might happen. But through the whole period during which I was the slave of my creature I allowed myself to be governed by the impulses of the moment; and my present sensations strongly intimated that the fiend would follow me and exempt my family from the danger of his machinations.

It was in the latter end of September that I again quitted my native country. My journey had been my own suggestion, and Elizabeth therefore acquiesced, but she was filled with disquiet at the idea of my suffering, away from her, the inroads of misery and grief. It had been her care which provided me a companion in Clerval – and yet a man is blind to a thousand minute circumstances which call forth a woman's sedulous attention. She longed to bid me hasten my return; a thousand conflicting emotions rendered her mute as she bade me a tearful, silent farewell.

I threw myself into the carriage that was to convey me away, hardly knowing whither I was going, and careless of what was passing around. I remembered only, and it was with a bitter anguish that I reflected on it, to order that my chemical instruments should be packed to go with me. Filled with dreary imaginations, I passed through many beautiful and majestic scenes, but my eyes were fixed and unobserving. I could only think of the bourne of my travels and the work which was to occupy me whilst they endured.

After some days spent in listless indolence, during which I traversed many leagues, I arrived at Strasbourg, where I waited two days for Clerval. He came. Alas, how great was the contrast between us! He was alive to every new scene, joyful when he saw the beauties of the setting sun, and more happy when he beheld it rise and recommence a new day. He pointed out to me the shifting colours of the landscape and the appearances of the sky. "This is what it is to live," he cried; "how I enjoy existence! But you, my dear Frankenstein, wherefore are you desponding and sorrowful!" In truth, I was occupied by gloomy thoughts and neither saw the descent of the evening star nor the golden sunrise reflected in the Rhine. And you, my friend, would be far more amused with the journal of Clerval, who observed the scenery with an eye of feeling and delight, than in listening to my reflections. I, a miserable wretch, haunted by a curse that shut up every avenue to enjoyment.

We had agreed to descend the Rhine in a boat from Strasbourg to Rotterdam, whence we might take shipping for London. During this voyage we passed many willowy islands and saw several beautiful towns. We stayed a day at Mannheim, and on the fifth from our departure from Strasbourg, arrived at Mainz. The course of the Rhine below Mainz becomes much more picturesque. The river descends rapidly and winds between hills, not high, but steep, and of beautiful forms. We saw many ruined castles standing on the edges of precipices, surrounded by black woods, high and inaccessible. This part of the Rhine, indeed, presents a singularly variegated landscape. In one spot you view rugged hills, ruined castles overlooking tremendous precipices, with the dark Rhine rushing beneath; and on the sudden turn of a promontory, flourishing vineyards with green sloping banks and a meandering river and populous towns occupy the scene.

We travelled at the time of the vintage and heard the song of the labourers as we glided down the stream. Even I, depressed in mind, and my spirits continually agitated by gloomy feelings, even I was pleased. I lay at the bottom of the boat, and as I gazed on the cloudless blue sky, I seemed to drink in a tranquillity to which I had long been a stranger. And if these were my sensations, who can describe those of Henry? He felt as if he had been transported to fairy-land and enjoyed a happiness seldom tasted by man. "I have seen," he said, "the most beautiful scenes of my own country; I have visited the lakes of Lucerne and Uri, where the snowy mountains descend almost perpendicularly to the water, casting black and impenetrable shades, which would cause a gloomy and mournful appearance were it not for the most verdant islands that believe the eye by their gay appearance; I have seen this lake agitated by a tempest, when the wind tore up whirlwinds of water and gave you an idea of what the water-spout must be on the great ocean; and the waves dash with fury the base of the mountain, where the priest and his mistress were overwhelmed by an avalanche and where their dying voices are still said to be heard amid the pauses of the nightly wind; I have seen the mountains of La Valais, and the Pays de Vaud; but this country, Victor, pleases me more than all those wonders. The mountains of Switzerland are more majestic and strange, but there is a charm in the banks of this divine river that I never before saw equalled. Look at that castle which overhangs yon precipice; and that also on the island, almost concealed amongst the foliage of those lovely trees; and now that group of labourers coming from among their vines; and that village half hid in the recess of the mountain. Oh, surely the spirit that inhabits and guards this place has a soul more in harmony with man than those who pile the glacier or retire to the inaccessible peaks of the mountains of our own country." Clerval! Beloved friend! Even now it delights me to record your words and to dwell on the praise of which you are so eminently deserving. He was a being formed in the "very poetry of nature." His wild and enthusiastic imagination was chastened by the sensibility of his heart. His soul overflowed with ardent affections, and his friendship was of that devoted and wondrous nature that the world-minded teach us to look for only in the imagination. But even human sympathies were not sufficient to satisfy his eager mind. The scenery of external nature, which others regard only with admiration, he loved with ardour:

> *The sounding cataract*
> *Haunted him like a passion: the tall rock,*
> *The mountain, and the deep and gloomy wood,*
> *Their colours and their forms, were then to him*
> *An appetite; a feeling, and a love,*
> *That had no need of a remoter charm,*
> *By thought supplied, or any interest*
> *Unborrow'd from the eye.*
> (William Wordsworth, 'Tintern Abbey')

And where does he now exist? Is this gentle and lovely being lost forever? Has this mind, so replete with ideas, imaginations fanciful and magnificent, which formed a world, whose existence depended on the life of its creator; – has this mind perished?

Does it now only exist in my memory? No, it is not thus; your form so divinely wrought, and beaming with beauty, has decayed, but your spirit still visits and consoles your unhappy friend.

Pardon this gush of sorrow; these ineffectual words are but a slight tribute to the unexampled worth of Henry, but they soothe my heart, overflowing with the anguish which his remembrance creates. I will proceed with my tale.

Beyond Cologne we descended to the plains of Holland; and we resolved to post the remainder of our way, for the wind was contrary and the stream of the river was too gentle to aid us. Our journey here lost the interest arising from beautiful scenery, but we arrived in a few days at Rotterdam, whence we proceeded by sea to England. It was on a clear morning, in the latter days of December, that I first saw the white cliffs of Britain. The banks of the Thames presented a new scene; they were flat but fertile, and almost every town was marked by the remembrance of some story. We saw Tilbury Fort and remembered the Spanish Armada, Gravesend, Woolwich, and Greenwich – places which I had heard of even in my country.

At length we saw the numerous steeples of London, St. Paul's towering above all, and the Tower famed in English history.

Chapter XIX

LONDON WAS our present point of rest; we determined to remain several months in this wonderful and celebrated city. Clerval desired the intercourse of the men of genius and talent who flourished at this time, but this was with me a secondary object; I was principally occupied with the means of obtaining the information necessary for the completion of my promise and quickly availed myself of the letters of introduction that I had brought with me, addressed to the most distinguished natural philosophers.

If this journey had taken place during my days of study and happiness, it would have afforded me inexpressible pleasure. But a blight had come over my existence, and I only visited these people for the sake of the information they might give me on the subject in which my interest was so terribly profound. Company was irksome to me; when alone, I could fill my mind with the sights of heaven and earth; the voice of Henry soothed me, and I could thus cheat myself into a transitory peace. But busy, uninteresting, joyous faces brought back despair to my heart. I saw an insurmountable barrier placed between me and my fellow men; this barrier was sealed with the blood of William and Justine, and to reflect on the events connected with those names filled my soul with anguish.

But in Clerval I saw the image of my former self; he was inquisitive and anxious to gain experience and instruction. The difference of manners which he observed was to him an inexhaustible source of instruction and amusement. He was also pursuing an object he had long had in view. His design was to visit India, in the belief that he had in his knowledge of its various languages, and in the views he had taken of its society, the means of materially assisting the progress of European colonization and trade. In Britain only could he further the execution of his plan. He was forever busy, and the only check to his enjoyments was my sorrowful and dejected mind. I tried to conceal this as much as possible, that I might not debar him from the pleasures natural to one who was entering on a new scene of life, undisturbed by any care or bitter recollection. I often refused to accompany him, alleging another engagement, that I might remain alone. I now also began to collect the materials necessary for my new creation, and this was to me like the torture of single drops of water continually falling on the head. Every thought that was devoted to it was an extreme anguish, and every word that I spoke in allusion to it caused my lips to quiver, and my heart to palpitate.

After passing some months in London, we received a letter from a person in Scotland who had formerly been our visitor at Geneva. He mentioned the beauties of his native country and asked us if those were not sufficient allurements to induce us to prolong our journey as far north as Perth, where he resided. Clerval eagerly desired to accept this invitation, and I, although I abhorred society, wished to view again mountains and streams and all the wondrous works with which Nature adorns her chosen dwelling-places. We had arrived in England at the beginning of October, and it was now February. We accordingly determined to commence our journey towards the north at the expiration of another month. In this expedition we did not intend to follow the great road to Edinburgh, but to visit Windsor, Oxford, Matlock, and the Cumberland lakes, resolving to arrive at the completion of this tour about the end of July. I packed up my chemical instruments and the materials I had collected, resolving to finish my labours in some obscure nook in the northern highlands of Scotland.

We quitted London on the 27th of March and remained a few days at Windsor, rambling in its beautiful forest. This was a new scene to us mountaineers; the majestic oaks, the quantity of game, and the herds of stately deer were all novelties to us.

From thence we proceeded to Oxford. As we entered this city our minds were filled with the remembrance of the events that had been transacted there more than a century and a half before. It was here that Charles I had collected his forces. This city had remained faithful to him, after the whole nation had forsaken his cause to join the standard of Parliament and liberty. The memory of that unfortunate king and his companions, the amiable Falkland, the insolent Goring, his queen, and son, gave a peculiar interest to every part of the city which they might be supposed to have inhabited. The spirit of elder days found a dwelling here, and we delighted to trace its footsteps. If these feelings had not found an imaginary gratification, the appearance of the city had yet in itself sufficient beauty to obtain our admiration. The colleges are ancient and picturesque; the streets are almost magnificent; and the lovely Isis, which flows beside it through meadows of exquisite verdure, is spread forth into a placid expanse of waters, which reflects its majestic assemblage of towers, and spires, and domes, embosomed among aged trees.

I enjoyed this scene, and yet my enjoyment was embittered both by the memory of the past and the anticipation of the future. I was formed for peaceful happiness. During my youthful days discontent never visited my mind, and if I was ever overcome by ennui, the sight of what is beautiful in nature or the study of what is excellent and sublime in the productions of man could always interest my heart and communicate elasticity to my spirits. But I am a blasted tree; the bolt has entered my soul; and I felt then that I should survive to exhibit what I shall soon cease to be – a miserable spectacle of wrecked humanity, pitiable to others and intolerable to myself.

We passed a considerable period at Oxford, rambling among its environs and endeavouring to identify every spot which might relate to the most animating epoch of English history. Our little voyages of discovery were often prolonged by the successive objects that presented themselves. We visited the tomb of the illustrious Hampden and the field on which that patriot fell. For a moment my soul was elevated from its debasing and miserable fears to contemplate the divine ideas of liberty and self sacrifice of which these sights were the monuments and the remembrancers. For an instant I dared to shake off my chains and look around me with a free and lofty spirit, but the iron had eaten into my flesh, and I sank again, trembling and hopeless, into my miserable self.

We left Oxford with regret and proceeded to Matlock, which was our next place of rest. The country in the neighbourhood of this village resembled, to a greater degree, the scenery of Switzerland; but everything is on a lower scale, and the green hills want the crown of distant white Alps which always attend on the piny mountains of my native country. We visited the wondrous cave and the little cabinets of natural history, where the curiosities are disposed in the same manner as in the collections at Servox and Chamounix. The latter name made me tremble when pronounced by Henry, and I hastened to quit Matlock, with which that terrible scene was thus associated.

From Derby, still journeying northwards, we passed two months in Cumberland and Westmorland. I could now almost fancy myself among the Swiss mountains. The little patches of snow which yet lingered on the northern sides of the mountains, the lakes, and the dashing of the rocky streams were all familiar and dear sights to me. Here also we made some acquaintances, who almost contrived to cheat me into happiness. The delight of Clerval was proportionably greater than mine; his mind expanded in the company of men of talent, and he found in his own nature greater capacities and resources than he could have imagined himself to have possessed while he associated with his inferiors. "I could pass my life here," said he to me; "and among these mountains I should scarcely regret Switzerland and the Rhine."

But he found that a traveller's life is one that includes much pain amidst its enjoyments. His feelings are forever on the stretch; and when he begins to sink into repose, he finds himself obliged to quit that on which he rests in pleasure for something new, which again engages his attention, and which also he forsakes for other novelties.

We had scarcely visited the various lakes of Cumberland and Westmorland and conceived an affection for some of the inhabitants when the period of our appointment with our Scotch friend approached, and we left them to travel on. For my own part I was not sorry. I had now neglected my promise for some time, and I feared the effects of the daemon's disappointment. He might remain in Switzerland and wreak his vengeance on my relatives. This idea pursued me and tormented me at every moment from which I might otherwise have snatched repose and peace. I waited for my letters with feverish impatience; if they were delayed I was miserable and overcome by a thousand fears; and when they arrived and I saw the superscription of Elizabeth or my father, I hardly dared to read and ascertain my fate. Sometimes I thought that the fiend followed me and might expedite my remissness by murdering my companion. When these thoughts possessed me, I would not quit Henry for a moment, but followed him as his shadow, to protect him from the fancied rage of his destroyer. I felt as if I had committed some great crime, the consciousness of which haunted me. I was guiltless, but I had indeed drawn down a horrible curse upon my head, as mortal as that of crime.

I visited Edinburgh with languid eyes and mind; and yet that city might have interested the most unfortunate being. Clerval did not like it so well as Oxford, for the antiquity of the latter city was more pleasing to him. But the beauty and regularity of the new town of Edinburgh, its romantic castle and its environs, the most delightful in the world, Arthur's Seat, St. Bernard's Well, and the Pentland Hills compensated him for the change and filled him with cheerfulness and admiration. But I was impatient to arrive at the termination of my journey.

We left Edinburgh in a week, passing through Coupar, St. Andrew's, and along the banks of the Tay, to Perth, where our friend expected us. But I was in no mood to laugh and talk with strangers or enter into their feelings or plans with the good humour expected from a guest; and accordingly I told Clerval that I wished to make the tour of Scotland alone. "Do you," said I, "enjoy yourself, and let this be our rendezvous. I may be absent a month or two; but do not interfere with my motions, I entreat you; leave me to peace and solitude for a short time; and when I return, I hope it will be with a lighter heart, more congenial to your own temper."

Henry wished to dissuade me, but seeing me bent on this plan, ceased to remonstrate. He entreated me to write often. "I had rather be with you," he said, "in your solitary rambles, than with these Scotch people, whom I do not know; hasten, then, my dear friend, to return, that I may again feel myself somewhat at home, which I cannot do in your absence."

Having parted from my friend, I determined to visit some remote spot of Scotland and finish my work in solitude. I did not doubt but that the monster followed me and would discover himself to me when I should have finished, that he might receive his companion. With this resolution I traversed the northern highlands and fixed on one of the remotest of the Orkneys as the scene of my labours. It was a place fitted for such a work, being hardly more than a rock whose high sides were continually beaten upon by the waves. The soil was barren, scarcely affording pasture for a few miserable cows, and oatmeal for its inhabitants, which consisted of five persons, whose gaunt and scraggy limbs gave tokens of their miserable fare. Vegetables and bread, when they indulged in such luxuries, and even fresh water, was to be procured from the mainland, which was about five miles distant.

On the whole island there were but three miserable huts, and one of these was vacant when I arrived. This I hired. It contained but two rooms, and these exhibited all the squalidness of the most miserable penury. The thatch had fallen in, the walls were unplastered, and the door was off its hinges. I ordered it to be repaired, bought some furniture, and took possession, an incident which would doubtless have occasioned some surprise had not all the senses of the cottagers been benumbed by want and squalid poverty. As it was, I lived ungazed at and unmolested, hardly thanked for the pittance of food and clothes which I gave, so much does suffering blunt even the coarsest sensations of men.

In this retreat I devoted the morning to labour; but in the evening, when the weather permitted, I walked on the stony beach of the sea to listen to the waves as they roared and dashed at my feet. It was a monotonous yet ever-changing scene. I thought of Switzerland; it was far different from this desolate and appalling landscape. Its hills are covered with vines, and its cottages are scattered thickly in the plains. Its fair lakes reflect a blue and gentle sky, and when troubled by the winds, their tumult is but as the play of a lively infant when compared to the roarings of the giant ocean.

In this manner I distributed my occupations when I first arrived, but as I proceeded in my labour, it became every day more horrible and irksome to me. Sometimes I could not prevail on myself to enter my laboratory for several days, and at other times I toiled day and night in order to complete my work. It was, indeed, a filthy process in which I was engaged. During my first experiment, a kind of enthusiastic frenzy had blinded me to the horror of my employment; my mind was intently fixed on the consummation of my labour, and my eyes were shut to the horror of my proceedings. But now I went to it in cold blood, and my heart often sickened at the work of my hands.

Thus situated, employed in the most detestable occupation, immersed in a solitude where nothing could for an instant call my attention from the actual scene in which I was engaged, my spirits became unequal; I grew restless and nervous. Every moment I feared to meet my persecutor. Sometimes I sat with my eyes fixed on the ground, fearing to raise them lest they should encounter the object which I so much dreaded to behold. I feared to wander from the sight of my fellow creatures lest when alone he should come to claim his companion.

In the mean time I worked on, and my labour was already considerably advanced. I looked towards its completion with a tremulous and eager hope, which I dared not trust myself to question but which was intermixed with obscure forebodings of evil that made my heart sicken in my bosom.

Chapter XX

I SAT ONE EVENING in my laboratory; the sun had set, and the moon was just rising from the sea; I had not sufficient light for my employment, and I remained idle, in a pause of consideration of whether I should leave my labour for the night or hasten its conclusion by an unremitting attention to it. As I sat, a train of reflection occurred to me which led me to consider the effects of what I was now doing. Three years before, I was engaged in the same manner and had created a fiend whose unparalleled barbarity had desolated my heart and filled it forever with the bitterest remorse. I was now about to form another being of whose dispositions I was alike ignorant; she might become ten thousand times more malignant than her mate and delight, for its own sake, in murder and wretchedness. He had sworn to quit the neighbourhood of man and hide himself in deserts, but she had not; and she, who in all probability was to become a thinking and reasoning animal, might refuse to comply with a compact made before her creation. They might even hate each other; the creature who already lived loathed his own deformity, and might he not conceive a greater abhorrence for it when it came before his eyes in the female form? She also might turn with disgust from him to the superior beauty of man; she might quit him, and he be again alone, exasperated by the fresh provocation of being deserted by one of his own species. Even if they were to leave Europe and inhabit the deserts of the new world, yet one of the first results of those sympathies for which the daemon thirsted would be children, and a race of devils would be propagated upon the earth who might make the very existence of the species of man a condition precarious and full of terror. Had I right, for my own benefit, to inflict this curse upon everlasting generations? I had before been moved by the sophisms of the being I had created; I had been struck senseless by his fiendish threats; but now, for the first time, the wickedness of my promise burst upon me; I shuddered to think that future ages might curse me as their pest, whose selfishness had not hesitated to buy its own peace at the price, perhaps, of the existence of the whole human race.

I trembled and my heart failed within me, when, on looking up, I saw by the light of the moon the daemon at the casement. A ghastly grin wrinkled his lips as he gazed on me, where I sat fulfilling the task which he had allotted to me. Yes, he had followed me in my travels; he had loitered in forests, hid himself in caves, or taken refuge in wide and desert heaths; and he now came to mark my progress and claim the fulfillment of my promise.

As I looked on him, his countenance expressed the utmost extent of malice and treachery. I thought with a sensation of madness on my promise of creating another like to him, and trembling with passion, tore to pieces the thing on which I was engaged. The wretch saw me destroy the creature on whose future existence he depended for happiness, and with a howl of devilish despair and revenge, withdrew.

I left the room, and locking the door, made a solemn vow in my own heart never to resume my labours; and then, with trembling steps, I sought my own apartment. I was alone; none were near me to dissipate the gloom and relieve me from the sickening oppression of the most terrible reveries.

Several hours passed, and I remained near my window gazing on the sea; it was almost motionless, for the winds were hushed, and all nature reposed under the eye of the quiet moon. A few fishing vessels alone specked the water, and now and then the gentle breeze wafted the sound of voices as the fishermen called to one another. I felt the silence, although I was hardly conscious of its extreme profundity, until my ear was suddenly arrested by the paddling of oars near the shore, and a person landed close to my house.

In a few minutes after, I heard the creaking of my door, as if someone endeavoured to open it softly. I trembled from head to foot; I felt a presentiment of who it was and wished to rouse one of the peasants who dwelt in a cottage not far from mine; but I was overcome by the sensation of helplessness, so often felt in frightful dreams, when you in vain endeavour to fly from an impending danger, and was rooted to the spot. Presently I heard the sound of footsteps along the passage; the door opened, and the wretch whom I dreaded appeared.

Shutting the door, he approached me and said in a smothered voice, "You have destroyed the work which you began; what is it that you intend? Do you dare to break your promise? I have endured toil and misery; I left Switzerland with you; I crept along the shores of the Rhine, among its willow islands and over the summits of its hills. I have dwelt many months in the heaths of England and among the deserts of Scotland. I have endured incalculable fatigue, and cold, and hunger; do you dare destroy my hopes?"

"Begone! I do break my promise; never will I create another like yourself, equal in deformity and wickedness."

"Slave, I before reasoned with you, but you have proved yourself unworthy of my condescension. Remember that I have power; you believe yourself miserable, but I can make you so wretched that the light of day will be hateful to you. You are my creator, but I am your master; obey!"

"The hour of my irresolution is past, and the period of your power is arrived. Your threats cannot move me to do an act of wickedness; but they confirm me in a determination of not creating you a companion in vice. Shall I, in cool blood, set loose upon the earth a daemon whose delight is in death and wretchedness? Begone! I am firm, and your words will only exasperate my rage."

The monster saw my determination in my face and gnashed his teeth in the impotence of anger. "Shall each man," cried he, "find a wife for his bosom, and each beast have his mate, and I be alone? I had feelings of affection, and they were requited by detestation and scorn. Man! You may hate, but beware! Your hours will pass in dread and misery, and soon the bolt will fall which must ravish from you your happiness forever. Are you to be happy while I grovel in the intensity of my wretchedness? You can blast my other passions, but revenge remains – revenge, henceforth dearer than light or food! I may die, but first you, my tyrant and tormentor, shall curse the sun that gazes on your misery. Beware, for I am fearless and therefore powerful. I will watch with the wiliness of a snake, that I may sting with its venom. Man, you shall repent of the injuries you inflict."

"Devil, cease; and do not poison the air with these sounds of malice. I have declared my resolution to you, and I am no coward to bend beneath words. Leave me; I am inexorable."

"It is well. I go; but remember, I shall be with you on your wedding-night."

I started forward and exclaimed, "Villain! Before you sign my death-warrant, be sure that you are yourself safe."

I would have seized him, but he eluded me and quitted the house with precipitation. In a few moments I saw him in his boat, which shot across the waters with an arrowy swiftness and was soon lost amidst the waves.

All was again silent, but his words rang in my ears. I burned with rage to pursue the murderer of my peace and precipitate him into the ocean. I walked up and down my room hastily and perturbed, while my imagination conjured up a thousand images to torment and sting me. Why had I not followed him and closed with him in mortal strife? But I had suffered him to depart, and he had directed his course towards the mainland. I shuddered to think who might be the next victim sacrificed to his insatiate revenge. And then I thought again of his words – "I will be with you on your wedding-night." That, then, was the period fixed for the fulfillment of my destiny. In that hour I should die and at once satisfy and extinguish his malice. The prospect did not move me to fear; yet when I thought of my beloved Elizabeth, of her tears and endless sorrow, when she should find her lover so barbarously snatched from her, tears, the first I had shed for many months, streamed from my eyes, and I resolved not to fall before my enemy without a bitter struggle.

The night passed away, and the sun rose from the ocean; my feelings became calmer, if it may be called calmness when the violence of rage sinks into the depths of despair. I left the house, the horrid scene of the last night's contention, and walked on the beach of the sea, which I almost regarded as an insuperable barrier between me and my fellow creatures; nay, a wish that such should prove the fact stole across me.

I desired that I might pass my life on that barren rock, wearily, it is true, but uninterrupted by any sudden shock of misery. If I returned, it was to be sacrificed or to see those whom I most loved die under the grasp of a daemon whom I had myself created.

I walked about the isle like a restless spectre, separated from all it loved and miserable in the separation. When it became noon, and the sun rose higher, I lay down on the grass and was overpowered by a deep sleep. I had been awake the whole of the preceding night, my nerves were agitated, and my eyes inflamed by watching and misery. The sleep into which I now sank refreshed me; and when I awoke, I again

MARY SHELLEY HORROR STORIES

felt as if I belonged to a race of human beings like myself, and I began to reflect upon what had passed with greater composure; yet still the words of the fiend rang in my ears like a death-knell; they appeared like a dream, yet distinct and oppressive as a reality.

The sun had far descended, and I still sat on the shore, satisfying my appetite, which had become ravenous, with an oaten cake, when I saw a fishing-boat land close to me, and one of the men brought me a packet; it contained letters from Geneva, and one from Clerval entreating me to join him. He said that he was wearing away his time fruitlessly where he was, that letters from the friends he had formed in London desired his return to complete the negotiation they had entered into for his Indian enterprise. He could not any longer delay his departure; but as his journey to London might be followed, even sooner than he now conjectured, by his longer voyage, he entreated me to bestow as much of my society on him as I could spare. He besought me, therefore, to leave my solitary isle and to meet him at Perth, that we might proceed southwards together. This letter in a degree recalled me to life, and I determined to quit my island at the expiration of two days. Yet, before I departed, there was a task to perform, on which I shuddered to reflect; I must pack up my chemical instruments, and for that purpose I must enter the room which had been the scene of my odious work, and I must handle those utensils the sight of which was sickening to me. The next morning, at daybreak, I summoned sufficient courage and unlocked the door of my laboratory. The remains of the half-finished creature, whom I had destroyed, lay scattered on the floor, and I almost felt as if I had mangled the living flesh of a human being. I paused to collect myself and then entered the chamber. With trembling hand I conveyed the instruments out of the room, but I reflected that I ought not to leave the relics of my work to excite the horror and suspicion of the peasants; and I accordingly put them into a basket, with a great quantity of stones, and laying them up, determined to throw them into the sea that very night; and in the meantime I sat upon the beach, employed in cleaning and arranging my chemical apparatus.

Nothing could be more complete than the alteration that had taken place in my feelings since the night of the appearance of the daemon. I had before regarded my promise with a gloomy despair as a thing that, with whatever consequences, must be fulfilled; but I now felt as if a film had been taken from before my eyes and that I for the first time saw clearly. The idea of renewing my labours did not for one instant occur to me; the threat I had heard weighed on my thoughts, but I did not reflect that a voluntary act of mine could avert it. I had resolved in my own mind that to create another like the fiend I had first made would be an act of the basest and most atrocious selfishness, and I banished from my mind every thought that could lead to a different conclusion.

Between two and three in the morning the moon rose; and I then, putting my basket aboard a little skiff, sailed out about four miles from the shore. The scene was perfectly solitary; a few boats were returning towards land, but I sailed away from them. I felt as if I was about the commission of a dreadful crime and avoided with shuddering anxiety any encounter with my fellow creatures. At one time the moon, which had before been clear, was suddenly overspread by a thick cloud, and I took advantage of the moment of darkness and cast my basket into the sea; I listened to the gurgling sound as it sank and then sailed away from the spot. The sky became clouded, but the air was pure, although chilled by the northeast breeze that was then rising. But it refreshed me and filled me with such agreeable sensations that I resolved to prolong my stay on the water, and fixing the rudder in a direct position, stretched myself at the bottom of the boat. Clouds hid the moon, everything was obscure, and I heard only the sound of the boat as its keel cut through the waves; the murmur lulled me, and in a short time I slept soundly. I do not know how long I remained in this situation, but when I awoke I found that the sun had already mounted considerably. The wind was high, and the waves continually threatened the safety of my little skiff. I found that the wind was northeast and must have driven me far from the coast from which I had embarked. I endeavoured to change my course but quickly found that if I again made the attempt the boat would be instantly filled with water. Thus situated, my only resource was to drive before the wind. I confess that I felt a few sensations of terror. I had no compass with me and was so slenderly acquainted with the geography of this part of the world that the sun was of little benefit to me. I might be driven into the wide Atlantic and feel all the tortures of starvation or be swallowed up in the immeasurable waters that roared and buffeted around me. I had already been out many hours and felt the torment of a burning thirst, a prelude to my other sufferings. I looked on the heavens, which were covered by clouds that flew before the wind, only to be replaced by others; I looked upon the sea; it was to be my grave. "Fiend," I exclaimed, "your task is already fulfilled!" I thought of Elizabeth, of my father, and of Clerval – all left behind, on whom the monster might satisfy his sanguinary and merciless passions. This idea plunged me into a reverie so despairing and frightful that even now, when the scene is on the point of closing before me forever, I shudder to reflect on it.

Some hours passed thus; but by degrees, as the sun declined towards the horizon, the wind died away into a gentle breeze and the sea became free from breakers. But these gave place to a heavy swell; I felt sick and hardly able to hold the rudder, when suddenly I saw a line of high land towards the south.

Almost spent, as I was, by fatigue and the dreadful suspense I endured for several hours, this sudden certainty of life rushed like a flood of warm joy to my heart, and tears gushed from my eyes.

How mutable are our feelings, and how strange is that clinging love we have of life even in the excess of misery! I constructed another sail with a part of my dress and eagerly steered my course towards the land. It had a wild and rocky appearance, but as I approached nearer I easily perceived the traces of cultivation. I saw vessels near the shore and found myself suddenly transported back to the neighbourhood of civilized man. I carefully traced the windings of the land and hailed a steeple which I at length saw issuing from behind a small promontory. As I was in a state of extreme debility, I resolved to sail directly towards the town, as a place where I could most easily procure nourishment. Fortunately I had money with me.

As I turned the promontory I perceived a small neat town and a good harbour, which I entered, my heart bounding with joy at my unexpected escape.

As I was occupied in fixing the boat and arranging the sails, several people crowded towards the spot. They seemed much surprised at my appearance, but instead of offering me any assistance, whispered together with gestures that at any other time might have produced in me a slight sensation of alarm. As it was, I merely remarked that they spoke English, and I therefore addressed them in that language. "My good friends," said I, "will you be so kind as to tell me the name of this town and inform me where I am?"

"You will know that soon enough," replied a man with a hoarse voice. "Maybe you are come to a place that will not prove much to your taste, but you will not be consulted as to your quarters, I promise you."

I was exceedingly surprised on receiving so rude an answer from a stranger, and I was also disconcerted on perceiving the frowning and angry countenances of his companions. "Why do you answer me so roughly?" I replied. "Surely it is not the custom of Englishmen to receive strangers so inhospitably."

"I do not know," said the man, "what the custom of the English may be, but it is the custom of the Irish to hate villains." While this strange dialogue continued, I perceived the crowd rapidly increase. Their faces expressed a mixture of curiosity and anger, which annoyed and in some degree alarmed me.

I inquired the way to the inn, but no one replied. I then moved forward, and a murmuring sound arose from the crowd as they followed and surrounded me, when an ill-looking man approaching tapped me on the shoulder and said, "Come, sir, you must follow me to Mr. Kirwin's to give an account of yourself."

"Who is Mr. Kirwin? Why am I to give an account of myself? Is not this a free country?"

"Ay, sir, free enough for honest folks. Mr. Kirwin is a magistrate, and you are to give an account of the death of a gentleman who was found murdered here last night."

This answer startled me, but I presently recovered myself. I was innocent; that could easily be proved; accordingly I followed my conductor in silence and was led to one of the best houses in the town. I was ready to sink from fatigue and hunger, but being surrounded by a crowd, I thought it politic to rouse all my strength, that no physical debility might be construed into apprehension or conscious guilt. Little did I then expect the calamity that was in a few moments to overwhelm me and extinguish in horror and despair all fear of ignominy or death. I must pause here, for it requires all my fortitude to recall the memory of the frightful events which I am about to relate, in proper detail, to my recollection.

Chapter XXI

I WAS SOON introduced into the presence of the magistrate, an old benevolent man with calm and mild manners. He looked upon me, however, with some degree of severity, and then, turning towards my conductors, he asked who appeared as witnesses on this occasion.

About half a dozen men came forward; and, one being selected by the magistrate, he deposed that he had been out fishing the night before with his son and brother-in-law, Daniel Nugent, when, about ten o'clock, they observed a strong northerly blast rising, and they accordingly put in for port. It was a very dark night, as the moon had not yet risen; they did not land at the harbour, but, as they had been accustomed, at a creek about two miles below. He walked on first, carrying a part of the fishing tackle, and his companions followed him at some distance.

As he was proceeding along the sands, he struck his foot against something and fell at his length on the ground. His companions came up to assist him, and by the light of their lantern they found that he had fallen on the body of a man, who was to all appearance dead. Their first supposition was that it was the corpse of some person who had been drowned and was thrown on shore by the waves, but on examination they found that the clothes were not wet and even that the body was not then cold. They instantly carried it to the cottage of an old woman near the spot and endeavoured, but in vain, to restore it to life. It appeared to be a handsome young man, about five and twenty years of age. He had apparently been strangled, for there was no sign of any violence except the black mark of fingers on his neck.

The first part of this deposition did not in the least interest me, but when the mark of the fingers was mentioned I remembered the murder of my brother and felt myself extremely agitated; my limbs trembled, and a mist came over my eyes, which obliged me to lean on a chair for support. The magistrate observed me with a keen eye and of course drew an unfavourable augury from my manner.

The son confirmed his father's account, but when Daniel Nugent was called he swore positively that just before the fall of his companion, he saw a boat, with a single man in it, at a short distance from the shore; and as far as he could judge by the light of a few stars, it was the same boat in which I had just landed. A woman deposed that she lived near the beach and was standing at the door of her cottage, waiting for the return of the fishermen, about an hour before she heard of the discovery of the body, when she saw a boat with only one man in it push off from that part of the shore where the corpse was afterwards found.

Another woman confirmed the account of the fishermen having brought the body into her house; it was not cold. They put it into a bed and rubbed it, and Daniel went to the town for an apothecary, but life was quite gone.

Several other men were examined concerning my landing, and they agreed that, with the strong north wind that had arisen during the night, it was very probable that I had beaten about for many hours and had been obliged to return nearly to the same spot from which I had departed. Besides, they observed that it appeared that I had brought the body from another place, and it was likely that as I did not appear to know the shore, I might have put into the harbour ignorant of the distance of the town of — from the place where I had deposited the corpse.

Mr. Kirwin, on hearing this evidence, desired that I should be taken into the room where the body lay for interment, that it might be observed what effect the sight of it would produce upon me. This idea was probably suggested by the extreme agitation I had exhibited when the mode of the murder had been described. I was accordingly conducted, by the magistrate and several other persons, to the inn. I could not help being struck by the strange coincidences that had taken place during this eventful night; but, knowing that I had been conversing with several persons in the island I had inhabited about the time that the body had been found, I was perfectly tranquil as to the consequences of the affair. I entered the room where the corpse lay and was led up to the coffin. How can I describe my sensations on beholding it? I feel yet parched with horror, nor can I reflect on that terrible moment without shuddering and agony. The examination, the presence of the magistrate and witnesses, passed like a dream from my memory when I saw the lifeless form of Henry Clerval stretched before me. I gasped for breath, and throwing myself on the body, I exclaimed, "Have my murderous machinations deprived you also, my dearest Henry, of life? Two I have already destroyed; other victims await their destiny; but you, Clerval, my friend, my benefactor –"

The human frame could no longer support the agonies that I endured, and I was carried out of the room in strong convulsions. A fever succeeded to this. I lay for two months on the point of death; my ravings, as I afterwards heard, were frightful; I called myself the murderer of William, of Justine, and of Clerval. Sometimes I entreated my attendants to assist me in the destruction of the fiend by whom I was tormented; and at others I felt the fingers of the monster already grasping my neck, and screamed aloud with agony and terror. Fortunately, as I spoke my native language, Mr. Kirwin alone understood me; but my gestures and bitter cries were sufficient to affright the other witnesses. Why did I not die? More miserable than man ever was before, why did I not sink into forgetfulness and rest? Death snatches away many blooming children, the only hopes of their doting parents; how many brides and youthful lovers have been one day in the bloom of health and hope, and the next a prey for worms and the decay of the tomb! Of what materials was I made that I could thus resist so many shocks, which, like the turning of the wheel, continually renewed the torture?

But I was doomed to live and in two months found myself as awaking from a dream, in a prison, stretched on a wretched bed, surrounded by jailers, turnkeys, bolts, and all the miserable apparatus of a dungeon. It was morning, I remember, when I thus awoke to understanding; I had forgotten the particulars of what had happened and only felt as if some great misfortune had suddenly overwhelmed me; but when I looked around and saw the barred windows and the squalidness of the room in which I was, all flashed across my memory and I groaned bitterly.

This sound disturbed an old woman who was sleeping in a chair beside me. She was a hired nurse, the wife of one of the turnkeys, and her countenance expressed all those bad qualities which often characterize that class. The lines of her face were hard and rude, like that of persons accustomed to see without sympathizing in sights of misery. Her tone expressed her entire indifference; she addressed me in English, and the voice struck me as one that I had heard during my sufferings. "Are you better now, sir?" said she.

I replied in the same language, with a feeble voice, "I believe I am; but if it be all true, if indeed I did not dream, I am sorry that I am still alive to feel this misery and horror."

"For that matter," replied the old woman, "if you mean about the gentleman you murdered, I believe that it were better for you if you were dead, for I fancy it will go hard with you! However, that's none of my business; I am sent to nurse you and get you well; I do my duty with a safe conscience; it were well if everybody did the same."

I turned with loathing from the woman who could utter so unfeeling a speech to a person just saved, on the very edge of death; but I felt languid and unable to reflect on all that had passed. The whole series of my life appeared to me as a dream; I sometimes doubted if indeed it were all true, for it never presented itself to my mind with the force of reality.

As the images that floated before me became more distinct, I grew feverish; a darkness pressed around me; no one was near me who soothed me with the gentle voice of love; no dear hand supported me. The physician came and prescribed medicines, and the old woman prepared them for me; but utter carelessness was visible in the first, and the expression of brutality was strongly marked in the visage of the second. Who could be interested in the fate of a murderer but the hangman who would gain his fee?

These were my first reflections, but I soon learned that Mr. Kirwin had shown me extreme kindness. He had caused the best room in the prison to be prepared for me (wretched indeed was the best); and it was he who had provided a physician and a nurse. It is true, he seldom came to see me, for although he ardently desired to relieve the sufferings of every human creature, he did not wish to be present at the agonies and miserable ravings of a murderer. He came, therefore, sometimes to see that I was not neglected, but his visits were short and with long intervals. One day, while I was gradually recovering, I was seated in a chair, my eyes half open and my cheeks livid like those in death. I was overcome by gloom and misery and often reflected I had better seek death than desire to remain in a world which to me was replete with wretchedness. At one time I considered whether I should not declare myself guilty and suffer the penalty of the law, less innocent than poor Justine had been. Such were my thoughts when the door of my apartment was opened and Mr. Kirwin entered. His countenance expressed sympathy and compassion; he drew a chair close to mine and addressed me in French, "I fear that this place is very shocking to you; can I do anything to make you more comfortable?"

"I thank you, but all that you mention is nothing to me; on the whole earth there is no comfort which I am capable of receiving."

"I know that the sympathy of a stranger can be but of little relief to one borne down as you are by so strange a misfortune. But you will, I hope, soon quit this melancholy abode, for doubtless evidence can easily be brought to free you from the criminal charge."

"That is my least concern; I am, by a course of strange events, become the most miserable of mortals. Persecuted and tortured as I am and have been, can death be any evil to me?"

"Nothing indeed could be more unfortunate and agonizing than the strange chances that have lately occurred. You were thrown, by some surprising accident, on this shore, renowned for its hospitality, seized immediately, and charged with murder. The first sight that was presented to your eyes was the body of your friend, murdered in so unaccountable a manner and placed, as it were, by some fiend across your path."

As Mr. Kirwin said this, notwithstanding the agitation I endured on this retrospect of my sufferings, I also felt considerable surprise at the knowledge he seemed to possess concerning me. I suppose some astonishment was exhibited in my countenance, for Mr. Kirwin hastened to say, "Immediately upon your being taken ill, all the papers that were on your person were brought me, and I examined them that I might discover some trace by which I could send to your relations an account of your misfortune and illness. I found several letters, and, among others, one which I discovered from its commencement to be from your father. I instantly wrote to Geneva; nearly two months have elapsed since the departure of my letter. But you are ill; even now you tremble; you are unfit for agitation of any kind."

"This suspense is a thousand times worse than the most horrible event; tell me what new scene of death has been acted, and whose murder I am now to lament?"

"Your family is perfectly well," said Mr. Kirwin with gentleness; "and someone, a friend, is come to visit you."

I know not by what chain of thought the idea presented itself, but it instantly darted into my mind that the murderer had come to mock at my misery and taunt me with the death of Clerval, as a new incitement for me to comply with his hellish desires. I put my hand before my eyes, and cried out in agony, "Oh! Take him away! I cannot see him; for God's sake, do not let him enter!"

Mr. Kirwin regarded me with a troubled countenance. He could not help regarding my exclamation as a presumption of my guilt and said in rather a severe tone, "I should have thought, young man, that the presence of your father would have been welcome instead of inspiring such violent repugnance."

"My father!" cried I, while every feature and every muscle was relaxed from anguish to pleasure. "Is my father indeed come? How kind, how very kind! But where is he, why does he not hasten to me?"

My change of manner surprised and pleased the magistrate; perhaps he thought that my former exclamation was a momentary return of delirium, and now he instantly resumed his former benevolence. He rose and quitted the room with my nurse, and in a moment my father entered it.

Nothing, at this moment, could have given me greater pleasure than the arrival of my father. I stretched out my hand to him and cried, "Are you, then, safe – and Elizabeth – and Ernest?" My father calmed me with assurances of their welfare and endeavoured, by dwelling on these subjects so interesting to my heart, to raise my desponding spirits; but he soon felt that a prison cannot be the abode of cheerfulness.

"What a place is this that you inhabit, my son!" said he, looking mournfully at the barred windows and wretched appearance of the room. "You travelled to seek happiness, but a fatality seems to pursue you. And poor Clerval –"

The name of my unfortunate and murdered friend was an agitation too great to be endured in my weak state; I shed tears. "Alas! Yes, my father," replied I; "some destiny of the most horrible kind hangs over me, and I must live to fulfil it, or surely I should have died on the coffin of Henry."

We were not allowed to converse for any length of time, for the precarious state of my health rendered every precaution necessary that could ensure tranquillity. Mr. Kirwin came in and insisted that my strength should not be exhausted by too much exertion. But the appearance of my father was to me like that of my good angel, and I gradually recovered my health.

As my sickness quitted me, I was absorbed by a gloomy and black melancholy that nothing could dissipate. The image of Clerval was forever before me, ghastly and murdered. More than once the agitation into which these reflections threw me made my friends dread a dangerous relapse. Alas! Why did they preserve so miserable and detested a life? It was surely that I might fulfil my destiny, which is now drawing to a close. Soon, oh, very soon, will death extinguish these throbbings and relieve me from the mighty weight of anguish that bears me to the dust; and, in executing the award of justice, I shall also sink to rest. Then the appearance of death was distant, although the wish was ever present to my thoughts; and I often sat for hours motionless and speechless, wishing for some mighty revolution that might bury me and my destroyer in its ruins.

The season of the assizes approached. I had already been three months in prison, and although I was still weak and in continual danger of a relapse, I was obliged to travel nearly a hundred miles to the country town where the court was held. Mr. Kirwin charged himself with every care of collecting witnesses and arranging my defence. I was spared the disgrace of appearing publicly as a criminal, as the case was not brought before the court that decides on life and death. The grand jury rejected the bill, on its being proved that I was on the Orkney Islands at the hour the body of my friend was found; and a fortnight after my removal I was liberated from prison.

My father was enraptured on finding me freed from the vexations of a criminal charge, that I was again allowed to breathe the fresh atmosphere and permitted to return to my native country. I did not participate in these feelings, for to me the walls of a dungeon or a palace were alike hateful. The cup of life was poisoned forever, and although the sun shone upon me, as upon the happy and gay of heart, I saw around me nothing but a dense and frightful darkness, penetrated by no light but the glimmer of two eyes that glared upon me. Sometimes they were the expressive eyes of Henry, languishing in death, the dark orbs nearly covered by the lids and the long black lashes that fringed them; sometimes it was the watery, clouded eyes of the monster, as I first saw them in my chamber at Ingolstadt.

My father tried to awaken in me the feelings of affection. He talked of Geneva, which I should soon visit, of Elizabeth and Ernest; but these words only drew deep groans from me. Sometimes, indeed, I felt a wish for happiness and thought with melancholy delight of my beloved cousin or longed, with a devouring maladie du pays, to see once more the blue lake and rapid Rhone, that had been so dear to me in early childhood; but my general state of feeling was a torpor in which a prison was as welcome a residence as the divinest scene in nature; and these fits were seldom interrupted but by paroxysms of anguish and despair. At these moments I often endeavoured to put an end to the existence I loathed, and it required unceasing attendance and vigilance to restrain me from committing some dreadful act of violence.

Yet one duty remained to me, the recollection of which finally triumphed over my selfish despair. It was necessary that I should return without delay to Geneva, there to watch over the lives of those I so fondly loved and to lie in wait for the murderer, that if any chance led me to the place of his concealment, or if he dared again to blast me by his presence, I might, with unfailing aim, put an end to the existence of the monstrous image which I had endued with the mockery of a soul still more monstrous. My father still desired to delay our departure, fearful that I could not sustain the fatigues of a journey, for I was a shattered wreck – the shadow of a human being. My strength was gone. I was a mere skeleton, and fever night and day preyed upon my wasted frame. Still, as I urged our leaving Ireland with such inquietude and impatience, my father thought it best to yield. We took our passage on board a vessel bound for Havre-de-Grace and sailed with a fair wind from the Irish shores. It was midnight. I lay on the deck looking at the stars and listening to the dashing of the waves. I hailed the darkness that shut Ireland from my sight, and my pulse beat with a feverish joy when I reflected that I should soon see Geneva. The past appeared to me in the light of a frightful dream; yet the vessel in which I was, the wind that blew me from the detested shore of Ireland, and the sea which surrounded me told me too forcibly that I was deceived by no vision and that Clerval, my friend and dearest companion, had fallen a victim to me and the monster of my creation. I repassed, in my memory, my whole life – my quiet happiness while residing with my family in Geneva, the death of my mother, and my departure for Ingolstadt. I remembered, shuddering, the mad enthusiasm that hurried me on to the creation of my hideous enemy, and I called to mind the night in which he first lived. I was unable to pursue the train of thought; a thousand feelings pressed upon me, and I wept bitterly. Ever since my recovery from the fever I had been in the custom of taking every night a small quantity of laudanum, for it was by means of this drug only that I was enabled to gain the rest necessary for the preservation of life. Oppressed by the recollection of my various misfortunes, I now swallowed double my usual quantity and soon slept profoundly. But sleep did not afford me respite from thought and misery; my dreams presented a thousand objects that scared me. Towards morning I was possessed by a kind of nightmare; I felt the fiend's grasp in my neck and could not free myself from it; groans and cries rang in my ears. My father, who was watching over me, perceiving my restlessness, awoke me; the dashing waves were around, the cloudy sky above, the fiend was not here: a sense of security, a feeling that a truce was established between the present hour and the irresistible, disastrous future imparted to me a kind of calm forgetfulness, of which the human mind is by its structure peculiarly susceptible.

Chapter XXII

THE VOYAGE came to an end. We landed, and proceeded to Paris. I soon found that I had overtaxed my strength and that I must repose before I could continue my journey. My father's care and attentions were indefatigable, but he did not know the origin of my sufferings and sought erroneous methods to remedy the incurable ill. He wished me to seek amusement in society. I abhorred the face of man. Oh, not abhorred! They were my brethren, my fellow beings, and I felt attracted even to the most repulsive among them, as to creatures of an angelic nature and celestial mechanism. But I felt that I had no right to share their intercourse. I had unchained an enemy among them whose joy it was to shed their blood and to revel in their groans. How they would, each and all, abhor me and hunt me from the world did they know my unhallowed acts and the crimes which had their source in me!

My father yielded at length to my desire to avoid society and strove by various arguments to banish my despair. Sometimes he thought that I felt deeply the degradation of being obliged to answer a charge of murder, and he endeavoured to prove to me the futility of pride.

"Alas! My father," said I, "how little do you know me. Human beings, their feelings and passions, would indeed be degraded if such a wretch as I felt pride. Justine, poor unhappy Justine, was as innocent as I, and she suffered the same charge; she died for it; and I am the cause of this – I murdered her. William, Justine, and Henry – they all died by my hands."

My father had often, during my imprisonment, heard me make the same assertion; when I thus accused myself, he sometimes seemed to desire an explanation, and at others he appeared to consider it as the offspring of delirium, and that, during my illness, some idea of this kind had presented itself to my imagination, the remembrance of which I preserved in my convalescence.

I avoided explanation and maintained a continual silence concerning the wretch I had created. I had a persuasion that I should be supposed mad, and this in itself would forever have chained my tongue. But, besides, I could not bring myself to disclose a secret which would fill my hearer with consternation and make fear and unnatural horror the inmates of his breast. I checked, therefore, my impatient thirst for sympathy and was silent when I would have given the world to have confided the fatal secret. Yet, still, words like those I have recorded would burst uncontrollably from me. I could offer no explanation of them, but their truth in part relieved the burden of my mysterious woe. Upon this occasion my father said, with an expression of unbounded wonder, "My dearest Victor, what infatuation is this? My dear son, I entreat you never to make such an assertion again."

"I am not mad," I cried energetically; "the sun and the heavens, who have viewed my operations, can bear witness of my truth. I am the assassin of those most innocent victims; they died by my machinations. A thousand times would I have shed my own blood, drop by drop, to have saved their lives; but I could not, my father, indeed I could not sacrifice the whole human race."

The conclusion of this speech convinced my father that my ideas were deranged, and he instantly changed the subject of our conversation and endeavoured to alter the course of my thoughts. He wished as much as possible to obliterate the memory of the scenes that had taken place in Ireland and never alluded to them or suffered me to speak of my misfortunes.

As time passed away I became more calm; misery had her dwelling in my heart, but I no longer talked in the same incoherent manner of my own crimes; sufficient for me was the consciousness of them. By the utmost self-violence I curbed the imperious voice of wretchedness, which sometimes desired to declare itself to the whole world, and my manners were calmer and more composed than they had ever been since my journey to the sea of ice. A few days before we left Paris on our way to Switzerland, I received the following letter from Elizabeth:

My dear Friend,

It gave me the greatest pleasure to receive a letter from my uncle dated at Paris; you are no longer at a formidable distance, and I may hope to see you in less than a fortnight. My poor cousin, how much you must have suffered! I expect to see you looking even more ill than when you quitted Geneva. This winter has been passed most miserably, tortured as I have been by anxious suspense; yet I hope to see peace in your countenance and to find that your heart is not totally void of comfort and tranquillity.

Yet I fear that the same feelings now exist that made you so miserable a year ago, even perhaps augmented by time. I would not disturb you at this period, when so many misfortunes weigh upon you, but a conversation that I had with my uncle previous to his departure renders some explanation necessary before we meet. Explanation! You may possibly say, What can Elizabeth have to explain? If you really say this, my questions are answered and all my doubts satisfied. But you are distant from me, and it is possible that you may dread and yet be pleased with this explanation; and in a probability of this being the case, I dare not any longer postpone writing what, during your absence, I have often wished to express to you but have never had the courage to begin.

You well know, Victor, that our union had been the favourite plan of your parents ever since our infancy. We were told this when young, and taught to look forward to it as an event that would certainly take place. We were affectionate playfellows during childhood, and, I believe, dear and valued friends to one another as we grew older. But as brother and sister often entertain a lively affection towards each other without desiring a more intimate union, may not such also be our case? Tell me, dearest Victor. Answer me, I conjure you by our mutual happiness, with simple truth – Do you not love another?

You have travelled; you have spent several years of your life at Ingolstadt; and I confess to you, my friend, that when I saw you last autumn so unhappy, flying to solitude from the society of every creature, I could not help supposing that you might regret our connection and believe yourself bound in honour to fulfil the wishes of your parents, although they opposed themselves to your inclinations. But this is false reasoning. I confess to you, my friend, that I love you and that in my airy dreams of futurity you have been my constant friend and companion. But it is your happiness I desire as well as my own when I declare to you that our marriage would render me eternally miserable unless it were the dictate of your own free choice. Even now I weep to think that, borne down as you are by the cruellest misfortunes, you may stifle, by the word "honour," all hope of that love and happiness which would alone restore you to yourself. I, who have so disinterested an affection for you, may increase your miseries tenfold by being an obstacle to your wishes. Ah! Victor, be assured that your cousin and playmate has too sincere a love for you not to be made miserable by this supposition. Be happy, my friend; and if you obey me in this one request, remain satisfied that nothing on earth will have the power to interrupt my tranquillity.

Do not let this letter disturb you; do not answer tomorrow, or the next day, or even until you come, if it will give you pain. My uncle will send me news of your health, and if I see but one smile on your lips when we meet, occasioned by this or any other exertion of mine, I shall need no other happiness.

Elizabeth Lavenza

Geneva, May 18th, 17—

This letter revived in my memory what I had before forgotten, the threat of the fiend – "*I will be with you on your wedding-night!*" Such was my sentence, and on that night would the daemon employ every art to destroy me and tear me from the glimpse of happiness which promised partly to console my sufferings. On that night he had determined to consummate his crimes by my death. Well, be it so; a deadly struggle would then assuredly take place, in which if he were victorious I should be at peace and his power over me be at an end. If he were vanquished, I should be a free man. Alas! What freedom? Such as the peasant enjoys when his family have been massacred before his eyes, his cottage burnt, his lands laid waste, and he is turned adrift, homeless, penniless, and alone, but free. Such would be my liberty except that in my Elizabeth I possessed a treasure, alas, balanced by those horrors of remorse and guilt which would pursue me until death.

Sweet and beloved Elizabeth! I read and reread her letter, and some softened feelings stole into my heart and dared to whisper paradisiacal dreams of love and joy; but the apple was already eaten, and the angel's arm bared to drive me from all hope. Yet I would die to make her happy. If the monster executed his threat, death was inevitable; yet, again, I considered whether my marriage would hasten my fate. My destruction might indeed arrive a few months sooner, but if my torturer should suspect that I postponed it, influenced by his menaces, he would surely find other and perhaps more dreadful means of revenge.

He had vowed *to be with me on my wedding-night*, yet he did not consider that threat as binding him to peace in the meantime, for as if to show me that he was not yet satiated with blood, he had murdered Clerval immediately after the enunciation of his threats. I resolved, therefore, that if my immediate union with my cousin would conduce either to hers or my father's happiness, my adversary's designs against my life should not retard it a single hour.

In this state of mind I wrote to Elizabeth. My letter was calm and affectionate.

I fear, my beloved girl, I said, little happiness remains for us on earth; yet all that I may one day enjoy is centred in you. Chase away your idle fears; to you alone do I consecrate my life and my endeavours for contentment. I have one secret, Elizabeth, a dreadful one; when revealed to you, it will chill your frame with horror, and then, far from being surprised at my misery, you will only wonder that I survive what I have endured. I will confide this tale of misery and terror to you the day after our marriage shall take place, for, my sweet cousin, there must be perfect confidence between us. But until then, I conjure you, do not mention or allude to it. This I most earnestly entreat, and I know you will comply.

In about a week after the arrival of Elizabeth's letter we returned to Geneva. The sweet girl welcomed me with warm affection, yet tears were in her eyes as she beheld my emaciated frame and feverish cheeks. I saw a change in her also. She was thinner and had lost much of that heavenly vivacity that had before charmed me; but her gentleness and soft looks of compassion made her a more fit companion for one blasted and miserable as I was. The tranquillity which I now enjoyed did not endure. Memory brought madness with it, and when I thought of what had passed, a real insanity possessed me; sometimes I was furious and burnt with rage, sometimes low and despondent. I neither spoke nor looked at anyone, but sat motionless, bewildered by the multitude of miseries that overcame me.

Elizabeth alone had the power to draw me from these fits; her gentle voice would soothe me when transported by passion and inspire me with human feelings when sunk in torpor. She wept with me and for me. When reason returned, she would remonstrate and endeavour to inspire me with resignation. Ah! It is well for the unfortunate to be resigned, but for the guilty there is no peace. The agonies of remorse poison the luxury there is otherwise sometimes found in indulging the excess of grief. Soon after my arrival my father spoke of my immediate marriage with Elizabeth. I remained silent.

"Have you, then, some other attachment?"

"None on earth. I love Elizabeth and look forward to our union with delight. Let the day therefore be fixed; and on it I will consecrate myself, in life or death, to the happiness of my cousin."

"My dear Victor, do not speak thus. Heavy misfortunes have befallen us, but let us only cling closer to what remains and transfer our love for those whom we have lost to those who yet live. Our circle will be small but bound close by the ties of affection and mutual misfortune. And when time shall have softened your despair, new and dear objects of care will be born to replace those of whom we have been so cruelly deprived."

Such were the lessons of my father. But to me the remembrance of the threat returned; nor can you wonder that, omnipotent as the fiend had yet been in his deeds of blood, I should almost regard him as invincible, and that when he had pronounced the words "I shall be with you on your wedding-night," I should regard the threatened fate as unavoidable. But death was no evil to me if the loss of Elizabeth were balanced with it, and I therefore, with a contented and even cheerful countenance, agreed with my father that if my cousin would consent, the ceremony should take place in ten days, and thus put, as I imagined, the seal to my fate.

Great God! If for one instant I had thought what might be the hellish intention of my fiendish adversary, I would rather have banished myself forever from my native country and wandered a friendless outcast over the earth than have consented to this miserable marriage. But, as if possessed of magic powers, the monster had blinded me to his real intentions; and when I thought that I had prepared only my own death, I hastened that of a far dearer victim.

As the period fixed for our marriage drew nearer, whether from cowardice or a prophetic feeling, I felt my heart sink within me. But I concealed my feelings by an appearance of hilarity that brought smiles and joy to the countenance of my father, but hardly deceived the everwatchful and nicer eye of Elizabeth. She looked forward to our union with placid contentment, not unmingled with a little fear, which past misfortunes had impressed, that what now appeared certain and tangible happiness might soon dissipate into an airy dream and leave no trace but deep and everlasting regret. Preparations were made for the event, congratulatory visits were received, and all wore a smiling appearance. I shut up, as well as I could, in my own heart the anxiety that preyed there and entered with seeming earnestness into the plans of my father, although they might only serve as the decorations of my tragedy. Through my father's exertions a part of the inheritance of Elizabeth had been restored to her by the Austrian government. A small possession on the shores of Como belonged to her. It was agreed that, immediately after our union, we should proceed to Villa Lavenza and spend our first days of happiness beside the beautiful lake near which it stood.

In the meantime I took every precaution to defend my person in case the fiend should openly attack me. I carried pistols and a dagger constantly about me and was ever on the watch to prevent artifice, and by these means gained a greater degree of tranquillity. Indeed, as the period approached, the threat appeared more as a delusion, not to be regarded as worthy to disturb my peace, while the happiness I hoped for in my marriage wore a greater appearance of certainty as the day fixed for its solemnization drew nearer and I heard it continually spoken of as an occurrence which no accident could possibly prevent.

Elizabeth seemed happy; my tranquil demeanour contributed greatly to calm her mind. But on the day that was to fulfil my wishes and my destiny, she was melancholy, and a presentiment of evil pervaded her; and perhaps also she thought of the dreadful secret which I had promised to reveal to her on the following day. My father was in the meantime overjoyed and in the bustle of preparation only recognized in the melancholy of his niece the diffidence of a bride.

After the ceremony was performed a large party assembled at my father's, but it was agreed that Elizabeth and I should commence our journey by water, sleeping that night at Evian and continuing our voyage on the following day. The day was fair, the wind favourable; all smiled on our nuptial embarkation.

Those were the last moments of my life during which I enjoyed the feeling of happiness. We passed rapidly along; the sun was hot, but we were sheltered from its rays by a kind of canopy while we enjoyed the beauty of the scene, sometimes on one side of the lake, where we saw Mont Saleve, the pleasant banks of Montalegre, and at a distance, surmounting all, the beautiful Mont Blanc and the assemblage of snowy mountains that in vain endeavour to emulate her; sometimes coasting the opposite banks, we saw the mighty Jura opposing its dark side to the ambition that would quit its native country, and an almost insurmountable barrier to the invader who should wish to enslave it.

I took the hand of Elizabeth. "You are sorrowful, my love. Ah! If you knew what I have suffered and what I may yet endure, you would endeavour to let me taste the quiet and freedom from despair that this one day at least permits me to enjoy."

"Be happy, my dear Victor," replied Elizabeth; "there is, I hope, nothing to distress you; and be assured that if a lively joy is not painted in my face, my heart is contented. Something whispers to me not to depend too much on the prospect that is opened before us, but I will not listen to such a sinister voice. Observe how fast we move along and how the clouds, which sometimes obscure and sometimes rise above the dome of Mont Blanc, render this scene of beauty still more interesting. Look also at the innumerable fish that are swimming in the clear waters, where we can distinguish every pebble that lies at the bottom. What a divine day! How happy and serene all nature appears!"

Thus Elizabeth endeavoured to divert her thoughts and mine from all reflection upon melancholy subjects. But her temper was fluctuating; joy for a few instants shone in her eyes, but it continually gave place to distraction and reverie.

The sun sank lower in the heavens; we passed the river Drance and observed its path through the chasms of the higher and the glens of the lower hills. The Alps here come closer to the lake, and we approached the amphitheatre of mountains which forms its eastern boundary. The spire of Evian shone under the woods that surrounded it and the range of mountain above mountain by which it was overhung.

The wind, which had hitherto carried us along with amazing rapidity, sank at sunset to a light breeze; the soft air just ruffled the water and caused a pleasant motion among the trees as we approached the shore, from which it wafted the most delightful scent of flowers and hay. The sun sank beneath the horizon as we landed, and as I touched the shore I felt those cares and fears revive which soon were to clasp me and cling to me forever.

Chapter XXIII

IT WAS EIGHT O'CLOCK when we landed; we walked for a short time on the shore, enjoying the transitory light, and then retired to the inn and contemplated the lovely scene of waters, woods, and mountains, obscured in darkness, yet still displaying their black outlines.

The wind, which had fallen in the south, now rose with great violence in the west. The moon had reached her summit in the heavens and was beginning to descend; the clouds swept across it swifter than the flight of the vulture and dimmed her rays, while the lake reflected the scene of the busy heavens, rendered still busier by the restless waves that were beginning to rise. Suddenly a heavy storm of rain descended.

I had been calm during the day, but so soon as night obscured the shapes of objects, a thousand fears arose in my mind. I was anxious and watchful, while my right hand grasped a pistol which was hidden in my bosom; every sound terrified me, but I resolved that I would sell my life dearly and not shrink from the conflict until my own life or that of my adversary was extinguished. Elizabeth observed my agitation for some time in timid and fearful silence, but there was something in my glance which communicated terror to her, and trembling, she asked, "What is it that agitates you, my dear Victor? What is it you fear?"

"Oh! Peace, peace, my love," replied I; "this night, and all will be safe; but this night is dreadful, very dreadful."

I passed an hour in this state of mind, when suddenly I reflected how fearful the combat which I momentarily expected would be to my wife, and I earnestly entreated her to retire, resolving not to join her until I had obtained some knowledge as to the situation of my enemy.

She left me, and I continued some time walking up and down the passages of the house and inspecting every corner that might afford a retreat to my adversary. But I discovered no trace of him and was beginning to conjecture that some fortunate chance had intervened to prevent the execution of his menaces when suddenly I heard a shrill and dreadful scream. It came from the room into which Elizabeth had retired. As I heard it, the whole truth rushed into my mind, my arms dropped, the motion of every muscle and fibre was suspended; I could feel the blood trickling in my veins and tingling in the extremities of my limbs. This state lasted but for an instant; the scream was repeated, and I rushed into the room. Great God! Why did I not then expire! Why am I here to relate the destruction of the best hope and the purest creature on earth? She was there, lifeless and inanimate, thrown across the bed, her head hanging down and her pale and distorted features half covered by her hair. Everywhere I turn I see the same figure – her bloodless arms and relaxed form flung by the murderer on its bridal bier. Could I behold this and live? Alas! Life is obstinate and clings closest where it is most hated. For a moment only did I lose recollection; I fell senseless on the ground.

When I recovered I found myself surrounded by the people of the inn; their countenances expressed a breathless terror, but the horror of others appeared only as a mockery, a shadow of the feelings that oppressed me. I escaped from them to the room where lay the body of Elizabeth, my love, my wife, so lately living, so dear, so worthy. She had been moved from the posture in which I had first beheld her, and now, as she lay, her head upon her arm and a handkerchief thrown across her face and neck, I might have supposed her asleep. I rushed towards her and embraced her with ardour, but the deadly languor and coldness of the limbs told me that what I now held in my arms had ceased to be the Elizabeth whom I had loved and cherished. The murderous mark of the fiend's grasp was on her neck, and the breath had ceased to issue from her lips. While I still hung over her in the agony of despair, I happened to look up. The windows of the room had before been darkened, and I felt a kind of panic on seeing the pale yellow light of the moon illuminate the chamber. The shutters had been thrown back, and with a sensation of horror not to be described, I saw at the open window a figure the most hideous and abhorred. A grin was on the face of the monster; he seemed to jeer, as with his fiendish finger he pointed towards the corpse of my wife. I rushed towards the window, and drawing a pistol from my bosom, fired; but he eluded me, leaped from his station, and running with the swiftness of lightning, plunged into the lake.

The report of the pistol brought a crowd into the room. I pointed to the spot where he had disappeared, and we followed the track with boats; nets were cast, but in vain. After passing several hours, we returned hopeless, most of my companions believing it to have been a form conjured up by my fancy. After having landed, they proceeded to search the country, parties going in different directions among the woods and vines.

I attempted to accompany them and proceeded a short distance from the house, but my head whirled round, my steps were like those of a drunken man, I fell at last in a state of utter exhaustion; a film covered my eyes, and my skin was parched with the heat of fever. In this state I was carried back and placed on a bed, hardly conscious of what had happened; my eyes wandered round the room as if to seek something that I had lost.

After an interval I arose, and as if by instinct, crawled into the room where the corpse of my beloved lay. There were women weeping around; I hung over it and joined my sad tears to theirs; all this time no distinct idea presented itself to my mind, but my thoughts rambled to various subjects, reflecting confusedly on my misfortunes and their cause. I was bewildered, in a cloud of wonder and horror. The death of William, the execution of Justine, the murder of Clerval, and lastly of my wife; even at that moment I knew not that my only remaining friends were safe from the malignity of the fiend; my father even now might be writhing under his grasp, and Ernest might be dead at his feet. This idea made me shudder and recalled me to action. I started up and resolved to return to Geneva with all possible speed.

There were no horses to be procured, and I must return by the lake; but the wind was unfavourable, and the rain fell in torrents. However, it was hardly morning, and I might reasonably hope to arrive by night. I hired men to row and took an oar myself, for I had always experienced relief from mental torment in bodily exercise. But the overflowing misery I now felt, and the excess of agitation that I endured rendered me incapable of any exertion. I threw down the oar, and leaning my head upon my hands, gave way to every gloomy idea that arose. If I looked up, I saw scenes which were familiar to me in my happier time and which I had contemplated but the day before in the company of her who was now but a shadow and a recollection. Tears streamed from my eyes. The rain had ceased for a moment, and I saw the fish play in the waters as they had done a few hours before; they had then been observed by Elizabeth. Nothing is so painful to the human mind as a great and sudden change. The sun might shine or the clouds might lower, but nothing could appear to me as it had done the day before. A fiend had snatched from me every hope of future happiness; no creature had ever been so miserable as I was; so frightful an event is single in the history of man. But why should I dwell upon the incidents that followed this last overwhelming event? Mine has been a tale of horrors; I have reached their acme, and what I must now relate can but be tedious to you. Know that, one by one, my friends were snatched away; I was left desolate. My own strength is exhausted, and I must tell, in a few words, what remains of my hideous narration. I arrived at Geneva. My father and Ernest yet lived, but the former sunk under the tidings that I bore. I see him now, excellent and venerable old man! His eyes wandered in vacancy, for they had lost their charm and their delight – his Elizabeth, his more than daughter, whom he doted on with all that affection which a man feels, who in the decline of life, having few affections, clings more earnestly to those that remain. Cursed, cursed be the fiend that brought misery on his grey hairs and doomed him to waste in wretchedness! He could not live under the horrors that were accumulated around him; the springs of existence suddenly gave way; he was unable to rise from his bed, and in a few days he died in my arms.

What then became of me? I know not; I lost sensation, and chains and darkness were the only objects that pressed upon me. Sometimes, indeed, I dreamt that I wandered in flowery meadows and pleasant vales with the friends of my youth, but I awoke and found myself in a dungeon. Melancholy followed, but by degrees I gained a clear conception of my miseries and situation and was then released from my prison. For they had called me mad, and during many months, as I understood, a solitary cell had been my habitation.

Liberty, however, had been a useless gift to me, had I not, as I awakened to reason, at the same time awakened to revenge. As the memory of past misfortunes pressed upon me, I began to reflect on their cause – the monster whom I had created, the miserable daemon whom I had sent abroad into the world for my destruction. I was possessed by a maddening rage when I thought of him, and desired and ardently prayed that I might have him within my grasp to wreak a great and signal revenge on his cursed head.

Nor did my hate long confine itself to useless wishes; I began to reflect on the best means of securing him; and for this purpose, about a month after my release, I repaired to a criminal judge in the town and told him that I had an accusation to make, that I knew the destroyer of my family, and that I required him to exert his whole authority for the apprehension of the murderer. The magistrate listened to me with attention and kindness.

"Be assured, sir," said he, "no pains or exertions on my part shall be spared to discover the villain."

"I thank you," replied I; "listen, therefore, to the deposition that I have to make. It is indeed a tale so strange that I should fear you would not credit it were there not something in truth which, however wonderful, forces conviction. The story is too connected to be mistaken for a dream, and I have no motive for falsehood." My manner as I thus addressed him was impressive but calm; I had formed in my own heart a resolution to pursue my destroyer to death, and this purpose quieted my agony and for an interval reconciled me to life. I now related my history briefly but with firmness and precision, marking the dates with accuracy and never deviating into invective or exclamation.

The magistrate appeared at first perfectly incredulous, but as I continued he became more attentive and interested; I saw him sometimes shudder with horror; at others a lively surprise, unmingled with disbelief, was painted on his countenance. When I had concluded my narration I said, "This is the being whom I accuse and for whose seizure and punishment I call upon you to exert your whole power. It is your duty as a magistrate, and I believe and hope that your feelings as a man will not revolt from the execution of those functions on this occasion." This address caused a considerable change in the physiognomy of my own auditor. He had heard my story with that half kind of belief that is given to a tale of spirits and supernatural events; but when he was called upon to act officially in consequence, the whole tide of his incredulity returned. He, however, answered mildly, "I would willingly afford you every aid in your pursuit, but the creature of whom you speak appears to have powers which would put all my exertions to defiance. Who can follow an animal which can traverse the sea of ice and inhabit caves and dens where no man would venture to intrude? Besides, some months have elapsed since the commission of his crimes, and no one can conjecture to what place he has wandered or what region he may now inhabit."

"I do not doubt that he hovers near the spot which I inhabit, and if he has indeed taken refuge in the Alps, he may be hunted like the chamois and destroyed as a beast of prey. But I perceive your thoughts; you do not credit my narrative and do not intend to pursue my enemy with the punishment which is his desert." As I spoke, rage sparkled in my eyes; the magistrate was intimidated. "You are mistaken," said he. "I will exert myself, and if it is in my power to seize the monster, be assured that he shall suffer punishment proportionate to his crimes. But I fear, from what you have yourself described to be his properties, that this will prove impracticable; and thus, while every proper measure is pursued, you should make up your mind to disappointment."

"That cannot be; but all that I can say will be of little avail. My revenge is of no moment to you; yet, while I allow it to be a vice, I confess that it is the devouring and only passion of my soul. My rage is unspeakable when I reflect that the murderer, whom I have turned loose upon society, still exists. You refuse my just demand; I have but one resource, and I devote myself, either in my life or death, to his destruction."

I trembled with excess of agitation as I said this; there was a frenzy in my manner, and something, I doubt not, of that haughty fierceness which the martyrs of old are said to have possessed. But to a Genevan magistrate, whose mind was occupied by far other ideas than those of devotion and heroism, this elevation of mind had much the appearance of madness. He endeavoured to soothe me as a nurse does a child and reverted to my tale as the effects of delirium.

"Man," I cried, "how ignorant art thou in thy pride of wisdom! Cease; you know not what it is you say."

I broke from the house angry and disturbed and retired to meditate on some other mode of action.

Chapter XXIV

MY PRESENT SITUATION was one in which all voluntary thought was swallowed up and lost. I was hurried away by fury; revenge alone endowed me with strength and composure; it moulded my feelings and allowed me to be calculating and calm at periods when otherwise delirium or death would have been my portion.

My first resolution was to quit Geneva forever; my country, which, when I was happy and beloved, was dear to me, now, in my adversity, became hateful. I provided myself with a sum of money, together with a few jewels which had belonged to my mother, and departed. And now my wanderings began which are to cease but with life. I have traversed a vast portion of the earth and have endured all the hardships which travellers in deserts and barbarous countries are wont to meet. How I have lived I hardly know; many times have I stretched my failing limbs upon the sandy plain and prayed for death. But revenge kept me alive; I dared not die and leave my adversary in being.

When I quitted Geneva my first labour was to gain some clue by which I might trace the steps of my fiendish enemy. But my plan was unsettled, and I wandered many hours round the confines of the town, uncertain what path I should pursue. As night approached I found myself at the entrance of the cemetery where William, Elizabeth, and my father reposed. I entered it and approached the tomb which marked their graves. Everything was silent except the leaves of the trees, which were gently agitated by the wind; the night was nearly dark, and the scene would have been solemn and affecting even to an uninterested observer. The spirits of the departed seemed to flit around and to cast a shadow, which was felt but not seen, around the head of the mourner.

The deep grief which this scene had at first excited quickly gave way to rage and despair. They were dead, and I lived; their murderer also lived, and to destroy him I must drag out my weary existence. I knelt on the grass and kissed the earth and with quivering lips exclaimed, "By the sacred earth on which I kneel, by the shades that wander near me, by the deep and eternal grief that I feel, I swear; and by thee, O Night, and the spirits that preside over thee, to pursue the daemon who caused this misery, until he or I shall perish in mortal conflict. For this purpose I will preserve my life; to execute this dear revenge will I again behold the sun and tread the green herbage of earth, which otherwise should vanish from my eyes forever. And I call on you, spirits of the dead, and on you, wandering ministers of vengeance, to aid and conduct me in my work. Let the cursed and hellish monster drink deep of agony; let him feel the despair that now torments me." I had begun my adjuration with solemnity and an awe which almost assured me that the shades of my murdered friends heard and approved my devotion, but the furies possessed me as I concluded, and rage choked my utterance.

I was answered through the stillness of night by a loud and fiendish laugh. It rang on my ears long and heavily; the mountains re-echoed it, and I felt as if all hell surrounded me with mockery and laughter. Surely in that moment I should have been possessed by frenzy and have destroyed my miserable existence but that my vow was heard and that I was reserved for vengeance. The laughter died away, when a well-known and abhorred voice, apparently close to my ear, addressed me in an audible whisper, "I am satisfied, miserable wretch! You have determined to live, and I am satisfied."

I darted towards the spot from which the sound proceeded, but the devil eluded my grasp. Suddenly the broad disk of the moon arose and shone full upon his ghastly and distorted shape as he fled with more than mortal speed.

I pursued him, and for many months this has been my task. Guided by a slight clue, I followed the windings of the Rhone, but vainly. The blue Mediterranean appeared, and by a strange chance, I saw the fiend enter by night and hide himself in a vessel bound for the Black Sea. I took my passage in the same ship, but he escaped, I know not how.

Amidst the wilds of Tartary and Russia, although he still evaded me, I have ever followed in his track. Sometimes the peasants, scared by this horrid apparition, informed me of his path; sometimes he himself, who feared that if I lost all trace of him I should despair and die, left some mark to guide me. The snows descended on my head, and I saw the print of his huge step on the white plain. To you first entering on life, to whom care is new and agony unknown, how can you understand what I have felt and still feel? Cold, want, and fatigue were the least pains which I was destined to endure; I was cursed by some devil and carried about with me my eternal hell; yet still a spirit of good followed and directed my steps and when I most murmured would suddenly extricate me from seemingly insurmountable difficulties. Sometimes, when nature, overcome by hunger, sank under the exhaustion, a repast was prepared for me in the desert that restored and inspirited me. The fare was, indeed, coarse, such as the peasants of the country ate, but I will not doubt that it was set there by the spirits that I had invoked to aid me. Often, when all was dry, the heavens cloudless, and I was parched by thirst, a slight cloud would bedim the sky, shed the few drops that revived me, and vanish.

I followed, when I could, the courses of the rivers; but the daemon generally avoided these, as it was here that the population of the country chiefly collected. In other places human beings were seldom seen, and I generally subsisted on the wild animals that crossed my path. I had money with me and gained the friendship of the villagers by distributing it; or I brought with me some food that I had killed, which, after taking a small part, I always presented to those who had provided me with fire and utensils for cooking.

My life, as it passed thus, was indeed hateful to me, and it was during sleep alone that I could taste joy. O blessed sleep! Often, when most miserable, I sank to repose, and my dreams lulled me even to rapture. The spirits that guarded me had provided these moments, or rather hours, of happiness that I might retain strength to fulfil my pilgrimage. Deprived of this respite, I should have sunk under my hardships. During the day I was sustained and inspirited by the hope of night, for in sleep I saw my friends, my wife, and my beloved country; again I saw the benevolent countenance of my father, heard the silver tones of my Elizabeth's voice, and beheld Clerval enjoying health and youth. Often, when wearied by a toilsome march, I persuaded myself that I was dreaming until night should come and that I should then enjoy reality in the arms of my dearest friends. What agonizing fondness did I feel for them! How did I cling to their dear forms, as sometimes they haunted even my waking hours, and persuade myself that they still lived! At such moments vengeance, that burned within me, died in my heart, and I pursued my path towards the destruction of the daemon more as a task enjoined by heaven, as the mechanical impulse of some power of which I was unconscious, than as the ardent desire of my soul. What his feelings were whom I pursued I cannot know. Sometimes, indeed, he left marks in writing on the barks of the trees or cut in stone that guided me and instigated my fury.

'My reign is not yet over' – these words were legible in one of these inscriptions – 'you live, and my power is complete. Follow me; I seek the everlasting ices of the north, where you will feel the misery of cold and frost, to which I am impassive. You will find near this place, if you follow not too tardily, a dead hare; eat and be refreshed. Come on, my enemy; we have yet to wrestle for our lives, but many hard and miserable hours must you endure until that period shall arrive.'

Scoffing devil! Again do I vow vengeance; again do I devote thee, miserable fiend, to torture and death. Never will I give up my search until he or I perish; and then with what ecstasy shall I join my Elizabeth and my departed friends, who even now prepare for me the reward of my tedious toil and horrible pilgrimage!

As I still pursued my journey to the northward, the snows thickened and the cold increased in a degree almost too severe to support. The peasants were shut up in their hovels, and only a few of the most hardy ventured forth to seize the animals whom starvation had forced from their hiding-places to seek for prey. The rivers were covered with ice, and no fish could be procured; and thus I was cut off from my chief article of maintenance. The triumph of my enemy increased with the difficulty of my labours. One inscription that he left was in these words: "Prepare! Your toils only begin; wrap yourself in furs and provide food, for we shall soon enter upon a journey where your sufferings will satisfy my everlasting hatred."

My courage and perseverance were invigorated by these scoffing words; I resolved not to fail in my purpose, and calling on heaven to support me, I continued with unabated fervour to traverse immense deserts, until the ocean appeared at a distance and formed the utmost boundary of the horizon. Oh! How unlike it was to the blue seasons of the south! Covered with ice, it was only to be distinguished from land by its superior wildness and ruggedness. The Greeks wept for joy when they beheld the Mediterranean from the hills of Asia, and hailed with rapture the boundary of their toils. I did not weep, but I knelt down and with a full heart thanked my guiding spirit for conducting me in safety to the place where I hoped, notwithstanding my adversary's gibe, to meet and grapple with him.

Some weeks before this period I had procured a sledge and dogs and thus traversed the snows with inconceivable speed. I know not whether the fiend possessed the same advantages, but I found that, as before I had daily lost ground in the pursuit, I now gained on him, so much so that when I first saw the ocean he was but one day's journey in advance, and I hoped to intercept him before he should reach the beach. With new courage, therefore, I pressed on, and in two days arrived at a wretched hamlet on the seashore. I inquired of the inhabitants concerning the fiend and gained accurate information. A gigantic monster, they said, had arrived the night before, armed with a gun and many pistols, putting to flight the inhabitants of a solitary cottage through fear of his terrific appearance. He had carried off their store of winter food, and placing it in a sledge, to draw which he had seized on a numerous drove of trained dogs, he had harnessed them, and the same night, to the joy of the horror-struck villagers, had pursued his journey across the sea in a direction that led to no land; and they conjectured that he must speedily be destroyed by the breaking of the ice or frozen by the eternal frosts.

On hearing this information I suffered a temporary access of despair. He had escaped me, and I must commence a destructive and almost endless journey across the mountainous ices of the ocean, amidst cold that few of the inhabitants could long endure and which I, the native of a genial and sunny climate, could not hope to survive. Yet at the idea that the fiend should live and be triumphant, my rage and vengeance returned, and like a mighty tide, overwhelmed every other feeling. After a slight repose, during which the spirits of the dead hovered round and instigated me to toil and revenge, I prepared for my journey. I exchanged my land-sledge for one fashioned for the inequalities of the frozen ocean, and purchasing a plentiful stock of provisions, I departed from land.

I cannot guess how many days have passed since then, but I have endured misery which nothing but the eternal sentiment of a just retribution burning within my heart could have enabled me to support. Immense and rugged mountains of ice often barred up my passage, and I often heard the thunder of the ground sea, which threatened my destruction. But again the frost came and made the paths of the sea secure.

By the quantity of provision which I had consumed, I should guess that I had passed three weeks in this journey; and the continual protraction of hope, returning back upon the heart, often wrung bitter drops of despondency and grief from my eyes. Despair had indeed almost secured her prey, and I should soon have sunk beneath this misery. Once, after the poor animals that conveyed me had with incredible toil gained the summit of a sloping ice mountain, and one, sinking under his fatigue, died, I viewed the expanse before me with anguish, when suddenly my eye caught a dark speck upon the dusky plain. I strained my sight to discover what it could be and uttered a wild cry of ecstasy when I distinguished a sledge and the distorted proportions of a well-known form within. Oh! With what a burning gush did hope revisit my heart! Warm tears filled my eyes, which I hastily wiped away, that they might not intercept the view I had of the daemon; but still my sight was dimmed by the burning drops, until, giving way to the emotions that oppressed me, I wept aloud.

But this was not the time for delay; I disencumbered the dogs of their dead companion, gave them a plentiful portion of food, and after an hour's rest, which was absolutely necessary, and yet which was bitterly irksome to me, I continued my route. The sledge was still visible, nor did I again lose sight of it except at the moments when for a short time some ice-rock concealed it with its intervening crags. I indeed perceptibly gained on it, and when, after nearly two days' journey, I beheld my enemy at no more than a mile distant, my heart bounded within me.

But now, when I appeared almost within grasp of my foe, my hopes were suddenly extinguished, and I lost all trace of him more utterly than I had ever done before. A ground sea was heard; the thunder of its progress, as the waters rolled and swelled beneath me, became every moment more ominous and terrific. I pressed on, but in vain. The wind arose; the sea roared; and, as with the mighty shock of an earthquake, it split and cracked with a tremendous and overwhelming sound. The work was soon finished; in a few minutes a tumultuous sea rolled between me and my enemy, and I was left drifting on a scattered piece of ice that was continually lessening and thus preparing for me a hideous death. In this manner many appalling hours passed; several of my dogs died, and I myself was about to sink under the accumulation of distress when I saw your vessel riding at anchor and holding forth to me hopes of succour and life. I had no conception that vessels ever came so far north and was astounded at the sight. I quickly destroyed part of my sledge to construct oars, and by these means was enabled, with infinite fatigue, to move my ice raft in the direction of your ship. I had determined, if you were going southwards, still to trust myself to the mercy of the seas rather than abandon my purpose. I hoped to induce you to grant me a boat with which I could pursue my enemy. But your direction was northwards. You took me on board when my vigour was exhausted, and I should soon have sunk under my multiplied hardships into a death which I still dread, for my task is unfulfilled.

Oh! When will my guiding spirit, in conducting me to the daemon, allow me the rest I so much desire; or must I die, and he yet live? If I do, swear to me, Walton, that he shall not escape, that you will seek him and satisfy my vengeance in his death. And do I dare to ask of you to undertake my pilgrimage, to endure the hardships that I have undergone? No; I am not so selfish. Yet, when I am dead, if he should appear, if the ministers of vengeance should conduct him to you, swear that he shall not live – swear that he shall not triumph over my accumulated woes and survive to add to the list of his dark crimes. He is eloquent and persuasive, and once his words had even power over my heart; but trust him not. His soul is as hellish as his form, full of treachery and fiendlike malice. Hear him not; call on the names of William, Justine, Clerval, Elizabeth, my father, and of the wretched Victor, and thrust your sword into his heart. I will hover near and direct the steel aright.

Walton, in Continuation

August 26th, 17—

You have read this strange and terrific story, Margaret; and do you not feel your blood congeal with horror, like that which even now curdles mine? Sometimes, seized with sudden agony, he could not continue his tale; at others, his voice broken, yet piercing, uttered with difficulty the words so replete with anguish. His fine and lovely eyes were now lighted up with indignation, now subdued to downcast sorrow and quenched in infinite wretchedness. Sometimes he commanded his countenance and tones and related the most horrible incidents with a tranquil voice, suppressing every mark of agitation; then, like a volcano bursting forth, his face would suddenly change to an expression of the wildest rage as he shrieked out imprecations on his persecutor.

His tale is connected and told with an appearance of the simplest truth, yet I own to you that the letters of Felix and Safie, which he showed me, and the apparition of the monster seen from our ship, brought to me a greater conviction of the truth of his narrative than his asseverations, however earnest and connected. Such a monster has, then, really existence! I cannot doubt it, yet I am lost in surprise and admiration. Sometimes I endeavoured to gain from Frankenstein the particulars of his creature's formation, but on this point he was impenetrable. "Are you mad, my friend?" said he. "Or whither does your senseless curiosity lead you? Would you also create for yourself and the world a demoniacal enemy? Peace, peace! Learn my miseries and do not seek to increase your own." Frankenstein discovered that I made notes concerning his history; he asked to see them and then himself corrected and augmented them in many places, but principally in giving the life and spirit to the conversations he held with his enemy. "Since you have preserved my narration," said he, "I would not that a mutilated one should go down to posterity."

Thus has a week passed away, while I have listened to the strangest tale that ever imagination formed. My thoughts and every feeling of my soul have been drunk up by the interest for my guest which this tale and his own elevated and gentle manners have created. I wish to soothe him, yet can I counsel one so infinitely miserable, so destitute of every hope of consolation, to live? Oh, no! The only joy that he can now know will be when he composes his shattered spirit to peace and death. Yet he enjoys one comfort, the offspring of solitude and delirium; he believes that when in dreams he holds converse with his friends and derives from that communion consolation for his miseries or excitements to his vengeance, that they are not the creations of his fancy, but the beings themselves who visit him from the regions of a remote world. This faith gives a solemnity to his reveries that render them to me almost as imposing and interesting as truth.

Our conversations are not always confined to his own history and misfortunes. On every point of general literature he displays unbounded knowledge and a quick and piercing apprehension. His eloquence is forcible and touching; nor can I hear him, when he relates a pathetic incident or endeavours to move the passions of pity or love, without tears. What a glorious *creature must he have been in the days of his prosperity, when he is thus noble and godlike in ruin! He seems to feel his own worth and the greatness of his fall.*

"When younger," said he, "I believed myself destined for some great enterprise. My feelings are profound, but I possessed a coolness of judgment that fitted me for illustrious achievements. This sentiment of the worth of my nature supported me when others would have been oppressed, for I deemed it criminal to throw away in useless grief those talents that might be useful to my fellow creatures. When I reflected on the work I had completed, no less a one than the creation of a sensitive and rational animal, I could not rank myself with the herd of common projectors. But this thought, which supported me in the commencement of my career, now serves only to plunge me lower in the dust. All my speculations and hopes are as nothing, and like the archangel who aspired to omnipotence, I am chained in an eternal hell. My imagination was vivid, yet my powers of analysis and application were intense; by the union of these qualities I conceived the idea and executed the creation of a man. Even now I cannot recollect without passion my reveries while the work was incomplete. I trod heaven in my thoughts, now exulting in my powers, now burning with the idea of their effects. From my infancy I was imbued with high hopes and a lofty ambition; but how am I sunk! Oh! My friend, if you had known me as I once was, you would not recognize me in this state of degradation. Despondency rarely visited my heart; a high destiny seemed to bear me on, until I fell, never, never again to rise." Must I then lose this admirable being? I have longed for a friend; I have sought one who would sympathize with and love me. Behold, on these desert seas I have found such a one, but I fear I have gained him only to know his value and lose him. I would reconcile him to life, but he repulses the idea.

"I thank you, Walton," he said, "for your kind intentions towards so miserable a wretch; but when you speak of new ties and fresh affections, think you that any can replace those who are gone? Can any man be to me as Clerval was, or any woman another Elizabeth? Even where the affections are not strongly moved by any superior excellence, the companions of our childhood always possess a certain power over our minds which hardly any later friend can obtain. They know our infantine dispositions, which, however they may be afterwards modified, are never eradicated; and they can judge of our actions with more certain conclusions as to the integrity of our motives. A sister or a brother can never, unless indeed such symptoms have been shown early, suspect the other of fraud or false dealing, when another friend, however strongly he may be attached, may, in spite of himself, be contemplated with suspicion. But I enjoyed friends, dear not only through habit and association, but from their own merits; and wherever I am, the soothing voice of my Elizabeth and the conversation of Clerval will be ever whispered in my ear. They are dead, and but one feeling in such a solitude can persuade me to preserve my life. If I were engaged in any high undertaking or design, fraught with extensive utility to my fellow creatures, then could I live to fulfil it. But such is not my destiny; I must pursue and destroy the being to whom I gave existence; then my lot on earth will be fulfilled and I may die."

* * *

September 2nd

My beloved Sister,

I write to you, encompassed by peril and ignorant whether I am ever doomed to see again dear England and the dearer friends that inhabit it. I am surrounded by mountains of ice which admit of no escape and threaten every moment to crush my vessel. The brave fellows whom I have persuaded to be my companions look towards me for aid, but I have none to bestow. There is something terribly appalling in our situation, yet my courage and hopes do not desert me. Yet it is terrible to reflect that the lives of all these men are endangered through me. If we are lost, my mad schemes are the cause.

And what, Margaret, will be the state of your mind? You will not hear of my destruction, and you will anxiously await my return. Years will pass, and you will have visitings of despair and yet be tortured by hope. Oh! My beloved sister, the sickening failing of your heart-felt expectations is, in prospect, more terrible to me than my own death.

But you have a husband and lovely children; you may be happy. Heaven bless you and make you so!

My unfortunate guest regards me with the tenderest compassion. He endeavours to fill me with hope and talks as if life were a possession which he valued. He reminds me how often the same accidents have happened to other navigators who have attempted this sea, and in spite of myself, he fills me with cheerful auguries. Even the sailors feel the power of his eloquence; when he speaks, they no longer despair; he rouses their energies, and while they hear his voice they believe these vast mountains of ice are mole – hills which will vanish before the resolutions of man. These feelings are transitory; each day of expectation delayed fills them with fear, and I almost dread a mutiny caused by this despair.

* * *

September 5th

A scene has just passed of such uncommon interest that, although it is highly probable that these papers may never reach you, yet I cannot forbear recording it.

We are still surrounded by mountains of ice, still in imminent danger of being crushed in their conflict. The cold is excessive, and many of my unfortunate comrades have already found a grave amidst this scene of desolation. Frankenstein has daily declined in health; a feverish fire still glimmers in his eyes, but he is exhausted, and when suddenly roused to any exertion, he speedily sinks again into apparent lifelessness.

I mentioned in my last letter the fears I entertained of a mutiny. This morning, as I sat watching the wan countenance of my friend – his eyes half closed and his limbs hanging listlessly – I was roused by half a dozen of the sailors, who demanded admission into the cabin. They entered, and their leader addressed me. He told me that he and his companions had been chosen by the other sailors to come in deputation to me to make me a requisition which, in justice, I could not refuse. We were immured in ice and should probably never escape, but they feared that if, as was possible, the ice should dissipate and a free passage be opened, I should be rash enough to continue my voyage and lead them into fresh dangers, after they might happily have surmounted this. They insisted, therefore, that I should engage with a solemn promise that if the vessel should be freed I would instantly direct my course southwards.

This speech troubled me. I had not despaired, nor had I yet conceived the idea of returning if set free. Yet could I, in justice, or even in possibility, refuse this demand? I hesitated before I answered, when Frankenstein, who had at first been silent, and indeed appeared hardly to have force enough to attend, now roused himself; his eyes sparkled, and his cheeks flushed with momentary vigour. Turning towards the men, he said, "What do you mean? What do you demand of your captain? Are you, then, so easily turned from your design? Did you not call this a glorious expedition?

"And wherefore was it glorious? Not because the way was smooth and placid as a southern sea, but because it was full of dangers and terror, because at every new incident your fortitude was to be called forth and your courage exhibited, because danger and death surrounded it, and these you were to brave and overcome. For this was it a glorious, for this was it an honourable undertaking. You were hereafter to be hailed as the benefactors of your species, your names adored as belonging to brave men who encountered death for honour and the benefit of mankind. And now, behold, with the first imagination of danger, or, if you will, the first mighty and terrific trial of your courage, you shrink away and are content to be handed down as men who had not strength enough to endure cold and peril; and so, poor souls, they were chilly and returned to their warm – firesides. Why, that requires not this preparation; ye need not have come thus far and dragged your captain to the shame of a defeat merely to prove yourselves cowards. Oh! Be men, or be more than men. Be steady to your purposes and firm as a rock. This ice is not made of such stuff as your hearts may be; it is mutable and cannot withstand you if you say that it shall not. Do not return to your families with the stigma of disgrace marked on your brows. Return as heroes who have fought and conquered and who know not what it is to turn their backs on the foe." He spoke this with a voice so modulated to the different feelings expressed in his speech, with an eye so full of lofty design and heroism, that can you wonder that these men were moved? They looked at one another and were unable to reply. I spoke; I told them to retire and consider of what had been said, that I would not lead them farther north if they strenuously desired the contrary, but that I hoped that, with reflection, their courage would return. They retired and I turned towards my friend, but he was sunk in languor and almost deprived of life.

How all this will terminate, I know not, but I had rather die than return shamefully, my purpose unfulfilled. Yet I fear such will be my fate; the men, unsupported by ideas of glory and honour, can never willingly continue to endure their present hardships.

* * *

September 7th

The die is cast; I have consented to return if we are not destroyed. Thus are my hopes blasted by cowardice and indecision; I come back ignorant and disappointed. It requires more philosophy than I possess to bear this injustice with patience.

* * *

September 12th

It is past; I am returning to England. I have lost my hopes of utility and glory; I have lost my friend. But I will endeavour to detail these bitter circumstances to you, my dear sister; and while I am wafted towards England and towards you, I will not despond.

September 9th, the ice began to move, and roarings like thunder were heard at a distance as the islands split and cracked in every direction. We were in the most imminent peril, but as we could only remain passive, my chief attention was occupied by my unfortunate guest whose illness increased in such a degree that he was entirely confined to his bed. The ice cracked behind us and was driven with force towards the north; a breeze sprang from the west, and on the 11th the passage towards the south became perfectly free. When the sailors saw this and that their return to their native country was apparently assured, a shout of tumultuous joy broke from them, loud and long-continued. Frankenstein, who was dozing, awoke and asked the cause of the tumult. "They shout," I said, "because they will soon return to England."

"Do you, then, really return?"

"Alas! Yes; I cannot withstand their demands. I cannot lead them unwillingly to danger, and I must return."

"Do so, if you will; but I will not. You may give up your purpose, but mine is assigned to me by heaven, and I dare not. I am weak, but surely the spirits who assist my vengeance will endow me with sufficient strength." Saying this, he endeavoured to spring from the bed, but the exertion was too great for him; he fell back and fainted.

It was long before he was restored, and I often thought that life was entirely extinct. At length he opened his eyes; he breathed with difficulty and was unable to speak. The surgeon gave him a composing draught and ordered us to leave him undisturbed. In the meantime he told me that my friend had certainly not many hours to live.

His sentence was pronounced, and I could only grieve and be patient. I sat by his bed, watching him; his eyes were closed, and I thought he slept; but presently he called to me in a feeble voice, and bidding me come near, said, "Alas! The strength I relied on is gone; I feel that I shall soon die, and he, my enemy and persecutor, may still be in being. Think not, Walton, that in the last moments of my existence I feel that burning hatred and ardent desire of revenge I once expressed; but I feel myself justified in desiring the death of my adversary. During these last days I have been occupied in examining my past conduct; nor do I find it blamable. In a fit of enthusiastic madness I created a rational creature and was bound towards him to assure, as far as was in my power, his happiness and well-being.

"This was my duty, but there was another still paramount to that. My duties towards the beings of my own species had greater claims to my attention because they included a greater proportion of happiness or misery. Urged by this view, I refused, and I did right in refusing, to create a companion for the first creature. He showed unparalleled malignity and selfishness in evil; he destroyed my friends; he devoted to destruction beings who possessed exquisite sensations, happiness, and wisdom; nor do I know where this thirst for vengeance may end. Miserable himself that he may render no other wretched, he ought to die. The task of his destruction was mine, but I have failed. When actuated by selfish and vicious motives, I asked you to undertake my unfinished work, and I renew this request now, when I am only induced by reason and virtue.

"Yet I cannot ask you to renounce your country and friends to fulfil this task; and now that you are returning to England, you will have little chance of meeting with him. But the consideration of these points, and the well balancing of what you may esteem your duties, I leave to you; my judgment and ideas are already disturbed by the near approach of death. I dare not ask you to do what I think right, for I may still be misled by passion.

"That he should live to be an instrument of mischief disturbs me; in other respects, this hour, when I momentarily expect my release, is the only happy one which I have enjoyed for several years. The forms of the beloved dead flit before me, and I hasten to their arms. Farewell, Walton! Seek happiness in tranquillity and avoid ambition, even if it be only the apparently innocent one of distinguishing yourself in science and discoveries. Yet why do I say this? I have myself been blasted in these hopes, yet another may succeed."

His voice became fainter as he spoke, and at length, exhausted by his effort, he sank into silence. About half an hour afterwards he attempted again to speak but was unable; he pressed my hand feebly, and his eyes closed forever, while the irradiation of a gentle smile passed away from his lips.

Margaret, what comment can I make on the untimely extinction of this glorious spirit? What can I say that will enable you to understand the depth of my sorrow? All that I should express would be inadequate and feeble. My tears flow; my mind is overshadowed by a cloud of disappointment. But I journey towards England, and I may there find consolation.

I am interrupted. What do these sounds portend? It is midnight; the breeze blows fairly, and the watch on deck scarcely stir. Again there is a sound as of a human voice, but hoarser; it comes from the cabin where the remains of Frankenstein still lie. I must arise and examine. Good night, my sister.

Great God! what a scene has just taken place! I am yet dizzy with the remembrance of it. I hardly know whether I shall have the power to detail it; yet the tale which I have recorded would be incomplete without this final and wonderful catastrophe. I entered the cabin where lay the remains of my ill-fated and admirable friend. Over him hung a form which I cannot find words to describe – gigantic in stature, yet uncouth and distorted in its proportions. As he hung over the coffin, his face was concealed by long locks of ragged hair; but one vast hand was extended, in colour and apparent texture like that of a mummy. When he heard the sound of my approach, he ceased to utter exclamations of grief and horror and sprung towards the window. Never did I behold a vision so horrible as his face, of such loathsome yet appalling hideousness. I shut my eyes involuntarily and endeavoured to recollect what were my duties with regard to this destroyer. I called on him to stay.

He paused, looking on me with wonder, and again turning towards the lifeless form of his creator, he seemed to forget my presence, and every feature and gesture seemed instigated by the wildest rage of some uncontrollable passion.

"That is also my victim!" he exclaimed. "In his murder my crimes are consummated; the miserable series of my being is wound to its close! Oh, Frankenstein! Generous and self-devoted being! What does it avail that I now ask thee to pardon me? I, who irretrievably destroyed thee by destroying all thou lovedst. Alas! He is cold, he cannot answer me." His voice seemed suffocated, and my first impulses, which had suggested to me the duty of obeying the dying request of my friend in destroying his enemy, were now suspended by a mixture of curiosity and compassion. I approached this tremendous being; I dared not again raise my eyes to his face, there was something so scaring and unearthly in his ugliness. I attempted to speak, but the words died away on my lips. The monster continued to utter wild and incoherent self-reproaches. At length I gathered resolution to address him in a pause of the tempest of his passion.

"Your repentance," I said, "is now superfluous. If you had listened to the voice of conscience and heeded the stings of remorse before you had urged your diabolical vengeance to this extremity, Frankenstein would yet have lived."

"And do you dream?" said the daemon. "Do you think that I was then dead to agony and remorse? He," he continued, pointing to the corpse, "he suffered not in the consummation of the deed. Oh! Not the ten-thousandth portion of the anguish that was mine during the lingering detail of its execution. A frightful selfishness hurried me on, while my heart was poisoned with remorse. Think you that the groans of Clerval were music to my ears? My heart was fashioned to be susceptible of love and sympathy, and when wrenched by misery to vice and hatred, it did not endure the violence of the change without torture such as you cannot even imagine.

"After the murder of Clerval I returned to Switzerland, heart-broken and overcome. I pitied Frankenstein; my pity amounted to horror; I abhorred myself. But when I discovered that he, the author at once of my existence and of its unspeakable torments, dared to hope for happiness, that while he accumulated wretchedness and despair upon me he sought his own enjoyment in feelings and passions from the indulgence of which I was forever barred, then impotent envy and bitter indignation filled me with an insatiable thirst for vengeance. I recollected my threat and resolved that it should be accomplished. I knew that I was preparing for myself a deadly torture, but I was the slave, not the master, of an impulse which I detested yet could not disobey. Yet when she died! Nay, then I was not miserable. I had cast off all feeling, subdued all *anguish, to riot in the excess of my despair. Evil thenceforth became my good. Urged thus far, I had no choice but to adapt my nature to an element which I had willingly chosen. The completion of my demoniacal design became an insatiable passion. And now it is ended; there is my last victim!"*

I was at first touched by the expressions of his misery; yet, when I called to mind what Frankenstein had said of his powers of eloquence and persuasion, and when I again cast my eyes on the lifeless form of my friend, indignation was rekindled within me. "Wretch!" I said. "It is well that you come here to whine over the desolation that you have made. You throw a torch into a pile of buildings, and when they are consumed, you sit among the ruins and lament the fall. Hypocritical fiend! If he whom you mourn still lived, still would he be the object, again would he become the prey, of your accursed vengeance. It is not pity that you feel; you lament only because the victim of your malignity is withdrawn from your power."

"Oh, it is not thus – not thus," interrupted the being. "Yet such must be the impression conveyed to you by what appears to be the purport of my actions. Yet I seek not a fellow feeling in my misery. No sympathy may I ever find. When I first sought it, it was the love of virtue, the feelings of happiness and affection with which my whole being overflowed, that I wished to be participated. But now that virtue has become to me a shadow, and that happiness and affection are turned into bitter and loathing despair, in what should I seek for sympathy? I am content to suffer alone while my sufferings shall endure; when I die, I am well satisfied that abhorrence and opprobrium should load my memory. Once my fancy was soothed with dreams of virtue, of fame, and of enjoyment. Once I falsely hoped to meet with beings who, pardoning my outward form, would love me for the excellent qualities which I was capable of unfolding. I was nourished with high thoughts of honour and devotion. But now crime has degraded me beneath the meanest animal. No guilt, no mischief, no malignity, no misery, can be found comparable to mine. When I run over the frightful catalogue of my sins, I cannot believe that I am the same creature whose thoughts were once filled with sublime and transcendent visions of the beauty and the majesty of goodness. But it is even so; the fallen angel becomes a malignant devil. Yet even that enemy of God and man had friends and associates in his desolation; I am alone. "You, who call Frankenstein your friend, seem to have a knowledge of my crimes and his misfortunes. But in the detail which he gave you of them he could not sum up the hours and months of misery which I endured wasting in impotent passions. For while I destroyed his hopes, I did not satisfy my own desires. They were forever ardent and craving; still I desired love and fellowship, and I was still spurned. Was there no injustice in this? Am I to be thought the only criminal, when all humankind sinned against me? Why do you not hate Felix, who drove his friend from his door with contumely? Why do you not execrate the rustic who sought to destroy the saviour of his child? Nay, these are virtuous and immaculate beings! I, the miserable and the abandoned, am an abortion, to be spurned at, and kicked, and trampled on. Even now my blood boils at the recollection of this injustice.

"But it is true that I am a wretch. I have murdered the lovely and the helpless; I have strangled the innocent as they slept and grasped to death his throat who never injured me or any other living thing. I have devoted my

creator, the select specimen of all that is worthy of love and admiration among men, to misery; I have pursued him even to that irremediable ruin.

"There he lies, white and cold in death. You hate me, but your abhorrence cannot equal that with which I regard myself. I look on the hands which executed the deed; I think on the heart in which the imagination of it was conceived and long for the moment when these hands will meet my eyes, when that imagination will haunt my thoughts no more.

"Fear not that I shall be the instrument of future mischief. My work is nearly complete. Neither yours nor any man's death is needed to consummate the series of my being and accomplish that which must be done, but it requires my own. Do not think that I shall be slow to perform this sacrifice. I shall quit your vessel on the ice raft which brought me thither and shall seek the most northern extremity of the globe; I shall collect my funeral pile and consume to ashes this miserable frame, that its remains may afford no light to any curious and unhallowed wretch who would create such another as I have been. I shall die. I shall no longer feel the agonies which now consume me or be the prey of feelings unsatisfied, yet unquenched. He is dead who called me into being; and when I shall be no more, the very remembrance of us both will speedily vanish. I shall no longer see the sun or stars or feel the winds play on my cheeks.

"Light, feeling, and sense will pass away; and in this condition must I find my happiness. Some years ago, when the images which this world affords first opened upon me, when I felt the cheering warmth of summer and heard the rustling of the leaves and the warbling of the birds, and these were all to me, I should have wept to die; now it is my only consolation. Polluted by crimes and torn by the bitterest remorse, where can I find rest but in death? "Farewell! I leave you, and in you the last of humankind whom these eyes will ever behold. Farewell, Frankenstein! If thou wert yet alive and yet cherished a desire of revenge against me, it would be better satiated in my life than in my destruction. But it was not so; thou didst seek my extinction, that I might not cause greater wretchedness; and if yet, in some mode unknown to me, thou hadst not ceased to think and feel, thou wouldst not desire against me a vengeance greater than that which I feel. Blasted as thou wert, my agony was still superior to thine, for the bitter sting of remorse will not cease to rankle in my wounds until death shall close them forever.

"But soon," he cried with sad and solemn enthusiasm, "I shall die, and what I now feel be no longer felt. Soon these burning miseries will be extinct. I shall ascend my funeral pile triumphantly and exult in the agony of the torturing flames. The light of that conflagration will fade away; my ashes will be swept into the sea by the winds. My spirit will sleep in peace, or if it thinks, it will not surely think thus. Farewell."

He sprang from the cabin window as he said this, upon the ice raft which lay close to the vessel. He was soon borne away by the waves and lost in darkness and distance.

If you enjoyed this, you might also like...
'The Fated Hour' by Friedrich Laun, see page 195
The Last Man, see page 331

A Fragment

Lord Byron

IN THE YEAR 17—, having for some time determined on a journey through countries not hitherto much frequented by travellers I set out, accompanied by a friend, whom I shall designate by the name of Augustus Darvell. He was a few years my elder, and a man of considerable fortune and ancient family – advantages which an extensive capacity prevented him alike from undervaluing or overrating. Some peculiar circumstances in his private history had rendered him to me an object of attention, of interest, and even of regard, which neither the reserve of his manners, nor occasional indications of an inquietude at times nearly approaching to alienation of mind, could extinguish.

I was yet young in life, which I had begun early; but my intimacy with him was of a recent date: we had been educated at the same schools and university; but his progress through these had preceded mine, and he had been deeply initiated into what is called the world, while I was yet in my noviciate. While thus engaged, I had heard much both of his past and present life; and although in these accounts there were many and irreconcileable contradictions, I could still gather from the whole that he was a being of no common order, and one who, whatever pains he might take to avoid remark, would still be remarkable. I had cultivated his acquaintance subsequently, and endeavoured to obtain his friendship, but this last appeared to be unattainable; whatever affections he might have possessed seemed now, some to have been extinguished, and others to be concentred: that his feelings were acute, I had sufficient opportunities of observing; for, although he could control, he could not altogether disguise them: still he had a power of giving to one passion the appearance of another in such a manner that it was difficult to define the nature of what was working within him; and the expressions of his features would vary so rapidly, though slightly, that it was useless to trace them to their sources. It was evident that he was a prey to some cureless disquiet; but whether it arose from ambition, love, remorse, grief, from one or all of these, or merely from a morbid temperament akin to disease, I could not discover: there were circumstances alleged, which might have justified the application to each of these causes; but, as I have before said, these were so contradictory and contradicted, that none could be fixed upon with accuracy. Where there is mystery, it is generally supposed that there must also be evil: I know not how this may be, but in him there certainly was the one, though I could not ascertain the extent of the other – and felt loth, as far as regarded himself, to believe in its existence. My advances were received with sufficient coldness; but I was young, and not easily discouraged, and at length succeeded in obtaining, to a certain degree, that common-place intercourse and moderate confidence of common and every day concerns, created and cemented by similarity of pursuit and frequency of meeting, which is called intimacy, or friendship, according to the ideas of him who uses those words to express them.

Darvell had already travelled extensively; and to him I had applied for information with regard to the conduct of my intended journey. It was my secret wish that he might be prevailed on to accompany me: it was also a probable hope, founded upon the shadowy restlessness which I had observed in him, and to which the animation which he appeared to feel on such subjects, and his apparent indifference to all by which he was more immediately surrounded, gave fresh strength. This wish I first hinted, and then expressed: his answer, though I had partly expected it, gave me all the pleasure of surprise – he consented; and, after the requisite arrangements, we commenced our voyages. After journeying through various countries of the south of Europe, our attention was turned towards the East, according to our original destination; and it was in my progress through those regions that the incident occurred upon which will turn what I may have to relate.

The constitution of Darvell, which must from his appearance have been in early life more than usually robust, had been for some time gradually giving way, without the intervention of any apparent disease: he had neither cough nor hectic, yet he became daily more enfeebled: his habits were temperate, and he neither declined nor complained of fatigue, yet he was evidently wasting away: he became more and more silent and sleepless, and at length so seriously altered, that my alarm grew proportionate to what I conceived to be his danger.

We had determined, on our arrival at Smyrna, on an excursion to the ruins of Ephesus and Sardis, from which I endeavoured to dissuade him in his present state of indisposition – but in vain: there appeared to be an oppression on his mind, and a solemnity in his manner, which ill corresponded with his eagerness to proceed on what I regarded as a mere party of pleasure, little suited to a valetudinarian; but I opposed him no longer – and in a few days we set off together, accompanied only by a serrugee and a single janizary.

We had passed halfway towards the remains of Ephesus, leaving behind us the more fertile environs of Smyrna, and were entering upon that wild and tenantless track through the marshes and defiles which lead to the few huts yet lingering over the broken columns of Diana – the roofless walls of expelled Christianlty, and the still more recent but complete desolation of abandoned mosques – when the sudden and rapid illness of my companion obliged us to halt at a Turkish cemetery, the turbaned tombstones of which were the sole indication that human life had ever been a sojourner in this wilderness. The only caravansera we had seen was left some hours behind us, not a vestige of a town or even cottage was within sight or hope, and this "city of the dead" appeared to be the sole refuge for my unfortunate friend, who seemed on the verge of becoming the last of its inhabitants.

In this situation, I looked round for a place where he might most conveniently repose: – contrary to the usual aspect of Mohometan burial-grounds, the cypresses were in this few in number, and these thinly scattered over its extent: the tombstones were mostly fallen, and worn with age: – upon one of the most considerable of these, and beneath one of the most spreading trees, Darvell supported himself, in a half-reclining posture, with great difficulty. He asked for water. I had some doubts of our being able to find any, and prepared to go in search of it with hesitating despondency – but he desired me to remain; and turning to Suleiman, our janizary, who stood by us smoking with great tranquillity, he said, "*Suleiman, verbana su,*" (i.e. bring some water,) and went on describing the spot where it was to be found with great minuteness, at a small well for camels, a few hundred yards to the right: the janizary obeyed. I said to Darvell, "How did you know this?" – He replied, "From our situation; you must perceive that this place was once inhabited, and could not have been so without springs: I have also been here before."

"You have been here before! – How came you never to mention this to me? and what could you be doing in a place where no one would remain a moment longer than they could help it?"

To this question I received no answer. In the mean time Suleiman returned with the water, leaving the serrugee and the horses at the fountain. The quenching of his thirst had the appearance of reviving him for a moment; and I conceived hopes of his being able to proceed, or at least to return, and I urged the attempt. He was silent – and appeared to be collecting his spirits for an effort to speak. He began.

"This is the end of my journey, and of my life – I came here "to die: but I have a request to make, a command – for such my "last words must be – You will observe it?"

"Most certainly; but have better hopes."

"I have no hopes, nor wishes, but this – conceal my death from every human being."

"I hope there will be no occasion; that you will recover, and –"

"Peace! – it must be so: promise this."

"I do."

"Swear it, by all that" – He here dictated an oath of great solemnity.

"There is no occasion for this – I will observe your request; and to doubt me is –"

"It cannot be helped, – you must swear."

I took the oath: it appeared to relieve him. He removed a seal ring from his finger, on which were some Arabic characters, and presented it to me. He proceeded –

"On the ninth day of the month, at noon precisely (what month you please, but this must be the day), you must fling this ring into the salt springs which run into the Bay of Eleusis: the day after, at the same hour, you must repair to the ruins of the temple of Ceres, and wait one hour."

"Why?"

"You will see."

"The ninth day of the month, you say?"

"The ninth."

As I observed that the present was the ninth day of the month, his countenance changed, and he paused. As he sate, evidently becoming more feeble, a stork, with a snake in her beak, perched upon a tombstone near us; and, without devouring her prey, appeared to be steadfastly regarding us. I know not what impelled me to drive it away, but the attempt was useless; she made a few circles in the air, and returned exactly to the same spot. Darvell pointed to it, and smiled: he spoke – I know not whether to himself or to me – but the words were only, "'Tis well!"

"What is well? what do you mean?"

"No matter: you must bury me here this evening, and exactly where that bird is now perched. You know the rest of my injunctions."

He then proceeded to give me several directions as to the manner in which his death might be best concealed. After these were finished, he exclaimed, "You perceive that bird?"

"Certainly."

"And the serpent writhing in her beak?"

"Doubtless: there is nothing uncommon in it; it is her natural prey. But it is odd that she does not devour it."

He smiled in a ghastly manner, and said, faintly, "It is not yet time!" As he spoke, the stork flew away. My eyes followed it for a moment, it could hardly be longer than ten might be counted. I felt Darvell's weight, as it were, increase upon my shoulder, and, turning to look upon his face, perceived that he was dead!

I was shocked with the sudden certainty which could not be mistaken – his countenance in a few minutes became nearly black. I should have attributed so rapid a change to poison, had I not been aware that he had no opportunity of receiving it unperceived. The day was declining, the body was rapidly altering, and nothing remained but to fulfil his request. With the aid of Suleiman's ataghan and my own sabre, we scooped a shallow grave upon the spot which Darvell had indicated: the earth easily gave way, having already received some Mahometan tenant. We dug as deeply as the time permitted us, and throwing the dry earth upon all that remained of the singular being so lately departed, we cut a few sods of greener turf from the less withered soil around us, and laid them upon his sepulchre.

Between astonishment and grief, I was tearless.

If you enjoyed this, you might also like...
'The Death's Head' by Friedrich Laun, see page 207
'The Pilgrims', see page 296

The Vampyre

John Polidori

Preface – Extract of a Letter from Geneva

I BREATHE FREELY in the neighbourhood of this lake; the ground upon which I tread has been subdued from the earliest ages; the principal objects which immediately strike my eye, bring to my recollection scenes, in which man acted the hero and was the chief object of interest. Not to look back to earlier times of battles and sieges, here is the bust of Rousseau – here is a house with an inscription denoting that the Genevan philosopher first drew breath under its roof. A little out of the town is Ferney, the residence of Voltaire; where that wonderful, though certainly in many respects contemptible, character, received, like the hermits of old, the visits of pilgrims, not only from his own nation, but from the farthest boundaries of Europe. Here too is Bonnet's abode, and, a few steps beyond, the house of that astonishing woman Madame de Stael: perhaps the first of her sex, who has really proved its often claimed equality with, the nobler man. We have before had women who have written interesting novels and poems, in which their tact at observing drawing-room characters has availed them; but never since the days of Heloise have those faculties which are peculiar to man, been developed as the possible inheritance of woman. Though even here, as in the case of Heloise, our sex have not been backward in alledging the existence of an Abeilard in the person of M. Schlegel as the inspirer of her works. But to proceed: upon the same side of the lake, Gibbon, Bonnivard, Bradshaw, and others mark, as it were, the stages for our progress; whilst upon the other side there is one house, built by Diodati, the friend of Milton, which has contained within its walls, for several months, that poet whom we have so often read together, and who – if human passions remain the same, and human feelings, like chords, on being swept by nature's impulses shall vibrate as before – will be placed by posterity in the first rank of our English Poets. You must have heard, or the Third Canto of Childe Harold will have informed you, that Lord Byron resided many months in this neighbourhood. I went with some friends a few days ago, after having seen Ferney, to view this mansion. I trod the floors with the same feelings of awe and respect as we did, together, those of Shakespeare's dwelling at Stratford. I sat down in a chair of the saloon, and satisfied myself that I was resting on what he had made his constant seat. I found a servant there who had lived with him; she, however, gave me but little information. She pointed out his bed-chamber upon the same level as the saloon and dining-room, and informed me that he retired to rest at three, got up at two, and employed himself a long time over his toilette; that he never went to sleep without a pair of pistols and a dagger by his side, and that he never ate animal food. He apparently spent some part of every day upon the lake in an English boat. There is a balcony from the saloon which looks upon the lake and the mountain Jura; and I imagine, that it must have been hence, he contemplated the storm so magnificently described in the Third Canto; for you have from here a most extensive view of all the points he has therein depicted. I can fancy him like the scathed pine, whilst all around was sunk to repose, still waking to observe, what gave but a weak image of the storms which had desolated his own breast.

> *The sky is changed! – and such a change; Oh, night!*
> *And storm and darkness, ye are wond'rous strong,*
> *Yet lovely in your strength, as is the light*
> *Of a dark eye in woman! Far along*
> *From peak to peak, the rattling crags among,*
> *Leaps the lire thunder! Not from one lone cloud,*
> *But every mountain now hath found a tongue,*
> *And Jura answers thro' her misty shroud,*
> *Back to the joyous Alps who call to her aloud!*
>
> *And this is in the night: – Most glorious night!*
> *Thou wer't not sent for slumber! let me be*
> *A sharer in thy far and fierce delight, –*
> *A portion of the tempest and of me!*
> *How the lit lake shines a phosphoric sea,*
> *And the big rain comet dancing to the earth!*
> *And now again 'tis black, – and now the glee*
> *Of the loud hills shakes with its mountain mirth,*
> *As if they did rejoice o'er a young; earthquake's birth,*
>
> *Now where the swift Rhine cleaves his way between*
> *Heights which appear, as lovers who have parted*
> *In haste, whose mining depths so intervene,*
> *That they can meet no more, tho' broken hearted;*
> *Tho' in their souls which thus each other thwarted,*
> *Love was the very root of the fond rage*
> *Which blighted their life's bloom, and then departed –*
> *Itself expired, but leaving; them an age*
> *Of years all winter – war within themselves to wage.*

I went down to the little port, if I may use the expression, wherein his vessel used to lay, and conversed with the cottager, who had the care of it. You may smile, but I have my pleasure in thus helping my personification of the individual I admire, by attaining to the knowledge of those circumstances which were daily around him. I have made numerous enquiries in the town concerning him, but can learn nothing. He only went into society there once, when M. Pictet took him to the house of a lady to spend the evening. They say he is a very singular man, and seem to think him very uncivil. Amongst other things they relate, that having invited M. Pictet and Bonstetten to dinner, he went on the lake to Chillon, leaving a gentleman who travelled with him to receive them and make his apologies. Another evening, being invited to the house of Lady D— H—, he promised to attend, but upon approaching the windows of her ladyship's villa, and perceiving the room to be full of company, he set down his friend, desiring him to plead his excuse, and immediately returned home. This will serve as a contradiction to the report which you tell me is current in England, of his having been avoided by his countrymen on the continent. The case happens to be directly the reverse, as he has been generally sought by them, though on most occasions, apparently without success. It is said, indeed, that upon paying his first visit at Coppet, following the servant who had announced his name, he was surprised to meet a lady carried out fainting; but before he had been seated many minutes, the same lady, who had been so affected at the sound of his name, returned and conversed with him a considerable time – such is female curiosity and affectation! He visited Coppet frequently, and of course associated there with several of his countrymen, who evinced no reluctance to meet him whom his enemies alone would represent as an outcast.

Though I have been so unsuccessful in this town, I have been more fortunate in my enquiries elsewhere. There is a society three or four miles from Geneva, the centre of which is the Countess of Breuss, a Russian lady, well acquainted with the agrémens de la Société, and who has collected them round herself at her mansion. It was chiefly here, I find, that the gentleman who travelled with Lord Byron, as physician, sought for society. He used almost every day to cross the lake by himself, in one of their flat-bottomed boats, and return after passing the evening with his friends, about eleven or twelve at night, often whilst the storms were raging in the circling summits of the mountains around. As he became intimate, from long acquaintance, with several of the families in this neighbourhood, I have gathered from their accounts some excellent traits of his lordship's character, which I will relate to you at some future opportunity. I must, however, free him from one imputation attached to him – of having in his house two sisters as the partakers of his revels. This is, like many other charges which have been brought against his lordship, entirely destitute of truth. His only companion was the physician I have already mentioned. The report originated from the following circumstance: Mr. Percy Bysshe Shelly, a gentleman well known for extravagance of doctrine, and for his daring, in their profession, even to sign himself with the title of Atheos in the Album at Chamouny, having taken a house below, in which he resided with Miss M. W. Godwin and Miss Clermont, (the daughters of the celebrated Mr. Godwin) they were frequently visitors at Diodati, and were often seen upon the lake with his Lordship, which gave rise to the report, the truth of which is here positively denied.

Among other things which the lady, from whom I procured these anecdotes, related to me, she mentioned the outline of a ghost story by Lord Byron. It appears that one evening Lord B., Mr. P.B. Shelly, the two ladies and the gentleman before alluded to, after having perused a German work, which was entitled Phantasmagoriana, began relating ghost stories; when his lordship having recited the beginning of Christabel, then unpublished, the whole took so strong a hold of Mr. Shelly's mind, that he suddenly started up and ran out of the room. The physician and Lord Byron followed, and discovered him leaning against a mantle-piece, with cold drops of perspiration trickling down his face. After having given him something to refresh him, upon enquiring into the cause of his alarm, they found that his wild imagination having pictured to him the bosom of one of the ladies with eyes (which was reported of a lady in the neighbourhood where he lived) he was obliged to leave the room in order to destroy the impression. It was afterwards proposed, in the course of conversation, that each of the company present should write a tale depending upon some supernatural agency, which was undertaken by Lord B., the physician, and Miss M.W. Godwin [since published under the title of *Frankenstein; or, The Modern Prometheus*. My friend, the lady above referred to, had in her possession the outline of each of these stories; I obtained them as a great favour, and herewith forward them to you, as I was assured you would feel as much curiosity as myself, to peruse the ebauches of so great a genius, and those immediately under his influence.

The Story

IT HAPPENED that in the midst of the dissipations attendant upon a London winter, there appeared at the various parties of the leaders of the ton a nobleman, more remarkable for his singularities, than his rank. He gazed upon the mirth around him, as if he could not participate therein. Apparently, the light laughter of the fair only attracted his attention, that he might by a look quell it, and throw fear into those breasts where thoughtlessness reigned. Those who felt this sensation of awe, could not explain whence it arose: some attributed it to the dead grey eye, which, fixing upon the object's face, did not seem to penetrate, and at one glance to pierce through to the inward workings of the heart; but fell upon the cheek with a leaden ray that weighed upon the skin it could not pass.

His peculiarities caused him to be invited to every house; all wished to see him, and those who had been accustomed to violent excitement, and now felt the weight of ennui, were pleased at having something in their presence capable of engaging their attention. In spite of the deadly hue of his face, which never gained a warmer tint, either from the blush of modesty, or from the strong emotion of passion, though its form and outline were beautiful, many of the female hunters after notoriety attempted to win his attentions, and gain, at least, some marks of what they might term affection: Lady Mercer, who had been the mockery of every monster shewn in drawing-rooms since her marriage, threw herself in his way, and did all but put on the dress of a mountebank, to attract his notice – though in vain: when she stood before him, though his eyes were apparently fixed upon hers, still it seemed as if they were unperceived – even her unappalled impudence was baffled, and she left the field.

But though the common adultress could not influence even the guidance of his eyes, it was not that the female sex was indifferent to him: yet such was the apparent caution with which he spoke to the virtuous wife and innocent daughter, that few knew he ever addressed himself to females. He had, however, the reputation of a winning tongue; and whether it was that it even overcame the dread of his singular character, or that they were moved by his apparent hatred of vice, he was as often among those females who form the boast of their sex from their domestic virtues, as among those who sully it by their vices.

About the same time, there came to London a young gentleman of the name of Aubrey: he was an orphan left with an only sister in the possession of great wealth, by parents who died while he was yet in childhood. Left also to himself by guardians, who thought it their duty merely to take care of his fortune, while they relinquished the more important charge of his mind to the care of mercenary subalterns, he cultivated more his imagination than his judgment. He had, hence, that high romantic feeling of honour and candour, which daily ruins so many milliners' apprentices. He believed all to sympathise with virtue, and thought that vice was thrown in by Providence merely for the picturesque effect of the scene, as we see in romances: he thought that the misery of a cottage merely consisted in the vesting of clothes, which were as warm, but which were better adapted to the painter's eye by their irregular folds and various coloured patches. He thought, in fine, that the dreams of poets were the realities of life.

He was handsome, frank, and rich: for these reasons, upon his entering into the gay circles, many mothers surrounded him, striving which should describe with least truth their languishing or romping favourites: the daughters at the same time, by their brightening countenances when he approached, and by their sparkling eyes, when he opened his lips, soon led him into false notions of his talents and his merit. Attached as he was to the romance of his solitary hours, he was startled at finding, that, except in the tallow and wax candles that flickered, not from the presence of a ghost, but from want of snuffing, there was no foundation in real life for any of that congeries of pleasing pictures and descriptions contained in those volumes, from which he had formed his study. Finding, however, some compensation in his gratified vanity, he was about to relinquish his dreams, when the extraordinary being we have above described, crossed him in his career.

He watched him; and the very impossibility of forming an idea of the character of a man entirely absorbed in himself, who gave few other signs of his observation of external objects, than the tacit assent to their existence, implied by the avoidance of their contact: allowing his imagination to picture every thing that flattered its propensity to extravagant ideas, he soon formed this object into the hero of a romance, and determined to observe the offspring of his fancy, rather than the person before him. He became acquainted with him, paid him attentions, and so far advanced upon his notice, that his presence was always recognised. He gradually learnt that Lord Ruthven's affairs were embarrassed, and soon found, from the notes of preparation in –Street, that he was about to travel.

Desirous of gaining some information respecting this singular character, who, till now, had only whetted his curiosity, he hinted to his guardians, that it was time for him to perform the tour, which for many generations has been thought necessary to enable the young to take some rapid steps in the career of vice towards putting themselves upon an equality with the aged, and not allowing them to appear as if fallen from the skies, whenever scandalous intrigues are mentioned as the subjects of pleasantry or of praise, according to the degree of skill shewn in carrying them on. They consented: and Aubrey immediately mentioning his intentions to Lord Ruthven, was surprised to receive from him a proposal to join him. Flattered by such a mark of esteem from him, who, apparently, had nothing in common with other men, he gladly accepted it, and in a few days they had passed the circling waters.

Hitherto, Aubrey had had no opportunity of studying Lord Ruthven's character, and now he found, that, though many more of his actions were exposed to his view, the results offered different conclusions from the apparent motives to his conduct. His companion was profuse in his liberality – the idle, the vagabond, and the beggar, received from his hand more than enough to relieve their immediate wants. But Aubrey could not avoid remarking, that it was not upon the virtuous, reduced to indigence by the misfortunes attendant even upon virtue, that he bestowed his alms – these were sent from the door with hardly suppressed sneers; but when the profligate came to ask something, not to relieve his wants, but to allow him to wallow in his lust, or to sink him still deeper in his iniquity, he was sent away with rich charity. This was, however, attributed by him to the greater importunity of the vicious, which generally prevails over the retiring bashfulness of the virtuous indigent. There was one circumstance about the charity of his Lordship, which was still more impressed upon his mind: all those upon whom it was bestowed, inevitably found that there was a curse upon it, for they were all either led to the scaffold, or sunk to the lowest and the most abject misery.

At Brussels and other towns through which they passed, Aubrey was surprised at the apparent eagerness with which his companion sought for the centres of all fashionable vice; there he entered into all the spirit of the faro table: he betted, and always gambled with success, except where the known sharper was his antagonist, and then he lost even more than he gained; but it was always with the same unchanging face, with which he generally watched the society around: it was not, however, so when he encountered the rash youthful novice, or the luckless father of a numerous family; then his very wish seemed fortune's law – this apparent abstractedness of mind was laid aside, and his eyes sparkled with more fire than that of the cat whilst dallying with the half-dead mouse.

In every town, he left the formerly affluent youth, torn from the circle he adorned, cursing, in the solitude of a dungeon, the fate that had drawn him within the reach of this fiend; whilst many a father sat frantic, amidst the speaking looks of mute hungry children, without a single farthing of his late immense wealth, wherewith to buy even sufficient to satisfy their present craving. Yet he took no money from the gambling table; but immediately lost, to the ruiner of many, the last gilder he had just snatched from the convulsive grasp of the innocent: this might but be the result of a certain degree of knowledge, which was not, however, capable of combating the cunning of the more experienced. Aubrey often wished to represent this to his friend, and beg him to resign that charity and pleasure which proved the ruin of all, and did not tend to his own profit; – but he delayed it – for each day he hoped his friend would give him some opportunity of speaking frankly and openly to him; however, this never occurred. Lord Ruthven in his carriage, and amidst the various wild and rich scenes of nature, was always the same: his eye spoke less than his lip; and though Aubrey was near the object of his curiosity, he obtained no greater gratification from it than the constant excitement of vainly wishing to break that mystery, which to his exalted imagination began to assume the appearance of something supernatural.

They soon arrived at Rome, and Aubrey for a time lost sight of his companion; he left him in daily attendance upon the morning circle of an Italian countess, whilst he went in search of the memorials of another almost deserted city. Whilst he was thus engaged, letters arrived from England, which he opened with eager impatience; the first was from his sister, breathing nothing but affection; the others were from his guardians, the latter astonished him; if it had before entered into his imagination that there was an evil power resident in his companion, these seemed to give him sufficient reason for the belief. His guardians insisted upon his immediately leaving his friend, and urged, that his character was dreadfully vicious, for that the possession of irresistible powers of seduction, rendered his licentious habits more dangerous to society. It had been discovered, that his contempt for the adultress had not originated in hatred of her character; but that he had required, to enhance his gratification, that his victim, the partner of his guilt, should be hurled from the pinnacle of unsullied virtue, down to the lowest abyss of infamy and degradation: in fine, that all those females whom he had sought, apparently on account of their virtue, had, since his departure, thrown even the mask aside, and had not scrupled to expose the whole deformity of their vices to the public gaze.

Aubrey determined upon leaving one, whose character had not yet shown a single bright point on which to rest the eye. He resolved to invent some plausible pretext for abandoning him altogether, purposing, in the meanwhile, to watch him more closely, and to let no slight circumstances pass by unnoticed. He entered into the same circle, and soon perceived, that his Lordship was endeavouring to work upon the inexperience of the daughter of the lady whose house he chiefly frequented. In Italy, it is seldom that an unmarried female is met with in society; he was therefore obliged to carry on his plans in secret; but Aubrey's eye followed him in all his windings, and soon discovered that an assignation had been appointed, which would most likely end in the ruin of an innocent, though thoughtless girl. Losing no time, he entered the apartment of Lord Ruthven, and abruptly asked him his intentions with respect to the lady, informing him at the same time that he was aware of his being about to meet her that very night.

Lord Ruthven answered, that his intentions were such as he supposed all would have upon such an occasion; and upon being pressed whether he intended to marry her, merely laughed. Aubrey retired; and, immediately writing a note, to say, that from that moment he must decline accompanying his Lordship in the remainder of their proposed tour, he ordered his servant to seek other apartments, and calling upon the mother of the lady, informed her of all he knew, not only with regard to her daughter, but also concerning the character of his Lordship. The assignation was prevented. Lord Ruthven next day merely sent his servant to notify his complete assent to a separation; but did not hint any suspicion of his plans having been foiled by Aubrey's interposition.

Having left Rome, Aubrey directed his steps towards Greece, and crossing the Peninsula, soon found himself at Athens. He then fixed his residence in the house of a Greek; and soon occupied himself in tracing the faded records of ancient glory upon monuments that apparently, ashamed of chronicling the deeds of freemen only before slaves, had hidden themselves beneath the sheltering soil or many coloured lichen. Under the same roof as himself, existed a being, so beautiful and delicate, that she might have formed the model for a painter wishing to portray on canvass the promised hope of the faithful in Mahomet's paradise, save that her eyes spoke too much mind for anyone to think she could belong to those who had no souls. As she danced upon the plain, or tripped along the mountain's side, one would have thought the gazelle a poor type of her beauties; for who would have exchanged her eye, apparently the eye of animated nature, for that sleepy luxurious look of the animal suited but to the taste of an epicure. The light step of Ianthe often accompanied Aubrey in his search after antiquities, and often would the unconscious girl, engaged in the pursuit of a Kashmere butterfly, show the whole beauty of her form, floating as it were upon the wind, to the eager gaze of him, who forgot the letters he had just decyphered upon an almost effaced tablet, in the contemplation of her sylph-like figure. Often would her tresses falling, as she flitted around, exhibit in the sun's ray such delicately brilliant and swiftly fading hues, it might well excuse the forgetfulness of the antiquary, who let escape from his mind the very object he had before thought of vital importance to the proper interpretation of a passage in Pausanias.

But why attempt to describe charms which all feel, but none can appreciate? It was innocence, youth, and beauty, unaffected by crowded drawing-rooms and stifling balls. Whilst he drew those remains of which he wished to preserve a memorial for his future hours, she would stand by, and watch the magic effects of his pencil, in tracing the scenes of her native place; she would then describe to him the circling dance upon the open plain, would paint, to him in all the glowing colours of youthful memory, the marriage pomp she remembered viewing in her infancy; and then, turning to subjects that had evidently made a greater impression upon her mind, would tell him all the supernatural tales of her nurse.

Her earnestness and apparent belief of what she narrated, excited the interest even of Aubrey; and often as she told him the tale of the living vampyre, who had passed years amidst his friends, and dearest ties, forced every year, by feeding upon the life of a lovely female to prolong his existence for the ensuing months, his blood would run cold, whilst he attempted to laugh her out of such idle and horrible fantasies; but Ianthe cited to him the names of old men, who had at last detected one living among themselves, after several of their near relatives and children had been found marked with the stamp of the fiend's appetite; and when she found him so incredulous, she begged of him to believe her, for it had been, remarked, that those who had dared to question their existence, always had some proof given, which obliged them, with grief and heartbreaking, to confess it was true. She detailed to him the traditional appearance of these monsters, and his horror was increased, by hearing a pretty accurate description of Lord Ruthven; he, however, still persisted in persuading her, that there could be no truth in her fears, though at the same time he wondered at the many coincidences which had all tended to excite a belief in the supernatural power of Lord Ruthven.

Aubrey began to attach himself more and more to Ianthe; her innocence, so contrasted with all the affected virtues of the women among whom he had sought for his vision of romance, won his heart; and while he ridiculed the idea of a young man of English habits, marrying an uneducated Greek girl, still he found himself more and more attached to the almost fairy form before him. He would tear himself at times from her, and, forming a plan for some antiquarian research, he would depart, determined not to return until his object was attained; but he always found it impossible to fix his attention upon the ruins around him, whilst in his mind he retained an image that seemed alone the rightful possessor of his thoughts. Ianthe was unconscious of his love, and was ever the same frank infantile being he had first known. She always seemed to part from him with reluctance; but it was because she had no longer anyone with whom she could visit her favourite haunts, whilst her guardian was occupied in sketching or uncovering some fragment which had yet escaped the destructive hand of time.

She had appealed to her parents on the subject of Vampyres, and they both, with several present, affirmed their existence, pale with horror at the very name. Soon after, Aubrey determined to proceed upon one of his excursions, which was to detain him for a few hours; when they heard the name of the place, they all at once begged of him not to return at night, as he must necessarily pass through a wood, where no Greek would ever remain, after the day had closed, upon any consideration. They described it as the resort of the vampyres in their nocturnal orgies, and denounced the most heavy evils as impending upon him who dared to cross their path. Aubrey made light of their representations, and tried to laugh them out of the idea; but when he saw them shudder at his daring thus to mock a superior, infernal power, the very name of which apparently made their blood freeze, he was silent.

Next morning Aubrey set off upon his excursion unattended; he was surprised to observe the melancholy face of his host, and was concerned to find that his words, mocking the belief of those horrible fiends, had inspired them with such terror. When he was about to depart, Ianthe came to the side of his horse, and earnestly begged of him to return, ere night allowed the power of these beings to be put in action; he promised. He was, however, so occupied in his research, that he did not perceive that daylight would soon end, and that in the horizon there was one of those specks which, in the warmer climates, so rapidly gather into a tremendous mass, and pour all their rage upon the devoted country. He at last, however, mounted his horse, determined to make up by speed for his delay: but it was too late. Twilight, in these southern climates, is almost unknown; immediately the sun sets, night begins: and ere he had advanced far, the power of the storm was above – its echoing thunders had scarcely an interval of rest – its thick heavy rain forced its way through the canopying foliage, whilst the blue forked lightning seemed to fall and radiate at his very feet. Suddenly his horse took fright, and he was carried with dreadful rapidity through the entangled forest. The animal at last, through fatigue, stopped, and he found, by the glare of lightning, that he was in the neighbourhood of a hovel that hardly lifted itself up from the masses of dead leaves and brushwood which surrounded it. Dismounting, he approached, hoping to find someone to guide him to the town, or at least trusting to obtain shelter from the pelting of the storm.

As he approached, the thunders, for a moment silent, allowed him to hear the dreadful shrieks of a woman mingling with the stifled, exultant mockery of a laugh, continued in one almost unbroken sound; he was startled, but, roused by the thunder which again rolled over his head, he, with a sudden effort, forced open the door of the hut. He found himself in utter darkness: the sound, however, guided him. He was apparently unperceived; for, though he called, still the sounds continued, and no notice was taken of him. He found himself in contact with someone, whom he immediately seized; when a voice cried, "Again baffled!" to which a loud laugh succeeded; and he felt himself grappled by one whose strength seemed superhuman: determined to sell his life as dearly as he could, he struggled; but it was in vain: he was lifted from his feet and hurled with enormous force against the ground: his enemy threw himself upon him, and kneeling upon his breast, had placed his hands upon his throat; when the glare of many torches penetrating through the hole that gave light in the day, disturbed him; he instantly rose, and, leaving his prey, rushed through the door, and in a moment the crashing of the branches, as he broke through the wood, was no longer heard.

The storm was now still; and Aubrey, incapable of moving, was soon heard by those without. They entered; the light of their torches fell upon the mud walls, and the thatch loaded on every individual straw with heavy flakes of soot. At the desire of Aubrey they searched for her who had attracted him by her cries; he was again left in darkness; but what was his horror, when the light of the torches once more burst upon him, to perceive the airy form of his fair conductress brought in a lifeless corpse. He shut his eyes, hoping that it was but a vision arising from his disturbed imagination; but he again saw the same form, when he unclosed them, stretched by his side. There was no colour upon her cheek, not even upon her lip; yet there was a stillness about her face that seemed almost as attaching as the life that once dwelt there: upon her neck and breast was blood, and upon her throat were the marks of teeth having opened the vein – to this the men pointed, crying, simultaneously struck with horror, "A Vampyre! A Vampyre!"

A litter was quickly formed, and Aubrey was laid by the side of her who had lately been to him the object of so many bright and fairy visions, now fallen with the flower of life that had died within her. He knew not what his thoughts were – his mind was benumbed and seemed to shun reflection, and take refuge in vacancy – he held almost unconsciously in his hand a naked dagger of a particular construction, which had been found in the hut. They were soon met by different parties who had been engaged in the search of her whom a mother had missed. Their lamentable cries, as they approached the city, forewarned the parents of some dreadful catastrophe. To describe their grief would be impossible; but when they ascertained the cause of their child's death, they looked at Aubrey, and pointed to the corpse. They were inconsolable; both died broken-hearted.

Aubrey being put to bed was seized with a most violent fever, and was often delirious; in these intervals he would call upon Lord Ruthven and upon Ianthe – by some unaccountable combination he seemed to beg of his former companion to spare the being he loved. At other times he would imprecate maledictions upon his head, and curse him as her destroyer. Lord Ruthven, chanced at this time to arrive at Athens, and, from whatever motive, upon hearing of the state of Aubrey, immediately placed himself in the same house, and became his constant attendant. When the latter recovered from his delirium, he was horrified and startled at the sight of him whose image he had now combined with that of a Vampyre; but Lord Ruthven, by his kind words, implying almost repentance for the fault that had caused their separation, and still more by the attention, anxiety, and care which he showed, soon reconciled him to his presence. His lordship seemed quite changed; he no longer appeared that apathetic being who had so astonished Aubrey; but as soon as his convalescence began to be rapid, he again gradually retired into the same state of mind, and Aubrey perceived no difference from the former man, except that at times he was surprised to meet his gaze fixed intently upon him, with a smile of malicious exultation playing upon his lips: he knew not why, but this smile haunted him. During the last stage of the invalid's recovery, Lord Ruthven was apparently engaged in watching the tideless waves raised by the cooling breeze, or in marking the progress of those orbs, circling, like our world, the moveless sun – indeed, he appeared to wish to avoid the eyes of all.

Aubrey's mind, by this shock, was much weakened, and that elasticity of spirit which had once so distinguished him now seemed to have fled forever. He was now as much a lover of solitude and silence as Lord Ruthven; but much as he wished for solitude, his mind could not find it in the neighbourhood of Athens; if he sought it amidst the ruins he had formerly frequented, Ianthe's form stood by his side – if he sought it in the woods, her light step would appear wandering amidst the underwood, in quest of the modest violet; then suddenly turning round, would show, to his wild imagination, her pale face and wounded throat, with a meek smile upon her lips. He determined to fly scenes, every feature of which created such bitter associations in his mind. He proposed to Lord Ruthven, to whom he held himself bound by the tender care he had taken of him during his illness, that they should visit those parts of Greece neither had yet seen. They travelled in every direction, and sought every spot to which a recollection could be attached: but though they thus hastened from place to place, yet they seemed not to heed what they gazed upon. They heard much of robbers, but they gradually began to slight these reports, which they imagined were only the invention of individuals, whose interest it was to excite the generosity of those whom they defended from pretended dangers.

In consequence of thus neglecting the advice of the inhabitants, on one occasion they travelled with only a few guards, more to serve as guides than as a defence. Upon entering, however, a narrow defile, at the bottom of which was the bed of a torrent, with large masses of rock brought down from the neighbouring precipices, they had reason to repent their negligence; for scarcely were the whole of the party engaged in the narrow pass, when they were startled by the whistling of bullets close to their heads, and by the echoed report of several guns. In an instant their guards had left them, and, placing themselves behind rocks, had begun to fire in the direction whence the report came. Lord Ruthven and Aubrey, imitating their example, retired for a moment behind the sheltering turn of the defile: but ashamed of being thus detained by a foe, who with insulting shouts bade them advance, and being exposed to unresisting slaughter, if any of the robbers should climb above and take them in the rear, they determined at once to rush forward in search of the enemy. Hardly had they lost the shelter of the rock, when Lord Ruthven received a shot in the shoulder, which brought him to the ground. Aubrey hastened to his assistance; and, no longer heeding the contest or his own peril, was soon surprised by seeing the robbers' faces around him – his guards having, upon Lord Ruthven's being wounded, immediately thrown up their arms and surrendered.

By promises of great reward, Aubrey soon induced them to convey his wounded friend to a neighbouring cabin; and having agreed upon a ransom, he was no more disturbed by their presence – they being content merely to guard the entrance till their comrade should return with the promised sum, for which he had an order. Lord Ruthven's strength rapidly decreased; in two days mortification ensued, and death seemed advancing with hasty steps. His conduct and appearance had not changed; he seemed as unconscious of pain as he had been of the objects about him: but towards the close of the last evening, his mind became apparently uneasy, and his eye often fixed upon Aubrey, who was induced to offer his assistance with more than usual earnestness: "Assist me! You may save me – you may do more than that – I mean not my life, I heed the death of my existence as little as that of the passing day; but you may save my honour, your friend's honour."

"How? Tell me how? I would do anything," replied Aubrey.

"I need but little – my life ebbs apace – I cannot explain the whole – but if you would conceal all you know of me, my honour were free from stain in the world's mouth – and if my death were unknown for some time in England – I – I – but life."

"It shall not be known."

"Swear!" cried the dying man, raising himself with exultant violence, "Swear by all your soul reveres, by all your nature fears, swear that, for a year and a day you will not impart your knowledge of my crimes or death to any living being in any way, whatever may happen, or whatever you may see."

His eyes seemed bursting from their sockets: "I swear!" said Aubrey; he sunk laughing upon his pillow, and breathed no more.

Aubrey retired to rest, but did not sleep; the many circumstances attending his acquaintance with this man rose upon his mind, and he knew not why; when he remembered his oath a cold shivering came over him, as if from the presentiment of something horrible awaiting him. Rising early in the morning, he was about to enter the hovel in which he had left the corpse, when a robber met him, and informed him that it was no longer there, having been conveyed by himself and comrades, upon his retiring, to the pinnacle of a neighbouring mount, according to a promise they had given his lordship, that it should be exposed to the first cold ray of the moon that rose after his death. Aubrey astonished, and taking several of the men, determined to go and bury it upon the spot where it lay. But, when he had mounted to the summit he found no trace of either the corpse or the clothes, though the robbers swore they pointed out the identical rock on which they had laid the body. For a time his mind was bewildered in conjectures, but he at last returned, convinced that they had buried the corpse for the sake of the clothes.

Weary of a country in which he had met with such terrible misfortunes, and in which all apparently conspired to heighten that superstitious melancholy that had seized upon his mind, he resolved to leave it, and soon arrived at Smyrna. While waiting for a vessel to convey him to Otranto, or to Naples, he occupied himself in arranging those effects he had with him belonging to Lord Ruthven. Amongst other things there was a case containing several weapons of offence, more or less adapted to ensure the death of the victim. There were several daggers and ataghans. Whilst turning them over, and examining their curious forms, what was his surprise at finding a sheath apparently ornamented in the same style as the dagger discovered in the fatal hut – he shuddered – hastening to gain further proof, he found the weapon, and his horror may be imagined when he discovered that it fitted, though peculiarly shaped, the sheath he held in his hand. His eyes seemed to need no further certainty – they seemed gazing to be bound to the dagger; yet still he wished to disbelieve; but the particular form, the same varying tints upon the haft and sheath were alike in splendour on both, and left no room for doubt; there were also drops of blood on each.

He left Smyrna, and on his way home, at Rome, his first inquiries were concerning the lady he had attempted to snatch from Lord Ruthven's seductive arts. Her parents were in distress, their fortune ruined, and she had not been heard of since the departure of his lordship. Aubrey's mind became almost broken under so many repeated horrors; he was afraid that this lady had fallen a victim to the destroyer of Ianthe. He became morose and silent; and his only occupation consisted in urging the speed of the postilions, as if he were going to save the life of someone he held dear. He arrived at Calais; a breeze, which seemed obedient to his will, soon wafted him to the English shores; and he hastened to the mansion of his fathers, and there, for a moment, appeared to lose, in the embraces and caresses of his sister, all memory of the past. If she before, by her infantine caresses, had gained his affection, now that the woman began to appear, she was still more attaching as a companion.

Miss Aubrey had not that winning grace which gains the gaze and applause of the drawing-room assemblies. There was none of that light brilliancy which only exists in the heated atmosphere of a crowded apartment. Her blue eye was never lit up by the levity of the mind beneath. There was a melancholy charm about it which did not seem to arise from misfortune, but from some feeling within, that appeared to indicate a soul conscious of a brighter realm. Her step was not that light footing, which strays where'er a butterfly or a colour may attract – it was sedate and pensive. When alone, her face was never brightened by the smile of joy; but when her brother breathed to her his affection, and would in her presence forget those griefs she knew destroyed his rest, who would have exchanged her smile for that of the voluptuary? It seemed as if those eyes – that face were then playing in the light of their own native sphere. She was yet only eighteen, and had not been presented to the world, it having been thought by her guardians more fit that her presentation should be delayed until her brother's return from the continent, when he might be her protector. It was now, therefore, resolved that the next drawing-room, which was fast approaching, should be the epoch of her entry into the 'busy scene'. Aubrey would rather have remained in the mansion of his fathers, and fed upon the melancholy which overpowered him. He could not feel interest about the frivolities of fashionable strangers, when his mind had been so torn by the events he had witnessed; but he determined to sacrifice his own comfort to the protection of his sister. They soon arrived in town, and prepared for the next day, which had been announced as a drawing-room.

The crowd was excessive – a drawing-room had not been held for a long time, and all who were anxious to bask in the smile of royalty, hastened thither. Aubrey was there with his sister. While he was standing in a corner by himself, heedless of all around him, engaged in the remembrance that the first time he had seen Lord Ruthven was in that very place – he felt himself suddenly seized by the arm, and a voice he recognized too well, sounded in his ear – "Remember your oath." He had hardly courage to turn, fearful of seeing a spectre that would blast him, when he perceived, at a little distance, the same figure which had attracted his notice on this spot upon his first entry into society. He gazed till his limbs almost refusing to bear their weight, he was obliged to take the arm of a friend, and forcing a passage through the crowd, he threw himself into his carriage, and was driven home. He paced the room with hurried steps, and fixed his hands upon his head, as if he were afraid his thoughts were bursting from his brain. Lord Ruthven again before him – circumstances started up in dreadful array – the dagger – his oath. He roused himself, he could not believe it possible – the dead rise again! He thought his imagination had conjured up the image his mind was resting upon. It was impossible that it could be real – he determined, therefore, to go again into society; for though he attempted to ask concerning Lord Ruthven, the name hung upon his lips, and he could not succeed in gaining information.

He went a few nights after with his sister to the assembly of a near relation. Leaving her under the protection of a matron, he retired into a recess, and there gave himself up to his own devouring thoughts. Perceiving, at last, that many were leaving, he roused himself, and entering another room, found his sister surrounded by several, apparently in earnest conversation; he attempted to pass and get near her, when one, whom he requested to move, turned round, and revealed to him those features he most abhorred. He sprang forward, seized his sister's arm, and, with hurried step, forced her towards the street: at the door he found himself impeded by the crowd of servants who were waiting for their lords; and while he was engaged in passing them, he again heard that voice whisper close to him – "Remember your oath!" He did not dare to turn, but, hurrying his sister, soon reached home.

Aubrey became almost distracted. If before his mind had been absorbed by one subject, how much more completely was it engrossed, now that the certainty of the monster's living again pressed upon his thoughts. His sister's attentions were now unheeded, and it was in vain that she intreated him to explain to her what had caused his abrupt conduct. He only uttered a few words, and those terrified her. The more he thought, the more he was bewildered. His oath startled him – was he then to allow this monster to roam, bearing ruin upon his breath, amidst all he held dear, and not avert its progress? His very sister might have been touched by him. But even if he were to break his oath, and disclose his suspicions, who would believe him? He thought of employing his own hand to free the world from such a wretch; but death, he remembered, had been already mocked. For days he remained in this state; shut up in his room, he saw no one, and ate only when his sister came, who, with eyes streaming with tears, besought him, for her sake, to support nature.

At last, no longer capable of bearing stillness and solitude, he left his house, roamed from street to street, anxious to fly that image which haunted him. His dress became neglected, and he wandered, as often exposed to the noon-day sun as to the midnight damps. He was no longer to be recognized; at first he returned with the evening to the house; but at last he laid him down to rest wherever fatigue overtook him. His sister, anxious for his safety, employed people to follow him; but they were soon distanced by him who fled from a pursuer swifter than any – from thought. His conduct, however, suddenly changed. Struck with the idea that he left by his absence the whole of his friends, with a fiend amongst them, of whose presence they were unconscious, he determined to enter again into society, and watch him closely, anxious to forewarn, in spite of his oath, all whom Lord Ruthven approached with intimacy. But when he entered into a room, his haggard and suspicious looks were so striking, his inward shudderings so visible, that his sister was at last obliged to beg of him to abstain from seeking, for her sake, a society which affected him so strongly. When, however, remonstrance proved unavailing, the guardians thought proper to interpose, and, fearing that his mind was becoming alienated, they thought it high time to resume again that trust which had been before imposed upon them by Aubrey's parents.

Desirous of saving him from the injuries and sufferings he had daily encountered in his wanderings, and of preventing him from exposing to the general eye those marks of what they considered folly, they engaged a physician to reside in the house, and take constant care of him. He hardly appeared to notice it, so completely was his mind absorbed by one terrible subject. His incoherence became at last so great, that he was confined to his chamber. There he would often lie for days, incapable of being roused. He had become emaciated, his eyes had attained a glassy lustre; the only sign of affection and recollection remaining displayed itself upon the entry of his sister; then he would sometimes start, and, seizing her hands, with looks that severely afflicted her, he would desire her not to touch him. "Oh, do not touch him – if your love for me is aught, do not go near him!" When, however, she inquired to whom he referred, his only answer was, "True! True!" and again he sank into a state, whence not even she could rouse him. This lasted many months: gradually, however, as the year was passing, his incoherences became less frequent, and his mind threw off a portion of its gloom, whilst his guardians observed, that several times in the day he would count upon his fingers a definite number, and then smile.

The time had nearly elapsed, when, upon the last day of the year, one of his guardians entering his room, began to converse with his physician upon the melancholy circumstance of Aubrey's being in so awful a situation, when his sister was going next day to be married. Instantly Aubrey's attention was attracted; he asked anxiously to whom. Glad of this mark of returning intellect, of which they feared he had been deprived, they mentioned the name of the Earl of Marsden. Thinking this was a young Earl whom he had met with in society, Aubrey seemed pleased, and astonished them still more by his expressing his intention to be present at the nuptials, and desiring to see his sister. They answered not, but in a few minutes his sister was with him. He was apparently again capable of being affected by the influence of her lovely smile; for he pressed her to his breast, and kissed her cheek, wet with tears, flowing at the thought of her brother's being once more alive to the feelings of affection.

He began to speak with all his wonted warmth, and to congratulate her upon her marriage with a person so distinguished for rank and every accomplishment; when he suddenly perceived a locket upon her breast; opening it, what was his surprise at beholding the features of the monster who had so long influenced his life. He seized the portrait in a paroxysm of rage, and trampled it under foot. Upon her asking him why he thus destroyed the resemblance of her future husband, he looked as if he did not understand her – then seizing her hands, and gazing on her with a frantic expression of countenance, he bade her swear that she would never wed this monster, for he – but he could not advance – it seemed as if that voice again bade him remember his oath – he turned suddenly round, thinking Lord Ruthven was near him but saw no one. In the meantime the guardians and physician, who had heard the whole, and thought this was but a return of his disorder, entered, and forcing him from Miss Aubrey, desired her to leave him. He fell upon his knees to them, he implored, he begged of them to delay but for one day. They, attributing this to the insanity they imagined had taken possession of his mind, endeavoured to pacify him, and retired.

Lord Ruthven had called the morning after the drawing-room, and had been refused with everyone else. When he heard of Aubrey's ill health, he readily understood himself to be the cause of it; but when he learned that he was deemed insane, his exultation and pleasure could hardly be concealed from those among whom he had gained this information. He hastened to the house of his former companion, and, by constant attendance, and the pretence of great affection for the brother and interest in his fate, he gradually won the ear of Miss Aubrey. Who could resist his power? His tongue had dangers and toils to recount – could speak of himself as of an individual having no sympathy with any being on the crowded earth, save with her to whom he addressed himself; could tell how, since he knew her, his existence, had begun to seem worthy of preservation, if it were merely that he might listen to her soothing accents; in fine, he knew so well how to use the serpent's art, or such was the will of fate, that he gained her affections. The title of the elder branch falling at length to him, he obtained an important embassy, which served as an excuse for hastening the marriage (in spite of her brother's deranged state), which was to take place the very day before his departure for the continent.

Aubrey, when he was left by the physician and his guardians, attempted to bribe the servants, but in vain. He asked for pen and paper; it was given him; he wrote a letter to his sister, conjuring her, as she valued her own happiness, her own honour, and the honour of those now in the grave, who once held her in their arms as their hope and the hope of their house, to delay but for a few hours that marriage, on which he denounced the most heavy curses. The servants promised they would deliver it; but giving it to the physician, he thought it better not to harass any more the mind of Miss Aubrey by, what he considered, the ravings of a maniac. Night passed on without rest to the busy inmates of the house; and Aubrey heard, with a horror that may more easily be conceived than described, the notes of busy preparation. Morning came, and the sound of carriages broke upon his ear. Aubrey grew almost frantic. The curiosity of the servants at last overcame their vigilance, they gradually stole away, leaving him in the custody of a helpless old woman. He seized the opportunity, with one bound was out of the room, and in a moment found himself in the apartment where all were nearly assembled. Lord Ruthven was the first to perceive him: he immediately approached, and, taking his arm by force, hurried him from the room, speechless with rage. When on the staircase, Lord Ruthven whispered in his ear – "Remember your oath, and know, if not my bride today, your sister is dishonoured. Women are frail!" So saying, he pushed him towards his attendants, who, roused by the old woman, had come in search of him. Aubrey could no longer support himself; his rage not finding vent, had broken a blood-vessel, and he was conveyed to bed. This was not mentioned to his sister, who was not present when he entered, as the physician was afraid of agitating her. The marriage was solemnized, and the bride and bridegroom left London.

Aubrey's weakness increased; the effusion of blood produced symptoms of the near approach of death. He desired his sister's guardians might be called, and when the midnight hour had struck, he related composedly what the reader has perused – he died immediately after.

The guardians hastened to protect Miss Aubrey; but when they arrived, it was too late. Lord Ruthven had disappeared, and Aubrey's sister had glutted the thirst of a Vampyre!

If you enjoyed this, you might also like...
'Christabel' by Samuel Coleridge Taylor, see opposite
'Transformation', see page 243

Christabel

Samuel Taylor Coleridge

Part the First

'Tis the middle of night by the castle clock,
And the owls have awakened the crowing cock;
Tu – whit! – Tu – whoo!
And hark, again! the crowing cock,
How drowsily it crew.
Sir Leoline; the Baron rich,
Hath a toothless mastiff, which
From her kennel beneath the rock
Maketh answer to the clock,
Four for the quarters, and twelve for the hour;
Ever and aye, by shine and shower,
Sixteen short howls, not over loud;
Some say, she sees my lady's shroud.

Is the night chilly and dark?
The night is chilly, but not dark.
The thin gray cloud is spread on high,
It covers but not hides the sky.
The moon is behind, and at the full;
And yet she looks both small and dull.
The night is chill, the cloud is gray:
'Tis a month before the month of May,
And the Spring comes slowly up this way.

The lovely lady, Christabel,
Whom her father loves so well,
What makes her in the wood so late,
A furlong from the castle gate?
She had dreams all yesternight
Of her own betrothed knight;
And she in the midnight wood will pray
For the weal of her lover that's far away.

She stole along, she nothing spoke,
The sighs she heaved were soft and low,
And naught was green upon the oak

But moss and rarest misletoe:
She kneels beneath the huge oak tree,
And in silence prayeth she.

The lady sprang up suddenly,
The lovely lady, Christabel!
It moaned as near, as near can be,
But what it is she cannot tell. –
On the other side it seems to be,
Of the huge, broad-breasted, old oak tree.

The night is chill; the forest bare;
Is it the wind that moaneth bleak?
There is not wind enough in the air
To move away the ringlet curl
From the lovely lady's cheek –
There is not wind enough to twirl
The one red leaf, the last of its clan,
That dances as often as dance it can,
Hanging so light, and hanging so high,
On the topmost twig that looks up at the sky.

Hush, beating heart of Christabel!
Jesu, Maria, shield her well!
She folded her arms beneath her cloak,
And stole to the other side of the oak.
What sees she there?

There she sees a damsel bright,
Drest in a silken robe of white,
That shadowy in the moonlight shone:
The neck that made that white robe wan,
Her stately neck, and arms were bare;
Her blue-veined feet unsandal'd were,
And wildly glittered here and there
The gems entangled in her hair.
I guess, 'twas frightful there to see
A lady so richly clad as she –
Beautiful exceedingly!

Mary mother, save me now!
(Said Christabel,) And who art thou?

The lady strange made answer meet,
And her voice was faint and sweet: –
Have pity on my sore distress,
I scarce can speak for weariness:

Stretch forth thy hand, and have no fear!
Said Christabel, How camest thou here?
And the lady, whose voice was faint and sweet,
Did thus pursue her answer meet: –

My sire is of a noble line,
And my name is Geraldine:
Five warriors seized me yestermorn,
Me, even me, a maid forlorn:
They choked my cries with force and fright,
And tied me on a palfrey white.
The palfrey was as fleet as wind,
And they rode furiously behind.
They spurred amain, their steeds were white:
And once we crossed the shade of night.
As sure as Heaven shall rescue me,
I have no thought what men they be;
Nor do I know how long it is
(For I have lain entranced I wis)
Since one, the tallest of the five,
Took me from the palfrey's back,
A weary woman, scarce alive.
Some muttered words his comrades spoke:
He placed me underneath this oak;
He swore they would return with haste;
Whither they went I cannot tell
I thought I heard, some minutes past,
Sounds as of a castle bell.
Stretch forth thy hand (thus ended she),
And help a wretched maid to flee.

Then Christabel stretched forth her hand,
And comforted fair Geraldine:
O well, bright dame! may you command
The service of Sir Leoline;
And gladly our stout chivalry
Will he send forth and friends withal
To guide and guard you safe and free
Home to your noble father's hall.

She rose: and forth with steps they passed
That strove to be, and were not, fast.
Her gracious stars the lady blest,
And thus spake on sweet Christabel:
All our household are at rest,
The hall as silent as the cell;
Sir Leoline is weak in health,

And may not well awakened be,
But we will move as if in stealth,
And I beseech your courtesy,
This night, to share your couch with me.

They crossed the moat, and Christabel
Took the key that fitted well;
A little door she opened straight,
All in the middle of the gate;
The gate that was ironed within and without
Where an army in battle array had marched out.
The lady sank, belike through pain,
And Christabel with might and main
Lifted her up, a weary weight,
Over the threshold of the gate:
Then the lady rose again,
And moved, as she were not in pain.

So free from danger, free from fear,
They crossed the court: right glad they were.
And Christabel devoutly cried
To the lady by her side,
Praise we the Virgin all divine
Who hath rescued thee from thy distress!
Alas! alas! said Geraldine,
I cannot speak for weariness.
So free from danger, free from fear,
They crossed the court: right glad they were.

Outside her kennel, the mastiff old
Lay fast asleep, in moonshine cold.
The mastiff old did not awake,
Yet she an angry moan did make!
And what can ail the mastiff bitch?
Never till now she uttered yell
Beneath the eye of Christabel.
Perhaps it is the owlet's scritch:
For what can ail the mastiff bitch?

They passed the hall, that echoes still,
Pass as lightly as you will!
The brands were flat, the brands were dying,
Amid their own white ashes lying;
But when the lady passed, there came
A tongue of light, a fit of flame
And Christabel saw the lady's eye,
And nothing else saw she thereby,

Save the boss of the shield of Sir Leoline tall,
Which hung in a murky old niche in the wall.
O softly tread, said Christabel,
My father seldom sleepeth well.

Sweet Christabel her feet doth bare,
And jealous of the listening air
They steal their way from stair to stair,
Now in glimmer, and now in gloom,
And now they pass the Baron's room,
As still as death with stifled breath!
And now have reached her chamber door;
And now doth Geraldine press down
The rushes of the chamber floor.

The moon shines dim in the open air,
And not a moonbeam enters here.
But they without its light can see
The chamber carved so curiously,
Carved with figures strange and sweet,
All made out of the carver's brain,
For a lady's chamber meet:
The lamp with twofold silver chain
Is fastened to an angel's feet.

The silver lamp burns dead and dim;
But Christabel the lamp will trim.
She trimmed the lamp, and made it bright,
And left it swinging to and fro,
While Geraldine, in wretched plight,
Sank down upon the floor below.

O weary lady, Geraldine,
I pray you, drink this cordial wine!
It is a wine of virtuous powers;
My mother made it of wild flowers.

And will your mother pity me,
Who am a maiden most forlorn?
Christabel answered – Woe is me!
She died the hour that I was born.
I have heard the grey-haired friar tell
How on her death-bed she did say,
That she should hear the castle-bell
Strike twelve upon my wedding-day.
O mother dear! that thou wert here!
I would, said Geraldine, she were!

But soon with altered voice, said she –
"Off, wandering mother! Peak and pine!
I have power to bid thee flee."
Alas! what ails poor Geraldine?
Why stares she with unsettled eye?
Can she the bodiless dead espy?

And why with hollow voice cries she,
"Off, woman, off! this hour is mine –
Though thou her guardian spirit be,
Off, woman, off! 'tis given to me."

Then Christabel knelt by the lady's side,
And raised to heaven her eyes so blue –,
Alas! said she, this ghastly ride –
Dear lady! it hath wildered you!
The lady wiped her moist cold brow,
And faintly said, "'tis over now!"

Again the wild-flower wine she drank:
Her fair large eyes 'gan glitter bright,
And from the floor whereon she sank,
The lofty lady stood upright:
She was most beautiful to see,
Like a lady of a far countrée.

And thus the lofty lady spake –
"All they who live in the upper sky,
Do love you, holy Christabel!
And you love them, and for their sake
And for the good which me befel,
Even I in my degree will try,
Fair maiden, to requite you well.
But now unrobe yourself; for I
Must pray, ere yet in bed I lie."

Quoth Christabel, So let it be!
And as the lady bade, did she.
Her gentle limbs did she undress,
And lay down in her loveliness.

But through her brain of weal and woe
So many thoughts moved to and fro,
That vain it were her lids to close;
So half-way from the bed she rose,
And on her elbow did recline
To look at the lady Geraldine.

Beneath the lamp the lady bowed,
And slowly rolled her eyes around
Then drawing in her breath aloud,
Like one that shuddered, she unbound
The cincture from beneath her breast:
Her silken robe, and inner vest,
Dropt to her feet, and full in view,
Behold! her bosom and half her side –
A sight to dream of, not to tell!
O shield her! shield sweet Christabel!

Yet Geraldine nor speaks nor stirs;
Ah! what a stricken look was hers!
Deep from within she seems half-way
To lift some weight with sick assay,
And eyes the maid and seeks delay;
Then suddenly, as one defied,
Collects herself in scorn and pride,
And lay down by the Maiden's side! –
And in her arms the maid she took,
Ah wel-a-day!
And with low voice and doleful look
These words did say:
In the touch of this bosom there worketh a spell,
Which is lord of thy utterance, Christabel!
Thou knowest tonight, and wilt know tomorrow,
This mark of my shame, this seal of my sorrow;
But vainly thou warrest,
For his is alone in
Thy power to declare,
That in the dim forest
Thou heard'st a low moaning,
And found'st a bright lady, surpassingly fair;
And didst bring her home with thee
in love and in charity,
To shield her and shelter her from the damp air."

The Conclusion to Part the First

It was a lovely sight to see
The lady Christabel, when she
Was praying at the old oak tree.
Amid the jagged shadows
Of mossy leafless boughs,
Kneeling in the moonlight,
To make her gentle vows;

Her slender palms together prest,
Heaving sometimes on her breast;
Her face resigned to bliss or bale –
Her face, oh call it fair not pale,
And both blue eyes more, bright than clear,
Each about to have a tear.

With open eyes (ah woe is me!)
Asleep, and dreaming fearfully,
Fearfully dreaming, yet, I wis,
Dreaming that alone, which is –
O sorrow and shame! Can this be she,
The lady, who knelt at the old oak tree?
And lo! the worker of these harms,
That holds the maiden in her arms,
Seems to slumber still and mild,
As a mother with her child.

A star hath set, a star hath risen,
O Geraldine! since arms of thine
Have been the lovely lady's prison.
O Geraldine! one hour was thine
Thou'st had thy will! By tairn and rill,
The night-birds all that hour were still.
But now they are jubilant anew,
From cliff and tower, tu-whoo! tu-whoo!
Tu-whoo! tu-whoo! from wood and fell!

And see! the lady Christabel
Gathers herself from out her trance;
Her limbs relax, her countenance
Grows sad and soft; the smooth thin lids
Close o'er her eyes; and tears she sheds
Large tears that leave the lashes bright!
And oft the while she seems to smile
As infants at a sudden light!

Yea, she doth smile, and she doth weep,
Like a youthful hermitess,
Beauteous in a wilderness,
Who, praying always, prays in sleep.
And, if she move unquietly,
Perchance,'tis but the blood so free
Comes back and tingles in her feet.
No doubt, she hath a vision sweet.
What if her guardian spirit 'twere,
What if she knew her mother near?

But this she knows, in joys and woes,
That saints will aid if men will call:
For the blue sky bends over all!

Part the Second

Each matin bell, the Baron saith,
Knells us back to a world of death.
These words Sir Leoline first said,
When he rose and found his lady dead:
These words Sir Leoline will say
Many a morn to his dying day!

And hence the custom and law began
That still at dawn the sacristan,
Who duly pulls the heavy bell,
Five and forty beads must tell
Between each stroke – a warning knell,
Which not a soul can choose but hear
From Bratha Head to Wyndermere.

Saith Bracy the bard, So let it knell!
And let the drowsy sacristan
Still count as slowly as he can!
There is no lack of such, I ween,
As well fill up the space between.
In Langdale Pike and Witch's Lair,
And Dungeon-ghyll so foully rent,
With ropes of rock and bells of air
Three sinful sextons' ghosts are pent,
Who all give back, one after t'other,
The death-note to their living brother;
And oft too, by the knell offended,
Just as their one! two! three! is ended,
The devil mocks the doleful tale
With a merry peal from Borrowdale.

The air is still! through mist and cloud
That merry peal comes ringing loud;
And Geraldine shakes off her dread,
And rises lightly from the bed;
Puts on her silken vestments white,
And tricks her hair in lovely plight,
And nothing doubting of her spell
Awakens the lady Christabel
"Sleep you, sweet lady Christabel?
I trust that you have rested well."

And Christabel awoke and spied
The same who lay down by her side –
O rather say, the same whom she
Raised up beneath the old oak tree!
Nay, fairer yet! and yet more fair!
For she belike hath drunken deep
Of all the blessedness of sleep!
And while she spake, her looks, her air,
Such gentle thankfulness declare,
That (so it seemed) her girded vests
Grew tight beneath her heaving breasts.
"Sure I have sinn'd!" said Christabel,
"Now heaven be praised if all be well!"

And in low faltering tones, yet sweet,
Did she the lofty lady greet
With such perplexity of mind
As dreams too lively leave behind.

So quickly she rose, and quickly arrayed
Her maiden limbs, and having prayed
That He, who on the cross did groan,
Might wash away her sins unknown,
She forthwith led fair Geraldine
To meet her sire, Sir Leoline.

The lovely maid and the lady tall
Are pacing both into the hall,
And pacing on through page and groom,
Enter the Baron's presence-room.

The Baron rose, and while he prest
His gentle daughter to his breast,
With cheerful wonder in his eyes
The lady Geraldine espies,
And gave such welcome to the same,
As might beseem so bright a dame!

But when he heard the lady's tale,
And when she told her father's name,
Why waxed Sir Leoline so pale,
Murmuring o'er the name again,
Lord Roland de Vaux of Tryermaine?
Alas! they had been friends in youth;
But whispering tongues can poison truth;
And constancy lives in realms above;
And life is thorny; and youth is vain;

And to be wroth with one we love
Doth work like madness in the brain.
And thus it chanced, as I divine,
With Roland and Sir Leoline.
Each spake words of high disdain
And insult to his heart's best brother:
They parted – ne'er to meet again!
But never either found another
To free the hollow heart from paining –
They stood aloof, the scars remaining,
Like cliffs which had been rent asunder;
A dreary sea now flows between.
But neither heat, nor frost, nor thunder,
Shall wholly do away, I ween,
The marks of that which once hath been.

Sir Leoline, a moment's space,
Stood gazing on the damsel's face:
And the youthful Lord of Tryermaine
Came back upon his heart again.

O then the Baron forgot his age,
His noble heart swelled high with rage;
He swore by the wounds in Jesu's side
He would proclaim it far and wide,
With trump and solemn heraldry,
That they, who thus had wronged the dame
Were base as spotted infamy!
"And if they dare deny the same,
My herald shall appoint a week,
And let the recreant traitors seek
My tourney court – that there and then
I may dislodge their reptile souls
From the bodies and forms of men!"
He spake: his eye in lightning rolls!
For the lady was ruthlessly seized; and he kenned
In the beautiful lady the child of his friend!

And now the tears were on his face,
And fondly in his arms he took
Fair Geraldine, who met the embrace,
Prolonging it with joyous look.
Which when she viewed, a vision fell
Upon the soul of Christabel,
The vision of fear, the touch and pain!
She shrunk and shuddered, and saw again –
(Ah, woe is me! Was it for thee,
Thou gentle maid! such sights to see?)

Again she saw that bosom old,
Again she felt that bosom cold,
And drew in her breath with a hissing sound:
Whereat the Knight turned wildly round,
And nothing saw, but his own sweet maid
With eyes upraised, as one that prayed.

The touch, the sight, had passed away,
And in its stead that vision blest,
Which comforted her after-rest,
While in the lady's arms she lay,
Had put a rapture in her breast,
And on her lips and o'er her eyes
Spread smiles like light!
With new surprise,
"What ails then my beloved child?"
The Baron said – His daughter mild
Made answer, "All will yet be well!"
I ween, she had no power to tell
Aught else: so mighty was the spell.

Yet he, who saw this Geraldine,
Had deemed her sure a thing divine.
Such sorrow with such grace she blended,
As if she feared she had offended
Sweet Christabel, that gentle maid!
And with such lowly tones she prayed
She might be sent without delay
Home to her father's mansion.
'Nay!
Nay, by my soul!" said Leoline.
"Ho! Bracy the bard, the charge be thine!
Go thou, with music sweet and loud,
And take two steeds with trappings proud,
And take the youth whom thou lov'st best
To bear thy harp, and learn thy song,
And clothe you both in solemn vest,
And over the mountains haste along,
Lest wandering folk, that are abroad,
Detain you on the valley road.

"And when he has crossed the Irthing flood,
My merry bard! he hastes, he hastes
Up Knorren Moor, through Halegarth Wood,
And reaches soon that castle good
Which stands and threatens Scotland's wastes.

"Bard Bracy! Bard Bracy! Your horses are fleet,
Ye must ride up the hall, your music so sweet,
More loud than your horses' echoing feet!
And loud and loud to Lord Roland call,
Thy daughter is safe in Langdale hall!
Thy beautiful daughter is safe and free –
Sir Leoline greets thee thus through me.
He bids thee come without delay
With all thy numerous array;
And take thy lovely daughter home:
And he will meet thee on the way
With all his numerous array
White with their panting palfreys' foam:
And, by mine honour! I will say,
That I repent me of the day
When I spake words of fierce disdain
To Roland de Vaux of Tryermaine! –
– For since that evil hour hath flown,
Many a summer's sun hath shone;
Yet ne'er found I a friend again
Like Roland de Vaux of Tryermaine."

The lady fell, and clasped his knees,
Her face upraised, her eyes o'erflowing;
And Bracy replied, with faltering voice,
His gracious hail on all bestowing;
"Thy words, thou sire of Christabel,
Are sweeter than my harp can tell;
Yet might I gain a boon of thee,
This day my journey should not be,
So strange a dream hath come to me;
That I had vowed with music loud
To clear yon wood from thing unblest,
Warn'd by a vision in my rest!
For in my sleep I saw that dove,
That gentle bird, whom thou dost love,
And call'st by thy own daughter's name –
Sir Leoline! I saw the same,
Fluttering, and uttering fearful moan,
Among the green herbs in the forest alone.
Which when I saw and when I heard,
I wonder'd what might ail the bird;
For nothing near it could I see,
Save the grass and green herbs underneath the old tree.

"And in my dream, methought, I went
To search out what might there be found;
And what the sweet bird's trouble meant,
That thus lay fluttering on the ground.
I went and peered, and could descry
No cause for her distressful cry;
But yet for her dear lady's sake
I stooped, methought, the dove to take,
When lo! I saw a bright green snake
Coiled around its wings and neck.
Green as the herbs on which it couched,
Close by the dove's its head it crouched;
And with the dove it heaves and stirs,
Swelling its neck as she swelled hers!
I woke; it was the midnight hour,
The clock was echoing in the tower;
But though my slumber was gone by,
This dream it would not pass away –
It seems to live upon my eye!

And thence I vowed this self-same day
With music strong and saintly song
To wander through the forest bare,
Lest aught unholy loiter there."

Thus Bracy said: the Baron, the while,
Half-listening heard him with a smile;
Then turned to Lady Geraldine,
His eyes made up of wonder and love;
And said in courtly accents fine,
"Sweet maid, Lord Roland's beauteous dove,
With arms more strong than harp or song,
Thy sire and I will crush the snake!"
He kissed her forehead as he spake,
And Geraldine in maiden wise
Casting down her large bright eyes,
With blushing cheek and courtesy fine
She turned her from Sir Leoline;
Softly gathering up her train,
That o'er her right arm fell again;
And folded her arms across her chest,
And couched her head upon her breast,
And looked askance at Christabel –
Jesu, Maria, shield her well!

A snake's small eye blinks dull and shy,
And the lady's eyes they shrunk in her head,
Each shrunk up to a serpent's eye,
And with somewhat of malice, and more of dread,
At Christabel she look'd askance! –
One moment – and the sight was fled!
But Christabel in dizzy trance
Stumbling on the unsteady ground
Shuddered aloud, with a hissing sound;
And Geraldine again turned round,
And like a thing, that sought relief,
Full of wonder and full of grief,
She rolled her large bright eyes divine
Wildly on Sir Leoline.

The maid, alas! her thoughts are gone,
She nothing sees – no sight but one!
The maid, devoid of guile and sin,
I know not how, in fearful wise,
So deeply had she drunken in
That look, those shrunken serpent eyes,
That all her features were resigned
To this sole image in her mind:
And passively did imitate
That look of dull and treacherous hate!
And thus she stood, in dizzy trance,
Still picturing that look askance
With forced unconscious sympathy
Full before her father's view –
As far as such a look could be
In eyes so innocent and blue!

And when the trance was o'er, the maid
Paused awhile, and inly prayed:
Then falling at the Baron's feet,
"By my mother's soul do I entreat
That thou this woman send away!"
She said: and more she could not say:
For what she knew she could not tell,
O'er-mastered by the mighty spell.

Why is thy cheek so wan and wild,
Sir Leoline? Thy only child
Lies at thy feet, thy joy, thy pride,
So fair, so innocent, so mild;
The same, for whom thy lady died!
O, by the pangs of her dear mother

Think thou no evil of thy child!
For her, and thee, and for no other,
She prayed the moment ere she died:
Prayed that the babe for whom she died,
Might prove her dear lord's joy and pride!
That prayer her deadly pangs beguiled,
Sir Leoline!
And wouldst thou wrong thy only child,
Her child and thine?

Within the Baron's heart and brain
If thoughts, like these, had any share,
They only swelled his rage and pain,
And did but work confusion there.
His heart was cleft with pain and rage,
His cheeks they quivered, his eyes were wild,
Dishonour'd thus in his old age;
Dishonour'd by his only child,
And all his hospitality
To the insulted daughter of his friend
By more than woman's jealousy
Brought thus to a disgraceful end –
He rolled his eye with stern regard
Upon the gentle minstrel bard,
And said in tones abrupt, austere –
"Why, Bracy! dost thou loiter here?
I bade thee hence!" The bard obeyed;
And turning from his own sweet maid,
The aged knight, Sir Leoline,
Led forth the lady Geraldine!

The Conclusion to Part the Second

A little child, a limber elf,
Singing, dancing to itself,
A fairy thing with red round cheeks,
That always finds, and never seeks,
Makes such a vision to the sight
As fills a father's eyes with light;
And pleasures flow in so thick and fast
Upon his heart, that he at last
Must needs express his love's excess
With words of unmeant bitterness.
Perhaps 'tis pretty to force together
Thoughts so all unlike each other;
To mutter and mock a broken charm,

To dally with wrong that does no harm.
Perhaps 'tis tender too and pretty
At each wild word to feel within
A sweet recoil of love and pity.
And what, if in a world of sin
(O sorrow and shame should this be true!)
Such giddiness of heart and brain
Comes seldom save from rage and pain,
So talks as it's most used to do.

If you enjoyed this, you might also like...
'The Spectre Barber' by Johann Karl August Musäus, see page 217
'On Ghosts', see page 238

Prefaces to Tales of the Dead

Sarah Elizabeth Utterson

[Publisher's Note: The collection of spooky tales which was read at that infamous party at the Villa Diodati was entitled Fantasmagoriana (1812) *– a French translation of selected German ghost stories. A year later, Sarah Elizabeth Utterson translated a selection of these stories into English, publishing them in her anthology* Tales of the Dead. *It is from this source that we have taken the following four stories.]*

Advertisement

ALTHOUGH THE PASSION for books of amusement founded on the marvellous relative to ghosts and spirits may be considered as having very much subsided; yet I cannot but think that the tales which form the bulk of this little volume, may still afford gratification in the perusal. From the period when the late Lord Orford first published The Castle of Otranto, till the production of Mrs. Ratcliffe's romances, the appetite for the species of reading in question gradually increased; and perhaps it would not have been now surfeited, but for the multitude of contemptible imitations which the popularity of the latter writer called forth, and which continually issued from the press, until the want of readers at length checked the inundation.

The Northern nations have generally discovered more of imagination in this description of writing than their neighbours in the South or West; and in proportion as they have been more the victims of credulity with respect to spirits, they have indulged in the wanderings of fancy on subjects of this kind, and have eagerly employed their invention in forming narrations founded on the supposed communication between the spiritual world and mankind. The productions of Schiller, and others of the modern German literati, of this nature, are well known in England.

The first four tales in this collection, and the last[1], are imitated from a small French work, which professes to be translated from the German. It contains several other stories of a similar cast; but which did not appear equally interesting, and they have therefore been omitted. The last tale[2] has been considerably curtailed, as it contained much matter relative to the loves of the hero and heroine, which in a compilation of this kind appeared rather misplaced.

The translation was the amusement of an idle hour; and if it afford an equal portion of gratification to the reader, the time has not been altogether misemployed.

Footnote 1. The following 4 tales which we have included in this collection are amongst those alluded to by Utterson here.
Footnote 2. 'The Spectre-Barber'.

Preface of the French Translator

IT IS GENERALLY BELIEVED that at this time of day no one puts any faith in ghosts and apparitions. Yet, on reflection, this opinion does not appear to me quite correct: for, without alluding to workmen in mines, and the inhabitants of mountainous countries – the former of whom believe in spectres and hobgoblins presiding over concealed treasures, and the latter in apparitions and phantoms announcing either agreeable or unfortunate tidings – may we not ask why amongst ourselves there are certain individuals who have a dread of passing through a church-yard after night-fall? Why others experience an involuntary shuddering at entering a church, or any other large uninhabited edifice, in the dark? And, in fine, why persons who are deservedly considered as possessing courage and good sense, dare not visit at night even places where they are certain of meeting with nothing they need dread from living beings? They are ever repeating, that the living are only to be dreaded; and yet fear night, because they believe, by tradition, that it is the time which phantoms choose for appearing to the inhabitants of the earth.

Admitting, therefore, as an undoubted fact, that, with few exceptions, ghosts are no longer believed in, and that the species of fear we have just mentioned arises from a natural horror of darkness incident to man – a horror which he cannot account for rationally – yet it is well known that he listens with much pleasure to stories of ghosts, spectres, and phantoms. The wonderful ever excites a degree of interest, and gains an attentive ear; consequently, all recitals relative to supernatural appearances please us. It was probably from this cause that the study of the sciences which was in former times intermixed with the marvellous, is now reduced to the simple observation of facts. This wise revolution will undoubtedly assist the progress of truth; but it has displeased many men of genius, who maintain that by so doing, the sciences are robbed of their greatest attractions, and that the new mode will tend to weary the mind and disenchant study; and they neglect no means in their power to give back to the supernatural, that empire of which it has been recently deprived: They loudly applaud their efforts, though they cannot pride themselves on their success: for in physic and natural history prodigies are entirely exploded.

But if in these classes of writing, the marvellous and supernatural would be improper, at least they cannot be considered as misplaced in the work we are now about to publish: and they cannot have any dangerous tendency on the mind; for the title-page announces extraordinary relations, to which more or less faith may be attached, according to the credulity of the person who reads them. Besides which, it is proper that some repertory should exist, in which we may discover the traces of those superstitions to which mankind have so long been subject. We now laugh at, and turn them into ridicule: and yet it is not clear to me, that recitals respecting phantoms have ceased to amuse; or that, so long as human nature exists, there will be wanting those who will attach faith to histories of ghosts and spectres.

I might in this preface have entered into a learned and methodical disquisition respecting apparitions; but should only have repeated what Dom Calmet and the Abbé Lenglet-Dufresnoy have already said on the subject, and which they have so thoroughly exhausted, that it would be almost impossible to advance anything new. Persons curious to learn everything relative to apparitions, will be amply recompensed by consulting the two writers above mentioned. They give to the full as strange recitals as any which are to be found in this work. Although the Abbé Lenglet-Dufresnoy says there really are apparitions;

yet he does not appear to believe in them himself: but Dom Calmet finishes (as Voltaire observes) as if he believed what he wrote, and especially with respect to the extraordinary histories of Vampires. And we may add, for the benefit of those anxious to make deeper search into the subject in question, that the Abbé Lenglet-Dufresnoy has given a list of the principal authors who have written on spirits, demons, apparitions, dreams, magic, and spectres.

Since this laborious writer has published this list, Swedenborg and St. Martin have rendered themselves notorious by their Works; and there have also appeared in Germany treatises on this question of the appearance of spirits. The two authors who have the most largely entered into the detail are Wagener and Jung. The first, whose book is entitled The Spectres, endeavours to explain apparitions by attributing them to natural causes. But the second, on the contrary, firmly believes in spirits; and his Theory on Phantasmatology furnishes us with an undoubted proof of this assertion. This work, the fruit of an ardent and exalted imagination, is in some degree a manual to the doctrines of the modern Seers, known in Germany under the denomination of Stillingianer. They take their name from Stilling, under which head Jung has written memoirs of his life, which forms a series of different works. This sect, which is actually in existence, is grafted on the Swedenborgians and Martinisme, and has a great number of adherents, especially in Switzerland. We also see in the number of the (English) Monthly Review for December 1811, that Mrs. Grant has given a pretty circumstantial detail of the apparitions and spirits to which the Scottish mountaineers attach implicit faith.

In making choice of the stories for my translations from the German, which I now offer to the public, I have neglected nothing to merit the approbation of those who take pleasure in this species of reading: and if this selection has the good fortune to meet with any success, it shall be followed by another; in which I shall equally endeavour to excite the curiosity of the lovers of romance; while to those who are difficult to please, and to whom it seems strange that any one should attach the slightest degree of faith to such relations, I merely say – Remember the words of Voltaire at the beginning of the article he wrote on 'Apparition,' in his Philosophical Dictionary: 'It is no uncommon thing for a person of lively feelings to fancy he sees what never really existed.'

The Family Portraits

Johann August Apel

> *"No longer shall you gaze on't; lest your fancy*
> *May think anon, it moves. –*
> *The fixure of her eye has motion in't."*
> **William Shakespeare, The Winter's Tale**

NIGHT HAD insensibly superseded day, when Ferdinand's carriage continued its slow course through the forest; the postilion uttering a thousand complaints on the badness of the roads, and Ferdinand employing the leisure which the tedious progress of his carriage allowed, with reflections to which the purpose of his journey gave rise.

As was usual with young men of rank, he had visited several universities; and after having travelled over the principal parts of Europe, he was now returning to his native country to take possession of the property of his father, who had died in his absence.

Ferdinand was an only son, and the last branch of the ancient family of Meltheim: it was on this account that his mother was the more anxious that he should form a brilliant alliance, to which both his birth and fortune entitled him; she frequently repeated that Clotilde of Hainthal was of all others the person she should be most rejoiced to have as a daughter-in-law, and who should give to the world an heir to the name and estates of Meltheim. In the first instance, she merely named her amongst other distinguished females whom she recommended to her son's attention: but after a short period she spoke of none but her: and at length declared, rather positively, that all her happiness depended on the completion of this alliance, and hoped her son would approve her choice.

Ferdinand, however, never thought of this union but with regret; and the urgent remonstrances which his mother ceased not to make on the subject, only contributed to render Clotilde, who was an entire stranger to him, less amiable in his eyes: he determined at last to take a journey to the capital, whither Mr. Hainthal and his daughter were attracted by the carnival. He wished at least to know the lady, ere he consented to listen to his mother's entreaties; and secretly flattered himself that he should find some more cogent reasons for opposing this union than mere caprice, which was the appellation the old lady gave to his repugnance.

Whilst travelling alone in his carriage, as night approached, the solitary forest, his imagination drew a picture of his early life, which happy recollections rendered still happier. It seemed, that the future presented no charms for him to equal the past; and the greater pleasure he took in retracing what no longer existed, the less wish he felt to bestow a thought on that futurity to which, contrary to his inclinations, he seemed destined. Thus, notwithstanding the slowness with which his carriage proceeded over the rugged ground, he found that he was too rapidly approaching the termination of his journey.

The postilion at length began to console himself; for one half of the journey was accomplished, and the remainder presented only good roads: Ferdinand, however, gave orders to his groom to stop at the approaching village, determining to pass the night there.

The road through the village which led to the inn was bordered by gardens, and the sound of different musical instruments led Ferdinand to suppose that the villagers were celebrating some rural fête. He already anticipated the pleasure of joining them, and hoped that this recreation would dissipate his melancholy thoughts. But on listening more attentively, he remarked that the music did not resemble that usually heard at inns; and the great light he perceived at the window of a pretty house from whence came the sounds that had arrested his attention, did not permit him to doubt that a more select party than are accustomed to reside in the country at that unfavourable season, were amusing themselves in performing a concert.

The carriage now stopped at the door of a small inn of mean appearance. Ferdinand, who counted on much inconvenience and few comforts, asked who was the lord of the village. They informed him that he occupied a château situated in an adjoining hamlet. Our traveller said no more, but was obliged to content himself with the best apartment the landlord could give him. To divert his thoughts, he determined to walk in the village, and directed his steps towards the spot where he had heard the music; to this the harmonious sounds readily guided him: he approached softly, and found himself close to the house where the concert was performing. A young girl, sitting at the door, was playing with a little dog, who began to bark. Ferdinand, drawn from his reverie by this singular accompaniment, begged the little girl to inform him who lived in that house. "It is my father," she replied, smiling; "come in, sir." And saying this, she slowly went up the steps.

Ferdinand hesitated for an instant whether to accept this unceremonious invitation. But the master of the house came down, saying to him in a friendly tone: "Our music, sir, has probably been the only attraction to this spot; no matter, it is the pastor's abode, and to it you are heartily welcome. My neighbours and I," continued he, whilst leading Ferdinand in, "meet alternately at each other's houses once a week, to form a little concert; and to-day it is my turn. Will you take a part in the performance, or only listen to it? Sit down in this apartment. Are you accustomed to hear better music than that performed simply by amateurs? or do you prefer an assemblage where they pass their time in conversation? If you like the latter, go into the adjoining room, where you will find my wife surrounded by a young circle: here is our musical party, there is their conversazióni." Saying this, he opened the door, made a gentle inclination of the head to Ferdinand, and seated himself before his desk. Our traveller would fain have made apologies; but the performers in an instant resumed the piece he had interrupted. At the same time the pastor's wife, a young and pretty woman, entreated Ferdinand, in the most gracious manner possible, entirely to follow his own inclinations, whether they led him to remain with the musicians, or to join the circle assembled in the other apartment. Ferdinand, after uttering some common-place terms of politeness, followed her into the adjoining room.

The chairs formed a semicircle round the sofa, and were occupied by several women and by some men. They all rose on Ferdinand's entering, and appeared a little disconcerted at the interruption. In the middle of the circle was a low chair, on which sat, with her back to the door, a young and sprightly female, who, seeing everyone rise, changed her position, and at sight of a stranger blushed and appeared embarrassed. Ferdinand entreated the company not to interrupt the conversation. They accordingly reseated themselves, and the mistress of the house invited the new guest to take a seat on the sofa by two elderly ladies, and drew her chair near him. "The music," she said to him, "drew you amongst us, and yet in this apartment we have none; I hear it nevertheless with pleasure myself: but I cannot participate in my husband's enthusiasm for simple quartets and symphonies; several of my friends are of the same way of thinking with me, which is the reason that, while our husbands are occupied with their favourite science, we here enjoy social converse, which sometimes, however, becomes too loud for our virtuoso neighbours. Today, I give a long-promised tea-drinking. Everyone is to relate a story of ghosts, or something of a similar nature. You see that my auditors are more numerous than the band of musicians."

"Permit me, madam," replied Ferdinand, "to add to the number of your auditors; although I have not much talent in explaining the marvellous."

"That will not be any hinderance to you here," answered a very pretty brunette; "for it is agreed amongst us that no one shall search for any explanation, even though it bears the stamp of truth, as explanations would take away all pleasure from ghost stories."

"I shall benefit by your instructions," answered Ferdinand: "but without doubt I interrupt a very interesting recital; – dare I entreat –?"

The young lady with flaxen hair, who rose from the little seat, blushed anew; but the mistress of the house drew her by the arm, and laughing, conducted her to the middle of the circle. "Come, child," said she, "don't make any grimace; reseat yourself, and relate your story. This gentleman will also give us his."

"Do you promise to give us one, sir?" said the young lady to Ferdinand. He replied by a low bow. She then reseated herself in the place destined for the narrator, and thus began:

"One of my youthful friends, named Juliana, passed every summer with her family at her father's estate. The château was situated in a romantic country; high mountains formed a circle in the distance; forests of oaks and fine groves surrounded it. It was an ancient edifice, and had descended through a long line of ancestry to Juliana's father; for which reason, instead of making any alterations, he was only anxious to preserve it in the same state they had left it to him.

"Among the number of antiquities most prized by him was the family picture gallery; a vaulted room, dark, high, and of gothic architecture, where hung the portraits of his forefathers, as large as the natural size, covering the walls, which were blackened by age. Conformable to an immemorial custom, they ate in this room: and Juliana has often told me, that she could not overcome, especially at supper-time, a degree of fear and repugnance; and that she had frequently feigned indisposition, to avoid entering this formidable apartment. Among the portraits there was one of a female, who, it would seem, did not belong to the family; for Juliana's father could neither tell whom it represented, nor how it had become ranged amongst his ancestry: but as to all appearance it had retained its station for ages, my friend's father was unwilling to remove it.

"Juliana never looked at this portrait without an involuntary shuddering: and she has told me, that from her earliest infancy she has felt this secret terror, without being able to define the cause. Her father treated this sentiment as puerile, and compelled her sometimes to remain alone in that room. But as Juliana grew up, the terror this singular portrait occasioned, increased; and she frequently supplicated her father, with tears in her eyes, not to leave her alone in that apartment – 'That portrait,' she would say, 'regards me not gloomily or terribly, but with looks full of a mild melancholy. It appears anxious to draw me to it, and as if the lips were about to open and speak to me. That picture will certainly cause my death.'

"Juliana's father at length relinquished all hope of conquering his daughter's fears. One night at supper, the terror she felt had thrown her into convulsions, for she fancied she saw the picture move its lips; and the physician enjoined her father in future to remove from her view all similar causes of fear. In consequence, the terrifying portrait was removed from the gallery, and it was placed over the door of an uninhabited room in the attic story.

"Juliana, after this removal, passed two years without experiencing any alarms. Her complexion resumed its brilliancy, which surprised everyone; for her continual fears had rendered her pale and wan: but the portrait and the fears it produced had alike disappeared, and Juliana –"

"Well," cried the mistress of the house, smiling, when she perceived that the narrator appeared to hesitate, "confess it, my dear child; Juliana found an admirer of her beauty – was it not so?"

"'Tis even so," resumed the young lady, blushing deeply; "she was affianced: and her intended husband coming to see her the day previous to that fixed on for her marriage, she conducted him over the château, and from the attic rooms was shewing him the beautiful prospect which extended to the distant mountains. On a sudden she found herself, without being aware of it, in the room where the unfortunate portrait was placed. And it was natural that a stranger, surprised at seeing it there alone, should ask who it represented. To look at it, recognise it, utter a piercing shriek, and run towards the door, were but the work of an instant with poor Juliana. But whether in effect owing to the violence with which she opened the door the picture was shaken, or whether the moment was arrived in which its baneful influence was to be exercised over Juliana, I know not; but at the moment this unfortunate girl was striving to get out of the room and avoid her destiny, the portrait fell; and Juliana, thrown down by her fears, and overpowered by the heavy weight of the picture, never rose more."

A long silence followed this recital, which was only interrupted by the exclamations of surprise and interest excited for the unfortunate Juliana. Ferdinand alone appeared untouched by the general emotions. At length, one of the ladies sitting near him broke the silence by saying, "This story is literally true; I knew the family where the fatal portrait caused the death of a charming young girl: I have also seen the picture; it has, as the young lady truly observed, an indescribable air of goodness which penetrates the heart, so that I could not bear to look on it long; and yet, as you say, its look is so full of tender melancholy, and has such infinite attractions, that it appears that the eyes move and have life."

"In general," resumed the mistress of the house, at the same time shuddering, "I don't like portraits, and I would not have any in the rooms I occupy. They say that they become pale when the original expires; and the more faithful the likeness, the more they remind me of those waxen figures I cannot look at without aversion."

"That is the reason," replied the young person who had related the history, "that I prefer those portraits where the individual is represented occupied in some employment, as then the figure is entirely independent of those who look at it; whereas in a simple portrait the eyes are inanimately fixed on everything that passes. Such portraits appear to me as contrary to the laws of illusion as painted statues."

"I participate in your opinion," replied Ferdinand; "for the remembrance of a terrible impression produced on my mind when young, by a portrait of that sort, will never be effaced."

"O! Pray relate it to us," said the young lady with flaxen hair, who had not as yet quitted the low chair; "you are obliged according to promise to take my place." She instantly arose, and jokingly forced Ferdinand to change seats with her.

"This history," said he, "will resemble a little too much the one you have just related; permit me therefore –"

"That does not signify," resumed the mistress of the house, "one is never weary with recitals of this kind; and the greater repugnance I feel in looking at these horrible portraits, the greater is the pleasure I take in listening to histories of their eyes or feet being seen to move."

"But seriously," replied Ferdinand, who would fain have retracted his promise, "my history is too horrible for so fine an evening. I confess to you that I cannot think of it without shuddering, although several years have elapsed since it happened."

"So much the better, so much the better!" cried nearly all present; "how you excite our curiosity! and its having happened to yourself will afford double pleasure, as we cannot entertain any doubt of the fact."

"It did not happen personally to me," answered Ferdinand, who reflected that he had gone too far, "but to one of my friends, on whose word I have as firm a reliance as if I had been myself a witness to it."

They reiterated their entreaties; and Ferdinand began in these words: – "One day, when I was arguing with the friend of whom I am about to make mention, on apparitions and omens, he told me the following story:"

"I had been invited," said he, "by one of my college companions, to pass my vacations with him at an estate of his father's. The spring was that year unusually late, owing to a long and severe winter, and appeared in consequence more gay and agreeable, which gave additional charms to our projected pleasures. We arrived at his father's in the pleasant month of April, animated by all the gaiety the season inspired.

"As my companion and I were accustomed to live together at the university, he had recommended to his family, in his letters, so to arrange matters that we might live together at his father's also: we in consequence occupied two adjoining rooms, from whence we enjoyed a view of the garden and a fine country, bounded in the distance by forests and vineyards. In a few days I found myself so completely at home in the house, and so familiarised with its inhabitants, that nobody, whether of the family or among the domesticks, made any difference between my friend and myself. His younger brothers, who were absent from me in the day, often passed the night in my room, or in that of their elder brother. Their sister, a charming girl about twelve years of age, lovely and blooming as a newly blown rose, gave me the appellation of brother, and fancied that under this title she was privileged to shew me all her favourite haunts in the garden, to gratify my wishes at table, and to furnish my apartment with all that was requisite. Her cares and attention will never be effaced from my recollection; they will long outlive the scenes of horror that château never ceases to recall to my recollection. From the first of my arrival, I had remarked a huge portrait affixed to the wall of an antechamber through which I was obliged to pass to go to my room; but, too much occupied by the new objects which on all sides attracted my attention, I had not particularly examined it. Meanwhile I could not avoid observing that, though the two younger brothers of my friend were so much attached to me, that they would never permit me to go at night into my room without them, yet they always evinced an unaccountable dread in crossing the hall where this picture hung. They clung to me, and embraced me that I might take them in my arms; and whichever I was compelled to take by the hand, invariably covered his face, in order that he might not see the least trace of the portrait.

"Being aware that the generality of children are afraid of colossal figures, or even of those of a natural height, I endeavoured to give my two young friends courage. However, on more attentively considering the portrait which caused them so much dread, I could not avoid feeling a degree of fear myself. The picture represented a knight in the costume of a very remote period; a full grey mantle descended from his shoulders to his knees; one of his feet placed in the foreground, appeared as if it was starting from the canvass; his countenance had an expression which petrified me with fear. I had never before seen anything at all like it in nature. It was a frightful mixture of the stillness of death, with the remains of a violent and baneful passion, which not even death itself was able to overcome. One would have thought the artist had copied the terrible features of one risen from the grave, in order to paint this terrific portrait. I was seized with a terror little less than the children, whenever I wished to contemplate this picture. Its aspect was disagreeable to my friend, but did not cause him any terror: his sister was the only one who could look at this hideous figure with a smiling countenance; and said to me with a compassionate air, when I discovered my aversion to it, 'That man is not wicked, but he is certainly very unhappy.' My friend told me that the picture represented the founder of his race, and that his father attached uncommon value to it; it had, in all probability, hung there from time immemorial, and it would not be possible to remove it from this chamber without destroying the regularity of its appearance.

"Meanwhile, the term of our vacation was speedily drawing to its close, and time insensibly wore away in the pleasures of the country. The old count, who remarked our reluctance to quit him, his amiable family, his château, and the fine country that surrounded it, applied himself with kind and unremitting care, to make the day preceding our departure a continual succession of rustic diversions: each succeeded the other without the slightest appearance of art; they seemed of necessity to follow each other. The delight that illumined the eyes of my friend's sister when she perceived her father's satisfaction; the joy that was painted in Emily's countenance (which was the name of this charming girl) when she surprised even her father by her arrangements, which outstripped his projects, led me to discover the entire confidence that existed between the father and daughter, and the active part Emily had taken in directing the order which reigned in that day's festivities.

"Night arrived; the company in the gardens dispersed; but my amiable companions never quitted my side. The two young boys skipped gaily before us, chasing the may-bug, and shaking the shrubs to make them come out. The dew arose, and aided by the light of the moon formed silver spangles on the flowers and grass. Emily hung on my arm; and an affectionate sister conducted me, as if to take leave, to all the groves and places I had been accustomed to visit with her, or with the family. On arriving at the door of the château, I was obliged to repeat the promise I had made to her father, of passing some weeks in the autumn with him. 'That season,' said she, 'is equally beautiful with the spring!' With what pleasure did I promise to decline all other engagements for this. Emily retired to her apartment, and, according to custom, I went up to mine, accompanied by my two little boys: they ran gaily up the stairs; and in crossing the range of apartments but faintly lighted, to my no small surprise their boisterous mirth was not interrupted by the terrible portrait.

"For my own part, my head and heart were full of the intended journey, and of the agreeable manner in which my time had passed at the count's château. The images of those happy days crowded on my recollection; my imagination, at that time possessing all the vivacity of youth, was so much agitated, that I could not enjoy the sleep which already overpowered my friend. Emily's image, so interesting by her sprightly grace, by her pure affection for me, was present to my mind like an amiable phantom shining in beauty. I placed myself at the window, to take another look at the country I had so frequently ranged with her, and traced our steps again probably for the last time. I remembered each spot illumined by the pale light the moon afforded. The nightingale was singing in the groves where we had delighted to repose; the little river on which while gaily singing we often sailed, rolled murmuringly her silver waves.

"Absorbed in a profound reverie, I mentally exclaimed: With the flowers of spring, this soft pure peaceful affection will probably fade; and as frequently the after seasons blight the blossoms and destroy the promised fruit, so possibly may the approaching autumn envelop in cold reserve that heart which, at the present moment, appears only to expand with mine!

"Saddened by these reflections, I withdrew from the window, and overcome by a painful agitation I traversed the adjoining rooms; and on a sudden found myself before the portrait of my friend's ancestor. The moon's beams darted on it in the most singular manner possible, insomuch as to give the appearance of a horrible moving spectre; and the reflexion of the light gave to it the appearance of a real substance about to quit the darkness by which it was surrounded. The inanimation of its features appeared to give place to the most profound melancholy; the sad and glazed look of the eyes appeared the only hinderance to its uttering its grief.

"My knees tremblingly knocked against each other, and with an unsteady step I regained my chamber: the window still remained open; I reseated myself at it, in order that the freshness of the night air, and the aspect of the beautiful surrounding country, might dissipate the terror I had experienced. My wandering eyes fixed on a long vista of ancient linden trees, which extended from my window to the ruins of an old tower, which had often been the scene of our pleasures and rural fêtes. The remembrance of the hideous portrait had vanished; when on a sudden there appeared to me a thick fog issuing from the ruined tower, which advancing through the vista of lindens came towards me.

"I regarded this cloud with an anxious curiosity: it approached; but again it was concealed by the thickly-spreading branches of the trees.

"On a sudden I perceived, in a spot of the avenue less dark than the rest, the same figure represented in the formidable picture, enveloped in the grey mantle I so well knew. It advanced towards the château, as if hesitating: no noise was heard of its footsteps on the pavement; it passed before my window without looking up, and gained a back door which led to the apartments in the colonnade of the château.

"Seized with trembling apprehension, I darted towards my bed, and saw with pleasure that the two children were fast asleep on either side. The noise I made awoke them; they started, but in an instant were asleep again. The agitation I had endured took from me the power of sleep, and I turned to awake one of the children to talk with me: but no powers can depict the horrors I endured when I saw the frightful figure at the side of the child's bed.

"I was petrified with horror, and dared neither move nor shut my eyes. I beheld the spectre stoop towards the child and softly kiss his forehead: he then went round the bed, and kissed the forehead of the other boy.

"I lost all recollection at that moment; and the following morning, when the children awoke me with their caresses, I was willing to consider the whole as a dream.

"Meanwhile, the moment for our departure was at hand. We once again breakfasted all together in a grove of lilacs and flowers. 'I advise you to take a little more care of yourself,' said the old count in the midst of other conversation; 'for I last night saw you walking rather late in the garden, in a dress ill suited to the damp air; and I was fearful such imprudence would expose you to cold and fever. Young people are apt to fancy they are invulnerable; but I repeat to you, Take advice from a friend.'

"'In truth,' I answered, 'I believe readily that I have been attacked by a violent fever, for never before was I so harassed by terrifying visions: I can now conceive how dreams afford to a heated imagination subjects for the most extraordinary stories of apparitions.'

"'What would you tell me?' demanded the count in a manner not wholly devoid of agitation. I related to him all that I had seen the preceding night; and to my great surprise he appeared to me in no way astonished, but extremely affected.

"'You say,' added he in a trembling voice, 'that the phantom kissed the two children's foreheads?' I answered him, that it was even so. He then exclaimed, in accents of the deepest despair, 'Oh heavens! they must then both die!'"

Till now the company had listened without the slightest noise or interruption to Ferdinand: but as he pronounced the last words, the greater part of his audience trembled; and the young lady who had previously occupied the chair on which he sat, uttered a piercing shriek.

"Imagine," continued Ferdinand, "how astonished my friend must have been at this unexpected exclamation. The vision of the night had caused him excess of agitation; but the melancholy voice of the count pierced his heart, and seemed to annihilate his being, by the terrifying conviction of the existence of the spiritual world, and the secret horrors with which this idea was accompanied. It was not then a dream, a chimera, the fruit of an over-heated imagination! but a mysterious and infallible messenger, which, dispatched from the world of spirits, had passed close to him, had placed itself by his couch, and by its fatal kiss had dropt the germ of death in the bosom of the two children.

"He vainly entreated the count to explain this extraordinary event. Equally fruitless were his son's endeavours to obtain from the count the developement of this mystery, which apparently concerned the whole family. 'You are as yet too young,' replied the count: 'too soon, alas! for your peace of mind, will you be informed of these terrible circumstances which you now think mysterious.'

"Just as they came to announce to my friend that all was ready, he recollected that during the recital the count had sent away Emily and her two younger brothers. Deeply agitated, he took leave of the count and the two young children who came towards him, and who would scarcely permit themselves to be separated from him. Emily, who had placed herself at a window, made a sign of adieu. Three days afterwards the young count received news of the death of his two younger brothers. They were both taken off in the same night.

"You see," continued Ferdinand, in a gayer tone, in order to counteract the impression of sadness and melancholy his story had produced on the company; "You see my history is very far from affording any natural explication of the wonders it contains; explanations which only tend to shock one's reason: it does not even make you entirely acquainted with the mysterious person, which one has a right to expect in all marvellous recitals. But I could learn nothing more; and the old count dying without revealing the mystery to his son, I see no other means of terminating the history of the portrait, which is undoubtedly by no means devoid of interest, than by inventing according to one's fancy a dénouement which shall explain all."

"That does not appear at all necessary to me," said a young man: "this history, like the one that preceded it, is in reality finished, and gives all the satisfaction one has any right to expect from recitals of this species."

"I should not agree with you," replied Ferdinand, "if I was capable of explaining the mysterious connection between the portrait and the death of the two children in the same night, or the terror of Juliana at sight of the other portrait, and her death, consequently caused by it. I am, however, not the less obliged to you for the entire satisfaction you evince."

"But," resumed the young man, "what benefit would your imagination receive, if the connections of which you speak were known to you?"

"Very great benefit, without doubt," replied Ferdinand; "for imagination requires the completion of the objects it represents, as much as the judgment requires correctness and accuracy in its ideas."

The mistress of the house, not being partial to these metaphysical disputes, took part with Ferdinand: "We ladies," said she, "are always curious; therefore don't wonder that we complain when a story has no termination. It appears to me like seeing the last scene of Mozart's Don Juan without having witnessed the preceding ones; and I am sure no one would be the better satisfied, although the last scene should possess infinite merit."

The young man remained silent, perhaps less through conviction than politeness. Several persons were preparing to retire; and Ferdinand, who had vainly searched with all his eyes for the young lady with flaxen hair, was already at the door, when an elderly gentleman, whom he remembered to have seen in the music-room, asked him whether the friend concerning whom he had related the story was not called Count Meltheim?

"That is his name," answered Ferdinand a little drily; "how did you guess it? Are you acquainted with his family?"

"You have advanced nothing but the simple truth," resumed the unknown. "Where is the count at this moment?"

"He is on his travels," replied Ferdinand. "But I am astonished –"

"Do you correspond with him?" demanded the unknown.

"I do," answered Ferdinand. "But I don't understand –"

"Well then," continued the old man, "tell him that Emily still continues to think of him, and that he must return as speedily as possible, if he takes any interest in a secret that very particularly concerns her family."

On this the old man stepped into his carriage, and had vanished from Ferdinand's sight ere he had recovered from his surprise. He looked around him in vain for someone who might inform him of the name of the unknown: everyone was gone; and he was on the point of risking being considered indiscreet, by asking for information of the pastor who had so courteously treated him, when they fastened the door of the house, and he was compelled to return in sadness to his inn, and leave his researches till the morning.

The frightful scenes of the night preceding Ferdinand's departure from the château of his friend's father, had tended to weaken the remembrance of Emily; and the distraction which his journey so immediately after had produced, had not contributed to recall it with any force: but all at once the recollection of Emily darted across his mind with fresh vigour, aided by the recital of the previous evening and the old man's conversation: it presented itself even with greater vivacity and strength than at the period of its birth. Ferdinand now fancied that he could trace Emily in the pretty girl with flaxen hair. The more he reflected on her figure, her eyes, the sound of her voice, the grace with which she moved; the more striking the resemblance appeared to him. The piercing shriek that had escaped her, when he mentioned the old count's explication of the phantom's appearance; her sudden disappearance at the termination of the recital; her connection with Ferdinand's family, (for the young lady, in her history of Juliana, had recounted the fatal accident which actually befell Ferdinand's sister), all gave a degree of certainty to his suppositions.

He passed the night in forming projects and plans, in resolving doubts and difficulties; and Ferdinand impatiently waited for the day which was to enlighten him. He went to the pastor's, whom he found in the midst of his quires of music; and by giving a natural turn to the conversation, he seized the opportunity of enquiring concerning the persons with whom he had passed the preceding evening.

He unfortunately, however, could not get satisfactory answers to his questions concerning the young lady with flaxen hair, and the mysterious old gentleman; for the pastor had been so absorbed in his music, that he had not paid attention to many persons who had visited him: and though Ferdinand in the most minute manner possible described their dress and other particulars, it was impossible to make the pastor comprehend the individuals whose names he was so anxious to learn. "It is unfortunate," said the pastor, "that my wife should be out; she would have given you all the information you desire. But according to your description, it strikes me the young person with flaxen hair must be Mademoiselle de Hainthal; but –"

"Mademoiselle de Hainthal!" reiterated Ferdinand, somewhat abruptly.

"I think so," replied the clergyman. "Are you acquainted with the young lady?"

"I know her family," answered Ferdinand; "but from her features bearing so strong a resemblance to the family, I thought it might have been the young countess of Wartbourg, who was so much like her brother."

"That is very possible," said the pastor. "You knew then the unfortunate count Wartbourg?"

"Unfortunate!" exclaimed Ferdinand, greatly surprised.

"You don't then know anything," continued the pastor, "of the deplorable event that has recently taken place at the château of Wartbourg? The young count, who had probably in his travels seen some beautifully laid-out gardens, was anxious to embellish the lovely country which surrounds his château; and as the ruins of an old tower seemed to be an obstacle to his plans, he ordered them to be pulled down. His gardener in vain represented to him, that seen from one of the wings of the château they presented, at the termination of a majestic and ancient avenue of linden trees, a magnificent coup d'oeil, and that they would also give a more romantic appearance to the new parts they were about to form. An old servant, grown grey in the service of his forefathers, supplicated him with tears in his eyes to spare the venerable remains of past ages. They even told him of an ancient tradition, preserved in the neighbourhood, which declared, that the existence of the house of Wartbourg was by supernatural means linked with the preservation of that tower.

"The count, who was a well-informed man, paid no attention to these sayings; indeed they possibly made him the more firmly adhere to his resolution. The workmen were put to their task: the walls, which were constructed of huge masses of rock, for a long while resisted the united efforts of tools and gunpowder; the architect of this place appeared to have built it for eternity.

"At length perseverance and labour brought it down. A piece of the rock separating from the rest, precipitated itself into an opening which had been concealed for ages by rubbish and loose sticks, and fell into a deep cavern. An immense subterranean vault was discovered by the rays of the setting sun, supported by enormous pillars – but ere they proceeded in their researches, they went to inform the young count of the discovery they had made.

"He came; and being curious to see this dark abode, descended into it with two servants. The first thing they discovered were chains covered with rust, which being fixed in the rock, plainly shewed the use formerly made of the cavern. On another side was a corpse, dressed in female attire of centuries past, which had surprisingly resisted the ravages of time: close to it was extended a human skeleton almost destroyed.

"The two servants related that the young count, on seeing the body, cried in an accent of extreme horror, 'Great God! it is she then whose portrait killed my intended wife.' Saying which, he fell senseless by the body. The shake which his fall occasioned reduced the skeleton to dust.

"They bore the count to his château, where the care of the physicians restored him to life; but he did not recover his senses. It is probable that this tragical event was caused by the confined and unwholesome air of the cavern. A very few days after, the count died in a state of total derangement.

"It is singular enough, that the termination of his life should coincide with the destruction of the ruined tower, and there no longer exists any male branch of that family. The deeds relative to the succession, ratified and sealed by the emperor Otho, are still amongst the archives of his house. Their contents have as yet only been transmitted verbally from father to son, as a hereditary secret, which will now, however, be made known. It is also true, that the affianced bride of the count was killed by the portrait's falling on her."

"I yesterday heard that fatal history recited by the lady with flaxen hair," replied Ferdinand.

"It is very possible that young person is the countess Emily," replied the pastor; "for she was the bosom-friend of the unfortunate bride."

"Does not then the countess Emily live at the castle of Wartbourg?" asked Ferdinand.

"Since her brother's death," answered the clergyman, "she has lived with a relation of her mother's at the château of Libinfelt, a short distance from hence. For as they yet know not with certainty to whom the castle of Wartbourg will belong, she prudently lives retired."

Ferdinand had learnt sufficient to make him abandon the projected journey to the capital. He thanked the pastor for the instructions he had given him, and was conducted to the château where Emily now resided.

It was still broad day when he arrived. The whole journey he was thinking of the amiable figure which he had recognised too late the preceding evening. He recalled to his idea her every word, the sound of her voice, her actions; and what his memory failed to represent, his imagination depicted with all the vivacity of youth, and all the fire of rekindled affection. He already addressed secret reproaches to Emily for not recognising him; as if he had himself remembered her; and in order to ascertain whether his features were entirely effaced from the recollection of her whom he adored, he caused himself to be announced as a stranger, who was anxious to see her on family matters.

While waiting impatiently in the room into which they had conducted him, he discovered among the portraits with which it was decorated, that of the young lady whose features had the over-night charmed him anew: he was contemplating it with rapture when the door opened and Emily entered. She instantly recognised Ferdinand; and in the sweetest accents accosted him as the friend of her youth.

Surprise rendered Ferdinand incapable of answering suitably to so gracious a reception: it was not the charming person with flaxen hair; it was not a figure corresponding with his imagination, which at this moment presented itself to his view. But it was Emily, shining in every possible beauty, far beyond what Ferdinand had expected: he recollected notwithstanding each feature which had already charmed him, but now clothed in every perfection which nature bestows on her most favoured objects. Ferdinand was lost in thought for some moments: he dared not make mention of his love, and still less did he dare speak of the portrait, and the other wonders of the castle of Wartbourg. Emily spoke only of the happiness she had experienced in her earlier days, and slightly mentioned her brother's death.

As the evening advanced, the young female with flaxen hair came in with the old stranger. Emily presented them both to Ferdinand, as the baron of Hainthal and his daughter Clotilde. They remembered instantly the stranger whom they had seen the preceding evening. Clotilde rallied him on his wish to be incognito; and he found himself on a sudden, by a short train of natural events, in the company of the person whom his mother intended for his wife; the object of his affection whom he had just discovered; and the interesting stranger who had promised him an explanation relative to the mysterious portraits.

Their society was soon augmented by the mistress of the château, in whom Ferdinand recognised one of those who sat by his side the preceding evening. In consideration for Emily, they omitted all the subjects most interesting to Ferdinand; but after supper the baron drew nearer to him.

"I doubt not," said he to him, "that you are anxious to have some light thrown on events, of which, according to your recital last night, you were a spectator. I knew you from the first; and I knew also, that the story you related as of a friend, was your own history. I cannot, however, inform you of more than I know: but that will perhaps be sufficient to save Emily, for whom I feel the affection of a daughter, from chagrin and uneasiness; and from your recital of last evening, I perceive you take a lively interest concerning her."

"Preserve Emily from uneasiness," replied Ferdinand with warmth; "explain yourself: what is there I ought to do?"

"We cannot," answered the baron, "converse here with propriety; tomorrow morning I will come and see you in your apartment."

Ferdinand asked him for an audience that night; but the baron was inflexible. "It is not my wish," said he, "to work upon your imagination by any marvellous recital, but to converse with you on the very important concerns of two distinguished families. For which reason, I think the freshness of morning will be better suited to lessen the horror that my recital must cause you: therefore, if not inconvenient to you, I wish you to attend me at an early hour in the morning: I am fond of rising with the sun; and yet I have never found the time till mid-day too long for arranging my affairs," added he, smiling, and turning half round towards the rest of the party, as if speaking on indifferent topics.

Ferdinand passed a night of agitation, thinking of the conference he was to have with the baron; who was at his window at dawn of day. "You know," said the baron, "that I married the old count of Wartbourg's sister; which alliance was less the cause, than the consequence, of our intimate friendship. We reciprocally communicated our most secret thoughts, and the one never undertook any thing, without the other taking an equal interest with himself in his projects. The count had, however, one secret from me, of which I should never have come at the knowledge but for an accident.

"On a sudden, a report was spread abroad, that the phantom of the Nun's rock had been seen, which was the name given by the peasantry to the old ruined tower which you knew. Persons of sense only laughed at the report: I was anxious the following night to unmask this spectre, and I already anticipated my triumph: but to my no small surprise, the count endeavoured to dissuade me from the attempt; and the more I persisted, the more serious his arguments became; and at length he conjured me in the name of friendship to relinquish the design.

"His gravity of manner excited my attention; I asked him several questions; I even regarded his fears in the light of disease, and urged him to take suitable remedies: but he answered me with an air of chagrin, 'Brother, you know my sincerity towards you; but this is a secret sacred to my family. My son can alone be informed of it, and that only on my death-bed. Therefore ask me no more questions.'

"I held my peace; but I secretly collected all the traditions known amongst the peasantry. The most generally believed one was, that the phantom of the Nun's rock was seen when any one of the count's family were about to die; and in effect, in a few days after the count's youngest son expired. The count seemed to apprehend it: he gave the strictest possible charge to the nurse to take care of him; and under pretext of feeling indisposed himself, sent for two physicians to the castle: but these extreme precautions were precisely the cause of the child's death; for the nurse passing over the stones near the ruins, in her extreme care took the child in her arms to carry him, and her foot slipping, she fell, and in her fall wounded the child so much, that he expired on the spot. She said she fancied that she saw the child extended, bleeding in the midst of the stones; that her fright had made her fall with her face on the earth; and that when she came to herself, the child was absolutely lying weltering in his blood, precisely on the same spot where she had seen his ghost.

"I will not tire you with a relation of all the sayings uttered by an illiterate woman to explain the cause of the vision, for under similar accidents invention far outstrips reality. I could not expect to gain much more satisfactory information from the family records; for the principal documents were preserved in an iron chest, the key of which was never out of the possession of the owner of the castle. I however discovered, by the genealogical register and other similar papers, that this family had never had collateral male branches; but further than this, my researches could not discover.

"At length, on my friend's death-bed I obtained some information, which, however, was far from being satisfactory. You remember, that while the son was on his travels, the father was attacked by the complaint which carried him off so suddenly. The evening previous to his decease, he sent for me express, dismissed all those who were with him, and turning towards me, said: 'I am aware that my end is fast approaching, and am the first of my family that has been carried off without communicating to his son the secret on which the safety of our house depends. Swear to me to reveal it only to my son, and I shall die contented.'

"In the names of friendship and honour, I promised what he exacted of me, and he thus began:

"'The origin of my race, as you know, is not to be traced. Ditmar, the first of my ancestry mentioned in the written records, accompanied the emperor Otho to Italy. His history is also very obscure. He had an enemy called count Bruno, whose only son he killed in revenge, according to ancient tradition, and then kept the father confined till his death in that tower, whose ruins, situated in the Nun's rock, still defy the hand of time. That portrait which hangs alone in the state-chamber, is Ditmar's; and if the traditions of the family are to be believed, it was painted by the Dead. In fact, it is almost impossible to believe that any human being could have contemplated sufficiently long to paint the portrait, the outline of features so hideous. My forefathers have frequently tried to plaster over this redoubtable figure; but in the night, the colours came through the plaster, and re-appeared as distinctly as before; and often in the night, this Ditmar has been seen wandering abroad dressed in the garb represented in the picture; and by kissing the descendants of the family, has doomed them to death. Three of my children have received this fatal kiss. It is said, a monk imposed on him this penance in expiation of his crimes. But he cannot destroy all the children of his race: for so long as the ruins of the old tower shall remain, and whilst one stone shall remain on another, so long shall the count de Wartbourg's family exist; and so long shall the spirit of Ditmar wander on earth, and devote to death the branches of his house, without being able to annihilate the trunk. His race will never be extinct; and his punishment will only cease when the ruins of the tower are entirely dispersed. He brought up, with a truly paternal care, the daughter of his enemy, and wedded her to a rich and powerful knight; but notwithstanding this, the monk never remitted his penance. Ditmar, however, foreseeing that one day or other his race would perish, was certainly anxious ere then, to prepare for an event on which his deliverance depended; and accordingly made a relative disposition of his hereditary property, in case of his family becoming extinct. The act which contained his will, was ratified by the emperor Otho: as yet it has not been opened, and nobody knows its contents. It is kept in the secret archives of our house.'

"The speaking thus much was a great effort to my friend. He required a little rest, but was shortly after incapable of articulating a single word. I performed the commission with which he charged me to his son."

"And he did, notwithstanding –" replied Ferdinand.

"Even so," answered the baron: "but judge more favourably of your excellent friend. I have often seen him alone in the great state-chamber, with his eyes fixed on this horrible portrait: he would then go into the other rooms, where the portraits of his ancestors were ranged for several successive generations; and after contemplating them with visible internal emotion, would return to that of the founder of his house. Broken sentences, and frequent soliloquies, which I overheard by accident, did not leave me a shadow of doubt, but that he was the first of his race who had magnanimity of soul sufficient to resolve on liberating the spirit of Ditmar from its penance, and of sacrificing himself to release his house from the malediction that hung over it. Possibly he was strengthened in his resolutions by the grief he experienced for the death of his dearly beloved."

"Oh!" cried Ferdinand deeply affected, "How like my friend!"

"He had, however, in the ardour of his enthusiasm, forgotten to guard his sister's sensibility," said the baron.

"How so?" demanded Ferdinand.

"It is in consequence of this," answered the baron, "that I now address myself to you, and reveal to you the secret. I have told you that Ditmar demonstrated a paternal affection to the daughter of his enemy, had given her a handsome portion, and had married her to a valiant knight. Learn then, that this knight was Adelbert de Meltheim, from whom the counts of this name descended in a direct line."

"Is it possible?" exclaimed Ferdinand, "the author of my race!"

"The same," answered the baron; "and according to appearances, Ditmar designed that the family of Meltheim should succeed him on the extinction of his own. Haste, then, in order to establish your probable right to the –"

"Never –" said Ferdinand "– so long as Emily –"

"This is no more than I expected from you," replied the baron; "but remember, that in Ditmar's time the girls were not thought of in deeds of this kind. Your inconsiderate generosity would be prejudicial to Emily. For the next of kin who lay claim to the fief, do not probably possess very gallant ideas."

"As a relation, though only on the female side, I have taken the necessary measures; and I think it right you should be present at the castle of Wartbourg when the seals are broken, that you may be immediately recognised as the only immediate descendant of Adelbert, and that you may take instant possession of the inheritance."

"And Emily?" demanded Ferdinand.

"As for what is to be done for her," replied the baron, "I leave to you; and feel certain of her being provided for suitably, since her destiny will be in the hands of a man whose birth equals her own, who knows how to appreciate the rank in which she is placed, and who will evince his claims to merit and esteem."

"Have I a right, then," said Ferdinand, "to flatter myself with the hope that Emily will permit me to surrender her the property to which she is actually entitled?"

"Consult Emily on the subject," said the baron. And here finished the conference.

Ferdinand, delighted, ran to Emily. She answered with the same frankness he had manifested; and they were neither of them slow to confess their mutual passion.

Several days passed in this amiable delirium. The inhabitants of the château participated in the joy of the young lovers; and Ferdinand at length wrote to his mother, to announce the choice he had made.

They were occupied in preparations for removing to the castle of Wartbourg, when a letter arrived, which at once destroyed Ferdinand's happiness. His mother refused to consent to his marriage with Emily: her husband having, she said, on his death-bed, insisted on his wedding the baron of Hainthal's daughter, and that she should refuse her consent to any other marriage. He had discovered a family secret, which forced him peremptorily to press this point, on which depended his son's welfare, and the happiness of his family; she had given her promise, and was obliged to maintain it, although much afflicted at being compelled to act contrary to her son's inclinations.

In vain did Ferdinand conjure his mother to change her determination; he declared to her that he would be the last of his race, rather than renounce Emily. She was not displeased with his entreaties, but remained inflexible.

The baron plainly perceived, from Ferdinand's uneasiness and agitation, that his happiness had fled; and as he possessed his entire confidence, he soon became acquainted with the cause of his grief. He wrote in consequence to the countess Meltheim, and expressed his astonishment at the singular disposition the count had made on his death-bed: but all he could obtain from her, was a promise to come to the castle of Wartbourg, to see the female whom she destined for her son, and the one whom he had himself chosen; and probably to elucidate by her arrival so singular and complicated an affair.

Spring was beginning to enliven all nature, when Ferdinand, accompanied by Emily, the baron, and his daughter, arrived at the castle of Wartbourg. The preparations which the principal cause of their journey required, occupied some days. Ferdinand and Emily consoled themselves in the hope that the countess of Meltheim's presence would remove every obstacle which opposed their love, and that at sight of the two lovers she would overcome her scruples.

A few days afterwards she arrived, embraced Emily in the most affectionate manner, and called her, her dear daughter, at the same time expressing her great regret that she could not really consider her such, being obliged to fulfil a promise made to her dying husband.

The baron at length persuaded her to reveal the motive for this singular determination: and after deliberating a short time, she thus expressed herself:

"The secret you are anxious I should reveal to you, concerns your family, Monsieur le Baron: consequently, if you release me from the necessity of longer silence, I am very willing to abandon my scruples. A fatal picture has, you know, robbed me of my daughter; and my husband, after this melancholy accident, determined on entirely removing this unfortunate portrait: he accordingly gave orders for it to be put in a heap of old furniture, where no one would think of looking for it; and in order to discover the best place to conceal it, he was present when it was taken there. In the removal, he perceived a piece of parchment behind the canvass which the fall had a little damaged: having removed it, he discovered it to be an old document, of a singular nature. The original of this portrait, (said the deed,) was called Bertha de Hainthal; she fixes her looks on her female descendants, in order that if any one of them should receive its death by this portrait, it may prove an expiatory sacrifice which will reconcile her to God. She will then see the families of Hainthal and Meltheim united by the bonds of love; and finding herself released, she will have cause to rejoice in the birth of her after-born descendants.

"This then is the motive which made my husband anxious to fulfil, by the projected marriage, the vows of Bertha; for the death of his daughter, caused by Bertha, had rendered her very name formidable to him. You see, therefore, I have the same reasons for adhering to the promise made my dying husband."

"Did not the count," demanded the baron, "allege any more positive reason for this command?"

"Nothing more, most assuredly," replied the countess.

"Well then," answered the baron, "in case the writing of which you speak should admit of an explanation wholly differing from, but equally clear with, the one attached thereto by the deceased, would you sooner follow the sense than the letter of the writing?"

"There is no doubt on that subject," answered the countess; "for no one is more anxious than myself to see that unfortunate promise set aside."

"Know then," said the baron, "that the corpse of that Bertha, who occasioned the death of your daughter, reposes here at Wartbourg; and that, on this subject, as well as all the other mysteries of the castle, we shall have our doubts satisfied."

The baron would not at this time explain himself further; but said to the countess, that the documents contained in the archives of the castle would afford the necessary information; and recommended that Ferdinand should, with all possible dispatch, hasten everything relative to the succession. Conformable to the baron's wish, it was requisite that, previous to any other research, the secret deeds contained in the archives should be opened. The law commissioners, and the next of kin who were present, who, most likely, promised themselves an ample compensation for their curiosity in the contents of the other parts of the records, were anxious to raise objections; but the baron represented to them, that the secrets of the family appertained to the unknown heir alone, and that consequently no one had a right to become acquainted with them, unless permitted by him.

These reasons produced the proper effect. They followed the baron into the immense vault in which were deposited the family records. They therein discovered an iron chest, which had not been opened for nearly a thousand years. A massive chain, which several times wound round it, was strongly fixed to the floor and to the wall; but the emperor's grand seal was a greater security for this sacred deposit, than all the chains and bolts which guarded it. It was instantly recognised and removed: the strong bolts yielded; and from the chest was taken the old parchment which had resisted the effects of time. This piece contained, as the baron expected, the disposition which confirmed the right of inheritance to the house of Meltheim, in case of the extinction of the house of Wartbourg: and Ferdinand, according to the baron's advice, having in readiness the deeds justifying and acknowledging him as the lawful heir to the house of Meltheim, the next of kin with regret permitted what they could not oppose; and he took possession of the inheritance. The baron having made him a signal, he immediately sealed the chest with his seal. He afterwards entertained the strangers in a splendid manner; and at night found himself in possession of his castle, with only his mother, Emily, the baron, and his daughter.

"It will be but just," said the baron, "to devote this night, which introduces a new name into this castle, to the memory of those who have hitherto possessed it. And we shall acquit ourselves most suitably in this duty, by reading in the council-chamber the documents which, without doubt, are destined to explain, as supplementary deeds, the will of Ditmar."

This arrangement was instantly adopted. The hearts of Emily and Ferdinand were divided between hope and fear; for they impatiently, yet doubtingly, awaited the denouement of Bertha's history, which, after so many successive generations, had in so incomprehensible a manner interfered with their attachment.

The chamber was lighted: Ferdinand opened the iron case; and the baron examined the old parchments.

"This," cried he, after having searched some short time, "will inform us." So saying, he drew from the chest some sheets of parchment. On the one which enveloped the rest was the portrait of a knight of an agreeable figure, and habited in the costume of the tenth century: and the inscription at the bottom called him Ditmar; but they could scarcely discover the slightest resemblance in it to the frightful portrait in the state-chamber.

The baron offered to translate, in reading to them the document written in Latin, provided they would make allowances for the errors which were likely to arise from so hasty a translation. The curiosity of his auditors was so greatly excited, that they readily consented; and he then read as follows:

"I the undersigned Tutilon, monk of St. Gall, have, with the lord Ditmar's consent, written the following narrative: I have omitted nothing, nor written aught of my own accord.

"Being sent for to Metz, to carve in stone the image of the Virgin Mary; and that mother of our blessed Saviour having opened my eyes and directed my hands, so that I could contemplate her celestial countenance, and represent it on stone to be worshipped by true believers, the lord Ditmar discovered me, and engaged me to follow him to his castle, in order that I might execute his portrait for his descendants. I began painting it in the state-chamber of his castle; and on returning the following day to resume my task, I found that a strange hand had been at work, and had given to the portrait quite a different countenance, which was horrible to look at, for it resembled one who had risen from the dead. I trembled with terror: however, I effaced these hideous features, and I painted anew the count Ditmar's figure, according to my recollection; but the following day I again discovered the nocturnal labour of the stranger hand. I was seized with still greater fear, but resolved to watch during the night; and I recommenced painting the knight's figure, such as it really was. At midnight I took a torch, and advancing softly into the chamber to examine the portrait, I perceived a spectre resembling the skeleton of a child; it held a pencil, and was endeavouring to give Ditmar's image the hideous features of death.

"On my entering, the spectre slowly turned its head towards me, that I might see its frightful visage. My terror became extreme: I advanced no further, but retired to my room, where I remained in prayer till morning; for I was unwilling to interrupt the work executed in the dead of night. In the morning, discovering the same strange features in Ditmar's portrait as that of the two preceding mornings, I did not again risk effacing the work of the nightly painter; but went in search of the knight, and related to him what I had seen. I shewed him the picture. He trembled with horror, and confessed his crimes to me, for which he required absolution. Having for three successive days invoked all the saints to my assistance, I imposed on him as a penance for the murder of his enemy, which he had avowed to me, to submit to the most rigid mortifications in a dungeon during the rest of his life. But I told him, that as he had murdered an innocent child, his spirit would never be at rest till it had witnessed the extermination of his race; for the Almighty would punish the death of that child by the death of the children of Ditmar, who, with the exception of one in each generation, would all be carried off in early life; and as for him, his spirit would wander during the night, resembling the portrait painted by the hand of the skeleton child; and that he would condemn to death, by a kiss, the children who were the sacrifices to his crimes, in the same manner as he had given one to his enemy's child before he killed it: and that, in fine, his race should not become extinct, so long as stone remained on stone in the tower where he had permitted his enemy to die of hunger. I then gave him absolution. He immediately made over his seigniory to his son; and married the daughter of his enemy, who had been brought up by him, to the brave knight Sir Adalbert. He bequeathed all his property, in case of his race becoming extinct, to this knight's descendants, and caused this will to be ratified by the emperor Otho. After having done so, he retired to a cave near the tower, where his corpse is interred; for he died like a pious recluse, and expiated his crimes by extreme penance. As soon as he was laid in his coffin, he resembled the portrait in the state-chamber; but during his life he was like the portrait depicted on this parchment, which I was able to paint without interruption, after having given him absolution: and by his command I have written and signed this document since his death; and I deposit it, with the emperor's letters patent, in an iron chest, which I have caused to be sealed. I pray God speedily to deliver his soul, and to cause his body to rise from the dead to everlasting felicity!"

"He is delivered," cried Emily, greatly affected; "and his image will no longer spread terror around. But I confess that the sight of that figure, and even that of the frightful portrait itself, would never have led me to dream of such horrible crimes as the monk Tutilon relates. Certain I am, his enemy must have mortally wounded his happiness, or he undoubtedly would have been incapable of committing such frightful crimes."

"Possibly," said the baron, continuing his researches, "we shall discover some explanation on that point."

"We must also find some respecting Bertha," replied Ferdinand in a low tone, and casting a timid look on Emily and his mother.

"This night," answered the baron, "is consecrated to the memory of the dead; let us therefore forget our own concerns, since those of the past call our attention."

"Assuredly," exclaimed Emily, "the unfortunate person who secured these sheets in the chest, ardently looked forward to the hope of their coming to light; let us therefore delay it no longer."

The baron, after having examined several, read aloud these words:

"The confession of Ditmar." And he continued thus: "Peace and health. When this sheet is drawn from the obscurity in which it is now buried, my soul will, I hope firmly in God and the saints, be at eternal rest and peace. But for your good I have ordered to be committed to paper the cause of my chastisement, in order that you may learn that vengeance belongs to God alone, and not to men; for the most just amongst them knows not how to judge: and again, that you may not in your heart condemn me, but rather that you may pity me; for my misery has nearly equalled my crimes; and my spirit would never have dreamt of evil, if man had not rent my heart."

"How justly," exclaimed Ferdinand, "has Emily's good sense divined thus much!"

The baron continued: "My name is Ditmar; they surnamed me The Rich, though I was then only a poor knight, and my only possession was a very small castle. When the emperor Otho departed for Italy, whither he was called by the beautiful Adelaide to receive her hand, I followed him; and I gained the affection of the most charming woman in Pavia, whom I conducted as my intended spouse to the castle of my forefathers. Already the day appointed for the celebration of my nuptials was at hand: the emperor sent for me. His favourite, the count Bruno de Hainthal had seen Bertha –"

"Bertha!" exclaimed everyone present. But the baron, without permitting them to interrupt him, continued his translation.

"One day, when the emperor had promised to grant him any recompence that he thought his services merited, he asked of him my intended bride. Otho was mute with astonishment – but his imperial word was given. I presented myself before the emperor, who offered me riches, lands, honours, if I would but consent to yield Bertha to the count: but she was dearer to me than every worldly good. The emperor yielded to a torrent of anger: he carried off my intended bride by force, ordered my castle to be pulled down, and caused me to be thrown into prison.

"I cursed his power and my destiny. The amiable figure of Bertha, however, appeared to me in a dream; and I consoled myself during the day by the sweet illusions of the night. At length my keeper said to me: 'I pity you, Ditmar; you suffer in a prison for your fidelity, while Bertha abandons you. Tomorrow she weds the count: accede then to the emperor's wish, ere it be too late; and ask of him what you think fit, as a recompence for the loss of the faithless fair.' These words froze my heart. The following night, instead of the gracious image of Bertha, the frightful spirit of vengeance presented itself to me. The following morning I said to my keeper: Go and tell the emperor, I yield Bertha to his Bruno; but as a recompence, I demand this tower, and as much land as will be requisite to build me a new castle.' The emperor was satisfied; for he frequently repented his violent passions, but he could not alter what he had already decided. He therefore gave me the tower in which I had been confined, and all the lands around it for the space of four leagues. He also gave me more gold and silver than was sufficient to build a castle much more magnificent than the one he had caused to be pulled down. I took unto myself a wife, in order to perpetuate my race; but Bertha still reigned sole mistress of my heart. I also built myself a castle, from which I made a communication, by subterranean and secret passages, with my former prison the tower, and with the castle of Bruno, the residence of my mortal enemy. As soon as the edifice was completed, I entered the fortress by the secret passage, and appeared as the spirit of one of his ancestors before the bed of his son, the heir with which Bertha had presented him. The women who lay beside him were seized with fear: I leaned over the child, who was the precise image of its mother, and kissed its forehead; but – it was the kiss of death; it carried with it a secret poison.

"Bruno and Bertha acknowledged the vengeance of Heaven: they received it as a punishment for the wrongs they had occasioned me; and they devoted their first child to the service of God. As it was a girl, I spared it: but Bertha had no more children; and Bruno, irritated to find his race so nearly annihilated, repudiated his wife, as if he repented the injustice of which he had been guilty in taking her, and married another. The unfortunate Bertha took refuge in a monastery, and consecrated herself to Heaven: but her reason fled; and one night she quitted her retreat, came to the tower in which I had been confined in consequence of her perfidy, there bewailed her crime, and there grief terminated her existence; which circumstance gave rise to that tower being called the Nun's Rock. I heard, during the night, her sobs; and on going to the tower found Bertha extended motionless; the dews of night had seized her: – she was dead. I then resolved to avenge her loss. I placed her corpse in a deep vault beneath the tower; and having by means of my subterranean passage discovered all the count's movements, I attacked him when unguarded; and dragging him to the vault which contained his wife's corpse, I there abandoned him. The emperor, irritated against him for having divorced Bertha, gave me all his possessions, as a remuneration for the injustice I had heretofore experienced.

"I caused all the subterranean passages to be closed. I took under my care his daughter Hildegarde, and brought her up as my child: she loved the count Adalbert de Meltheim. But one night her mother's ghost appeared to her, and reminded her that she was consecrated to the Almighty: this vision, however, could not deter her from marrying Adalbert. The night of her marriage the phantom appeared again before her bed, and thus addressed her:

"'Since you have infringed the vow I made, my spirit can never be at rest, till one of your female descendants receives its death from me.'

"This discourse occasioned me to send for the venerable Tutilon, monk of St. Gall, who was very celebrated, in order that he might paint a portrait of Bertha, as she had painted herself in the monastery during her insanity; and I gave it to her daughter.

"Tutilon concealed behind that portrait a writing on parchment, the contents of which were as follows:

"'I am Bertha; and I look at my daughters, to see whether one of them will not die for me, in expiation of my crimes, and thus reconcile me to God. Then shall I see the two families of Meltheim and Hainthal reunited by love, and in the birth of their descendants I shall enjoy happiness.'"

"This then," exclaimed Ferdinand, "is the fatal writing that is to separate me from Emily; but which, in fact, only unites me to her more firmly! and Bertha, delivered from her penance, blesses the alliance; for by my marriage with Emily, the descendants of Bertha and Ditmar will be reunited."

"Do you think," demanded the baron of the countess, "that this explanation can admit of the slightest doubt?"

The only answer the countess made, was by embracing Emily, and placing her hand in that of her son.

The joy was universal. Clotilde in particular had an air of extreme delight; and her father several times, in a jocular manner, scolded her for expressing her joy so vehemently. The following morning they removed the seals from the state-chamber, in order to contemplate the horrible portrait with somewhat less of sadness than heretofore: but they found that it had faded in a singular manner, and the colours, which formerly appeared so harsh, had blended and become softened.

Shortly after arrived the young man who was anxious to enter into an argument with Ferdinand on the explication of the mysteries relative to the portraits. Clotilde did not conceal that he was far from indifferent to her; and they discovered the joy she had evinced, in discovering the favourable turn Emily's attachment had taken, was not altogether disinterested, but occasioned by the prospect it afforded of happiness to herself. Her father, in fact, would never have approved her choice, had not the countess Meltheim removed all pretensions to Clotilde.

"But," asked Ferdinand of Clotilde's intended, "do you not forgive our having searched into certain mysteries which concerned us?"

"Completely," he answered; "but not less disinterestedly than formerly, when I maintained a contrary opinion. I ought now to confess to you, that I was present at the fatal accident which caused your sister's death, and that I then discovered the writing concealed behind the portrait. I naturally explained it as your father did afterwards; but

I held my peace; for the consequences have brought to light what the discovery of that writing had caused me to apprehend for my love."

"Unsatisfactory explanations are bad," replied Ferdinand, laughing.

The happy issue of these discoveries spread universal joy amongst the inhabitants of the castle, which was in some degree heightened by the beauty of the season. The lovers were anxious to celebrate their marriage ere the fall of the leaf. And when next the primrose's return announced the approach of spring, Emily gave birth to a charming boy.

Ferdinand's mother, Clotilde and her husband, and all the friends of the family, among whom were the pastor who was so fond of music, and his pretty little wife, assembled at the fête given in honour of the christening. When the priest who was performing the ceremony asked what name he was to give the child, that of Ditmar was uttered by every mouth, as if they had previously agreed on it. The christening over, Ferdinand, elate with joy, accompanied by his relations and guests, carried his son to the state-chamber, before his forefather's portrait; but it was no longer perceptible; the colours, figure, – all had disappeared; not the slightest trace remained.

If you enjoyed this, you might also like...
Frankenstein, see page 11
'The Mourner', see page 264

The Fated Hour

Friedrich Laun

Chapter I
Mirdath the Beautiful

– Wan the maiden was,
Of saintly paleness, and there seem'd to dwell
In the strong beauties of her countenance
Something that was not earthly.
Robert Southey, 'Joan of Arc'

The clock has toll'd; and, hark! The bell
Of death beats slow.
William Mason, Elegies

A HEAVY RAIN prevented the three friends from taking the morning's walk they had concerted: notwithstanding which, Amelia and Maria failed not to be at Florentina's house at the appointed hour. The latter had for some time past been silent, pensive, and absorbed in thought; and the anxiety of her friends made them very uneasy at the visible impression left on her mind by the violent tempest of the preceding night.

Florentina met her friends greatly agitated, and embraced them with more than usual tenderness.

"Fine weather for a walk!" cried Amelia: "How have you passed this dreadful night?"

"Not very well, you may easily imagine. My residence is in too lonely a situation."

"Fortunately," replied Maria, laughing, "it will not long be yours."

"That's true," answered Florentina, sighing deeply. "The count returns from his travels tomorrow, in the hope of soon conducting me to the altar."

"Merely in the hope?" replied Maria: "the mysterious manner in which you uttered these words, leads me to apprehend you mean to frustrate those hopes."

"I? – But how frequently in this life does hope prove only an untimely flower?"

"My dear Florentina," said Maria, embracing her, "for some time past my sister and I have vainly attempted to account for your lost gaiety; and have been tormented with the idea, that possibly family reasons have induced you, contrary to your wishes, to consent to this marriage which is about to take place."

"Family reasons! Am I not then the last of our house; the only remaining one, whom the tombs of my ancestors have not as yet enclosed? And have I not for my Ernest that ardent affection which is natural to my time of life? Or do you think me capable of such duplicity, when I have so recently depicted to you, in the most glowing colours, the man of my heart's choice?"

"What then am I to believe?" inquired Maria. "Is it not a strange contradiction, that a young girl, handsome and witty, rich and of high rank, and who, independently of these advantages, will not by her marriage be estranged from her family, should approach the altar with trembling?"

Florentina, holding out her hand to the two sisters, said to them:

"How kind you are! I ought really to feel quite ashamed in not yet having placed entire confidence in your friendship, even on a subject which is to me, at this moment, incomprehensible. At this moment I am not equal to the task; but in the course of the day I hope to be sufficiently recovered. In the mean while let us talk on less interesting subjects."

The violent agitation of Florentina's mind was so evident at this moment, that the two sisters willingly assented to her wishes. Thinking that the present occasion required trifling subjects of conversation, they endeavoured to joke with her on the terrors of the preceding night. However, Maria finished by saying, with rather a serious air:

"I must confess, that more than once I have been tempted to think something extraordinary occurred. At first it appeared as if someone opened and shut the window of the room in which we slept, and then as if they approached my bed. I distinctly heard footsteps: an icy trembling seized me, and I covered my face over with the clothes."

"Alas!" exclaimed Amelia, "I cannot tell you how frequently I have heard similar noises. But as yet nothing have I seen."

"Most fervently do I hope," replied Florentina in an awful tone of voice, "that neither of you will ever, in this life, be subject to a proof of this nature!"

The deep sigh which accompanied these words, and the uneasy look she cast on the two sisters, produced evident emotions in them both.

"Possibly you have experienced such proof?" replied Amelia.

"Not precisely so: but – suspend your curiosity. This evening – if I am still alive – I mean to say – that this evening I shall be better able to communicate all to you."

Maria made a sign to Amelia, who instantly understood her sister; and thinking that Florentina wished to be alone, though evidently disturbed in her mind, they availed themselves of the first opportunity which her silence afforded. Her prayer-book was lying open on the table, which, now perceiving for the first time, confirmed Maria in the idea she had conceived. In looking for her shawl she removed a handkerchief which covered this book, and saw that the part which had most probably occupied Florentina before their arrival was the Canticle on Death. The three friends separated, overcome and almost weeping, as if they were never to meet again.

Amelia and Maria awaited with the greatest impatience the hour of returning to Florentina. They embraced her with redoubled satisfaction, for she seemed to them more gay than usual.

"My dear girls," said she to them, "pardon, I pray you, my abstraction of this morning. Depressed by having passed so bad a night, I thought myself on the brink of the grave; and fancied it needful to make up my accounts in this world, and prepare for the next. I have made my will, and have placed it in the magistrate's hands: however, since I have taken a little repose this afternoon, I find myself so strong, and in such good spirits, that I feel as if I had escaped the danger which threatened me."

"But, my dear," replied Maria, in a mild yet affectionate tone of reproach, "how could one sleepless night fill your mind with such gloomy thoughts?"

"I agree with you on the folly of permitting it so to do; and had I encouraged sinister thoughts, that dreadful night would not have been the sole cause, for it found me in such a frame of mind that its influence was not at all necessary to add to my horrors. But no more of useless mystery. I will fulfil my promise, and clear up your doubts on many parts of my manner and conduct, which at present must appear to you inexplicable. Prepare yourselves for the strangest and most surprising events. But the damp and cold evening air has penetrated this room, it will therefore be better to have a fire lighted, that the chill which my recital may produce be not increased by any exterior cause."

While they were lighting the fire, Maria and her sister expressed great joy at seeing such a happy change in Florentina's manner; and the latter could scarcely describe the satisfaction she felt, at having resolved to develop to them the secret which she had so long concealed.

The three friends being alone, Florentina began as follows:

"You were acquainted with my sister Seraphina, whom I had the misfortune to lose; but I alone can boast of possessing her confidence; which is the cause of my mentioning many things relative to her, before I begin the history I have promised, in which she is the principal personage.

"From her infancy, Seraphina was remarkable for several singularities. She was a year younger than myself; but frequently, while seated by her side I was amusing myself with the playthings common to our age, she would fix her eyes, by the half hour together, as if absorbed in thought: she seldom took any part in our infantine amusements. This disposition greatly chagrined our parents; for they attributed Seraphina's indifference to stupidity; and they were apprehensive this defect would necessarily prove an obstacle in the education requisite for the distinguished rank we held in society, my father being, next the prince, the first person in the country. They had already thought of procuring for her a canonry from some noble chapel, when things took an entirely different turn.

"Her preceptor, an aged man, to whose care they had confided her at a very early age, assured them, that in his life he had never met with so astonishing an intellect as Seraphina's. My father doubted the assertion: but an examination, which he caused to be made in his presence, convinced him that it was founded in truth.

"Nothing was then neglected to give Seraphina every possible accomplishment: masters of different languages, of music, and of dancing, every day filled the house.

"But in a short time my father perceived that he was again mistaken: for Seraphina made so little progress in the study of the different languages, that the masters shrugged their shoulders; and the dancing-master pretended, that though her feet were extremely pretty, he could do nothing with them, as her head seldom took the trouble to guide them.

"By way of retaliation, she made such wonderful progress in music that she soon excelled her masters. She sang in a manner superior to that of the best opera-singers.

"My father acknowledged that his plans for the education of this extraordinary child were now as much too enlarged, as they were before too circumscribed; and that it would not do to keep too tight a hand over her, but let her follow the impulse of her own wishes.

"This new arrangement afforded Seraphina the opportunity of more particularly studying the science of astronomy; which was one they had never thought of as needful for her. You can, my friends, form but a very indifferent idea of the avidity with which (if so I may express myself) she devoured those books which treated on celestial bodies; or what rapture the globes and telescopes occasioned her, when her father presented them to her on her thirteenth birthday.

"But the progress made in this science in our days did not long satisfy Seraphina's curiosity. To my father's great grief, she was wrapped up in reveries of astrology; and more than once she was found in the morning occupied in studying books which treated on the influence of the stars, and which she had begun to peruse the preceding evening.

"My mother, being at the point of death, was anxious, I believe, to remonstrate with Seraphina on this whim; but her death was too sudden. My father thought that at this tender age Seraphina's whimsical fancy would wear off: however, time passed on, and he found that she still remained constant to a study she had cherished from her infancy.

"You cannot forget the general sensation her beauty produced at court: how much the fashionable versifiers of the day sang her graceful figure and beautiful flaxen locks; and how often they failed, when they attempted to describe the particular and indefinable character which distinguished her fine blue eyes. I must say, I have often embraced my sister, whom I loved with the greatest affection, merely to have the pleasure of getting nearer, if possible, to her soft angelic eyes, from which Seraphina's pale countenance borrowed almost all its sublimity.

"She received many extremely advantageous proposals of marriage, but declined them all. You know her predilection in favour of solitude, and that she never went out but to enjoy my society. She took no pleasure in dress; nay, she even avoided all occasions which required more than ordinary expense. Those who were not acquainted with the singularity of her character might have accused her of affectation.

"But a very extraordinary particularity, which I by chance discovered in her just as she attained her fifteenth year, created an impression of fear on my mind which will never be effaced.

"On my return from making a visit, I found Seraphina in my father's cabinet, near the window, with her eyes fixed and immoveable. Accustomed from her earliest infancy to see her in this situation, without being perceived by her I pressed her to my bosom, without producing on her the least sensation of my presence. At this moment I looked towards the garden, and I there saw my father walking with this same Seraphina whom I held in my arms.

"In the name of God, my sister –!" exclaimed I, equally cold with the statue before me; who now began to recover.

"At the same time my eye involuntarily returned towards the garden, where I had seen her; and there perceived my father alone, looking with uneasiness, as it appeared to me, for her, who, but an instant before, was with him. I endeavoured to conceal this event from my sister; but in the most affectionate tone she loaded me with questions to learn the cause of my agitation.

"I eluded them as well as I could; and asked her how long she had been in the closet. She answered me, smiling, that I ought to know best; as she came in after me; and that if she was not mistaken, she had before that been walking in the garden with my father.

"This ignorance of the situation in which she was but an instant before, did not astonish me on my sister's account, as she had often shewn proofs of this absence of mind. At that instant my father came in, exclaiming: 'Tell me, my dear Seraphina, how you so suddenly escaped from my sight, and came here? We were, as you know, conversing; and scarcely had you finished speaking, when, looking round, I found myself alone. I naturally thought that you had concealed yourself in the adjacent thicket; but in vain I looked there for you; and on coming into this room, here I find you.'

"'It is really strange,' replied Seraphina; 'I know not myself how it has happened.'

"From that moment I felt convinced of what I had heard from several persons, but what my father always contradicted; which was, that while Seraphina was in the house, she had been seen elsewhere. I secretly reflected also on what my sister had repeatedly told me, that when a child (she was ignorant whether sleeping or awake), she had been transported to heaven, where she had played with angels; to which incident she attributed her disinclination to all infantine games.

"My father strenuously combated this idea, as well as the event to which I had been witness, of her sudden disappearance from the garden.

"'Do not torment me any longer,' said he, 'with these phaenomena, which appear complaisantly renewed every day, in order to gratify your eager imagination. It is true, that your sister's person and habits present many singularities; but all your idle talk will never persuade me that she holds any immediate intercourse with the world of spirits.'

"My father did not then know, that where there is any doubt of the future, the weak mind of man ought not to allow him to profane the word never, by uttering it.

"About a year and half afterwards, an event occurred which had power to shake even my father's determined manner of thinking to its very foundation. It was on a Sunday, that Seraphina and I wished at last to pay a visit which we had from time to time deferred: for notwithstanding my sister was very fond of being with me, she avoided even my society whenever she could not enjoy it but in the midst of a large assembly, where constraint destroyed all pleasure.

"To adorn herself for a party, was to her an anticipated torment; for she said, she only submitted to this trouble to please those whose frivolous and dissipated characters greatly offended her. On similar occasions she sometimes met with persons to whom she could not speak without shuddering, and whose presence made her ill for several days.

"The hour of assembling approached; she was anxious that I should go without her: my father doubting her, came into our room, and insisted on her changing her determination.

"'I cannot permit you to infringe every duty.'

"He accordingly desired her to dress as quickly as possible, and accompany me.

"The waiting-maid was just gone out on an errand with which I had commissioned her. My sister took a light to fetch her clothes from a wardrobe in the upper story. She remained much longer absent than was requisite. At length she returned without a light: I screamed with fright. My father asked her in an agitated manner, what had happened to her. In fact, she had scarcely been absent a quarter of an hour, and yet during that time her face had undergone a complete alteration; her habitual paleness had given place to a death-like hue; her ruby lips were turned blue.

"My arms involuntarily opened to embrace this sister whom I adored. I almost doubted my sight, for I could get no answer from her; but for a long while she leaned against my bosom, mute and inanimate. The look, replete with infinite softness, which she gave my father and me, alone informed us, that during her continuance in this incomprehensible trance, she still belonged to the material world.

"'I was seized with a sudden indisposition,' she at length said in a low voice; 'but I now find myself better.'

"She asked my father whether he still wished her to go into society. He thought, that after an occurrence of this nature her going out might be dangerous: but he would not dispense with my making the visit, although I endeavoured to persuade him that my attention might be needful to Seraphina. I left her with an aching heart.

"I had ordered the carriage to be sent for me at a very early hour: but the extreme anxiety I felt would not allow me to wait its arrival, and I returned home on foot. The servant could scarcely keep pace with me, such was my haste to return to Seraphina.

* * *

"On my arrival in her room, my impatience was far from being relieved.

"'Where is she?' I quickly asked.

"'Who mademoiselle?'

"'Why, Seraphina.'

"'Mademoiselle, Seraphina is in your father's closet.'

"'Alone?'

"'No with his excellency.'

"I ran to the boudoir: the door, which was previously shut, at that instant opened, and my father with Seraphina came out: the latter was in tears. I remarked that my father had an air of chagrin and doubt which not even the storms of public life had ever produced in his countenance.

"He made us a sign full of gentleness, and Seraphina followed me into another room: but she first assured my father she would remember the promise he had exacted, and of which I was still ignorant.

"Seraphina appeared to me so tormented by the internal conflicts she endured, that I several times endeavoured, but in vain, to draw from her the mysterious event which had so recently thrown her into so alarming a situation. At last I overcame her scruples, and she answered me as follows:

"'Your curiosity shall be satisfied, in part. I will develop some of the mystery to you; but only on one irrevocable condition.'

"I entreated her instantly to name the condition: and she thus continued:

"'Swear to me, that you will rest satisfied with what I shall disclose to you, and that you will never urge nor use that power which you possess over my heart, to obtain a knowledge of what I am obliged to conceal from you.'

"I swore it to her.

"'Now, my dear Florentina, forgive me, if, for the first time in my life, I have a secret from you; and also for not being satisfied with your mere word for the promise I have exacted from you. My father, to whom I have confided everything, has imposed these two obligations on me, and his last words were to that effect.'

"I begged her to come to the point.

"'Words are inadequate to describe,' said she, 'the weight I felt my soul oppressed with when I went to get my clothes. I had no sooner closed the door of the room in which you and my father were, than I fancied I was about to be separated from life and all that constituted my happiness; and that I had many dreadful nights to linger through, ere I could arrive at a better and more peaceful abode. The air which I breathed on the staircase was not such as usually circulates around us; it oppressed my breathing, and caused large drops of icy perspiration to fall from my forehead. Certain it is, I was not alone on the staircase; but for a long while I dared not look around me.

"'You know, my dear Florentina, with what earnestness I wished and prayed, but in vain, that my mother would appear to me after her death, if only for once. I fancied that on the stairs I heard my mother's spirit behind me. I was apprehensive it was come to punish me for the vows I had already made.'

"'A strange thought, certainly!'

"'But how could I imagine that a mother, who was goodness itself, could be offended by the natural wishes of a tenderly beloved child, or have imputed them to indiscreet curiosity? It was no less foolish to think that she, who had been so long since enclosed in the tomb, should occupy herself in inflicting chastisement on me, for faults which were nearly obliterated from my recollection. I was so immediately convinced of the weakness of giving way to such ideas, that I summoned courage and turned my head.

"'Although my affrighted survey could discover nothing, I again heard the footsteps following me, but more distinctly than before. At the door of the room I was about to enter, I felt my gown held. Overpowered by terror, I was unable to proceed, and fell on the threshold of the door.

"'I lost no time, however, in reproaching myself for suffering terror so to overcome me; and recollected that there was nothing supernatural in this accident, for my gown had caught on the handle of an old piece of furniture which had been placed in the passage, to be taken out of the house the following day.

"'This discovery inspired me with fresh courage. I approached the wardrobe: but judge my consternation, when, preparing to open it, the two doors unclosed of themselves, without making the slightest noise; the lamp which I held in my hand was extinguished, and – as if I was standing before a looking-glass, – my exact image came out of the wardrobe: the light which it spread, illumined great part of the room.

"'I then heard these words: Why tremble you at the sight of your own spirit, which appears to give you warning of your approaching dissolution, and to reveal to you the fate of your house?'

"'The phantom then informed me of several future events. But when, after having deeply meditated on its prophetic words, I asked a question relative to you, the room became as dark as before, and the spirit had vanished. This, my dear, is all I am permitted to reveal.'

"'Your approaching death!' cried I: That thought had in an instant effaced all other.

"Smiling, she made me a sign in the affirmative; and gave me to understand, at the same time, that I ought to press her no further on this subject. 'My father,' added she, 'has promised to make you acquainted, in proper time, with all it concerns you to know.'

"'At a proper time!' repeated I, in a plaintive voice; for it appeared to me, that since I had learned so much, it was high time that I should be made acquainted with the whole.

"The same evening I mentioned my wishes to my father: but he was inexorable. He fancied that possibly what had happened to Seraphina might have arisen from her disordered and overheated imagination. However, three days afterwards, my sister finding herself so ill as to be obliged to keep her bed, my father's doubts began to be shaken; and although the precise day of Seraphina's death had not been named to me, I could not avoid observing by her paleness, and the more than usually affectionate manner of embracing my father and me, that the time of our eternal separation was not far off.

"'Will the clock soon strike nine?' asked Seraphina, while we were sitting near her bed in the evening.

"'Yes, soon,' replied my father.

"'Well then! Think of me, dear objects of my affection: we shall meet again.' She pressed our hands; and the clock no sooner struck, than she fell back in her bed, never to rise more.

"My father has since related to me every particular as it happened; for at that time I was so much overcome that my senses had forsaken me.

"Seraphina's eyes were scarcely closed, when I returned to a life which then appeared to me insupportable. I was apprehensive that the state of stupefaction into which I was thrown by the dread of the loss that threatened me, had appeared to my sister a want of attachment. And from that time I have never thought of the melancholy scene without experiencing a violent shuddering.

"'You must be aware,' said my father to me (it was at the precise hour, and before the same chimney we are at this moment placed) – you must be aware, that the pretended vision should still be kept quite secret.' I was of his opinion; but could not help adding, 'What! still, my father, though one part of the prediction has in so afflicting a manner been verified, you continue to call it a pretended vision?'

"'Yes, my child; you know not what a dangerous enemy to man is his own imagination. Seraphina will not be the last of its victims.'

"We were seated, as I before said, just as we now are; and I was about to name a motive which I had before omitted, when I perceived that his eyes were fixed in a disturbed manner on the door. I was ignorant of the cause, and could discover nothing extraordinary there: notwithstanding, however, an instant afterwards it opened of its own accord."

Here Florentina stopped, as if overcome anew by the remembrance of her terror. At the same moment Amelia rose from her seat uttering a loud scream.

Her sister and her friend inquired what ailed her. For a long while she made them no reply, and would not resume her seat on the chair, the back of which was towards the door. At length, however, she confessed (casting an inquiring and anxious look around her) that a hand, cold as ice, had touched her neck.

"This is truly the effect of imagination," said Maria, reseating herself. "It was my hand: for some time my arm has been resting on your chair; and when mention was made of the door opening of its own accord, I felt a wish to rest on some living object –"

"But à-propos – And the door –?"

"Strange incident! I trembled with fear; and clinging to my father, asked him if he did not see a sort of splendid light, a something brilliant, penetrate the apartment.

"'Tis well!' answered he, in a low and tremulous voice, 'we have lost a being whom we cherished; and consequently, in some degree, our minds are disposed to exalted ideas, and our imaginations may very easily be duped by the same illusions: besides, there is nothing very unnatural in a door opening of its own accord.'

"'It ought to be closely shut now,' replied I; without having the courage to do it.

"'Tis very easy to shut it,' said my father. But he rose in visible apprehension, walked a few paces, and then returned, adding, 'The door may remain open; for the room is too warm.'

"It is impossible for me to describe, even by comparison, the singular light I had perceived: and I do assure you, that if, instead of the light, I had seen my sister's spirit enter, I should have opened my arms to receive it; for it was only the mysterious and vague appearance of this strange vision which caused me so much fear.

"The servants coming in at this instant with supper, put an end to the conversation.

"Time could not efface the remembrance of Seraphina; but it wore off all recollection of the last apparition. My daily intercourse with you, my friends, since the loss of Seraphina, has been for me a fortunate circumstance, and has insensibly become an indispensable habit. I no longer thought deeply of the prediction relative to our house, uttered by the phantom to my sister; and in the arms of friendship gave myself up entirely to the innocent gaiety which youth inspires. The beauties of spring contributed to the restoration of my peace of mind. One evening, just as you had left me, I continued walking in the garden, as if intoxicated with the delicious vapours emitted from the flowers, and the magnificent spectacle which the serenity of the sky presented to my view.

"Absorbed entirely by the enjoyment of my existence, I did not notice that it was later than my usual hour for returning. And I know not why, but that evening no one appeared to think of me; for my father, whose solicitude for everything concerning me was redoubled since my sister's death, and who knew I was in the garden, had not, as was his usual custom, sent me any garment to protect me from the chilling night air.

"While thus reflecting, I was seized with a violent feverish shivering, which I could by no means attribute to the night air. My eyes accidentally fixed on the flowering shrubs; and the same brilliant light which I had seen at the door of the room on the day of Seraphina's burial, appeared to me to rest on these shrubs, and dart its rays towards me. The avenue in which I was happened to have been Seraphina's favourite walk.

"The recollection of this inspired me with courage, and I approached the shrubs in the hope of meeting my sister's shade beneath the trees. But my hopes being frustrated, I returned to the house with trembling steps.

"I there found many extraordinary circumstances: nobody had thought of supper, which I imagined would have been half over. All the servants were running about in confusion, and were hastening to pack up the clothes and furniture.

"'Who is going away?' I demanded.

"'Why surely, mademoiselle!' exclaimed the steward, 'are you not acquainted with his excellency's wish to have us all?'

"'Wherefore then?'

"'This very night we are to set out for his excellency's estate.'

"'Why so?'

"They shrugged their shoulders. I ran into my father's cabinet, and there found him with his eyes fixed on the ground.

"'Seraphina's second prophecy is also accomplished,' said he to me, 'though precisely the least likely thing possible. I am in disgrace.'

"'What! Did she predict this?'

"'Yes, my child; but I concealed it from you. I resign myself to my fate, and leave others better to fill this perilous post. I am about to retire to my own estates, there to live for you, and to constitute the happiness of my vassals.'

"In spite of the violent emotions which were created by my father's misfortune, and the idea of separating from all the friends I loved, his apparent tranquillity produced a salutary effect on my mind. At midnight we set off. My father was so much master of himself under his change of condition, that by the time he arrived at his estate he was calm and serene.

"He found many things to arrange and improve; and his active turn of mind soon led him to find a train of pleasing occupations.

"In a short time, however, he was withdrawn from them, by an illness which the physicians regarded as very serious. My father conformed to all they prescribed: he abstained from all occupation, though he entertained very little hope of any good resulting from it. 'Seraphina,' he said to me (entirely changing his former opinion), 'Seraphina has twice predicted true; and will a third time.'

"This conversation made me very miserable; for I understood from it that my father believed he should shortly die.

"In fact, he visibly declined, and was at length forced to keep his bed. He one evening sent for me; and after having dismissed his attendants, he, in a feeble voice, and with frequent interruptions, thus addressed me:

"'Experience has cured me of incredulity; When the clock strikes nine according to Seraphina's prediction) I shall be no more. For this reason, my dear child, I am anxious to address a few words of advice to you. If possible, remain in your present state; never marry. Destiny appears to have conspired against our race. But no more of this. To proceed: if ever you seriously think of marrying, do not, I beseech you, neglect to read this paper; but my express desire is, that you do not open it beforehand, as in that case its contents would cause you unnecessary misery.'

"Saying these words, which with sobbing I listened to, he drew from under his pillow a sealed paper, which he gave me. The moment was not favourable for reflecting on the importance of the condition which he imposed on me. The clock, which announced the fated hour, at which my father, resting on my shoulder, drew his last gasp, deprived me of my senses.

"The day of his interment was also marked by the brilliant and extraordinary light of which I have before made mention.

"You know, that shortly after this melancholy loss I returned to the capital, in hopes of finding consolation in your beloved society. You also know, that youth seconded your efforts to render existence desirable, and that by degrees I felt a relish for life. Neither are you ignorant that the result of this intercourse was an attachment between the count Ernest and me, which rendered my father's exhortations abortive. The count loved me, and I returned his affection, and nothing more was wanting to make me think that I ought not to lead a life of celibacy: besides, my father had only made this request conditionally.

"My marriage appeared certain; and I did not hesitate to open the mysterious paper. There it is, I will read it to you:

"'Seraphina has undoubtedly already told you, that when she endeavoured to question the phantom concerning your destiny, it suddenly disappeared. The incomprehensible being seen by your sister had made mention of you, and its afflicting decree was, that three days before that fixed on for your marriage, you would die at the same ninth hour which has been so fatal to us. Your sister recovering a little from her first alarm, asked it, if you could not escape this dreadful mandate by remaining single.

"'Unhappily, Seraphina did not receive any answer: but I feel assured, that by marrying you will die. For this reason I entreat you to remain single: I add, however – if it accords with your inclinations; as I do not feel confident that even this will ensure you from the effect of the prediction.

"'In order, my dear child, to save you from all premature uneasiness, I have avoided this communication till the hour of danger: reflect, therefore, seriously on what you ought to do.

"'My spirit, when you read these lines, shall hover over and bless you, whatever way you decide.'"

Florentina folded up the paper again in silence; and, after a pause which her two friends sensibly felt, added:

"Possibly, my dear friends, this has caused the change in me which you have sometimes condemned. But tell me whether, situated as I am, you would not become troubled, and almost annihilated, by the prediction which announced your death on the very eve of your happiness?

"Here my recital ends. Tomorrow the count returns from his travels. The ardour of his affection has induced him to fix on the third day after his arrival for the celebration of our marriage."

"Then 'tis this very day!" exclaimed Amelia and Maria at the same moment; paleness and inquietude depicted on every feature, when their eyes glanced to a clock on the point of striking nine.

"Yes, this is indeed the decisive day," replied Florentina, with a grave yet serene air. "The morning has been to me a frightful one; but at this moment I find myself composed, my health is excellent, and gives me a confidence that death would with difficulty overcome me to-day. Besides, a secret but lively presentiment tells me that this very evening the wish I have so long formed will be accomplished. My beloved sister will appear to me, and will defeat the prediction concerning me.

"Dear Seraphina! you were so suddenly, so cruelly snatched from me! Where are you, that I may return, with tenfold interest, the love that I have not the power of proving towards you?"

The two sisters, transfixed with horror, had their eyes riveted on the clock, which struck the fated hour.

"You are welcome!" cried Florentina, seeing the fire in the chimney, to which they had paid no attention, suddenly extinguished. She then rose from her chair; and with open arms walked towards the door which Maria and Amelia anxiously regarded, whilst sighs escaped them both; and at which entered the figure of Seraphina, illumined by the moon's rays. Florentina folded her sister in her arms. "I am thine forever!"

These words, pronounced in a soft and melancholy tone of voice, struck Amelia and Maria's ears; but they knew not whether they were uttered by Florentina or the phantom, or whether by both the sisters together.

Almost at the same moment the servants came in, alarmed, to learn what had happened. They had heard a noise as if all the glasses and porcelain in the house were breaking. They found their mistress extended at the door, but not the slightest trace of the apparition remained.

Every means of restoring Florentina to life were used, but in vain. The physicians attributed her death to a ruptured blood-vessel. Maria and Amelia will carry the remembrance of this heart-rending scene to their graves.

If you enjoyed this, you might also like...

'A Fragment' by Lord Byron, see page 133
'A Dirge', see page 277

The Death's Head

Friedrich Laun

– What guilt
Can equal violations of the dead?
The dead how sacred! –
Edward Young, Night Thoughts

THE BEAUTY of the evening which succeeded to a very sultry day tempted colonel Kielholm to sit, surrounded by his little family, on the stone bench placed before the door of the noble mansion he had recently purchased. In order to become acquainted by degrees with his new tenants, he took pleasure in questioning on their occupations and conditions the greater part of those who passed by; he alleviated their little sufferings by his advice as well as by his bounty. His family enjoyed particular pleasure in seeing the little inn situated in front of the château, which, instead of presenting a disgusting object, as when the late owner lived there, became each succeeding day better and more orderly. Their pleasure was heightened from the circumstance that the new landlord, who had been many years a servant in the family, was loud in praises of its amended condition, and delighted himself in his new calling, with the idea of the happy prospects it held forth to himself, his wife, and children.

Formerly, though the road was greatly frequented, nobody ventured to pass a night at this inn; but now each day there was a succession of travellers; carriages were constantly seen at the door or in the court-yard; and the air of general satisfaction of each party as they proceeded on their route, incontestably proved to the landlord, (who always, hat in hand, was at the door of their carriages as they drove off,) that his efforts to give the various travellers satisfaction were completely successful.

A moving scene of this nature had just disappeared, which furnished conversation for the moment, when a whimsical equipage, which arrived from another quarter, attracted the attention of the colonel and his family. A long carriage, loaded with trunks and all sorts of luggage, and drawn by two horses, whose form and colour presented the most grotesque contrast imaginable, but which in point of meagreness were an excellent match, was succeeded by a second long and large vehicle, which they had, most probably at the expense of the adjacent forest, converted into a travelling thicket. The four steeds which drew it, did not in any respect make a better appearance than the two preceding. But the colonel and his family were still more struck by the individuals who filled this second carriage: it was a strange medley of children and grown persons, closely wedged together; but not one of their countenances bore the slightest mark of similarity of ideas. Discontent, aversion, and hatred, were legible in the face of each of these sun-burnt strangers. It was not a family, but a collection of individuals which fear or necessity kept together without uniting.

The colonel's penetrating eye led him to discover thus much, though the distance was considerable. He at length saw descend from the back part of the carriage a man of better appearance than the others. At something which he said, the whole troop turned their eyes towards the inn; they assumed an air of greater content, and appeared a little better satisfied.

The first carriage had already stopped at the door of the inn, while the second was passing the château; and the extremely humble salutations from the passengers in the latter, seemed to claim the good-will of the colonel and his family.

The second carriage had scarcely stopped, ere the troop were out of it, each appearing anxious to quit those next to whom they had been sitting with all possible speed. The spruce and agile manner in which they leapt out of the vehicle, left no doubt on the mind what their profession was, – they could be none other than rope-dancers.

The colonel remarked, that "notwithstanding the humble salutations they had made, he did not think they would exhibit in these parts; but according to appearances they would proceed to the capital with all possible dispatch; as it was hardly to be expected that they would be delayed a single day, by the very trivial profit to be expected from exhibiting in a mere country village."

"We have," said he, "seen the worst side of these gentry, without the probability of ascertaining whether they have any thing to recommend them to our notice."

His wife was on the point of expressing her dislike to all those tricks which endanger the neck, when the person whom they had observed as being superior to the rest, advanced towards them, and after making a low bow, asked permission to remain there a few days. The colonel was unable to refuse this request, as he shewed him a passport properly signed.

"I beg you," replied the colonel, "to declare most positively to your company, that every equivocal action is punished in my villages; as I am anxious to avoid all possibility of quarrels."

"Do not in the least alarm yourself, Monsieur; an extremely severe discipline is kept up in my troop, which has in some respects the effect of a secret police among ourselves: all can answer for one, and one can answer for all. Each is bound to communicate any misconduct on the part of another to me, and is always rewarded for such communication; but, on the contrary, if he omits so to do, he is severely punished."

The colonel's lady could not conceal her aversion to such a barbarous regulation; which the stranger perceiving, shrugged his shoulders.

"We must all accommodate our ideas to our condition. I have found, that if persons of this stamp are not so treated, there is no possibility of governing them. And you may the more confidently rely on my vigilance, as I had the happiness of being born in this place, and in consequence feel a double obligation: first, to the place of my birth; secondly, to his worship."

"Were you born here?" demanded the colonel's wife with surprise.

"Yes, my lady; my father was Schurster the schoolmaster, who died lately. But I call myself Calzolaro, finding that my profession succeeds better under an Italian than a German name."

This explanation redoubled the interest the colonel and his lady already felt for this man, who appeared to have received a tolerable education. They knew that the schoolmaster, whose profession had been pretty lucrative, owing to the numerous population of the village, had died worth some considerable property; but that he had named a distant female relation as his sole heiress, leaving his only son an extremely scanty pittance.

"My father," continued Calzolaro, "did not behave to me as he ought: and I cannot but think I should be justified in availing myself of some important informalities in his will, and endeavouring to set it aside, which is my present intention. But excuse, I pray you, my having tired your patience with relations to which the conversation has involuntarily given rise. I have still one more request to make: Permit me to return you my best thanks for your gracious condescension, and to shew you some of the exercises for which my troop is famous."

The colonel acceded to Calzolaro's request, and a day was fixed for the performance.

Calzolaro went that very evening to the village pastor, and communicated to him his intentions relative to his father's will. The worthy minister condemned such procedure, and endeavoured to convince Calzolaro that his father's anger was just. "Picture to yourself, young man," said he, "a father who has grown old in an honest profession, and who rejoices in having a son to whom he can leave it: added to which, this son has great talents, a good understanding, and is well-disposed. It was natural that the father should use every possible exertion to obtain for this son his own situation at his death. The son is in truth nominated to succeed him. The father, thinking himself secure from misfortune, feels quite happy. It was at this period that the son, enticed by hair-brained companions, gave up a certain and respectable, though not very brilliant provision. My dear Schurster, if, when shaking off the salutary yoke, and quitting your venerable father, to ramble over the world, you could lightly forget the misery it would occasion him, you ought at least in the present instance to behave differently; or, in plain terms, I shall say you are a good-for-nothing fellow. Did not your father, even after this, do all he could to reclaim you? but you were deaf to his remonstrances."

"Because the connexion which I had formed imposed obligations on me, from which I could not free myself, as from a garment of which one is tired. For had I then been my own master, as I now am – "

"Here let us stop, if you please: I have only one request to make of you. You ought, from respect to your father's memory, not to dispute his will."

This conversation and the venerable air of the pastor had a little shaken Calzolaro's resolutions: but the next day they returned with double force; for he heard several persons say, that shortly before his death, his father was heard to speak of him with great bitterness.

This discourse rendered him so indignant, that he would not even accede to a proposal of accommodation with the heiress, made to him by the pastor.

The colonel tried equally, but without success, to become a mediator, and at length determined to let the matter take its course.

He however assisted at the rehearsals made by the troop; and took so much pleasure in the performances prepared for the amusement of him and his family by Calzolaro, that he engaged him to act again, and invited several of his neighbours to witness them.

Calzolaro said to him on this occasion: "You have as yet seen very trifling proofs of our abilities. But do not fancy that I am an idle spectator, and merely stand by to criticize: – I, as well as each individual of my troop, have a sphere of action; and I reserve myself to give you, before we take our leave, some entertaining experiments in electricity and magnetism."

The colonel then told him, that he had recently seen in the capital a man who exhibited experiments of that sort, which had greatly delighted him; and above all, he had been singularly astonished by his powers of ventriloquism.

"It is precisely in that particular point," replied Calzolaro, that I think myself equal to any one, be they whom they may."

"I am very glad of it," answered the colonel. "But what would produce the most astonishing effect on those who have never heard a ventriloquist, would be a dialogue between the actor and a death's head – the man of whom I made mention gave us one."

"If you command it, I can undertake it."

"Delightful!" exclaimed the colonel. And Calzolaro having given some unequivocal proofs of his powers as a ventriloquist, the colonel added: "The horror of the scene must be augmented by every possible means: for instance, we must hang the room with black; the lights must be extinguished; we must fix on midnight. It will be a species of phantasmagoria dessert after supper; an unexpected spectacle. We must contrive to throw the audience into a cold perspiration, in order that when the explanation takes place they may have ample reason to laugh at their fears. For if all succeeds, no one will be exempt from a certain degree of terror."

Calzolaro entered into the project, and promised that nothing should be neglected to make it successful. They unfurnished a closet, and hung it with black.

The colonel's wife was the only one admitted to their confidence, as they could rely on her discretion. Her husband had even a little altercation on the subject with her. She wished, that for the ventriloquist scene they should use the model of a head in plaster, which her son used to draw from; whereas the colonel maintained that they must have a real skull: "Otherwise," said he, "the spectators' illusion will speedily be at an end; but after they have heard the death's head speak, we will cause it to be handed round, in order to convince them that it is in truth but a skull."

"And where can we procure this skull?" asked the colonel's wife.

"The sexton will undertake to provide us with it."

"And whose corpse will you thus disturb, for a frivolous amusement?"

"How sentimental you are!" replied Kielholm, who did not consider the subject in so serious a light: "We may easily see you are not accustomed to the field of battle, where no further respect is paid to the repose of the dead, than suits the convenience of the labourer in the fields where they are buried."

"God preserve me from such a spectacle!" exclaimed the colonel's lady in quitting them, when she perceived her husband was insensible to her representations.

According to the orders which he received, the sexton one night brought a skull in good preservation.

The morning of the day destined for the representation, Calzolaro went into the adjacent forest to rehearse the dialogue which he was to have with the death's head. He considered in what way to place the head, so as to avoid all suspicion of the answers given by it being uttered by a person concealed. In the mean while the pastor arrived at the spot from a neighbouring hamlet, where he had been called to attend a dying person: and believing that the interposition of Providence was visible in this accidental meeting, the good man stopped, in order once again to exhort Calzolaro to agree to an accommodation with the heiress.

"I yesterday," said he, "received a letter from her, in which she declares that, rather than any disrespect should be paid to your father's last will and testament, she will give up to you half the inheritance to which she is thereby entitled. Ought you not to prefer this to a process at law, the issue of which is doubtful, and which at all events will never do you credit?"

Calzolaro persisted in declaring that the law should decide between him and the testator. The poor young man was not in a state to see in a proper point of view his father's conduct towards him. The pastor, finding all his representations and entreaties fruitless, left him. Calzolaro proceeded slowly to the inn, to assign to each of his band their particular part. He told them that he should not be with them; but notwithstanding he should have an eye over their conduct. He was not willing to appear as the manager of these mountebanks, to the party assembled at the colonel's, thinking that if he appeared for the first time in the midnight scene, as an entire stranger, it would add still more to the marvellous.

The tumblers' tricks and rope-dancing were performed to admiration. And those of the spectators whose constant residence in the country prevented their having witnessed similar feats, were the most inclined to admire and praise the agility of the troop. The little children in particular were applauded. The compassion excited by their unhappy destiny, mingled with the approbation bestowed on them; and the ladies were subjects of envy, in giving birth to the satisfaction depicted in the countenances of these little wretches by their liberal donations.

The agility of the troop formed the subject of general conversation the whole afternoon. They were even speaking in their praise after supper, when the master of the house said to the company assembled:

"I am rejoiced, my dear friends, to see the pleasure you have received from the little spectacle that I have been enabled to give you. My joy is so much the greater, since I find you doubting the possibility of things which are very natural; for I have it in my power to submit for your examination something of a very incomprehensible nature. At this very moment I have in my house a person who entertains a most singular intercourse with the world of spirits, and who can compel the dead to answer his questions."

"O!" exclaimed a lady smiling, "Don't terrify us."

"You jest now," replied the colonel; "but I venture to affirm your mirth will be a little changed when the scene takes place."

"I accept the challenge," answered the incredulous fair one. All the party was of her opinion, and declared themselves so openly and so loudly against the truth of these terrific scenes, that the colonel began to be really apprehensive for the effects likely to be produced by those he had prepared. He would have even relinquished his project, if his guests, one and all, had not entreated him to the contrary. They even went further: they besought him not long to delay the wonderful things he promised. But the colonel, keeping his own counsel, feigned ignorance that they were laughing at him; and with a grave air declared that the experiment could not take place till midnight.

The clock at length struck twelve. The colonel gave his servants orders to place chairs facing the door of a closet which had been hitherto kept shut: he invited the company to sit down, and gave orders for all the lights to be put out. While these preparations were making, he thus addressed the company:

"I entreat you, my friends, to abstain from all idle curiosity." The grave and solemn tone in which he uttered these words made a deep impression on the party, whose incredulity was not a little lessened by the striking of the clock, and the putting out the lights one after the other. Presently they heard from the closet facing them the hoarse and singular sounds by which it is pretended spirits are conjured up; and which were interrupted at intervals by loud strokes of a hammer. All on a sudden the door of the closet opened: and as by slow degrees the cloud of incense which filled it evaporated, they gradually discovered the black trappings with which it was hung, and an altar in the middle also hung with black drapery. On this altar was placed a skull, which cast its terrifying regards on all the company present.

Meanwhile the spectators' breathing became more audible and difficult, and their embarrassment increased in proportion as the vapour gave place to a brilliant light issuing from an alabaster lamp suspended from the ceiling. Many of them indeed turned their heads away in alarm on hearing a noise behind them; which, however, they discovered simply proceeded from some of the servants, whom the colonel had given permission to be present during the exhibition, at a respectful distance.

After a moment of profound silence, Calzolaro entered. A long beard had so effectually altered his youthful appearance, that though several of the spectators had previously seen him, they could not possibly recognize him under this disguise. And his Oriental costume added so much to the deceit, that his entrance had an excellent effect.

In order that his art should impose the more, the colonel recommended to him a degree of haughtiness in addressing the company; and that he should not salute them according to any prescribed forms of politeness, but to announce himself in terms foreign from all ordinary modes of conversation. They both agreed that a mysterious jargon would best answer their purpose.

In consequence of such determination, Calzolaro, assuming a deep sepulchral tone, thus began: – "After our present state of existence, we are swallowed up in the obscure abyss which we call death, in order that we may become incorporated in an entirely new and peaceful state. It is in order to emancipate the soul from this state, that the sublime arts are exercised; and to create among fools and weak persons the idea of its being impossible! The wise and learned pity them for their ignorance, in not knowing what is possible and impossible, true or false, light or dark; because they do not know and cannot comprehend the exalted spirits, who, from the silence of the vault and the grave, from the mouldering bones of the dead, speak to the living in a voice no less formidable than true. As to you, who are now here assembled, listen to a word of advice: Avoid provoking by any indiscreet question the vengeance of the spirit, who at my command will be invisibly stationed beneath this human skull. Endeavour to moderate your fear: listen to everything with calmness and submission; for I take under my especial care all those who are obedient, and only leave the guilty as a prey to the destruction they merit."

The colonel remarked with secret satisfaction the impression produced on the company, hitherto so incredulous, by this pompous harangue.

"Everything succeeds better than I could have hoped," said he, in an under tone to his wife, who was not at all amused by the performance, and who was only present to please her husband.

Meanwhile Calzolaro continued: "Look on this pitiful and neglected head: my magic art has removed the bolts of the tomb to which it was consigned, and in which reposes a long line of princes. The owner of it is now actually there, rendering up to the spirits an exact account of the life he had led. Don't be alarmed, even though it should burst forth in terrible menaces against you: and against me his impotency will be manifest, as, spite of his former grandeur, he cannot resist the power I have over him, provided no culpable precipitation on your part interrupt the solemnity of my questions."

He then opened a door of the closet hitherto concealed from the company, brought a chafing-dish filled with red-hot coals, threw thereon some incense, and walked three times round the altar, pronouncing at each circle a spell. He then drew from its scabbard a sword which hung in his girdle, plunged it in the smoke issuing from the incense, and making frightful contortions of his face and limbs, pretended to endeavour to cleave the head, which, however, he did not touch. At last he took the head up on the point of his sword, held it up in the air before him, and advanced towards the spectators a little moved.

"Who art thou, miserable dust, that I hold at the point of my sword?" demanded Calzolaro with a confident air and a firm voice. But scarcely had he uttered this question, when he turned pale; his arm trembled; his knees shook; his haggard eyes, which were fixed on the head, were horror-struck: he had hardly strength sufficient to place the head and the sword on the altar, ere he suddenly fell on the floor with every symptom of extreme terror.

The spectators, frightened out of their wits, looked at the master of the house, who in his turn looked at them. No one seemed to know whether this was to be considered part of the scene, nor whether it was possible to explain it. The curiosity of the audience was raised to its utmost pitch: they waited still a considerable time, but no explanation took place. At length Calzolaro, half-raising himself, asked if his father's shadow had disappeared.

Stupefaction succeeded astonishment. The colonel was anxious to know whether he was still attempting to impose on the company by a pretended dialogue with the death's head?

Calzolaro answered that he would do anything, and that he would willingly submit to any punishment they chose to inflict on him for his frightful crime: but he entreated they would instantly carry back the head to its place of repose.

His countenance had undergone a complete change, and only resumed its wonted appearance on the colonel's wife acquiescing in his wish: she ordered the head to be instantly conveyed to the church-yard, and to be replaced in the grave.

During this unexpected denouement, every eye was turned on Calzolaro; he, who not long ago was talking with so much emphasis and in such a lofty strain, could now scarcely draw his breath; and from time to time threw supplicating looks on the spectators, as if entreating them to wait patiently till he had recovered strength sufficient to continue his performance.

The colonel informed them in the meanwhile of the species of jest that he had projected to play on them, and for the failure of which he could not at that moment account. At last Calzolaro, with an abashed air, spoke as follows: –

"The spectacle which I designed to have given, has terminated in a terrible manner for me. But, happily for the honourable company present, I perceive they did not see the frightful apparition which caused me a temporary privation of my reason. Scarcely had I raised the death's head on the point of my sword, and had begun to address it, than it appeared to me in my father's features: and whether my ears deceived me or not, I am ignorant; neither do I know how I was restored to my senses; but I heard it say, 'Tremble, parricide, whom nothing can convert, and who wilt not turn to the path thou hast abandoned!'"

The very recollection produced such horror on Calzolaro's mind as to stop his respiration and prevent his proceeding. The colonel briefly explained to the spectators what appeared to them mysterious in his words, and then said to the penitent juggler:

"Since your imagination has played you so strange a trick, I exhort you in future to avoid all similar accidents, and to accept the arrangement proposed to you by the person whom your father has named as his heir."

"No, monsieur," answered he, "no agreement, no bargain; else I shall only half fulfil my duty. Everything shall belong to this heiress, and the law-suit shall be abandoned."

He at the same time declared that he was weary of the mode of life he had adopted, and that every wish of his father's should be fulfilled.

The colonel told him that such a resolution compensated for what had failed in the evening's amusement.

The company, however, did not cease making numberless inquiries of Calzolaro, many of which were very ludicrous. They were anxious to know, among other things, whether the head which had appeared to him, resembled that of a corpse or a living being.

"It most probably belongs to a corpse," he replied. "I was so thunderstruck with the horrible effect of it, that I cannot remember minutiae. Imagine an only son, with the point of a sword which he holds in his hand, piercing his father's skull! The bare idea is sufficient to deprive one of one's senses."

"I did not believe," answered the colonel, after having for some time considered Calzolaro, "that the conscience of a man, who like you has rambled the world over, could still be so much overcome by the powers of imagination."

"What! Monsieur, do you still doubt the reality of the apparition, though I am ready to attest it by the most sacred oaths?"

"Your assertion contradicts itself. We have also our eyes to see what really exists; and nobody, excepting yourself, saw any other than a simple skull."

"That is what I cannot explain: but this I can add, that I am firmly persuaded, although even now I cannot account for my so thinking, that as sure as I exist, that head is actually and truly the head of my father: I am ready to attest it by my most solemn oath."

"To prevent your perjuring yourself, they shall instantly go to the sexton, and learn the truth."

Saying this, the colonel went out to give the necessary orders. He returned an instant afterwards, saying:

"Here is another strange phenomenon. The sexton is in this house, but is not able to answer my questions. Anxious to enjoy the spectacle I was giving my friends, he mixed with some of my servants, who, possessing the same degree of curiosity, had softly opened the door through which the chaffing-dish was conveyed. But at the moment of the conjurer falling on the floor, the same insensibility overcame the sexton; who even now has not recovered his reason, although they have used every possible method to restore him."

One of the party said, that, being subject to fainting himself, he constantly carried about him a liquor, the effect of which was wonderful in such cases, and that he would go and try it now on the sexton. They all followed him: but this did not succeed better than the methods previously resorted to.

"This man must indeed be dead," said the person who had used the liquor without effect on him.

The clock in the tower had just struck one, and every person thought of retiring; but slight symptoms of returning life being perceptible in the sexton, they still remained.

"God be praised!" exclaimed the sexton awaking; "he is at length restored to rest!"

"Who, old dad?" said the colonel.

"Our late schoolmaster."

"What then, that head was actually his?"

"Alas! If you will only promise not to be angry with me, I will confess – it was his."

The colonel then asked him how the idea of disturbing the schoolmaster's corpse in particular came into his head.

"Owing to a diabolical boldness. It is commonly believed, that when a child speaks to the head of its deceased parent at the midnight hour, the head comes to life again. I was anxious to prove the fact, but shall never recover from its effects: happily, however, the head is actually restored to rest."

They asked him how he knew it. He answered, that he had seen it all the while he was in a state of lethargy; that as the clock struck one, his wife had finished re-interring the head in its grave. And he described in the most minute manner how she held it.

The curiosity of the company assembled was so much excited by witnessing these inexplicable events, that they awaited the return of the servant whom the colonel had dispatched to the sexton's wife. Every thing had happened precisely as he described – the clock struck one at the very moment the head was laid in the grave.

These events had produced to the spectators a night of much greater terrors than the colonel had prepared for them. Nay, even his imagination was raised to such a pitch, that the least breath of wind, or the slightest noise, appeared to him as a forerunner to some disagreeable visitor from the world of spirits.

He was out of his bed at dawn of day, to look out of his window and see the occasion of the noise which at that hour was heard at the inn-door. He saw the rope-dancers seated in the carriage, about to take their departure. Calzolaro was not with them; but presently afterwards came to the side of the vehicle, where he took leave of them: the children seemed to leave him behind with regret.

The carriage drove off; and the colonel made a signal to Calzolaro to come and speak to him.

"I apprehend," said he to him, when he came in, "that you have taken entire leave of your troop."

"Well, monsieur, ought I not so to do?"

"It appears to me a procedure in which you have acted with as little reflection as the one which tempted you first to join them. You ought rather to have availed yourself of some favourable occasion for withdrawing the little capital that you have in their funds."

"Do you then, monsieur colonel, forget what has happened to me; and that I could not have enjoyed another moment of repose in the society of persons who are only externally men? Every time I recall the scene of last night to my recollection, my very blood freezes in my veins. From this moment I must do all in my power to appease my father's shade, which is now so justly incensed against me. Without much effort I have withdrawn myself from a profession which never had any great charms for me. Reflect only on the misery of being the chief of a troop, who, to earn a scanty morsel of bread, are compelled every moment to risk their lives! – and even this morsel of bread not always attainable. Moreover, I know that the clown belonging to the troop, who is a man devoid of all sentiment, has for a long while aspired to become the chief: and I know that he has for some time been devising various means to remove me from this world; therefore it appears to me that I have not been precipitate in relinquishing my rights to him for a trifling sum of money. I only feel for the poor children; and would willingly have purchased them, to save them from so unhappy a career; but he would not take any price for them. I have only one consolation, which is, the hope that the inhuman treatment they will experience at his hands will induce them to make their escape, and follow a better course of life."

"And what do you purpose doing yourself?"

"I have told you, that I shall retire to some obscure corner of Germany, and follow the profession to which my father destined me."

The colonel made him promise to wait a little; and, if possible, he would do something for him.

In the interim, the heiress to his father's property arrived, to have a conference on the subject with him. As soon as he had made known his intentions to her, she entreated him no longer to refuse half the inheritance, or at least to receive it as a voluntary gift on her part. The goodness, the sweetness of this young person, (who was pretty also), so pleased Calzolaro, that a short time afterwards he asked her hand in marriage. She consented to give it to him. And the colonel then exerted himself more readily in behalf of this man, who had already gained his favour. He fulfilled his wishes, by sending him to a little property belonging to his wife, to follow the profession his father had fixed on for him.

Ere he set off, Calzolaro resumed his German name of Schurster. The good pastor, who had so recently felt indignant at his obstinacy, gave the nuptial benediction to the happy couple in presence of the colonel and his family, who on this occasion gave an elegant entertainment at the château.

In the evening, a little after sun-set, the bride and bridegroom were walking in the garden, at some little distance from the rest of the company, and appeared plunged in a deep reverie. All on a sudden they looked at each other; for it seemed to them, that someone took a hand of each and united them. They declared, at least, that the idea of this action having taken place came to them both so instantaneously and so involuntarily, that they were astonished at it themselves.

An instant afterwards, they distinctly heard these words:

"May God bless your union!" pronounced by the voice of Calzolaro's father.

The bridegroom told the colonel, some time afterwards, that without these consolatory words, the terrible apparition which he saw on the memorable night, would assuredly have haunted him all his life, and have impoisoned his happiest moments.

If you enjoyed this, you might also like...
'The Vampyre' by John Polidori, see page 137
The Last Man, see page 331

The Spectre-Barber

Johann Karl August Musäus

"Sir Ryence of North-Gales greeteth well thee,
And bids thee thy beard anon to him send,
Or else from thy jaws he will it off rend."
Bishop Thomas Percy, *Reliques of Ancient English Poetry*

THERE FORMERLY LIVED at Bremen a wealthy merchant named Melchior, who, it was remarked, invariably stroked his chin with complacency, whenever the subject of the sermon was the rich man in the Gospel; who, by the bye, in comparison with him, was only a petty retail dealer. This said Melchior possessed such great riches, that he had caused the floor of his dining-room to be paved with crown-pieces. This ridiculous luxury gave great offence to Melchior's fellow-citizens and relations. They attributed it to vanity and ostentation, but did not guess its true motive: however, it perfectly answered the end Melchior designed by it; for, by their constantly expressing their disapprobation of this ostentatious species of vanity, they spread abroad the report of their neighbour's immense riches, and thereby augmented his credit in a most astonishing manner.

Melchior died suddenly while at a corporation dinner, and consequently had not time to make a disposition of his property by will; so that his only son Francis, who was just of age, came into possession of the whole. This young man was particularly favoured by fortune, both with respect to his personal advantages and his goodness of heart; but this immense inheritance caused his ruin. He had no sooner got into the possession of so considerable a fortune, than he squandered it, as if it had been a burthen to him; ran into every possible extravagance, and neglected his concerns. Two or three years passed over without his perceiving that, owing to his dissipations, his funds were considerably diminished; but at length his coffers were emptied: and one day when Francis had drawn a draft to a very considerable amount on his banker, who had no funds to meet it, it was returned to him protested. This disappointment greatly vexed our prodigal, but only as it caused a temporary check to his wishes; for he did not even then give himself the trouble to inquire into the reason of it. After swearing and blustering for some time, he gave his steward a positive but laconic order to get money.

All the brokers, bankers, money-changers, and usurers, were put in requisition, and the empty coffers were soon filled; for the dining-room floor was in the eyes of the lenders a sufficient security.

This palliative had its effect for a time: but all at once a report was spread abroad in the city that the celebrated silver floor had been taken up; the consequence of which was, that the lenders insisted on examining into and proving the fact, and then became urgent for payment: but as Francis had not the means to meet their demands, they seized on all his goods and chattels; everything was sold by auction, and he had nothing left excepting a few jewels which had formed part of his heritage, and which might for a short time keep him from starving.

He now took up his abode in a small street in one of the most remote quarters of the city, where he lived on his straitened means. He, however, accommodated himself to his situation: but the only resource he found against the ennui which overpowered him, was to play on the lute; and when fatigued by this exercise, he used to stand at his window and make observations on the weather; and his intelligent mind was not long in discovering an object which soon entirely engrossed his thoughts.

Opposite his window there lived a respectable woman, who was at her spinning-wheel from morning till night, and by her industry earned a subsistence for herself and her daughter. Meta was a young girl of great beauty and attraction: she had known happier times; for her father had been the proprietor of a vessel freighted by himself, in which he annually made trading voyages to Antwerp: but he, as well as his ship and all its cargo, was lost in a violent storm. His widow supported this double loss with resignation and firmness, and resolved to support herself and her daughter by her own industry. She made over her house and furniture to the creditors of her husband, and took up her abode in the little bye street in which Francis lodged, where by her assiduity she acquired a subsistence without laying herself under an obligation to anyone. She brought up her daughter to spinning and other work, and lived with so much economy, that by her savings she was enabled to set up a little trade in linen.

Mother Bridget, (which was the appellation given to our widow), did not, however, calculate on terminating her existence in this penurious situation; and the hope of better prospects sustained her courage. The beauty and excellent qualities of her daughter, whom she brought up with every possible care and attention, led her to think that some advantageous offer would one day present itself. Meta lived tranquilly and lonely with her mother, was never seen in any of the public walks, and indeed never went out but to mass once a day.

One day while Francis was making his meteorological observations at the window, he saw the beautiful Meta, who, under her mother's watchful eye, was returning from church. The heart of Francis was as yet quite free; for the boisterous pleasures of his past life did not leave him leisure for a true affection; but at this time, when all his senses were calm, the appearance of one of the most enchanting female forms he had ever seen, ravished him, and he henceforth thought solely of the adorable object which his eyes had thus discovered. He questioned his landlord respecting the two females who lived in the opposite house, and from him learned the particulars we have just related.

He now regretted his want of economy, since his present miserable state prevented him from making an offer to the charming Meta. He was, however, constantly at the window, in hopes of seeing her, and in that consisted his greatest delight. The mother very soon discovered the frequent appearance of her new neighbour at his window, and attributed it to its right cause. In consequence, she rigorously enjoined her daughter not to shew herself at the windows, which were now kept constantly shut.

Francis was not much versed in the arts of finesse, but love awakened all the energies of his soul. He soon discovered that if he appeared much at the window, his views would be suspected, and he resolved therefore studiously to refrain from coming near it. He determined, however, to continue his observation of what occurred in the opposite dwelling without being perceived. He accordingly purchased a large mirror, and fixed it in his chamber in such a position that it distinctly presented to his view what passed in the abode of his opposite neighbour. Francis not being seen at the window, the old lady relaxed in her rigour, and Meta's windows were once more opened. Love more than ever reigned triumphant in the bosom of Francis: but how was he to make known his attachment to its object? he could neither speak nor write to her. Love, however, soon suggested a mode of communication which succeeded. Our prodigal took his lute, and drew from it tones the best adapted to express the subject of his passion; and by perseverance, in less than a month he made a wonderful progress. He soon had the gratification of seeing the fair hand of Meta open the little casement, when he began to tune the instrument. When she made her appearance, he testified his joy by an air lively and gay; but if she did not shew herself, the melancholy softness of his tones discovered the disappointment he experienced.

In the course of a short time he created a great interest in the bosom of his fair neighbour; and various modes which love suggested shortly convinced our prodigal that Meta shared a mutual attachment. She now endeavoured to justify him, when her mother with acrimony spoke of his prodigality and past misconduct, by attributing his ruin to the effect of bad example. But in so doing, she cautiously avoided exciting the suspicions of the old lady; and seemed less anxious to excuse him, than to take a part in the conversation which was going on.

Circumstances which our limits will not allow us to narrate rendered the situation of Francis more and more difficult to be supported: his funds had now nearly failed him; and an offer of marriage from a wealthy brewer, who was called in the neighbourhood the 'King of Hops,' and which Meta, much to her mother's disappointment, refused, excited still more the apprehensions of poor Francis, lest some more fortunate suitor might yet be received, and blast his hopes forever.

When he received the information that this opulent lover had been rejected for his sake, with what bitterness did he lament his past follies!

"Generous girl!" said he, "you sacrifice yourself for a miserable creature, who has nothing but a heart fondly attached to you, and which is riven with despair that its possessor cannot offer you the happiness you so truly merit."

The King of Hops soon found another female, who listened more kindly to his vows, and whom he wedded with great splendour.

Love, however, did not leave his work incomplete; for its influence created in the mind of Francis a desire of exerting his faculties and actively employing himself, in order, if possible, to emerge from the state of nothingness into which he was at present plunged· and it inspired him also with courage to prosecute his good intentions. Among various projects which he formed, the most rational appeared that of overlooking his father's books, taking an account of the claimable debts, and from that source to get all he possibly could. The produce of this procedure would, he thought, furnish him with the means of beginning in some small way of business; and his imagination led him to extend this to the most remote corners of the earth. In order to equip himself for the prosecution of his plans, he sold all the remainder of his father's effects, and with the money purchased a horse to commence his travels.

The idea of a separation from Meta was almost more than he could endure. "What will she think," said he, "of this sudden disappearance, when she no longer meets me in her way to church? Will she not think me perfidious, and banish me from her heart?" Such ideas as these caused him infinite pain: and for a long while he could not devise any means of acquainting Meta with his plans; but at length the fertile genius of love furnished him with the following idea: – Francis went to the curate of the church which his mistress daily frequented, and requested him before the sermon and during mass to put up prayers for a happy issue to the affairs of a young traveller; and these prayers were to be continued till the moment of his return, when they were to be changed into those of thanks.

Everything being arranged for his departure, he mounted his steed, and passed close under Meta's window. He saluted her with a very significant air, and with much less caution than heretofore. The young girl blushed deeply; and mother Bridget took this opportunity of loudly expressing her dislike to this bold adventurer, whose impertinence and foppery induced him to form designs on her daughter.

From this period the eyes of Meta in vain searched for Francis. She constantly heard the prayer which was put up for him; but was so entirely absorbed by grief at no longer perceiving the object of her affection, that she paid no attention to the words of the priest. In no way could she account for his disappearing. Some months afterwards, her grief being somewhat ameliorated, and her mind more tranquillized, when she was one day thinking of the last time she had seen Francis, the prayer arrested her attention; she reflected for an instant, and quickly divined for whom it was said; she naturally joined in it with great fervour, and strongly recommended the young traveller to the protection of her guardian angel.

Meanwhile Francis continued his journey, and had travelled the whole of a very sultry day over one of the desert cantons of Westphalia without meeting with a single house. As night approached, a violent storm came on: the rain fell in torrents; and poor Francis was soaked to the very skin. In this miserable situation he anxiously looked around, and fortunately discovered in the distance a light, towards which he directed his horse's steps; but as he drew near, he beheld a miserable cottage, which did not promise him much succour, for it more resembled a stable than the habitation of a human being. The unfeeling wretch who inhabited it refused him fire or water as if he had been a banished man – he was just about to extend himself on the straw in the midst of the cattle, and his indolence prevented his lighting a fire for the stranger. Francis vainly endeavoured to move the peasant to pity: the latter was inexorable, and blew out his candle with the greatest nonchalance possible, without bestowing a thought on Francis. However, as the traveller hindered him from sleeping, by his incessant lamentations and prayers, he was anxious to get rid of him.

"Friend," said he to him, "if you wish to be accommodated, I promise you it will not be here; but ride through the little wood to your left-hand, and you will find the castle belonging to the chevalier Eberhard Bronkhorst, who is very hospitable to travellers; but he has a singular mania, which is, to flagellate all whom he entertains: therefore decide accordingly."

Francis, after considering for some minutes what he had best do, resolved on hazarding the adventure. "In good faith," said he, "there is no great difference between having one's back broken by the miserable accommodation of a peasant, or by the chevalier Bronkhorst: friction disperses fever; possibly its effects may prove beneficial to me, if I am compelled to keep on my wet garments."

Accordingly he put spurs to his horse, and very shortly found himself before a gothic castle, at the iron gate of which he loudly knocked: and was answered from within by "Who's there?" But ere he was allowed time to reply, the gate was opened. However, in the first court he was compelled to wait with patience, till they could learn whether it was the lord of the castle's pleasure to flagellate a traveller, or send him out to pass the night under the canopy of heaven.

This lord of the castle had from his earliest infancy served in the Imperial army, under command of George of Frunsberg, and had himself led a company of infantry against the Venetians. At length, however, fatigued with warfare, he had retired to his own territory, where, in order to expiate the crimes he had committed during the several campaigns he had been in, he did all the good and charitable acts in his power. But his manner still preserved all the roughness of his former profession. The newly arrived guest, although disposed to submit to the usages of the house for the sake of the good fare, could not help feeling a certain trembling of fear as he heard the bolts grating, ere the doors were opened to him; and the very doors by their groaning noise seemed to presage the catastrophe which awaited him. A cold perspiration came over him as he passed the last door; but finding that he received the utmost attention, his fears a little abated. The servants assisted him in getting off his horse, and unfastened his cloak-bag; some of them led his horse to the stable, while others preceding him with flambeaux conducted Francis to their master, who awaited his arrival in a room magnificently lighted up.

Poor Francis was seized with a universal tremor when he beheld the martial air and athletic form of the lord of the castle, who came up to him and shook him by the hand with so much force that he could scarcely refrain from crying out, and in a thundering voice enough to stun him, told him "he was welcome." Francis shook like an aspen-leaf in every part of his body.

"What ails you, my young comrade?" cried the chevalier Bronkhorst, in his voice of thunder: "What makes you thus tremble, and renders you as pale as if death had actually seized you by the throat?"

Francis recovered himself; and knowing that his shoulders would pay the reckoning, his fears gave place to a species of audacity.

"My lord," answered he with confidence, "you see that I am so soaked with rain that one might suppose I had swam through the Wezer; order me therefore some dry clothes instead of those I have on, and let us then drink a cup of hot wine, that I may, if possible, prevent the fever which otherwise may probably seize me. It will comfort my heart."

"Admirable!" replied the chevalier; "ask for whatever you want, and consider yourself here as at home."

Accordingly Francis gave his orders like a baron of high degree: he sent away the wet clothes, made choice of others, and, in fine, made himself quite at his ease. The chevalier, so far from expressing any dissatisfaction at his free and easy manners, commanded his people to execute whatever he ordered with promptitude, and condemned some of them as blockheads who did not appear to know how to wait on a stranger. As soon as the table was spread, the chevalier seated himself at it with his guest: they drank a cup of hot wine together.

"Do you wish for anything to eat?" demanded the lord of Francis.

The latter desired he would order up what his house afforded, that he might see whether his kitchen was good.

No sooner had he said this, than the steward made his appearance, and soon furnished up a most delicious repast. Francis did not wait for his being requested to partake of it: but after having made a hearty meal, he said to the lord of the castle, "Your kitchen is by no means despicable; if your cellar is correspondent, I cannot but say you treat your guests nobly."

The chevalier made a sign to his butler, who brought up some inferior wine, and filled a large glass of it to his master, who drank to his guest. Francis instantly returned the compliment.

"Well, young man, what say you to my wine?" asked the chevalier.

"'Faith," replied Francis, "I say it is bad, if it is the best you have in your cellar; but if you have none worse, I do not condemn it."

"You are a connoisseur;" answered the chevalier. "Butler, bring us a flask of older wine."

His orders being instantly attended to, Francis tasted it. "This is indeed some good old wine, and we will stick to it if you please."

The servants brought in a great pitcher of it, and the chevalier, being in high good-humour, drank freely with his guest; and then launched out into a long history of his several feats of prowess in the war against the Venetians. He became so overheated by the recital, that in his enthusiasm he overturned the bottles and glasses, and flourishing his knife as if it were a sword, passed it so near the nose and ears of Francis, that he dreaded he should lose them in the action.

Though the night wore away, the chevalier did not manifest any desire to sleep; for he was quite in his element, whenever he got on the topic of the Venetian war. Each succeeding glass added to the heat of his imagination as he proceeded in his narration, till at length Francis began to apprehend that it was the prologue to the tragedy in which he was to play the principal part; and feeling anxious to learn whether he was to pass the night in the castle, or to be turned out, he asked for a last glass of wine to enable him to sleep well. He feared that they would commence by filling him with wine, and that if he did not consent to continue drinking, a pretext would be laid hold of for driving him out of the castle with the usual chastisement.

However, contrary to his expectation, the lord of the castle broke the thread of his narration, and said to him: "Good friend, everything in its place: tomorrow we will resume our discourse."

"Excuse me, sir knight," replied Francis; "tomorrow, before sunrise, I shall be on my road. The distance from hence to Brabant is very considerable, and I cannot tarry here longer, therefore permit me to take leave of you now, that I may not disturb you in the morning."

"Just as you please about that: but you will not leave the castle before I am up; we will breakfast together, and I shall accompany you to the outer gate, and take leave of you according to my usual custom."

Francis needed no comment to render these words intelligible. Most willingly would he have dispensed with the chevalier's company to the gate; but the latter did not appear at all inclined to deviate from his usual custom. He ordered his servants to assist the stranger in undressing, and to take care of him till he was in bed.

Francis found his bed an excellent one; and ere he went to sleep, he owned that so handsome a reception was not dearly bought at the expense of a trifling beating. The most delightful dreams (in which Meta bore the sway) occupied him the whole night; and he would have gone on (thus dreaming) till mid-day, if the sonorous voice of the chevalier and the clanking of his spurs had not disturbed him.

It needed all Francis's efforts to quit this delightful bed, in which he was so comfortable, and where he knew himself to be in safety: he turned from side to side; but the chevalier's tremendous voice was like a death-stroke to him, and at length he resolved to get up. Several servants assisted him in dressing, and the chevalier waited for him at a small but well-served table; but Francis, knowing the moment of trial was at hand, had no great inclination to feast. The chevalier tried to persuade him to eat, telling him it was the best thing to keep out the fog and damp air of the morning.

"Sir knight," replied Francis, "my stomach is still loaded from your excellent supper of last evening; but my pockets are empty, and I should much like to fill them, in order to provide against future wants."

The chevalier evinced his pleasure at his frankness by filling his pockets with as much as they could contain. As soon as they brought him his horse, which he discovered had been well groomed and fed, he drank the last glass of wine to say Adieu, expecting that at that signal the chevalier would take him by the collar and make him pay his welcome. But, to his no small surprise, the chevalier contented himself with heartily shaking him by the hand as on his arrival: and as soon as the gate was opened, Francis rode off safe and sound.

In no way could our traveller account for his host permitting him thus to depart without paying the usual score. At length he began to imagine that the peasant had simply told him the story to frighten him; and feeling a curiosity to learn whether or not it had any foundation in fact, he rode back to the castle. The chevalier had not yet quitted the gate, and was conversing with his servants on the pace of Francis's horse, who appeared to trot very roughly: and seeing the traveller return, he supposed that he had forgotten something, and by his looks seemed to accuse his servants of negligence.

"What do you want, young man?" demanded he: "Why do you, who were so much pressed for time, return?"

"Allow me, most noble sir," replied Francis, "to ask you one question, for there are reports abroad which tend to vilify you: It is said, that, after having hospitably received and entertained strangers, you make them at their departure feel the weight of your arm. And although I gave credence to this rumour, I have omitted nothing which might have entitled me to this mark of your favour. But, strange to say, you have permitted me to depart in peace, without even the slightest mark of your strength. You see my surprise; therefore do pray inform me whether there is any foundation for the report, or whether I shall chastise the impudent story-teller who related the false tale to me."

"Young man," replied Bronkhorst, "you have heard nothing but the truth: but it needs some explanations. I open my door hospitably to every stranger, and in Christian charity I give them a place at my table; but I am a man who hates form or disguise; I say all I think, and only wish in return that my guests openly and undisguisedly ask for all they want. There are unfortunately, however, a tribe of people who fatigue by their mean complaisance and ceremonies without end; who wear me out by their dissimulation, and stun me by propositions devoid of sense, or who do not conduct themselves with decency during the repast. Gracious heavens! I lose all patience when they carry their fooleries to such excesses, and I exert my right as master of the castle, by taking hold of their collars, and giving them tolerably severe chastisement ere I turn them out of my gates. – But a man of your sort, my young friend, will ever be welcome under my roof; for you boldly and openly ask for what you require, and say what you think; and such are the persons I admire. If in your way back you pass through this canton, promise me you will pay me another visit. Good bye! Let me caution you never to place implicit confidence in anything you hear; believe only that there may be a single grain of truth in the whole story: be always frank, and you will succeed through life. Heaven's blessings attend you."

Francis continued his journey towards Anvers most gaily, wishing, as he went, that he might everywhere meet with as good a reception as at the chevalier Bronkhorst's.

Nothing remarkable occurred during the rest of his journey: and he entered the city full of the most sanguine hopes and expectations. In every street his fancied riches stared him in the face. "It appears to me," said he, "that some of my father's debtors must have succeeded in business, and that they will only require my presence to repay their debts with honour."

After having rested from the fatigue of his journey, he made himself acquainted with every particular relative to the debtors, and learnt that the greater part had become rich, and were doing extremely well. This intelligence reanimated his hopes: he arranged his papers, and paid a visit to each of the persons who owed him anything. But his success was by no means what he had expected: some of the debtors pretended that they had paid everything; others, that they had never heard mention of Melchior of Bremen; and the rest produced accounts precisely contradictory to those he had, and which tended to prove they were creditors instead of debtors. In fine, ere three days had elapsed, Francis found himself in the debtors-prison, from whence he stood no chance of being released till he had paid the uttermost farthing of his father's debts.

How pitiable was this poor young man's condition! Even the horrors of the prison were augmented by the remembrance of Meta – nay, to such a pitch of desperation was he carried, that he resolved to starve himself. Fortunately, however, at twenty-seven years of age such determinations are more easily formed than practised.

The intention of those who put him into confinement was not merely with a view of exacting payment of his pretended debts, but to avoid paying him his due: so, whether the prayers put up for poor Francis at Bremen were effectual, or that the pretended creditors were not disposed to maintain him during his life, I know not; but after a detention of three months they liberated Francis from prison, with a particular injunction to quit the territories of Anvers within four-and-twenty hours, and never to set his foot within that city again: – They gave him at the same time five florins to defray his expenses on the road. As one may well imagine, his horse and baggage had been sold to defray the costs incident to the proceedings.

With a heart overloaded with grief he quitted Anvers, in a very different frame of mind to what he experienced at entering it. Discouraged and irresolute, he mechanically followed the road which chance directed: he paid no attention to the various travellers, or indeed to any object on the road, till hunger or thirst caused him to lift his eyes to discover a steeple or some other token announcing the habitation of human beings. In this state of mind did he continue journeying on for several days incessantly; nevertheless a secret instinct impelled him to take the road leading to his own country.

All on a sudden he roused as if from a profound sleep, and recollected the place in which he was: he stopped an instant to consider whether he should continue the road he was then in, or return; "For," said he, "what a shame to return to my native city a beggar!" How could he thus return to that city in which he formerly felt equal to the richest of its inhabitants? How could he as a beggar present himself before Meta, without causing her to blush for the choice she had made? He did not allow time for his imagination to complete this miserable picture, for he instantly turned back, as if already he had found himself before the gates of Bremen, followed by the shouts of the children. His mind was soon made up as to what he should do: he resolved to go to one of the ports of the Low-Countries, there to engage himself as sailor on board a Spanish vessel, to go to the newly discovered world; and not to return to his native country till he had amassed as much wealth as he had formerly so thoughtlessly squandered. In the whole of this project, Meta was only thought of at an immeasurable distance: but Francis contented himself with connecting her in idea with his future plans, and walked, or rather strode along, as if by hurrying his pace he should sooner gain possession of her.

Having thus attained the frontiers of the Low-Countries, he arrived at sun-set in a village situated near Rheinburg; but since entirely destroyed in the thirty years' war. A caravan of carriers from Liege filled the inn so entirely, that the landlord told Francis he could not give him a lodging; adding, that at the adjoining village he would find accommodations. Possibly he was actuated to this refusal by Francis's appearance, who certainly in point of garb might well be mistaken for a vagabond.

The landlord took him for a spy to a band of thieves, sent probably to rob the carriers: so that poor Francis, spite of his extreme lassitude, was compelled with his wallet at his back to proceed on his road; and having at his departure muttered through his teeth some bitter maledictions against the cruel and unfeeling landlord, the latter appeared touched with compassion for the poor stranger, and from the door of the inn called after him: "Young man; a word with you! If you resolve on passing the night here, I will procure you a lodging in that castle you now see on the hill; there you will have rooms in abundance, provided you are not afraid of being alone, for it is uninhabited. See, here are the keys belonging to it."

Francis joyfully accepted the landlord's proposition, and thanked him for it as if it had been an act of great charity.

"It is to me a matter of little moment where I pass the night, provided I am at my ease, and have something to eat." But the landlord was an ill-tempered fellow; and wishing to revenge the invectives Francis had poured forth against him, he sent him to the castle in order that he might be tormented by the spirits which were said to frequent it.

This castle was situated on a steep rock, and was only separated from the village by the high-road and a little rivulet. Its delightful prospects caused it to be kept in good repair, and to be well furnished, as its owner made use of it as a hunting-seat: but no sooner did night come on than he quitted it, in order to avoid the apparitions and ghosts which haunted it; but during the day nothing of the sort was visible, and all was tranquil.

When it was quite dark, Francis with a lantern in his hand proceeded towards the castle. The landlord accompanied him, and carried a little basket of provisions, to which he had added a bottle of wine (which he said would stand the test), as well as two candles and two wax-tapers for the night. Francis, not thinking he should require so many things, and being apprehensive he should have to pay for them, asked why they were all brought.

"The light from my lantern," said he, "will suffice me till the time of my getting into bed; and ere I shall get out of it, the sun will have risen, for I am quite worn out with fatigue."

"I will not endeavour to conceal from you," replied the landlord, "that according to the current reports this castle is haunted by evil spirits: but do not let that frighten you; you see I live sufficiently near, that, in case any thing extraordinary should happen to you, I can hear you call, and shall be in readiness with my people to render you any assistance. At my house there is somebody stirring all night, and there is also someone constantly on the watch. I have lived on this spot for thirty years, and cannot say that I have ever seen anything to alarm me: indeed, I believe that you may with safety attribute any noises you hear during the night in this castle, to cats and weazels, with which the granaries are overrun. I have only provided you with the means of keeping up a light in case of need, for, at best, night is but a gloomy season; and, in addition, these candles are consecrated, and their light will undoubtedly keep off any evil spirits, should there be such in the castle."

The landlord spoke only the truth, when he said he had not seen any ghosts in the castle; for he never had the courage to set his foot within its doors after dark; and though he now spoke so courageously, the rogue would not have ventured on any account to enter. After having opened the door, he gave the basket into Francis's hand, pointed out the way he was to turn, and wished him good night: while the latter, fully satisfied that the story of the ghosts must be fabulous, gaily entered. He recollected all that had been told him to the prejudice of the chevalier Bronkhorst, but unfortunately forgot what that brave Castellan had recommended to him at parting.

Conformably to the landlord's instructions, he went upstairs and came to a door, which the key in his possession soon unlocked: it opened into a long dark gallery, where his very steps re-echoed; this gallery led to a large hall, from which issued a suite of apartments furnished in a costly manner: he surveyed them all; and made choice of one in which to pass the night, that appeared rather more lively than the rest. The windows looked to the high-road, and everything that passed in front of the inn could be distinctly heard from them. He lighted two candles, spread the cloth, ate very heartily, and felt completely at his ease so long as he was thus employed; for while eating, no thought or apprehension of spirits molested him; but he no sooner arose from table, than he began to feel a sensation strongly resembling fear.

In order to render himself secure, he locked the door, drew the bolts, and looked out from each window; but nothing was to be seen. Everything along the high-road and in front of the inn was tranquil, where, contrary to the landlord's assertions, not a single light was discernible. The sound of the horn belonging to the night-guard was the only thing that interrupted the silence which universally prevailed.

Francis closed the windows, once again looked round the room, and after snuffing the candles that they might burn the better, he threw himself on the bed, which he found good and comfortable: but although greatly fatigued, he could not get to sleep so soon as he had hoped. A slight palpitation of the heart, which he attributed to the agitation produced by the heat of his journey, kept him awake for a considerable time, till at length sleep came to his aid. After having as he imagined been asleep somewhat about an hour, he awoke and started up in a state of horror possibly not unusual to a person whose blood is overheated: this idea in some degree allayed his apprehensions; and he listened attentively, but could hear nothing excepting the clock, which struck the hour of midnight. Again he listened for an instant; and turning on his side, he was just going off to sleep again, when he fancied he heard a distant door grinding on its hinges, and then shut with a heavy noise. In an instant the idea of the ghost approaching caused him no little fear: but he speedily got the better of his alarm, by fancying it was only the wind; however, he could not comfort himself long with this idea, for the sound approached nearer and nearer, and resembled the noise made by the clanking of chains, or the rattling of a large bunch of keys.

The terror which Francis experienced was beyond all description, and he put his head under the clothes. The doors continued to open with a frightful noise, and at last he heard someone trying different keys at the door of his room; one of them seemed perfectly to fit the lock, but the bolts kept the door fast; however, a violent shock like a clap of thunder caused them to give way, and in stalked a tall thin figure with a black beard, whose appearance was indicative of chagrin and melancholy. He was habited in the antique style, and on his left shoulder wore a red cloak or mantle, while his head was covered with a high-crowned hat. Three times with slow and measured steps he walked round the room, examined the consecrated candles, and snuffed them: he then threw off his cloak, unfolded a shaving apparatus, and took from it the razors, which he sharpened on a large leather strop hanging to his belt.

No powers are adequate to describe the agonies Francis endured: he recommended himself to the Virgin Mary, and endeavoured, as well as his fears would permit, to form an idea of the spectre's designs on him. Whether he purposed to cut his throat, or only take off his beard, he was at a loss to determine. The poor traveller, however, was a little more composed, when he saw the spectre take out a silver shaving-pot, and in a basin of the same metal put some water; after which he made a lather, and then placed a chair. But a cold perspiration came over Francis, when the spectre with a grave air, made signs for him to sit in that chair.

He knew it was useless to resist this mandate, which was but too plainly given: and thinking it most prudent to make a virtue of necessity, and to put a good face on the matter, Francis obeyed the order, jumped nimbly out of bed, and seated himself as directed.

The spirit placed the shaving-bib round his neck: then taking a comb and scissors, cut off his hair and whiskers; after which he lathered, according to rule, his beard, his eye-brows and head, and shaved them all off completely from his chin to the nape of his neck. This operation ended, he washed his head, wiped and dried it very nicely, made him a low bow, folded up his case, put his cloak on his shoulder, and made towards the door to go away.

The consecrated candles had burnt most brilliantly during the whole of this operation; and by their clear light Francis discovered, on looking into the glass, that he had not a single hair remaining on his head. Most bitterly did he deplore the loss of his beautiful brown hair: but he regained courage on remarking, that, however great the sacrifice, all was now over, and that the spirit had no more power over him.

In effect, the ghost walked towards the door with as grave an air as he had entered: but after going a few steps, he stopped, looked at Francis with a mournful air, and stroked his beard. He three times repeated this action; and was on the point of quitting the room, when Francis began to fancy he wanted something. With great quickness of thought he imagined it might be, that he wished him to perform a like service for him to that which he had just been executing on himself.

As the spectre, spite of his woe-begone aspect, appeared more inclined to raillery than gravity, and as his proceedings towards Francis appeared more a species of frolic than absolute ill treatment, the latter no longer appeared to entertain any apprehension of him; and in consequence determined to hazard the adventure. He therefore beckoned the phantom to seat himself in the chair. It instantly returned, and obeyed: taking off its cloak, and unfolding the case, it placed it on the table, and seated itself in the chair, in the attitude of one about to be shaved. Francis imitated precisely all he had seen it do: he cut off its hair and whiskers, and then lathered its head. The spirit did not move an inch. Our barber's apprentice did not handle the razor very dexterously; so that having taken hold of the ghost's beard against the grain, the latter made a horrible grimace. Francis did not feel much assured by this action: however, he got through the job as well as he could, and rendered the ghost's head as completely bald as his own.

Hitherto the scene between the two performers had passed in profound silence; but on a sudden the silence was interrupted by the ghost exclaiming with a smiling countenance: "Stranger, I heartily thank you for the eminent service you have rendered me; for to you am I indebted for deliverance from my long captivity. During the space of three hundred years I have been immersed within these walls, and my soul has been condemned to submit to this chastisement as a punishment for my crimes, until some living being had the courage to exercise retaliation on me, by doing to me what I have done by others during my life.

"Count Hartmann formerly resided in this castle: he was a man who recognized no law nor superior; was of an arrogant and overbearing disposition; committed every species of wickedness, and violated the most sacred rights of hospitality: he played all sorts of malicious tricks to strangers who sought refuge under his roof, and to the poor who solicited his charity. I was his barber, and did everything to please him. No sooner did I perceive a pious pilgrim, than in an endearing tone I urged him to come into the castle, and prepared a bath for him; and while he was enjoying the idea of being taken care of, I shaved his beard and head quite close, and then turned him out of the bye door, with raillery and ridicule. All this was seen by count Hartmann from his window with a sort of devilish pleasure, while the children would assemble round the abused stranger, and pursue him with cries of derision.

"One day there came a holy man from a far distant country; he wore a penitentiary cross at his back, and his devotion had imprinted scars on his feet, hands, and sides; his head was shaved, excepting a circle of hair left to resemble the crown of thorns worn by our Saviour. He asked some water to wash his feet as he passed by, and some bread to eat. I instantly put him into the bath; but did not respect even his venerable head. Upon which the pilgrim pronounced this terrible curse on me: 'Depraved wretch,' said he, 'know that at your death, the formidable gates of heaven, of hell, and of purgatory will alike be closed against your sinful soul, which shall wander through this castle, in the form of a ghost, until some man, without being invited or constrained, shall do to you, what you have so long done to others.'

"From that moment the marrow in my bones dried up, and I became a perfect shadow; my soul quitted my emaciated body, and remained wandering within these walls, according to the prediction of the holy man. In vain did I look and hope for release from the painful ties which held me to earth; for know, that no sooner is the soul separated from the body, than it aspires to the blissful regions of peace, and the ardour of its wishes causes years to appear as long as centuries, while it languishes in a strange element. As a punishment, I am compelled to continue the trade that I had exercised during my life; but, alas! my nocturnal appearance soon rendered this castle deserted. Now and then a poor pilgrim entered to pass the night here: when they did, however, I treated them all as I have done you; but not one has understood me, or rendered me the only service which could deliver my soul from this sad servitude. Henceforth no spirit will haunt this castle; for I shall now enjoy that repose of which I have been so long in search. Once again let me thank you, gallant youth; and believe, that had I power over the hidden treasures of the globe, I would give them all to you; but, unfortunately, during my life riches did not fall to my lot, and this castle contains no store: however, listen to the advice I am now about to give you.

"Remain here till your hair has grown again; then return to your own country; and at that period of the year when the days and nights are of equal length, go on the bridge which crosses the Weser, and there remain till a friend, whom you will there meet, shall tell you what you ought to do to get possession of terrestrial wealth. When you are rolling in riches and prosperity, remember me; and on every anniversary of the day on which you released me from the heavy maledictions which overwhelmed me, cause a mass to be said for the repose of my soul. Adieu! I must now leave you."

Thus saying, the phantom vanished, and left his liberator perfectly astonished at the strange history he had just related. For a considerable time Francis remained immoveable, and reasoned with himself as to the reality of what he had seen; for he could not help fancying still that it was only a dream: but his closely shaved head soon convinced him that the event had actually taken place. He got into bed again, and slept soundly till midday.

The malicious inn-keeper had been on the watch from dawn of day for the appearance of the traveller, in order that he might enjoy a laugh at his expense, and express his surprise at the night's adventure. But after waiting till his patience was nearly exhausted, and finding it approached to noon, he began to apprehend that the spirit had either strangled the stranger, or that he had died of fright. He therefore called his servants together, and ran with them to the castle, passing through every room till he reached the one in which he had observed the light the over-night: there he found a strange key in the door, which was still bolted; for Francis had drawn the bolts again after the ghost had vanished. The landlord, who was all anxiety, knocked loudly; and Francis on awaking, at first thought it was the phantom come to pay him a second visit; but at length recognising the landlord's voice, he got up and opened the door.

The landlord, affecting the utmost possible astonishment, clasped his hands together, and exclaimed, "Great God and all the saints! then the red cloak has actually been here and shaved you completely? I now see that the story was but too well founded. But pray relate to me all the particulars: tell me what the spirit was like; how he came thus to shave you; and what he said to you?"

Francis, having sense enough to discover his roguery, answered him by saying: "The spirit resembled a man wearing a red cloak; you know full well how he performed the operation: and his conversation I perfectly remember – listen attentively – 'Stranger,' said he to me, 'do not trust to a certain inn-keeper who has a figure of malice for his sign; the rogue knew well what would happen to you. Adieu! I now quit this abode, as my time is come; and in future no spirit will make its appearance here. I am now about to be transformed into a night-mare, and shall constantly torment and haunt this said inn-keeper, unless he does penance for his villany, by lodging, feeding, and furnishing you with everything needful, till your hair shall grow again and fall in ringlets over your shoulders.'"

At these words the landlord was seized with a violent trembling: he crossed himself, and vowed to the Virgin Mary that he would take care of the young stranger, lodge him, and give him everything he required free of cost. He then conducted him to his house, and faithfully fulfilled what he promised.

The spirit being no longer heard or seen, Francis was naturally looked on as a conjuror. He several times passed a night in the castle; and one evening a courageous villager accompanied him, and returned without having lost his hair. The lord of the castle, hearing that the formidable red cloak was no longer to be seen, was quite delighted, and gave orders that the stranger who had delivered him from this spirit should be well taken care of.

Early in the month of September, Francis's hair began to form into ringlets, and he prepared to depart; for all his thoughts were directed towards the bridge over the Weser, where he hoped, according to the barber's predictions, to find the friend who would point out to him the way to make his fortune.

When Francis took leave of the landlord, the latter presented him with a handsome horse well appointed, and loaded with a large cloak-bag on the back of the saddle, and gave him at the same time a sufficient sum of money to complete his journey. This was a present from the lord of the castle, expressive of his thanks for having delivered him from the spirit, and rendered his castle again habitable.

Francis arrived at his native place in high spirits. He returned to his lodging in the little street, where he lived very retired, contenting himself for the present with secret information respecting Meta. All the tidings he thus gained were of a satisfactory nature; but he would neither visit her, nor make her acquainted with his return, till his fate was decided.

He waited with the utmost impatience for the equinox; till which, time seemed immeasurably long. The night preceding the eventful day, he could not close his eyes to sleep; and that he might be sure of not missing the friend with whom as yet he was unacquainted, he took his station ere sun-rise on the bridge, where no human being but himself was to be discovered. Replete with hopes of future good fortune, he formed a thousand projects in what way to spend his money.

Already had he, during the space of nearly an hour, traversed the bridge alone, giving full scope to his imagination; when on a sudden the bridge presented a moving scene, and amongst others, many beggars took their several stations on it, to levy contributions on the passengers. The first of this tribe who asked charity of Francis was a poor devil with a wooden leg, who, being a pretty good physiognomist, judged from the gay and contented air of the young man that his request would be crowned with success; and his conjecture was not erroneous, for he threw a demi-florin into his hat.

Francis, meanwhile, feeling persuaded that the friend he expected must belong to the highest class of society, was not surprised at not seeing him at so early an hour, and waited therefore with patience. But as the hour for visiting the Exchange and the Courts of Justice drew near, his eyes were in constant motion. He discovered at an immense distance every well-dressed person who came on the bridge, and his blood was in a perfect ferment as each approached him, for in some one of them did he hope to discover the author of his good fortune; but it was in vain his looking the people in the face, no one paid attention to him. The beggars, who at noon were seated on the ground eating their dinner, remarking that the young man they had seen from the first of the morning was the only person remaining with them on the bridge, and that he had not spoken to any one, or appeared to have any employment, took him for a lazy vagabond; and although they had received marks of his beneficence, they began to make game of him, and in derision called him the provost of the bridge. The physiognomist with the wooden leg remarked that his air was no longer so gay as in the morning, and that having drawn his hat over his face he appeared entirely lost in thought, for he walked slowly along, nibbling an apple with an abstracted air. The observer, resolving to benefit by what he had remarked, went to the further extremity of the bridge, and after well examining the visionary, came up to him as a stranger, asked his charity, and succeeded to his utmost wish; for Francis, without turning round his head, gave him another demi-florin.

In the afternoon a crowd of new faces presented themselves to Francis's observation, while he became quite weary at his friend's tardiness; but hope still kept up his attention. However, the fast declining sun gave notice of the approach of night, and yet scarcely any of the many passers-by had noticed Francis. Some few, perhaps, had returned his salutation, but not one had, as he expected and hoped, embraced him. At length, the day so visibly declined that the bridge became nearly deserted; for even the beggars went away. A profound melancholy seized the heart of poor Francis, when he found his hopes thus deceived; and giving way to despair, he would have precipitated himself into the Weser, had not the recollection of Meta deterred him. He felt anxious, ere he terminated his days in so tragical a manner, to see her once again as she went to mass, and feast on the contemplation of her features.

He was preparing to quit the bridge, when the beggar with the wooden leg accosted him, for he had in vain puzzled his brains to discover what could possibly have caused the young man to remain on the bridge from morning till night. The poor cripple had waited longer than usual on account of Francis, in order to see when he went; but as he remained longer than he wished, curiosity at length induced him openly to address him, in order to learn what he so ardently desired to know.

"Pray excuse me, worthy sir," said he; "and permit me to ask you a question."

Francis, who was by no means in a mood to talk, and who now heard from the mouth of a beggar the words which he had so anxiously expected from a friend, answered him in rather an angry tone: "Well then! what is it you want to know, old man?"

"Sir, you and I were the two first persons on this bridge to-day; and here we are still the only remaining two. As for me and my companions, it is pretty clear that we only come to ask alms: but it is equally evident you do not belong to our profession; and yet you have not quitted the bridge the whole day. My dear sir, for the love of God, if it is no secret, tell me I entreat you for what purpose you came, and what is the grief that rends your heart?"

"What can it concern you, old dotard, to know where the shoe pinches me, or what afflictions I am labouring under?"

"My good sir, I wish you well; you have twice bestowed your charity on me, which I hope the Almighty will return to you with interest. I could not but observe, however, that this evening your countenance no longer looked gay and happy as in the morning; and, believe me, I was sorry to see the change."

The unaffected interest evinced by the old man pleased Francis. "Well," replied he, "since you attach so much importance to the knowledge of the reason I have for remaining the whole day here plaguing myself, I will inform you that I came in search of a friend who appointed to meet me on this bridge, but whom I have expected in vain."

"With your permission I should say your friend is a rogue, to play the fool with you in this manner. If he had so served me, I should make him feel the weight of my crutch whenever I met him: for if he has been prevented from keeping his word by any unforeseen obstacle, he ought at least to have sent to you, and not have kept you here on your feet a whole day."

"And yet I have no reason to complain of his not coming, for he promised me nothing. In fact, it was only in a dream that I was told I should meet a friend here."

Francis spoke of it as a dream, because the history of the ghost was too long to relate.

"That alters the case," replied the old man. "Since you rest your hopes on dreams, I am not astonished at your being deceived. I have also had many dreams in my life; but I was never fool enough to pay attention to them. If I had all the treasures that have been promised me in dreams, I could purchase the whole city of Bremen: but I have never put faith in dreams, and have not taken a single step to prove whether they were true or false; for I know full well, it would be useless trouble: and I am astonished that you should have lost so fine a day, which you might have employed so much more usefully, merely on the strength of a dream which appears to me so wholly devoid of sense or meaning."

"The event proves the justness of your remark, old father; and that dreams generally are deceitful. But it is rather more than three months since I had a very circumstantial dream relative to my meeting a friend on this particular day, here on this bridge; and it was so clearly indicated that he should communicate things of the utmost importance, that I thought it worthwhile to ascertain whether this dream had any foundation in truth."

"Ah! sir, no one has had clearer dreams than myself; and one of them I shall never forget. I dreamt, several years since, that my good angel stood at the foot of my bed, in the form of a young man, and addressed me as follows: – 'Berthold, listen attentively to my words, and do not lose any part of what I am about to say. A treasure is allotted you; go and secure it, that you may be enabled to live happily the rest of your days. Tomorrow evening, when the sun is setting, take a pick-axe and spade over your shoulder, and go out of the city by the gate leading to Hamburgh: when you arrive facing the convent of Saint Nicholas, you will see a garden, the entrance to which is ornamented by two pillars; conceal yourself behind one of these until the moon rises: then push the door hard, and it will yield to your efforts; go without fear into the garden, follow a walk covered by a treillage of vines, and to the left you will see a great apple-tree: place yourself at the foot of this tree, with your face turned towards the moon, and you will perceive, at fifteen feet distance, two bushy rose-trees: search between these two shrubs, and at the depth of about six feet you will discover a great flag-stone, which covers the treasure inclosed within an iron chest; and although it is heavy and difficult to handle, do not regret the labour it will occasion you to move it from the hole where it now is. You will be well rewarded for your pains and trouble, if you look for the key which is hid under the box.'"

Francis remained like one stupified at this recital; and certainly would have been unable to conceal his astonishment, if the darkness of the night had not favoured him. The various particulars pointed out by the beggar brought to his recollection a little garden which he had inherited from his father, and which garden was the favourite spot of that good man; but possibly for that very reason it was not held in estimation by the son. Melchior had caused it to be laid out according to his own taste, and his son in the height of his extravagance had sold it at a very low price.

The beggar with his wooden leg was now become a very interesting personage to Francis, who perceived that he was the friend alluded to by the ghost in the castle of Rummelsbourg. The first impulse of joy would have led him to embrace the mendicant; but he restrained his feelings, thinking it best not to communicate the result of his intelligence to him.

"Well, my good man," said he, "what did you when you awoke? did you not attend to the advice given by your good angel?"

"Why should I undertake a hopeless labour? It was only a vague dream; and if my good angel was anxious to appear to me, he might choose a night when I am not sleeping, which occurs but too frequently: but he has not troubled his head much about me; for if he had, I should not have been reduced, as I now am, to his shame, to beg my bread."

Francis took from his pocket another piece of money, and gave it to the old man, saying: "Take this to procure half a pint of wine, and drink it ere you retire to rest. Your conversation has dispelled my sorrowful thoughts; do not fail to come regularly to this bridge, where I hope we shall meet again."

The old lame man, not having for a long while made so good a day's work, overwhelmed Francis with his grateful benedictions. They separated, and each went their way. Francis, whose joy was at its height from the near prospect of his hopes being realised, very speedily reached his lodging in the bye street.

The following day he ran to the purchaser of the little garden, and proposed to re-purchase it. The latter, to whom this property was of no particular value, and indeed who began to be tired of it, willingly consented to part with it. They very soon agreed as to the conditions of the purchase, and went immediately to sign the contract: with the money he had found in his bag, as a gift from the lord of Rummelsbourg, Francis paid down half the price: he then procured the necessary tools for digging a hole in the earth, conveyed them to the garden, waited till the moon was up, strictly adhered to the instructions given him by the old beggar, set to work, and without any unlucky adventure he obtained the hidden treasure.

His father, as a precaution against necessity, had buried this money, without any intention to deprive his son of this considerable portion of his inheritance; but dying suddenly, he had carried the secret to his grave, and nothing but a happy combination of circumstances could have restored this lost treasure to its rightful owner.

The chest filled with gold pieces was too heavy for Francis to remove to his lodging without employing some person to assist him: and feeling unwilling to become a topic of general conversation, he preferred concealing it in the summer-house belonging to the garden, and fetching it at several times. On the third day the whole was safely conveyed to his lodging in the little back street.

Francis dressed himself in the best possible style, and went to the church to request that the priest would substitute for the prayers which had been previously offered up, a thanksgiving for the safe return of a traveller to his native country, after having happily terminated his business. He concealed himself in a corner, where, unseen, he could observe Meta. The sight of her gave him inexpressible delight, especially when he saw the beautiful blush which overspread her cheeks, and the brilliancy of her eyes, when the priest offered up the thanksgiving. A secret meeting took place as had been formerly arranged; and so much was Meta affected by it, that any indifferent person might have divined the cause.

Francis repaired to the Exchange, set up again in business, and in a very short time had enough to do; his fortune each succeeding day becoming better known, his neighbours judged that he had had greater luck than sense in his journey to collect his father's debts. He hired a large house in the best part of the town, engaged clerks, and continued his business with laudable and indefatigable assiduity; he conducted himself with the utmost propriety and sagacity, and abstained from the foolish extravagancies which had formerly been his ruin.

The re-establishment of Francis's fortune formed the general topic of conversation. Everyone was astonished at the success of his foreign voyage: but in proportion to the spreading fame of his riches, did Meta's tranquillity and happiness diminish; for it appeared that her silent lover was now in a condition to declare himself openly, and yet he remained dumb, and only manifested his love by the usual rencontre on coming out of church; and even this species of rendezvous became less frequent, which appeared to evince a diminution of his affection.

Poor Meta's heart was now torn by jealousy; for she imagined that the inconstant Francis was offering up his vows to some other beauty. She had experienced secret transports of delight on learning the change of fortune of the man she loved, not from interested motives and the wish to participate in his bettered fortune herself, but from affection to her mother, who, since the failure of the match with the rich brewer, absolutely seemed to despair of ever enjoying happiness or comfort in this world. When she thought Francis faithless, she wished that the prayers put up for him in the church had not been heard, and that his journey had not been attended with such entire success; for had he been reduced to means merely sufficient to procure the necessaries of life, in all probability he would have shared them with her.

Mother Bridget failed not to perceive her daughter's uneasiness, and easily guessed the cause; for she had heard of her old neighbour's surprising return, and she knew he was now considered an industrious intelligent merchant; therefore she thought if his love for her daughter was what it ought to be, he would not be thus tardy in declaring it; for she well knew Meta's sentiments towards him. However, feeling anxious to avoid the probability of wounding her daughter's feelings, she avoided mentioning the subject to her: but the latter, no longer able to confine her grief to her own bosom, disclosed it to her mother, and confided the whole to her.

Mother Bridget did not reproach her daughter for her past conduct, but employed all her eloquence to console her, and entreated her to bear up with courage under the loss of all her hopes:

"You must resign him," said she: "you scorned at the happiness which presented itself to your acceptance, therefore you must now endeavour to be resigned at its departure. Experience has taught me that those hopes which appear the best founded are frequently the most delusive; follow my example, and never again deliver up your heart. Do not reckon on any amelioration of your condition, and you will be contented with your lot. Honour this spinning-wheel which produces the means of your subsistence, and then fortune and riches will be immaterial to you: you may do without them."

Thus saying, mother Bridget turned her wheel round with redoubled velocity, in order to make up for the time lost in conversation. She spoke nothing but the truth to her daughter: for since the opportunity was gone by when she hoped it was possible to have regained her lost comforts, she had in such a manner simplified her present wants and projects of future life, that it was not in the power of destiny to produce any considerable derangement in them. But as yet Meta was not so great a philosopher; so that her mother's exhortations, consolations, and doctrines, produced a precisely different effect on her from what they were intended. Meta looked on herself as the destroyer of the flattering hopes her mother had entertained. Although she did not formerly accept the offer of marriage proposed to her, and even then could not have reckoned on possessing beyond the common necessaries of life; yet, since she had heard the tidings of the great fortune obtained by the man of her heart, her views had become enlarged, and she anticipated with pleasure that by her choice she might realize her mother's wishes.

Now, however, this golden dream had vanished: Francis would not come again; and indeed they even began to talk in the city of an alliance about to take place between him and a very rich young lady of Anvers. This news was a death-blow to poor Meta:

she vowed she would banish him from her thoughts; but still moistened her work with her tears.

Contrary, however, to her vow, she was one day thinking of the faithless one: for whenever she filled her spinning-wheel, she thought of the following distich, which her mother had frequently repeated to her to encourage her in her work:

"Spin the thread well; spin, spin it more,
For see your intended is now at the door."

Someone did in reality knock gently at the door; and mother Bridget went to see who it was. Francis entered, attired as for the celebration of a wedding. Surprise for a while suspended mother Bridget's faculties of speech. Meta, blushing deeply and trembling, arose from her seat, but was equally unable with her mother to say a word. Francis was the only one of the three who could speak; and he candidly declared his love, and demanded of Bridget the hand of her daughter. The good mother, ever attentive to forms, asked eight days to consider the matter, although the tears of joy which she shed, plainly evinced her ready and prompt acquiescence: but Francis, all impatience, would not hear of delay: finding which, she, conformable to her duty as a mother, and willing to satisfy Francis's ardour, adopted a mid-way, and left the decision to her daughter. The latter, obeying the dictates of her heart, placed herself by the side of the object of her tenderest affection; and Francis, transported with joy, thanked her by a kiss.

The two lovers then entertained themselves with talking over the delights of the time when they so well communicated their sentiments by signs. Francis had great difficulty in tearing himself away from Meta and such 'converse sweet,' but he had an important duty to fulfil.

He directed his steps towards the bridge over the Weser, where he hoped to find his old friend with the wooden leg, whom he had by no means forgotten, although he had delayed making the promised visit. The latter instantly recognised Francis; and no sooner saw him at the foot of the bridge, than he came to meet him, and shewed evident marks of pleasure at sight of him.

"Can you, my friend," said Francis to him, after returning his salutation, "come with me into the new town and execute a commission? You will be well rewarded for your trouble."

"Why not? With my wooden leg I walk about just as well as other people; and indeed have an advantage over them, for it is never fatigued. I beg you, however, my good sir, to have the kindness to wait till the man with the grey great-coat arrives."

"What has this man in the grey great-coat to do with you?"

"He every day comes as evening approaches and gives me a demi-florin; I know not from whom. It is not indeed always proper to learn all things; so I do not breathe a word. I am sometimes tempted to believe, that it is the devil who is anxious to buy my soul; but it matters little, I have not consented to the bargain, therefore it cannot be valid."

"I verily believe that grey surtout has some malice in his head; so follow me, and you shall have a quarter-florin over and above the bargain."

Francis conducted the old man to a distant corner, near the ramparts of the city, stopped before a newly built house, and knocked at the door. As soon as the door was opened, he thus addressed the old beggar: "You have procured a very agreeable evening for me in the course of my life; it is but just, therefore, that I should shed some comforts over your declining days. This house and everything appertaining thereto belongs to you. The kitchen and cellar are both well stocked; there is a person to take care of you, and every day at dinner you will find a quarter-florin under your plate. It is now time for you to know that the man in the grey surtout is my servant, whom I every day sent with my alms till this house was ready to receive you. You may, if you please, consider me as your guardian angel, since your good angel did not acquit himself uprightly in return for your gratitude."

Saying this, he made the old man go into his house; where the latter found everything he could possibly desire or want. The table was spread; and the old man was so much astonished at this unexpected good fortune, that he thought it must be a dream; for he could in no way imagine why a rich man should feel so much interest for a miserable beggar. Francis having again assured him that everything he saw was his own, a torrent of tears expressed his thanks; and before he could sufficiently recover from his astonishment to express his gratitude by words, Francis had vanished.

The following day, mother Bridget's house was filled with merchants and shopkeepers of all descriptions, whom Francis had sent to Meta, in order that she might purchase and get ready everything she required for her appearance in the world with suitable éclat. Three weeks afterwards he conducted her to the altar. The splendour of the wedding far exceeded that of the King of Hops. Mother Bridget enjoyed the satisfaction of adorning her daughter's forehead with the nuptial crown, and thereby obtained the accomplishment of all her desires, and was recompensed for her virtuous and active life. She witnessed her daughter's happiness with delight, and proved the very best of grand-mothers to her daughter's children.

If you enjoyed this, you might also like...
'The Dream', see page 278
'Roger Dodsworth', see page 466

Eerie Supernatural

Tales by Mary Shelley

On Ghosts

I look for ghosts – but none will force
Their way to me; 'tis falsely said
That there was ever intercourse
Between the living and the dead.
William Wordsworth, 'The Affliction of Margaret'

WHAT A DIFFERENT EARTH do we inhabit from that on which our forefathers dwelt! The antediluvian world, strode over by mammoths, preyed upon by the megatherion, and peopled by the offspring of the Sons of God, is a better type of the earth of Homer, Herodotus, and Plato, than the hedged-in cornfields and measured hills of the present day. The globe was then encircled by a wall which paled in the bodies of men, whilst their feathered thoughts soared over the boundary; it had a brink, and in the deep profound which it overhung, men's imaginations, eagle-winged, dived and flew, and brought home strange tales to their believing auditors. Deep caverns harboured giants; cloud-like birds cast their shadows upon the plains; while far out at sea lay islands of bliss, the fair paradise of Atlantis or El Dorado sparkling with untold jewels. Where are they now? The Fortunate Isles have lost the glory that spread a halo round them; for who deems himself nearer to the golden age, because he touches at the Canaries on his voyage to India? Our only riddle is the rise of the Niger; the interior of New Holland, our only terra incognita; and our sole mare incognitum, the north-west passage. But these are tame wonders, lions in leash; we do not invest Mungo Park, or the Captain of the Hecla, with divine attributes; no one fancies that the waters of the unknown river bubble up from hell's fountains, no strange and weird power is supposed to guide the ice-berg, nor do we fable that a stray pick-pocket from Botany Bay has found the gardens of the Hesperides within the circuit of the Blue Mountains. What have we left to dream about? The clouds are no longer the charioted servants of the sun, nor does he any more bathe his glowing brow in the bath of Thetis; the rainbow has ceased to be the messenger of the Gods, and thunder longer their awful voice, warning man of that which is to come. We have the sun which has been weighed and measured, but not understood; we have the assemblage of the planets, the congregation of the stars, and the yet unshackled ministration of the winds: – such is the list of our ignorance.

Nor is the empire of the imagination less bounded in its own proper creations, than in those which were bestowed on it by the poor blind eyes of our ancestors. What has become of enchantresses with their palaces of crystal and dungeons of palpable darkness? What of fairies and their wands? What of witches and their familiars? and, last, what of ghosts, with beckoning hands and fleeting shapes, which quelled the soldier's brave heart, and made the murderer disclose to the astonished noon the veiled work of midnight? These which were realities to our fore-fathers, in our wiser age –

> – *Characterless are grated*
> *To dusty nothing.*

Yet is it true that we do not believe in ghosts? There used to be several traditionary tales repeated, with their authorities, enough to stagger us when we consigned them to that place where that is which 'is as though it had never been.' But these are gone out of fashion. Brutus's dream has become a deception of his over-heated brain, Lord Lyttleton's vision is called a cheat; and one by one these inhabitants of deserted houses, moonlight glades, misty mountain tops, and midnight church-yards, have been ejected from their immemorial seats, and small thrill is felt when the dead majesty of Denmark blanches the cheek and unsettles the reason of his philosophic son.

But do none of us believe in ghosts? If this question be read at noon-day, when –

> *Every little corner, nook, and hole,*
> *Is penetrated with the insolent light –*

at such a time derision is seated on the features of my reader. But let it be twelve at night in a lone house; take up, I beseech you, the story of the Bleeding Nun; or of the Statue, to which the bridegroom gave the wedding ring, and she came in the dead of night to claim him, tall, and cold; or of the Grandsire, who with shadowy form and breathless lips stood over the couch and kissed the foreheads of his sleeping grandchildren, and thus doomed them to their fated death; and let all these details be assisted by solitude, flapping curtains, rushing wind, a long and dusky passage, an half open door – O, then truly, another answer may be given, and many will request leave to sleep upon it, before they decide whether there be such a thing as a ghost in the world, or out of the world, if that phraseology be more spiritual. What is the meaning of this feeling?

For my own part, I never saw a ghost except once in a dream. I feared it in my sleep; I awoke trembling, and lights and the speech of others could hardly dissipate my fear. Some years ago I lost a friend, and a few months afterwards visited the house where I had last seen him. It was deserted, and though in the midst of a city, its vast halls and spacious apartments occasioned the same sense of loneliness as if it had been situated on an uninhabited heath. I walked through the vacant chambers by twilight, and none save I awakened the echoes of their pavement. The far mountains (visible from the upper windows) had lost their tinge of sunset; the tranquil atmosphere grew leaden coloured as the golden stars appeared in the firmament; no wind ruffled the shrunk-up river which crawled lazily through the deepest channel of its wide and empty bed; the chimes of the Ave Maria had ceased, and the bell hung moveless in the open belfry: beauty invested a reposing world, and awe was inspired by beauty only. I walked through the rooms filled with sensations of the most poignant grief. He had been there; his living frame had been caged by those walls, his breath had mingled with that atmosphere, his step had been on those stones, I thought: – the earth is a tomb, the gaudy sky a vault, we but walking corpses. The wind rising in the east rushed through the open casements, making them shake; – methought, I heard, I felt – I know not what – but I trembled. To have seen him but for a moment, I would have knelt until the stones had been worn by the impress, so I told myself, and so I knew a moment after, but then I trembled, awe-struck and fearful. Wherefore? There is something beyond us of which we are ignorant. The sun drawing up the vaporous air makes a void, and the wind rushes in to fill it, – thus beyond our soul's ken there is an empty space; and our hopes and fears, in gentle gales or terrific whirlwinds, occupy the vacuum; and if it does no more, it bestows on the feeling heart a belief that influences do exist to watch and guard us, though they be impalpable to the coarser faculties.

I have heard that when Coleridge was asked if he believed in ghosts, he replied that he had seen too many to put any trust in their reality; and the person of the most lively imagination that I ever knew echoed this reply. But these were not real ghosts (pardon, unbelievers, my mode of speech) that they saw; they were shadows, phantoms unreal; that while they appalled the senses, yet carried no other feeling to the mind of others than delusion, and were viewed as we might view an optical deception which we see to be true with our eyes, and know to be false with our understandings. I speak of other shapes. The returning bride, who claims the fidelity of her betrothed; the murdered man who shakes to remorse the murderer's heart; ghosts that lift the curtains at the foot of your bed as the clock chimes one; who rise all pale and ghastly from the churchyard and haunt their ancient abodes; who, spoken to, reply; and whose cold unearthly touch makes the hair stand stark upon the head; the true old-fashioned, foretelling, flitting, gliding ghost, – who has seen such a one?

I have known two persons who at broad daylight have owned that they believed in ghosts, for that they had seen one. One of these was an Englishman, and the other an Italian. The former had lost a friend he dearly loved, who for awhile appeared to him nightly, gently stroking his cheek and spreading a serene calm over his mind. He did not fear the appearance, although he was somewhat awe-stricken as each night it glided into his chamber, and –

Ponsi del letto insula sponda manca.
[placed itself on the left side of the bed]

This visitation continued for several weeks, when by some accident he altered his residence, and then he saw it no more. Such a tale may easily be explained away; but several years had passed, and he, a man of strong and virile intellect, said that 'he had seen a ghost.'

The Italian was a noble, a soldier, and by no means addicted to superstition: he had served in Napoleon's armies from early youth, and had been to Russia, had fought and bled, and been rewarded, and he unhesitatingly, and with deep relief, recounted his story.

This Chevalier, a young, and (somewhat a miraculous incident) a gallant Italian, was engaged in a duel with a brother officer, and wounded him in the arm. The subject of the duel was frivolous; and distressed therefore at its consequences he attended on his youthful adversary during his consequent illness, so that when the latter recovered they became firm and dear friends. They were quartered together at Milan, where the youth fell desperately in love with the wife of a musician, who disdained his passion, so that it preyed on his spirits and his health; he absented himself from all amusements, avoided all his brother officers, and his only consolation was to pour his love-sick plaints into the ear of the Chevalier, who strove in vain to inspire him either with indifference towards the fair disdainer, or to inculcate lessons of fortitude and heroism. As a last resource he urged him to ask leave of absence; and to seek, either in change of scene, or the amusement of hunting, some diversion to his passion. One evening the youth came to the Chevalier, and said, "Well, I have asked leave of absence, and am to have it early tomorrow morning, so lend me your fowling-piece and cartridges, for I shall go to hunt for a fortnight." The

Chevalier gave him what he asked; among the shot there were a few bullets. "I will take these also," said the youth, "to secure myself against the attack of any wolf, for I mean to bury myself in the woods."

Although he had obtained that for which he came, the youth still lingered. He talked of the cruelty of his lady, lamented that she would not even permit him a hopeless attendance, but that she inexorably banished him from her sight, "so that," said he, "I have no hope but in oblivion." At length lie rose to depart. He took the Chevalier's hand and said, "You will see her tomorrow, you will speak to her, and hear her speak; tell her, I entreat you, that our conversation tonight has been concerning her, and that her name was the last that I spoke." "Yes, yes," cried the Chevalier, "I will say anything you please; but you must not talk of her any more, you must forget her." The youth embraced his friend with warmth, but the latter saw nothing more in it than the effects of his affection, combined with his melancholy at absenting himself from his mistress, whose name, joined to a tender farewell, was the last sound that he uttered.

When the Chevalier was on guard that night, he heard the report of a gun. He was at first troubled and agitated by it, but afterwards thought no more of it, and when relieved from guard went to bed, although he passed a restless, sleepless night. Early in the morning someone knocked at his door. It was a soldier, who said that he had got the young officer's leave of absence, and had taken it to his house; a servant had admitted him, and he had gone up stairs, but the room door of the officer was locked, and no one answered to his knocking, but something oozed through from under the door that looked like blood. The Chevalier, agitated and frightened at this account, hurried to his friend's house, burst open the door, and found him stretched on the ground – he had blown out his brains, and the body lay a headless trunk, cold, and stiff.

The shock and grief which the Chevalier experienced in consequence of this catastrophe produced a fever which lasted for some days. When he got well, he obtained leave of absence, and went into the country to try to divert his mind. One evening at moonlight, he was returning home from a walk, and passed through a lane with a hedge on both sides, so high that he could not see over them. The night was balmy; the bushes gleamed with fireflies, brighter than the stars which the moon had veiled with her silver light. Suddenly he heard a rustling near him, and the figure of his friend issued from the hedge and stood before him, mutilated as he had seen him after his death. This figure he saw several times, always in the same place. It was impalpable to the touch, motionless, except in its advance, and made no sign when it was addressed. Once the Chevalier took a friend with him to the spot. The same rustling was heard, the same shadow slept forth, his companion fled in horror, but the Chevalier staid, vainly endeavouring to discover what called his friend from his quiet tomb, and if any act of his might give repose to the restless shade.

Such are my two stories, and I record them the more willingly, since they occurred to men, and to individuals distinguished the one for courage and the other for sagacity. I will conclude my 'modern instances,' with a story told by M.G. Lewis, not probably so authentic as these, but perhaps more amusing. I relate it as nearly as possible in his own words.

"A gentleman journeying towards the house of a friend, who lived on the skirts of an extensive forest, in the east of Germany, lost his way. He wandered for some time among the trees, when he saw a light at a distance. On approaching it he was surprised to observe that it proceeded from the interior of a ruined monastery. Before he knocked at the gate he thought it proper to look through the window. He saw a number of cats assembled round a small grave, four of whom were at that moment letting down a coffin with a crown upon it. The gentleman startled at this unusual sight, and, imagining that he had arrived at the retreats of fiends or witches, mounted his horse and rode away with the utmost precipitation. He arrived at his friend's house at a late hour, who sate up waiting for him. On his arrival his friend questioned him as to the cause of the traces of agitation visible in his face. He began to recount his adventures after much hesitation, knowing that it was scarcely possible that his friend should give faith to his relation. No sooner had he mentioned the coffin with the crown upon it, than his friend's cat, who seemed to have been lying asleep before the fire, leaped up, crying out, "Then I am king of the cats;" and then scrambled up the chimney, and was never seen more."

If you enjoyed this, you might also like...
'The Family Portraits' by Johann August Apel, see page 173
'The Spectre-Barber' by Johann Karl August Musäus, see page 217

Transformation

Forthwith this frame of mine was wrench'd
With a woful agony,
Which forced me to begin my tale,
And then it set me free.

Since then, at an uncertain hour,
That agony returns;
And till my ghastly tale is told
This heart within me burns.
Samuel Coleridge, 'The Rime of the Ancient Mariner'

I HAVE HEARD IT SAID, that, when any strange, supernatural, and necromantic adventure has occurred to a human being, that being, however desirous he may be to conceal the same, feels at certain periods torn up as it were by an intellectual earthquake, and is forced to bare the inner depths of his spirit to another. I am a witness of the truth of this. I have dearly sworn to myself never to reveal to human ears the horrors to which I once, in excess of fiendly pride, delivered myself over. The holy man who heard my confession, and reconciled me to the church, is dead. None knows that once –

Why should it not be thus? Why tell a tale of impious tempting of Providence, and soul-subduing humiliation? Why? answer me, ye who are wise in the secrets of human nature! I only know that so it is; and in spite of strong resolve – of a pride that too much masters me – of shame, and even of fear, so to render myself odious to my species – I must speak.

Genoa! My birth-place-proud city! looking upon the blue waves of the Mediterranean Sea – dost thou remember me in my boyhood, when thy cliffs and promontories, thy bright sky and gay vineyards, were my world? Happy time! when to the young heart the narrow-bounded universe, which leaves, by its very limitation, free scope to the imagination, enchains our physical energies, and, sole period in our lives, innocence and enjoyment are united. Yet, who can look back to childhood, and not remember its sorrows and its harrowing fears? I was born with the most imperious, haughty, tameless spirit, with which ever mortal was gifted. I quailed before my father only; and he, generous and noble, but capricious and tyrannical, at once fostered and checked the wild impetuosity of my character, making obedience necessary, but inspiring no respect for the motives which guided his commands. To be a man, free, independent; or, in better words, insolent and domineering, was the hope and prayer of my rebel heart.

My father had one friend, a wealthy Genoese noble, who in a political tumult was suddenly sentenced to banishment, and his property confiscated. The Marchese Torella went into exile alone. Like my father, he was a widower: he had one child, the almost infant Juliet, who was left under my father's guardianship. I should certainly have been an unkind master to the lovely girl, but that I was forced by my position to become her protector. A variety of childish incidents all tended to one point – to make Juliet see in me a rock of refuge; I in her, one, who must perish through the soft sensibility of her nature too rudely visited, but for my guardian care. We grew up together. The opening rose in May was not more sweet than this dear girl. An irradiation of beauty was spread over her face. Her form, her step, her voice – my heart weeps even now, to think of all of relying, gentle, loving, and pure, that was enshrined in that celestial tenement. When I was eleven and Juliet eight years of age, a cousin of mine, much older than either – he seemed to us a man – took great notice of my playmate; he called her his bride, and asked her to marry him. She refused, and he insisted, drawing her unwillingly towards him. With the countenance and emotions of a maniac I threw myself on him – I strove to draw his sword – I clung to his neck with the ferocious resolve to strangle him: he was obliged to call for assistance to disengage himself from me. On that night I led Juliet to the chapel of our house: I made her touch the sacred relics – I harrowed her child's heart, and profaned her child's lips with an oath, that she would be mine, and mine only.

Well, those days passed away. Torella returned in a few years, and became wealthier and more prosperous than ever. When I was seventeen my father died; he had been magnificent to prodigality; Torella rejoiced that my minority would afford an opportunity for repairing my fortunes. Juliet and I had been affianced beside my father's deathbed – Torella was to be a second parent to me.

I desired to see the world, and I was indulged. I went to Florence, to Rome, to Naples; thence I passed to Toulon, and at length reached what had long been the bourne of my wishes, Paris. There was wild work in Paris then. The poor king, Charles the Sixth, now sane, now mad, now a monarch, now an abject slave, was the very mockery of humanity. The queen, the dauphin, the Duke of Burgundy, alternately friends and foes now meeting in prodigal feasts, now shedding blood in rivalry-were blind to the miserable state of their country, and the dangers that impended over it, and gave themselves wholly up to dissolute enjoyment or savage strife. My character still followed me. I was arrogant and selfwilled; I loved display, and above all, I threw all control far from me. Who could control me in Paris? My young friends were eager to foster passions which furnished them with pleasures. I was deemed handsome – I was master of every knightly accomplishment. I was disconnected with any political party. I grew a favourite with all: my presumption and arrogance were pardoned in one so young: I became a spoiled child. Who could control me? not the letters and advice of Torella – only strong necessity visiting me in the abhorred shape of an empty purse. But there were means to refill this void. Acre after acre, estate after estate, I sold. My dress, my jewels, my horses and their caparisons, were almost unrivalled in gorgeous Paris, while the lands of my inheritance passed into possession of others.

The Duke of Orleans was waylaid and murdered by the Duke of Burgundy. Fear and terror possessed all Paris. The dauphin and the queen shut themselves up; every pleasure was suspended. I grew weary of this state of things, and my heart yearned for my boyhood's haunts. I was nearly a beggar, yet still I would go there, claim my bride, and rebuild my fortunes. A few happy ventures as a merchant would make me rich again. Nevertheless, I would not return in humble guise. My last act was to dispose of my remaining estate near Albaro for half its worth, for ready money. Then I despatched all kinds of artificers, arras, furniture of regal splendour, to fit up the last relic of my inheritance, my palace in Genoa. I lingered a little longer yet, ashamed at the part of the prodigal returned, which I feared I should play. I sent my horses. One matchless Spanish jennet I despatched to my promised bride; its caparisons flamed with jewels and cloth of gold. In every part I caused to be entwined the initials of Juliet and her Guido. My present found favour in hers and in her father's eyes.

Still to return a proclaimed spendthrift, the mark of impertinent wonder, perhaps of scorn, and to encounter singly the reproaches or taunts of my fellow-citizens, was no alluring prospect. As a shield between me and censure, I invited some few of the most reckless of my comrades to accompany me: thus I went armed against the world, hiding a rankling feeling, half fear and half penitence, by bravado and an insolent display of satisfied vanity.

I arrived in Genoa. I trod the pavement of my ancestral palace. My proud step was no interpreter of my heart, for I deeply felt that, though surrounded by every luxury, I was a beggar. The first step I took in claiming Juliet must widely declare me such. I read contempt or pity in the looks of all. I fancied, so apt is conscience to imagine what it deserves, that rich and poor, young and old, all regarded me with derision. Torella came not near me. No wonder that my second father should expect a son's deference from me in waiting first on him. But, galled and stung by a sense of my follies and demerit, I strove to throw the blame on others. We kept nightly orgies in Palazzo Carega. To sleepless, riotous nights, followed listless, supine mornings. At the Ave Maria we showed our dainty persons in the streets, scoffing at the sober citizens, casting insolent glances on the shrinking women. Juliet was not among them – no, no; if she had been there, shame would have driven me away, if love had not brought me to her feet.

I grew tired of this. Suddenly I paid the Marchese a visit. He was at his villa, one among the many which deck the suburb of San Pietro d'Arena. It was the month of May – a month of May in that garden of the world the blossoms of the fruit trees were fading among thick, green foliage; the vines were shooting forth; the ground strewed with the fallen olive blooms; the fire-fly was in the myrtle hedge; heaven and earth wore a mantle of surpassing beauty. Torella welcomed me kindly, though seriously; and even his shade of displeasure soon wore away. Some resemblance to my father–some look and tone of youthful ingenuousness, lurking still in spite of my misdeeds, softened the good old man's heart. He sent for his daughter – he presented me to her as her betrothed. The chamber became hallowed by a holy light as she entered. Hers was that cherub look, those large, soft eyes, full dimpled cheeks, and mouth of infantine sweetness, that expresses the rare union of happiness and love. Admiration first possessed me; she is mine! was the second proud emotion, and my lips curled with haughty triumph. I had not been the enfant gâté of the beauties of France not to have learnt the art of pleasing the soft heart of woman. If towards men I was overbearing, the deference I paid to them was the more in contrast. I commenced my courtship by the display of a thousand gallantries to Juliet, who, vowed to me from infancy, had never admitted the devotion of others; and who, though accustomed to expressions of admiration, was uninitiated in the language of lovers.

For a few days all went well. Torella never alluded to my extravagance; he treated me as a favourite son. But the time came, as we discussed the preliminaries to my union with his daughter, when this fair face of things should be overcast. A contract had been drawn up in my father's lifetime. I had rendered this, in fact, void, by having squandered the whole of the wealth which was to have been shared by Juliet and myself. Torella, in consequence, chose to consider this bond as cancelled, and proposed another, in which, though the wealth he bestowed was immeasurably increased, there were so many restrictions as to the mode of spending it, that I, who saw independence only in free career being given to my own imperious will, taunted him as taking advantage of my situation, and refused utterly to subscribe to his conditions. The old man mildly strove to recall me to reason. Roused pride became the tyrant of my thought: I listened with indignation – I repelled him with disdain.

"Juliet, thou art mine! Did we not interchange vows in our innocent childhood? are we not one in the sight of God? and shall thy cold-hearted, cold-blooded father divide us? Be generous, my love, be just; take not away a gift, last treasure of thy Guido – retract not thy vows – let us defy the world, and setting at nought the calculations of age, find in our mutual affection a refuge from every ill."

Fiend I must have been, with such sophistry to endeavour to poison that sanctuary of holy thought and tender love. Juliet shrank from me affrighted. Her father was the best and kindest of men, and she strove to show me how, in obeying him, every good would follow. He would receive my tardy submission with warm affection; and generous pardon would follow my repentance. Profitless words for a young and gentle daughter to use to a man accustomed to make his will, law; and to feel in his own heart a despot so terrible and stern, that he could yield obedience to nought save his own imperious desires! My resentment grew with resistance; my wild companions were ready to add fuel to the flame. We laid a plan to carry off Juliet. At first it appeared to be crowned with success. Midway, on our return, we were overtaken by the agonized father and his attendants. A conflict ensued. Before the city guard came to decide the victory in favour of our antagonists, two of Torella's servitors were dangerously wounded.

This portion of my history weighs most heavily with me. Changed man as I am, I abhor myself in the recollection. May none who hear this tale ever have felt as I. A horse driven to fury by a rider armed with barbed spurs, was not more a slave than I, to the violent tyranny of my temper. A fiend possessed my soul, irritating it to madness. I felt the voice of conscience within me; but if I yielded to it for a brief interval, it was only to be a moment after torn, as by a whirlwind, away – borne along on the stream of desperate rage – the plaything of the storms engendered by pride. I was imprisoned, and, at the instance of Torella, set free. Again I returned to carry off both him and his child to France; which hapless country, then preyed on by freebooters and gangs of lawless soldiery, offered a grateful refuge to a criminal like me. Our plots were discovered. I was sentenced to banishment; and, as my debts were already enormous, my remaining property was put in the hands of commissioners for their payment. Torella again offered his mediation, requiring only my promise not to renew my abortive attempts on himself and his daughter. I spurned his offers, and fancied that I triumphed when I was thrust out from Genoa, a solitary and penniless exile. My companions were gone: they had been dismissed the city some weeks before, and were already in France. I was alone – friendless; with nor sword at my side, nor ducat in my purse.

I wandered along the sea-shore, a whirlwind of passion possessing and tearing my soul. It was as if a live coal had been set burning in my breast. At first I meditated on what I should do. I would join a band of freebooters. Revenge! – the word seemed balm to me – I hugged it – caressed it – till, like a serpent, it stung me. Then again I would abjure and despise Genoa, that little corner of the world. I would return to Paris, where so many of my friends swarmed; where my services would be eagerly accepted; where I would carve out fortune with my sword, and might, through success, make my paltry birth-place, and the false Torella, rue the day when they drove me, a new Coriolanus, from her walls. I would return to Paris – thus on foot – a beggar – and present myself in my poverty to those I had formerly entertained sumptuously? There was gall in the mere thought of it.

The reality of things began to dawn upon my mind, bringing despair in its train. For several months I had been a prisoner: the evils of my dungeon had whipped my soul to madness, but they had subdued my corporeal frame. I was weak and wan. Torella. had used a thousand artifices to administer to my comfort; I had detected and scorned them all-and I reaped the harvest of my obduracy. What was to be done? Should I crouch before my foe, and sue for forgiveness? – Die rather ten thousand deaths! – Never should they obtain that victory! Hate – I swore eternal hate! Hate from whom? – to whom? – From a wandering outcast to a mighty noble. I and my feelings were nothing to them: already had they forgotten one so unworthy. And Juliet! – her angel-face and sylphlike form gleamed among the clouds of my despair with vain beauty; for I had lost her – the glory and flower of the world! Another will call her his! – that smile of paradise will bless another!

Even now my heart fails within me when I recur to this rout of grim-visaged ideas. Now subdued almost to tears, now raving in my agony, still I wandered along the rocky shore, which grew at each step wilder and more desolate. Hanging rocks and hoar precipices overlooked the tideless ocean; black caverns yawned; and forever, among the seaworn recesses, murmured and dashed the unfruitful waters. Now my way was almost barred by an abrupt promontory, now rendered nearly impracticable by fragments fallen from the cliff. Evening was at hand, when, seaward, arose, as if on the waving of a wizard's wand, a murky web of clouds, blotting the late azure sky, and darkening and disturbing the till now placid deep. The clouds had strange fantastic shapes; and they changed, and mingled, and seemed to be driven about by a mighty spell. The waves raised their white crests; the thunder first muttered, then roared from across the waste of waters, which took a deep purple dye, flecked with foam. The spot where I stood, looked, on one side, to the wide-spread ocean; on the other, it was barred by a rugged promontory.

Round this cape suddenly came, driven by the wind, a vessel. In vain the mariners tried to force a path for her to the open sea – the gale drove her on the rocks. It will perish! – all on board will perish! – Would I were among them! And to my young heart the idea of death came for the first time blended with that of joy. It was an awful sight to behold that vessel struggling with her fate. Hardly could I discern the sailors, but I heard them. It was soon all over! – A rock, just covered by the tossing waves, and so unperceived, lay in wait for its prey. A crash of thunder broke over my head at the moment that, with a frightful shock, the skiff dashed upon her unseen enemy. In a brief space of time she went to pieces There I stood in safety; and there were my fellow-creatures, battling, how hopelessly, with annihilation. Methought I saw them struggling – too truly did I hear their shrieks, conquering the barking surges in their shrill agony. The dark breakers threw hither and thither the fragments of the wreck: soon it disappeared. I had been fascinated to gaze till the end: at last I sank on my knees – I covered my face with my hands: I again looked up; something was floating on the billows towards the shore. It neared and neared. Was that a human form? – It grew more distinct; and at last a mighty wave, lifting the whole freight, lodged it upon a rock. A human being bestriding a sea-chest! – A human being! – Yet was it one? Surely never such had existed before-a misshapen dwarf, with squinting eyes, distorted features, and body deformed, till it became a horror to behold. My blood, lately warming towards a fellow-being so snatched from a watery tomb, froze in my heart. The dwarf got off his chest; he tossed his straight, straggling hair from his odious visage:

"By St. Beelzebub!" he exclaimed, "I have been well bested." He looked round and saw me. "Oh, by the fiend! Here is another ally of the mighty one. To what saint did you offer prayers, friend – if not to mine? Yet I remember you not on board."

I shrank from the monster and his blasphemy. Again he questioned me, and I muttered some inaudible reply. He continued:

"Your voice is drowned by this dissonant roar. What a noise the big ocean makes! Schoolboys bursting from their prison are not louder than these waves set free to play. They disturb me. I will no more of their illtimed brawling. – Silence, hoary One! – Winds, avaunt! – to your homes! Clouds, fly to the antipodes, and leave our heaven clear!"

As he spoke, he stretched out his two long lank arms, that looked like spider's claws, and seemed to embrace with them the expanse before him. Was it a miracle? The clouds became broken, and fled; the azure sky first peeped out, and then was spread a calm field of blue above us; the stormy gale was exchanged to the softly breathing west; the sea grew calm; the waves dwindled to riplets.

"I like obedience even in these stupid elements," said the dwarf. "How much more in the tameless mind of man! It was a well got up storm, you must allow – and all of my own making."

It was tempting Providence to interchange talk with this magician. But Power, in all its shapes, is venerable to man. Awe, curiosity, a clinging fascination, drew me towards him.

"Come, don't be frightened, friend," said the wretch: "I am good humoured when pleased; and something does please me in your well proportioned body and handsome face, though you look a little woebegone. You have suffered a land – I, a sea wreck. Perhaps I can allay the tempest of your fortunes as I did my own. Shall we be friends?" – And he held out his hand; I could not touch it. "Well, then, companions – that will do as well. And now, while I rest after the buffeting I underwent just now, tell me why, young and gallant as you seem, you wander thus alone and downcast on this wild sea-shore."

The voice of the wretch was screeching and horrid, and his contortions as he spoke were frightful to behold. Yet he did gain a kind of influence over me, which I could not master, and I told him my tale. When it was ended, he laughed long and loud: the rocks echoed back the sound: hell seemed yelling around me.

"Oh, thou cousin of Lucifer!" said he; "So thou too hast fallen through thy pride; and, though bright as the son of Morning, thou art ready to give up thy good looks, thy bride, and thy well-being, rather than submit thee to the tyranny of good. I honour thy choice, by my soul! – So thou hast fled, and yield the day; and mean to starve on these rocks, and to let the birds peck out thy dead eyes, while thy enemy and thy betrothed rejoice in thy ruin. Thy pride is strangely akin to humility, methinks."

As he spoke, a thousand fanged thoughts stung me to the heart.

"What would you that I should do?" I cried.

"I! – Oh, nothing, but lie down and say your prayers before you die. But, were I you, I know the deed that should be done."

I drew near him. His supernatural powers made him an oracle in my eyes; yet a strange unearthly thrill quivered through my frame as I said, "Speak! – Teach me – what act do you advise?"

"Revenge thyself, man! – humble thy enemies! – set thy foot on the old man's neck, and possess thyself of his daughter!"

"To the east and west I turn," cried I, "and see no means! Had I gold, much could I achieve; but, poor and single, I am powerless."

The dwarf had been seated on his chest as he listened to my story. Now he got off; he touched a spring; it flew open! – What a mine of wealth – of blazing jewels, beaming gold, and pale silver-was displayed therein. A mad desire to possess this treasure was born within me.

"Doubtless," I said, "one so powerful as you could do all things."

"Nay," said the monster, humbly, "I am less omnipotent than I seem. Some things I possess which you may covet; but I would give them all for a small share, or even for a loan of what is yours."

"My possessions are at your service," I replied, bitterly – "my poverty, my exile, my disgrace – I make a free gift of them all."

"Good! I thank you. Add one other thing to your gift, and my treasure is yours."

"As nothing is my sole inheritance, what besides nothing would you have?"

"Your comely face and well-made limbs."

I shivered. Would this all-powerful monster murder me? I had no dagger. I forgot to pray – but I grew pale.

"I ask for a loan, not a gift," said the frightful thing: "lend me your body for three days – you shall have mine to cage your soul the while, and, in payment, my chest. What say you to the bargain? – Three short days."

We are told that it is dangerous to hold unlawful talk; and well do I prove the same. Tamely written down, it may seem incredible that I should lend any ear to this proposition; but, in spite of his unnatural ugliness, there was something fascinating in a being whose voice could govern earth, air, and sea. I felt a keen desire to comply; for with that chest I could command the world. My only hesitation resulted from a fear that he would not be true to his bargain. Then, I thought, I shall soon die here on these lonely sands, and the limbs he covets will be mine no more: – it is worth the chance. And, besides, I knew that, by all the rules of art-magic, there were formula and oaths which none of its practisers dared break. I hesitated to reply; and he went on, now displaying his wealth, now speaking of the petty price he demanded, till it seemed madness to refuse. Thus is it: place our bark in the current of the stream, and down, over fall and cataract it is hurried; give up our conduct to the wild torrent of passion, and we are away, we know not whither.

He swore many an oath, and I adjured him by many a sacred name; till I saw this wonder of power, this ruler of the elements, shiver like an autumn leaf before my words; and as if the spirit spake unwillingly and per force within him, at last, lie, with broken voice, revealed the spell whereby he might be obliged, did he wish to play me false, to render up the unlawful spoil. Our warm life blood must mingle to make and to mar the charm.

Enough of this unholy theme. I was persuaded – the thing was done. The morrow dawned upon me as I lay upon the shingles, and I knew not my own shadow as it fell from me. I felt myself changed to a shape of horror, and cursed my easy faith and blind credulity. The chest was there – there the gold and precious stones for which I had sold the frame of flesh which nature had given me. The sight a little stilled my emotions: three days would soon be gone.

They did pass. The dwarf had supplied me with a plenteous store of food. At first I could hardly walk, so strange and out of joint were all my limbs; and my voice – it was that of the fiend. But I kept silent, and turned my face to the sun, that I might not see my shadow, and counted the hours, and ruminated on my future conduct. To bring Torella to my feet – to possess my Juliet in spite of him – all this my wealth could easily achieve.

During dark night I slept, and dreamt of the accomplishment of my desires. Two suns had set-the third dawned. I was agitated, fearful. Oh expectation, what a frightful thing art thou, when kindled more by fear than hope! How dost thou twist thyself round the heart, torturing its pulsations! How dost thou dart unknown pangs all through our feeble mechanism, now seeming to shiver us like broken glass, to nothingness now giving us a fresh strength, which can do nothing, and so torments us by a sensation, such as the strong man must feel who cannot break his fetters, though they bend in his grasp. Slowly paced the bright, bright orb up the eastern sky; long it lingered in the zenith, and still more slowly wandered down the west: it touched the horizon's verge – it was lost! Its glories were on the summits of the cliff – they grew dun and grey. The evening star shone bright. He will soon be here.

He came not! – By the living heavens, he came not! – And night dragged out its weary length, and, in its decaying age, 'day began to grizzle its dark hair;' and the sun rose again on the most miserable wretch that ever upbraided its light. Three days thus I passed. The jewels and the gold – oh, how I abhorred them!

Well, well – I will not blacken these pages with demoniac ravings. All too terrible were the thoughts, the raging tumult of ideas that filled my soul. At the end of that time I slept; I had not before since the third sunset; and I dreamt that I was at Juliet's feet, and she smiled, and then she shrieked – for she saw my transformation – and again she smiled, for still her beautiful lover knelt before her. But it was not I – it was he, the fiend, arrayed in my limbs, speaking with my voice, winning her with my looks of love. I strove to warn her, but my tongue refused its office; I strove to tear him from her, but I was rooted to the ground – I awoke with the agony. There were the solitary hoar precipices – there the plashing sea, the quiet strand, and the blue sky over all. What did it mean? was my dream but a mirror of the truth? was he wooing and winning my betrothed? I would on the instant back to Genoa – but I was banished. I laughed – the dwarf's yell burst from my lips – I banished! O, no! they had not exiled the foul limbs I wore; I might with these enter, without fear of incurring the threatened penalty of death, my own, my native city.

I began to walk towards Genoa. I was somewhat accustomed to my distorted limbs; none were ever so ill adapted for a straight-forward movement; it was with infinite difficulty that I proceeded. Then, too, I desired to avoid all the hamlets strewed here and there on the sea-beach, for I was unwilling to make a display of my hideousness. I was not quite sure that, if seen, the mere boys would not stone me to death as I passed, for a monster: some ungentle salutations I did receive from the few peasants or fishermen I chanced to meet. But it was dark night before I approached Genoa. The weather was so balmy and sweet that it struck me that the Marchese and his daughter would very probably have quitted the city for their country retreat. It was from Villa Torella that I had attempted to carry off Juliet; I had spent many an hour reconnoitering the spot, and knew each inch of ground in its vicinity. It was beautifully situated, embosomed in trees, on the margin of a stream. As I drew near, it became evident that my conjecture was right; nay, moreover, that the hours were being then devoted to feasting and merriment. For the house was lighted up; strains of soft and gay music were wafted towards me by the breeze. My heart sank within me. Such was the generous kindness of Torella's heart that I felt sure that he would not have indulged in public manifestations of rejoicing just after my unfortunate banishment, but for a cause I dared not dwell upon.

The country people were all alive and flocking about; it became necessary that I should study to conceal myself; and yet I longed to address some one, or to hear others discourse, or in any way to gain intelligence of what was really going on. At length, entering the walks that were in immediate vicinity to the mansion, I found one dark enough to veil my excessive frightfulness; and yet others as well as I were loitering in its shade. I soon gathered all I wanted to know – all that first made my very heart die with horror, and then boil with indignation. Tomorrow Juliet was to be given to the penitent, reformed, beloved Guido – tomorrow my bride was to pledge her vows to a fiend from hell! And I did this! – my accursed pride – my demoniac violence and wicked self-idolatry had caused this act. For if I had acted as the wretch who had stolen my form had acted– if, with a mien at once yielding and dignified, I had presented myself to Torella, saying, I have done wrong, forgive me; I am unworthy of your angel-child, but permit me to claim her hereafter, when my altered conduct shall manifest that I abjure my vices, and endeavour to become in some sort worthy of her. I go to serve against the infidels; and when my zeal for religion and my true penitence for the past shall appear to you to cancel my crimes, permit me again to call myself your son. Thus had he spoken; and the penitent was welcomed even as the prodigal son of scripture: the fatted calf was killed for him; and he, still pursuing the same path, displayed such open-hearted regret for his follies, so humble a concession of all his rights, and so ardent a resolve to reacquire them by a life of contrition and virtue, that he quickly conquered the kind, old man; and full pardon, and the gift of his lovely child, followed in swift succession.

Oh, had an angel from Paradise whispered to me to act thus! But now, what would be the innocent Juliet's fate? Would God permit the foul union – or, some prodigy destroying it, link the dishonoured name of Carega with the worst of crimes? Tomorrow at dawn they were to be married: there was but one way to prevent this – to meet mine enemy, and to enforce the ratification of our agreement. I felt that this could only be done by a mortal struggle. I had no sword – if indeed my distorted arms could wield a soldier's weapon – but I had a dagger, and in that lay my every hope. There was no time for pondering or balancing nicely the question: I might die in the attempt; but besides the burning jealousy and despair of my own heart, honour, mere humanity, demanded that I should fall rather than not destroy the machinations of the fiend.

The guests departed – the lights began to disappear; it was evident that the inhabitants of the villa were seeking repose. I hid myself among the trees – the garden grew desert – the gates were closed – I wandered round and came under a window-ah! well did I know the same! – a soft twilight glimmered in the room – the curtains were half withdrawn. It was the temple of innocence and beauty. Its magnificence was tempered, as it were, by the slight disarrangements occasioned by its being dwelt in, and all the objects scattered around displayed the taste of her who hallowed it by her presence. I saw her enter with a quick light step – I saw her approach the window – she drew back the curtain yet further, and looked out into the night. Its breezy freshness played among her ringlets, and wafted them from the transparent marble of her brow. She clasped her hands, she raised her eyes to Heaven. I heard her voice. "Guido!" she softly murmured, "Mine own Guido!" and then, as if overcome by the fullness of her own heart, she sank on her knees: – her upraised eyes – her negligent but graceful attitude – the beaming thankfulness that lighted up her face – oh, these are tame words! Heart of mine, thou imagest ever, though thou canst not portray, the celestial beauty of that child of light and love.

I heard a step – a quick firm step along the shady avenue. Soon I saw a cavalier, richly dressed, young and, methought, graceful to look on, advance. – I hid myself yet closer. – The youth approached; he paused beneath the window. She arose, and again looking out she saw him, and said – I cannot, no, at this distant time I cannot record her terms of soft silver tenderness; to me they were spoken, but they were replied to by him.

"I will not go," he cried: "here where you have been, where your memory glides like some Heaven-visiting ghost, I will pass the long hours till we meet, never, my Juliet, again, day or night, to part. But do thou, my love, retire; the cold morn and fitful breeze will make thy cheek pale, and fill with languor thy love-lighted eyes. Ah, sweetest! could I press one kiss upon them, I could, methinks, repose."

And then he approached still nearer, and methought lie was about to clamber into her chamber. I had hesitated, not to terrify her; now I was no longer master of myself. I rushed forward – I threw myself on him – I tore him away – I cried, "O loathsome and foul-shaped wretch!"

I need not repeat epithets, all tending, as it appeared, to rail at a person I at present feel some partiality for. A shriek rose from Juliet's lips. I neither heard nor saw – I felt only mine enemy, whose throat I grasped, and my dagger's hilt; he struggled, but could not escape: at length hoarsely he breathed these words: "Do! – Strike home! Destroy this body – you will still live: may your life be long and merry!"

The descending dagger was arrested at the word, and he, feeling my hold relax, extricated himself and drew his sword, while the uproar in the house, and flying of torches from one room to the other, showed that soon we should be separated – and I – oh! far better die: so that he did not survive, I cared not. In the midst of my frenzy there was much calculation: – fall I might, and so that he did not survive, I cared not for the death-blow I might deal against myself. While still, therefore, he thought I paused, and while I saw the villanous resolve to take advantage of my hesitation, in the sudden thrust he made at me, I threw myself on his sword, and at the same moment plunged my dagger, with a true desperate aim, in his side. We fell together, rolling over each other, and the tide of blood that flowed from the gaping wound of each mingled on the grass. More I know not – I fainted.

Again I returned to life: weak almost to death, I found myself stretched upon a bed – Juliet was kneeling beside it. Strange! My first broken request was for a mirror. I was so wan and ghastly, that my poor girl hesitated, as she told me afterwards; but, by the mass! I thought myself a right proper youth when I saw the dear reflection of my own well-known features. I confess it is a weakness, but I avow it, I do entertain a considerable affection for the countenance and limbs I behold, whenever I look at a glass; and have more mirrors in my house, and consult them oftener than any beauty in Venice. Before you too much condemn me, permit me to say that no one better knows than I the value of his own body; no one, probably, except myself, ever having had it stolen from him.

Incoherently I at first talked of the dwarf and his crimes, and reproached Juliet for her too easy admission of his love. She thought me raving, as well she might, and yet it was some time before I could prevail on myself to admit that the Guido whose penitence had won her back for me was myself; and while I cursed bitterly the monstrous dwarf, and blest the well-directed blow that had deprived him of life, I suddenly checked myself when I heard her say – "Amen!" – knowing that him whom she reviled was my very self. A little reflection taught me silence-a little practice enabled me to speak of that frightful night without any very excessive blunder. The wound I had given myself was no mockery of one – it was long before I recovered – and as the benevolent and generous Torella sat beside me, talking such wisdom as might win friends to repentance, and mine own dear Juliet hovered near me, administering to my wants, and cheering me by her smiles, the work of my bodily cure and mental reform went on together. I have never, indeed, wholly recovered my strength my cheek is paler since – my person a little bent. Juliet sometimes ventures to allude bitterly to the malice that caused this change, but I kiss her on the moment, and tell her all is for the best. I am a fonder and more faithful husband – and true is this – but for that wound, never had I called her mine.

I did not revisit the sea-shore, nor seek for the fiend's treasure; yet, while I ponder on the past, I often think, and my confessor was not backward in favouring the idea, that it might be a good rather than an evil spirit, sent by my guardian angel, to show me the folly and misery of pride. So well at least did I learn this lesson, roughly taught as I was, that I am known now by all my friends and fellow-citizens by the name of Guido il Cortese.

If you enjoyed this, you might also like...
'The Dream', see page 278
'The Mortal Immortal', see page 254

The Mortal Immortal

July 16, 1833

THIS IS A MEMORABLE ANNIVERSARY for me; on it I complete my three hundred and twenty-third year!

The Wandering Jew? – certainly not. More than eighteen centuries have passed over his head. In comparison with him, I am a very young Immortal.

Am I, then, immortal? This is a question which I have asked myself, by day and night, for now three hundred and three years, and yet cannot answer it. I detected a grey hair amidst my brown locks this very day – that surely signifies decay. Yet it may have remained concealed there for three hundred years – for some persons have become entirely white headed before twenty years of age.

I will tell my story, and my reader shall judge for me. I will tell my story, and so contrive to pass some few hours of a long eternity, become so wearisome to me. Forever! Can it be? to live forever! I have heard of enchantments, in which the victims were plunged into a deep sleep, to wake, after a hundred years, as fresh as ever: I have heard of the Seven Sleepers – thus to be immortal would not be so burthensome: but, oh! the weight of never-ending time – the tedious passage of the still-succeeding hours! How happy was the fabled Nourjahad! But to my task.

All the world has heard of Cornelius Agrippa. His memory is as immortal as his arts have made me. All the world has also heard of his scholar, who, unawares, raised the foul fiend during his master's absence, and was destroyed by him. The report, true or false, of this accident, was attended with many inconveniences to the renowned philosopher. All his scholars at once deserted him – his servants disappeared. He had no one near him to put coals on his ever-burning fires while he slept, or to attend to the changeful colours of his medicines while he studied. Experiment after experiment failed, because one pair of hands was insufficient to complete them: the dark spirits laughed at him for not being able to retain a single mortal in his service.

I was then very young – very poor – and very much. in love. I had been for about a year the pupil of Cornelius, though I was absent when this accident took place. On my return, my friends implored me not to return to the alchymist's abode. I trembled as I listened to the dire tale they told; I required no second warning; and when Cornelius came and offered me a purse of gold if I would remain under his roof, I felt as if Satan himself tempted me. My teeth chattered – my hair stood on end: – I ran off as fast as my trembling knees would permit.

My failing steps were directed whither for two years they had every evening been attracted, – a gently bubbling spring of pure living waters, beside which lingered a dark-haired girl, whose beaming eyes were fixed on the path I was accustomed each night to tread. I cannot remember the hour when I did not love Bertha; we had been neighbours and playmates from infancy – her parents, like mine, were of humble life, yet respectable – our attachment had been a source of pleasure to them. In an evil hour, a malignant fever carried off both her father and mother, and Bertha became an orphan. She would have found a home beneath my paternal roof, but, unfortunately, the old lady of the near castle, rich, childless, and solitary, declared her intention to adopt her. Henceforth Bertha was clad in silk – inhabited a marble palace – and was looked on as being highly favoured by fortune. But in her new situation among her new associates, Bertha remained true to the friend of her humbler days; she often visited the cottage of my father, and when forbidden to go thither, she would stray towards the neighbouring wood, and meet me beside its shady fountain.

She often declared that she owed no duty to her new protectress equal in sanctity to that which bound us. Yet still I was too poor to marry, and she grew weary of being tormented on my account. She had a haughty but an impatient spirit, and grew angry at the obstacles that prevented our union. We met now after an absence, and she had been sorely beset while I was away; she complained bitterly, and almost reproached me for being poor. I replied hastily:

"I am honest, if I am poor! – Were I not, I might soon become rich!"

This exclamation produced a thousand questions. I feared to shock her by owning the truth, but she drew it from me; and then, casting a look of disdain on me, she said:

"You pretend to love, and you fear to face the Devil for my sake!"

I protested that I had only dreaded to offend her; – while she dwelt on the magnitude of the reward that I should receive. Thus encouraged –shamed by her – led on by love and hope, laughing at my late fears, with quick steps and a light heart, I returned to accept the offers of the alchymist, and was instantly installed in my office.

A year passed away. I became possessed of no insignificant sum of money. Custom had banished my fears. In spite of the most painful vigilance, I had never detected the trace of a cloven foot; nor was the studious silence of our abode ever disturbed by demoniac howls. I still continued my stolen interviews with Bertha, and Hope dawned on me – Hope – but not perfect joy; for Bertha fancied that love and security were enemies, and her pleasure was to divide them in my bosom. Though true of heart, she was somewhat of a coquette in manner; and I was jealous as a Turk. She slighted me in a thousand ways, yet would never acknowledge herself to be in the wrong. She would drive me mad with anger, and then force me to beg her pardon. Sometimes she fancied that I was not sufficiently submissive, and then she had some story of a rival, favoured by her protectress. She was surrounded by silk-clad youths – the rich and gay – What chance had the sad-robed scholar of Cornelius compared with these?

On one occasion, the philosopher made such large demands upon my time, that I was unable to meet her as I was wont. He was engaged in some mighty work, and I was forced to remain, day and night, feeding his furnaces and watching his chemical preparations. Bertha waited for me in vain at the fountain. Her haughty spirit fired at this neglect; and when at last I stole out during the few short minutes allotted to me for slumber, and hoped to be consoled by her, she received me with disdain, dismissed me in scorn, and vowed that any man should possess her hand rather than he who could not be in two places at once for her sake. She would be revenged! – And truly she was. In my dingy retreat I heard that she had been hunting, attended by Albert Hoffer. Albert Hoffer was favoured by her protectress, and the three passed in cavalcade before my smoky window. Methought that they mentioned my name – it was followed by a laugh of derision, as her dark eyes glanced contemptuously towards my abode.

Jealousy, with all its venom, and all its misery, entered my breast. Now I shed a torrent of tears, to think that I should never call her mine; and, anon, I imprecated a thousand curses on her inconstancy. Yet, still I must stir the fires of the alchymist, still attend on the changes of his unintelligible medicines.

Cornelius had watched for three days and nights, nor closed his eyes. The progress of his alembics was slower than he expected: in spite of his anxiety, sleep weighed upon his eyelids. Again and again he threw off drowsiness with more than human energy; again and again it stole away his senses. He eyed his crucibles wistfully. "Not ready yet," he murmured; "will another night pass before the work is accomplished? Winzy, you are vigilant – you are faithful – you have slept, my boy – you slept last night. Look at that glass vessel. The liquid it contains is of a soft rose-colour: the moment it begins to change its hue, awaken me – till then I may close my eyes. First, it will turn white, and then emit golden flashes; but wait not till then; when the rose-colour fades, rouse me." I scarcely heard the last words, muttered, as they were, in sleep. Even then he did not quite yield to nature. "Winzy, my boy," he again said, "do not touch the vessel – do not put it to your lips; it is a philter – a philter to cure love; you would not cease to love your Bertha – beware to drink!"

And he slept. His venerable head sunk on his breast, and I scarce heard his regular breathing. For a few minutes I watched the vessel – the rosy hue of the liquid remained unchanged. Then my thoughts wandered– they visited the fountain, and dwelt on a thousand charming scenes never to be renewed – never! Serpents and adders were in my heart as the word "Never!" half formed itself on my lips. False girl! – false and cruel! Never more would she smile on me as that evening she smiled on Albert. Worthless, detested woman! I would not remain unrevenged – she should see Albert expire at her feet – she should die beneath my vengeance. She had smiled in disdain and triumph – she knew my wretchedness and her power. Yet what power had she? – the power of exciting my hate – my utter scorn – my – oh, all but indifference! Could I attain that – could I regard her with careless eyes, transferring my rejected love to one fairer and more true, that were indeed a victory!

A bright flash darted before my eyes. I had forgotten the medicine of the adept; I gazed on it with wonder: flashes of admirable beauty, more bright than those which the diamond emits when the sun's rays are on it, glanced from the surface of the liquid; an odour the most fragrant and grateful stole over my sense; the vessel seemed one globe of living radiance, lovely to the eye, and most inviting to the taste. The first thought, instinctively inspired by the grosser sense, was, I will – I must drink. I raised the vessel to my lips. "It will cure me of love – of torture!" Already I had quaffed half of the most delicious liquor ever tasted by the palate of man, when the philosopher stirred. I started – I dropped the glass – the fluid flamed and glanced along the floor, while I felt Cornelius's gripe at my throat, as he shrieked aloud, "Wretch! you have destroyed the labour of my life!"

The philosopher was totally unaware that I had drunk any portion of his drug. His idea was, and I gave a tacit assent to it, that I had raised the vessel from curiosity, and that, frighted at its brightness, and the flashes of intense light it gave forth, I had let it fall. I never undeceived him. The fire of the medicine was quenched – the fragrance died away – he grew calm, as a philosopher should under the heaviest trials, and dismissed me to rest.

I will not attempt to describe the sleep of glory and bliss which bathed my soul in paradise during the remaining hours of that memorable night. Words would be faint and shallow types of my enjoyment, or of the gladness that possessed my bosom when I woke. I trod air – my thoughts were in heaven. Earth appeared heaven, and my inheritance upon it was to be one trance of delight. "This it is to be cured of love," I thought; "I will see Bertha this day, and she will find her lover cold and regardless: too happy to be disdainful, yet how utterly indifferent to her!"

The hours danced away. The philosopher, secure that he had once succeeded, and believing that he might again, began to concoct the same medicine once more. He was shut up with his books and drugs, and I had a holiday. I dressed myself with care; I looked in an old but polished shield, which served me for a mirror; methought my good looks had wonderfully improved. I hurried beyond the precincts of the town, joy in my soul, the beauty of heaven and earth around me. I turned my steps towards the castle – I could look on its lofty turrets with lightness of heart, for I was cured of love. My Bertha saw me afar off, as I came up the avenue. I know not what sudden impulse animated her bosom, but at the sight, she sprung with a light fawn-like bound down the marble steps, and was hastening towards me. But I had been perceived by another person. The old high-born hag, who called herself her protectress, and was her tyrant, had seen me, also; she hobbled, panting, up the terrace; a page, as ugly as herself, held up her train, and fanned her as she hurried along, and stopped my fair girl with a "How, now, my bold mistress? whither so fast? Back to your cage – hawks are abroad!"

Bertha clasped her hands – her eyes were still bent on my approaching figure. I saw the contest. How I abhorred the old crone who checked the kind impulses of my Bertha's softening heart. Hitherto, respect for her rank had caused me to avoid the lady of the castle; now I disdained such trivial considerations. I was cured of love, and lifted above all human fears; I hastened forwards, and soon reached the terrace. How lovely Bertha looked! her eyes flashing fire, her cheeks glowing with impatience and anger, she was a thousand times more graceful and charming than ever – I no longer loved – Oh! no, I adored – worshipped – idolized her!

She had that morning been persecuted, with more than usual vehemence, to consent to an immediate marriage with my rival. She was reproached with the encouragement that she had shown him – she was threatened with being turned out of doors with disgrace and shame. Her proud spirit rose in arms at the threat; but when she remembered the scorn that she had heaped upon me, and how, perhaps, she had thus lost one whom she now regarded as her only friend, she wept with remorse and rage. At that moment I appeared. "O, Winzy!" she exclaimed, "take me to your mother's cot; swiftly let me leave the detested luxuries and wretchedness of this noble dwelling – take me to poverty and happiness."

I clasped her in my arms with transport. The old lady was speechless with fury, and broke forth into invective only when we were far on our road to my natal cottage. My mother received the fair fugitive, escaped from a gilt cage to nature and liberty, with tenderness and joy; my father, who loved her, welcomed her heartily; it was a day of rejoicing, which did not need the addition of the celestial potion of the alchymist to steep me in delight.

Soon after this eventful day, I became the husband of Bertha. I ceased to be the scholar of Cornelius, but I continued his friend. I always felt grateful to him for having, unawares, procured me that delicious draught of a divine elixir, which, instead of curing me of love (sad cure! solitary and joyless remedy for evils which seem blessings to the memory), had inspired me with courage and resolution, thus winning for me an inestimable treasure in my Bertha.

I often called to mind that period of trance-like inebriation with wonder. The drink of Cornelius had not fulfilled the task for which he affirmed that it had been prepared, but its effects were more potent and blissful than words can express.

They had faded by degrees, yet they lingered long – and painted life in hues of splendour. Bertha often wondered at my lightness of heart and unaccustomed gaiety; for, before, I had been rather serious, or even sad, in my disposition. She loved me the better for my cheerful temper, and our days were winged by joy.

Five years afterwards I was suddenly summoned to the bedside of the dying Cornelius. He had sent for me in haste, conjuring my instant presence. I found him stretched on his pallet, enfeebled even to death; all of life that yet remained animated his piercing eyes, and they were fixed on a glass vessel, full of a roseate liquid.

"Behold," he said, in a broken and inward voice, "the vanity of human wishes! a second time my hopes are about to be crowned, a second time they are destroyed. Look at that liquor – you remember five years ago I had prepared the same, with the same success; – then, as now, my thirsting lips expected to taste the immortal elixir – you dashed it from me! and at present it is too late."

He spoke with difficulty, and fell back on his pillow. I could not help saying:

"How, revered master, can a cure for love restore you to life?"

A faint smile gleamed across his face as I listened earnestly to his scarcely intelligible answer. "A cure for love and for all things – the Elixir of Immortality. Ah! If now I might drink, I should live forever!"

As he spoke, a golden flash gleamed from the fluid; a well-remembered fragrance stole over the air; he raised himself, all weak as he was – strength seemed miraculously to re-enter his frame – he stretched forth his hand – a loud explosion startled me – a ray of fire shot up from the elixir, and the glass vessel which contained it was shivered to atoms! I turned my eyes towards the philosopher; he had fallen back – his eyes were glassy – his features rigid – he was dead!

But I lived, and was to live forever! So said the unfortunate alchymist, and for a few days I believed his words. I remembered the glorious drunkenness that had followed my stolen draught. I reflected on the change I had felt in my frame – in my soul. The bounding elasticity of the one – the buoyant lightness of the other. I surveyed myself in a mirror, and could perceive no change in my features during the space of the five years which had elapsed. I remembered the radiant hues and grateful scent of that delicious beverage – worthy the gift it was capable of bestowing – I was, then, immortal!

A few days after I laughed at my credulity. The old proverb, that "a prophet is least regarded in his own country," was true with respect to me and my defunct master. I loved him as a man – I respected him as a sage – but I derided the notion that he could command the powers of darkness, and laughed at the superstitious fears with which he was regarded by the vulgar. He was a wise philosopher, but had no acquaintance with any spirits but those clad in flesh and blood. His science was simply human; and human science, I soon persuaded myself, could never conquer nature's laws so far as to imprison the soul forever within its carnal habitation. Cornelius had brewed a soul-refreshing drink – more inebriating than wine – sweeter and more fragrant than any fruit: it possessed probably strong medicinal powers, imparting gladness to the heart and vigour to the limbs; but its effects would wear out; already were they diminished in my frame. I was a lucky fellow to have quaffed health and joyous spirits, and perhaps long life, at my master's hands; but my good fortune ended there: longevity was far different from immortality.

I continued to entertain this belief for many years. Sometimes a thought stole across me – Was the alchymist indeed deceived? But my habitual credence was, that I should meet the fate of all the children of Adam at my appointed time – a little late, but still at a natural age. Yet it was certain that I retained a wonderfully youthful look. I was laughed at for my vanity in consulting the mirror so often, but I consulted it in vain – my brow was untrenched – my cheeks – my eyes – my whole person continued as untarnished as in my twentieth year.

I was troubled. I looked at the faded beauty of Bertha – I seemed more like her son. By degrees our neighbours began to make similar observations, and I found at last that I went by the name of the Scholar bewitched. Bertha herself grew uneasy. She became jealous and peevish, and at length she began to question me. We had no children; we were all in all to each other; and though, as she grew older, her vivacious spirit became a little allied to ill-temper, and her beauty sadly diminished, I cherished her in my heart as the mistress I had idolized, the wife I had sought and won with such perfect love.

At last our situation became intolerable: Bertha was fifty – I twenty years of age. I had, in very shame, in some measure adopted the habits of a more advanced age; I no longer mingled in the dance among the young and gay, but my heart bounded along with them while I restrained my feet; and a sorry figure I cut among the Nestors of our village. But before the time I mention, things were altered – we were universally shunned; we were – at least, I was – reported to have kept up an iniquitous acquaintance with some of my former master's supposed friends. Poor Bertha was pitied, but deserted. I was regarded with horror and detestation.

What was to be done? we sat by our winter fire – poverty had made itself felt, for none would buy the produce of my farm; and often I had been forced to journey twenty miles, to some place where I was not known, to dispose of our property. It is true we had saved something for an evil day – that day was come.

We sat by our lone fireside – the old-hearted youth and his antiquated wife. Again Bertha insisted on knowing the truth; she recapitulated all she had ever heard said about me, and added her own observations. She conjured me to cast off the spell; she described how much more comely grey hairs were than my chestnut locks; she descanted on the reverence and respect due to age – how preferable to the slight regard paid to mere children: could I imagine that the despicable gifts of youth and good looks outweighed disgrace, hatred, and scorn? Nay, in the end I should be burnt as a dealer in the black art, while she, to whom I had not deigned to communicate any portion of my good fortune, might be stoned as my accomplice. At length she insinuated that I must share my secret with her, and bestow on her like benefits to those I myself enjoyed, or she would denounce me – and then she burst into tears.

Thus beset, methought it was the best way to tell the truth. I revealed it as tenderly as I could, and spoke only of a very long life, not of immortality – which representation, indeed, coincided best with my own ideas. When I ended, I rose and said,

"And now, my Bertha, will you denounce the lover of your youth? – You will not, I know. But it is too hard, my poor wife, that you should suffer from my ill-luck and the accursed arts of Cornelius. I will leave you – you have wealth enough, and friends will return in my absence. I will go; young as I seem, and strong as I am, I can work and gain my bread among strangers, unsuspected and unknown. I loved you in youth; God is my witness that I would not desert you in age, but that your safety and happiness require it."

I took my cap and moved towards the door; in a moment Bertha's arms were round my neck, and her lips were pressed to mine. "No, my husband, my Winzy," she said, "you shall not go alone – take me with you; we will remove from this place, and, as you say, among strangers we shall be unsuspected and safe. I am not so very old as quite to shame you, my Winzy; and I dare say the charm will soon wear off, and, with the blessing of God, you will become more elderly-looking, as is fitting; you shall not leave me."

I returned the good soul's embrace heartily. "I will not, my Bertha; but for your sake I had not thought of such a thing. I will be your true, faithful husband while you are spared to me, and do my duty by you to the last."

The next day we prepared secretly for our emigration. We were obliged to make great pecuniary sacrifices – it could not be helped. We realised a sum sufficient, at least, to maintain us while Bertha lived; and, without saying adieu to any one, quitted our native country to take refuge in a remote part of western France.

It was a cruel thing to transport poor Bertha from her native village, and the friends of her youth, to a new country, new language, new customs. The strange secret of my destiny rendered this removal immaterial to me; but I compassionated her deeply, and was glad to perceive that she found compensation for her misfortunes in a variety of little ridiculous circumstances. Away from all tell-tale chroniclers, she sought to decrease the apparent disparity of our ages by a thousand feminine arts – rouge, youthful dress, and assumed juvenility of manner. I could not be angry – Did not I myself wear a mask? Why quarrel with hers, because it was less successful? I grieved deeply when I remembered that this was my Bertha, whom I had loved so fondly, and won with such transport – the dark eyed, dark-haired girl, with smiles of enchanting archness and a step like a fawn – this mincing, simpering, jealous old woman. I should have revered her grey locks and withered cheeks; but thus! – It was my, work, I knew; but I did not the less deplore this type of human weakness.

Her jealousy never slept. Her chief occupation was to discover that, in spite of outward appearances, I was myself growing old. I verily believe that the poor soul loved me truly in her heart, but never had woman so tormenting a mode of displaying fondness. She would discern wrinkles in my face and decrepitude in my walk, while I bounded along in youthful vigour, the youngest looking of twenty youths. I never dared address another woman: on one occasion, fancying that the belle of the village regarded me with favouring eyes, she bought me a grey wig. Her constant discourse among her acquaintances was, that though I looked so young, there was ruin at work within my frame; and she affirmed that the worst symptom about me was my apparent health. My youth was a disease, she said, and I ought at all times to prepare, if not for a sudden and awful death, at least to awake some morning white-headed, and bowed down with all the marks of advanced years. I let her talk – I often joined in her conjectures. Her warnings chimed in with my never-ceasing speculations concerning my state, and I took an earnest, though painful, interest in listening to all that her quick wit and excited imagination could say on the subject.

Why dwell on these minute circumstances? We lived on for many long years. Bertha became bed-rid and paralytic: I nursed her as mother might a child. She grew peevish, and still harped upon one string – of how long I should survive her. It has ever been a source of consolation to me, that I performed my duty scrupulously towards her. She had been mine in youth, she was mine in age, and at last, when I heaped the sod over her corpse, I wept to feel that I had lost all that really bound me to humanity.

Since then how many have been my cares and woes, how few and empty my enjoyments! I pause here in my history – I will pursue it no further. A sailor without rudder or compass, tossed on a stormy sea – a traveller lost on a wide-spread heath, without landmark or star to him – such have I been: more lost, more hopeless than either. A nearing ship, a gleam from some far cot, may save them; but I have no beacon except the hope of death.

Death! mysterious, ill-visaged friend of weak humanity! Why alone of all mortals have you cast me from your sheltering fold? O, for the peace of the grave! the deep silence of the iron-bound tomb! that thought would cease to work in my brain, and my heart beat no more with emotions varied only by new forms of sadness!

Am I immortal? I return to my first question. In the first place, is it not more probable that the beverage of the alchymist was fraught rather with longevity than eternal life? Such is my hope. And then be it remembered that I only drank half of the potion prepared by him. Was not the whole necessary to complete the charm? To have drained half the Elixir of Immortality is but to be half immortal – my Forever is thus truncated and null.

But again, who shall number the years of the half of eternity? I often try to imagine by what rule the infinite may be divided. Sometimes I fancy age advancing upon me. One grey hair I have found. Fool! Do I lament? Yes, the fear of age and death often creeps coldly into my heart; and the more I live, the more I dread death, even while I abhor life. Such an enigma is man – born to perish – when he wars, as I do, against the established laws of his nature.

But for this anomaly of feeling surely I might die: the medicine of the alchymist would not be proof against fire – sword – and the strangling waters. I have gazed upon the blue depths of many a placid lake, and the tumultuous rushing of many a mighty river, and have said, peace inhabits those waters; yet I have turned my steps away, to live yet another day. I have asked myself, whether suicide would be a crime in one to whom thus only the portals of the other world could be opened. I have done all, except presenting myself as a soldier or duellist, an object of destruction to my – no, not my fellow-mortals, and therefore I have shrunk away. They are not my fellows. The inextinguishable power of life in my frame, and their ephemeral existence, place us wide as the poles asunder. I could not raise a hand against the meanest or the most powerful among them.

Thus I have lived on for many a year – alone, and weary of myself – desirous of death, yet never dying – a mortal immortal. Neither ambition nor avarice can enter my mind, and the ardent love that gnaws at my heart, never to be returned – never to find an equal on which to expend itself – lives there only to torment me.

This very day I conceived a design by which I may end all – without self-slaughter, without making another man a Cain – an expedition, which mortal frame can never survive, even endued with the youth and strength that inhabits mine. Thus I shall put my immortality to the test, and rest forever – or return, the wonder and benefactor of the human species.

Before I go, a miserable vanity has caused me to pen these pages. I would not die, and leave no name behind. Three centuries have passed since I quaffed the fatal beverage: another year shall not elapse before, encountering gigantic dangers – warring with the powers of frost in their home – beset by famine, toil, and tempest – I yield this body, too tenacious a cage for a soul which thirsts for freedom, to the destructive elements of air and water – or, if I survive, my name shall be recorded as one of the most famous among the sons of men; and, my task achieved, I shall adopt more resolute means, and, by scattering and annihilating the atoms that compose my frame, set at liberty the life imprisoned within, and so cruelly prevented from soaring from this dim earth to a sphere more congenial to its immortal essence.

If you enjoyed this, you might also like...
'The Heir of Mondolfo', see page 311
The Last Man, see page 331

Gothic Tales

Stories by Mary Shelley

The Mourner

One fatal remembrance, one sorrow that throws
Its bleak shade alike o er our joys and our woes,
To which life nothing darker or brighter can bring,
For which joy has no balm, and affliction no sting!"
Thomas Moore, 'As a Beam O'er the Face of the Waters May Glow'

A GORGEOUS SCENE of kingly pride is the prospect now before us! The offspring of art, the nursling of nature where can the eye rest on a landscape more deliciously lovely than the fair expanse of Virginia Water, now an open mirror to the sky, now shaded by umbrageous banks, which wind into dark recesses, or are rounded into soft promontories? Looking down on it, now that the sun is low in the west, the eye is dazzled, the soul oppressed, by excess of beauty. Earth, water, air, drink to overflowing the radiance that streams from yonder well of light; the foliage of the trees seems dripping with the golden flood; while the lake, filled with no earthly dew, appears but an imbasining of the sun-tinctured atmosphere; and trees and gay pavilion float in its depth, more clear, more distinct than their twins in the upper air. Nor is the scene silent: strains more sweet than those that lull Venus to her balmy rest, more inspiring than the song of Tiresias which awoke Alexander to the deed of ruin, more solemn than the chantings of St. Cecilia, float along the waves and mingle with the lagging breeze, which ruffles not the lake. Strange, that a few dark scores should be the key to this fountain of sound; the unconscious link between unregarded noise and harmonies which unclose paradise to our entranced senses!

The sun touches the extreme boundary, and a softer, milder light mingles a roseate tinge with the fiery glow. Our boat has floated long on the broad expanse; now let it approach the umbrageous bank. The green tresses of the graceful willow dip into the waters, which are checked by them into a ripple. The startled teal dart from their recess, skimming the waves with splashing wing. The stately swans float onward; while innumerable water fowl cluster together out of the way of the oars. The twilight is blotted by no dark shades; it is one subdued, equal receding of the great tide of day. We may disembark, and wander yet amid the glades, long before the thickening shadows speak of night. The plantations are formed of every English tree, with an old oak or two standing out in the walks. There the glancing foliage obscures heaven, as the silken texture of a veil a woman s lovely features. Beneath such fretwork we may indulge in light-hearted thoughts; or, if sadder meditations lead us to seek darker shades, we may pass the cascade towards the large groves of pine, with their vast undergrowth of laurel, reaching up to the Belvidere; or, on the opposite side of the water, sit under the shadow of the silver-stemmed birch, or beneath the leafy pavilions of those fine old beeches, whose high fantastic roots seem formed in nature's sport; and the near jungle of sweet-smelling myrica leaves no sense unvisited by pleasant ministration.

Now this splendid scene is reserved for the royal possessor; but in past years, while the lodge was called the Regent's Cottage, or before, when the under-ranger inhabited it, the mazy paths of Chapel Wood were open, and the iron gates enclosing the plantations and Virginia Water were guarded by no Cerberus untamable by sops. It was here, on a summer's evening, that Horace Neville and his two fair cousins floated idly on the placid lake:

> In that sweet mood when pleasant thoughts
> Bring sad thoughts to the mind.

Seville had been eloquent in praise of English scenery. "In distant climes," he said, "we may find landscapes grand in barbaric wildness, or rich in the luxuriant vegetation of the south, or sublime in Alpine magnificence. We may lament, though it is ungrateful to say so on such a night as this, the want of a more genial sky; but where find scenery to be compared to the verdant, well-wooded, well-watered groves of our native land; the clustering cottages, shadowed by fine old elms; each garden blooming with early flowers, each lattice gay with geraniums and roses; the blue-eyed child devouring his white bread, while he drives a cow to graze; the hedge redolent with summer blooms; the enclosed cornfields, seas of golden grain, weltering in the breeze; the stile, the track across the meadow, leading through the copse, under which the path winds, and the meeting branches overhead, which give, by their dimming tracery, a cathedral-like solemnity to the scene; the river, winding with sweet inland murmur; and, as additional graces, spots like these oases of taste gardens of Eden the works of wealth, which evince at once the greatest power and the greatest will to create beauty?"

"And yet," continued Neville, "it was with difficulty that I persuaded myself to reap the best fruits of my uncle's will, and to inhabit this spot, familiar to my boyhood, associated with unavailing regrets and recollected pain."

Horace Neville was a man of birth of wealth; but he could hardly be termed a man of the world. There was in his nature a gentleness, a sweetness, a winning sensibility, allied to talent and personal distinction, that gave weight to his simplest expressions, and excited sympathy for all his emotions. His younger cousin, his junior by several years, was attached to him by the tenderest sentiments secret long but they were now betrothed to each other a lovely, happy pair. She looked inquiringly, but he turned away. "No more of this," he said, and, giving a swifter impulse to their boat, they speedily reached the shore, landed, and walked through the long extent of Chapel Wood. It was dark night before they met their carriage at Bishopsgate.

A week or two after, Horace received letters to call him to a distant part of the country. A few days before his departure, he requested his cousin to walk with him. They bent their steps across several meadows to Old Windsor Churchyard. At first he did not deviate from the usual path; and as they went they talked cheerfully gaily. The beauteous sunny day might well exhilarate them; the dancing waves sped onwards at their feet; the country church lifted its rustic spire into the bright pure sky. There was nothing in their conversation that could induce his cousin to think that Neville had led her hither for any saddening purpose; but when they were about to quit the churchyard, Horace, as if he had suddenly recollected himself, turned from the path, crossed the greensward, and paused beside a grave near the river. No stone was there to commemorate the being who reposed beneath it was thickly grown with grass, starred by a luxuriant growth of humble daisies: a few dead leaves, a broken bramble twig, defaced its neatness. Neville removed these, and then said, "Juliet, I commit this sacred spot to your keeping while I am away."

"There is no monument," he continued; "for her commands were implicitly obeyed by the two beings to whom she addressed them. One day another may lie near, and his name will be her epitaph. I do not mean myself," he said, half-smiling at the terror his cousin's countenance expressed; "but promise me, Juliet, to preserve this grave from every violation. I do not wish to sadden you by the story; yet, if I have excited your interest, I will satisfy it; but not now not here."

It was not till the following day, when, in company with her sister, they again visited Virginia Water, that, seated under the shadow of its pines, whose melodious swinging in the wind breathed unearthly harmony, Neville, unasked, commenced his story.

"I was sent to Eton at eleven years of age. I will not dwell upon my sufferings there; I would hardly refer to them, did they not make a part of my present narration. I was a fag to a hard taskmaster; every labour he could invent and the youthful tyrant was ingenious he devised for my annoyance; early and late, I was forced to be in attendance, to the neglect of my school duties, so incurring punishment. There were worse things to bear than these: it was his delight to put me to shame, and, finding that I had too much of my mother in my blood, to endeavour to compel me to acts of cruelty from which my nature revolted, I refused to obey. Speak of West Indian slavery! I hope things may be better now; in my days, the tender years of aristocratic childhood were yielded up to a capricious, unrelenting, cruel bondage, far beyond the measured despotism of Jamaica.

"One day – I had been two years at school, and was nearly thirteen – my tyrant, I will give him no other name, issued a command, in the wantonness of power, for me to destroy a poor little bullfinch I had tamed and caged. In a hapless hour he found it in my room, and was indignant that I should dare to appropriate a single pleasure. I refused, stubbornly, dauntlessly, though the consequence of my disobedience was immediate and terrible. At this moment a message came from my tormentor s tutor his father had arrived. Well, old lad, he cried, I shall pay you off some day! Seizing my pet at the same time, he wrung its neck, threw it at my feet, and, with a laugh of derision, quitted the room.

"Never before – never may I again feel the same swelling, boiling fury in my bursting heart; the sight of my nursling expiring at my feet my desire of vengeance my impotence, created a Vesuvius within me, that no tears flowed to quench. Could I have uttered acted my passion, it would have been less torturous: it was so when I burst into a torrent of abuse and imprecation. My vocabulary – it must have been a choice collection – was supplied by him against whom it was levelled. But words were air. I desired to give more substantial proof of my resentment I destroyed everything in the room belonging to him; I tore them to pieces, I stamped on them, crushed them with more than childish strength. My last act was to seize a timepiece, on which my tyrant infinitely prided himself, and to dash it to the ground. The sight of this, as it lay shattered at my feet, recalled me to my senses, and something like an emotion of fear allayed the tumult in my heart. I began to meditate an escape: I got out of the house, ran down a lane, and across some meadows, far out of bounds, above Eton. I was seen by an elder boy, a friend of my tormentor. He called to me, thinking at first that I was performing some errand for him; but seeing that I shirked, he repeated his 'Come up!' in an authoritative voice. It put wings to my heels; he did not deem it necessary to pursue. But I grow tedious, my dear Juliet; enough that fears the most intense, of punishment both from my masters and the upper boys, made me resolve to run away. I reached the banks of the Thames, tied my clothes over my head, swam across, and, traversing several fields, entered Windsor Forest, with a vague childish feeling of being able to hide myself forever in the unexplored obscurity of its immeasurable wilds. It was early autumn; the weather was mild, even warm; the forest oaks yet showed no sign of winter change, though the fern beneath wore a yellowy tinge. I got within Chapel Wood; I fed upon chestnuts and beech nuts; I continued to hide myself from the gamekeepers and woodmen. I lived thus two days.

"But chestnuts and beechnuts were sorry fare to a growing lad of thirteen years old. A day's rain occurred, and I began to think myself the most unfortunate boy on record. I had a distant, obscure idea of starvation: I thought of the Children in the Wood, of their leafy shroud, gift of the pious robin; this brought my poor bullfinch to my mind, and tears streamed in torrents down my cheeks. I thought of my father and mother; of you, then my little baby cousin and playmate; and I cried with renewed fervour, till, quite exhausted, I curled myself up under a huge oak among some dry leaves, the relics of a hundred summers, and fell asleep.

"I ramble on in my narration as if I had a story to tell; yet I have little except a portrait a sketch to present, for your amusement or interest. When I awoke, the first object that met my opening eyes was a little foot, delicately clad in silk and soft kid. I looked up in dismay, expecting to behold some gaily dressed appendage to this indication of high-bred elegance; but I saw a girl, perhaps seventeen, simply clad in a dark cotton dress, her face shaded by a large, very coarse straw hat; she was pale even to marmoreal whiteness; her chestnut-coloured hair was parted in plain tresses across a brow which wore traces of extreme suffering; her eyes were blue, full, large, melancholy, often even suffused with tears; but her mouth had an infantine sweetness and innocence in its expression, that softened the otherwise sad expression of her countenance.

"She spoke to me. I was too hungry, too exhausted, too unhappy, to resist her kindness, and gladly permitted her to lead me to her home. We passed out of the wood by some broken palings on to Bishopsgate Heath, and after no long walk arrived at her habitation. It was a solitary, dreary-looking cottage; the palings were in disrepair, the garden waste, the lattices unadorned by flowers or creepers; within, all was neat, but sombre, and even mean. The diminutiveness of a cottage requires an appearance of cheerfulness and elegance to make it pleasing; the bare floor, clean, it is true, the rush chairs, deal table, checked curtains of this cot, were beneath even a peasant s rusticity; yet it was the dwelling of my lovely guide, whose little white hand, delicately gloved, contrasted with her unadorned attire, as did her gentle self with the clumsy appurtenances of her too humble dwelling.

"Poor child! she had meant entirely to hide her origin, to degrade herself to a peasant s state, and little thought that she forever betrayed herself by the strangest incongruities. Thus, the arrangements of her table were mean, her fare meagre for a hermit; but the linen was matchlessly fine, and wax lights stood in candlesticks which a beggar would almost have disdained to own. But I talk of circumstances I observed afterwards; then I was chiefly aware of the plentiful breakfast she caused her single attendant, a young girl, to place before me, and of the sweet soothing voice of my hostess, which spoke a kindness with which lately I had been little conversant. When my hunger was appeased, she drew my story from me, encouraged me to write to my father, and kept me at her abode till, after a few days, I returned to school pardoned. No long time elapsed before I got into the upper forms, and my woful slavery ended.

"Whenever I was able, I visited my disguised nymph. I no longer associated with my schoolfellows; their diversions, their pursuits appeared vulgar and stupid to me; I had but one object in view to accomplish my lessons, and to steal to the cottage of Ellen Burnet.

"Do not look grave, love! True, others as young as I then was have loved, and I might also; but not Ellen. Her profound, her intense melancholy, sister to despair her serious, sad discourse her mind, estranged from all worldly concerns, forbade that; but there was an enchantment in her sorrow, a fascination in her converse, that lifted me above commonplace existence; she created a magic circle, which I entered as holy ground: it was not akin to heaven, for grief was the presiding spirit; but there was an exaltation of sentiment, an enthusiasm, a view beyond the grave, which made it unearthly, singular, wild, enthralling. You have often observed that I strangely differ from all other men; I mingle with them, make one in their occupations and diversions, but I have a portion of my being sacred from them: a living well, sealed up from their contamination, lies deep in my heart it is of little use, but there it is; Ellen opened the spring, and it has flowed ever since.

"Of what did she talk? She recited no past adventures, alluded to no past intercourse with friend or relative; she spoke of the various woes that wait on humanity, on the intricate mazes of life, on the miseries of passion, of love, remorse, and death, and that which we may hope or fear beyond the tomb; she spoke of the sensation of wretchedness alive in her own broken heart, and then she grew fearfully eloquent, till, suddenly pausing, she reproached herself for making me familiar with such wordless misery. 'I do you harm,' she often said; 'I unfit you for society; I have tried, seeing you thrown upon yonder distorted miniature of a bad world, to estrange you from its evil contagion; I fear that I shall be the cause of greater harm to you than could spring from association with your fellow-creatures in the ordinary course of things. This is not well – avoid the stricken deer.' There were darker shades in the picture than those which I have already developed. Ellen was more miserable than the imagination of one like you, dear girl, unacquainted with woe, can portray. Sometimes she gave words to her despair it was so great as to confuse the boundary between physical and mental sensation and every pulsation of her heart was a throb of pain. She has suddenly broken off in talking of her sorrows, with a cry of agony bidding me leave her hiding her face on her arms, shivering with the anguish some thought awoke. The idea that chiefly haunted her, though she earnestly endeavoured to put it aside, was self-destruction to snap the silver cord that bound together so much grace, wisdom, and sweetness to rob the world of a creation made to be its ornament. Sometimes her piety checked her; oftener a sense of unendurable suffering made her brood with pleasure over the dread resolve. She spoke of it to me as being wicked; yet I often fancied this was done rather to prevent her example from being of ill effect to me, than from any conviction that the Father of all would regard angrily the last act of His miserable child. Once she had prepared the mortal beverage; it was on the table before her when I entered; she did not deny its nature, she did not attempt to justify herself; she only besought me not to hate her, and to soothe by my kindness her last moments. 'I cannot live!' was all her explanation, all her excuse; and it was spoken with such fervent wretched ness that it seemed wrong to attempt to persuade her to prolong the sense of pain. I did not act like a boy; I wonder I did not; I made one simple request, to which she instantly acceded, that she should walk with me to this Belvidere. It was a glorious sunset; beauty and the spirit of love breathed in the wind, and hovered over the softened hues of the landscape. 'Look, Ellen,' I cried, 'if only such loveliness of nature existed, it were worth living for!'

"'True, if a latent feeling did not blot this glorious scene with murky shadows. Beauty is as we see it – my eyes view all things deformed and evil.' She closed them as she said this; but, young and sensitive, the visitings of the soft breeze already began to minister consolation. 'Dearest Ellen,' I continued, 'what do I not owe to you? I am your boy, your pupil; I might have gone on blindly as others do, but you opened my eyes; you have given me a sense of the just, the good, the beautiful and have you done this merely for my misfortune? If you leave me, what can become of me?' The last words came from my heart, and tears gushed from my eyes. 'Do not leave me, Ellen,' I said; 'I cannot live without you and I cannot die, for I have a mother a father.' She turned quickly round, saying, 'You are blessed sufficiently.' Her voice struck me as unnatural; she grew deadly pale as she spoke, and was obliged to sit down. Still I clung to her, prayed, cried; till she – I had never seen her shed a tear before – burst into passionate weeping. After this she seemed to forget her resolve. We returned by moonlight, and our talk was even more calm and cheerful than usual. When in her cottage, I poured away the fatal draught. Her goodnight bore with it no traces of her late agitation; and the next day she said, I have thoughtlessly, even wickedly, created a new duty to myself, even at a time when I had forsworn all; but I will be true to it. Pardon me for making you familiar with emotions and scenes so dire; I will behave better I will preserve myself, if I can, till the link between us is loosened, or broken, and I am free again.

"One little incident alone occurred during our intercourse that appeared at all to connect her with the world. Sometimes I brought her a newspaper, for those were stirring times; and though, before I knew her, she had forgotten all except the world her own heart enclosed, yet, to please me, she would talk of Napoleon Russia, from whence the emperor now returned overthrown and the prospect of his final defeat. The paper lay one day on her table; some words caught her eye; she bent eagerly down to read them, and her bosom heaved with violent palpitation; but she subdued herself, and after a few moments told me to take the paper away. Then, indeed, I did feel an emotion of even impertinent inquisitiveness; I found nothing to satisfy it though afterwards I became aware that it contained a singular advertisement, saying:

> If these lines meet the eye of any one of the passengers who were on board the St. Mary, bound for Liverpool from Barbadoes, which sailed on the third of May last, and was destroyed by fire in the high seas, a part of the crew only having been saved by his Majesty's frigate the Bellerophon, they are entreated to communicate with the advertiser; and if anyone be acquainted with the particulars of the Hon. Miss Eversham s fate and present abode, they are earnestly requested to disclose them, directing to L. E., Stratton Street, Park Lane.

"It was after this event, as winter came on, that symptoms of decided ill-health declared themselves in the delicate frame of my poor Ellen. I have often suspected that, without positively attempting her life, she did many things that tended to abridge it and to produce mortal disease. Now, when really ill, she refused all medical attendance;

but she got better again, and I thought her nearly well when I saw her for the last time, before going home for the Christmas holidays. Her manner was full of affection: she relied, she said, on the continuation of my friendship; she made me promise never to forget her, though she refused to write to me, and forbade any letters from me.

"Even now I see her standing at her humble doorway. If an appearance of illness and suffering can ever be termed lovely, it was in her. Still she was to be viewed as the wreck of beauty. What must she not have been in happier days, with her angel expression of face, her nymph-like figure, her voice, whose tones were music? 'So young – so lost!' was the sentiment that burst even from me, a young lad, as I waved my hand to her as a last adieu. She hardly looked more than fifteen, but none could doubt that her very soul was impressed by the sad lines of sorrow that rested so unceasingly on her fair brow. Away from her, her figure forever floated before my eyes; I put my hands before them, still she was there: my day, my night dreams were filled by my recollections of her.

"During the winter holidays, on a fine soft day, I went out to hunt: you, dear Juliet, will remember the sad catastrophe; I fell and broke my leg. The only person who saw me fall was a young man who rode one of the most beautiful horses I ever saw, and I believe it was by watching him as he took a leap, that I incurred my disaster: he dismounted, and was at my side in a minute. My own animal had fled; he called his; it obeyed his voice; with ease he lifted my light figure on to the saddle, contriving to support my leg, and so conducted me a short distance to a lodge situated in the woody recesses of Elmore Park, the seat of the Earl of D—, whose second son my preserver was. He was my sole nurse for a day or two, and during the whole of my illness passed many hours of each day by my bedside. As I lay gazing on him, while he read to me, or talked, narrating a thousand strange adventures which had occurred during his service in the Peninsula, I thought is it forever to be my fate to fall in with the highly gifted and excessively unhappy?

"The immediate neighbour of Lewis' family was Lord Eversham. He had married in very early youth, and became a widower young. After this misfortune, which passed like a deadly blight over his prospects and possessions, leaving the gay view utterly sterile and bare, he left his surviving infant daughter under the care of Lewis mother, and travelled for many years in far distant lands. He returned when Clarice was about ten, a lovely sweet child, the pride and delight of all connected with her. Lord Eversham, on his return – he was then hardly more than thirty – devoted himself to her education. They were never separate: he was a good musician, and she became a proficient under his tutoring. They rode, walked, read together. When a father is all that a father may be, the sentiments of filial piety, entire dependence, and perfect confidence being united, the love of a daughter is one of the deepest and strongest, as it is the purest passion of which our natures are capable. Clarice worshipped her parent, who came, during the transition from mere childhood to the period when reflection and observation awaken, to adorn a commonplace existence with all the brilliant adjuncts which enlightened and devoted affection can bestow. He appeared to her like an especial gift of Providence, a guardian angel but far dearer, as being akin to her own nature. She grew, under his eye, in loveliness and refinement both of intellect and heart. These feelings were not divided almost strengthened, by the engagement that had taken place between her and Lewis: Lewis was destined for the army, and, after a few years' service, they were to be united.

"It is hard, when all is fair and tranquil, when the world, opening before the ardent gaze of youth, looks like a well-kept demesne, unencumbered by let or hindrance for the annoyance of the young traveller, that we should voluntarily stray into desert wilds and tempest-visited districts. Lewis Elmore was ordered to Spain; and, at the same time, Lord Eversham found it necessary to visit some estates he possessed in Barbadoes. He was not sorry to revisit a scene, which had dwelt in his memory as an earthly paradise, nor to show to his daughter a new and strange world, so to form her understanding and enlarge her mind. They were to return in three months, and departed as on a summer tour. Clarice was glad that, while her lover gathered experience and knowledge in a distant land, she should not remain in idleness; she was glad that there would be some diversion for her anxiety during his perilous absence; and in every way she enjoyed the idea of travelling with her beloved father, who would fill every hour, and adorn every new scene, with pleasure and delight. They sailed. Clarice wrote home, with enthusiastic expressions of rapture and delight from Madeira: yet, without her father, she said, the fair scene had been blank to her. More than half her letter was filled by the expressions of her gratitude and affection for her adored and revered parent. While he, in his, with fewer words, perhaps, but with no less energy, spoke of his satisfaction in her improvement, his pride in her beauty, and his grateful sense of her love and kindness.

"Such were they, a matchless example of happiness in the dearest connection in life, as resulting from the exercise of their reciprocal duties and affections. A father and daughter; the one all care, gentleness, and sympathy, consecrating his life for her happiness; the other fond, duteous, grateful: such had they been, and where were they now, the noble, kind, respected parent, and the beloved and loving child? They had departed from England as on a pleasure voyage down an inland stream; but the ruthless car of destiny had overtaken them on their unsuspecting way, crushing them under its heavy wheels scattering love, hope, and joy as the bellowing avalanche overwhelms and grinds to mere spray the streamlet of the valley. They were gone; but whither? Mystery hung over the fate of the most helpless victim; and my friend s anxiety was, to penetrate the clouds that hid poor Clarice from his sight.

"After an absence of a few months, they had written, fixing their departure in the St. Mary, to sail from Barbadoes in a few days. Lewis, at the same time, returned from Spain: he was invalided, in his very first action, by a bad wound in his side. He arrived, and each day expected to hear of the landing of his friends, when that common messenger, the newspaper, brought him tidings to fill him with more than anxiety with fear and agonizing doubt. The St. Mary had caught fire, and had burned in the open sea. A frigate, the Bellerophon, had saved a part of the crew. In spite of illness and a physician's commands, Lewis set out the same day for London to ascertain as speedily as possible the fate of her he loved. There he heard that the frigate was expected in the Downs. Without alighting from his travelling chaise, he posted thither, arriving in a burning fever. He went on board, saw the commander, and spoke with the crew. They could give him few particulars as to whom they had saved; they had touched at Liverpool, and left there most of the persons, including all the passengers rescued from the St. Mary. Physical suffering for awhile disabled Mr. Elmore; he was confined by his wound and consequent fever, and only recovered to give himself up to his exertions to discover the fate of his friends; they did not appear nor write; and all Lewis inquiries only tended to confirm his worst fears; yet still he hoped, and still continued indefatigable in his perquisitions. He visited Liverpool and Ireland, whither some of the passengers had gone, and learnt only scattered, incongruous details of the fearful tragedy, that told nothing of Miss Eversham s present abode, though much that confirmed his suspicion that she still lived.

"The fire on board the St. Mary had raged long and fearfully before the Bellerophon hove in sight, and boats came off for the rescue of the crew. The women were to be first embarked; but Clarice clung to her father, and refused to go till he should accompany her. Some fearful presentiment that, if she were saved, he would remain and die, gave such energy to her resolve, that not the entreaties of her father, nor the angry expostulations of the captain, could shake it. Lewis saw this man, after the lapse of two or three months, and he threw most light on the dark scene. He well remembered that, transported with anger by her obstinacy, he had said to her, 'You will cause your father s death and be as much a parricide as if you put poison into his cup; you are not the first girl who has murdered her father in her wilful mood.' Still Clarice passionately refused to go – there was no time for long parley – the point was yielded, and she remained pale, but firm, near her parent, whose arm was around her, supporting her during the awful interval. It was no period for regular action and calm order; a tempest was rising, the scorching waves blew this way and that, making a fearful day of the night which veiled all except the burning ship. The boats returned with difficulty, and one only could contrive to approach; it was nearly full; Lord Eversham and his daughter advanced to the deck s edge to get in. 'We can only take one of you,' vociferated the sailors; 'keep back on your life! Throw the girl to us – we will come back for you if we can.' Lord Eversham cast with a strong arm his daughter, who had now entirely lost her self-possession, into the boat; she was alive again in a minute; she called to her father, held out her arms to him, and would have thrown herself into the sea, but was held back by the sailors. Meanwhile Lord Eversham, feeling that no boat could again approach the lost vessel, contrived to heave a spar overboard, and threw himself into the sea, clinging to it. The boat, tossed by the huge waves, with difficulty made its way to the frigate; and as it rose from the trough of the sea, Clarice saw her father struggling with his fate battling with the death that at last became the victor; the spar floated by, his arms had fallen from it; were those his pallid features? She neither wept nor fainted, but her limbs grew rigid, her face colourless, and she was lifted as a log on to the deck of the frigate.

"The captain allowed that on her homeward voyage the people had rather a horror of her, as having caused her father s death; her own servants had perished, few people remembered who she was; but they talked together with no careful voices as they passed her, and a hundred times she must have heard herself accused of having destroyed her parent. She spoke to no one, or only in brief reply when addressed; to avoid the rough remonstrances of those around, she appeared at table, ate as well as she could; but there was a settled wretchedness in her face that never changed. When they landed at Liverpool, the captain conducted her to a hotel; he left her, meaning to return, but an opportunity of sailing that night for the Downs occurred, of which he availed himself, without again visiting her. He knew, he said, and truly, that she was in her native country, where she had but to write a letter to gather crowds of friends about her; and where can greater civility be found than at an English hotel, if it is known that you are perfectly able to pay your bill?

"This was all that Mr. Elmore could learn, and it took many months to gather together these few particulars. lie went to the hotel at Liverpool. It seemed that as soon as there appeared some hope of rescue from the frigate, Lord Eversham had given his pocket-book to his daughter s care, containing bills on a banking-house at Liverpool to the amount of a few hundred pounds. On the second day after Clarice's arrival there, she had sent for the master of the hotel, and showed him these. He got the cash for her; and the next day she quitted Liverpool in a little coasting vessel. In vain Lewis endeavoured to trace her. Apparently she had crossed to Ireland; but whatever she had done, wherever she had gone, she had taken infinite pains to conceal herself, and all clue was speedily lost.

"Lewis had not yet despaired; he was even now perpetually making journeys, sending emissaries, employing every possible means for her discovery. From the moment he told me this story, we talked of nothing else. I became deeply interested, and we ceaselessly discussed the probabilities of the case, and where she might be concealed. That she did not meditate suicide was evident from her having possessed herself of money; yet, unused to the world, young, lovely, and inexperienced, what could be her plan? What might not have been her fate?

"Meanwhile I continued for nearly three months confined by the fracture of my limb; before the lapse of that time, I had begun to crawl about the ground, and now I considered myself as nearly recovered. It had been settled that I should not return to Eton, but be entered at Oxford; and this leap from boyhood to man's estate elated me considerably. Yet still I thought of my poor Ellen, and was angry at her obstinate silence. Once or twice I had, disobeying her command, written to her, mentioning my accident, and the kind attentions of Mr. Elmore. Still she wrote not; and I began to fear that her illness might have had a fatal termination. She had made me vow so solemnly never to mention her name, never to inquire about her during my absence, that, considering obedience the first duty of a young inexperienced boy to one older than himself, I resisted each suggestion of my affection or my fears to transgress her orders.

"And now spring came, with its gift of opening buds, odoriferous flowers, and sunny genial days. I returned home, and found my family on the eve of their departure for London; my long confinement had weakened me; it was deemed inadvisable for me to encounter the bad air and fatigues of the metropolis, and I remained to rusticate. I rode and hunted, and thought of Ellen; missing the excitement of her conversation, and feeling a vacancy in my heart which she had filled. I began to think of riding across the country from Shropshire to Berks for the purpose of seeing her. The whole landscape haunted my imagination the fields round Eton the silver Thames the majestic forest this lovely scene of Virginia Water the heath and her desolate cottage she herself pale, slightly bending from weakness of health, awakening from dark abstraction to bestow on me a kind smile of welcome. It grew into a passionate desire of my heart to behold her, to cheer her as I might by my affectionate attentions, to hear her, and to hang upon her accents of inconsolable despair as if it had been celestial harmony. As I meditated on these things, a voice seemed forever to repeat, Now go, or it will be too late; while another yet more mournful tone responded, You can never see her more!

"I was occupied by these thoughts, as, on a summer moonlight night, I loitered in the shrubbery, unable to quit a scene of entrancing beauty, when I was startled at hearing myself called by Mr. Elmore. He came on his way to the coast; he had received a letter from Ireland, which made him think that Miss Eversham was residing near Enniscorthy, a strange place for her to select, but as concealment was evidently her object, not an improbable one. Yet his hopes were not high; on the contrary, he performed this journey more from the resolve to leave nothing undone, than in expectation of a happy result. He asked me if I would accompany him; I was delighted with the offer, and we departed together on the following morning.

"We arrived at Milford Haven, where we were to take our passage. The packet was to sail early in the morning we walked on the beach, and beguiled the time by talk. I had never mentioned Ellen to Lewis; I felt now strongly inclined to break my vow, and to relate my whole adventure with her; but restrained myself, and we spoke only of the unhappy Clarice of the despair that must have been hers, of her remorse and unavailing regret.

"We retired to rest; and early in the morning I was called to prepare for going on board. I got ready, and then knocked at Lewis door; he admitted me, for he was dressed, though a few of his things were still unpacked, and scattered about the room. The morocco case of a miniature was on his table; I took it up. 'Did I never show you that?' said Elmore; 'poor dear Clarice! She was very happy when that was painted!'

"I opened it; rich, luxuriant curls clustered on her brow and the snow-white throat; there was a light zephyr appearance in the figure; an expression of unalloyed exuberant happiness in the countenance; but those large dove s eyes, the innocence that dwelt on her mouth, could not be mistaken, and the name of Ellen Burnet burst from my lips.

"There was no doubt: why had I ever doubted? The thing was so plain! Who but the survivor of such a parent, and she the apparent cause of his death, could be so miserable as Ellen? A torrent of explanation followed, and a thousand minute circumstances, forgotten before, now assured us that my sad hermitess was the beloved of Elmore. No more sea voyage not a second of delay our chaise, the horses heads turned to the east, rolled on with lightning rapidity, yet far too slowly to satisfy our impatience. It was not until we arrived at Worcester that the tide of expectation, flowing all one way, ebbed. Suddenly, even while I was telling Elmore some anecdote to prove that, in spite of all, she would be accessible to consolation, I remembered her ill-health and my fears. Lewis saw the change my countenance underwent; for some time I could not command my voice; and when at last I spoke, my gloomy anticipations passed like an electric shock into my friend s soul.

"When we arrived at Oxford we halted for an hour or two, unable to proceed; yet we did not converse on the subject so near our hearts, nor until we arrived in sight of Windsor did a word pass between us; then Elmore said, 'Tomorrow morning, dear Neville, you shall visit Clarice; we must not be too precipitate.'

"The morrow came. I arose with that intolerable weight at my breast, which it is grief's worst heritage to feel. A sunny day it was; yet the atmosphere looked black to me; my heart was dead within me. We sat at the breakfast-table, but neither ate, and after some rest less indecision, we left our inn, and (to protract the interval) walked to Bishopsgate. Our conversation belied our feelings: we spoke as if we expected all to be well; we felt that there was no hope. We crossed the heath along the accustomed path. On one side was the luxuriant foliage of the forest, on the other the widespread moor; her cottage was situated at one extremity, and could hardly be distinguished, until we should arrive close to it. When we drew near, Lewis bade me go on alone; he would wait my return. I obeyed, and reluctantly approached the confirmation of my fears. At length it stood before me, the lonely cot and desolate garden; the unfastened wicket swung in the breeze; every shutter was closed.

"To stand motionless and gaze on these symbols of my worst forebodings was all that I could do. My heart seemed to me to call aloud for Ellen, for such was she to me, her other name might be a fiction but silent as her own life-deserted lips were mine. Lewis grew impatient, and advanced. My stay had occasioned a transient ray of hope to enter his mind; it vanished when he saw me and her deserted dwelling. Slowly we turned away, and were directing our steps back again, when my name was called by a child. A little girl came running across some fields towards us, whom at last I recognised as having seen before with Ellen. 'Mr. Neville, there is a letter for you!' cried the child. 'A letter; where? Who?' 'The lady left a letter for you. You must go to Old Windsor, to Mr. Cooke's; he has got it for you'.

"She had left a letter: was she then departed on an earthly journey? 'I will go for it immediately. Mr. Cooke! Old Windsor! Where shall I find him? Who is he?'

"'Oh, sir, everybody knows him,' said the child; 'he lives close to the churchyard; he is the sexton. After the burial, Nancy gave him the letter to take care of.'

"Had we hoped? Had we for a moment indulged the expectation of ever again seeing our miserable friend? Never! Never! Our hearts had told us that the sufferer was at peace the unhappy orphan with her father in the abode of spirits! Why, then, were we here? Why had a smile dwelt on our lips, now wreathed into the expression of anguish? Our full hearts demanded one consolation to weep upon her grave; her sole link now with us, her mourners. There at last my boy's grief found vent in tears, in lamentation. You saw the spot; the grassy mound rests lightly on the bosom of fair Clarice, of my own poor Ellen. Stretched upon this, kissing the scarcely springing turf; for many hours no thought visited me but the wretched one, that she had lived, and was lost to me forever!

"If Lewis had ever doubted the identity of my friend with her he loved, the letter put into our hands un deceived him; the handwriting was Miss Eversham's, it was directed to me, and contained words like these:

April 11

I have vowed never to mention certain beloved names, never to communicate with beings who cherished me once, to whom my deepest gratitude is due; and, as well as poor bankrupt can, is paid. Perhaps it is a mere prevarication to write to you, dear Horace, concerning them; but Heaven pardon me! my disrobed spirit would not repose, I fear, if I did not thus imperfectly bid them a last farewell.

You know him, Neville; and know that he forever laments her whom he has lost. Describe your poor Ellen to him, and he will speedily see that she died on the waves of the murderous Atlantic. Ellen had nothing in common with her, save love for, and interest in him. Tell him it had been well for him, perhaps, to have united himself to the child of prosperity, the nursling of deep love; but it had been destruction, even could he have meditated such an act, to wed the parrici.

I will not write that word. Sickness and near death have taken the sting from my despair. The agony of woe which you witnessed is melted into tender affliction and pious hope. I am not miserable now. Now! When you read these words, the hand that writes, the eye that sees, will be a little dust, becoming one with the earth around it. You, perhaps he, will visit my quiet retreat, bestow a few tears on my fate, but let them be secret; they may make green my grave, but do not let a misplaced feeling adorn it with any other tribute. It is my last request; let no stone, no name, mark that spot.

Farewell, dear Horace! Farewell to one other whom I may not name. May the God to whom I am about to resign my spirit in confidence and hope, bless your earthly career! Blindly, perhaps, you will regret me for your own sakes; but for mine, you will be grateful to the Providence which has snapt the heavy chain binding me to unutterable sorrow, and which permits me from my lowly grass-grown tomb to say to you. I am at peace.

Ellen.

If you enjoyed this, you might also like...
'A Fragment' by Lord Byron, see page 133
'The Invisible Girl', see page 287

A Dirge

This morn thy gallant bark, love,
Sailed on a sunny sea;
'Tis noon, and tempests dark, love,
Have wrecked it on the lee.
Ah woe! Ah woe! Ah woe!
By spirits of the deep
He's cradled on the billow
To his unwaking sleep.

Thou liest upon the shore, love,
Beside the knelling surge,
But sea-nymphs evermore, love,
Shall sadly chaunt thy dirge.
Oh come! Oh come! Oh come!
Ye spirits of the deep,
While near his seaweed pillow
My lonely watch I keep.

From far across the sea, love,
I hear a wild lament,
By Echo's voice for thee, love,
From ocean's caverns sent:
Oh list! Oh list! Oh list!
The spirits of the deep –
Loud sounds their wail of sorrow,
While I forever weep.

If you enjoyed this, you might also like...
'Christabel', see page 153
'The Fated Hour' by Friedrich Laun, see page 195

The Dream

THE TIME OF the occurrence of the little legend about to be narrated, was that of the commencement of the reign of Henry IV of France, whose accession and conversion, while they brought peace to the kingdom whose throne he ascended, were inadequate to heal the deep wounds mutually inflicted by the inimical parties. Private feuds, and the memory of mortal injuries, existed between those now apparently united; and often did the hands that had clasped each other in seeming friendly greeting, involuntarily, as the grasp was released, clasp the dagger's hilt, as fitter spokesman to their passions than the words of courtesy that had just fallen from their lips. Many of the fiercer Catholics retreated to their distant provinces; and while they concealed in solitude their rankling discontent, not less keenly did they long for the day when they might show it openly. In a large and fortified château built on a rugged steep overlooking the Loire, not far from the town of Nantes, dwelt the last of her race, and the heiress of their fortunes, the young and beautiful Countess de Villeneuve. She had spent the preceding year in complete solitude in her secluded abode; and the mourning she wore for a father and two brothers, the victims of the civil wars, was a graceful and good reason why she did not appear at court, and mingle with its festivities. But the orphan countess inherited a high name and broad lands; and it was soon signified to her that the king, her guardian, desired that she should bestow them, together with her hand, upon some noble whose birth and accomplishments should entitle him to the gift. Constance, in reply, expressed her intention of taking vows, and retiring to a convent. The king earnestly and resolutely forbade this act, believing such an idea to be the result of sensibility overwrought by sorrow, and relying on the hope that, after a time, the genial spirit of youth would break through this cloud.

A year passed, and still the countess persisted; and at last Henry, unwilling, to exercise compulsion – desirous, too, of judging for himself of the motives that led one so beautiful, young, and gifted with fortune's favours, to desire to bury herself in a cloister – announced his intention, now that the period of her mourning was expired, of visiting her château; and if he brought not with him, the monarch said, inducement sufficient to change her design, he would yield his consent to its fulfilment.

Many a sad hour had Constance passed – many a day of tears, and many a night of restless misery. She had closed her gates against every visitant; and, like the Lady Olivia in 'Twelfth Night', vowed herself to loneliness and weeping. Mistress of herself, she easily silenced the entreaties and remonstrances of underlings, and nursed her grief as it had been the thing she loved. Yet it was too keen, too bitter, too burning, to be a favoured guest. In fact, Constance, young, ardent, and vivacious, battled with it, struggled and longed to cast it off; but all that was joyful in itself, or fair in outward show, only served to renew it; and she could best support the burden of her sorrow with patience, when, yielding to it, it oppressed but did not torture her.

Constance had left the castle to wander in the neighbouring grounds. Lofty and extensive as were the apartments of her abode, she felt pent up within their walls, beneath their fretted roofs. The spreading uplands and the antique wood, associated to her with every dear recollection of her past life, enticed her to spend hours and days beneath their leafy coverts. The motion and change eternally working, as the wind stirred among the boughs, or the journeying sun rained its beams through them, soothed and called her out of that dull sorrow which clutched her heart with so unrelenting a pang beneath her castle roof.

There was one spot on the verge of the well-wooded park, one nook of ground, whence she could discern the country extended beyond, yet which was in itself thick set with tall umbrageous trees – a spot which she had forsworn, yet whither unconsciously her steps forever tended, and where again for the twentieth time that day, she had unaware found herself. She sat upon a grassy mound, and looked wistfully on the flowers she had herself planted to adorn the verdurous recess – to her the temple of memory and love. She held the letter from the king which was the parent to her of so much despair. Dejection sat upon her features, and her gentle heart asked fate why, so young, unprotected, and forsaken, she should have to struggle with this new form of wretchedness.

"I but ask," she thought, "to live in my father's halls – in the spot familiar to my infancy – to water with my frequent tears the graves of those I loved; and here in these woods, where such a mad dream of happiness was mine, to celebrate forever the obsequies of Hope!"

A rustling among the boughs now met her ear – her heart beat quick – all again was still.

"Foolish girl!" she half muttered; "Dupe of thine own passionate fancy: because here we met; because seated here I have expected, and sounds like these have announced, his dear approach; so now every coney as it stirs, and every bird as it awakens silence, speaks of him. O Gaspar! – mine once – never again will this beloved spot be made glad by thee – never more!"

Again the bushes were stirred, and footsteps were heard in the brake. She rose; her heart beat high; it must be that silly Manon, with her impertinent entreaties for her to return. But the steps were firmer and slower than would be those of her waiting-woman; and now emerging from the shade, she too plainly discerned the intruder. He first impulse was to fly: but once again to see him – to hear his voice: – once again before she placed eternal vows between them, to stand together, and find the wide chasm filled which absence had made, could not injure the dead, and would soften the fatal sorrow that made her cheek so pale.

And now he was before, her, the same beloved one with whom she had exchanged vows of constancy. He, like her, seemed sad; nor could she resist the imploring glance that entreated her for one moment to remain.

"I come, lady," said the young knight, "without a hope to bend your inflexible will. I come but once again to see you, and to bid you farewell before I depart for the Holy Land. I come to beseech you not to immure yourself in the dark cloister to avoid one as hateful as myself, – one you will never see more. Whether I die or live, France and I are parted forever!"

"That were fearful, were it true," said Constance; "but King Henry will never so lose his favourite cavalier. The throne you helped to build, you still will guard. Nay, as I ever had power over thought of thine, go not to Palestine."

"One word of yours could detain me – one smile – Constance" – and the youthful lover knelt before her; but her harsher purpose was recalled by the image once so dear and familiar, now so strange and so forbidden.

"Linger no longer here!" she cried. "No smile, no word of mine will ever again be yours. Why are you here – here, where the spirits of the dead wander, and claiming these shades as their own, curse the false girl who permits their murderer to disturb their sacred repose?"

"When love was young and you were kind," replied the knight, "you taught me to thread the intricacies of these woods you welcomed me to this dear spot, where once you vowed to be my own – even beneath these ancient trees."

"A wicked sin it was," said Constance, "to unbar my father's doors to the son of his enemy, and dearly is it punished!"

The young knight gained courage as she spoke; yet he dared not move, lest she, who, every instant, appeared ready to take flight, should be startled from her momentary tranquillity, but he slowly replied: – "Those were happy days, Constance, full of terror and deep joy, when evening brought me to your feet; and while hate and vengeance were as its atmosphere to yonder frowning castle, this leafy, starlit bower was the shrine of love."

"Happy? – Miserable days!" echoed Constance; "When I imagined good could arise from failing in my duty, and that disobedience would be rewarded of God. Speak not of love, Gaspar! – a sea of blood divides us forever! Approach me not! The dead and the beloved stand even now between us: their pale shadows warn me of my fault, and menace me for listening to their murderer."

"That am not I!" exclaimed the youth. "Behold, Constance, we are each the last of our race. Death has dealt cruelly with us, and we are alone. It was not so when first we loved – when parent, kinsman, brother, nay, my own mother breathed curses on the house of Villeneuve; and in spite of all I blessed it. I saw thee, my lovely one, and blessed it. The God of peace planted love in our hearts, and with mystery and secrecy we met during many a summer night in the moonlit dells; and when daylight was abroad, in this sweet recess we fled to avoid its scrutiny, and here, even here, where now I kneel in supplication, we both knelt and made our vows. Shall they be broken?"

Constance wept as her lover recalled the images of happy hours. "Never," she exclaimed, "O never! Thou knowest, or wilt soon know, Gaspar, the faith and resolves of one who dare not be yours. Was it for us to talk of love and happiness, when war, and hate, and blood were raging around! The fleeting flowers our young hands strewed were trampled by the deadly encounter of mortal foes. By your father's hand mine died; and little boots it to know whether, as my brother swore, and you deny, your hand did or did not deal the blow that destroyed him. You fought among those by whom he died. Say no more – no other word: it is impiety towards the unreposing dead to hear you. Go, Gaspar; forget me. Under the chivalrous and gallant Henry your career may be glorious; and some fair girl will listen, as once I did, to your vows, and be made happy by them. Farewell! May the Virgin bless you! In my cell and cloister-home I will not forget the best Christian lesson – to pray for our enemies. Gaspar, farewell!"

She glided hastily from the bower: with swift steps she threaded the glade and sought the castle. Once within the seclusion of her own apartment she gave way to the burst of grief that tore her gentle bosom like a tempest; for hers was that worst sorrow, which taints past joys, making wait upon the memory of bliss, and linking love and fancied guilt in such fearful society as that of the tyrant when he bound a living body to a corpse. Suddenly a thought darted into her mind. At first she rejected it as puerile and superstitious; but it would not be driven away. She called hastily for her attendant. "Manon," she said, "didst thou ever sleep on St. Catherine's couch?"

Manon crossed herself. "Heaven forefend! None ever did, since I was born, but two: one fell into the Loire and was drowned; the other only looked upon the narrow bed, and turned to her own home without a word. It is an awful place; and if the votary have not led a pious and good life, woe betide the hour when she rests her head on the holy stone!"

Constance crossed herself also. "As for our lives, it is only through our Lord and the blessed saints that we can any of us hope for righteousness. I will sleep on that couch tomorrow night!"

"Dear, my lady! And the king arrives tomorrow."

"The more need that I resolve. It cannot be that misery so intense should dwell in any heart, and no cure be found. I had hoped to be the bringer of peace to our houses; and if the good work to be for me a crown of thorns Heaven shall direct me. I will rest tomorrow night on St. Catherine's bed: and if, as I have heard, the saint deigns to direct her votaries in dreams, I will be guided by her; and, believing that I act according to the dictates of Heaven, I shall feel resigned even to the worst."

The king was on his way to Nantes from Paris, and he slept in this night at a castle but a few miles distant Before dawn a young cavalier was introduced into his chamber. The knight had a serious, nay, a sad aspect; and all beautiful as he was in feature and limb, looked wayworn and haggard. He stood silent in Henry's presence, who, alert and gay, turned his lively blue eyes upon his guest, saying gently, "So thou foundest her obdurate, Gaspar?"

"I found her resolved on our mutual misery. Alas! my liege, it is not, credit me, the least of my grief, that Constance sacrifices her own happiness when she destroys mine."

"And thou believest that she will say nay to the gaillard chevalier whom we ourselves present to her?"

"Oh, my liege, think not that thought! it cannot be. My heart deeply, most deeply, thanks you for your generous condescension. But she whom her lover's voice in solitude – whose entreaties, when memory and seclusion aided the spell – could not persuade, will resist even your majesty's commands. She is bent upon entering a cloister; and I, so please you, will now take my leave: – I am henceforth a soldier of the cross."

"Gaspar," said the monarch, "I know woman better than thou. It is not by submission nor tearful plaints she is to be won. The death of her relatives naturally sits heavy at the young countess's heart; and nourishing in solitude her regret and her repentance, she fancies that Heaven itself forbids your union. Let the voice of the world reach her – the voice of earthly power and earthly kindness – the one commanding, the other pleading, and both finding response in her own heart – and by my say and the Holy Cross. she will be yours. Let our plan still hold. And now to horse: the morning wears, and the sun is risen."

The king arrived at the bishop's palace, and proceeded forthwith to mass in the cathedral. A sumptuous dinner succeeded, and it was afternoon before the monarch proceeded through the town beside the Loire to where, a little above Nantes, the Chateau Villeneuve was situated. The, young countess received him at the gate. Henry looked in vain for the cheek blanched by misery, the aspect of downcast despair which he had been taught to expect. Her cheek was flushed, her manner animated, her voice scarce tremulous. "She loves him not," thought Henry, or already her heart has consented."

A collation was prepared for the monarch; and after some little hesitation, arising from the cheerfulness of her mien, he mentioned the name of Gaspar. Constance blushed instead of turning pale, and replied very quickly, "Tomorrow, good my liege; I ask for a respite but until tomorrow; – all will then be decided; – tomorrow I am vowed to God – or –."

She looked confused, and the king, at once surprised and pleased, said, "Then you hate not young De Vaudemont; – you forgive him for the inimical blood that warms his veins."

"We are taught that we should forgive, that we should love our enemies," the countess replied, with some trepidation.

"Now, by Saint Denis, that is a right welcome answer for the novice," said the king, laughing. "What ho! my faithful servingman, Don Apollo in disguise! Come forward, and thank your lady for her love."

In such disguise as had concealed him from all, the cavalier had hung behind, and viewed with infinite surprise the demeanour and calm countenance of the lady. He could not hear her words: but was this even she whom he had seen trembling and weeping the evening before? this she whose very heart was torn by conflicting passion? – who saw the pale ghosts of parent and kinsman stand between her and the lover whom more than her life she adored? It was a riddle hard to solve. The king's call was in unison with his impatience, and he sprang forward. He was at her feet; while she, still passion-driven overwrought by the very calmness she had assumed, uttered one cry as she recognized him and sank senseless on the floor.

All this was very unintelligible. Even when her attendants had brought her to life, another fit succeeded, and then passionate floods of tears; while the monarch, waiting in the hall, eyeing the half-eaten collation, and, humming some romance in commemoration of woman's waywardness, knew not how to reply to Vaudemont's look of bitter disappointment and anxiety. At length the countess's chief attendant came with an apology. "Her lady was ill, very ill. The next day she would throw herself at the king's feet, at once to solicit his excuse, and to disclose her purpose."

"Tomorrow – again tomorrow! Does tomorrow bear some charm, maiden?" said the king. "Can you read us the riddle pretty one? What strange tale belongs to tomorrow, that all rests on its advent?"

Manon coloured, looked down, and hesitated. But Henry was no tyro in the art of enticing ladies' attendants to disclose their ladies' council. Manon was besides, frightened by the countess's scheme, on which she was still obstinately bent, so she was the more readily induced to betray it. To sleep in St. Catherine's bed, to rest on a narrow ledge overhanging the deep rapid Loire, and if, as was most probable, the luckless dreamer escaped from falling into it, to take the disturbed visions that, such uneasy slumber might produce for the dictate of Heaven, was a madness of which even Henry himself could scarcely deem any woman capable. But could Constance, her whose beauty was so highly intellectual, and whom he had heard perpetually praised for her strength of mind and talents, could she be so strangely infatuated! And can passion play such freaks with us? – like death, levelling even the aristocracy of the soul, and bringing noble and peasant, the wise and foolish, under one thraldom? It was strange – yes she must have her way. That she hesitated in her decision was much; and it was to be hoped that St. Catherine would play no ill-natured part. Should it be otherwise, a purpose to be swayed by a dream might be influenced by other waking thoughts. To the more material kind of danger some safeguard should be brought.

There is no feeling more awful than that which invades a weak human heart bent upon gratifying its ungovernable impulses in contradiction to the dictates of conscience.

Forbidden pleasures are said to be the most agreeable – it may be so to rude natures, to those who love to struggle, combat, and contest; who find happiness in a fray, and joy in the conflict of passion. But softer and sweeter was the gentle spirit of Constance; and love and duty contending crushed and tortured her poor heart. To commit her conduct to the inspirations of religion, or, if it was so to be named, of superstition, was a blessed relief. The very perils that threatened her undertaking gave zest to it – to dare for his sake was happiness; – the very difficulty of the way that led to the completion of her wishes at once gratified her love and distracted her thoughts from her despair. Or if it was decreed that she must sacrifice all, the risk of danger and of death were of trifling import in comparison with the anguish which would then be her portion forever.

The night threatened to be stormy, the raging wind shook the casements, and the trees waved their huge shadowy arms, as giants might in fantastic dance and mortal broil. Constance and Manon, unattended, quitted the chateau by a postern, and began to descend the hillside. The moon had not yet risen; and though the way was familiar to both, Manon tottered and trembled; while the countess, drawing her silken cloak around her, walked with a firm step down the steep. They came to the river's side, where a small boat was moored, and one man was in waiting. Constance stepped lightly in, and then aided her fearful companion. In a few moments they were in the middle of the stream. The warm, tempestuous, animating, equinoctial wind swept over them. For the first time since her mourning, a thrill of pleasure swelled the bosom of Constance. She hailed the emotion with double joy. It cannot be, she thought, that Heaven will forbid me to love one so brave, so generous, and so good as the noble Gaspar. Another I can never love; I shall die if divided from him; and this heart, these limbs, so alive with glowing sensation, are they already predestined to an early grave? Oh no! life speaks aloud within them: I shall live to love. Do not all things love? – The winds as they whisper to the rushing waters? the waters as they kiss the flowery banks, and speed to mingle with the sea? Heaven and earth are sustained by, and live through, love; and shall Constance alone, whose heart has ever been a deep, gushing, overflowing well of true affection, be compelled to set a stone upon the fount to lock it up forever?

These thoughts bade fair for pleasant dreams; and perhaps the countess, an adept in the blind god's lore, therefore indulged them the more readily. But as thus she was engrossed by soft emotions, Manon caught her arm: – "Lady, look," she cried; "it comes yet the oars have no sound. Now the Virgin shield us! Would we were at home!"

A dark boat glided by them. Four rowers, habited in black cloaks, pulled at oars which, as Manon said, gave no sound; another sat at the helm: like the rest, his person was veiled in a dark mantle, but he wore no cap; and though his face was turned from them, Constance recognized her lover. "Gaspar," she cried aloud, "dost thou live?" – but the figure in the boat neither turned its head nor replied, and quickly it was lost. in the shadowy waters.

How changed now was the fair countess's reverie! Already Heaven had begun its spell, and unearthly forms were around, as she strained her eyes through the gloom. Now she saw and now she lost view of the bark that occasioned her terror; and now it seemed that another was there, which held the spirits of the dead; and her father waved to her from shore, and her brothers frowned on her.

Meanwhile they neared the landing. Her bark was moored in a little cove, and Constance stood upon the bank. Now she trembled, and half yielded to Manon's entreaty to return; till the unwise suivante mentioned the king's and De Vaudemont's name, and spoke of the answer to be given tomorrow. What answer, if she turned back from her intent?

She now hurried forward up the broken ground of the bank, and then along its edge, till they came to a bill which abruptly hung over the tide. A small chapel stood near. With trembling fingers the countess drew forth the key and unlocked its door. They entered. It was dark – save that a little lamp, flickering in the wind, showed an uncertain light from before the figure of Saint Catherine. The two women knelt; they prayed; and then rising, with a cheerful accent the countess bade her attendant goodnight. She unlocked a little low iron door. It opened on a narrow cavern. The roar of waters was heard beyond. "Thou mayest not follow, my poor Manon," said Constance, – "nor dost thou much desire: – this adventure is for me alone."

It was hardly fair to leave the trembling servant in the chapel alone, who had neither hope nor fear, nor love, nor grief to beguile her; but, in those days, esquires and waiting-women often played the part of subalterns in the army, gaming knocks and no fame. Besides, Manon was safe in holy ground. The countess meanwhile pursued her way groping in the dark through the narrow tortuous passage. At length what seemed light to her long darkened sense gleamed on her. She reached an open cavern in the overhanging hill's side, looking over the rushing tide beneath. She looked out upon the night. The waters of the Loire were speeding, as since that day have they ever sped – changeful, yet the same; the heavens were thickly veiled with clouds, and the wind in the trees was as mournful and ill-omened as if it rushed round a murderer's tomb. Constance shuddered a little, and looked upon her, bed, – a narrow ledge of earth and a grown stone bordering on the very verge of the precipice. She doffed her mantle – such was one of the conditions of the spell – she bowed her head, and loosened the tresses of her dark hair; she bared her feet; and thus, fully prepared for suffering to the utmost the chill influence of the cold night, she stretched herself on the narrow couch that scarce afforded room for her repose, and whence, if she moved in sleep, she must he precipitated into the cold waters below.

At first it seemed to her as if she never should sleep again. No great wonder that exposure to the blast and her perilous position should forbid her eyelids to close. At length she fell into a reverie so soft and soothing that she wished even to watch; and then by degrees her senses became confused; and now she was on St. Catherine's bed – the Loire rushing beneath, and the wild wind sweeping by – and now – oh whither? – and what dreams did the saint send, to drive her to despair, or to bid her be blest forever?

Beneath the rugged hill, upon the dark tide, another watched, who feared a thousand things, and scarce dared hope. He had meant to precede the lady on her way, but when he found that he had outstayed his time, with muffled oars and breathless haste he had shot by the bark that contained his Constance, nor even turned at her voice, fearful to incur her blame, and her commands to return. He had seen her emerge from the passage, and shuddered as she leant over the cliff. He saw her step forth, clad as she was in white, and could mark her as she lay on the edge beetling above. What a vigil did the lovers keep! – she given up to visionary thoughts, he knowing – and the consciousness thrilled his bosom with strange emotion – that love, and love for him, had led her to that perilous couch; and that while angers surrounded her in every shape, she was alive only to a small still voice that whispered to her heart the dream which was to decide their destinies. She slept perhaps – but he waked rid watched; and night wore away, as now praying, now entranced by alternating hope and fear, he sat in his boat, his eyes fixed on the white garb of the slumberer above.

Morning – was it morning that struggled in the clouds? Would morning ever come to waken her? And had she slept? and what dreams of weal or woe had peopled her sleep?

Gaspar grew impatient. He commanded his boatmen still to wait, and he sprang forward, intent on clambering the precipice. In vain they urged the danger, nay, the impossibility of the attempt; he clung to the rugged face of the hill, and found footing where it would seem no footing was. The acclivity, indeed, was not high; the dangers of St. Catherine's bed arising from the likelihood that any one who slept on so narrow a couch would be precipitated into the waters beneath. Up the steep ascent Gaspar continued to toil, and at last reached the roots of a tree that grew near the summit. Aided by its branches, he made good his stand at the very extremity of the ledge, near the pillow on which lay the uncovered head of his beloved. Her hands were folded on her bosom; her dark hair fell round her throat and pillowed her cheek; her face was serene: sleep was there in all its innocence and in all its helplessness; every wilder emotion was hushed, and her bosom heaved in regular breathing. He could see her heart beat as it lifted her fair hands crossed above. No statue hewn of marble in monumental effigy was ever half so fair; and within that surpassing form dwelt a soul true, tender, self-devoted, and affectionate as ever warmed a human breast.

With what deep passion did Gaspar gaze, gathering hope from the placidity of her angel countenance! A smile wreathed her lips, and he too involuntarily smiled, as he hailed the happy omen; when suddenly her cheek was flushed, her bosom heaved, a tear stole from her dark lashes, and then a whole shower fell, as starting up she cried, "No! – He shall not die! – I will unloose his chains! – I will save him!" Gaspar's hand was there. He caught her light form ready to fall from the perilous couch. She opened her eyes and beheld her lover, who had watched over her dream of fate, and who had saved her.

Manon also had slept well, dreaming or not, and was startled in the morning to find that she waked surrounded by a crowd. The little desolate chapel was hung with tapestry, the altar adorned with golden chalices – the priest was chanting mass to a goodly array of kneeling knights. Manon saw that King Henry was there; and she looked for another whom she found not, when the iron door of the cavern passage opened, and Gaspar de Vaudemont entered from it, leading the fair form of Constance; who, in her white robes and dark dishevelled hair, with a face in which smiles and blushes contended with deeper emotion, approached the altar, and, kneeling with her lover, pronounced the vows that united them forever.

It was long before the happy Gaspar could win from his lady the secret of her dream. In spite of the happiness she now enjoyed, she had suffered too much not to look back even with terror to those days when she thought love a crime, and every event connected with them wore an awful aspect. "Many a vision," she said, "she had that fearful night. She had seen the spirits of her father and brothers in Paradise; she had beheld Gaspar victoriously combating among the infidels; she had beheld him in King Henry's court, favoured and beloved; and she herself – now pining in a cloister, now a bride, now grateful to Heaven for the full measure of bliss presented to her, now weeping away her sad days – till suddenly she thought herself in Paynim land; and the saint herself, St. Catherine, guiding her unseen through the city of the infidels. She entered a palace, and beheld the miscreants rejoicing in victory; and then, descending to the dungeons beneath, they groped their way through damp vaults, and low, mildewed passages, to one cell, darker more frightful than the rest. On the floor lay one with soiled tattered garments, with unkempt locks and wild, matted beard. His cheek was worn and thin; his eyes had lost their fire; his form was a mere skeleton; the chains hung loosely on the fleshless bones."

"And was it my appearance in that attractive state and winning costume that softened the hard heart of Constance?" asked Gaspar, smiling at this painting of what would never be.

"Even so," replied Constance; "for my heart whispered me that this was my doing; and who could recall the life that waned in your pulses – who restore, save the destroyer? My heart never warmed to my living, happy knight as then it did to his wasted image as it lay, in the visions of night, at my feet. A veil fell from my eyes; a darkness was dispelled from before me. Methought I then knew for the first time what life and what death was. I was bid believe that to make the living happy was not to injure the dead; and I felt how wicked and how vain was that false philosophy which placed virtue and good in hatred, and unkindness. You should not die; I would loosen your chains and save you, and bid you live for love. I sprang forward, and the death I deprecated for you would, in my presumption, have been mine, – then, when first I felt the real value of life, – but that your arm was there to save me, your dear voice to bid me be blest for evermore."

If you enjoyed this, you might also like...
'The Pilgrims', see page 296
'Roger Dodsworth', see page 466

The Invisible Girl

THIS SLENDER NARRATIVE has no pretensions on the regularity of a story, or the development of situations and feelings; it is but a slight sketch, delivered nearly as it was narrated to me by one of the humblest of the actors concerned: nor will I spin out a circumstance interesting principally from its singularity and truth, but narrate, as concisely as I can, how I was surprised on visiting what seemed a ruined tower, crowning a bleak promontory overhanging the sea, that flows between Wales and Ireland, to find that though the exterior preserved all the savage rudeness that betokened many a war with the elements, the interior was fitted up somewhat in the guise of a summer-house, for it was too small to deserve any other name. It consisted but of the ground-floor, which served as an entrance, and one room above, which was reached by a staircase made out of the thickness of the wall.

This chamber was floored and carpeted, decorated with elegant furniture; and, above all, to attract the attention and excite curiosity, there hung over the chimney-piece – for to preserve the apartment from damp a fire-place had been built evidently since it had assumed a guise so dissimilar to the object of its construction – a picture simply painted in water-colours, which seemed more than any part of the adornments of the room to be at war with the rudeness of the building, the solitude in which it was placed, and the desolation of the surrounding scenery. This drawing represented a lovely girl in the very pride and bloom of youth; her dress was simple, in the fashion of the day – (remember, reader, I write at the beginning of the eighteenth century), her countenance was embellished by a look of mingled innocence and intelligence, to which was added the imprint of serenity of soul and natural cheerfulness. She was reading one of those folio romances which have so long been the delight of the enthusiastic and young; her mandoline was at her feet – her parroquet perched on a huge mirror near her; the arrangement of furniture and hangings gave token of a luxurious dwelling, and her attire also evidently that of home and privacy, yet bore with it an appearance of ease and girlish ornament, as if she wished to please. Beneath this picture was inscribed in golden letters, 'The Invisible Girl.'

Rambling about a country nearly uninhabited, having lost my way, and being overtaken by a shower, I had lighted on this dreary looking tenement, which seemed to rock in the blast, and to be hung up there as the very symbol of desolation. I was gazing wistfully and cursing inwardly my stars which led me to a ruin that could afford no shelter, though the storm began to pelt more seriously than before, when I saw an old woman's head popped out from a kind of loophole, and as suddenly withdrawn – a minute after a feminine voice called to me from within, and penetrating a little brambly maze that skreened a door, which I had not before observed, so skilfully had the planter succeeded in concealing art with nature I found the good dame standing on the threshold and inviting me to take refuge within. "I had just come up from our cot hard by," she said, "to look after the things, as I do every day, when the rain came on – will ye walk up till it is over?" I was about to observe that the cot hard by, at the venture of a few rain drops, was better than a ruined tower, and to ask my kind hostess whether 'the things' were pigeons or crows that she was come to look after, when the matting of the floor and the carpeting of the staircase struck my eye. I was still more surprised when I saw the room above; and beyond all, the picture and its singular inscription, naming her invisible, whom the painter had coloured forth into very agreeable visibility, awakened my most lively curiosity: the result of this, of my exceeding politeness towards the old woman, and her own natural garrulity, was a kind of garbled narrative which my imagination eked out, and future inquiries rectified, till it assumed the following form.

Some years before in the afternoon of a September day, which, though tolerably fair, gave many tokens of a tempestuous evening, a gentleman arrived at a little coast town about ten miles from this place; he expressed his desire to hire a boat to carry him to the town of about fifteen miles further on the coast. The menaces which the sky held forth made the fishermen loathe to venture, till at length two, one the father of a numerous family, bribed by the bountiful reward the stranger promised – the other, the son of my hostess, induced by youthful daring, agreed to undertake the voyage. The wind was fair, and they hoped to make good way before nightfall, and to get into port ere the rising of the storm. They pushed off with good cheer, at least the fishermen did; as for the stranger, the deep mourning which he wore was not half so black as the melancholy that wrapt his mind. He looked as if he had never smiled – as if some unutterable thought, dark as night and bitter as death, had built its nest within his bosom, and brooded therein eternally; he did not mention his name; but one of the villagers recognised him as Henry Vernon, the son of a baronet who possessed a mansion about three miles distant from the town for which be was bound. This mansion was almost abandoned by the family; but Henry had, in a romantic fit, visited it about three years before, and Sir Peter had been down there during the previous spring for about a couple of months.

The boat did not make so much way as was expected; the breeze failed them as they got out to sea, and they were fain with oar as well as sail, to try to weather the promontory that jutted out between them and the spot they desired to reach. They were yet far distant when the shifting wind began to exert its strength, and to blow with violent though unequal puffs. Night came on pitchy dark, and the howling waves rose and broke with frightful violence, menacing to overwhelm the tiny bark that dared resist their fury. They were forced to lower every sail, and take to their oars; one man was obliged to bale out the water, and Vernon himself took an oar, and rowing with desperate energy, equalled the force of the more practised boatmen. There had been much talk between the sailors before the tempest came on; now, except a brief command, all were silent. One thought of his wife and children, and silently cursed the caprice of the stranger that endangered in its effects, not only his life, but their welfare; the other feared less, for he was a daring lad, but he worked hard, and had no time for speech; while Vernon bitterly regretting the thoughtlessness which had made him cause others to share a peril, unimportant as far as he himself was concerned, now tried to cheer them with a voice full of animation and courage, and now pulled yet more strongly at the oar he held. The only person who did not seem wholly intent on the work he was about, was the man who baled; every now and then he gazed intently round, as if the sea held afar off, on its tumultuous waste, some object that he strained his eyes to discern. But all was blank, except as the crests of the high waves showed themselves, or far out on the verge of the horizon, a kind of lifting of the clouds betokened greater violence for the blast. At length he exclaimed – "Yes, I see it! – The larboard oar! – Now! If we can make yonder light, we are saved!" Both the rowers instinctively turned their heads, – but cheerless darkness answered their gaze.

"You cannot see it," cried their companion, "but we are nearing it; and, please God, we shall outlive this night." Soon he took the oar from Vernon's hand, who, quite exhausted, was failing in his strokes. He rose and looked for the beacon which promised them safety – it glimmered with so faint a ray, that now he said, "I see it;" and again, "it is nothing:" still, as they made way, it dawned upon his sight, growing more steady and distinct as it beamed across the lurid waters, which themselves became smoother, so that safety seemed to arise from the bosom of the ocean under the influence of that flickering gleam.

"What beacon is it that helps us at our need?" asked Vernon, as the men, now able to manage their oars with greater ease, found breath to answer his question.

"A fairy one, I believe," replied the elder sailor, "yet no less a true: it burns in an old tumble-down tower, built on the top of a rock which looks over the sea. We never saw it before this summer; and now each night it is to be seen, – at least when it is looked for, for we cannot see it from our village – and it is such an out of the way place that no one has need to go near it, except through a chance like this. Some say it is burnt by witches, some say by smugglers; but this I know, two parties have been to search, and found nothing but the bare walls of the tower.

All is deserted by day, and dark by night; for no light was to be seen while we were there, though it burned sprightly enough when we were out at sea.

"I have heard say," observed the younger sailor, "it is burnt by the ghost of a maiden who lost her sweetheart in these parts; he being wrecked, and his body found at the foot of the tower: she goes by the name among us of the 'Invisible Girl.'"

The voyagers had now reached the landing-place at the foot of the tower. Vernon cast a glance upward, – the light was still burning. With some difficulty, struggling with the breakers, and blinded by night, they contrived to get their little bark to shore, and to draw her up on the beach: they then scrambled up the precipitous pathway, overgrown by weeds and underwood, and, guided by the more experienced fishermen, they found the entrance to the tower, door or gate there was none, and all was dark as the tomb, and silent and almost as cold as death.

"This will never do," said Vernon; "surely our hostess will show her light, if not herself, and guide our darkling steps by some sign of life and comfort."

"We will get to the upper chamber," said the sailor, "if I can but hit upon the broken down steps: but you will find no trace of the Invisible Girl nor her light either, I warrant."

"Truly a romantic adventure of the most disagreeable kind," muttered Vernon, as he stumbled over the unequal ground: "she of the beacon-light must be both ugly and old, or she would not be so peevish and inhospitable."

With considerable difficulty, and, after divers knocks and bruises, the adventurers at length succeeded in reaching the upper story; but all was blank and bare, and they were fain to stretch themselves on the hard floor, when weariness, both of mind and body, conduced to steep their senses in sleep.

Long and sound were the slumbers of the mariners. Vernon but forgot himself for an hour; then, throwing off drowsiness, and finding his roughcouch uncongenial to repose, he got up and placed himself at the hole that served for a window, for glass there was none, and there being not even a rough bench, he leant his back against the embrasure, as the only rest he could find. He had forgotten his danger, the mysterious beacon, and its invisible guardian: his thoughts were occupied on the horrors of his own fate, and the unspeakable wretchedness that sat like a night-mare on his heart.

It would require a good-sized volume to relate the causes which had changed the once happy Vernon into the most woeful mourner that ever clung to the outer trappings of grief, as slight though cherished symbols of the wretchedness within. Henry was the only child of Sir Peter Vernon, and as much spoiled by his father's idolatry as the old baronet's violent and tyrannical temper would permit. A young orphan was educated in his father's house, who in the same way was treated with generosity and kindness, and yet who lived in deep awe of Sir Peter's authority, who was a widower; and these two children were all he had to exert his power over, or to whom to extend his affection. Rosina was a cheerful-tempered girl, a little timid, and careful to avoid displeasing her protector; but so docile, so kind-hearted, and so affectionate, that she felt even less than Henry the discordant spirit of his parent.

It is a tale often told; they were playmates and companions in childhood, and lovers in after days. Rosina was frightened to imagine that this secret affection, and the vows they pledged, might be disapproved of by Sir Peter. But sometimes she consoled herself by thinking that perhaps she was in reality her Henry's destined bride, brought up with him under the design of their future union; and Henry, while he felt that this was not the case, resolved to wait only until he was of age to declare and accomplish his wishes in making the sweet Rosina his wife. Meanwhile he was careful to avoid premature discovery of his intentions, so to secure his beloved girl from persecution and insult. The old gentleman was very conveniently blind; he lived always in the country, and the lovers spent their lives together, unrebuked and uncontrolled. It was enough that Rosina played on her mandoline, and sang Sir Peter to sleep every day after dinner; she was the sole female in the house above the rank of a servant, and had her own way in the disposal of her time. Even when Sir Peter frowned, her innocent caresses and sweet voice were powerful to smooth the rough current of his temper. If ever human spirit lived in an earthly paradise, Rosina did at this time: her pure love was made happy by Henry's constant presence; and the confidence they felt in each other, and the security with which they looked forward to the future, rendered their path one of roses under a cloudless sky. Sir Peter was the slight drawback that only rendered their tête-à-tête more delightful, and gave value to the sympathy they each bestowed on the other.

All at once an ominous personage made its appearance in Vernon-Place, in the shape of a widow sister of Sir Peter, who, having succeeded in killing her husband and children with the effects of her vile temper, came, like a harpy, greedy for new prey, under her brother's roof. She too soon detected the attachment of the unsuspicious pair. She made all speed to impart her discovery to her brother, and at once to restrain and inflame his rage. Through her contrivance Henry was suddenly despatched on his travels abroad, that the coast might be clear for the persecution of Rosina; and then the richest of the lovely girl's many admirers, whom, under Sir Peter's single reign, she was allowed, nay, almost commanded, to dismiss, so desirous was he of keeping her for his own comfort, was selected, and she was ordered to marry him. The scenes of violence to which she was now exposed, the bitter taunts of the odious Mrs. Bainbridge, and the reckless fury of Sir Peter, were the more frightful and overwhelming from their novelty. To all she could only oppose a silent, tearful, but immutable steadiness of purpose: no threats, no rage could extort from her more than a touching prayer that they would not hate her, because she could not obey.

"There must he something we don't see under all this," said Mrs. Bainbridge, "take my word for it, brother, she corresponds secretly with Henry. Let us take her down to your seat in Wales, where she will have no pensioned beggars to assist her; and we shall see if her spirit be not bent to our purpose."

Sir Peter consented, and they all three posted down to —shire, and took up their abode in the solitary and dreary looking house before alluded to as belonging to the family. Here poor Rosina's sufferings grew intolerable: – before, surrounded by well-known scenes, and in perpetual intercourse with kind and familiar faces, she had not despaired in the end of conquering by her patience the cruelty of her persecutors; – nor had she written to Henry, for his name had not been mentioned by his relatives, nor their attachment alluded to, and she felt an instinctive wish to escape the dangers about her without his being annoyed, or the sacred secret of her love being laid bare, and wronged by the vulgar abuse of his aunt or the bitter curses of his father. But when she was taken to Wales, and made a prisoner in her apartment, when the flinty mountains about her seemed feebly to imitate the stony hearts she had to deal with, her courage began to fail. The only attendant permitted to approach her was Mrs. Bainbridge's maid; and under the tutelage of her fiend-like mistress, this woman was used as a decoy to entice the poor prisoner into confidence, and then to be betrayed. The simple, kind-hearted Rosina was a facile dupe, and at last, in the excess of her despair, wrote to Henry, and gave the letter to this woman to be forwarded. The letter in itself would have softened marble; it did not speak of their mutual vows, it but asked him to intercede with his father, that he would restore her to the kind place she had formerly held in his affections, and cease from a cruelty that would destroy her. "For I may die," wrote the hapless girl, "but marry another – never!" That single word, indeed, had sufficed to betray her secret, had it not been already discovered; as it was, it gave increased fury to Sir Peter, as his sister triumphantly pointed it out to him, for it need hardly be said that while the ink of the address was yet wet, and the seal still warm, Rosina's letter was carried to this lady. The culprit was summoned before them; what ensued none could tell; for their own sakes the cruel pair tried to palliate their part. Voices were high, and the soft murmur of Rosina's tone was lost in the howling of Sir Peter and the snarling of his sister. "Out of doors you shall go," roared the old man; "under my roof you shall not spend another night." And the words "infamous seductress," and worse, such as had never met the poor girl's ear before, were caught by listening servants; and to each angry speech of the baronet, Mrs. Bainbridge added an envenomed point worse than all.

More dead than alive, Rosina was at last dismissed. Whether guided by despair, whether she took Sir Peter's threats literally, or whether his sister's orders were more decisive, none knew, but Rosina left the house; a servant saw her cross the park, weeping, and wringing her hands as she went. What became of her none could tell; her disappearance was not disclosed to Sir Peter till the following day, and then he showed by his anxiety to trace her steps and to find her, that his words had been but idle threats. The truth was, that though Sir Peter went to frightful lengths to prevent the marriage of the heir of his house with the portionless orphan, the object of his charity, yet in his heart he loved Rosina, and half his violence to her rose from anger at himself for treating her so ill. Now remorse began to sting him, as messenger after messenger came back without tidings of his victim; he dared not confess his worst fears to himself; and when his inhuman sister, trying to harden her conscience by angry words, cried, "The vile hussy has too surely made away with herself out of revenge to us;" an oath, the most tremendous, and a look sufficient to make even her tremble, commanded her silence. Her conjecture, however, appeared too true: a dark and rushing stream that flowed at the extremity of the park had doubtless received the lovely form, and quenched the life of this unfortunate girl.

Sir Peter, when his endeavours to find her proved fruitless, returned to town, haunted by the image of his victim, and forced to acknowledge in his own heart that he would willingly lay down his life, could he see her again, even though it were as the bride of his son – his son, before whose questioning he quailed like the veriest coward; for when Henry was told of the death of Rosina, he suddenly returned from abroad to ask the cause – to visit her grave, and mourn her loss in the groves and valleys which had been the scenes of their mutual happiness. He made a thousand inquiries, and an ominous silence alone replied. Growing more earnest and more anxious, at length he drew from servants and dependants, and his odious aunt herself, the whole dreadful truth. From that moment despair struck his heart, and misery named him her own. He fled from his father's presence; and the recollection that one whom he ought to revere was guilty of so dark a crime, haunted him, as of old the Eumenides tormented the souls of men given up to their torturings.

His first, his only wish, was to visit Wales, and to learn if any new discovery had been made, and whether it were possible to recover the mortal remains of the lost Rosina, so to satisfy the unquiet longings of his miserable heart. On this expedition was he bound, when he made his appearance at the village before named; and now in the deserted tower, his thoughts were busy with images of despair and death, and what his beloved one had suffered before her gentle nature had been goaded to such a deed of woe.

While immersed in gloomy reverie, to which the monotonous roaring of the sea made fit accompaniment, hours flew on, and Vernon was at last aware that the light of morning was creeping from out its eastern retreat, and dawning over the wild ocean, which still broke in furious tumult on the rocky beach. His companions now roused themselves, and prepared to depart. The food they had brought with them was damaged by sea water, and their hunger, after hard labour and many hours fasting, had become ravenous. It was impossible to put to sea in their shattered boat; but there stood a fisher's cot about two miles off, in a recess in the bay, of which the promontory on which the tower stood formed one side, and to this they hastened to repair; they did not spend a second thought on the light which had saved them, nor its cause, but left the ruin in search of a more hospitable asylum. Vernon cast his eyes round as he quitted it, but no vestige of an inhabitant met his eye, and he began to persuade himself that the beacon had been a creation of fancy merely. Arriving at the cottage in question, which was inhabited by a fisherman and his family, they made a homely breakfast, and then prepared to return to the tower, to refit their boat, and if possible bring her round. Vernon accompanied them, together with their host and his son. Several questions were asked concerning the Invisible Girl and her light, each agreeing that the apparition was novel, and not one being able to give even an explanation of how the name had become affixed to the unknown cause of this singular appearance; though both of the men of the cottage affirmed that once or twice they had seen a female figure in the adjacent wood, and that now and then a stranger girl made her appearance at another cot a mile off, on the other side of the promontory, and bought bread; they suspected both these to be the same, but could not tell. The inhabitants of the cot, indeed, appeared too stupid even to feel curiosity, and had never made any attempt at discovery. The whole day was spent by the sailors in repairing the boat; and the sound of hammers, and the voices of the men at work, resounded along the coast, mingled with the dashing of the waves. This was no time to explore the ruin for one who whether human or supernatural so evidently withdrew herself from intercourse with every living being. Vernon, however, went over the tower, and searched every nook in vain; the dingy bare walls bore no token of serving as a shelter; and even a little recess in the wall of the staircase, which he had not before observed, was equally empty and desolate.

Quitting the tower, he wandered in the pine wood that surrounded it, and giving up all thought of solving the mystery, was soon engrossed by thoughts that touched his heart more nearly, when suddenly there appeared on the ground at his feet the vision of a slipper. Since Cinderella so tiny a slipper had never been seen; as plain as shoe could speak, it told a tale of elegance, loveliness, and youth. Vernon picked it up; he had often admired Rosina's singularly small foot, and his first thought was a question whether this little slipper would have fitted it. It was very strange! – It must belong to the Invisible Girl. Then there was a fairy form that kindled that light, a form of such material substance, that its foot needed to be shod – and yet how shod? – with kid so fine, and of shape so exquisite, that it exactly resembled such as Rosina wore! Again the recurrence of the image of the beloved dead came forcibly across him; and a thousand home-felt associations, childish yet sweet, and lover-like though trifling, so filled Vernon's heart, that he threw himself his length on the ground, and wept more bitterly than ever the miserable fate of the sweet orphan.

In the evening the men quitted their work, and Vernon returned with them to the cot where they were to sleep, intending to pursue their voyage, weather permitting, the following morning.

Vernon said nothing of his slipper, but returned with his rough associates. Often he looked back; but the tower rose darkly over the dim waves, and no light appeared. Preparations had been made in the cot for their accommodation, and the only bed in it was offered Vernon; but he refused to deprive his hostess, and spreading his cloak on a heap of dry leaves, endeavoured to give himself up to repose. He slept for some hours; and when he awoke, all was still, save that the hard breathing of the sleepers in the same room with him interrupted the silence. He rose, and going to the window, looked out over the now placid sea towards the mystic tower; the light burning there, sending its slender rays across the waves. Congratulating himself on a circumstance he had not anticipated, Vernon softly left the cottage, and, wrapping his cloak round him, walked with a swift pace round the bay towards the tower.

He reached it; still the light was burning. To enter and restore the maiden her shoe, would be but an act of courtesy; and Vernon intended to do this with such caution, as to come unaware, before its wearer could, with her accustomed arts, withdraw herself from his eyes; but, unluckily, while yet making his way up the narrow pathway, his foot dislodged a loose fragment, that fell with crash and sound down the precipice. He sprung forward, on this, to retrieve by speed the advantage he had lost by this unlucky accident. He reached the door; he entered: all was silent, but also all was dark. He paused in the room below; he felt sure that a slight sound met his ear. He ascended the steps, and entered the upper chamber; but blank obscurity met his penetrating gaze, the starless night admitted not even a twilight glimmer through the only aperture. He closed his eyes, to try, on opening them again, to be able to catch some faint, wandering ray on the visual nerve; but it was in vain. He groped round the room: he stood still, and held his breath; and then, listening intently, he felt sure that another occupied the chamber with him, and that its atmosphere was slightly agitated by another's respiration. He remembered the recess in the staircase; but, before he approached it, he spoke – he hesitated a moment what to say. "I must believe," he said, "that misfortune alone can cause your seclusion; and if the assistance of a man – of a gentleman –"

An exclamation interrupted him; a voice from the grave spoke his name – the accents of Rosina syllabled, "Henry! – Is it indeed Henry whom I hear?"

He rushed forward, directed by the sound, and clasped in his arms the living form of his own lamented girl – his own Invisible Girl he called her; for even yet, as he felt her heart beat near his, and as he entwined her waist with his arm, supporting her as she almost sank to the ground with agitation, he could not see her; and, as her sobs prevented her speech, no sense, but the instinctive one that filled his heart with tumultuous gladness, told him that the slender, wasted form he pressed so fondly was the living shadow of the Hebe beauty he had adored.

The morning saw this pair thus strangely restored to each other on the tranquil sea, sailing with a fair wind for L—, whence they were to proceed to Sir Peter's seat, which, three months before, Rosina had quitted in such agony and terror. The morning light dispelled the shadows that had veiled her, and disclosed the fair person of the Invisible Girl. Altered indeed she was by suffering and woe, but still the same sweet smile played on her lips, and the tender light of her soft blue eyes were all her own. Vernon drew out the slipper, and shoved the cause that had occasioned him to resolve to discover the guardian of the mystic beacon; even now he dared not inquire how she had existed in that desolate spot, or wherefore she had so sedulously avoided observation, when the right thing to have been done was, to have sought him immediately, under whose care, protected by whose love, no danger need be feared. But Rosina shrunk from him as he spoke, and a death-like pallor came over her cheek, as she faintly whispered, "Your father's curse – your father's dreadful threats!" It appeared, indeed, that Sir Peter's violence, and the cruelty of Mrs. Bainbridge, had succeeded in impressing Rosina with wild and unvanquishable terror. She had fled from their house without plan or forethought – driven by frantic horror and overwhelming fear, she had left it with scarcely any money, and there seemed to her no possibility of either returning or proceeding onward. She had no friend except Henry in the wide world; whither could she go? – to have sought Henry would have sealed their fates to misery; for, with an oath, Sir Peter had declared he would rather see them both in their coffins than married. After wandering about, hiding by day, and only venturing forth at night, she had come to this deserted tower, which seemed a place of refuge. How she had lived since then she could hardly tell; – she had lingered in the woods by day, or slept in the vault of the tower, an asylum none were acquainted with or had discovered: by night she burned the pine-cones of the wood, and night was her dearest time; for it seemed to her as if security came with darkness. She was unaware that Sir Peter had left that part of the country, and was terrified lest her hiding-place should be revealed to him. Her only hope was that Henry would return – that Henry would never rest till he had found her. She confessed that the long interval and the approach of winter had visited her with dismay; she feared that, as her strength was failing, and her form wasting to a skeleton, that she might die, and never see her own Henry more.

An illness, indeed, in spite of all his care, followed her restoration to security and the comforts of civilized life; many months went by before the bloom revisiting her cheeks, and her limbs regaining their roundness, she resembled once more the picture drawn of her in her days of bliss, before any visitation of sorrow. It was a copy of this portrait that decorated the tower, the scene of her suffering, in which I had found shelter. Sir Peter, overjoyed to be relieved from the pangs of remorse, and delighted again to see his orphan-ward, whom he really loved, was now as eager as before he had been averse to bless her union with his son: Mrs. Bainbridge they never saw again. But each year they spent a few months in their Welch mansion, the scene of their early wedded happiness, and the spot where again poor Rosina had awoke to life and joy after her cruel persecutions. Henry's fond care had fitted up the tower, and decorated it as I saw; and often did he come over, with his 'Invisible Girl,' to renew, in the very scene of its occurrence, the remembrance of all the incidents which had led to their meeting again, during the shades of night, in that sequestered ruin.

If you enjoyed this, you might also like...
'A Dirge', see page 277
The Last Man, see page 331

The Pilgrims

THE TWILIGHT of one of those burning days of summer whose unclouded sky seems to speak to man of happier realms, had already flung broad shadows over the valley of Unspunnen; whilst the departing rays of a gorgeous sunset continued to glitter on the summits of the surrounding hills. Gradually, however, the glowing tints deepened; then grew darker and darker; until they finally yielded to the still more sober hues of night.

Beneath an avenue of lime-trees, which, from their size and luxuriance, appeared almost coeval with the soil in which they grew, Burkhardt of Unspunnen wandered to and fro with uneasy step, as if some recent sorrow occupied his troubled mind. At times he stood with his eyes steadfastly fixed on the earth, as if he expected to see the object of his contemplation start forth from its bosom; at other times he would raise his eyes to the summits of the trees, whose branches, now gently agitated by the night breeze, seemed to breathe sighs of compassion in remembrance of those happy hours which had once been passed beneath their welcome shade. When, however, advancing from beneath them, he beheld the deep blue heavens with the bright host of stars, hope sprang up within him at the thoughts of that glory to which those heavens and those stars, all lovely and beauteous as they seem, are but the faint heralds, and for a time dissipated the grief which had so long weighed heavily upon his heart.

From these reflections he was suddenly aroused by the tones of a manly voice addressing him. Burkhardt advancing, beheld, standing in the light of the moon, two pilgrims, clothed in the usual coarse and sombre garb, with their broad hats drawn over their brows.

"Praise be to God!" said the pilgrim who had just before awakened Burkhardt's attention, and who, from his height and manner, appeared to be the elder of the two. His words were echoed by a voice whose gentle and faultering accents showed the speaker to be still but of tender years.

"Whither are you going, friends? What seek you here, at this late hour?" said Burkhardt. "If you wish to rest you after your journey enter, and with God's blessing, and my hearty welcome, recruit yourselves."

"Noble sir, you have more than anticipated our petition," replied the elder pilgrim; "our duty has led us far from our native land, being bound on a pilgrimage to fulfil the vow of a beloved parent. We have been forced during the heat of the day to climb the steep mountain paths; and the strength of my brother, whose youth but ill befits him for such fatigues, began to fail, when the sight of your castle's towers, which the moon's clear beams discovered to us, revived our hopes. We resolved to beg a night's lodging under your hospitable roof, that we might be enabled, on tomorrow's dawn, to pursue our weary way."

"Follow me, my friends," said Burkhardt, as he, with quickened step, preceded them, that he might give some orders for their entertainment. The pilgrims rejoicing in so kind a reception, followed the knight in silence into a high-vaulted saloon, over which the tapers that were placed in branches against the walls cast a solemn but pleasing light, well in accordance with the present feelings of the parties.

The knight then discerned two countenances, the pleasing impression of which was considerably heightened by the modest yet easy manner with which the youthful pair received their host's kind attentions. Much struck with their appearance and demeanour, Burkhardt was involuntarily led back into the train of thoughts from which their approach had aroused him; and the scenes of former days flitted before him as he recollected that in this hall his beloved child was ever wont to greet him with her welcome smile on his return from the battle or the chase; brief scenes of happiness, which had been followed by events that had cankered his heart, and rendered memory but an instrument of bitterness and chastisement.

Supper was soon after served, and the pilgrims were supplied with the greatest attention, yet conversation wholly languished; for his melancholy reflections occupied Burkhardt, and respect, or perhaps a more kindly feeling, towards their host and benefactor, seemed to have sealed the lips of his youthful guests. After supper, however, a flask of the baron's old wine cheered his flagging spirits, and emboldened the elder pilgrim to break through the spell which had chained them.

"Pardon me, noble sir," said he, "for I feel it must seem intrusive in me to seek the cause of that sorrow which renders you so sad a spectator of the bounty and happiness which you liberally bestow upon others. Believe me, it is not the impulse of a mere idle curiosity that makes me express my wonder that you can thus dwell alone in this spacious and noble mansion, the prey to a deeply-rooted sorrow. Would that it were in our power to alleviate the cares of one who with such bounteous hand relieves the wants of his poorer brethren!"

"I thank you for your sympathy, good pilgrim," said the old noble, "but what can it avail you to know the story of those griefs which have made this earth a desert? And which are, with rapid pace, conducting me where alone I can expect to find rest. Spare me, then, the pain of recalling scenes which I would fain bury in oblivion. As yet, you are in the spring of life, when no sad remembrance gives a discordant echo of past follies, or of joys irrecoverably lost. Seek not to darken the sunshine of your youth with a knowledge of those fierce, guilty beings who, in listening to the fiend-like suggestions of their passions, are led astray from the paths of rectitude, and tear asunder the ties of nature."

Burkhardt thus sought to avoid the entreaty of the pilgrim. But the request was still urged with such earnest though delicate persuasion, and the rich tones of the stranger's voice awoke within him so many thoughts of days long, long past, that the knight felt himself almost irresistibly impelled to unburden his long- closed heart to one who seemed to enter into its feelings with a sincere cordiality.

"Your artless sympathy has won my confidence, my young friends," said he, "and you shall learn the cause of my sorrow.

"You see me here, lonely and forsaken. But fortune once looked upon me with her blandest smiles; and I felt myself rich in the consciousness of my prosperity, and the gifts which bounteous Heaven had bestowed. My powerful vassals made me a terror to those enemies which the protection that I was ever ready to afford to the oppressed and helpless brought against me. My broad and fertile possessions enabled me, with liberal hand, to relieve the wants of the poor, and to exercise the rights of hospitality in a manner becoming my state and my name. But of all the gifts which Heaven had showered upon me, that which I most prized was a wife, whose virtues had made her the idol of both the rich and the poor. But she who was already an angel, and unfitted for this grosser world, was too soon, alas! claimed by her kindred spirits. One brief year alone had beheld our happiness.

"My grief and anguish were most bitter, and would soon have laid me in the same grave with her, but that she had left me a daughter, for whose dear sake I struggled earnestly against my affliction. In her were now centred all my cares, all my hopes, all my happiness. As she grew in years, so did her likeness to her sainted mother increase; and every look and gesture reminded me of my Agnes. With her mother's beauty I had, with fond presumption, dared to cherish the hope that Ida would inherit her mother's virtues.

"Greatly did I feel the void that my irreparable loss had made; but the very thought of marrying again seemed to me a profanation. If, however, even for a single instant I had entertained this disposition, one look at our child would have crushed it, and made me cling with still fonder hope to her, in the fond confidence that she would reward me for every sacrifice that I could make. Alas! my friends, this hope was built on an unsure foundation! and my heart is even now tortured when I think on those delusive dreams.

"Ida, with the fondest caresses, would dispel each care from my brow; in sickness and in health she watched me with the tenderest solicitude; her whole endeavour seemed to be to anticipate my wishes. But, alas! like the serpent, which only fascinates to destroy, she lavished these caresses and attentions to blind me, and wrap me in fatal security.

"Many and deep were the affronts, revenged indeed, but not forgotten, which had long since caused (with shame I avow it) a deadly hatred between myself and Rupert, Lord of Wadischwyl, which the slightest occasion seemed to increase to a degree of madness. As he dared no longer throw down the gauntlet, he found means, much harder than steel or iron, to glut his revenge upon me.

"Duke Berchtold of Zähringen, one of those wealthy and powerful tyrants who are the very pests of that society of whose rights they ought to be the ready guardians, had made a sudden irruption on the peaceful inhabitants of the mountains, seizing their herds and flocks, and insulting their wives and daughters. Though possessed of great courage, yet being not much used to warfare, these unhappy men found it impossible to resist the tyrant, and hastened to entreat my instant succour. Without a moment's delay, I assembled my brave vassals, and marched against the spoiler. After a long and severe struggle, God blessed our cause, and our victory was complete.

"On the morning that I was to depart on my return to my castle, one of my followers announced to me that the duke had arrived in my camp, and wished an immediate interview with me. I instantly went forth to meet him; and Berchtold, hastening towards me with a smile, offered me his hand in token of reconciliation. I frankly accepted it, not suspecting that falsehood could lurk beneath so open and friendly an aspect.

"'My friend,' said he, 'for such I must call you; your valour in this contest has won my esteem, although I could at once convince you that I have just cause of quarrel with the insolent mountaineers. But, in spite of your victory in this unjust strife, into which doubtless you were induced to enter by the misrepresentations of those villains, yet as my nature abhors to prolong dissensions, I would willingly cease to think that we are enemies, and commence a friendship which, on my part, at least, shall not be broken. In token, therefore, that you do not mistrust a fellow-soldier, return with me to my castle, that we may there drown all remembrance of our past dissensions'.

"During a long time I resisted his importunity, for I had now been more than a year absent from my home, and was doubly impatient to return, as I fondly imagined that my delay would occasion much anxiety to my daughter. But the duke, with such apparent kindness and in such a courteous manner, renewed and urged his solicitations, that I could resist no longer.

"His Highness entertained me with the greatest hospitality and unremitted attention. But I soon perceived that an honest man is more in his element amidst the toils of the battle than amongst the blandishments of a Court, where the lip and the gesture carry welcome, but where the heart, to which the tongue is never the herald, is corroded by the unceasing strifes of jealousy and envy. I soon, too, saw that my rough and undisguised manners were an occasion of much mirth to the perfumed and essenced nothings who crowded the halls of the duke. I however stifled my resentment, when I considered that these creatures lived but in his favour, like those swarms of insects which are warmed into existence from the dunghill, by the sun's rays.

"I had remained the unwilling guest of the duke during some days, when the arrival of a stranger of distinction was announced with much ceremony; this stranger I found to be my bitterest foe, Rupert of Wadischwyl. The duke received him with the most marked politeness and attention, and more than once I fancied that I perceived the precedence of me was studiously given to my enemy. My frank yet haughty nature could ill brook this disparagement; and, besides, it seemed to me that I should but play the hypocrite if I partook of the same cup with the man for whom I entertained a deadly hatred.

"I resolved therefore to depart, and sought his Highness to bid him farewell. He appeared much distressed at my resolution, and earnestly pressed me to avow the cause of my abrupt departure. I candidly confessed that the undue favour which I thought he showed to my rival, was the cause.

"'I am hurt, deeply hurt,' said the duke, affecting an air of great sorrow, 'that my friend, and that friend the valiant Unspunnen, should think thus unjustly, dare I add, thus meanly of me. No, I have not even in thought wronged you; and to prove my sincerity and my regard for your welfare, know that it was not chance which conducted your adversary to my court. He comes in consequence of my eager wish to reconcile two men whom I so much esteem, and whose worth and excellence place them amongst the brightest ornaments of our favoured land. Let me,' therefore, said he, taking my hand and the hand of Rupert, who had entered during our dis course, 'let me have the satisfaction of reconciling two such men, and of terminating your ancient discord. You cannot refuse a request so congenial to that holy faith which we all profess. Suffer me therefore to be the minister of peace, and to suggest that, in token and in confirmation of an act which will draw down Heaven's blessing on us all, you will permit our holy Church to unite in one your far-famed lovely daughter with Lord Rupert's only son, whose virtues, if reports speak truly, render him no undeserving object of her love.'

"A rage, which seemed in an instant to turn my blood into fire, and which almost choked my utterance, took possession of me.

"'What!' exclaimed I, 'What, think you that I would thus sacrifice, thus cast away my precious jewel! Thus debase my beloved Ida? No, by her sainted mother, I swear that rather than see her married to his son, I would devote her to the cloister! Nay, I would rather see her dead at my feet than suffer her purity to be sullied by such contamination!'

"'But for the presence of his Highness,' cried Rupert wrathfully, 'your life should instantly answer for this insult! Nathless, I will well mark you, and watch you, too, my lord; and if you escape my revenge, you are more than man.'

"'Indeed, indeed, my Lord of Unspunnen,' said the duke, 'you are much too rash. Your passion has clouded your reason; and, believe me, you will live to repent having so scornfully refused my friendly proposal.'

"'You may judge me rash, my Lord Duke, and perhaps think me somewhat too hold, because I dare assert the truth in the courts of princes. But since my tongue cannot frame itself to speak that which my heart does not dictate, arid my plain but honest manner seems to displease you, I will, with your Highness's permission, withdraw to my own domain, whence I have been but too long absent.'

"'Undoubtedly, my lord, you have my permission,' said the duke haughtily, and at the same time turning coldly from me.

"My horse was brought, I mounted him with as much composure as I could command, and I breathed more freely as I left the castle far behind.

"During the second day's journey I arrived within a near view of my own native mountains, and I felt doubly invigorated as their pure breezes were wafted towards me. Still the fond anxiety of a father for his beloved child, and that child his only treasure, made the way seem doubly long. But as I approached the turn of the road which is immediately in front of my castle, I almost then wished the way lengthened; for my joy, my hopes, and my apprehensions crowded upon me almost to suffocation. A few short minutes, however, I thought, and then the truth, ill or good, will be known to me.

"When I came in full sight of my dwelling, all seemed in peace; nought exhibited any change since I had left it. I spurred my horse on to the gate, but as I advanced the litter stillness and desertion of all around surprised me. Not a domestic, not a peasant, was to be seen in the courts; it appeared as if the inhabitants of the castle were still asleep.

"'Merciful Heaven!' I thought, 'what can this stillness forebode! Is she, is my beloved child dead?'

"I could not summon courage to pull the bell. Thrice I attempted, yet thrice the dread of learning the awful truth prevented me. One moment, one word, even one sign, and I might be a forlorn, childless, wretched man, forever! None but a father can feel or fully sympathize in the agony of those moments! none but a father can ever fitly describe them!

"I was aroused from this inactive state by my faithful dog springing towards me to welcome my return with his boisterous caresses, and deep and loud-toned expressions of his joy. Then the old porter, attracted by the noise, came to the gate, which he instantly opened; but, as he was hurrying forward to meet me, I readily perceived that some sudden and painful recollection checked his eagerness. I leaped from my horse quickly, and entered the hall. All the other domestics now came forward, except my faithful steward Wilfred, he who had been always the foremost to greet his master.

"'Where is my daughter? Where is your mistress?' I eagerly exclaimed; 'Let me but know that she lives!'

"The faithful Wilfred, who had now entered the hall, threw himself at my feet, and with the tears rolling down his furrowed cheeks, earnestly pressed my hand, and hesitatingly informed me that my daughter lived: was well, he believed, but had quitted the castle.

"'Now, speak more quickly, old man,' said I hastily, and passionately interrupting him. 'What is it you can mean? My daughter lives; my Ida is well, but she is not here. Now, have you and my vassals proved recreants, and suffered my castle in my absence to be robbed of its greatest treasure? Speak! Speak plainly, I command ye!'

"'It is with anguish, as great almost as your own can be, my beloved master, that I make known to you the sad truth that your daughter has quitted her father's roof to become the wife of Conrad, the son of the Lord of Wadischwyl.'

"'The wife of Lord Rupert's son! My Ida the wife of the son of him whose very name my soul loathes!'

"My wrath now knew no bounds; the torments of hell seemed to have changed the current of my blood. In the madness of my passion I even cursed my own dear daughter! Yes, pilgrim, I even cursed her on whom I so fondly doted; for whose sake alone life for me had any charms. Oh! how often since have I attempted to recall that curse! and these bitter tears, which even now I cannot control, witness how severe has been my repentance of that awful and unnatural act!

"Dreadful were the imprecations which I heaped upon my enemy; and deep was the revenge I swore. I know not to what fearful length my unbridled passion would have hurried me, had I not, from its very excess, sunk senseless into the arms of my domestics. When I recovered, I found myself in my own chamber, and Wilfred seated near me. Some time, however, elapsed before I came to a clear recollection of the past events; and when I did, it seemed as if an age of crime and misery had weighed me down, and chained my tongue. My eye involuntarily wandered to that part of the chamber where hung my daughter's portrait. But this the faithful old man – who had not removed it, no doubt thinking that to do so would have offended me – had contrived to hide, by placing before it a piece of armour, which seemed as though it had accidentally fallen into that position.

"Many more days elapsed ere I was enabled to listen to the particulars of my daughter's flight, which I will, not to detain you longer with my griefs, now briefly relate. It appeared that, urged by the fame of her beauty, and by a curiosity most natural, I confess to youth, Conrad of Wadischwyl had, for a long time sought, but sought in vain, to see my Ida. Chance at length, however, favoured him. On her way to hear mass at our neighbouring monastery, he beheld her; and beheld her but to love. Her holy errand did not prevent him from addressing her; and well he knew how to gain the ear of one so innocent, so unsuspicious as my Ida! Too soon, alas! did his flatteries win their way to her guiltless heart.

"My child's affection for her father was unbounded; and readily would she have sacrificed her life for mine. But when love has once taken possession of the female heart, too quickly drives he thence those sterner guests, reason and duty. Suffice it therefore to say she was won, and induced to unite herself to Wadischwyl, before my return, by his crafty and insidious argument that I should be more easily persuaded to give them my pardon and my blessing, when I found that the step that she had taken was irrevocable. With almost equal art, he pleaded too that their union would doubtless heal the breach between the families of Wadischwyl and Unspunnen; and thus terminate that deadly hatred which my gentle Ida, ever the intercessor for peace, had always condemned. By this specious of sophistry my poor child was prevailed upon to tear herself from the heart of u fond parent, to unite herself with the son of that parent's most bitter enemy."

The pain of these recollections so overcame Burkhardt, that some time elapsed ere he could master his feelings. At length he proceeded.

"My soul seemed now to have but one feeling, revenge.

All other passions were annihilated by this master one; and I instantly prepared myself and my vassals to chastise this worse than robber. But such satisfaction was (I now thank God) denied me; for the Duke of Zähringen soon gave me memorable cause to recollect his parting words. Having attached himself with his numerous followers to my rival's party, these powerful chiefs suddenly invaded my domain. A severe struggle against most unequal numbers ensued. But, at length, though my brave retainers would fain have prolonged the hopeless strife, resolved to stop a needless waste of blood, I left the field to my foes; and, with the remnant of my faithful soldiers, hastened, in deep mortification, to bury myself within these walls. This galling repulse prevented all possibility of reconciliation with my daughter, whom I now regarded as the cause of my disgrace; and, consequently, I forbade her name even to be mentioned in my presence.

"Years rolled on; and I had no intelligence of her until I learned by a mere chance that she had with her husband quitted her native land. Altogether, more than twenty, to me long, long years, have now passed since her flight; and though, when time brought repentance, and my anger and revenge yielded to better feelings, I made every effort to gain tidings of my poor child, I have not yet been able to discover any further traces of her. Here therefore have I lived a widowed, childless, heartbroken old man. But I have at least learned to bow to the dispensations of an all-wise Providence, which has in its justice stricken me, for thus remorselessly cherishing that baneful passion which Holy Law so expressly forbids. Oh! how I have yearned to see my beloved child! how I have longed to clasp her to this withered, blighted heart! With scalding tears of the bitterest repentance have I revoked those deadly curses, which, in the plenitude of my unnatural wrath, I dared to utter daily. Ceaselessly do I now weary Heaven with my prayers to obliterate all memory of those fatal imprecations; or to let them fall on my own head, and shower down only its choicest blessings on that of my beloved child! But a fear, which freezes my veins with horror, constantly haunts me lest the maledictions which I dared to utter in my moments of demoniac vindictiveness, should, in punishment for my impiety, have been fulfilled.

"Often, in my dreams, do I behold my beloved child; but her looks are always in sadness, and she ever seems mildly but most sorrowfully to upbraid me for having so inhumanly cast her from me. Yet she must, I fear, have died long ere now; for, were she living, she would not, I think, have ceased to endeavour to regain the affections of a father who once loved her so tenderly. It is true that at first she made many efforts to obtain my forgiveness. Nay, I have subsequently learned that she even knelt at the threshold of my door, and piteously supplicated to be allowed to see me. But my commands had been so peremptory, and the steward who had replaced Wilfred, after his death, was of so stern and unbending a disposition, that, just and righteous as was this her last request, it was unfeelingly denied to her. Eternal Heaven! She whom I had loved as perhaps never father loved before – she whom I had fondly watched almost hourly lest the rude breeze of winter should chill her, or the summer's heat should scorch her – she whom I had cherished in sickness through many a livelong night, with a mother's devotion, and more than a mother's solicitude, even she, the only child of my beloved Agnes, and the anxious object of the last moments of her life, was spurned from my door! From this door whence no want goes unrelieved, and where the very beggar finds rest! And now, when I would bless the lips that even could say to me 'she lives,' I can nowhere gather the slightest tidings of my child. Ah, had I listened to the voice of reason, had I not suffered my better feelings to be mastered by the wildest and fellest passions, I might have seen herself, and perhaps her children, happy around me, cheering the evening of my life. And when my last hour shall come, they would have closed my eyes in peace, and, in unfeigned sorrow have daily addressed to Heaven their innocent prayers for my soul's eternal rest.

"You now know, pilgrims, the cause of my grief; and I see by the tears which you have so abundantly shed, that you truly pity the forlorn being before you. Remember him and his sorrows therefore ever in your prayers; and when you kneel at the shrine to which you are bound, let not those sorrows be forgotten."

The elder pilgrim in vain attempted to answer; the excess of his feelings overpowered his utterance. At length, throwing himself at the feet of Burkhardt, and casting off his pilgrim's habits, he with difficulty exclaimed:

"See here, thine Ida's son! And behold in my youthful companion, thine Ida's daughter! Yes, before you kneel the children of her whom you so much lament. We came to sue for that pardon, for that love, which we had feared would have been denied us. But, thanks be to God, who has mollified your heart, we have only to implore that you will suffer us to use our poor efforts to alleviate your sorrows, and render more bright and cheerful your declining years."

In wild and agitated surprise, Burkhardt gazed intently upon them. It seemed to him as if a beautiful vision were before him, which he feared even a breath might dispel. When, however, he became assured that he was under the influence of no delusion, the tumult of his feelings overpowered him, and he sank senselessly on the neck of the elder pilgrim; who, with his sister's assistance, quickly raised the old man, and by their united efforts restored him, ere long, to his senses. But when Burkhardt beheld the younger pilgrim, the very image of his lost Ida, bending over him with the most anxious and tender solicitude, he thought that death had ended all his worldly sufferings, and that heaven had already opened to his view.

"Great God!" at length he exclaimed, "I am unworthy of these Thy mercies! Grant me to receive them as I ought! I need not ask," added he after a pause, and pressing the pilgrims to his bosom, "for a confirmation of your statement, or of my own sensations of joy. All, all tells me that you are the children of my beloved Ida. Say, therefore, is your mother dead? Or dare I hope once more to clasp her to my heart?"

The elder pilgrim, whose name was Hermann, then stated to him that two years had passed since his parent had breathed her last in his arms. Her latest prayer was. that Heaven would forgive her the sorrow she had caused her father, and forbear to visit her own error on her children's heads. He then added that his father had been dead many years.

"My mother," continued Hermann, drawing from his bosom a small sealed packet, "commanded me, on her deathbed, to deliver this into your own hands. 'My son,' she said, 'when I am dead, if my father still lives, cast yourself at his feet, and desist not your supplications until you have obtained from him a promise that he will read this prayer. It will acquaint him with a repentance that may incite him to recall his curse; and thus cause the earth to lie lightly on all that will shortly remain of his once loved Ida. Paint to him the hours of anguish which even your tender years have witnessed. Weary him, my son, with your entreaties; cease them not until you have wrung from him his forgiveness.'

"As you may suppose, I solemnly engaged to perform my mother's request; and as soon as our grief for the loss of so dear, so fond a parent, would permit us, my sister and myself resolved, in these pilgrim's habits, to visit your castle; and, by gradual means, attempt to win your affections, if we found you still relentless, and unwilling to listen to our mother's prayer."

"Praise be to God, my son," said Burkhardt, "at whose command the waters spring from the barren rock, that He has bidden the streams of love and repentance to flow once more from my once barren and flinty heart. But let me not delay to open this sad memorial of your mother's griefs. I wish you, my children, to listen to it, that you may hear both her exculpation and her wrongs."

Burkhardt hid his face in his hands, and remained for some moments earnestly struggling with his feelings. At length he broke the seal, and, with a voice which at times was almost overpowered, read aloud the contents.

"My beloved father, if by that fond title your daughter may still address you, feeling that my sad days are now numbered, I make this last effort, ere my strength shall fail me, to obtain at least your pity for her you once so much loved; and to beseech you to recall that curse which has weighed too heavily upon her heart. Indeed, my father, I am not quite that guilty wretch you think me. Do not imagine that, neglecting every tie of duty and gratitude, I could have left the tenderest of parents to his widowed lonely home, and have united myself with the son of his sworn foe, had I not fondly, most ardently, hoped, nay, had cherished the idea almost to certainty, that you would, when you found that I was a wife, have quickly pardoned a fault, which the fears of your refusal to our union had alone tempted me to commit. I firmly believed that my husband would then have shared with me my father's love, and have, with his child, the pleasing task of watching over his happiness and comfort. But never did I for an instant imagine that I was permanently wounding the heart of that father. My youth, and the ardour of my husband's persuasions, must plead some extenuation of my fault.

"The day that I learnt the news of your having pronounced against me that fatal curse, and your fixed determination never more to admit me to your presence, has been marked in characters indelible on my memory. At that moment it appeared as if Heaven had abandoned me, had marked me for its reprobation as a parricide! My brain and my heart seemed on fire, whilst my blood froze in my veins. The dullness of death crept over every limb, and my

tongue refused all utterance. I would have wept, but the source of my tears was dried within me.

"How long I remained in this state I know not, as I became insensible, and remained so for some days. On returning to a full consciousness of my wretchedness, I would instantly have rushed to you, and cast myself at your feet, to wring from you, if possible, your forgiveness; but my limbs were incapable of all motion. Soon, too, I learned that the letters which I dictated were returned unopened; and my husband at last informed me that all his efforts to see you had been utterly fruitless.

"Yet the moment I had gained sufficient strength, I went to the castle, but, unfortunately for me, even as I entered, I encountered a stern wretch, to whom my person was not unknown; and he instantly told me that my efforts to see his master would be useless. I used prayers and entreaties; I even knelt upon the bare ground to him. But so far from listening to me, he led me to the gate, and, in my presence, dismissed the old porter who had admitted me, and who afterwards followed my fortunes until the hour of his death. Finding that all my attempts were fruitless, and that several of the old servants had been discarded on my account, with a heart completely broken, I succumbed to my fate, and abandoned all further attempt.

"After the birth of my son (to whose fidelity and love I trust this sad memorial), my husband, with the tenderest solicitude, employed every means in his power to divert my melancholy, and having had a valuable property in Italy bequeathed to him, prevailed upon me to repair to that favoured and beauteous country. But neither the fond attentions of my beloved Conrad, nor the bright sunshine and luxurious breezes, could overcome a grief so deeply rooted as mine; and I soon found that Italy had less charms for me than my own dear native land, with its dark pine-clad mountains.

"Shortly after we had arrived at Rome, I gave birth to a daughter; an event which was only too soon followed by the death of my affectionate husband. The necessity of ceaseless attention to my infant in some measure alleviated the intense anguish which I suffered from that most severe loss. Nevertheless, in the very depth of this sorrow, which almost overcharged my heart, Heaven only knows how often, and how remorsefully, while bending over my own dear children in sickness, have I called to mind the anxious fondness with which the tenderest and best of fathers used to watch over me!

"I struggled long and painfully with my feelings, and often did I beseech God to spare my life, that I might be enabled to instruct my children in His holy love and fear, and teach them to atone for the error of their parent. My prayer has in mercy been heard; the boon I supplicated has been granted; and I trust, my beloved father, that if these children should be admitted to your affections, you will find that I have trained up two blessed intercessors for your forgiveness, when it shall have pleased Heaven to have called your daughter to her account before that dread tribunal where a sire's curse will plead so awfully against her. Recall then, oh, father! recall your dreadful malediction from your poor repentant Ida! and send your blessing as an angel of mercy to plead for her eternal rest. Farewell, my father, forever! forever, farewell! By the cross, whose emblem her fevered lips now press; by Him, who in His bound *less mercy hung upon that cross, your daughter, your once much loved Ida, implores you, supplicates you, not to let her plead in vain!"*

"My child, my child!" sobbed Burkhardt, as the letter dropped from his hand, "May the Father of All forgive me as freely as I from the depths of my wrung heart forgive you! Would that your remorseful father could have pressed you to his heart, with his own lips have assured you of his affection, and wiped away the tears of sorrow from your eyes! But he will cherish these beloved remembrances of you, and will more jealously guard them than his own life."

Burkhardt passed the whole of the following day in his chamber, to which the good Father Jerome alone was admitted, as the events of the preceding day rendered a long repose absolutely necessary. The following morning, however, he entered the hall, where Hermann and Ida were impatiently waiting for him. His pale countenance still exhibited deep traces of the agitation he had experienced; but having kissed his children most affectionately, he smilingly flung round Ida's neck a massive gold chain, richly wrought, with a bunch of keys appended to it.

"We must duly install our Lady of the Castle," said he, "and invest her with her appropriate authorities. But, hark! from the sound of the porter's horn it seems as if our hostess would have early calls upon her hospitality. Whom have we here?" continued he, looking out up the avenue. "By St. Hubert, a gay and gallant knight is approaching, who shall be right welcome – that is, if my lady approve. Well, Willibald, what bring you? A letter from our good friend the Abbot of St. Anselm. What says he?"

"I am sure that you will not refuse your welcome to a young knight, who is returning by your castle to his home, from the Emperor's wars. He is well known to me, and I can vouch for his being a guest worthy of your hospitality, which will not be the less freely granted to him because he does not bask in the golden smiles of fortune."

"No, no, that it shall not, my good friend; and if fortune frown upon him, he shall be doubly welcome. Conduct him hither instantly, good Willibald."

The steward hastened to usher in the stranger, who advanced into the hall with a modest but manly air. He was apparently about twenty-five years of age; his person was such as might well, in the dreams of a young maiden, occupy no unconspicuous place.

"Sir Knight," said Burkhardt, taking him cordially by the hand, "you are right welcome to my castle, and such poor entertainment as it can afford. We must make you forget your wounds, and the rough usage of a soldier's life. But, soft, I already neglect my duty in not first introducing our hostess," added the aged knight, presenting Ida. "By my faith," he continued, "judging from my lady's blushing smile, you seem not to have met for the first time. Am I right in my conjecture?"

"We have met, sir," replied Ida, with such confusion as pleasantly implied that the meeting was not in differently recollected, "in the parlour of the abbess of the Ursulines, at Munich, where I have sometimes been to visit a much valued friend."

"The abbess," said the young knight, "was my cousin; and my good fortune more than once gave me the happiness of seeing in her convent this lady. But little did I expect that amongst these mountains the fickle goddess would again have so favoured a homeless wanderer."

"Well, Sir Knight," replied Burkhardt, "we trust that fortune has been equally favourable to us. And now we will make bold to ask your name; and then, without useless and tedious ceremony, on the part of ourselves and our hostess, bid you again a hearty welcome."

"My name," said the stranger, "is Walter de Blumfeldt; though humble, it has never been disgraced; and with the blessing of Heaven, I hope to hand it down as honoured as I have received it."

* * *

Weeks, months rolled on, and Walter de Blumfeldt was still the guest of the Lord of Unspunnen; till, by his virtues, and the many excellent qualities which daily more and more developed themselves, he wound himself around Burkhardt's heart, which the chastened life of the old knight had rendered particularly susceptible of the kindlier feelings. Frequently would he now, with tears in his eyes, declare that he wished he could convince each and all with whom his former habits had caused any difference, how truly he forgave them, and desired their forgiveness.

"Would," said he one day, in allusion to this subject, "that I could have met my old enemy, the Duke of Zähringen, and with a truly heartfelt pleasure and joy have embraced him, and numbered him amongst my friends. But he is gathered to his fathers, and I know not whether he has left any one to bear his honours."

Each time that Walter had offered to depart, Burkhardt had found some excuse to detain him; for it seemed to him that in separating from his young guest he should lose a link of that chain which good fortune had so lately woven for him. Hermann, too, loved Walter as a brother; and Ida fain would have imagined that she loved him as a sister; but her heart more plainly told her what her colder reasoning sought to hide. Unspunnen, who had for some time perceived the growing attachment between Walter and Ida, was not displeased at the discovery, as he had long ceased to covet riches; and had learnt to prize the sterling worth of the young knight, who fully answered the high terms in which the Prior of St. Anselm always spoke of him. Walking one evening under the shade of that very avenue where he had first encountered Hermann and Ida, he perceived the latter, at some little distance, in conversation with Walter. It was evident to Burkhardt that the young knight was not addressing himself to a very unwilling ear, as Ida was totally regardless of the loud cough with which Burkhardt chose to be seized at that moment; nor did she perceive him, until he exclaimed, or rather vociferated, "Do you know, Walter, that, under this very avenue, two pilgrims, bound to some holy shrine, once accosted me; but that, in pity to my sins and forlorn condition, they exchanged their penitential journey for an act of greater charity, and have ever since remained to extend their kind cares to an aged and helpless relative. One, however, of these affectionate beings is now about to quit my abode, and to pass through the rest of this life's pilgrimage with a helpmate, in the person of the fair daughter of the Baron de Leichtfeldt, and thus leave his poor companion with only the tedious society of an old man. Say, Sir Knight, will thy valour suffer that such wrong be done; or wilt thou undertake to conduct this forsaken pilgrim on her way, and guide her through the chequered paths of this variable life? I see by the lowliness with which you bend, and the colour which mantles in your cheek, that I speak not to one insensible to an old man's appeal. But soft, soft, Sir Knight, my Ida is not yet canonized, and therefore cannot afford to lose a hand, which inevitably must occur if you continue to press it with such very ardent devotion. But what says our pilgrim; does she accept of thy conduct and service, Sir Knight?"

Ida, scarcely able to support herself, threw herself on Burkhardt's neck. We will not raise the veil which covers the awful moment that renders a man, as he supposes, happy or miserable forever. Suffice is to say that the day which made Hermann the husband of the daughter of the Baron de Leichtfeldt, saw Ida the wife of Walter de Blumfeldt.

* * *

Six months had passed rapidly away to the happy inhabitants of Unspunnen, and Burkhardt seemed almost to have grown young again. He was one of the most active in the preparations which were necessary in consequence of Walter suggesting that they should spend Ida's birthday in a favourite retreat of his and hers. This chosen spot was a beautiful meadow, in front of which meandered a small limpid stream; at the back was a gorgeous amphitheatre of trees, the wide-spreading branches of which cast a refreshing shade over the richly enamelled grass.

In this beauteous retreat were Burkhardt, Walter, and his Ida passing the sultry hours of noon, when Walter, who had been relating some of his adventures at the court of the Emperor, and recounting the magnificence of the tournaments, turning to his bride, said:

"But what avails all that pomp, my Ida. How happy are we in this peaceful vale! We envy neither princes nor dukes their palaces or their states. What say you, my Ida, could you brook the ceremony of a court, and the pride of royalty? Methinks even the coronet of a duchess would but ill replace the wreath of blushing roses on your head."

"Gently, my good husband," replied Ida, laughing; "they say, you know, that a woman loves these vanities too dearly in her heart ever to despise them. Then how can you expect so frail a mortal as your poor wife to hold them in contempt? Indeed, I think," added she, assuming an air of burlesque dignity, "that I should make a lofty duchess, and wear my coronet with most becoming grace. And now, by my faith, Walter, I recollect that you have this day, like a true and gallant knight, promised to grant whatever boon I shall ask. On my bended knee, therefore, I humbly sue that if you know any spell or magic wile, to make a princess or a duchess for only a single day, that you will forthwith exercise your art upon me; just in order to enable me to ascertain with how much or how little dignity I could sustain such honours. It is no very difficult matter, Sir Knight: you have only to call in the aid of Number Nip, or some such handy workman of the woods. Answer, most chivalrous husband, for thy disconsolate wife rises not until her prayer is granted."

"Why, Ida, you have indeed craved a rare boon," replied Walter; "and how to grant it may well puzzle my brain till it becomes crazed with the effort. But, let me see, let me see," continued he musingly; "I have it! Come hither, love, here is your throne," said he, placing her on a gentle eminence richly covered with the fragrant wild thyme and the delicate harebell; "kings might now envy you the incense which is offered to you. And you, noble sir," added he, addressing Burkhardt, "must stand beside her Highness, in quality of chief counsellor. There are your attendants around you; behold that tall oak, he must be your Highness's pursuivant, and yonder slender mountain ashes, your trusty pages."

"This is but a poor fulfilment of the task you have undertaken, Sir mummer," said Ida, with a playful and arch affectation of disappointment.

"Have patience for a brief while, fair dame," replied Walter, laughing; "for now I must awaken your Highness's men-at-arms."

Then, taking from his side a silver horn, he loudly sounded the melodious reveille. As he withdrew the instrument from his lips, a trumpet thrillingly answered to the call; and scarcely had its last notes died away, when, from the midst of the woods, as if the very trees were gifted with life, came forth a troop of horsemen, followed by a body of archers on foot. They had but just entirely emerged, when numerous peasants, both male and female, appeared in their gayest attire; and, together with the horsemen and the archers, rapidly and picturesquely ranged themselves in front of the astonished Ida, who had already abdicated her throne, and clung to the arm. of Walter. They then suddenly divided, and twelve pages in richly - emblazoned dresses advanced. After them followed six young girls, whose forms and features the Graces might have envied, bearing two coronets placed on embroidered cushions. In the rear of these, supporting his steps with his abbatial staff, walked the venerable Abbot of St. Anselm, who, with his white beard flowing almost to his girdle, and his benign looks that showed the pure commerce of the soul which gave life to an eye the brightness of which seventy years had scarcely diminished, seemed to Ida a being of another world. The young girls then advancing, and kneeling before Walter and his wife, presented the coronets.

Ida, who had remained almost breathless with wonder, could now scarcely articulate: "Dear, dear Walter, what is all this pomp what does – what can – it mean?"

"Mean! My beloved," replied her husband; "did you not bid me make you a duchess? I have but obeyed your high commands, and I now salute you, Duchess of Zähringen!"

The whole multitude then made the woods resound with the acclamation:

"Long live the Duke and Duchess of Zähringen!"

Walter, having for some moments enjoyed the unutterable amazement of the now breathless Ida, and the less evident but perhaps equally intense surprise of Burkhardt, turning to the latter, said:

"My more than father, you see in me the son of your once implacable enemy, the Duke of Zähringen. He has been many years gathered to his fathers; and I, as his only son, have succeeded to his title and his possessions. My heart, my liberty, were entirely lost in the parlour of the Abbess of the Ursulines. But when I learnt whose child my Ida was, and your sad story, I resolved ere I would make her mine to win not only her love, but also your favour and esteem. How well I have succeeded, this little magic circle on my Ida's finger is my witness. It will add no small measure to your happiness to know that my father had for many years repented of the wrongs which he had done you; and, as much as possible to atone for them, entrusted the education of his son to the care of this my best of friends, the Abbot of St. Anselm, that he might learn to shun the errors into which his sire had unhappily fallen. And now," continued he, advancing, and leading Ida towards the abbot, "I have only to beg your blessing, and that this lady, whom through Heaven's goodness I glory to call my wife, be invested with those insignia of the rank which she is so fit to adorn."

Walter, or, as we must now call him, the Duke of Zähringen, with Ida, then lowly knelt before the venerable abbot, whilst the holy man, with tears in his eyes, invoked upon them the blessings of Heaven. His High ness then rising, took one of the coronets, and placing it on Ida's head, said:

"Mayst thou be as happy under this glittering coronet, as thou wert under the russet hood in which I first beheld thee."

"God and our Lady aid me!" replied the agitated Ida; "And may He grant that I may wear it with as much humility. Yet thorns, they say, spring up beneath a crown."

"True, my beloved," said the duke, "and they also grow beneath the peasant's homely cap. But the rich alchemy of my Ida's virtues will ever convert all thorns into the brightest jewels of her diadem."

If you enjoyed this, you might also like...
'The Dream', see page 278
'The Mourner', see page 264

The Heir of Mondolfo

IN THE BEAUTIFUL and wild country near Sorrento, in the Kingdom of Naples, at the time it was governed by monarchs of the house of Anjou, there lived a territorial noble, whose wealth and power overbalanced that of the neighbouring nobles. His castle, itself a stronghold, was built on a rocky eminence, toppling over the blue and lovely Mediterranean. The hills around were covered with ilex-forests, or subdued to the culture of the olive and vine. Under the sun no spot could be found more favoured by nature.

If at eventide you had passed on the placid wave beneath the castellated rock that bore the name of Mondolfo, you would have imagined that all happiness and bliss must reside within its walls, which, thus nestled in beauty, overlooked a scene of such surpassing loveliness; yet if by chance you saw its lord issue from the portal, you shrunk from his frowning brow, you wondered what could impress on his worn cheek the combat of passions. More piteous sight was it to behold his gentle lady, who, the slave of his unbridled temper, the patient sufferer of many wrongs, seemed on the point of entering upon that only repose 'where the wicked cease from troubling and the weary are at rest'. The Prince Mondolfo had been united early in life to a princess of the regal family of Sicily. She died in giving birth to a son. Many years subsequently, after a journey to the northern Italian states, he returned to his castle, married. The speech of his bride declared her to be a Florentine. The current tale was that he married her for love, and then hated her as the hindrance of his ambitious views. She bore all for the sake of her only child – a child born to its father's hate; a boy of gallant spirit, brave even to wildness. As he grew up, he saw with anger the treatment his mother received from the haughty Prince. He dared come forward as her defender; he dared oppose his boyish courage to his father's rage: the result was natural – he became the object of his father's dislike. Indignity was heaped on him; the vassals were taught to disobey him, the menials to scorn him, his very brother to despise him as of inferior blood and birth. Yet the blood of Mondolfo was his; and, though tempered by the gentle Isabel's more kindly tide, it boiled at the injustice to which he was a victim. A thousand times he poured forth the overflowings of his injured spirit in eloquent complaints to his mother. As her health decayed, he nurtured the project, in case of her death, of flying his paternal castle, and becoming a wanderer, a soldier of fortune. He was now thirteen. The Lady Isabel soon, with a mother's penetration, discovered his secret, and on her death-bed made him swear not to quit his father's protection until he should have attained the age of twenty. Her heart bled for the wretchedness that she foresaw would be his lot; but she looked forward with still greater horror to the picture her active fancy drew of her son at an early age wandering forth in despair, alone and helpless, suffering all the extremities of famine and wretchedness; or, almost worse, yielding to the temptations that in such a situation would be held out to him. She extracted this vow, and died satisfied that he would keep it. Of all the world, she alone knew the worth of her Ludovico – had penetrated beneath the rough surface, and become acquainted with the rich store of virtue and affectionate feeling that lay like unsunned ore in his sensitive heart.

Fernando hated his son. From his earliest boyhood he had felt the sentiment of aversion, which, far from endeavouring to quell, he allowed to take deep root, until Ludovico's most innocent action became a crime, and a system of denial and resistance was introduced that called forth all of sinister that there was in the youth's character, and engendered an active spirit of detestation in his father's mind. Thus Ludovico grew, hated and hating. Brought together through their common situation, the father and son, lord and vassal, oppressor and oppressed, the one was continually ready to exert his power of inflicting evil, the other perpetually on the alert to resist even the shadow of tyranny. After the death of his mother, Ludovico's character greatly changed.

The smile that, as the sun, had then often irradiated his countenance, now never shone; suspicion, irritability, and dogged resolution, seemed his master-feelings. He dared his father to the worst, endured that worst, and prevented from flying by his sacred observance of his vow, nurtured all angry and even revengeful feelings till the cup of wrath seemed ready to overflow. He was loved by none, and loving none his good qualities expired, or slept as if they would never more awaken.

His father had intended him for the Church; and Ludovico, until he was sixteen, wore the priestly garb. That period past, be cast it aside, and appeared habited as a cavalier of those days, and in short words told his parent that he refused to comply with his wishes; that he should dedicate himself to arms and enterprise. All that followed this declaration – menace, imprisonment, and even ignominy – he bore, but he continued firm; and the haughty Fernando was obliged to submit his towering will to the firmer will of a stripling. And now, for the first time, while rage seemed to burst his heart, he felt to its highest degree the sentiment of hatred; he expressed this passion – words of contempt and boundless detestation replied; and the bystanders feared that a personal encounter would ensue. Once Fernando put his hand on his sword, and the unarmed Ludovico drew in and collected himself, as if ready to spring and seize the arm that might be uplifted against him.

Fernando saw and dreaded the mad ferocity his son's eye expressed. In all personal encounters of this kind the victory rests not with the strong, but the most fearless. Fernando was not ready to stake his own life, or even with his own hand to shed his son's blood; Ludovico, not as aggressor, but in self-defence, was careless of the consequences of an attack – he would resist to the death; and this dauntless feeling gave him an ascendency his father felt and could not forgive.

From this time Fernando's conduct toward his son changed. He no longer punished, imprisoned, or menaced him. This was usage for a boy, but the Prince felt that they were man to man, and acted accordingly. He was the gainer by the change; for he soon acquired all the ascendency that experience, craft, and a court education, must naturally give him over a hot-headed youth, who, nerved to resist all personal violence, neither saw nor understood a more covert mode of proceeding. Fernando hoped to drive his son to desperation. He set spies over him, paid the tempters that were to lead him to crime, and by a continued system of restraint and miserable thwarting hoped to reduce him to such despair that he would take refuge in any line of conduct that promised freedom from so irksome and degrading a slavery. His observance of his vow saved the youth; and this steadiness of purpose gave him time to read and understand the motives of the tempters. He saw his father's master-hand in all, and his heart sickened at the discovery.

He had reached his eighteenth year. The treatment he had endured and the constant exertion of fortitude and resolution had already given him the appearance of manhood.

He was tall, well made, and athletic. His person and demeanour were more energetic than graceful, and his manners were haughty and reserved. He had few accomplishments, for his father had been at no pains for his education; feats of horsemanship and arms made up the whole catalogue. He hated books, as being a part of a priest's insignia; he was averse to all occupation that brought bodily repose with it. His complexion was dark – hardship had even rendered it sallow; his eyes, once soft, now glared with fierceness; his lips, formed to express tenderness, were now habitually curled in contempt; his dark hair, clustering in thick curls round his throat, completed the wild but grand and interesting appearance of his person.

It was winter, and the pleasures of the chase began. Every morning the huntsmen assembled to attack the wild-boars or stags which the dogs might arouse in the fastnesses of the Apennines.

This was the only pleasure that Ludovico ever enjoyed. During these pursuits he felt himself free. Mounted on a noble horse, which he urged to its full speed, his blood danced in his veins, and his eyes shone with rapture as he cast his eagle glance to Heaven; with a smile of ineffable disdain, he passed his false friends or open tormentors, and gained a solitary precedence in the pursuit.

The plain at the foot of Vesuvius and its neighbouring hills was stripped bare by winter; the full stream rushed impetuously from the hills; and there was mingled with it the baying of the dogs and the cries of the hunters; the sea, dark under a lowering sky, made a melancholy dirge as its waves broke on the shore; Vesuvius groaned heavily, and the birds answered it by wailing shrieks; a heavy sirocco hung upon the atmosphere, rendering it damp and cold. This wind seems at once to excite and depress the human mind: it excites it to thought, but colours those thoughts, as it does the sky, with black. Ludovico felt this; but he tried to surmount the natural feelings with which the ungenial air filled him.

The temperature of the air changed as the day advanced. The clouded sky spent itself in snow, which fell in abundance; it then became clear, and sharp frost succeeded. The aspect of earth was changed. Snow covered the ground and lay on the leafless trees, sparkling, white, and untrod.

Early in the morning a stag had been roused, and, as he was coursed along the plain skirting the hills, the hunters went at speed. All day the chase endured. At length the stag, who from the beginning had directed his course toward the hills, began to ascend them, and, with various windings and evolutions, almost put the hounds to fault. Day was near its close when Ludovico alone followed the stag, as it made for the edge of a kind of platform of the mountain, which, isthmus-like, was connected with the hill by a small tongue of land, and on three sides was precipitous to the plain below. Ludovico balanced his spear, and his dogs drew in, expecting that the despairing animal would there turn to bay. He made one bound, which conducted him to the very brow of the precipice – another, and he was seen no more. He sprang downward, expecting more pity from the rocks beneath than from his human adversary. Ludovico was fatigued by the chase and angry at the escape of his prey. He sprang from his horse, tied him to a tree, and sought a path by which he might safely descend to the plain. Snow covered and hid the ground, obliterating the usual traces that the flocks or herds might have left as they descended from their pastures on the hills to the hamlets beneath; but Ludovico had passed his boyhood among mountains: while his hunting-spear found sure rest on the ground, he did not fear, or while a twig afforded him sufficient support as he held it, he did not doubt to secure his passage; but the descent was precipitous, and necessary caution obliged him to be long. The sun approached the horizon, and the glow of its departure was veiled by swift-rising clouds which the wind blew upward from the sea – a cold wind, which whirled the snow from its resting-place and shook it from the trees. Ludovico at length arrived at the foot of the precipice. The snow reflected and enhanced the twilight, and he saw four deep marks that must have been made by the deer. The precipice was high above, and its escape appeared a miracle. It must have escaped; but those were the only marks it had left. Around lay a forest of ilex, beset by thick, entangled underwood, and it seemed impossible that any animal so large as the stag in pursuit could have broken its way through the apparently impenetrable barrier it opposed. The desire to find his quarry became almost a passion in the heart of Ludovico. He walked round to seek for an opening, and at last found a narrow pathway through the forest, and some few marks seemed to indicate that the stag must have sought for refuge up the glen. With a swiftness characteristic even of his prey, Ludovico rushed up the pathway, and thought not of how far he ran, until, breathless, he stopped before a cottage that opposed itself to his further progress. He stopped and looked around. There was something singularly mournful in the scene. It was not dark, but the shades of evening seemed to descend from the vast woof of cloud that climbed the sky from the West. The black and shining leaves of the ilex and those of the laurel and myrtle underwood were strongly contrasted with the white snow that lay upon them. A breeze passed among the boughs, and scattered the drift that fell in flakes, and disturbed by fits the silence around; or, again, a bird twittered, or flew with melancholy flap of wing, beneath the trees to its nest in some hollow trunk. The house seemed desolate; its windows were glassless, and small heaps of snow lay upon the sills. There was no print of footing on the equal surface of the path that led right up to the door, yet a little smoke now and then struggled upward from its chimney, and, on paying fixed attention, Prince Ludovico thought he heard a voice. He called, but received no answer. He put his hand on the latch; it yielded, and he entered. On the floor, strewed with leaves, lay a person sick and dying; for, though there was a slight motion in the eyes that showed that life had not yet deserted his throne, the paleness of the visage was that of death only. It was an aged woman, and her white hair showed that she descended to no untimely grave. But a figure knelt beside her which might have been mistaken for the angel of heaven waiting to receive and guide the departing soul to eternal rest, but for the sharp agony that was stamped on the features, and the glazed but earnest gaze of her eye. She was very young, and beautiful as the star of evening. She had apparently despoiled herself to bestow warmth on her dying friend, for her arms and neck were bare but for the quantity of dark and flowing hair that clustered on her shoulders. She was absorbed in one feeling, that of watching the change in the sick person. Her cheeks, even her lips, were pale; her eyes seemed to gaze as if her whole life reigned in their single perception.

She did not hear Ludovico enter, or, at least, she made no sign that indicated that she was conscious of it. The sick person murmured; as she bent her head down to catch the sound, she replied, in an accent of despair:

"I can get no more leaves, for the snow is on the ground; nor have I any other earthly thing to place over you."

"Is she cold?" said Ludovico, creeping near, and bending down beside the afflicted girl.

"Oh, very cold!" she replied, "And there is no help."

Ludovico had gone to the chase in a silken mantle lined with the choicest furs: he had thrown it off, and left it with his horse that it might not impede his descent. He hastened from the cottage, he ran down the lane, and, following the marks of his footsteps, he arrived where his steed awaited him. He did not again descend by the same path, reflecting that it might be necessary for him to seek assistance for the dying woman. He led his horse down the bill by a circuitous path, and, although he did this with all possible speed, night closed in, and the glare of the snow alone permitted him to see the path that he desired to follow. When he arrived at the lane he saw that the cottage, before so dark, was illuminated, and, as he approached, he heard the solemn hymn of death as it was chanted by the priests who filled it. The change had taken place, the soul had left its mortal mansion, and the deserted ruin was attended with more of solemnity than had been paid to the mortal struggle. Amid the crowd of priests Ludovico entered unperceived, and he looked around for the lovely female he had left She sat, retired from the priests, on a heap of leaves in a corner of the cottage. Her clasped hands lay on her knees, her head was bent downward, and every now and then she wiped away her fast-falling tears with her hair. Ludovico threw his cloak over her. She looked up, and drew the covering round her, more to hide her person than for the sake of warmth, and then, again turning away, was absorbed in her melancholy thoughts.

Ludovico gazed on her in pity. For the first time since his mother's death, tears filled his eyes, and his softened countenance beamed with tender sympathy. He said nothing, but he continued to look on as a wish arose in his mind that he might wipe the tears that one by one fell from the shrouded eyes of the unfortunate girl. As he was thus engaged, he heard his name called by one of the attendants of the castle, and, throwing the few pieces of gold he possessed into the lap of the sufferer, he suddenly left the cottage, and, joining the servant who had been in search of him, rode rapidly toward his home.

As Ludovico rode along, and the first emotions of pity having, as it were, ceased to throb in his mind, these feelings merged into the strain of thought in which he habitually indulged, and turned its course to something new.

"I call myself wretched," he cried – "I, the well-clad and fed, and this lovely peasant-girl, half famished, parts with her necessary clothing to cover the dying limbs of her only friend. I also have lost my only friend, and that is my true misfortune, the cause of all my real misery – sycophants would assume that name – spies and traitors usurp that office. I have cast these aside – shaken them from me as yon bough shakes to earth its incumbrance of snow, not as cold as their iced hearts, but I am alone – solitude gnaws my heart and makes me savage – miserable – worthless."

Yet, although he thought in this manner, the heart of Ludovico was softened by what he had seen, and milder feelings pressed upon him. He had felt sympathy for one who needed it; he had conferred a benefit on the necessitous; tenderness moulded his lips to a smile, and the pride of utility gave dignity to the fire of his eye. The people about him saw the change, and, not meeting with the usual disdain of his manner, they also became softened, and the alteration apparent in his character seemed ready to effect as great a metamorphosis in his external situation. But the time was not come when this change would become permanent.

On the day that succeeded to this hunt, Prince Fernando removed to Naples, and commanded his son to accompany him. The residence at Naples was peculiarly irksome to Ludovico. In the country he enjoyed comparative freedom. Satisfied that he was in the castle, his father sometimes forgot him for days together; but it was otherwise here. Fearful that he should form friends and connections, and knowing that his commanding figure and peculiar manners excited attention and often curiosity, he kept him ever in sight; or, if he left him for a moment, he first made himself sure of the people around him, and left such of his own confidants whose very presence was venom to the eye of Ludovico. Add to which, Prince Mondolfo delighted to insult and browbeat his son in public, and, aware of his deficiencies in the more elegant accomplishments, he exposed him even to the derision of his friends. They remained two months at Naples, and then returned to Mondolfo.

It was spring; the air was genial and spirit-stirring. The white blossoms of the almond-trees and the pink ones of the peach just began to be contrasted with the green leaves that shot forth among them. Ludovico felt little of the exhilarating effects of spring. Wounded in his heart's core, he asked nature why she painted a sepulchre; he asked the airs why they fanned the sorrowful and the dead. He wandered forth to solitude. He rambled down the path that led to the sea; he sat on the beach, watching the monotonous flow of the waves; they danced and sparkled; his gloomy thoughts refused to imbibe cheerfulness from wave or sun.

A form passed near him – a peasant-girl, who balanced a pitcher, urn-shaped, upon her head; she was meanly clad, but she attracted Ludovico's regard, and when, having approached the fountain, she took her pitcher and turned to fill it, he recognized the cottager of the foregoing winter. She knew him also, and, leaving her occupation, she approached him and kissed his hand with that irresistible grace that southern climes seem to instill into the meanest of their children.

At first she hesitated, and began to thank him in broken accents, but words came as she spoke, and Ludovico listened to her eloquent thanks – the first he had heard addressed to him by any human being. A smile of pleasure stole over his face – a smile whose beauty sank deep into the gazer's heart. In a minute they were seated on the bank beside the fountain, and Viola told the story of her poverty-stricken youth – her orphan lot – the death of her best friend – and it was now only the benign climate which, in diminishing human wants, made her appear less wretched than then. She was alone in the world – living in that desolate cottage – providing for her daily fare with difficulty. Her pale cheek, the sickly languor that pervaded her manner, gave evidence of the truth of her words; but she did not weep, she spoke words of good heart, and it was only when she alluded to the benefaction of Ludovico that her soft dark eyes swam with tears.

The youth visited her cottage the next day. He rode up the lane, now grass-grown and scented by violets, which Viola was gathering from the banks. She presented her nosegay to him. They entered the cottage together. It was dilapidated and miserable. A few flowers placed in a broken vase was a type only of poor Viola herself – a lovely blossom in the midst of utter poverty; and the rose-tree that shaded the window could only tell that sweet Italy, even in the midst of wretchedness, spares her natural wealth to adorn her children.

Ludovico made Viola sit down on a bench by the window, and stood opposite to her, her flowers in his hand, listening. She did not talk of her poverty, and it would be difficult to recount what was said. She seemed happy and smiled and spoke with a gleeful voice, which softened the heart of her friend, so that he almost wept with pity and admiration. After this, day by day, Ludovico visited the cottage and bestowed all his time on Viola. He came and talked with her, gathered violets with her, consoled and advised her, and became happy. The idea that he was of use to a single human being instilled joy into his heart; and yet he was wholly unconscious how entirely he was necessary to the happiness of his protégée. He felt happy beside her, he was delighted to bestow benefits on her, and to see her profit by them; but he did not think of love, and his mind, unawakened to passion, reposed from its long pain without a thought for the future. It was not so with the peasant-girl. She could not see his eyes bent in gentleness on her, his mouth lighted by its tender smile, or listen to his voice as he bade her trust in him, for that he would be father, brother, all to her, without deeply, passionately loving him. He became the sun of her day, the breath of her life – her hope, joy, and sole possession. She watched for his coming, she watched him as he went, and for a long time she was happy. She would not repine that he replied to her earnest love with calm affection only – she was a peasant, he a noble – and she could claim and expect no more; he was a god – she might adore him; and it were blasphemy to hope for more than a benign acceptation of her worship.

Prince Mondolfo was soon made aware of Ludovico's visits to the cottage of the forest, and he did not doubt that Viola had become the mistress of his son. He did not endeavour to interrupt the connection, or put any bar to his visits. Ludovico, indeed, enjoyed more liberty than ever, and his cruel father confined himself alone to the restricting of him more than ever in money. His policy was apparent: Ludovico had resisted every temptation of gambling and other modes of expense thrown in his way. Fernando had long wished to bring his son to a painful sense of his poverty and dependence, and to oblige him to seek the necessary funds in such a career as would necessitate his desertion of the paternal roof. He had wound many snares around the boy, and all were snapped by his firm but almost unconscious resistance; but now, without seeking, without expectation, the occasion came of itself which would lead him to require far more than his father had at any time allowed him, and now that allowance was restricted, yet Ludovico did not murmur – and until now he had had enough.

A long time Fernando abstained from all allusion to the connection of his son; but one evening, at a banquet, gayety overcame his caution – a gayety which ever led him to sport with his son's feelings, and to excite a pain which might repress the smile that his new state of mind ceased to make frequent visits to his countenance.

"Here," cried Fernando, as he filled a goblet – "here, Ludovico, is to the health of your violet-girl!" – and he concluded his speech with some indecorous allusion that suffused Ludovico's cheek with red. Without replying he arose to depart.

"And whither are you going, sir?" cried his father. "Take yon cup to answer my pledge, for, by Bacchus! none that sit at my table shall pass it uncourteously by."

Ludovico, still standing, filled his cup and raised it as he was about to speak and retort to his father's speech, but the memory of his words and the innocence of Viola pressed upon him and filled his heart almost to bursting. He put down his cup, pushed aside the people who sought to detain him, and left the castle, and soon the laughter of the revellers was no more heard by him, though it had loudly rung and was echoed through the lofty halls. The words of Fernando had awakened a strange spirit in Ludovico. "Viola! Can she love me? Do I love her?" The last question was quickly answered. Passion, suddenly awake, made every artery tingle by its thrilling presence. His cheeks burned and his heart danced with strange exultation as he hastened toward the cottage, unheeding all but the universe of sensation that dwelt within him. He reached its door. Blank and dark the walls rose before him, and the boughs of the wood waved and sighed over him. Until now he had felt impatience alone – the sickness of fear – fear of finding a cold return to his passion's feeling now entered his heart; and, retreating a little from the cottage, he sat on a bank, and hid his face in his hands, while passionate tears gushed from his eyes and trickled from between his fingers. Viola opened the door of her cottage; Ludovico had failed in his daily visit, and she was unhappy. She looked on the sky – the sun had set, and Hesperus glowed in the West; the dark ilex-trees made a deep shade, which was broken by innumerable fire-flies, which flashed now low on the ground, discovering the flowers as they slept hushed and closed in night, now high among the branches, and their light was reflected by the shining leaves of ilex and laurel. Viola's wandering eye unconsciously selected one and followed it as it flew, and ever and anon cast aside its veil of darkness and shed a wide pallor around its own form. At length it nestled itself in a bower of green leaves formed by a clump of united laurels and myrtles; and there it stayed, flashing its beautiful light, which, coming from among the boughs, seemed as if the brightest star of the heavens had wandered from its course, and, trembling at its temerity, sat panting on its earthly perch. Ludovico sat near the laurel – Viola saw him – her breath came quick – she spoke not – but stepped lightly to him – and looked with such mazed ecstasy of thought that she felt, nay, almost heard, her heart beat with her emotion. At length she spoke – she uttered his name, and he looked up on her gentle face, her beaming eyes and her sylph-like form bent over him. He forgot his fears, and his hopes were soon confirmed. For the first time he pressed the trembling lips of Viola, and then tore himself away to think with rapture and wonder on all that had taken place.

Ludovico ever acted with energy and promptness. He returned only to plan with Viola when they might be united. A small chapel in the Apennines, sequestered and unknown, was selected; a priest was easily procured from a neighbouring convent and easily bribed to silence. Ludovico led back his bride to the cottage in the forest. There she continued to reside; for worlds he would not have had her change her habitation; all his wealth was expended in decorating it; yet his all only sufficed to render it tolerable. But they were happy. The small circlet of earth's expanse that held in his Viola was the universe to her husband. His heart and imagination widened and filled it until it encompassed all of beautiful, and was inhabited by all of excellent, this world contains.

She sang to him; he listened, and the notes built around him a magic bower of delight. He trod the soil of paradise, and its winds fed his mind to intoxication. The inhabitants of Mondolfo could not recognize the haughty, resentful Ludovico in the benign and gentle husband of Viola.

His father's taunts were unheeded, for he did not hear them. He no longer trod the earth, but, angel-like, sustained by the wings of love, skimmed over it, so that he felt not its inequalities nor was touched by its rude obstacles. And Viola, with deep gratitude and passionate tenderness, repaid his love. She thought of him only, lived for him, and with unwearied attention kept alive in his mind the first dream of passion.

Thus nearly two years passed, and a lovely child appeared to bind the lovers with closer ties, and to fill their humble roof with smiles and joy.

Ludovico seldom went to Mondolfo; and his father, continuing his ancient policy, and glad that in his attachment to a peasant-girl he had relieved his mind from the fear of brilliant connections and able friends, even dispensed with his attendance when he visited Naples. Fernando did not suspect that his son had married his low-born favourite; if he had, his aversion for him would not have withheld him from resisting so degrading an alliance; and, while his blood flowed in Ludovico's veins, he would never have avowed offspring who were contaminated by a peasant's less highly-sprung tide.

Ludovico had nearly completely his twentieth year when his elder brother died. Prince Mondolfo at that time spent four months at Naples, endeavouring to bring to a conclusion a treaty of marriage he had entered into between his heir and the daughter of a noble Neapolitan house, when this death overthrew his hopes, and he retired in grief and mourning to his castle. A few weeks of sorrow and reason restored him to himself. He had loved even this favoured eldest son more as the heir of his name and fortune than as his child; and the web destroyed that he had woven for him, he quickly began another.

Ludovico was summoned to his father's presence. Old habit yet rendered such a summons momentous; but the youth, with a proud smile, threw off these boyish cares, and stood with a gentle dignity before his altered parent.

"Ludovico," said the Prince, "four years ago you refused to take a priest's vows, and then you excited my utmost resentment; now I thank you for that resistance."

A slight feeling of suspicion crossed Ludovico's mind that his father was about to cajole him for some evil purpose. Two years before he would have acted on such a thought, but the habit of happiness made him unsuspicious. He bent his head gently.

"Ludovico," continued his father, while pride and a wish to conciliate disturbed his mind and even his countenance, "my son, I have used you hardly; but that time is now past."

Ludovico gently replied:

"My father, I did not deserve your ill-treatment; I hope I shall merit your kindness when I know –"

"Yes, yes," interrupted Fernando, uneasily, "you do not understand – you desire to know why – in short, you, Ludovico, are now all my hope – Olympio is dead – the house of Mondolfo has no support but you –"

"Pardon me," replied the youth. "Mondolfo is in no danger; you, my lord, are fully able to support and even to augment its present dignity."

"You do not understand. Mondolfo has no support but you. I am old, I feel my age, and these grey hairs announce it to me too glaringly. There is no collateral branch, and my hope must rest in your children –"

"My children, my lord!" replied Ludovico. "I have only one; and if the poor little boy –"

"What folly is this?" cried Fernando, impatiently. "I speak of your marriage and not –"

"My lord, my wife is ever ready to pay her dutious respects to you –"

"Your wife, Ludovico! But you speak without thought. How? Who?"

"The violet-girl, my lord."

A tempest had crossed the countenance of Fernando. That his son, unknown to him, should have made an unworthy alliance, convulsed every fibre of his frame, and the lowering of his brows and his impatient gesture told the intolerable anguish of such a thought. The last words of Ludovico restored him. It was not his wife that he thus named – he felt assured that it was not.

He smiled somewhat gloomily, still it was a smile of satisfaction.

"Yes," he replied, "I understand; but you task my patience – you should not trifle with such a subject or with me. I talk of your marriage. Now that Olympio is dead, and you are, in his place, heir of Mondolfo, you may, in his stead, conclude the advantageous, nay, even princely, alliance I was forming for him."

Ludovico replied with earnestness:

"You are pleased to misunderstand me. I am already married. Two years ago, while I was still the despised, insulted Ludovico, I formed this connection, and it will be my pride to show the world how, in all but birth, my peasant-wife is able to follow the duties of her distinguished situation."

Fernando was accustomed to command himself. He felt as if stabbed by a poniard; but he paused till calm and voice returned, and then he said:

"You have a child?"

"An heir, my lord," replied Ludovico, smiling – for his father's mildness deceived him – "a lovely, healthy boy."

"They live near here?"

"I can bring them to Mondolfo in an hour's space. Their cottage is in the forest, about a quarter of a mile east of the convent of Santa Chiara."

"Enough, Ludovico; you have communicated strange tidings, and I must consider of them. I will see you again this evening."

Ludovico bowed and disappeared. He hastened to his cottage, and related all that he remembered or understood of this scene, and bade Viola prepare to come to the castle at an instant's notice. Viola trembled; it struck her that all was not so fair as Ludovico represented; but she hid her fears, and even smiled as her husband with a kiss hailed his boy as heir of Mondolfo.

Fernando had commanded both look and voice while his son was within hearing. He had gone to the window of his chamber, and stood steadily gazing on the drawbridge until Ludovico crossed it and disappeared. Then, unrestrained, he strode up and down the apartment, while the roof rang with his impetuous tread. He uttered cries and curses, and struck his head with his clenched fist. It was long ere he could think – he felt only, and feeling was torture. The tempest at length subsided, and he threw himself in his chair. His contracted brows and frequently-convulsed lips showed how entirely he was absorbed in consideration. All at first was one frightful whirl; by degrees, the motion was appeased; his thoughts flowed with greater calmness; they subsided into one channel whose course he warily traced until he thought that he saw the result, Hours passed during this contemplation. When he arose from his chair, as one who had slept and dreamed uneasily, his brows became by degrees smooth; he stretched out his arm, and, spreading his hand, cried:

"So it is! And I have vanquished him!"

Evening came, and Ludovico was announced. Fernando feared his son. He had ever dreaded his determined and fearless mode of action. He dreaded to encounter the boy's passions with his own, and felt in the clash that his was not the master-passion. So, subduing all of hate, revenge, and wrath, he received him with a smile. Ludovico smiled also; yet there was no similarity in their look: one was a smile of frankness, joy, and affection – the other the veiled grimace of smothered malice. Fernando said:

"My son, you have entered lightly into a marriage as if it were a child's game, but, where principalities and noble blood are at stake, the loss or gain is too momentous to be trifled with. Silence, Ludovico! Listen to me, I entreat. You have made a strange marriage with a peasant, which, though I may acknowledge, I cannot approve, which must be displeasing to your sovereign, and derogatory to all who claim alliance with the house of Mondolfo."

Cold dew stood on the forehead of Fernando as he spoke; he paused, recovered his self-command, and continued:

"It will be difficult to reconcile these discordant interests, and a moment of rashness might cause us to lose our station, fortune, everything! Your interests are in my hands. I will be careful of them. I trust, before the expiration of a very few months, the future Princess Mondolfo will be received at the court of Naples with due honour and respect. But you must leave it to me. You must not move in the affair. You must promise that you will not, until I permit, mention your marriage to any one, or acknowledge it if you are taxed with it."

Ludovico, after a moment's hesitation, replied:

"I promise that, for the space of six months, I will not mention my marriage to anyone. I will not be guilty of falsehood, but for that time I will not affirm it or bring it forward in any manner so as to annoy you."

Fernando again paused; but prudence conquered, and he said no more. He entered on other topics with his son; they supped together, and the mind of Ludovico, now attuned to affection, received all the marks of his father's awakening love with gratitude and joy. His father thought that he held him in his toils, and was ready to sweeten the bitterness of his intended draft by previous kindness.

A week passed thus in calm. Ludovico and Viola were perfectly happy. Ludovico only wished to withdraw his wife from obscurity from that sensation of honest pride which makes us desire to declare to the whole world the excellence of a beloved object. Viola shrank from such an exhibition; she loved her humble cottage – humble still though adorned with all that taste and love could bestow on it. The trees bent over Its low roof and shaded its windows, which were filled with flowering shrubs; its floor shone with marble, and vases of antique shape and exquisite beauty stood in the niches of the room.

Every part was consecrated by the memory of their first meeting and their loves – the walks in snow and violets; the forest of ilex with its underwood of myrtle and its population of fire-flies; the birds; the wild and shy animals that sometimes came in sight, and, seen, retreated; the changes of the seasons, of the hues of nature influenced by them; the alterations of the sky; the walk of the moon; and the moving of the stars – all were dear, known, and commented on by this pair, who saw the love their own hearts felt reflected in the whole scene around, and in their child, their noisy but speechless companion, whose smiles won hopes, and whose bright form seemed as if sent from Heaven to reward their constant affection.

A week passed, and Fernando and Ludovico were riding together, when the Prince said:

"Tomorrow, early, my son, you must go to Naples. It is time that you should show yourself there as my heir, and the best representative of a princely house. The sooner you do this the quicker will arrive the period for which, no doubt, you long, when the unknown Princess Mondolfo will be acknowledged by all. I cannot accompany you. In fact, circumstances which you may guess make me desire that you should appear at first without me. You will be distinguished by your sovereign, courted by all, and you will remember your promise as the best means of accomplishing your object. In a very few days I will join you."

Ludovico readily assented to this arrangement, and went the same evening to take leave of Viola. She was seated beneath the laurel tree where first they had made their mutual vows; her child was in her arms, gazing with wonder and laughter on the light of the flies. Two years had passed. It was summer again, and as the beams from their eyes met and mingled each drank in the joyous certainty that they were still as dear to one another as when he, weeping from intense emotion, sat under that tree. He told her of his visit to Naples which his father had settled for him, and a cloud passed over her countenance, but she dismissed it. She would not fear; yet again and again a thrilling sense of coming evil made her heart beat, and each time was resisted with greater difficulty. As night came on, she carried the sleeping child into the cottage, and placed him on his bed, and then walked up and down the pathway of the forest with Ludovico until the moment of his departure should arrive, for the heat of the weather rendered it necessary that he should travel by night. Again the fear of danger crossed her, and again she with a smile shook off the thought; but, when he turned to give her his parting embrace, it returned with full force on her. Weeping bitterly, she clung to him, and entreated him not to go. Startled by her earnestness, he eagerly sought an explanation, but the only explanation she could give excited a gentle smile as he caressed and bade her to be calm; and then, pointing to the crescent moon that gleamed through the trees and checkered the ground with their moving shades, he told her he would be with her ere its full, and with one more embrace left her weeping. And thus it is a strange prophecy often creeps about, and the spirit of Cassandra inhabits many a hapless human heart, and utters from many lips unheeded forebodings of evils that are to be: the hearers heed them not – the speaker hardly gives them credit – the evil comes which, if it could have been avoided, no Cassandra could have foretold, for if that spirit were not a sure harbinger so would it not exist; nor would these half revealings have place if the to come did not fulfil and make out the sketch.

Viola beheld him depart with hopeless sorrow, and then turned to console herself beside the couch of her child. Yet, gazing on him, her fears came thicker; and in a transport of terror she rushed from the cottage, ran along the pathway, calling on Ludovico's name, and sometimes listening if she might hear the tread of his horse, and then again shrieking aloud for him to return.

But he was far out of hearing, and she returned again to her cot, and, lying down beside her child, clasping his little hand in hers, at length slept peacefully.

Her sleep was light and short. She arose before the sun, and hardly had he begun to cast long shadows on the ground when, attiring herself in her veil, she was about to go with the infant to the neighbouring chapel of Santa Chiara, when she heard the trampling of horses come up the pathway; her heart beat quick, and still quicker when she saw a stranger enter the cottage. His form was commanding, and age, which had grizzled his hair, had not tempered the fire of his eye nor marred the majesty of his carriage; but every lineament was impressed by pride and even cruelty. Self-will and scorn were even more apparent. He was somewhat like what Ludovico had been, and so like what he then was that Viola did not doubt that his father stood before her. She tried to collect her courage, but the surprise, his haughty mien, and, above all, the sound of many horses, and the voices of men who had remained outside the cottage, so disturbed and distracted her that her heart for a moment failed her, and she leaned trembling and ashy white against the wall, straining her child to her heart with convulsive energy. Fernando spoke:

"You are Viola Amaldi, and you call yourself, I believe, the wife of Ludovico Mandolfo?"

"I am so" – her lips formed themselves to these words, but the sound died away.

Fernando continued:

"I am Prince Mondolfo, father of the rash boy who has entered into this illegal and foolish contract. When I heard of it my plan was easily formed, and I am now about to put it into execution. I could easily have done so without coming to you, without enduring the scene which, I suppose, I shall endure; but benevolence has prompted me to the line of conduct I adopt, and I hope that I shall not repent it."

Fernando paused; Viola had heard little of what he had said. She was employed in collecting her scattered spirits, in bidding her heart be still, and arming herself with the pride and courage of innocence and helplessness. Every word he spoke was thus of use to her, as it gave her time to recollect herself. She only bowed her head as he paused, and he continued:

"While Ludovico was a younger son, and did not seek to obtrude his misalliance into notice, I was content that he should enjoy what he termed happiness unmolested; but circumstances have changed. He has become the heir of Mondolfo, and must support that family and title by a suitable marriage. Your dream has passed. I mean you no ill. You will be conducted hence with your child, placed on board a vessel, and taken to a town in Spain. You will receive a yearly stipend, and, as long as you seek no communication with Ludovico, or endeavour to leave the asylum provided for you, you are safe; but the slightest movement, the merest yearning for a station you may never fill, shall draw upon you and that boy the vengeance of one whose menaces are but the uplifted arm – the blow quickly follows!"

The excess of danger that threatened the unprotected Viola gave her courage. She replied:

"I am alone and feeble, you are strong, and have ruffians waiting on you to execute such crimes as your imagination suggests. I care not for Mondolfo, nor the title, nor the possession, but I will never, oh! never, never! renounce my Ludovico – never do aught to derogate from our plighted faith. Torn from him, I will seek him, though it be barefoot and a-hungered, through the wide world. He is mine by that love be has been pleased to conceive for me; I am his by the sentiment of devotion and eternal attachment that now animates my voice. Tear us asunder, yet we shall meet again, and, unless you put the grave between us, you cannot separate us."

Fernando smiled in scorn.

"And that boy," he said, pointing to die infant, "will you lead him, innocent lamb, a sacrifice to the altar of your love, and plant the knife yourself in the victim's heart?"

Again the lips of Viola became pale as she clasped her boy and exclaimed, in almost inarticulate accents:

"There is a God in Heaven!" Fernando left the cottage, and it was soon filled by men, one of whom threw a cloak over Viola and her boy, and, dragging them from the cottage, placed them in a kind of litter, and the cavalcade proceeded silently. Viola had uttered one shriek when she beheld her enemies, but, knowing their power and her own impotence, she stifled all further cries. When in the litter she strove in vain to disengage herself from the cloak that enveloped her, and then tried to hush her child, who, frightened at his strange situation, uttered piercing cries. At length he slept; and Viola, darkling and fearful, with nothing to sustain her spirits or hopes, felt her courage vanish.

She wept long with despair and misery. She thought of Ludovico and what his grief would be, and her tears were redoubled. There was no hope, for her enemy was relentless, her child torn from her, a cloister her prison. Such were the images constantly before her. They subdued her courage, and filled her with terror and dismay.

The cavalcade entered the town of Salerno, and the roar of the sea announced to poor Viola that they were on its shores.

"O bitter waves!" she cried. "My tears are as bitter as ye, and they will soon mingle!"

Her conductors now entered a building. It was a watch-tower at some distance from the town, on the sea-beach. They lifted Viola from the litter and led her to one of the dreary apartments of the tower. The window, which was not far from the ground, was grated with iron; it bore the appearance of a guardroom. The chief of her conductors addressed her, courteously asked her to excuse the rough lodging; the wind was contrary, he said, but change was expected, and the next day he hoped they would be able to embark. He pointed to the destined vessel in the offing.

Viola, excited to hope by his mildness, began to entreat his compassion, but he immediately left her. Soon after another man brought in food, with a flask of wine and a jug of water. He also retired; her massive door was locked, the sound of retreating footsteps died away.

Viola did not despair; she felt, however, that it would need all her courage to extricate herself from her prison. She ate a part of the food which had been provided, drank some water, and then, a little refreshed, she spread the cloak her conductors had left on the floor, placed her child on it to play, and then stationed herself at the window to see if any one might pass whom she might address, and, if he were not able to assist her in any other way, he might at least bear a message to Ludovico, that her fate might not be veiled in the fearful mystery that threatened it; but probably the way past her window was guarded, for no one drew near. As she looked, however, and once advanced her head to gaze more earnestly, it struck her that her person would pass between the iron grates of her window, which was not high from the ground. The cloak, fastened to one of the stanchions, promised a safe descent. She did not dare make the essay; nay, she was so fearful that she might be watched, and that, if she were seen near the window, her jailers might be struck with the same idea, that she retreated to the farther end of the room, and sat looking at the bars with fluctuating hope and fear, that now dyed her cheeks with crimson, and again made them pale as when Ludovico had first seen her.

Her boy passed his time in alternate play and sleep. The ocean still roared, and the dark clouds brought up by the sirocco blackened the sky and hastened the coming evening. Hour after hour passed; she, heard no clock; there was no sun to mark the time, but by degrees the room grew dark, and at last the Ave Maria tolled, heard by fits between the howling of the winds and the dashing of the waves. She knelt, and put up a fervent prayer to the Madonna, protector of innocence – prayer for herself and her boy – no less innocent than the Mother and Divine Child, to whom she made her orisons. Still she paused. Drawing near to the window, she listened for the sound of any human being: that sound, faint and intermittent, died away, and with darkness came rain that poured in torrents, accompanied by thunder and lightning that drove every creature to shelter. Viola shuddered. Could she expose her child during such a night? Yet again she gathered courage. It only made her meditate on some plan by which she might get the cloak as a shelter for her boy after it had served for their descent. She tried the bars, and found that, with some difficulty, she could pass, and, gazing downward from the outside, a flash of lightning revealed the ground not far below. Again she commended herself to divine protection; again she called upon and blessed her Ludovico; and then, not fearless but determined, she began her operations.

She fastened the cloak by means of her long veil, which, hanging to the ground, was tied by a slip-knot, and gave way when pulled. She took her child in her arms, and, having got without the bars, bound him with the sash to her waist, and then, without accident, she reached the ground.

Having then secured the cloak, and enveloped herself and her child in its dark and ample folds, she paused breathlessly to listen. Nature was awake with its loudest voice – the sea roared – and the incessant flashes of lightning that discovered that solitude around her were followed by such deafening peals as almost made her fear. She crossed the field, and kept the sight of the white sea-foam to her right hand, knowing that she thus proceeded in an opposite direction from Mondolfo. She walked as fast as her burden permitted her, keeping the beaten road, for the darkness made her fear to deviate. The rain ceased, and she walked on, until, her limbs falling under her, she was fain to rest, and refresh herself with the bread she had brought with her from the prison. Action and success had inspired her with unusual energy. She would not fear – she believed herself free and secure. She wept, but it was the overflowing emotion that found no other expression. She doubted not that she should rejoin Ludovico. Seated thus in the dark night – having for hours been the sport of the elements, which now for an instant paused in their fury – seated on a stone by the roadside – a wide, dreary, unknown country about her – her helpless child in her arms – herself having just finished eating the only food she possessed – she felt triumph, and joy, and love, descend into her heart, prophetic of future reunion with her beloved.

It was summer, and the air consequently warm. Her cloak had protected her from the wet, so her limbs were free and unnumbed. At the first ray of dawn she arose, and at the nearest pathway she struck out of the road, and took her course nearer the bordering Apennines. From Salerno as far south as the eye could reach, a low plain stretched itself along the seaside, and the hills at about the distance of ten miles bound it in. These mountains are high and singularly beautiful in their shape; their crags point to Heaven and streams flow down their sides and water the plain below. After several hours' walking, Viola reached a pine forest, which descended from the heights and stretched itself in the plain. She sought its friendly shelter with joy, and, penetrating its depths until she saw trees only on all sides of her, she again reposed. The sirocco had been dissipated by the thunderstorm, and the sun, vanquishing the clouds that at first veiled its splendour, glowed forth in the clear majesty of noon. Southern born, Viola did not fear the heat.

She collected pine nuts, she contrived to make a fire, and ate them with appetite; and then, seeking a covert, she lay down and slept, her boy in her arms, thanking Heaven and the Virgin for her escape. When she awoke, the triumph of her heart somewhat died away. She felt the solitude, she felt her helplessness, she feared pursuers, yet she dashed away the tears, and then reflecting that she was too near Salerno – the sun being now at the sea's verge – she arose and pursued her way through the intricacies of the wood. She got to the edge of it so far as to be able to direct her steps by the neighbouring sea. Torrents intercepted her path, and one rapid river threatened to impede it altogether; but, going somewhat lower down, she found a bridge; and then, approaching still nearer to the sea, she passed through a wide and desolate kind of pasture-country, which seemed to afford neither shelter nor sustenance to any human being. Night closed in, and she was fearful to pursue her way, but, seeing some buildings dimly in the distance, she directed her steps thither, hoping to discover a hamlet where she might get shelter and such assistance as would enable her to retrace her steps and reach Naples without being discovered by her powerful enemy. She kept these high buildings before her, which appeared like vast cathedrals, but that they were untopped by any dome or spire; and she wondered much what they could be, when suddenly they disappeared. She would have thought some rising ground had intercepted them, but all before her was plain. She paused, and at length resolved to wait for dawn. All day she had seen no human being; twice or thrice she had heard the bark of a dog, and once the whistle of a shepherd, but she saw no one. Desolation was around her; this, indeed, had lulled her into security at first. Where no men were, there was no danger for her. But at length the strange solitude became painful-she longed to see a cottage, or to find some peasant, however uncouth, who might answer her inquiries and provide for her wants. She had viewed with surprise the buildings which had been as beacons to her. She did not wish to enter a large town, and she wondered how one could exist in such a desert; but she had left the wood far behind her, and required food. Night passed – balmy and sweet night – the breezes fanned her, the glowing atmosphere encompassed her, the fire-flies flitted round her, bats wheeled about in the air, and the heavy-winged owl hooped anigh, while the beetle's constant hum filled the air. She lay on the ground, her babe pillowed on her arm, looking upon the starry heavens. Many thoughts crowded upon her: the thought of Ludovico, of her reunion with him, of joy after sorrow; and she forgot that she was alone, half-famished, encompassed by enemies in a desert plain of Calabria – she slept.

She awoke not until the sun had risen high – it had risen above the temples of Pastum, and the columns threw short shadows on the ground. They were near her, unseen during night, and were now revealed as the edifices that had attracted her the evening before. They stood on a rugged plain, despoiled of all roof, their columns and cornices encompassing a space of high and weed-grown grass; the deep-blue sky canopied them and filled them with light and cheerfulness. Viola looked on them with wonder and reverence; they were temples to some god who still seemed to deify them with his presence; he clothed them still with beauty, and what was called their ruin might, in its picturesque wildness and sublime loneliness, be more adapted to his nature than when, roofed and gilded, they stood in pristine strength; and the silent worship of air and happy animals might be more suited to him than the concourse of the busy and heartless. The most benevolent of spirit-gods seemed to inhabit that desert, weed-grown area; the spirit of beauty flitted between those columns embrowned by time, painted with strange colour, and raised a genial atmosphere on the deserted altar. Awe and devotion filled the heart of lonely Viola; she raised her eyes and heart to Heaven in thanksgiving and prayer – not that her lips formed words, or her thoughts suggested connected sentences, but the feeling of worship and gratitude animated her; and, as the sunlight streamed through the succession of columns, so – did joy, dove-shaped, fall on and illumine her soul.

With such devotion as seldom before she had visited a saint-dedicated church, she ascended the broken and rude steps of the larger temple, and entered the plot that it inclosed. An inner circuit of smaller columns formed a smaller area, which she entered, and, sitting on a huge fragment of the broken cornice that had fallen to the ground, she silently waited as if for some oracle to visit her sense and guide her.

Thus sitting, she heard the near bark of a dog, followed by the bleating of sheep, and she saw a little flock spread itself in the field adjoining the farther temple. They were shepherded by a girl clothed in rags, but the season required little covering; and these poor people, moneyless, possessing only what their soil gives them, are in the articles of clothing poor even to nakedness.

In inclement weather they wrap rudely-formed clothes of undressed sheepskin around them – during the heats of summer they do little more than throw aside these useless garments. The shepherd-girl was probably about fifteen years of age; a large black straw hat shaded her head from the intense rays of the sun; her feet and legs were bare; and her petticoat, tucked up, Diana-like, above one knee, gave a picturesque appearance to her rags, which, bound at her waist by a girdle, bore some resemblance to the costume of a Greek maiden. Rags have a costume of their own, as fine in their way, in their contrast of rich colours and the uncouth boldness of their drapery, as kingly robes. Viola approached the shepherdess and quietly entered into conversation with her; without making any appeal to her charity or feelings, she asked the name of the place where she was, and her boy, awake and joyous, soon attracted attention. The shepherd-girl was pretty, and, above all, good-natured; she caressed the child, seemed delighted to have found a companion for her solitude, and, when Viola said that she was hungry, unloaded her scrip of roasted pine nuts, boiled chestnuts, and coarse bread. Viola ate with joy and gratitude. They remained together all day; the sun went down, the glowing light of its setting faded, and the shepherdess would have taken Viola home with her. But she dreaded a human dwelling, still fearing that, wherever there appeared a possibility of shelter, there her pursuers would seek her.

She gave a few small silver-pieces, part of what she had about her when seized, to her new friend, and, bidding her bring sufficient food for the next day, entreated her not to mention her adventure to anyone. The girl promised, and, with the assistance of her dog, drove the flock toward their fold. Viola passed the night within the area of the larger temple.

Not doubting the success of his plan, on the very evening that followed its execution, Prince Mondolfo had gone to Naples. He found his son at the Mondolfo Palace. Despising the state of a court, and careless of the gaieties around him, Ludovico longed to return to the cottage of Viola.

So, after the expiration of two days, he told his father that he should ride over to Mondolfo, and return the following morning. Fernando did not oppose him, but, two hours after his departure, followed him, and arrived at the castle just after Ludovico, leaving his attendants there, quitted it to proceed alone to his cottage. The first person Prince Mondolfo saw was the chief of the company who had had the charge of Viola. His story was soon told: the unfavorable wind, the imprisonment in a room barricaded with the utmost strength, her incomprehensible escape, and the vain efforts that had subsequently been made to find her. Fernando listened as if in a dream; convinced of the truth, he saw no clue to guide him – no hope of recovering possession of his prisoner. He foamed with rage, then endeavoured to suppress as useless his towering passion. He overwhelmed the bearer of the news with execrations; sent out parties of men in pursuit in all directions, promising every reward, and urging the utmost secrecy, and then, left alone, paced his chamber in fury and dismay. His solitude was of no long duration. Ludovico burst into his room, his countenance lighted up with rage.

"Murderer!" he cried. "Where is my Viola?"

Fernando remained speechless.

"Answer!" said Ludovico. "Speak with those lips that pronounced her death-sentence – or raise against me that hand from which her blood is scarcely washed – Oh, my Viola! thou and my angel-child, descend with all thy sweetness into my heart, that this hand write not parricide on my brow!"

Fernando attempted to speak.

"No!" shrieked the miserable Ludovico; "I will not listen to her murderer. Yet – is she dead? I kneel – I call you father – I appeal to that savage heart – I take in peace that hand that often struck me, and now has dealt the death-blow – oh, tell me, does she yet live?"

Fernando seized on this interval of calm to relate his story. He told the simple truth; but could such a tale gain belief? It awakened the wildest rage in poor Ludovico's heart. He doubted not that Viola had been murdered; and, after every expression of despair and hatred, he bade his father seek his heir among the clods of the earth, for that such he should soon become, and rushed from his presence.

He wandered to the cottage, he searched the country round, he heard the tale of those who had witnessed any part of the carrying off of his Viola. He went to Salerno. He heard the tale there told with the most determined incredulity. It was the tale, he doubted not, that his father forged to free himself from accusation, and to throw an impenetrable veil over the destruction of Viola.

His quick imagination made out for itself the scene of her death. The very house in which she had been confined had at the extremity of it a tower jutting out over the sea; a river flowed at its base, making its confluence with the ocean deep and dark. He was convinced that the fatal scene had been acted there. He mounted the tower; the higher room was windowless, the iron grates of the windows had for some cause been recently taken out. He was persuaded that Viola and her child had been thrown from that window into the deep and gurgling waters below.

He resolved to die! In those days of simple Catholic faith, suicide was contemplated with horror. But there were other means almost as sure. He would go a pilgrim to the Holy Land, and fight and die beneath the walls of Jerusalem. Rash and energetic, his purpose was no sooner formed than he hastened to put it in execution. He procured a pilgrim's weeds at Salerno, and at midnight, advising none of his intentions, he left that city, and proceeded southward. Alternate rage and grief swelled his heart. Rage at length died away. She whose murderer he execrated was an angel in Heaven, looking down on him, and he in the Holy Land would win his right to join her. Tender grief dimmed his eyes. The world's great theatre closed before him-of all its trappings his pilgrim's cloak was alone gorgeous, his pilgrim's staff the only sceptre – they were the symbols and signs of the power he possessed beyond the earth, and the pledges of his union with Viola. He bent his steps toward Brundusium. He walked on fast, as if he grudged all space and time that lay between him and his goal. Dawn awakened the earth and he proceeded on his way. The sun of noon darted its ray upon him, but his march was uninterrupted. He entered a pine wood, and, following the track of flocks, he heard the murmurs of a fountain. Oppressed with thirst, he hastened toward it. The water welled up from the ground and filled a natural basin; flowers grew on its banks and looked on the waters unreflected, for the stream paused not, but whirled round and round, spending its superabundance in a small rivulet that, dancing over stones and glancing in the sun, went on its way to its eternity – the sea. The trees had retreated from the mountain, and formed a circle about it; the grass was green and fresh, starred with summer flowers. At one extremity was a silent pool that formed a strange contrast with the fountain that, ever in motion, showed no shape, and reflected only the colour of the objects around it. The pool reflected the scene with greater distinctness and beauty than its real existence. The trees stood distinct, the ambient air between, all grouped and pictured by the hand of a divine artist. Ludovico drank from the fount, and then approached the pool. He looked with half wonder on the scene depicted there. A bird now flitted across in the air, and its form, feathers, and motion, were shown in the waters. An ass emerged from among the trees, where in vain it sought herb-age, and came to grass near these waters; Ludovico saw it depicted therein, and then looked on the living animal, almost appearing less real, less living, than its semblance in the stream.

Under the trees from which the ass had come lay someone on the ground, enveloped in a mantle, sleeping. Ludovico looked carelessly – he hardly at first knew why his curiosity was roused; then an eager thought, which he deemed madness, yet resolved to gratify, carried him forward.

Rapidly he approached the sleeper, knelt down, and drew aside the cloak, and saw Viola, her child within her arms, the warm breath issued from her parted lips, her lovebeaming eyes hardly veiled by the transparent lids, which soon were lifted up.

Ludovico and Viola, each too happy to feel the earth they trod, returned to their cottage-their cottage dearer than any palace – yet only half believing the excess of their own joy. By turns they wept, and gazed on each other and their child, holding each other's hands as if grasping reality and fearful it would vanish.

Prince Mondolfo heard of their arrival. He had long suffered keenly from the fear of losing his son. The dread of finding himself childless, heirless, had tamed him. He feared the world's censure, his sovereign's displeasure – perhaps worse accusation and punishment. He yielded to fate. Not daring to appear before his intended victim, he sent his confessor to mediate for their forgiveness, and to entreat them to take up their abode at Mondolfo. At first, little credit was given to these offers. They loved their cottage, and had small inclination to risk happiness, liberty, and life, for worthless luxury. The Prince, by patience and perseverance, at length convinced them. Time softened painful recollections; they paid him the duty of children, and cherished and honoured him in his old age; while he caressed his lovely grandchild, he did not re-pine that the violet-girl should be the mother of the heir of Mondolfo.

If you enjoyed this, you might also like...
'The Vampyre' by John Polidori, page 137
'The Mortal Immortal', see page 254

The Horrors of Isolation

Long Tales by Mary Shelley

The Last Man
(Volume II, Chapter IV–The End)

[*Publisher's Note: Mary Shelley's* The Last Man *takes place in a future setting, where the Earth is being devastated by a plague. Volume I of the novel follows the burgeoning friendship, romantic entanglements and political aspirations of Lionel Verney – a man who has grown up hating the aristocracy; Lionel's sister Perdita – who has come to embrace isolation; Adrian, Earl of Windsor – who opposes his mother's wishes to claim the throne; and Lord Raymond – a man full of ambition but also passion. Volume II opens with the death of both Raymond and his then wife Perdita. We join the action some time after that, following the surviving Lionel and Adrian as the state of the world takes a turn for the worse.*]

Volume II

Chapter IV

I RETURNED to my family estate in the autumn of the year 2092. My heart had long been with them; and I felt sick with the hope and delight of seeing them again. The district which contained them appeared the abode of every kindly spirit. Happiness, love and peace, walked the forest paths, and tempered the atmosphere. After all the agitation and sorrow I had endured in Greece, I sought Windsor, as the storm-driven bird does the nest in which it may fold its wings in tranquillity.

How unwise had the wanderers been, who had deserted its shelter, entangled themselves in the web of society, and entered on what men of the world call 'life,' – that labyrinth of evil, that scheme of mutual torture. To live, according to this sense of the word, we must not only observe and learn, we must also feel; we must not be mere spectators of action, we must act; we must not describe, but be subjects of description. Deep sorrow must have been the inmate of our bosoms; fraud must have lain in wait for us; the artful must have deceived us; sickening doubt and false hope must have chequered our days; hilarity and joy, that lap the soul in ecstasy, must at times have possessed us. Who that knows what 'life' is, would pine for this feverish species of existence? I have lived. I have spent days and nights of festivity; I have joined in ambitious hopes, and exulted in victory: now – shut the door on the world, and build high the wall that is to separate me from the troubled scene enacted within its precincts. Let us live for each other and for happiness; let us seek peace in our dear home, near the inland murmur of streams, and the gracious waving of trees, the beauteous vesture of earth, and sublime pageantry of the skies. Let us leave 'life,' that we may live.

Idris was well content with this resolve of mine. Her native sprightliness needed no undue excitement, and her placid heart reposed contented on my love, the well-being of her children, and the beauty of surrounding nature. Her pride and blameless ambition was to create smiles in all around her, and to shed repose on the fragile existence of her brother. In spite of her tender nursing, the health of Adrian perceptibly declined. Walking, riding, the common occupations of life, overcame him: he felt no pain, but seemed to tremble forever on the verge of annihilation. Yet, as he had lived on for months nearly in the same state, he did not inspire us with any immediate fear; and, though he talked of death as an event most familiar to his thoughts, he did not cease to exert himself to render others happy, or to cultivate his own astonishing powers of mind. Winter passed away; and spring, led by the months, awakened life in all nature. The forest was dressed in green; the young calves frisked on the new-sprung grass; the wind-winged shadows of light clouds sped over the green cornfields; the hermit cuckoo repeated his monotonous all-hail to the season; the nightingale, bird of love and minion of the evening star, filled the woods with song; while Venus lingered in the warm sunset, and the young green of the trees lay in gentle relief along the clear horizon.

Delight awoke in every heart, delight and exultation; for there was peace through all the world; the temple of Universal Janus was shut, and man died not that year by the hand of man.

"Let this last but twelve months," said Adrian; "and earth will become a Paradise. The energies of man were before directed to the destruction of his species: they now aim at its liberation and preservation. Man cannot repose, and his restless aspirations will now bring forth good instead of evil. The favoured countries of the south will throw off the iron yoke of servitude; poverty will quit us, and with that, sickness. What may not the forces, never before united, of liberty and peace achieve in this dwelling of man?"

"Dreaming, forever dreaming, Windsor!" said Ryland, the old adversary of Raymond, and candidate for the Protectorate at the ensuing election. "Be assured that earth is not, nor ever can be heaven, while the seeds of hell are natives of her soil. When the seasons have become equal, when the air breeds no disorders, when its surface is no longer liable to blights and droughts, then sickness will cease; when men's passions are dead, poverty will depart. When love is no longer akin to hate, then brotherhood will exist: we are very far from that state at present."

"Not so far as you may suppose," observed a little old astronomer, by name Merrival, "the poles precede slowly, but securely; in a hundred thousand years –"

"We shall all be underground," said Ryland.

"The pole of the earth will coincide with the pole of the ecliptic," continued the astronomer, "an universal spring will be produced, and earth become a paradise."

"And we shall of course enjoy the benefit of the change," said Ryland, contemptuously.

"We have strange news here," I observed. I had the newspaper in my hand, and, as usual, had turned to the intelligence from Greece. "It seems that the total destruction of Constantinople, and the supposition that winter had purified the air of the fallen city, gave the Greeks courage to visit its site, and begin to rebuild it. But they tell us that the curse of God is on the place, for everyone who has ventured within the walls has been tainted by the plague; that this disease has spread in Thrace and Macedonia; and now, fearing the virulence of infection during the coming heats, a cordon has been drawn on the frontiers of Thessaly, and a strict quarantine exacted." This intelligence brought us back from the prospect of paradise, held out after the lapse of a hundred thousand years, to the pain and misery at present existent upon earth. We talked of the ravages made last year by pestilence in every quarter of the world; and of the dreadful consequences of a second visitation. We discussed the best means of preventing infection, and of preserving health and activity in a large city thus afflicted – London, for instance. Merrival did not join in this conversation; drawing near Idris, he proceeded to assure her that the joyful prospect of an earthly paradise after a hundred thousand years, was clouded to him by the knowledge that in a certain period of time after, an earthly hell or purgatory, would occur, when the ecliptic and equator would be at right angles. Our party at length broke up; "We are all dreaming this morning," said Ryland, "it is as wise to discuss the probability of a visitation of the plague in our well-governed metropolis, as to calculate the centuries which must escape before we can grow pineapples here in the open air."

But, though it seemed absurd to calculate upon the arrival of the plague in London, I could not reflect without extreme pain on the desolation this evil would cause in Greece. The English for the most part talked of Thrace and Macedonia, as they would of a lunar territory, which, unknown to them, presented no distinct idea or interest to the minds. I had trod the soil. The faces of many of the inhabitants were familiar to me; in the towns, plains, hills, and defiles of these countries, I had enjoyed unspeakable delight, as I journied through them the year before. Some romantic village, some cottage, or elegant abode there situated, inhabited by the lovely and the good, rose before my mental sight, and the question haunted me, is the plague there also? – That same invincible monster, which hovered over and devoured Constantinople – that fiend more cruel than tempest, less tame than fire, is, alas, unchained in that beautiful country – these reflections would not allow me to rest.

The political state of England became agitated as the time drew near when the new Protector was to be elected. This event excited the more interest, since it was the current report, that if the popular candidate (Ryland) should be chosen, the question of the abolition of hereditary rank, and other feudal relics, would come under the consideration of parliament. Not a word had been spoken during the present session on any of these topics. Everything would depend upon the choice of a Protector, and the elections of the ensuing year. Yet this very silence was awful, shewing the deep weight attributed to the question; the fear of either party to hazard an ill-timed attack, and the expectation of a furious contention when it should begin.

But although St. Stephen's did not echo with the voice which filled each heart, the newspapers teemed with nothing else; and in private companies the conversation however remotely begun, soon verged towards this central point, while voices were lowered and chairs drawn closer. The nobles did not hesitate to express their fear; the other party endeavoured to treat the matter lightly. "Shame on the country," said Ryland, "to lay so much stress upon words and frippery; it is a question of nothing; of the new painting of carriage-pannels and the embroidery of footmen's coats."

Yet could England indeed doff her lordly trappings, and be content with the democratic style of America? Were the pride of ancestry, the patrician spirit, the gentle courtesies and refined pursuits, splendid attributes of rank, to be erased among us? We were told that this would not be the case; that we were by nature a poetical people, a nation easily duped by words, ready to array clouds in splendour, and bestow honour on the dust. This spirit we could never lose; and it was to diffuse this concentrated spirit of birth, that the new law was to be brought forward. We were assured that, when the name and title of Englishman was the sole patent of nobility, we should all be noble; that when no man born under English sway, felt another his superior in rank, courtesy and refinement would become the birthright of all our countrymen. Let not England be so far disgraced, as to have it imagined that it can be without nobles, nature's true nobility, who bear their patent in their mien, who are from their cradle elevated above the rest of their species, because they are better than the rest. Among a race of independent, and generous, and well educated men, in a country where the imagination is empress of men's minds, there needs be no fear that we should want a perpetual succession of the high-born and lordly. That party, however, could hardly yet be considered a minority in the kingdom, who extolled the ornament of the column, 'the Corinthian capital of polished society;' they appealed to prejudices without number, to old attachments and young hopes; to the expectation of thousands who might one day become peers; they set up as a scarecrow, the spectre of all that was sordid, mechanic and base in the commercial republics.

The plague had come to Athens. Hundreds of English residents returned to their own country. Raymond's beloved Athenians, the free, the noble people of the divinest town in Greece, fell like ripe corn before the merciless sickle of the adversary. Its pleasant places were deserted; its temples and palaces were converted into tombs; its energies, bent before towards the highest objects of human ambition, were now forced to converge to one point, the guarding against the innumerous arrows of the plague.

At any other time this disaster would have excited extreme compassion among us; but it was now passed over, while each mind was engaged by the coming controversy. It was not so with me; and the question of rank and right dwindled to insignificance in my eyes, when I pictured the scene of suffering Athens. I heard of the death of only sons; of wives and husbands most devoted; of the rending of ties twisted with the heart's fibres, of friend losing friend, and young mothers mourning for their first born; and these moving incidents were grouped and painted in my mind by the knowledge of the persons, by my esteem and affection for the sufferers. It was the admirers, friends, fellow soldiers of Raymond, families that had welcomed Perdita to Greece, and lamented with her the loss of her lord, that were swept away, and went to dwell with them in the undistinguishing tomb.

The plague at Athens had been preceded and caused by the contagion from the East; and the scene of havoc and death continued to be acted there, on a scale of fearful magnitude. A hope that the visitation of the present year would prove the last, kept up the spirits of the merchants connected with these countries; but the inhabitants were driven to despair, or to a resignation which, arising from fanaticism, assumed the same dark hue. America had also received the taint; and, were it yellow fever or plague, the epidemic was gifted with a virulence before unfelt. The devastation was not confined to the towns, but spread throughout the country; the hunter died in the woods, the peasant in the corn-fields, and the fisher on his native waters.

A strange story was brought to us from the East, to which little credit would have been given, had not the fact been attested by a multitude of witnesses, in various parts of the world. On the twenty-first of June, it was said that an hour before noon, a black sun arose: an orb, the size of that luminary, but dark, defined, whose beams were shadows, ascended from the west; in about an hour it had reached the meridian, and eclipsed the bright parent of day. Night fell upon every country, night, sudden, rayless, entire. The stars came out, shedding their ineffectual glimmerings on the light-widowed earth. But soon the dim orb passed from over the sun, and lingered down the eastern heaven. As it descended, its dusky rays crossed the brilliant ones of the sun, and deadened or distorted them. The shadows of things assumed strange and ghastly shapes. The wild animals in the woods took fright at the unknown shapes figured on the ground. They fled they knew not whither; and the citizens were filled with greater dread, at the convulsion which "shook lions into civil streets;" — birds, strong-winged eagles, suddenly blinded, fell in the market-places, while owls and bats shewed themselves welcoming the early night. Gradually the object of fear sank beneath the horizon, and to the last shot up shadowy beams into the otherwise radiant air. Such was the tale sent us from Asia, from the eastern extremity of Europe, and from Africa as far west as the Golden Coast. Whether this story were true or not, the effects were certain. Through Asia, from the banks of the Nile to the shores of the Caspian, from the Hellespont even to the sea of Oman, a sudden panic was driven. The men filled the mosques; the women, veiled, hastened to the tombs, and carried offerings to the dead, thus to preserve the living. The plague was forgotten, in this new fear which the black sun had spread; and, though the dead multiplied, and the streets of Ispahan, of Pekin, and of Delhi were strewed with pestilence-struck corpses, men passed on, gazing on the ominous sky, regardless of the death beneath their feet. The Christians sought their churches – Christian maidens, even at the feast of roses, clad in white, with shining veils, sought, in long procession, the places consecrated to their religion, filling the air with their hymns; while, ever and anon, from the lips of some poor mourner in the crowd, a voice of wailing burst, and the rest looked up, fancying they could discern the sweeping wings of angels, who passed over the earth, lamenting the disasters about to fall on man.

In the sunny clime of Persia, in the crowded cities of China, amidst the aromatic groves of Cashmere, and along the southern shores of the Mediterranean, such scenes had place. Even in Greece the tale of the sun of darkness increased the fears and despair of the dying multitude. We, in our cloudy isle, were far removed from danger, and the only circumstance that brought these disasters at all home to us, was the daily arrival of vessels from the east, crowded with emigrants, mostly English; for the Moslems, though the fear of death was spread keenly among them, still clung together; that, if they were to die (and if they were, death would as readily meet them on the homeless sea, or in far England, as in Persia,) – if they were to die, their bones might rest in earth made sacred by the relics of true believers. Mecca had never before been so crowded with pilgrims; yet the Arabs neglected to pillage the caravans, but, humble and weaponless, they joined the procession, praying Mahomet to avert plague from their tents and deserts.

I cannot describe the rapturous delight with which I turned from political brawls at home, and the physical evils of distant countries, to my own dear home, to the selected abode of goodness and love; to peace, and the interchange of every sacred sympathy. Had I never quitted Windsor, these emotions would not have been so intense; but I had in Greece been the prey of fear and deplorable change; in Greece, after a period of anxiety and sorrow, I had seen depart two, whose very names were the symbol of greatness and virtue. But such miseries could never intrude upon the domestic circle left to me, while, secluded in our beloved forest, we passed our lives in tranquillity. Some small change indeed the progress of years brought here; and time, as it is wont, stamped the traces of mortality on our pleasures and expectations. Idris, the most affectionate wife, sister and friend, was a tender and loving mother. The feeling was not with her as with many, a pastime; it was a passion. We had had three children; one, the second in age, died while I was in Greece. This had dashed the triumphant and rapturous emotions of maternity with grief and fear. Before this event, the little beings, sprung from herself, the young heirs of her transient life, seemed to have a sure lease of existence; now she dreaded that the pitiless destroyer might snatch her remaining darlings, as it had snatched their brother. The least illness caused throes of terror; she was miserable if she were at all absent from them; her treasure of happiness she had garnered in their fragile being, and kept forever on the watch, lest the insidious thief should as before steal these valued gems. She had fortunately small cause for fear. Alfred, now nine years old, was an upright, manly little fellow, with radiant brow, soft eyes, and gentle, though independent disposition. Our youngest was yet in infancy; but his downy cheek was sprinkled with the roses of health, and his unwearied vivacity filled our halls with innocent laughter.

Clara had passed the age which, from its mute ignorance, was the source of the fears of Idris. Clara was dear to her, to all. There was so much intelligence combined with innocence, sensibility with forbearance, and seriousness with perfect good-humour, a beauty so transcendant, united to such endearing simplicity, that she hung like a pearl in the shrine of our possessions, a treasure of wonder and excellence.

At the beginning of winter our Alfred, now nine years of age, first went to school at Eton. This appeared to him the primary step towards manhood, and he was proportionably pleased. Community of study and amusement developed the best parts of his character, his steady perseverance, generosity, and well-governed firmness. What deep and sacred emotions are excited in a father's bosom, when he first becomes convinced that his love for his child is not a mere instinct, but worthily bestowed, and that others, less akin, participate his approbation! It was supreme happiness to Idris and myself, to find that the frankness which Alfred's open brow indicated, the intelligence of his eyes, the tempered sensibility of his tones, were not delusions, but indications of talents and virtues, which would 'grow with his growth, and strengthen with his strength.' At this period, the termination of an animal's love for its offspring – the true affection of the human parent commences. We no longer look on this dearest part of ourselves, as a tender plant which we must cherish, or a plaything for an idle hour. We build now on his intellectual faculties, we establish our hopes on his moral propensities. His weakness still imparts anxiety to this feeling, his ignorance prevents entire intimacy; but we begin to respect the future man, and to endeavour to secure his esteem, even as if he were our equal. What can a parent have more at heart than the good opinion of his child? In all our transactions with him our honour must be inviolate, the integrity of our relations untainted: fate and circumstance may, when he arrives at maturity, separate us forever – but, as his aegis in danger, his consolation in hardship, let the ardent youth forever bear with him through the rough path of life, love and honour for his parents.

We had lived so long in the vicinity of Eton, that its population of young folks was well known to us. Many of them had been Alfred's playmates, before they became his school-fellows. We now watched this youthful congregation with redoubled interest. We marked the difference of character among the boys, and endeavoured to read the future man in the stripling. There is nothing more lovely, to which the heart more yearns than a free-spirited boy, gentle, brave, and generous. Several of the Etonians had these characteristics; all were distinguished by a sense of honour, and spirit of enterprize; in some, as they verged towards manhood, this degenerated into presumption; but the younger ones, lads a little older than our own, were conspicuous for their gallant and sweet dispositions.

Here were the future governors of England; the men, who, when our ardour was cold, and our projects completed or destroyed forever, when, our drama acted, we doffed the garb of the hour, and assumed the uniform of age, or of more equalizing death; here were the beings who were to carry on the vast machine of society; here were the lovers, husbands, fathers; here the landlord, the politician, the soldier; some fancied that they were even now ready to appear on the stage, eager to make one among the dramatis personae of active life. It was not long since I was like one of these beardless aspirants; when my boy shall have obtained the place I now hold, I shall have tottered into a grey-headed, wrinkled old man. Strange system! riddle of the Sphynx, most awe-striking! that thus man remains, while we the individuals pass away. Such is, to borrow the words of an eloquent and philosophic writer, 'the mode of existence decreed to a permanent body composed of transitory parts; wherein, by the disposition of a stupendous wisdom, moulding together the great mysterious incorporation of the human race, the whole, at one time, is never old, or middle-aged, or young, but, in a condition of unchangeable constancy, moves on through the varied tenour of perpetual decay, fall, renovation, and progression.

Willingly do I give place to thee, dear Alfred! advance, offspring of tender love, child of our hopes; advance a soldier on the road to which I have been the pioneer! I will make way for thee. I have already put off the carelessness of childhood, the unlined brow, and springy gait of early years, that they may adorn thee. Advance; and I will despoil myself still further for thy advantage. Time shall rob me of the graces of maturity, shall take the fire from my eyes, and agility from my limbs, shall steal the better part of life, eager expectation and passionate love, and shower them in double portion on thy dear head. Advance! avail thyself of the gift, thou and thy comrades; and in the drama you are about to act, do not disgrace those who taught you to enter on the stage, and to pronounce becomingly the parts assigned to you! May your progress be uninterrupted and secure; born during the spring-tide of the hopes of man, may you lead up the summer to which no winter may succeed!

Chapter V

SOME DISORDER had surely crept into the course of the elements, destroying their benignant influence. The wind, prince of air, raged through his kingdom, lashing the sea into fury, and subduing the rebel earth into some sort of obedience.

> *The God sends down his angry plagues from high,*
> *Famine and pestilence in heaps they die.*
> *Again in vengeance of his wrath he falls*
> *On their great hosts, and breaks their tottering walls;*
> *Arrests their navies on the ocean's plain,*
> *And whelms their strength with mountains of the main.*

Their deadly power shook the flourishing countries of the south, and during winter, even, we, in our northern retreat, began to quake under their ill effects.

That fable is unjust, which gives the superiority to the sun over the wind. Who has not seen the lightsome earth, the balmy atmosphere, and basking nature become dark, cold and ungenial, when the sleeping wind has awoke in the east? Or, when the dun clouds thickly veil the sky, while exhaustless stores of rain are poured down, until, the dank earth refusing to imbibe the superabundant moisture, it lies in pools on the surface; when the torch of day seems like a meteor, to be quenched; who has not seen the cloud-stirring north arise, the streaked blue appear, and soon an opening made in the vapours in the eye of the wind, through which the bright azure shines? The clouds become thin; an arch is formed forever rising upwards, till, the universal cope being unveiled, the sun pours forth its rays, re-animated and fed by the breeze.

Then mighty art thou, O wind, to be throned above all other vicegerents of nature's power; whether thou comest destroying from the east, or pregnant with elementary life from the west; thee the clouds obey; the sun is subservient to thee; the shoreless ocean is thy slave! Thou sweepest over the earth, and oaks, the growth of centuries, submit to thy viewless axe; the snow-drift is scattered on the pinnacles of the Alps, the avalanche thunders down their vallies. Thou holdest the keys of the frost, and canst first chain and then set free the streams; under thy gentle governance the buds and leaves are born, they flourish nursed by thee.

Why dost thou howl thus, O wind? By day and by night for four long months thy roarings have not ceased – the shores of the sea are strewn with wrecks, its keel-welcoming surface has become impassable, the earth has shed her beauty in obedience to thy command; the frail balloon dares no longer sail on the agitated air; thy ministers, the clouds, deluge the land with rain; rivers forsake their banks; the wild torrent tears up the mountain path; plain and wood, and verdant dell are despoiled of their loveliness; our very cities are wasted by thee. Alas, what will become of us? It seems as if the giant waves of ocean, and vast arms of the sea, were about to wrench the deep-rooted island from its centre; and cast it, a ruin and a wreck, upon the fields of the Atlantic.

What are we, the inhabitants of this globe, least among the many that people infinite space? Our minds embrace infinity; the visible mechanism of our being is subject to merest accident. Day by day we are forced to believe this. He whom a scratch has disorganized, he who disappears from apparent life under the influence of the hostile agency at work around us, had the same powers as I – I also am subject to the same laws. In the face of all this we call ourselves lords of the creation, wielders of the elements, masters of life and death, and we allege in excuse of this arrogance, that though the individual is destroyed, man continues forever.

Thus, losing our identity, that of which we are chiefly conscious, we glory in the continuity of our species, and learn to regard death without terror. But when any whole nation becomes the victim of the destructive powers of exterior agents, then indeed man shrinks into insignificance, he feels his tenure of life insecure, his inheritance on earth cut off.

I remember, after having witnessed the destructive effects of a fire, I could not even behold a small one in a stove, without a sensation of fear. The mounting flames had curled round the building, as it fell, and was destroyed. They insinuated themselves into the substances about them, and the impediments to their progress yielded at their touch. Could we take integral parts of this power, and not be subject to its operation? Could we domesticate a cub of this wild beast, and not fear its growth and maturity?

Thus we began to feel, with regard to many-visaged death let loose on the chosen districts of our fair habitation, and above all, with regard to the plague. We feared the coming summer. Nations, bordering on the already infected countries, began to enter upon serious plans for the better keeping out of the enemy. We, a commercial people, were obliged to bring such schemes under consideration; and the question of contagion became matter of earnest disquisition.

That the plague was not what is commonly called contagious, like the scarlet fever, or extinct small-pox, was proved. It was called an epidemic. But the grand question was still unsettled of how this epidemic was generated and increased. If infection depended upon the air, the air was subject to infection. As for instance, a typhus fever has been brought by ships to one sea-port town; yet the very people who brought it there, were incapable of communicating it in a town more fortunately situated. But how are we to judge of airs, and pronounce – in such a city plague will die unproductive; in such another, nature has provided for it a plentiful harvest? In the same way, individuals may escape ninety-nine times, and receive the death-blow at the hundredth; because bodies are sometimes in a state to reject the infection of malady, and at others, thirsty to imbibe it. These reflections made our legislators pause, before they could decide on the laws to be put in force. The evil was so wide-spreading, so violent and immedicable, that no care, no prevention could be judged superfluous, which even added a chance to our escape.

These were questions of prudence; there was no immediate necessity for an earnest caution. England was still secure. France, Germany, Italy and Spain, were interposed, walls yet without a breach, between us and the plague. Our vessels truly were the sport of winds and waves, even as Gulliver was the toy of the Brobdignagians; but we on our stable abode could not be hurt in life or limb by these eruptions of nature. We could not fear – we did not. Yet a feeling of awe, a breathless sentiment of wonder, a painful sense of the degradation of humanity, was introduced into every heart. Nature, our mother, and our friend, had turned on us a brow of menace. She shewed us plainly, that, though she permitted us to assign her laws and subdue her apparent powers, yet, if she put forth but a finger, we must quake. She could take our globe, fringed with mountains, girded by the atmosphere, containing the condition of our being, and all that man's mind could invent or his force achieve; she could take the ball in her hand, and cast it into space, where life would be drunk up, and man and all his efforts forever annihilated.

These speculations were rife among us; yet not the less we proceeded in our daily occupations, and our plans, whose accomplishment demanded the lapse of many years. No voice was heard telling us to hold! When foreign distresses came to be felt by us through the channels of commerce, we set ourselves to apply remedies. Subscriptions were made for the emigrants, and merchants bankrupt by the failure of trade. The English spirit awoke to its full activity, and, as it had ever done, set itself to resist the evil, and to stand in the breach which diseased nature had suffered chaos and death to make in the bounds and banks which had hitherto kept them out.

At the commencement of summer, we began to feel, that the mischief which had taken place in distant countries was greater than we had at first suspected. Quito was destroyed by an earthquake. Mexico laid waste by the united effects of storm, pestilence and famine. Crowds of emigrants inundated the west of Europe; and our island had become the refuge of thousands. In the meantime Ryland had been chosen Protector. He had sought this office with eagerness, under the idea of turning his whole forces to the suppression of the privileged orders of our community. His measures were thwarted, and his schemes interrupted by this new state of things. Many of the foreigners were utterly destitute; and their increasing numbers at length forbade a recourse to the usual modes of relief. Trade was stopped by the failure of the interchange of cargoes usual between us, and America, India, Egypt and Greece. A sudden break was made in the routine of our lives. In vain our Protector and his partizans sought to conceal this truth; in vain, day after day, he appointed a period for the discussion of the new laws concerning hereditary rank and privilege; in vain he endeavoured to represent the evil as partial and temporary. These disasters came home to so many bosoms, and, through the various channels of commerce, were carried so entirely into every class and division of the community, that of necessity they became the first question in the state, the chief subjects to which we must turn our attention.

Can it be true, each asked the other with wonder and dismay, that whole countries are laid waste, whole nations annihilated, by these disorders in nature? The vast cities of America, the fertile plains of Hindostan, the crowded abodes of the Chinese, are menaced with utter ruin. Where late the busy multitudes assembled for pleasure or profit, now only the sound of wailing and misery is heard. The air is empoisoned, and each human being inhales death, even while in youth and health, their hopes are in the flower. We called to mind the plague of 1348, when it was calculated that a third of mankind had been destroyed. As yet western Europe was uninfected; would it always be so?

O, yes, it would – Countrymen, fear not! In the still uncultivated wilds of America, what wonder that among its other giant destroyers, Plague should be numbered! It is of old a native of the East, sister of the tornado, the earthquake, and the simoon. Child of the sun, and nursling of the tropics, it would expire in these climes. It drinks the dark blood of the inhabitant of the south, but it never feasts on the pale-faced Celt. If perchance some stricken Asiatic come among us, plague dies with him, uncommunicated and innoxious. Let us weep for our brethren, though we can never experience their reverse. Let us lament over and assist the children of the garden of the earth. Late we envied their abodes, their spicy groves, fertile plains, and abundant loveliness. But in this mortal life extremes are always matched; the thorn grows with the rose, the poison tree and the cinnamon mingle their boughs. Persia, with its cloth of gold, marble halls, and infinite wealth, is now a tomb. The tent of the Arab is fallen in the sands, and his horse spurns the ground unbridled and unsaddled. The voice of lamentation fills the valley of Cashmere; its dells and woods, its cool fountains, and gardens of roses, are polluted by the dead; in Circassia and Georgia the spirit of beauty weeps over the ruin of its favourite temple – the form of woman.

Our own distresses, though they were occasioned by the fictitious reciprocity of commerce, increased in due proportion. Bankers, merchants, and manufacturers, whose trade depended on exports and interchange of wealth, became bankrupt. Such things, when they happen singly, affect only the immediate parties; but the prosperity of the nation was now shaken by frequent and extensive losses. Families, bred in opulence and luxury, were reduced to beggary. The very state of peace in which we gloried was injurious; there were no means of employing the idle, or of sending any overplus of population out of the country. Even the source of colonies was dried up, for in New Holland, Van Diemen's Land, and the Cape of Good Hope, plague raged. O, for some medicinal vial to purge unwholesome nature, and bring back the earth to its accustomed health!

Ryland was a man of strong intellects and quick and sound decision in the usual course of things, but he stood aghast at the multitude of evils that gathered round us. Must he tax the landed interest to assist our commercial population? To do this, he must gain the favour of the chief land-holders, the nobility of the country; and these were his vowed enemies – he must conciliate them by abandoning his favourite scheme of equalization; he must confirm them in their manorial rights; he must sell his cherished plans for the permanent good of his country, for temporary relief. He must aim no more at the dear object of his ambition; throwing his arms aside, he must for present ends give up the ultimate object of his endeavours. He came to Windsor to consult with us. Every day added to his difficulties; the arrival of fresh vessels with emigrants, the total cessation of commerce, the starving multitude that thronged around the palace of the Protectorate, were circumstances not to be tampered with. The blow was struck; the aristocracy obtained all they wished, and they subscribed to a twelvemonths' bill, which levied twenty per cent on all the rent-rolls of the country. Calm was now restored to the metropolis, and to the populous cities, before driven to desperation; and we returned to the consideration of distant calamities, wondering if the future would bring any alleviation to their excess. It was August; so there could be small hope of relief during the heats. On the contrary, the disease gained virulence, while starvation did its accustomed work. Thousands died unlamented; for beside the yet warm corpse the mourner was stretched, made mute by death.

On the eighteenth of this month news arrived in London that the plague was in France and Italy. These tidings were at first whispered about town; but no one dared express aloud the soul-quailing intelligence. When any one met a friend in the street, he only cried as he hurried on, "You know!" – while the other, with an ejaculation of fear and horror, would answer – "What will become of us?" At length it was mentioned in the newspapers. The paragraph was inserted in an obscure part: 'We regret to state that there can be no longer a doubt of the plague having been introduced at Leghorn, Genoa, and Marseilles.' No word of comment followed; each reader made his own fearful one. We were as a man who hears that his house is burning, and yet hurries through the streets, borne along by a lurking hope of a mistake, till he turns the corner, and sees his sheltering roof enveloped in a flame. Before it had been a rumour; but now in words uneraseable, in definite and undeniable print, the knowledge went forth. Its obscurity of situation rendered it the more conspicuous: the diminutive letters grew gigantic to the bewildered eye of fear: they seemed graven with a pen of iron, impressed by fire, woven in the clouds, stamped on the very front of the universe.

The English, whether travellers or residents, came pouring in one great revulsive stream, back on their own country; and with them crowds of Italians and Spaniards. Our little island was filled even to bursting. At first an unusual quantity of specie made its appearance with the emigrants; but these people had no means of receiving back into their hands what they spent among us. With the advance of summer, and the increase of the distemper, rents were unpaid, and their remittances failed them. It was impossible to see these crowds of wretched, perishing creatures, late nurslings of luxury, and not stretch out a hand to save them. As at the conclusion of the eighteenth century, the English unlocked their hospitable store, for the relief of those driven from their homes by political revolution; so now they were not backward in affording aid to the victims of a more wide-spreading calamity. We had many foreign friends whom we eagerly sought out, and relieved from dreadful penury. Our Castle became an asylum for the unhappy. A little population occupied its halls. The revenue of its possessor, which had always found a mode of expenditure congenial to his generous nature, was now attended to more parsimoniously, that it might embrace a wider portion of utility. It was not however money, except partially, but the necessaries of life, that became scarce. It was difficult to find an immediate remedy. The usual one of imports was entirely cut off. In this emergency, to feed the very people to whom we had given refuge, we were obliged to yield to the plough and the mattock our pleasure-grounds and parks. Live stock diminished sensibly in the country, from the effects of the great demand in the market. Even the poor deer, our antlered proteges, were obliged to fall for the sake of worthier pensioners. The labour necessary to bring the lands to this sort of culture, employed and fed the offcasts of the diminished manufactories.

Adrian did not rest only with the exertions he could make with regard to his own possessions. He addressed himself to the wealthy of the land; he made proposals in parliament little adapted to please the rich; but his earnest pleadings and benevolent eloquence were irresistible. To give up their pleasure-grounds to the agriculturist, to diminish sensibly the number of horses kept for the purposes of luxury throughout the country, were means obvious, but unpleasing. Yet, to the honour of the English be it recorded, that, although natural disinclination made them delay awhile, yet when the misery of their fellow-creatures became glaring, an enthusiastic generosity inspired their decrees. The most luxurious were often the first to part with their indulgencies. As is common in communities, a fashion was set. The high-born ladies of the country would have deemed themselves disgraced if they had now enjoyed, what they before called a necessary, the ease of a carriage. Chairs, as in olden time, and Indian palanquins were introduced for the infirm; but else it was nothing singular to see females of rank going on foot to places of fashionable resort. It was more common, for all who possessed landed property to secede to their estates, attended by whole troops of the indigent, to cut down their woods to erect temporary dwellings, and to portion out their parks, parterres and flower-gardens, to necessitous families. Many of these, of high rank in their own countries, now, with hoe in hand, turned up the soil. It was found necessary at last to check the spirit of sacrifice, and to remind those whose generosity proceeded to lavish waste, that, until the present state of things became permanent, of which there was no likelihood, it was wrong to carry change so far as to make a reaction difficult. Experience demonstrated that in a year or two pestilence would cease; it were well that in the meantime we should not have destroyed our fine breeds of horses, or have utterly changed the face of the ornamented portion of the country.

It may be imagined that things were in a bad state indeed, before this spirit of benevolence could have struck such deep roots. The infection had now spread in the southern provinces of France. But that country had so many resources in the way of agriculture, that the rush of population from one part of it to another, and its increase through foreign emigration, was less felt than with us. The panic struck appeared of more injury, than disease and its natural concomitants.

Winter was hailed, a general and never-failing physician. The embrowning woods, and swollen rivers, the evening mists, and morning frosts, were welcomed with gratitude. The effects of purifying cold were immediately felt; and the lists of mortality abroad were curtailed each week. Many of our visitors left us: those whose homes were far in the south, fled delightedly from our northern winter, and sought their native land, secure of plenty even after their fearful visitation. We breathed again. What the coming summer would bring, we knew not; but the present months were our own, and our hopes of a cessation of pestilence were high.

Chapter VI

I HAVE LINGERED thus long on the extreme bank, the wasting shoal that stretched into the stream of life, dallying with the shadow of death. Thus long, I have cradled my heart in retrospection of past happiness, when hope was. Why not forever thus? I am not immortal; and the thread of my history might be spun out to the limits of my existence. But the same sentiment that first led me to portray scenes replete with tender recollections, now bids me hurry on. The same yearning of this warm, panting heart, that has made me in written words record my vagabond youth, my serene manhood, and the passions of my soul, makes me now recoil from further delay. I must complete my work.

Here then I stand, as I said, beside the fleet waters of the flowing years, and now away! Spread the sail, and strain with oar, hurrying by dark impending crags, adown steep rapids, even to the sea of desolation I have reached. Yet one moment, one brief interval before I put from shore – once, once again let me fancy myself as I was in 2094 in my abode at Windsor, let me close my eyes, and imagine that the immeasurable boughs of its oaks still shadow me, its castle walls anear. Let fancy portray the joyous scene of the twentieth of June, such as even now my aching heart recalls it.

Circumstances had called me to London; here I heard talk that symptoms of the plague had occurred in hospitals of that city. I returned to Windsor; my brow was clouded, my heart heavy; I entered the Little Park, as was my custom, at the Frogmore gate, on my way to the Castle. A great part of these grounds had been given to cultivation, and strips of potatoe-land and corn were scattered here and there. The rooks cawed loudly in the trees above; mixed with their hoarse cries I heard a lively strain of music. It was Alfred's birthday. The young people, the Etonians, and children of the neighbouring gentry, held a mock fair, to which all the country people were invited. The park was speckled by tents, whose flaunting colours and gaudy flags, waving in the sunshine, added to the gaiety of the scene. On a platform erected beneath the terrace, a number of the younger part of the assembly were dancing. I leaned against a tree to observe them. The band played the wild eastern air of Weber introduced in Abon Hassan; its volatile notes gave wings to the feet of the dancers, while the lookers-on unconsciously beat time. At first the tripping measure lifted my spirit with it, and for a moment my eyes gladly followed the mazes of the dance. The revulsion of thought passed like keen steel to my heart. Ye are all going to die, I thought; already your tomb is built up around you. Awhile, because you are gifted with agility and strength, you fancy that you live: but frail is the 'bower of flesh' that encaskets life; dissoluble the silver cord than binds you to it. The joyous soul, charioted from pleasure to pleasure by the graceful mechanism of well-formed limbs, will suddenly feel the axle-tree give way, and spring and wheel dissolve in dust. Not one of you, O! fated crowd, can escape – not one! not my own ones! not my Idris and her babes! Horror and misery! Already the gay dance vanished, the green sward was strewn with corpses, the blue air above became fetid with deathly exhalations. Shriek, ye clarions! ye loud trumpets, howl! Pile dirge on dirge; rouse the funereal chords; let the air ring with dire wailing; let wild discord rush on the wings of the wind! Already I hear it, while guardian angels, attendant on humanity, their task achieved, hasten away, and their departure is announced by melancholy strains; faces all unseemly with weeping, forced open my lids; faster and faster many groups of these woe-begone countenances thronged around, exhibiting every variety of wretchedness – well known faces mingled with the distorted creations of fancy. Ashy pale, Raymond and Perdita sat apart, looking on with sad smiles. Adrian's countenance flitted across, tainted by death – Idris, with eyes languidly closed and livid lips, was about to slide into the wide grave. The confusion grew – their looks of sorrow changed to mockery; they nodded their heads in time to the music, whose clang became maddening.

I felt that this was insanity – I sprang forward to throw it off; I rushed into the midst of the crowd. Idris saw me: with light step she advanced; as I folded her in my arms, feeling, as I did, that I thus enclosed what was to me a world, yet frail as the waterdrop which the noon-day sun will drink from the water lily's cup; tears filled my eyes, unwont to be thus moistened. The joyful welcome of my boys, the soft gratulation of Clara, the pressure of Adrian's hand, contributed to unman me. I felt that they were near, that they were safe, yet methought this was all deceit; – the earth reeled, the firm-enrooted trees moved – dizziness came over me – I sank to the ground.

My beloved friends were alarmed – nay, they expressed their alarm so anxiously, that I dared not pronounce the word plague, that hovered on my lips, lest they should construe my perturbed looks into a symptom, and see infection in my languor. I had scarcely recovered, and with feigned hilarity had brought back smiles into my little circle, when we saw Ryland approach.

Ryland had something the appearance of a farmer; of a man whose muscles and full grown stature had been developed under the influence of vigorous exercise and exposure to the elements. This was to a great degree the case: for, though a large landed proprietor, yet, being a projector, and of an ardent and industrious disposition, he had on his own estate given himself up to agricultural labours. When he went as ambassador to the Northern States of America, he, for some time, planned his entire migration; and went so far as to make several journies far westward on that immense continent, for the purpose of choosing the site of his new abode. Ambition turned his thoughts from these designs – ambition, which labouring through various lets and hindrances, had now led him to the summit of his hopes, in making him Lord Protector of England.

His countenance was rough but intelligent – his ample brow and quick grey eyes seemed to look out, over his own plans, and the opposition of his enemies. His voice was stentorian: his hand stretched out in debate, seemed by its gigantic and muscular form, to warn his hearers that words were not his only weapons. Few people had discovered some cowardice and much infirmity of purpose under this imposing exterior. No man could crush a "butterfly on the wheel" with better effect; no man better cover a speedy retreat from a powerful adversary. This had been the secret of his secession at the time of Lord Raymond's election. In the unsteady glance of his eye, in his extreme desire to learn the opinions of all, in the feebleness of his hand-writing, these qualities might be obscurely traced, but they were not generally known. He was now our Lord Protector. He had canvassed eagerly for this post. His protectorate was to be distinguished by every kind of innovation on the aristocracy. This his selected task was exchanged for the far different one of encountering the ruin caused by the convulsions of physical nature. He was incapable of meeting these evils by any comprehensive system; he had resorted to expedient after expedient, and could never be induced to put a remedy in force, till it came too late to be of use.

Certainly the Ryland that advanced towards us now, bore small resemblance to the powerful, ironical, seemingly fearless canvasser for the first rank among Englishmen. Our native oak, as his partisans called him, was visited truly by a nipping winter. He scarcely appeared half his usual height; his joints were unknit, his limbs would not support him; his face was contracted, his eye wandering; debility of purpose and dastard fear were expressed in every gesture.

In answer to our eager questions, one word alone fell, as it were involuntarily, from his convulsed lips: The Plague. – "Where?" – "Everywhere – we must fly – all fly – but whither? No man can tell – there is no refuge on earth, it comes on us like a thousand packs of wolves – we must all fly – where shall you go? Where can any of us go?"

These words were syllabled trembling by the iron man. Adrian replied, "Whither indeed would you fly? We must all remain; and do our best to help our suffering fellow-creatures."

"Help!" said Ryland, "There is no help! – great God, who talks of help! All the world has the plague!"

"Then to avoid it, we must quit the world," observed Adrian, with a gentle smile.

Ryland groaned; cold drops stood on his brow. It was useless to oppose his paroxysm of terror: but we soothed and encouraged him, so that after an interval he was better able to explain to us the ground of his alarm. It had come sufficiently home to him. One of his servants, while waiting on him, had suddenly fallen down dead. The physician declared that he died of the plague. We endeavoured to calm him – but our own hearts were not calm. I saw the eye of Idris wander from me to her children, with an anxious appeal to my judgment. Adrian was absorbed in meditation. For myself, I own that Ryland's words rang in my ears; all the world was infected; – in what uncontaminated seclusion could I save my beloved treasures, until the shadow of death had passed from over the earth? We sunk into silence: a silence that drank in the doleful accounts and prognostications of our guest. We had receded from the crowd; and ascending the steps of the terrace, sought the Castle. Our change of cheer struck those nearest to us; and, by means of Ryland's servants, the report soon spread that he had fled from the plague in London. The sprightly parties broke up – they assembled in whispering groups. The spirit of gaiety was eclipsed; the music ceased; the young people left their occupations and gathered together. The lightness of heart which had dressed them in masquerade habits, had decorated their tents, and assembled them in fantastic groups, appeared a sin against, and a provocative to, the awful destiny that had laid its palsying hand upon hope and life. The merriment of the hour was an unholy mockery of the sorrows of man. The foreigners whom we had among us, who had fled from the plague in their own country, now saw their last asylum invaded; and, fear making them garrulous, they described to eager listeners the miseries they had beheld in cities visited by the calamity, and gave fearful accounts of the insidious and irremediable nature of the disease.

We had entered the Castle. Idris stood at a window that over-looked the park; her maternal eyes sought her own children among the young crowd. An Italian lad had got an audience about him, and with animated gestures was describing some scene of horror. Alfred stood immoveable before him, his whole attention absorbed. Little Evelyn had endeavoured to draw Clara away to play with him; but the Italian's tale arrested her, she crept near, her lustrous eyes fixed on the speaker. Either watching the crowd in the park, or occupied by painful reflection, we were all silent; Ryland stood by himself in an embrasure of the window; Adrian paced the hall, revolving some new and overpowering idea – suddenly he stopped and said: "I have long expected this; could we in reason expect that this island should be exempt from the universal visitation? The evil is come home to us, and we must not shrink from our fate. What are your plans, my Lord Protector, for the benefit of our country?"

"For heaven's love! Windsor," cried Ryland, "do not mock me with that title. Death and disease level all men. I neither pretend to protect nor govern an hospital – such will England quickly become."

"Do you then intend, now in time of peril, to recede from your duties?"

"Duties! Speak rationally, my Lord! – When I am a plague-spotted corpse, where will my duties be? Every man for himself! The devil take the protectorship, say I, if it expose me to danger!"

"Faint-hearted man!" cried Adrian indignantly – "Your countrymen put their trust in you, and you betray them!"

"I betray them!" said Ryland, "the plague betrays me. Faint-hearted! It is well, shut up in your castle, out of danger, to boast yourself out of fear. Take the Protectorship who will; before God I renounce it!"

"And before God," replied his opponent, fervently, "do I receive it! No one will canvass for this honour now – none envy my danger or labours. Deposit your powers in my hands. Long have I fought with death, and much" (he stretched out his thin hand) "much have I suffered in the struggle. It is not by flying, but by facing the enemy, that we can conquer. If my last combat is now about to be fought, and I am to be worsted – so let it be!"

"But come, Ryland, recollect yourself! Men have hitherto thought you magnanimous and wise, will you cast aside these titles? Consider the panic your departure will occasion. Return to London. I will go with you. Encourage the people by your presence. I will incur all the danger. Shame! shame! if the first magistrate of England be foremost to renounce his duties."

Meanwhile among our guests in the park, all thoughts of festivity had faded. As summer-flies are scattered by rain, so did this congregation, late noisy and happy, in sadness and melancholy murmurs break up, dwindling away apace. With the set sun and the deepening twilight the park became nearly empty. Adrian and Ryland were still in earnest discussion. We had prepared a banquet for our guests in the lower hall of the castle; and thither Idris and I repaired to receive and entertain the few that remained. There is nothing more melancholy than a merry-meeting thus turned to sorrow: the gala dresses – the decorations, gay as they might otherwise be, receive a solemn and funereal appearance. If such change be painful from lighter causes, it weighed with intolerable heaviness from the knowledge that the earth's desolator had at last, even as an arch-fiend, lightly over-leaped the boundaries our precautions raised, and at once enthroned himself in the full and beating heart of our country. Idris sat at the top of the half-empty hall. Pale and tearful, she almost forgot her duties as hostess; her eyes were fixed on her children. Alfred's serious air shewed that he still revolved the tragic story related by the Italian boy. Evelyn was the only mirthful creature present: he sat on Clara's lap; and, making matter of glee from his own fancies, laughed aloud. The vaulted roof echoed again his infant tone. The poor mother who had brooded long over, and suppressed the expression of her anguish, now burst into tears, and folding her babe in her arms, hurried from the hall. Clara and Alfred followed. While the rest of the company, in confused murmur, which grew louder and louder, gave voice to their many fears.

The younger part gathered round me to ask my advice; and those who had friends in London were anxious beyond the rest, to ascertain the present extent of disease in the metropolis. I encouraged them with such thoughts of cheer as presented themselves. I told them exceedingly few deaths had yet been occasioned by pestilence, and gave them hopes, as we were the last visited, so the calamity might have lost its most venomous power before it had reached us. The cleanliness, habits of order, and the manner in which our cities were built, were all in our favour. As it was an epidemic, its chief force was derived from pernicious qualities in the air, and it would probably do little harm where this was naturally salubrious. At first, I had spoken only to those nearest me; but the whole assembly gathered about me, and I found that I was listened to by all. "My friends," I said, "our risk is common; our precautions and exertions shall be common also. If manly courage and resistance can save us, we will be saved. We will fight the enemy to the last. Plague shall not find us a ready prey; we will dispute every inch of ground; and, by methodical and inflexible laws, pile invincible barriers to the progress of our foe. Perhaps in no part of the world has she met with so systematic and determined an opposition. Perhaps no country is naturally so well protected against our invader; nor has nature anywhere been so well assisted by the hand of man. We will not despair. We are neither cowards nor fatalists; but, believing that God has placed the means for our preservation in our own hands, we will use those means to our utmost. Remember that cleanliness, sobriety, and even good-humour and benevolence, are our best medicines."

There was little I could add to this general exhortation; for the plague, though in London, was not among us. I dismissed the guests therefore; and they went thoughtful, more than sad, to await the events in store for them.

I now sought Adrian, anxious to hear the result of his discussion with Ryland. He had in part prevailed; the Lord Protector consented to return to London for a few weeks; during which time things should be so arranged, as to occasion less consternation at his departure. Adrian and Idris were together. The sadness with which the former had first heard that the plague was in London had vanished; the energy of his purpose informed his body with strength, the solemn joy of enthusiasm and self-devotion illuminated his countenance; and the weakness of his physical nature seemed to pass from him, as the cloud of humanity did, in the ancient fable, from the divine lover of Semele. He was endeavouring to encourage his sister, and to bring her to look on his intent in a less tragic light than she was prepared to do; and with passionate eloquence he unfolded his designs to her.

"Let me, at the first word," he said, "relieve your mind from all fear on my account. I will not task myself beyond my powers, nor will I needlessly seek danger. I feel that I know what ought to be done, and as my presence is necessary for the accomplishment of my plans, I will take especial care to preserve my life.

"I am now going to undertake an office fitted for me. I cannot intrigue, or work a tortuous path through the labyrinth of men's vices and passions; but I can bring patience, and sympathy, and such aid as art affords, to the bed of disease; I can raise from earth the miserable orphan, and awaken to new hopes the shut heart of the mourner. I can enchain the plague in limits, and set a term to the misery it would occasion; courage, forbearance, and watchfulness, are the forces I bring towards this great work.

"O, I shall be something now! From my birth I have aspired like the eagle – but, unlike the eagle, my wings have failed, and my vision has been blinded. Disappointment and sickness have hitherto held dominion over me; twin born with me, my would, was forever enchained by the shall not, of these my tyrants. A shepherd-boy that tends a silly flock on the mountains, was more in the scale of society than I. Congratulate me then that I have found fitting scope for my powers. I have often thought of offering my services to the pestilence-stricken towns of France and Italy; but fear of paining you, and expectation of this catastrophe, withheld me. To England and to Englishmen I dedicate myself. If I can save one of her mighty spirits from the deadly shaft; if I can ward disease from one of her smiling cottages, I shall not have lived in vain."

Strange ambition this! Yet such was Adrian. He appeared given up to contemplation, averse to excitement, a lowly student, a man of visions – but afford him worthy theme, and –

> *Like to the lark at break of day arising,*
> *From sullen earth, sings hymns at heaven's gate.*

– so did he spring up from listlessness and unproductive thought, to the highest pitch of virtuous action.

With him went enthusiasm, the high-wrought resolve, the eye that without blenching could look at death. With us remained sorrow, anxiety, and unendurable expectation of evil. The man, says Lord Bacon, who hath wife and children, has given hostages to fortune. Vain was all philosophical reasoning – vain all fortitude – vain, vain, a reliance on probable good. I might heap high the scale with logic, courage, and resignation – but let one fear for Idris and our children enter the opposite one, and, over-weighed, it kicked the beam.

The plague was in London! Fools that we were not long ago to have foreseen this. We wept over the ruin of the boundless continents of the east, and the desolation of the western world; while we fancied that the little channel between our island and the rest of the earth was to preserve us alive among the dead. It were no mighty leap methinks from Calais to Dover. The eye easily discerns the sister land; they were united once; and the little path that runs between looks in a map but as a trodden footway through high grass. Yet this small interval was to save us: the sea was to rise a wall of adamant – without, disease and misery – within, a shelter from evil, a nook of the garden of paradise – a particle of celestial soil, which no evil could invade – truly we were wise in our generation, to imagine all these things!

But we are awake now. The plague is in London; the air of England is tainted, and her sons and daughters strew the unwholesome earth. And now, the sea, late our defence, seems our prison bound; hemmed in by its gulphs, we shall die like the famished inhabitants of a besieged town. Other nations have a fellowship in death; but we, shut out from all neighbourhood, must bury our own dead, and little England become a wide, wide tomb.

This feeling of universal misery assumed concentration and shape, when I looked on my wife and children; and the thought of danger to them possessed my whole being with fear. How could I save them? I revolved a thousand and a thousand plans. They should not die – first I would be gathered to nothingness, ere infection should come anear these idols of my soul. I would walk barefoot through the world, to find an uninfected spot; I would build my home on some wave-tossed plank, drifted about on the barren, shoreless ocean. I would betake me with them to some wild beast's den, where a tyger's cubs, which I would slay, had been reared in health. I would seek the mountain eagle's eirie, and live years suspended in some inaccessible recess of a sea-bounding cliff – no labour too great, no scheme too wild, if it promised life to them. O! ye heart-strings of mine, could ye be torn asunder, and my soul not spend itself in tears of blood for sorrow!

Idris, after the first shock, regained a portion of fortitude. She studiously shut out all prospect of the future, and cradled her heart in present blessings. She never for a moment lost sight of her children. But while they in health sported about her, she could cherish contentment and hope. A strange and wild restlessness came over me – the more intolerable, because I was forced to conceal it. My fears for Adrian were ceaseless; August had come; and the symptoms of plague increased rapidly in London. It was deserted by all who possessed the power of removing; and he, the brother of my soul, was exposed to the perils from which all but slaves enchained by circumstance fled. He remained to combat the fiend – his side unguarded, his toils unshared – infection might even reach him, and he die unattended and alone. By day and night these thoughts pursued me. I resolved to visit London, to see him; to quiet these agonizing throes by the sweet medicine of hope, or the opiate of despair.

It was not until I arrived at Brentford, that I perceived much change in the face of the country. The better sort of houses were shut up; the busy trade of the town palsied; there was an air of anxiety among the few passengers I met, and they looked wonderingly at my carriage – the first they had seen pass towards London, since pestilence sat on its high places, and possessed its busy streets. I met several funerals; they were slenderly attended by mourners, and were regarded by the spectators as omens of direst import. Some gazed on these processions with wild eagerness – others fled timidly – some wept aloud.

Adrian's chief endeavour, after the immediate succour of the sick, had been to disguise the symptoms and progress of the plague from the inhabitants of London. He knew that fear and melancholy forebodings were powerful assistants to disease; that desponding and brooding care rendered the physical nature of man peculiarly susceptible of infection. No unseemly sights were therefore discernible: the shops were in general open, the concourse of passengers in some degree kept up. But although the appearance of an infected town was avoided, to me, who had not beheld it since the commencement of the visitation, London appeared sufficiently changed. There were no carriages, and grass had sprung high in the streets; the houses had a desolate look; most of the shutters were closed; and there was a ghast and frightened stare in the persons I met, very different from the usual business-like demeanour of the Londoners. My solitary carriage attracted notice, as it rattled along towards the Protectoral Palace – and the fashionable streets leading to it wore a still more dreary and deserted appearance. I found Adrian's anti-chamber crowded – it was his hour for giving audience. I was unwilling to disturb his labours, and waited, watching the ingress and egress of the petitioners. They consisted of people of the middling and lower classes of society, whose means of subsistence failed with the cessation of trade, and of the busy spirit of money-making in all its branches, peculiar to our country. There was an air of anxiety, sometimes of terror in the new-comers, strongly contrasted with the resigned and even satisfied mien of those who had had audience. I could read the influence of my friend in their quickened motions and cheerful faces. Two o'clock struck, after which none were admitted; those who had been disappointed went sullenly or sorrowfully away, while I entered the audience-chamber.

I was struck by the improvement that appeared in the health of Adrian. He was no longer bent to the ground, like an over-nursed flower of spring, that, shooting up beyond its strength, is weighed down even by its own coronal of blossoms. His eyes were bright, his countenance composed, an air of concentrated energy was diffused over his whole person, much unlike its former languor. He sat at a table with several secretaries, who were arranging petitions, or registering the notes made during that day's audience. Two or three petitioners were still in attendance. I admired his justice and patience. Those who possessed a power of living out of London, he advised immediately to quit it, affording them the means of so doing. Others, whose trade was beneficial to the city, or who possessed no other refuge, he provided with advice for better avoiding the epidemic; relieving overloaded families, supplying the gaps made in others by death. Order, comfort, and even health, rose under his influence, as from the touch of a magician's wand.

"I am glad you are come," he said to me, when we were at last alone; "I can only spare a few minutes, and must tell you much in that time. The plague is now in progress – it is useless closing one's eyes to the fact – the deaths increase each week. What will come I cannot guess. As yet, thank God, I am equal to the government of the town; and I look only to the present. Ryland, whom I have so long detained, has stipulated that I shall suffer him to depart before the end of this month. The deputy appointed by parliament is dead; another therefore must be named; I have advanced my claim, and I believe that I shall have no competitor. Tonight the question is to be decided, as there is a call of the house for the purpose. You must nominate me, Lionel; Ryland, for shame, cannot shew himself; but you, my friend, will do me this service?

How lovely is devotion! Here was a youth, royally sprung, bred in luxury, by nature averse to the usual struggles of a public life, and now, in time of danger, at a period when to live was the utmost scope of the ambitious, he, the beloved and heroic Adrian, made, in sweet simplicity, an offer to sacrifice himself for the public good. The very idea was generous and noble – but, beyond this, his unpretending manner, his entire want of the assumption of a virtue, rendered his act ten times more touching. I would have withstood his request; but I had seen the good he diffused; I felt that his resolves were not to be shaken, so, with an heavy heart, I consented to do as he asked. He grasped my hand affectionately: "Thank you," he said, "you have relieved me from a painful dilemma, and are, as you ever were, the best of my friends. Farewell – I must now leave you for a few hours. Go you and converse with Ryland. Although he deserts his post in London, he may be of the greatest service in the north of England, by receiving and assisting travellers, and contributing to supply the metropolis with food. Awaken him, I entreat you, to some sense of duty."

Adrian left me, as I afterwards learnt, upon his daily task of visiting the hospitals, and inspecting the crowded parts of London. I found Ryland much altered, even from what he had been when he visited Windsor. Perpetual fear had jaundiced his complexion, and shrivelled his whole person. I told him of the business of the evening, and a smile relaxed the contracted muscles. He desired to go; each day he expected to be infected by pestilence, each day he was unable to resist the gentle violence of Adrian's detention. The moment Adrian should be legally elected his deputy, he would escape to safety. Under this impression he listened to all I said; and, elevated almost to joy by the near prospect of his departure, he entered into a discussion concerning the plans he should adopt in his own county, forgetting, for the moment, his cherished resolution of shutting himself up from all communication in the mansion and grounds of his estate.

In the evening, Adrian and I proceeded to Westminster. As we went he reminded me of what I was to say and do, yet, strange to say, I entered the chamber without having once reflected on my purpose. Adrian remained in the coffee-room, while I, in compliance with his desire, took my seat in St. Stephen's. There reigned unusual silence in the chamber. I had not visited it since Raymond's protectorate; a period conspicuous for a numerous attendance of members, for the eloquence of the speakers, and the warmth of the debate. The benches were very empty, those by custom occupied by the hereditary members were vacant; the city members were there – the members for the commercial towns, few landed proprietors, and not many of those who entered parliament for the sake of a career. The first subject that occupied the attention of the house was an address from the Lord Protector, praying them to appoint a deputy during a necessary absence on his part.

A silence prevailed, till one of the members coming to me, whispered that the Earl of Windsor had sent him word that I was to move his election, in the absence of the person who had been first chosen for this office. Now for the first time I saw the full extent of my task, and I was overwhelmed by what I had brought on myself. Ryland had deserted his post through fear of the plague: from the same fear Adrian had no competitor. And I, the nearest kinsman of the Earl of Windsor, was to propose his election. I was to thrust this selected and matchless friend into the post of danger – impossible! the die was cast – I would offer myself as candidate.

The few members who were present, had come more for the sake of terminating the business by securing a legal attendance, than under the idea of a debate. I had risen mechanically – my knees trembled; irresolution hung on my voice, as I uttered a few words on the necessity of choosing a person adequate to the dangerous task in hand. But, when the idea of presenting myself in the room of my friend intruded, the load of doubt and pain was taken from off me. My words flowed spontaneously – my utterance was firm and quick. I adverted to what Adrian had already done – I promised the same vigilance in furthering all his views. I drew a touching picture of his vacillating health; I boasted of my own strength. I prayed them to save even from himself this scion of the noblest family in

England. My alliance with him was the pledge of my sincerity, my union with his sister, my children, his presumptive heirs, were the hostages of my truth.

This unexpected turn in the debate was quickly communicated to Adrian. He hurried in, and witnessed the termination of my impassioned harangue. I did not see him: my soul was in my words – my eyes could not perceive that which was; while a vision of Adrian's form, tainted by pestilence, and sinking in death, floated before them. He seized my hand, as I concluded – "Unkind!" he cried, "you have betrayed me!" then, springing forwards, with the air of one who had a right to command, he claimed the place of deputy as his own. He had bought it, he said, with danger, and paid for it with toil. His ambition rested there; and, after an interval devoted to the interests of his country, was I to step in, and reap the profit? Let them remember what London had been when he arrived: the panic that prevailed brought famine, while every moral and legal tie was loosened. He had restored order – this had been a work which required perseverance, patience, and energy; and he had neither slept nor waked but for the good of his country. – Would they dare wrong him thus? Would they wrest his hard-earned reward from him, to bestow it on one, who, never having mingled in public life, would come a tyro to the craft, in which he was an adept. He demanded the place of deputy as his right. Ryland had shewn that he preferred him. Never before had he, who was born even to the inheritance of the throne of England, never had he asked favour or honour from those now his equals, but who might have been his subjects. Would they refuse him? Could they thrust back from the path of distinction and laudable ambition, the heir of their ancient kings, and heap another disappointment on a fallen house.

No one had ever before heard Adrian allude to the rights of his ancestors. None had ever before suspected, that power, or the suffrage of the many, could in any manner become dear to him. He had begun his speech with vehemence; he ended with unassuming gentleness, making his appeal with the same humility, as if he had asked to be the first in wealth, honour, and power among Englishmen, and not, as was the truth, to be the foremost in the ranks of loathsome toils and inevitable death. A murmur of approbation rose after his speech. "Oh, do not listen to him," I cried, "he speaks false – false to himself," – I was interrupted: and, silence being restored, we were ordered, as was the custom, to retire during the decision of the house. I fancied that they hesitated, and that there was some hope for me – I was mistaken – hardly had we quitted the chamber, before Adrian was recalled, and installed in his office of Lord Deputy to the Protector.

We returned together to the palace. "Why, Lionel," said Adrian, "what did you intend? you could not hope to conquer, and yet you gave me the pain of a triumph over my dearest friend."

"This is mockery," I replied, "you devote yourself – you, the adored brother of Idris, the being, of all the world contains, dearest to our hearts – you devote yourself to an early death. I would have prevented this; my death would be a small evil – or rather I should not die; while you cannot hope to escape."

"As to the likelihood of escaping," said Adrian, "ten years hence the cold stars may shine on the graves of all of us; but as to my peculiar liability to infection, I could easily prove, both logically and physically, that in the midst of contagion I have a better chance of life than you.

"This is my post: I was born for this – to rule England in anarchy, to save her in danger – to devote myself for her. The blood of my forefathers cries aloud in my veins, and bids me be first among my countrymen. Or, if this mode of speech offend you, let me say, that my mother, the proud queen, instilled early into me a love of distinction, and all that, if the weakness of my physical nature and my peculiar opinions had not prevented such a design, might have made me long since struggle for the lost inheritance of my race. But now my mother, or, if you will, my mother's lessons, awaken within me. I cannot lead on to battle; I cannot, through intrigue and faithlessness rear again the throne upon the wreck of English public spirit. But I can be the first to support and guard my country, now that terrific disasters and ruin have laid strong hands upon her.

"That country and my beloved sister are all I have. I will protect the first – the latter I commit to your charge. If I survive, and she be lost, I were far better dead. Preserve her – for her own sake I know that you will – if you require any other spur, think that, in preserving her, you preserve me. Her faultless nature, one sum of perfections, is wrapt up in her affections – if they were hurt, she would droop like an unwatered floweret, and the slightest injury they receive is a nipping frost to her. Already she fears for us. She fears for the children she adores, and for you, the father of these, her lover, husband, protector; and you must be near her to support and encourage her. Return to Windsor then, my brother; for such you are by every tie – fill the double place my absence imposes on you, and let me, in all my sufferings here, turn my eyes towards that dear seclusion, and say – There is peace."

Chapter VII

I DID PROCEED to Windsor, but not with the intention of remaining there. I went but to obtain the consent of Idris, and then to return and take my station beside my unequalled friend; to share his labours, and save him, if so it must be, at the expence of my life. Yet I dreaded to witness the anguish which my resolve might excite in Idris. I had vowed to my own heart never to shadow her countenance even with transient grief, and should I prove recreant at the hour of greatest need? I had begun my journey with anxious haste; now I desired to draw it out through the course of days and months. I longed to avoid the necessity of action; I strove to escape from thought – vainly   futurity, like a dark image in a phantasmagoria, came nearer and more near, till it clasped the whole earth in its shadow.

A slight circumstance induced me to alter my usual route, and to return home by Egham and Bishopgate. I alighted at Perdita's ancient abode, her cottage; and, sending forward the carriage, determined to walk across the park to the castle. This spot, dedicated to sweetest recollections, the deserted house and neglected garden were well adapted to nurse my melancholy. In our happiest days, Perdita had adorned her cottage with every aid art might bring, to that which nature had selected to favour. In the same spirit of exaggeration she had, on the event of her separation from Raymond, caused it to be entirely neglected. It was now in ruin: the deer had climbed the broken palings, and reposed among the flowers; grass grew on the threshold, and the swinging lattice creaking to the wind, gave signal of utter desertion. The sky was blue above, and the air impregnated with fragrance by the rare flowers that grew among the weeds. The trees moved overhead, awakening nature's favourite melody – but the melancholy appearance of the choaked paths, and weed-grown flower-beds, dimmed even this gay summer scene. The time when in proud and happy security we assembled at this cottage, was gone – soon the present hours would join those past, and shadows of future ones rose dark and menacing from the womb of time, their cradle and their bier. For the first time in my life I envied the sleep of the dead, and thought with pleasure of one's bed under the sod, where grief and fear have no power. I passed through the gap of the broken paling – I felt, while I disdained, the choking tears – I rushed into the depths of the forest. O death and change, rulers of our life, where are ye, that I may grapple with you! What was there in our tranquillity, that excited your envy – in our happiness, that ye should destroy it? We were happy, loving, and beloved; the horn of Amalthea contained no blessing unshowered upon us, but, alas!

> *la fortuna*
> *deidad barbara importuna,*
> *oy cadaver y ayer flor,*
> *no permanece jamas!*[1]

As I wandered on thus ruminating, a number of country people passed me. They seemed full of careful thought, and a few words of their conversation that reached me, induced me to approach and make further enquiries. A party of people flying from London, as was frequent in those days, had come up the Thames in a boat. No one at Windsor would afford them shelter; so, going a little further up, they remained all night in a deserted hut near Bolter's lock. They pursued their way the following morning, leaving one of their company behind them, sick of the plague. This circumstance once spread abroad, none dared approach within half a mile of the infected neighbourhood, and the deserted wretch was left to fight with disease and death in solitude, as he best might. I was urged by compassion to hasten to the hut, for the purpose of ascertaining his situation, and administering to his wants.

As I advanced I met knots of country-people talking earnestly of this event: distant as they were from the apprehended contagion, fear was impressed on every countenance. I passed by a group of these terrorists, in a lane in the direct road to the hut. One of them stopped me, and, conjecturing that I was ignorant of the circumstance, told me not to go on, for that an infected person lay but at a short distance.

"I know it," I replied, "and I am going to see in what condition the poor fellow is."

A murmur of surprise and horror ran through the assembly. I continued:

"This poor wretch is deserted, dying, succourless; in these unhappy times, God knows how soon any or all of us may be in like want. I am going to do, as I would be done by."

"But you will never be able to return to the Castle – Lady Idris – his children –" in confused speech were the words that struck my ear.

"Do you not know, my friends," I said, "that the Earl himself, now Lord Protector, visits daily, not only those probably infected by this disease, but the hospitals and pest houses, going near, and even touching the sick? yet he was never in better health. You labour under an entire mistake as to the nature of the plague; but do not fear, I do not ask any of you to accompany me, nor to believe me, until I return safe and sound from my patient."

So I left them, and hurried on. I soon arrived at the hut: the door was ajar. I entered, and one glance assured me that its former inhabitant was no more – he lay on a heap of straw, cold and stiff; while a pernicious effluvia filled the room, and various stains and marks served to shew the virulence of the disorder.

I had never before beheld one killed by pestilence. While every mind was full of dismay at its effects, a craving for excitement had led us to peruse De Foe's account, and the masterly delineations of the author of Arthur Mervyn. The pictures drawn in these books were so vivid, that we seemed to have experienced the results depicted by them. But cold were the sensations excited by words, burning though they were, and describing the death and misery of thousands, compared to what I felt in looking on the corpse of this unhappy stranger. This indeed was the plague. I raised his rigid limbs, I marked the distortion of his face, and the stony eyes lost to perception. As I was thus occupied, chill horror congealed my blood, making my flesh quiver and my hair to stand on end. Half insanely I spoke to the dead. So the plague killed you, I muttered. How came this? Was the coming painful? You look as if the enemy had tortured, before he murdered you. And now I leapt up precipitately, and escaped from the hut, before nature could revoke her laws, and inorganic words be breathed in answer from the lips of the departed.

On returning through the lane, I saw at a distance the same assemblage of persons which I had left. They hurried away, as soon as they saw me; my agitated mien added to their fear of coming near one who had entered within the verge of contagion.

At a distance from facts one draws conclusions which appear infallible, which yet when put to the test of reality, vanish like unreal dreams. I had ridiculed the fears of my countrymen, when they related to others; now that they came home to myself, I paused. The Rubicon, I felt, was passed; and it behoved me well to reflect what I should do on this hither side of disease and danger. According to the vulgar superstition, my dress, my person, the air I breathed, bore in it mortal danger to myself and others. Should I return to the Castle, to my wife and children, with this taint upon me? Not surely if I were infected; but I felt certain that I was not – a few hours would determine the question – I would spend these in the forest, in reflection on what was to come, and what my future actions were to be. In the feeling communicated to me by the sight of one struck by the plague, I forgot the events that had excited me so strongly in London; new and more painful prospects, by degrees were cleared of the mist which had hitherto veiled them. The question was no longer whether I should share Adrian's toils and danger; but in what manner I could, in Windsor and the neighbourhood, imitate the prudence and zeal which, under his government, produced order and plenty in London, and how, now pestilence had spread more widely, I could secure the health of my own family.

I spread the whole earth out as a map before me. On no one spot of its surface could I put my finger and say, here is safety. In the south, the disease, virulent and immedicable, had nearly annihilated the race of man; storm and inundation, poisonous winds and blights, filled up the measure of suffering. In the north it was worse – the lesser population gradually declined, and famine and plague kept watch on the survivors, who, helpless and feeble, were ready to fall an easy prey into their hands.

I contracted my view to England. The overgrown metropolis, the great heart of mighty Britain, was pulseless. Commerce had ceased. All resort for ambition or pleasure was cut off – the streets were grass-grown – the houses empty – the few, that from necessity remained, seemed already branded with the taint of inevitable pestilence. In the larger manufacturing towns the same tragedy was acted on a smaller, yet more disastrous scale. There was no Adrian to superintend and direct, while whole flocks of the poor were struck and killed. Yet we were not all to die. No truly, though thinned, the race of man would continue, and the great plague would, in after years, become matter of history and wonder. Doubtless this visitation was for extent unexampled – more need that we should work hard to dispute its progress; ere this men have gone out in sport, and slain their thousands and tens of thousands; but now man had become a creature of price; the life of one of them was of more worth than the so called treasures of kings. Look at his thought-endued countenance, his graceful limbs, his majestic brow, his wondrous mechanism – the type and model of this best work of God is not to be cast aside as a broken vessel – he shall be preserved, and his children and his children's children carry down the name and form of man to latest time.

Above all I must guard those entrusted by nature and fate to my especial care. And surely, if among all my fellow-creatures I were to select those who might stand forth examples of the greatness and goodness of man, I could choose no other than those allied to me by the most sacred ties. Some from among the family of man must survive, and these should be among the survivors; that should be my task – to accomplish it my own life were a small sacrifice. There then in that castle – in Windsor Castle, birth-place of Idris and my babes, should be the haven and retreat for the wrecked bark of human society. Its forest should be our world – its garden afford us food; within its walls I would establish the shaken throne of health. I was an outcast and a vagabond, when Adrian gently threw over me the silver net of love and civilization, and linked me inextricably to human charities and human excellence. I was one, who, though an aspirant after good, and an ardent lover of wisdom, was yet unenrolled in any list of worth, when Idris, the princely born, who was herself the personification of all that was divine in woman, she who walked the earth like a poet's dream, as a carved goddess endued with sense, or pictured saint stepping from the canvas – she, the most worthy, chose me, and gave me herself – a priceless gift.

During several hours I continued thus to meditate, till hunger and fatigue brought me back to the passing hour, then marked by long shadows cast from the descending sun. I had wandered towards Bracknel, far to the west of Windsor. The feeling of perfect health which I enjoyed, assured me that I was free from contagion. I remembered that Idris had been kept in ignorance of my proceedings. She might have heard of my return from London, and my visit to Bolter's Lock, which, connected with my continued absence, might tend greatly to alarm her. I returned to Windsor by the Long Walk, and passing through the town towards the Castle, I found it in a state of agitation and disturbance.

"It is too late to be ambitious," says Sir Thomas Browne. "We cannot hope to live so long in our names as some have done in their persons; one face of Janus holds no proportion to the other." Upon this text many fanatics arose, who prophesied that the end of time was come. The spirit of superstition had birth, from the wreck of our hopes, and antics wild and dangerous were played on the great theatre, while the remaining particle of futurity dwindled into a point in the eyes of the prognosticators. Weak-spirited women died of fear as they listened to their denunciations; men of robust form and seeming strength fell into idiotcy and madness, racked by the dread of coming eternity. A man of this kind was now pouring forth his eloquent despair among the inhabitants of Windsor. The scene of the morning, and my visit to the dead, which had been spread abroad, had alarmed the country-people, so they had become fit instruments to be played upon by a maniac.

The poor wretch had lost his young wife and lovely infant by the plague. He was a mechanic; and, rendered unable to attend to the occupation which supplied his necessities, famine was added to his other miseries. He left the chamber which contained his wife and child – wife and child no more, but "dead earth upon the earth" – wild with hunger, watching and grief, his diseased fancy made him believe himself sent by heaven to preach the end of time to the world. He entered the churches, and foretold to the congregations their speedy removal to the vaults below. He appeared like the forgotten spirit of the time in the theatres, and bade the spectators go home and die. He had been seized and confined; he had escaped and wandered from London among the neighbouring towns, and, with frantic gestures and thrilling words, he unveiled to each their hidden fears, and gave voice to the soundless thought they dared not syllable. He stood under the arcade of the town-hall of Windsor, and from this elevation harangued a trembling crowd.

"Hear, O ye inhabitants of the earth," he cried, "hear thou, all seeing, but most pitiless Heaven! hear thou too, O tempest-tossed heart, which breathes out these words, yet faints beneath their meaning! Death is among us! The earth is beautiful and flower-bedecked, but she is our grave! The clouds of heaven weep for us – the pageantry of the stars is but our funeral torchlight. Grey headed men, ye hoped for yet a few years in your long-known abode – but the lease is up, you must remove – children, ye will never reach maturity, even now the small grave is dug for ye – mothers, clasp them in your arms, one death embraces you!"

Shuddering, he stretched out his hands, his eyes cast up, seemed bursting from their sockets, while he appeared to follow shapes, to us invisible, in the yielding air – "There they are," he cried, "the dead! They rise in their shrouds, and pass in silent procession towards the far land of their doom – their bloodless lips move not – their shadowy limbs are void of motion, while still they glide onwards. We come," he exclaimed, springing forwards, "for what should we wait? Haste, my friends, apparel yourselves in the court-dress of death. Pestilence will usher you to his presence. Why thus long? they, the good, the wise, and the beloved, are gone before. Mothers, kiss you last – husbands, protectors no more, lead on the partners of your death! Come, O come! while the dear ones are yet in sight, for soon they will pass away, and we never never shall join them more."

From such ravings as these, he would suddenly become collected, and with unexaggerated but terrific words, paint the horrors of the time; describe with minute detail, the effects of the plague on the human frame, and tell heart-breaking tales of the snapping of dear affinities – the gasping horror of despair over the death-bed of the last beloved – so that groans and even shrieks burst from the crowd. One man in particular stood in front, his eyes fixt on the prophet, his mouth open, his limbs rigid, while his face changed to various colours, yellow, blue, and green, through intense fear. The maniac caught his glance, and turned his eye on him – one has heard of the gaze of the rattle-snake, which allures the trembling victim till he falls within his jaws. The maniac became composed; his person rose higher; authority beamed from his countenance. He looked on the peasant, who began to tremble, while he still gazed; his knees knocked together; his teeth chattered. He at last fell down in convulsions. "That man has the plague," said the maniac calmly. A shriek burst from the lips of the poor wretch; and then sudden motionlessness came over him; it was manifest to all that he was dead.

Cries of horror filled the place – everyone endeavoured to effect his escape – in a few minutes the market place was cleared – the corpse lay on the ground; and the maniac, subdued and exhausted, sat beside it, leaning his gaunt cheek upon his thin hand. Soon some people, deputed by the magistrates, came to remove the body; the unfortunate being saw a jailor in each – he fled precipitately, while I passed onwards to the Castle.

Death, cruel and relentless, had entered these beloved walls. An old servant, who had nursed Idris in infancy, and who lived with us more on the footing of a revered relative than a domestic, had gone a few days before to visit a daughter, married, and settled in the neighbourhood of London. On the night of her return she sickened of the plague. From the haughty and unbending nature of the Countess of Windsor, Idris had few tender filial associations with her. This good woman had stood in the place of a mother, and her very deficiencies of education and knowledge, by rendering her humble and defenceless, endeared her to us – she was the especial favourite of the children. I found my poor girl, there is no exaggeration in the expression, wild with grief and dread. She hung over the patient in agony, which was not mitigated when her thoughts wandered towards her babes, for whom she feared infection. My arrival was like the newly discovered lamp of a lighthouse to sailors, who are weathering some dangerous point. She deposited her appalling doubts in my hands; she relied on my judgment, and was comforted by my participation in her sorrow. Soon our poor nurse expired; and the anguish of suspense was changed to deep regret, which though at first more painful, yet yielded with greater readiness to my consolations. Sleep, the sovereign balm, at length steeped her tearful eyes in forgetfulness.

She slept; and quiet prevailed in the Castle, whose inhabitants were hushed to repose. I was awake, and during the long hours of dead night, my busy thoughts worked in my brain, like ten thousand mill-wheels, rapid, acute, untameable. All slept – all England slept; and from my window, commanding a wide prospect of the star-illumined country, I saw the land stretched out in placid rest. I was awake, alive, while the brother of death possessed my race. What, if the more potent of these fraternal deities should obtain dominion over it? The silence of midnight, to speak truly, though apparently a paradox, rung in my ears. The solitude became intolerable – I placed my hand on the beating heart of Idris, I bent my head to catch the sound of her breath, to assure myself that she still existed – for a moment I doubted whether I should not awake her; so effeminate an horror ran through my frame. – Great God! would it one day be thus? One day all extinct, save myself, should I walk the earth alone? Were these warning voices, whose inarticulate and oracular sense forced belief upon me?

Yet I would not call them
Voices of warning, that announce to us
Only the inevitable. As the sun,
Ere it is risen, sometimes paints its image
In the atmosphere – so often do the spirits
Of great events stride on before the events,
And in to-day already walks tomorrow.

Footnote 1. Calderon de la Barca's El príncipe constante In an edition of *The Last Man*, ed. Jane Blumberg with Nora Crook, it is translated as: 'Troublesome fortune / Barbarous deity / Today a cadaver and yesterday a flower / Never permanent!'

Chapter VIII

AFTER A LONG INTERVAL, I am again impelled by the restless spirit within me to continue my narration; but I must alter the mode which I have hitherto adopted. The details contained in the foregoing pages, apparently trivial, yet each slightest one weighing like lead in the depressed scale of human afflictions; this tedious dwelling on the sorrows of others, while my own were only in apprehension; this slowly laying bare of my soul's wounds: this journal of death; this long drawn and tortuous path, leading to the ocean of countless tears, awakens me again to keen grief. I had used this history as an opiate; while it described my beloved friends, fresh with life and glowing with hope, active assistants on the scene, I was soothed; there will be a more melancholy pleasure in painting the end of all. But the intermediate steps, the climbing the wall, raised up between what was and is, while I still looked back nor saw the concealed desert beyond, is a labour past my strength. Time and experience have placed me on an height from which I can comprehend the past as a whole; and in this way I must describe it, bringing forward the leading incidents, and disposing light and shade so as to form a picture in whose very darkness there will be harmony.

It would be needless to narrate those disastrous occurrences, for which a parallel might be found in any slighter visitation of our gigantic calamity. Does the reader wish to hear of the pest-houses, where death is the comforter – of the mournful passage of the death-cart – of the insensibility of the worthless, and the anguish of the loving heart – of harrowing shrieks and silence dire – of the variety of disease, desertion, famine, despair, and death? There are many books which can feed the appetite craving for these things; let them turn to the accounts of Boccaccio, De Foe, and Browne. The vast annihilation that has swallowed all things – the voiceless solitude of the once busy earth – the lonely state of singleness which hems me in, has deprived even such details of their stinging reality, and mellowing the lurid tints of past anguish with poetic hues, I am able to escape from the mosaic of circumstance, by perceiving and reflecting back the grouping and combined colouring of the past.

I had returned from London possessed by the idea, with the intimate feeling that it was my first duty to secure, as well as I was able, the well-being of my family, and then to return and take my post beside Adrian. The events that immediately followed on my arrival at Windsor changed this view of things. The plague was not in London alone, it was everywhere – it came on us, as Ryland had said, like a thousand packs of wolves, howling through the winter night, gaunt and fierce. When once disease was introduced into the rural districts, its effects appeared more horrible, more exigent, and more difficult to cure, than in towns. There was a companionship in suffering there, and, the neighbours keeping constant watch on each other, and inspired by the active benevolence of Adrian, succour was afforded, and the path of destruction smoothed. But in the country, among the scattered farm-houses, in lone cottages, in fields, and barns, tragedies were acted harrowing to the soul, unseen, unheard, unnoticed. Medical aid was less easily procured, food was more difficult to obtain, and human beings, unwithheld by shame, for they were unbeheld of their fellows, ventured on deeds of greater wickedness, or gave way more readily to their abject fears.

Deeds of heroism also occurred, whose very mention swells the heart and brings tears into the eyes. Such is human nature, that beauty and deformity are often closely linked. In reading history we are chiefly struck by the generosity and self-devotion that follow close on the heels of crime, veiling with supernal flowers the stain of blood. Such acts were not wanting to adorn the grim train that waited on the progress of the plague.

The inhabitants of Berkshire and Bucks had been long aware that the plague was in London, in Liverpool, Bristol, Manchester, York, in short, in all the more populous towns of England. They were not however the less astonished and dismayed when it appeared among themselves. They were impatient and angry in the midst of terror. They would do something to throw off the clinging evil, and, while in action, they fancied that a remedy was applied. The inhabitants of the smaller towns left their houses, pitched tents in the fields, wandering separate from each other careless of hunger or the sky's inclemency, while they imagined that they avoided the death-dealing disease. The farmers and cottagers, on the contrary, struck with the fear of solitude, and madly desirous of medical assistance, flocked into the towns.

But winter was coming, and with winter, hope. In August, the plague had appeared in the country of England, and during September it made its ravages. Towards the end of October it dwindled away, and was in some degree replaced by a typhus, of hardly less virulence. The autumn was warm and rainy: the infirm and sickly died off – happier they: many young people flushed with health and prosperity, made pale by wasting malady, became the inhabitants of the grave. The crop had failed, the bad corn, and want of foreign wines, added vigour to disease. Before Christmas half England was under water. The storms of the last winter were renewed; but the diminished shipping of this year caused us to feel less the tempests of the sea. The flood and storms did more harm to continental Europe than to us – giving, as it were, the last blow to the calamities which destroyed it. In Italy the rivers were unwatched by the diminished peasantry; and, like wild beasts from their lair when the hunters and dogs are afar, did Tiber, Arno, and Po, rush upon and destroy the fertility of the plains. Whole villages were carried away. Rome, and Florence, and Pisa were overflowed, and their marble palaces, late mirrored in tranquil streams, had their foundations shaken by their winter-gifted power. In Germany and Russia the injury was still more momentous.

But frost would come at last, and with it a renewal of our lease of earth. Frost would blunt the arrows of pestilence, and enchain the furious elements; and the land would in spring throw off her garment of snow, released from her menace of destruction. It was not until February that the desired signs of winter appeared. For three days the snow fell, ice stopped the current of the rivers, and the birds flew out from crackling branches of the frost-whitened trees. On the fourth morning all vanished. A south-west wind brought up rain – the sun came out, and mocking the usual laws of nature, seemed even at this early season to burn with solsticial force. It was no consolation, that with the first winds of March the lanes were filled with violets, the fruit trees covered with blossoms, that the corn sprung up, and the leaves came out, forced by the unseasonable heat. We feared the balmy air – we feared the cloudless sky, the flower-covered earth, and delightful woods, for we looked on the fabric of the universe no longer as our dwelling, but our tomb, and the fragrant land smelled to the apprehension of fear like a wide church-yard.

> *Pisando la tierra dura*
> *de continuo el hombre esta*
> *y cada passo que da*
> *es sobre su sepultura.*[2]

Yet notwithstanding these disadvantages winter was breathing time; and we exerted ourselves to make the best of it. Plague might not revive with the summer; but if it did, it should find us prepared. It is a part of man's nature to adapt itself through habit even to pain and sorrow. Pestilence had become a part of our future, our existence; it was to be guarded against, like the flooding of rivers, the encroachments of ocean, or the inclemency of the sky. After long suffering and bitter experience, some panacea might be discovered; as it was, all that received infection died – all however were not infected; and it became our part to fix deep the foundations, and raise high the barrier between contagion and the sane; to introduce such order as would conduce to the well-being of the survivors, and as would preserve hope and some portion of happiness to those who were spectators of the still renewed tragedy. Adrian had introduced systematic modes of proceeding in the metropolis, which, while they were unable to stop the progress of death, yet prevented other evils, vice and folly, from rendering the awful fate of the hour still more tremendous. I wished to imitate his example, but men are used to

– move all together, if they move at all,

and I could find no means of leading the inhabitants of scattered towns and villages, who forgot my words as soon as they heard them not, and veered with every baffling wind, that might arise from an apparent change of circumstance.

I adopted another plan. Those writers who have imagined a reign of peace and happiness on earth, have generally described a rural country, where each small township was directed by the elders and wise men. This was the key of my design. Each village, however small, usually contains a leader, one among themselves whom they venerate, whose advice they seek in difficulty, and whose good opinion they chiefly value. I was immediately drawn to make this observation by occurrences that presented themselves to my personal experience.

In the village of Little Marlow an old woman ruled the community. She had lived for some years in an alms-house, and on fine Sundays her threshold was constantly beset by a crowd, seeking her advice and listening to her admonitions. She had been a soldier's wife, and had seen the world; infirmity, induced by fevers caught in unwholesome quarters, had come on her before its time, and she seldom moved from her little cot. The plague entered the village; and, while fright and grief deprived the inhabitants of the little wisdom they possessed, old Martha stepped forward and said – "Before now I have been in a town where there was the plague." – "And you escaped?" – "No, but I recovered." – After this Martha was seated more firmly than ever on the regal seat, elevated by reverence and love. She entered the cottages of the sick; she relieved their wants with her own hand; she betrayed no fear, and inspired all who saw her with some portion of her own native courage. She attended the markets – she insisted upon being supplied with food for those who were too poor to purchase it. She shewed them how the well-being of each included the prosperity of all. She would not permit the gardens to be neglected, nor the very flowers in the cottage lattices to droop from want of care. Hope, she said, was better than a doctor's prescription, and everything that could sustain and enliven the spirits, of more worth than drugs and mixtures.

It was the sight of Little Marlow, and my conversations with Martha, that led me to the plan I formed. I had before visited the manor houses and gentlemen's seats, and often found the inhabitants actuated by the purest benevolence, ready to lend their utmost aid for the welfare of their tenants. But this was not enough. The intimate sympathy generated by similar hopes and fears, similar experience and pursuits, was wanting here. The poor perceived that the rich possessed other means of preservation than those which could be partaken of by themselves, seclusion, and, as far as circumstances permitted, freedom from care. They could not place reliance on them, but turned with tenfold dependence to the succour and advice of their equals. I resolved therefore to go from village to village, seeking out the rustic archon of the place, and by systematizing their exertions, and enlightening their views, increase both their power and their use among their fellow-cottagers. Many changes also now occurred in these spontaneous regal elections: depositions and abdications were frequent, while, in the place of the old and prudent, the ardent youth would step forward, eager for action, regardless of danger. Often too, the voice to which all listened was suddenly silenced, the helping hand cold, the sympathetic eye closed, and the villagers feared still more the death that had selected a choice victim, shivering in dust the heart that had beat for them, reducing to incommunicable annihilation the mind forever occupied with projects for their welfare.

Whoever labours for man must often find ingratitude, watered by vice and folly, spring from the grain which he has sown. Death, which had in our younger days walked the earth like 'a thief that comes in the night,' now, rising from his subterranean vault, girt with power, with dark banner floating, came a conqueror. Many saw, seated above his vice-regal throne, a supreme Providence, who directed his shafts, and guided his progress, and they bowed their heads in resignation, or at least in obedience. Others perceived only a passing casualty; they endeavoured to exchange terror for heedlessness, and plunged into licentiousness, to avoid the agonizing throes of worst apprehension. Thus, while the wise, the good, and the prudent were occupied by the labours of benevolence, the truce of winter produced other effects among the young, the thoughtless, and the vicious. During the colder months there was a general rush to London in search of amusement – the ties of public opinion were loosened; many were rich, heretofore poor – many had lost father and mother, the guardians of their morals, their mentors and restraints. It would have been useless to have opposed these impulses by barriers, which would only have driven those actuated by them to more pernicious indulgencies. The theatres were open and thronged; dance and midnight festival were frequented – in many of these decorum was violated, and the evils, which hitherto adhered to an advanced state of civilization, were doubled. The student left his books, the artist his study: the occupations of life were gone, but the amusements remained; enjoyment might be protracted to the verge of the grave. All factitious colouring disappeared – death rose like night, and, protected by its murky shadows the blush of modesty, the reserve of pride, the decorum of prudery were frequently thrown aside as useless veils. This was not universal. Among better natures, anguish and dread, the fear of eternal separation, and the awful wonder produced by unprecedented calamity, drew closer the ties of kindred and friendship. Philosophers opposed their principles, as barriers to the inundation of profligacy or despair, and the only ramparts to protect the invaded territory of human life; the religious, hoping now for their reward, clung fast to their creeds, as the rafts and planks which over the tempest-vexed sea of suffering, would bear them in safety to the harbour of the Unknown Continent. The loving heart, obliged to contract its view, bestowed its overflow of affection in triple portion on the few that remained. Yet, even among these, the present, as an unalienable possession, became all of time to which they dared commit the precious freight of their hopes.

The experience of immemorial time had taught us formerly to count our enjoyments by years, and extend our prospect of life through a lengthened period of progression and decay; the long road threaded a vast labyrinth, and the Valley of the Shadow of Death, in which it terminated, was hid by intervening objects. But an earthquake had changed the scene – under our very feet the earth yawned – deep and precipitous the gulph below opened to receive us, while the hours charioted us towards the chasm. But it was winter now, and months must elapse before we are hurled from our security. We became ephemera, to whom the interval between the rising and setting sun was as a long drawn year of common time. We should never see our children ripen into maturity, nor behold their downy cheeks roughen, their blithe hearts subdued by passion or care; but we had them now – they lived, and we lived – what more could we desire? With such schooling did my poor Idris try to hush thronging fears, and in some measure succeeded. It was not as in summer-time, when each hour might bring the dreaded fate – until summer, we felt sure; and this certainty, short lived as it must be, yet for awhile satisfied her maternal tenderness. I know not how to express or communicate the sense of concentrated, intense, though evanescent transport, that imparadized us in the present hour. Our joys were dearer because we saw their end; they were keener because we felt, to its fullest extent, their value; they were purer because their essence was sympathy – as a meteor is brighter than a star, did the felicity of this winter contain in itself the extracted delights of a long, long life.

How lovely is spring! As we looked from Windsor Terrace on the sixteen fertile counties spread beneath, speckled by happy cottages and wealthier towns, all looked as in former years, heart-cheering and fair. The land was ploughed, the slender blades of wheat broke through the dark soil, the fruit trees were covered with buds, the husbandman was abroad in the fields, the milk-maid tripped home with well-filled pails, the swallows and martins struck the sunny pools with their long, pointed wings, the new dropped lambs reposed on the young grass, the tender growth of leaves –

> *Lifts its sweet head into the air, and feeds*
> *A silent space with ever sprouting green.*

Man himself seemed to regenerate, and feel the frost of winter yield to an elastic and warm renewal of life – reason told us that care and sorrow would grow with the opening year – but how to believe the ominous voice breathed up with pestiferous vapours from fear's dim cavern, while nature, laughing and scattering from her green lap flowers, and fruits, and sparkling waters, invited us to join the gay masque of young life she led upon the scene?

Where was the plague? "Here – everywhere!" one voice of horror and dismay exclaimed, when in the pleasant days of a sunny May the Destroyer of man brooded again over the earth, forcing the spirit to leave its organic chrysalis, and to enter upon an untried life. With one mighty sweep of its potent weapon, all caution, all care, all prudence were levelled low: death sat at the tables of the great, stretched itself on the cottager's pallet, seized the dastard who fled, quelled the brave man who resisted: despondency entered every heart, sorrow dimmed every eye.

Sights of woe now became familiar to me, and were I to tell all of anguish and pain that I witnessed, of the despairing moans of age, and the more terrible smiles of infancy in the bosom of horror, my reader, his limbs quivering and his hair on end, would wonder how I did not, seized with sudden frenzy, dash myself from some precipice, and so close my eyes forever on the sad end of the world. But the powers of love, poetry, and creative fancy will dwell even beside the sick of the plague, with the squalid, and with the dying. A feeling of devotion, of duty, of a high and steady purpose, elevated me; a strange joy filled my heart. In the midst of saddest grief I seemed to tread air, while the spirit of good shed round me an ambrosial atmosphere, which blunted the sting of sympathy, and purified the air of sighs. If my wearied soul flagged in its career, I thought of my loved home, of the casket that contained my treasures, of the kiss of love and the filial caress, while my eyes were moistened by purest dew, and my heart was at once softened and refreshed by thrilling tenderness.

Maternal affection had not rendered Idris selfish; at the beginning of our calamity she had, with thoughtless enthusiasm, devoted herself to the care of the sick and helpless. I checked her; and she submitted to my rule. I told her how the fear of her danger palsied my exertions, how the knowledge of her safety strung my nerves to endurance. I shewed her the dangers which her children incurred during her absence; and she at length agreed not to go beyond the inclosure of the forest. Indeed, within the walls of the Castle we had a colony of the unhappy, deserted by their relatives, and in themselves helpless, sufficient to occupy her time and attention, while ceaseless anxiety for my welfare and the health of her children, however she strove to curb or conceal it, absorbed all her thoughts, and undermined the vital principle. After watching over and providing for their safety, her second care was to hide from me her anguish and tears. Each night I returned to the Castle, and found there repose and love awaiting me. Often I waited beside the bed of death till midnight, and through the obscurity of rainy, cloudy nights rode many miles, sustained by one circumstance only, the safety and sheltered repose of those I loved. If some scene of tremendous agony shook my frame and fevered my brow, I would lay my head on the lap of Idris, and the tumultuous pulses subsided into a temperate flow – her smile could raise me from hopelessness, her embrace bathe my sorrowing heart in calm peace. Summer advanced, and, crowned with the sun's potent rays, plague shot her unerring shafts over the earth. The nations beneath their influence bowed their heads, and died. The corn that sprung up in plenty, lay in autumn rotting on the ground, while the melancholy wretch who had gone out to gather bread for his children, lay stiff and plague-struck in the furrow. The green woods waved their boughs majestically, while the dying were spread beneath their shade, answering the solemn melody with inharmonious cries. The painted birds flitted through the shades; the careless deer reposed unhurt upon the fern – the oxen and the horses strayed from their unguarded stables, and grazed among the wheat, for death fell on man alone.

With summer and mortality grew our fears. My poor love and I looked at each other, and our babes. – "We will save them, Idris," I said, "I will save them. Years hence we shall recount to them our fears, then passed away with their occasion. Though they only should remain on the earth, still they shall live, nor shall their cheeks become pale nor their sweet voices languish." Our eldest in some degree understood the scenes passing around, and at times, he with serious looks questioned me concerning the reason of so vast a desolation. But he was only ten years old; and the hilarity of youth soon chased unreasonable care from his brow. Evelyn, a laughing cherub, a gamesome infant, without idea of pain or sorrow, would, shaking back his light curls from his eyes, make the halls re-echo with his merriment, and in a thousand artless ways attract our attention to his play. Clara, our lovely gentle Clara, was our stay, our solace, our delight. She made it her task to attend the sick, comfort the sorrowing, assist the aged, and partake the sports and awaken the gaiety of the young. She flitted through the rooms, like a good spirit, dispatched from the celestial kingdom, to illumine our dark hour with alien splendour. Gratitude and praise marked where her footsteps had been. Yet, when she stood in unassuming simplicity before us, playing with our children, or with girlish assiduity performing little kind offices for Idris, one wondered in what fair lineament of her pure loveliness, in what soft tone of her thrilling voice, so much of heroism, sagacity and active goodness resided.

The summer passed tediously, for we trusted that winter would at least check the disease. That it would vanish altogether was an hope too dear – too heartfelt, to be expressed. When such a thought was heedlessly uttered, the hearers, with a gush of tears and passionate sobs, bore witness how deep their fears were, how small their hopes. For my own part, my exertions for the public good permitted me to observe more closely than most others, the virulence and extensive ravages of our sightless enemy. A short month has destroyed a village, and where in May the first person sickened, in June the paths were deformed by unburied corpses – the houses tenantless, no smoke arising from the chimneys; and the housewife's clock marked only the hour when death had been triumphant. From such scenes I have sometimes saved a deserted infant – sometimes led a young and grieving mother from the lifeless image of her first born, or drawn the sturdy labourer from childish weeping over his extinct family.

July is gone. August must pass, and by the middle of September we may hope. Each day was eagerly counted; and the inhabitants of towns, desirous to leap this dangerous interval, plunged into dissipation, and strove, by riot, and what they wished to imagine to be pleasure, to banish thought and opiate despair. None but Adrian could have tamed the motley population of London, which, like a troop of unbitted steeds rushing to their pastures, had thrown aside all minor fears, through the operation of the fear paramount. Even Adrian was obliged in part to yield, that he might be able, if not to guide, at least to set bounds to the license of the times. The theatres were kept open; every place of public resort was frequented; though he endeavoured so to modify them, as might best quiet the agitation of the spectators, and at the same time prevent a reaction of misery when the excitement was over. Tragedies deep and dire were the chief favourites. Comedy brought with it too great a contrast to the inner despair: when such were attempted, it was not unfrequent for a comedian, in the midst of the laughter occasioned by his disporportioned buffoonery, to find a word or thought in his part that jarred with his own sense of wretchedness, and burst from mimic merriment into sobs and tears, while the spectators, seized with irresistible sympathy, wept, and the pantomimic revelry was changed to a real exhibition of tragic passion.

It was not in my nature to derive consolation from such scenes; from theatres, whose buffoon laughter and discordant mirth awakened distempered sympathy, or where fictitious tears and wailings mocked the heart-felt grief within; from festival or crowded meeting, where hilarity sprung from the worst feelings of our nature, or such enthralment of the better ones, as impressed it with garish and false varnish; from assemblies of mourners in the guise of revellers. Once however I witnessed a scene of singular interest at one of the theatres, where nature overpowered art, as an overflowing cataract will tear away the puny manufacture of a mock cascade, which had before been fed by a small portion of its waters.

I had come to London to see Adrian. He was not at the palace; and, though the attendants did not know whither he had gone, they did not expect him till late at night. It was between six and seven o'clock, a fine summer afternoon, and I spent my leisure hours in a ramble through the empty streets of London; now turning to avoid an approaching funeral, now urged by curiosity to observe the state of a particular spot; my wanderings were instinct with pain, for silence and desertion characterized every place I visited, and the few beings I met were so pale and woe-begone, so marked with care and depressed by fear, that weary of encountering only signs of misery, I began to retread my steps towards home.

I was now in Holborn, and passed by a public house filled with uproarious companions, whose songs, laughter, and shouts were more sorrowful than the pale looks and silence of the mourner. Such an one was near, hovering round this house. The sorry plight of her dress displayed her poverty, she was ghastly pale, and continued approaching, first the window and then the door of the house, as if fearful, yet longing to enter. A sudden burst of song and merriment seemed to sting her to the heart; she murmured, "Can he have the heart?" and then mustering her courage, she stepped within the threshold. The landlady met her in the passage; the poor creature asked, "Is my husband here? Can I see George?"

"See him," cried the woman, "yes, if you go to him; last night he was taken with the plague, and we sent him to the hospital."

The unfortunate inquirer staggered against a wall, a faint cry escaped her – "O! were you cruel enough," she exclaimed, "to send him there?"

The landlady meanwhile hurried away; but a more compassionate bar-maid gave her a detailed account, the sum of which was, that her husband had been taken ill, after a night of riot, and sent by his boon companions with all expedition to St. Bartholomew's Hospital. I had watched this scene, for there was a gentleness about the poor woman that interested me; she now tottered away from the door, walking as well as she could down Holborn Hill; but her strength soon failed her; she leaned against a wall, and her head sunk on her bosom, while her pallid cheek became still more white. I went up to her and offered my services. She hardly looked up – "You can do me no good," she replied; "I must go to the hospital; if I do not die before I get there."

There were still a few hackney-coaches accustomed to stand about the streets, more truly from habit than for use. I put her in one of these, and entered with her that I might secure her entrance into the hospital. Our way was short, and she said little; except interrupted ejaculations of reproach that he had left her, exclamations on the unkindness of some of his friends, and hope that she would find him alive. There was a simple, natural earnestness about her that interested me in her fate, especially when she assured me that her husband was the best of men – had been so, till want of business during these unhappy times had thrown him into bad company. "He could not bear to come home," she said, "only to see our children die. A man cannot have the patience a mother has, with her own flesh and blood."

We were set down at St. Bartholomew's, and entered the wretched precincts of the house of disease. The poor creature clung closer to me, as she saw with what heartless haste they bore the dead from the wards, and took them into a room, whose half-opened door displayed a number of corpses, horrible to behold by one unaccustomed to such scenes. We were directed to the ward where her husband had been first taken, and still was, the nurse said, if alive. My companion looked eagerly from one bed to the other, till at the end of the ward she espied, on a wretched bed, a squalid, haggard creature, writhing under the torture of disease. She rushed towards him, she embraced him, blessing God for his preservation.

The enthusiasm that inspired her with this strange joy, blinded her to the horrors about her; but they were intolerably agonizing to me. The ward was filled with an effluvia that caused my heart to heave with painful qualms. The dead were carried out, and the sick brought in, with like indifference; some were screaming with pain, others laughing from the influence of more terrible delirium; some were attended by weeping, despairing relations, others called aloud with thrilling tenderness or reproach on the friends who had deserted them, while the nurses went from bed to bed, incarnate images of despair, neglect, and death. I gave gold to my luckless companion; I recommended her to the care of the attendants; I then hastened away; while the tormentor, the imagination, busied itself in picturing my own loved ones, stretched on such beds, attended thus. The country afforded no such mass of horrors; solitary wretches died in the open fields; and I have found a survivor in a vacant village, contending at once with famine and disease; but the assembly of pestilence, the banqueting hall of death, was spread only in London.

I rambled on, oppressed, distracted by painful emotions – suddenly I found myself before Drury Lane Theatre. The play was Macbeth – the first actor of the age was there to exert his powers to drug with irreflection the auditors; such a medicine I yearned for, so I entered. The theatre was tolerably well filled. Shakspeare, whose popularity was established by the approval of four centuries, had not lost his influence even at this dread period; but was still "Ut magus," the wizard to rule our hearts and govern our imaginations. I came in during the interval between the third and fourth act. I looked round on the audience; the females were mostly of the lower classes, but the men were of all ranks, come hither to forget awhile the protracted scenes of wretchedness, which awaited them at their miserable homes. The curtain drew up, and the stage presented the scene of the witches' cave. The wildness and supernatural machinery of Macbeth, was a pledge that it could contain little directly connected with our present circumstances. Great pains had been taken in the scenery to give the semblance of reality to the impossible. The extreme darkness of the stage, whose only light was received from the fire under the cauldron, joined to a kind of mist that floated about it, rendered the unearthly shapes of the witches obscure and shadowy. It was not three decrepid old hags that bent over their pot throwing in the grim ingredients of the magic charm, but forms frightful, unreal, and fanciful. The entrance of Hecate, and the wild music that followed, took us out of this world. The cavern shape the stage assumed, the beetling rocks, the glare of the fire, the misty shades that crossed the scene at times, the music in harmony with all witch-like fancies, permitted the imagination to revel, without fear of contradiction, or reproof from reason or the heart. The entrance of Macbeth did not destroy the illusion, for he was actuated by the same feelings that inspired us, and while the work of magic proceeded we sympathized in his wonder and his daring, and gave ourselves up with our whole souls to the influence of scenic delusion. I felt the beneficial result of such excitement, in a renewal of those pleasing flights of fancy to which I had long been a stranger. The effect of this scene of incantation communicated a portion of its power to that which followed. We forgot that Malcolm and Macduff were mere human beings, acted upon by such simple passions as warmed our own breasts. By slow degrees however we were drawn to the real interest of the scene. A shudder like the swift passing of an electric shock ran through the house, when Rosse exclaimed, in answer to "Stands Scotland where it did?"

> Alas, poor country;
> Almost afraid to know itself! It cannot
> Be called our mother, but our grave: where nothing,
> But who knows nothing, is once seen to smile;
> Where sighs, and groans, and shrieks that rent the air,
> Are made, not marked; where violent sorrow seems
> A modern extasy: the dead man's knell
> Is there scarce asked, for who; and good men's lives
> Expire before the flowers in their caps,
> Dying, or ere they sicken.

Each word struck the sense, as our life's passing bell; we feared to look at each other, but bent our gaze on the stage, as if our eyes could fall innocuous on that alone. The person who played the part of Rosse, suddenly became aware of the dangerous ground he trod. He was an inferior actor, but truth now made him excellent; as he went on to announce to Macduff the slaughter of his family, he was afraid to speak, trembling from apprehension of a burst of grief from the audience, not from his fellow-mime. Each word was drawn out with difficulty; real anguish painted his features; his eyes were now lifted in sudden horror, now fixed in dread upon the ground. This shew of terror increased ours, we gasped with him, each neck was stretched out, each face changed with the actor's changes – at length while Macduff, who, attending to his part, was unobservant of the high wrought sympathy of the house, cried with well acted passion:

> *All my pretty ones?*
> *Did you say all? – O hell kite! All?*
> *What! all my pretty chickens, and their dam,*
> *At one fell swoop!*

A pang of tameless grief wrenched every heart, a burst of despair was echoed from every lip. – I had entered into the universal feeling – I had been absorbed by the terrors of Rosse – I re-echoed the cry of Macduff, and then rushed out as from an hell of torture, to find calm in the free air and silent street.

Free the air was not, or the street silent. Oh, how I longed then for the dear soothings of maternal Nature, as my wounded heart was still further stung by the roar of heartless merriment from the public-house, by the sight of the drunkard reeling home, having lost the memory of what he would find there in oblivious debauch, and by the more appalling salutations of those melancholy beings to whom the name of home was a mockery. I ran on at my utmost speed until I found myself I knew not how, close to Westminster Abbey, and was attracted by the deep and swelling tone of the organ. I entered with soothing awe the lighted chancel, and listened to the solemn religious chaunt, which spoke peace and hope to the unhappy. The notes, freighted with man's dearest prayers, re-echoed through the dim aisles, and the bleeding of the soul's wounds was staunched by heavenly balm. In spite of the misery I deprecated, and could not understand; in spite of the cold hearths of wide London, and the corpse-strewn fields of my native land; in spite of all the variety of agonizing emotions I had that evening experienced, I thought that in reply to our melodious adjurations, the Creator looked down in compassion and promise of relief; the awful peal of the heaven-winged music seemed fitting voice wherewith to commune with the Supreme; calm was produced by its sound, and by the sight of many other human creatures offering up prayers and submission with me. A sentiment approaching happiness followed the total resignation of one's being to the guardianship of the world's ruler. Alas! with the failing of this solemn strain, the elevated spirit sank again to earth. Suddenly one of the choristers died – he was lifted from his desk, the vaults below were hastily opened – he was consigned with a few muttered prayers to the darksome cavern, abode of thousands who had gone before – now wide yawning to receive even all who fulfilled the funeral rites. In vain I would then have turned from this scene, to darkened aisle or lofty dome, echoing with melodious praise. In the open air alone I found relief; among nature's beauteous works, her God reassumed his attribute of benevolence, and again I could trust that he who built up the mountains, planted the forests, and poured out the rivers, would erect another state for lost humanity, where we might awaken again to our affections, our happiness, and our faith.

Fortunately for me those circumstances were of rare occurrence that obliged me to visit London, and my duties were confined to the rural district which our lofty castle overlooked; and here labour stood in the place of pastime, to occupy such of the country people as were sufficiently exempt from sorrow or disease. My endeavours were directed towards urging them to their usual attention to their crops, and to the acting as if pestilence did not exist. The mower's scythe was at times heard; yet the joyless haymakers after they had listlessly turned the grass, forgot to cart it; the shepherd, when he had sheared his sheep, would let the wool lie to be scattered by the winds, deeming it useless to provide clothing for another winter. At times however the spirit of life was awakened by these employments; the sun, the refreshing breeze, the sweet smell of the hay, the rustling leaves and prattling rivulets brought repose to the agitated bosom, and bestowed a feeling akin to happiness on the apprehensive. Nor, strange to say, was the time without its pleasures. Young couples, who had loved long and hopelessly, suddenly found every impediment removed, and wealth pour in from the death of relatives. The very danger drew them closer. The immediate peril urged them to seize the immediate opportunity; wildly and passionately they sought to know what delights existence afforded, before they yielded to death, and

> Snatching their pleasures with rough strife
> Thorough the iron gates of life,

they defied the conquering pestilence to destroy what had been, or to erase even from their death-bed thoughts the sentiment of happiness which had been theirs.

One instance of this kind came immediately under our notice, where a high-born girl had in early youth given her heart to one of meaner extraction. He was a schoolfellow and friend of her brother's, and usually spent a part of the holidays at the mansion of the duke her father. They had played together as children, been the confidants of each other's little secrets, mutual aids and consolers in difficulty and sorrow. Love had crept in, noiseless, terrorless at first, till each felt their life bound up in the other, and at the same time knew that they must part. Their extreme youth, and the purity of their attachment, made them yield with less resistance to the tyranny of circumstances. The father of the fair Juliet separated them; but not until the young lover had promised to remain absent only till he had rendered himself worthy of her, and she had vowed to preserve her virgin heart, his treasure, till he returned to claim and possess it.

Plague came, threatening to destroy at once the aim of the ambitious and the hopes of love. Long the Duke of L— derided the idea that there could be danger while he pursued his plans of cautious seclusion; and he so far succeeded, that it was not till this second summer, that the destroyer, at one fell stroke, overthrew his precautions, his security, and his life. Poor Juliet saw one by one, father, mother, brothers, and sisters, sicken and die. Most of the servants fled on the first appearance of disease, those who remained were infected mortally; no neighbour or rustic ventured within the verge of contagion. By a strange fatality Juliet alone escaped, and she to the last waited on her relatives, and smoothed the pillow of death. The moment at length came, when the last blow was given to the last of the house: the youthful survivor of her race sat alone among the dead. There was no living being near to soothe her, or withdraw her from this hideous company. With the declining heat of a September night, a whirlwind of storm, thunder, and hail, rattled round the house, and with ghastly harmony sung the dirge of her family. She sat upon the ground absorbed in wordless despair, when through the gusty wind and bickering rain she thought she heard her name called. Whose could that familiar voice be? Not one of her relations, for they lay glaring on her with stony eyes. Again her name was syllabled, and she shuddered as she asked herself, am I becoming mad, or am I dying, that I hear the voices of the departed? A second thought passed, swift as an arrow, into her brain; she rushed to the window; and a flash of lightning shewed to her the expected vision, her lover in the shrubbery beneath; joy lent her strength to descend the stairs, to open the door, and then she fainted in his supporting arms.

A thousand times she reproached herself, as with a crime, that she should revive to happiness with him. The natural clinging of the human mind to life and joy was in its full energy in her young heart; she gave herself impetuously up to the enchantment: they were married; and in their radiant features I saw incarnate, for the last time, the spirit of love, of rapturous sympathy, which once had been the life of the world.

I envied them, but felt how impossible it was to imbibe the same feeling, now that years had multiplied my ties in the world. Above all, the anxious mother, my own beloved and drooping Idris, claimed my earnest care; I could not reproach the anxiety that never for a moment slept in her heart, but I exerted myself to distract her attention from too keen an observation of the truth of things, of the near and nearer approaches of disease, misery, and death, of the wild look of our attendants as intelligence of another and yet another death reached us; for to the last something new occurred that seemed to transcend in horror all that had gone before. Wretched beings crawled to die under our succouring roof; the inhabitants of the Castle decreased daily, while the survivors huddled together in fear, and, as in a famine-struck boat, the sport of the wild, interminable waves, each looked in the other's face, to guess on whom the death-lot would next fall. All this I endeavoured to veil, so that it might least impress my Idris; yet, as I have said, my courage survived even despair: I might be vanquished, but I would not yield.

One day, it was the ninth of September, seemed devoted to every disaster, to every harrowing incident. Early in the day, I heard of the arrival of the aged grandmother of one of our servants at the Castle. This old woman had reached her hundredth year; her skin was shrivelled, her form was bent and lost in extreme decrepitude; but as still from year to year she continued in existence, out-living many younger and stronger, she began to feel as if she were to live forever. The plague came, and the inhabitants of her village died. Clinging, with the dastard feeling of the aged, to the remnant of her spent life, she had, on hearing that the pestilence had come into her neighbourhood, barred her door, and closed her casement, refusing to communicate with any. She would wander out at night to get food, and returned home, pleased that she had met no one, that she was in no danger from the plague. As the earth became more desolate, her difficulty in acquiring sustenance increased; at first, her son, who lived near, had humoured her by placing articles of food in her way: at last he died. But, even though threatened by famine, her fear of the plague was paramount; and her greatest care was to avoid her fellow creatures. She grew weaker each day, and each day she had further to go. The night before, she had reached Datchet; and, prowling about, had found a baker's shop open and deserted. Laden with spoil, she hastened to return, and lost her way. The night was windless, hot, and cloudy; her load became too heavy for her; and one by one she threw away her loaves, still endeavouring to get along, though her hobbling fell into lameness, and her weakness at last into inability to move.

She lay down among the tall corn, and fell asleep. Deep in midnight, she was awaked by a rustling near her; she would have started up, but her stiff joints refused to obey her will. A low moan close to her ear followed, and the rustling increased; she heard a smothered voice breathe out, Water, Water! several times; and then again a sigh heaved from the heart of the sufferer. The old woman shuddered, she contrived at length to sit upright; but her teeth chattered, and her knees knocked together – close, very close, lay a half-naked figure, just discernible in the gloom, and the cry for water and the stifled moan were again uttered. Her motions at length attracted the attention of her unknown companion; her hand was seized with a convulsive violence that made the grasp feel like iron, the fingers like the keen teeth of a trap. – "At last you are come!" were the words given forth – but this exertion was the last effort of the dying – the joints relaxed, the figure fell prostrate, one low moan, the last, marked the moment of death. Morning broke; and the old woman saw the corpse, marked with the fatal disease, close to her; her wrist was livid with the hold loosened by death. She felt struck by the plague; her aged frame was unable to bear her away with sufficient speed; and now, believing herself infected, she no longer dreaded the association of others; but, as swiftly as she might, came to her grand-daughter, at Windsor Castle, there to lament and die. The sight was horrible; still she clung to life, and lamented her mischance with cries and hideous groans; while the swift advance of the disease shewed, what proved to be the fact, that she could not survive many hours.

While I was directing that the necessary care should be taken of her, Clara came in; she was trembling and pale; and, when I anxiously asked her the cause of her agitation, she threw herself into my arms weeping and exclaiming – "Uncle, dearest uncle, do not hate me forever! I must tell you, for you must know, that Evelyn, poor little Evelyn" – her voice was choked by sobs. The fear of so mighty a calamity as the loss of our adored infant made the current of my blood pause with chilly horror; but the remembrance of the mother restored my presence of mind. I sought the little bed of my darling; he was oppressed by fever; but I trusted, I fondly and fearfully trusted, that there were no symptoms of the plague. He was not three years old, and his illness appeared only one of those attacks incident to infancy. I watched him long – his heavy half-closed lids, his burning cheeks and restless twining of his small fingers – the fever was violent, the torpor complete – enough, without the greater fear of pestilence, to awaken alarm. Idris must not see him in this state. Clara, though only twelve years old, was rendered, through extreme sensibility, so prudent and careful, that I felt secure in entrusting the charge of him to her, and it was my task to prevent Idris from observing their absence. I administered the fitting remedies, and left my sweet niece to watch beside him, and bring me notice of any change she should observe.

I then went to Idris, contriving in my way, plausible excuses for remaining all day in the Castle, and endeavouring to disperse the traces of care from my brow. Fortunately she was not alone. I found Merrival, the astronomer, with her. He was far too long sighted in his view of humanity to heed the casualties of the day, and lived in the midst of contagion unconscious of its existence. This poor man, learned as La Place, guileless and unforeseeing as a child, had often been on the point of starvation, he, his pale wife and numerous offspring, while he neither felt hunger, nor observed distress. His astronomical theories absorbed him; calculations were scrawled with coal on the bare walls of his garret: a hard-earned guinea, or an article of dress, was exchanged for a book without remorse; he neither heard his children cry, nor observed his companion's emaciated form, and the excess of calamity was merely to him as the occurrence of a cloudy night, when he would have given his right hand to observe a celestial phenomenon. His wife was one of those wondrous beings, to be found only among women, with affections not to be diminished by misfortune. Her mind was divided between boundless admiration for her husband, and tender anxiety for her children – she waited on him, worked for them, and never complained, though care rendered her life one long-drawn, melancholy dream.

He had introduced himself to Adrian, by a request he made to observe some planetary motions from his glass. His poverty was easily detected and relieved. He often thanked us for the books we lent him, and for the use of our instruments, but never spoke of his altered abode or change of circumstances. His wife assured us, that he had not observed any difference, except in the absence of the children from his study, and to her infinite surprise he complained of this unaccustomed quiet.

He came now to announce to us the completion of his Essay on the Pericyclical Motions of the Earth's Axis, and the precession of the equinoctial points. If an old Roman of the period of the Republic had returned to life, and talked of the impending election of some laurel-crowned consul, or of the last battle with Mithridates, his ideas would not have been more alien to the times, than the conversation of Merrival. Man, no longer with an appetite for sympathy, clothed his thoughts in visible signs; nor were there any readers left: while each one, having thrown away his sword with opposing shield alone, awaited the plague, Merrival talked of the state of mankind six thousand years hence. He might with equal interest to us, have added a commentary, to describe the unknown and unimaginable lineaments of the creatures, who would then occupy the vacated dwelling of mankind. We had not the heart to undeceive the poor old man; and at the moment I came in, he was reading parts of his book to Idris, asking what answer could be given to this or that position.

Idris could not refrain from a smile, as she listened; she had already gathered from him that his family was alive and in health; though not apt to forget the precipice of time on which she stood, yet I could perceive that she was amused for a moment, by the contrast between the contracted view we had so long taken of human life, and the seven league strides with which Merrival paced a coming eternity. I was glad to see her smile, because it assured me of her total ignorance of her infant's danger: but I shuddered to think of the revulsion that would be occasioned by a discovery of the truth. While Merrival was talking, Clara softly opened a door behind Idris, and beckoned me to come with a gesture and look of grief. A mirror betrayed the sign to Idris – she started up. To suspect evil, to perceive that, Alfred being with us, the danger must regard her youngest darling, to fly across the long chambers into his apartment, was the work but of a moment. There she beheld her Evelyn lying fever-stricken and motionless. I followed her, and strove to inspire more hope than I could myself entertain; but she shook her head mournfully. Anguish deprived her of presence of mind; she gave up to me and Clara the physician's and nurse's parts; she sat by the bed, holding one little burning hand, and, with glazed eyes fixed on her babe, passed the long day in one unvaried agony. It was not the plague that visited our little boy so roughly; but she could not listen to my assurances; apprehension deprived her of judgment and reflection; every slight convulsion of her child's features shook her frame – if he moved, she dreaded the instant crisis; if he remained still, she saw death in his torpor, and the cloud on her brow darkened.

The poor little thing's fever increased towards night. The sensation is most dreary, to use no stronger term, with which one looks forward to passing the long hours of night beside a sick bed, especially if the patient be an infant, who cannot explain its pain, and whose flickering life resembles the wasting flame of the watch-light,

Whose narrow fire
Is shaken by the wind, and on whose edge
Devouring darkness hovers.

With eagerness one turns toward the east, with angry impatience one marks the unchequered darkness; the crowing of a cock, that sound of glee during day-time, comes wailing and untuneable – the creaking of rafters, and slight stir of invisible insect is heard and felt as the signal and type of desolation. Clara, overcome by weariness, had seated herself at the foot of her cousin's bed, and in spite of her efforts slumber weighed down her lids; twice or thrice she shook it off; but at length she was conquered and slept. Idris sat at the bedside, holding Evelyn's hand; we were afraid to speak to each other; I watched the stars – I hung over my child – I felt his little pulse – I drew near the mother – again I receded. At the turn of morning a gentle sigh from the patient attracted me, the burning spot on his cheek faded – his pulse beat softly and regularly – torpor yielded to sleep. For a long time I dared not hope; but when his unobstructed breathing and the moisture that suffused his forehead, were tokens no longer to be mistaken of the departure of mortal malady, I ventured to whisper the news of the change to Idris, and at length succeeded in persuading her that I spoke truth.

But neither this assurance, nor the speedy convalescence of our child could restore her, even to the portion of peace she before enjoyed. Her fear had been too deep, too absorbing, too entire, to be changed to security. She felt as if during her past calm she had dreamed, but was now awake; she was

> As one
> In some lone watch-tower on the deep, awakened
> From soothing visions of the home he loves,
> Trembling to hear the wrathful billows roar;

as one who has been cradled by a storm, and awakes to find the vessel sinking. Before, she had been visited by pangs of fear – now, she never enjoyed an interval of hope. No smile of the heart ever irradiated her fair countenance; sometimes she forced one, and then gushing tears would flow, and the sea of grief close above these wrecks of past happiness. Still while I was near her, she could not be in utter despair – she fully confided herself to me – she did not seem to fear my death, or revert to its possibility; to my guardianship she consigned the full freight of her anxieties, reposing on my love, as a wind-nipped fawn by the side of a doe, as a wounded nestling under its mother's wing, as a tiny, shattered boat, quivering still, beneath some protecting willow-tree. While I, not proudly as in days of joy, yet tenderly, and with glad consciousness of the comfort I afforded, drew my trembling girl close to my heart, and tried to ward every painful thought or rough circumstance from her sensitive nature.

One other incident occurred at the end of this summer. The Countess of Windsor, Ex-Queen of England, returned from Germany. She had at the beginning of the season quitted the vacant city of Vienna; and, unable to tame her haughty mind to anything like submission, she had delayed at Hamburgh, and, when at last she came to London, many weeks elapsed before she gave Adrian notice of her arrival. In spite of her coldness and long absence, he welcomed her with sensibility, displaying such affection as sought to heal the wounds of pride and sorrow, and was repulsed only by her total apparent want of sympathy. Idris heard of her mother's return with pleasure. Her own maternal feelings were so ardent, that she imagined her parent must now, in this waste world, have lost pride and harshness, and would receive with delight her filial attentions. The first check to her duteous demonstrations was a formal intimation from the fallen majesty of England, that I was in no manner to be intruded upon her. She consented, she said, to forgive her daughter, and acknowledge her grandchildren; larger concessions must not be expected.

To me this proceeding appeared (if so light a term may be permitted) extremely whimsical. Now that the race of man had lost in fact all distinction of rank, this pride was doubly fatuitous; now that we felt a kindred, fraternal nature with all who bore the stamp of humanity, this angry reminiscence of times forever gone, was worse than foolish. Idris was too much taken up by her own dreadful fears, to be angry, hardly grieved; for she judged that insensibility must be the source of this continued rancour. This was not altogether the fact: but predominant self-will assumed the arms and masque of callous feeling; and the haughty lady disdained to exhibit any token of the struggle she endured; while the slave of pride, she fancied that she sacrificed her happiness to immutable principle.

False was all this – false all but the affections of our nature, and the links of sympathy with pleasure or pain. There was but one good and one evil in the world – life and death. The pomp of rank, the assumption of power, the possessions of wealth vanished like morning mist. One living beggar had become of more worth than a national peerage of dead lords – alas the day! – than of dead heroes, patriots, or men of genius. There was much of degradation in this: for even vice and virtue had lost their attributes – life – life – the continuation of our animal mechanism – was the Alpha and Omega of the desires, the prayers, the prostrate ambition of human race.

Footnote 2. Calderon de la Barca. Calderon de la Barca's El príncipe constante. In an edition of *The Last Man*, ed. Jane Blumberg with Nora Crook, it is translated as: 'Man endlessly walks / On the earth's hard ground / And each step he takes / is on his tomb.'

Chapter IX

HALF ENGLAND was desolate, when October came, and the equinoctial winds swept over the earth, chilling the ardours of the unhealthy season. The summer, which was uncommonly hot, had been protracted into the beginning of this month, when on the eighteenth a sudden change was brought about from summer temperature to winter frost. Pestilence then made a pause in her death-dealing career. Gasping, not daring to name our hopes, yet full even to the brim with intense expectation, we stood, as a ship-wrecked sailor stands on a barren rock islanded by the ocean, watching a distant vessel, fancying that now it nears, and then again that it is bearing from sight. This promise of a renewed lease of life turned rugged natures to melting tenderness, and by contrast filled the soft with harsh and unnatural sentiments. When it seemed destined that all were to die, we were reckless of the how and when – now that the virulence of the disease was mitigated, and it appeared willing to spare some, each was eager to be among the elect, and clung to life with dastard tenacity. Instances of desertion became more frequent; and even murders, which made the hearer sick with horror, where the fear of contagion had armed those nearest in blood against each other. But these smaller and separate tragedies were about to yield to a mightier interest – and, while we were promised calm from infectious influences, a tempest arose wilder than the winds, a tempest bred by the passions of man, nourished by his most violent impulses, unexampled and dire.

A number of people from North America, the relics of that populous continent, had set sail for the East with mad desire of change, leaving their native plains for lands not less afflicted than their own. Several hundreds landed in Ireland, about the first of November, and took possession of such vacant habitations as they could find; seizing upon the superabundant food, and the stray cattle. As they exhausted the produce of one spot, they went on to another. At length they began to interfere with the inhabitants, and strong in their concentrated numbers, ejected the natives from their dwellings, and robbed them of their winter store. A few events of this kind roused the fiery nature of the Irish; and they attacked the invaders. Some were destroyed; the major part escaped by quick and well ordered movements; and danger made them careful. Their numbers ably arranged; the very deaths among them concealed; moving on in good order, and apparently given up to enjoyment, they excited the envy of the Irish. The Americans permitted a few to join their band, and presently the recruits outnumbered the strangers – nor did they join with them, nor imitate the admirable order which, preserved by the Trans-Atlantic chiefs, rendered them at once secure and formidable. The Irish followed their track in disorganized multitudes; each day increasing; each day becoming more lawless. The Americans were eager to escape from the spirit they had roused, and, reaching the eastern shores of the island, embarked for England. Their incursion would hardly have been felt had they come alone; but the Irish, collected in unnatural numbers, began to feel the inroads of famine, and they followed in the wake of the Americans for England also. The crossing of the sea could not arrest their progress. The harbours of the desolate sea-ports of the west of Ireland were filled with vessels of all sizes, from the man of war to the small fishers' boat, which lay sailorless, and rotting on the lazy deep. The emigrants embarked by hundreds, and unfurling their sails with rude hands, made strange havoc of buoy and cordage. Those who modestly betook themselves to the smaller craft, for the most part achieved their watery journey in safety. Some, in the true spirit of reckless enterprise, went on board a ship of a hundred and twenty guns; the vast hull drifted with the tide out of the bay, and after many hours its crew of landsmen contrived to spread a great part of her enormous canvass – the wind took it, and while a thousand mistakes of the helmsman made her present her head now to one point, and now to another, the vast fields of canvass that formed her sails flapped with a sound like that of a huge cataract; or such as a sea-like forest may give forth when buffeted by an equinoctial north-wind. The port-holes were open, and with every sea, which as she lurched, washed her decks, they received whole tons of water. The difficulties were increased by a fresh breeze which began to blow, whistling among the shrouds, dashing the sails this way and that, and rending them with horrid split, and such whir as may have visited the dreams of Milton, when he imagined the winnowing of the arch-fiend's van-like wings, which increased the uproar of wild chaos. These sounds were mingled with the roaring of the sea, the splash of the chafed billows round the vessel's sides, and the gurgling up of the water in the hold. The crew, many of whom had never seen the sea before, felt indeed as if heaven and earth came ruining together, as the vessel dipped her bows in the waves, or rose high upon them. Their yells were drowned in the clamour of elements, and the thunder rivings of their unwieldy habitation – they discovered at last that the water gained on them, and they betook themselves to their pumps; they might as well have laboured to empty the ocean by bucketfuls. As the sun went down, the gale increased; the ship seemed to feel her danger, she was now completely water-logged, and presented other indications of settling before she went down. The bay was crowded with vessels, whose crews, for the most part, were observing the uncouth sportings of this huge unwieldy machine – they saw her gradually sink; the waters now rising above her lower decks – they could hardly wink before she had utterly disappeared, nor could the place where the sea had closed over her be at all discerned. Some few of her crew were saved, but the greater part clinging to her cordage and masts went down with her, to rise only when death loosened their hold.

This event caused many of those who were about to sail, to put foot again on firm land, ready to encounter any evil rather than to rush into the yawning jaws of the pitiless ocean. But these were few, in comparison to the numbers who actually crossed. Many went up as high as Belfast to ensure a shorter passage, and then journeying south through Scotland, they were joined by the poorer natives of that country, and all poured with one consent into England.

Such incursions struck the English with affright, in all those towns where there was still sufficient population to feel the change. There was room enough indeed in our hapless country for twice the number of invaders; but their lawless spirit instigated them to violence; they took a delight in thrusting the possessors from their houses; in seizing on some mansion of luxury, where the noble dwellers secluded themselves in fear of the plague; in forcing these of either sex to become their servants and purveyors; till, the ruin complete in one place, they removed their locust visitation to another. When unopposed they spread their ravages wide; in cases of danger they clustered, and by dint of numbers overthrew their weak and despairing foes. They came from the east and the north, and directed their course without apparent motive, but unanimously towards our unhappy metropolis.

Communication had been to a great degree cut off through the paralyzing effects of pestilence, so that the van of our invaders had proceeded as far as Manchester and Derby, before we received notice of their arrival. They swept the country like a conquering army, burning – laying waste – murdering. The lower and vagabond English joined with them. Some few of the Lords Lieutenant who remained, endeavoured to collect the militia – but the ranks were vacant, panic seized on all, and the opposition that was made only served to increase the audacity and cruelty of the enemy. They talked of taking London, conquering England – calling to mind the long detail of injuries which had for many years been forgotten. Such vaunts displayed their weakness, rather than their strength – yet still they might do extreme mischief, which, ending in their destruction, would render them at last objects of compassion and remorse.

We were now taught how, in the beginning of the world, mankind clothed their enemies in impossible attributes – and how details proceeding from mouth to mouth, might, like Virgil's ever-growing Rumour, reach the heavens with her brow, and clasp Hesperus and Lucifer with her outstretched hands. Gorgon and Centaur, dragon and iron-hoofed lion, vast sea-monster and gigantic hydra, were but types of the strange and appalling accounts brought to London concerning our invaders. Their landing was long unknown, but having now advanced within a hundred miles of London, the country people flying before them arrived in successive troops, each exaggerating the numbers, fury, and cruelty of the assailants. Tumult filled the before quiet streets – women and children deserted their homes, escaping they knew not whither – fathers, husbands, and sons, stood trembling, not for themselves, but for their loved and defenceless relations. As the country people poured into London, the citizens fled southwards – they climbed the higher edifices of the town, fancying that they could discern the smoke and flames the enemy spread around them. As Windsor lay, to a great degree, in the line of march from the west, I removed my family to London, assigning the Tower for their sojourn, and joining Adrian, acted as his Lieutenant in the coming struggle.

We employed only two days in our preparations, and made good use of them. Artillery and arms were collected; the remnants of such regiments, as could be brought through many losses into any show of muster, were put under arms, with that appearance of military discipline which might encourage our own party, and seem most formidable to the disorganized multitude of our enemies. Even music was not wanting: banners floated in the air, and the shrill fife and loud trumpet breathed forth sounds of encouragement and victory. A practised ear might trace an undue faltering in the step of the soldiers; but this was not occasioned so much by fear of the adversary, as by disease, by sorrow, and by fatal prognostications, which often weighed most potently on the brave, and quelled the manly heart to abject subjection.

Adrian led the troops. He was full of care. It was small relief to him that our discipline should gain us success in such a conflict; while plague still hovered to equalize the conqueror and the conquered, it was not victory that he desired, but bloodless peace. As we advanced, we were met by bands of peasantry, whose almost naked condition, whose despair and horror, told at once the fierce nature of the coming enemy. The senseless spirit of conquest and thirst of spoil blinded them, while with insane fury they deluged the country in ruin. The sight of the military restored hope to those who fled, and revenge took place of fear. They inspired the soldiers with the same sentiment. Languor was changed to ardour, the slow step converted to a speedy pace, while the hollow murmur of the multitude, inspired by one feeling, and that deadly, filled the air, drowning the clang of arms and sound of music. Adrian perceived the change, and feared that it would be difficult to prevent them from wreaking their utmost fury on the Irish. He rode through the lines, charging the officers to restrain the troops, exhorting the soldiers, restoring order, and quieting in some degree the violent agitation that swelled every bosom.

We first came upon a few stragglers of the Irish at St. Albans. They retreated, and, joining others of their companions, still fell back, till they reached the main body. Tidings of an armed and regular opposition recalled them to a sort of order. They made Buckingham their head-quarters, and scouts were sent out to ascertain our situation. We remained for the night at Luton. In the morning a simultaneous movement caused us each to advance. It was early dawn, and the air, impregnated with freshest odour, seemed in idle mockery to play with our banners, and bore onwards towards the enemy the music of the bands, the neighings of the horses, and regular step of the infantry. The first sound of martial instruments that came upon our undisciplined foe, inspired surprise, not unmingled with dread. It spoke of other days, of days of concord and order; it was associated with times when plague was not, and man lived beyond the shadow of imminent fate. The pause was momentary. Soon we heard their disorderly clamour, the barbarian shouts, the untimed step of thousands coming on in disarray. Their troops now came pouring on us from the open country or narrow lanes; a large extent of unenclosed fields lay between us; we advanced to the middle of this, and then made a halt: being somewhat on superior ground, we could discern the space they covered. When their leaders perceived us drawn out in opposition, they also gave the word to halt, and endeavoured to form their men into some imitation of military discipline. The first ranks had muskets; some were mounted, but their arms were such as they had seized during their advance, their horses those they had taken from the peasantry; there was no uniformity, and little obedience, but their shouts and wild gestures showed the untamed spirit that inspired them. Our soldiers received the word, and advanced to quickest time, but in perfect order: their uniform dresses, the gleam of their polished arms, their silence, and looks of sullen hate, were more appalling than the savage clamour of our innumerous foe. Thus coming nearer and nearer each other, the howls and shouts of the Irish increased; the English proceeded in obedience to their officers, until they came near enough to distinguish the faces of their enemies; the sight inspired them with fury: with one cry, that rent heaven and was re-echoed by the furthest lines, they rushed on; they disdained the use of the bullet, but with fixed bayonet dashed among the opposing foe, while the ranks opening at intervals, the matchmen lighted the cannon, whose deafening roar and blinding smoke filled up the horror of the scene. I was beside Adrian; a moment before he had again given the word to halt, and had remained a few yards distant from us in deep meditation: he was forming swiftly his plan of action, to prevent the effusion of blood; the noise of cannon, the sudden rush of the troops, and yell of the foe, startled him: with flashing eyes he exclaimed, "Not one of these must perish!" and plunging the rowels into his horse's sides, he dashed between the conflicting bands. We, his staff, followed him to surround and protect him; obeying his signal, however, we fell back somewhat. The soldiery perceiving him, paused in their onset; he did not swerve from the bullets that passed near him, but rode immediately between the opposing lines. Silence succeeded to clamour; about fifty men lay on the ground dying or dead. Adrian raised his sword in act to speak: "By whose command," he cried, addressing his own troops, "do you advance? Who ordered your attack? Fall back; these misguided men shall not be slaughtered, while I am your general. Sheath your weapons; these are your brothers, commit not fratricide; soon the plague will not leave one for you to glut your revenge upon: will you be more pitiless than pestilence? As you honour me – as you worship God, in whose image those also are created – as your children and friends are dear to you – shed not a drop of precious human blood."

He spoke with outstretched hand and winning voice, and then turning to our invaders, with a severe brow, he commanded them to lay down their arms: "Do you think," he said, "that because we are wasted by plague, you can overcome us; the plague is also among you, and when ye are vanquished by famine and disease, the ghosts of those you have murdered will arise to bid you not hope in death. Lay down your arms, barbarous and cruel men – men whose hands are stained with the blood of the innocent, whose souls are weighed down by the orphan's cry! We shall conquer, for the right is on our side; already your cheeks are pale – the weapons fall from your nerveless grasp. Lay down your arms, fellow men! brethren! Pardon, succour, and brotherly love await your repentance. You are dear to us, because you wear the frail shape of humanity; each one among you will find a friend and host among these forces. Shall man be the enemy of man, while plague, the foe to all, even now is above us, triumphing in our butchery, more cruel than her own?"

Each army paused. On our side the soldiers grasped their arms firmly, and looked with stern glances on the foe. These had not thrown down their weapons, more from fear than the spirit of contest; they looked at each other, each wishing to follow some example given him – but they had no leader. Adrian threw himself from his horse, and approaching one of those just slain: "He was a man," he cried, "and he is dead. O quickly bind up the wounds of the fallen – let not one die; let not one more soul escape through your merciless gashes, to relate before the throne of God the tale of fratricide; bind up their wounds – restore them to their friends. Cast away the hearts of tigers that burn in your breasts; throw down those tools of cruelty and hate; in this pause of exterminating destiny, let each man be brother, guardian, and stay to the other. Away with those blood-stained arms, and hasten some of you to bind up these wounds."

As he spoke, he knelt on the ground, and raised in his arms a man from whose side the warm tide of life gushed – the poor wretch gasped – so still had either host become, that his moans were distinctly heard, and every heart, late fiercely bent on universal massacre, now beat anxiously in hope and fear for the fate of this one man. Adrian tore off his military scarf and bound it round the sufferer – it was too late – the man heaved a deep sigh, his head fell back, his limbs lost their sustaining power. – "He is dead!" said Adrian, as the corpse fell from his arms on the ground, and he bowed his head in sorrow and awe. The fate of the world seemed bound up in the death of this single man. On either side the bands threw down their arms, even the veterans wept, and our party held out their hands to their foes, while a gush of love and deepest amity filled every heart. The two forces mingling, unarmed and hand in hand, talking only how each might assist the other, the adversaries conjoined; each repenting, the one side their former cruelties, the other their late violence, they obeyed the orders of the General to proceed towards London.

Adrian was obliged to exert his utmost prudence, first to allay the discord, and then to provide for the multitude of the invaders. They were marched to various parts of the southern counties, quartered in deserted villages – a part were sent back to their own island, while the season of winter so far revived our energy, that the passes of the country were defended, and any increase of numbers prohibited.

On this occasion Adrian and Idris met after a separation of nearly a year. Adrian had been occupied in fulfilling a laborious and painful task. He had been familiar with every species of human misery, and had forever found his powers inadequate, his aid of small avail. Yet the purpose of his soul, his energy and ardent resolution, prevented any re-action of sorrow. He seemed born anew, and virtue, more potent than Medean alchemy, endued him with health and strength. Idris hardly recognized the fragile being, whose form had seemed to bend even to the summer breeze, in the energetic man, whose very excess of sensibility rendered him more capable of fulfilling his station of pilot in storm-tossed England.

It was not thus with Idris. She was uncomplaining; but the very soul of fear had taken its seat in her heart. She had grown thin and pale, her eyes filled with involuntary tears, her voice was broken and low. She tried to throw a veil over the change which she knew her brother must observe in her, but the effort was ineffectual; and when alone with him, with a burst of irrepressible grief she gave vent to her apprehensions and sorrow. She described in vivid terms the ceaseless care that with still renewing hunger ate into her soul; she compared this gnawing of sleepless expectation of evil, to the vulture that fed on the heart of Prometheus; under the influence of this eternal excitement, and of the interminable struggles she endured to combat and conceal it, she felt, she said, as if all the wheels and springs of the animal machine worked at double rate, and were fast consuming themselves. Sleep was not sleep, for her waking thoughts, bridled by some remains of reason, and by the sight of her children happy and in health, were then transformed to wild dreams, all her terrors were realized, all her fears received their dread fulfilment. To this state there was no hope, no alleviation, unless the grave should quickly receive its destined prey, and she be permitted to die, before she experienced a thousand living deaths in the loss of those she loved. Fearing to give me pain, she hid as best she could the excess of her wretchedness, but meeting thus her brother after a long absence, she could not restrain the expression of her woe, but with all the vividness of imagination with which misery is always replete, she poured out the emotions of her heart to her beloved and sympathizing Adrian.

Her present visit to London tended to augment her state of inquietude, by shewing in its utmost extent the ravages occasioned by pestilence. It hardly preserved the appearance of an inhabited city; grass sprung up thick in the streets; the squares were weed-grown, the houses were shut up, while silence and loneliness characterized the busiest parts of the town. Yet in the midst of desolation Adrian had preserved order; and each one continued to live according to law and custom – human institutions thus surviving as it were divine ones, and while the decree of population was abrogated, property continued sacred. It was a melancholy reflection; and in spite of the diminution of evil produced, it struck on the heart as a wretched mockery. All idea of resort for pleasure, of theatres and festivals had passed away. "Next summer," said Adrian as we parted on our return to Windsor, "will decide the fate of the human race. I shall not pause in my exertions until that time; but, if plague revives with the coming year, all contest with her must cease, and our only occupation be the choice of a grave."

I must not forget one incident that occurred during this visit to London. The visits of Merrival to Windsor, before frequent, had suddenly ceased. At this time where but a hair's line separated the living from the dead, I feared that our friend had become a victim to the all-embracing evil. On this occasion I went, dreading the worst, to his dwelling, to see if I could be of any service to those of his family who might have survived. The house was deserted, and had been one of those assigned to the invading strangers quartered in London. I saw his astronomical instruments put to strange uses, his globes defaced, his papers covered with abstruse calculations destroyed. The neighbours could tell me little, till I lighted on a poor woman who acted as nurse in these perilous times. She told me that all the family were dead, except Merrival himself, who had gone mad – mad, she called it, yet on questioning her further, it appeared that he was possessed only by the delirium of excessive grief. This old man, tottering on the edge of the grave, and prolonging his prospect through millions of calculated years – this visionary who had not seen starvation in the wasted forms of his wife and children, or plague in the horrible sights and sounds that surrounded him – this astronomer, apparently dead on earth, and living only in the motion of the spheres – loved his family with unapparent but intense affection. Through long habit they had become a part of himself; his want of worldly knowledge, his absence of mind and infant guilelessness, made him utterly dependent on them. It was not till one of them died that he perceived their danger; one by one they were carried off by pestilence; and his wife, his helpmate and supporter, more necessary to him than his own limbs and frame, which had hardly been taught the lesson of self-preservation, the kind companion whose voice always spoke peace to him, closed her eyes in death. The old man felt the system of universal nature which he had so long studied and adored, slide from under him, and he stood among the dead, and lifted his voice in curses. – No wonder that the attendant should interpret as phrensy the harrowing maledictions of the grief-struck old man.

I had commenced my search late in the day, a November day, that closed in early with pattering rain and melancholy wind. As I turned from the door, I saw Merrival, or rather the shadow of Merrival, attenuated and wild, pass me, and sit on the steps of his home. The breeze scattered the grey locks on his temples, the rain drenched his uncovered head, he sat hiding his face in his withered hands. I pressed his shoulder to awaken his attention, but he did not alter his position. "Merrival," I said, "it is long since we have seen you – you must return to Windsor with me – Lady Idris desires to see you, you will not refuse her request – come home with me."

He replied in a hollow voice, "Why deceive a helpless old man, why talk hypocritically to one half crazed? Windsor is not my home; my true home I have found; the home that the Creator has prepared for me."

His accent of bitter scorn thrilled me – "Do not tempt me to speak," he continued, "my words would scare you – in an universe of cowards I dare think – among the church-yard tombs – among the victims of His merciless tyranny I dare reproach the Supreme Evil. How can he punish me? Let him bare his arm and transfix me with lightning – this is also one of his attributes" – and the old man laughed.

He rose, and I followed him through the rain to a neighbouring church-yard – he threw himself on the wet earth. "Here they are," he cried, "beautiful creatures – breathing, speaking, loving creatures. She who by day and night cherished the age-worn lover of her youth – they, parts of my flesh, my children – here they are: call them, scream their names through the night; they will not answer!" He clung to the little heaps that marked the graves. "I ask but one thing; I do not fear His hell, for I have it here; I do not desire His heaven, let me but die and be laid beside them; let me but, when I lie dead, feel my flesh as it moulders, mingle with theirs. Promise," and he raised himself painfully, and seized my arm, "promise to bury me with them."

"So God help me and mine as I promise," I replied, "on one condition: return with me to Windsor."

"To Windsor!" he cried with a shriek, "Never! – from this place I never go – my bones, my flesh, I myself, are already buried here, and what you see of me is corrupted clay like them. I will lie here, and cling here, till rain, and hail, and lightning and storm, ruining on me, make me one in substance with them below."

In a few words I must conclude this tragedy. I was obliged to leave London, and Adrian undertook to watch over him; the task was soon fulfilled; age, grief, and inclement weather, all united to hush his sorrows, and bring repose to his heart, whose beats were agony. He died embracing the sod, which was piled above his breast, when he was placed beside the beings whom he regretted with such wild despair.

I returned to Windsor at the wish of Idris, who seemed to think that there was greater safety for her children at that spot; and because, once having taken on me the guardianship of the district, I would not desert it while an inhabitant survived. I went also to act in conformity with Adrian's plans, which was to congregate in masses what remained of the population; for he possessed the conviction that it was only through the benevolent and social virtues that any safety was to be hoped for the remnant of mankind.

It was a melancholy thing to return to this spot so dear to us, as the scene of a happiness rarely before enjoyed, here to mark the extinction of our species, and trace the deep uneraseable footsteps of disease over the fertile and cherished soil. The aspect of the country had so far changed, that it had been impossible to enter on the task of sowing seed, and other autumnal labours. That season was now gone; and winter had set in with sudden and unusual severity. Alternate frosts and thaws succeeding to floods, rendered the country impassable. Heavy falls of snow gave an arctic appearance to the scenery; the roofs of the houses peeped from the white mass; the lowly cot and stately mansion, alike deserted, were blocked up, their thresholds uncleared; the windows were broken by the hail, while the prevalence of a north-east wind rendered out-door exertions extremely painful. The altered state of society made these accidents of nature, sources of real misery. The luxury of command and the attentions of servitude were lost. It is true that the necessaries of life were assembled in such quantities, as to supply to superfluity the wants of the diminished population; but still much labour was required to arrange these, as it were, raw materials; and depressed by sickness, and fearful of the future, we had not energy to enter boldly and decidedly on any system.

I can speak for myself – want of energy was not my failing. The intense life that quickened my pulses, and animated my frame, had the effect, not of drawing me into the mazes of active life, but of exalting my lowliness, and of bestowing majestic proportions on insignificant objects – I could have lived the life of a peasant in the same way – my trifling occupations were swelled into important pursuits; my affections were impetuous and engrossing passions, and nature with all her changes was invested in divine attributes. The very spirit of the Greek mythology inhabited my heart; I deified the uplands, glades, and streams, I

Had sight of Proteus coming from the sea;
And heard old Triton blow his wreathed horn.

Strange, that while the earth preserved her monotonous course, I dwelt with ever-renewing wonder on her antique laws, and now that with excentric wheel she rushed into an untried path, I should feel this spirit fade; I struggled with despondency and weariness, but like a fog, they choked me. Perhaps, after the labours and stupendous excitement of the past summer, the calm of winter and the almost menial toils it brought with it, were by natural re-action doubly irksome. It was not the grasping passion of the preceding year, which gave life and individuality to each moment – it was not the aching pangs induced by the distresses of the times. The utter inutility that had attended all my exertions took from them their usual effects of exhilaration, and despair rendered abortive the balm of self applause – I longed to return to my old occupations, but of what use were they? To read were futile – to write, vanity indeed. The earth, late wide circus for the display of dignified exploits, vast theatre for a magnificent drama, now presented a vacant space, an empty stage – for actor or spectator there was no longer aught to say or hear.

Our little town of Windsor, in which the survivors from the neighbouring counties were chiefly assembled, wore a melancholy aspect. Its streets were blocked up with snow – the few passengers seemed palsied, and frozen by the ungenial visitation of winter. To escape these evils was the aim and scope of all our exertions. Families late devoted to exalting and refined pursuits, rich, blooming, and young, with diminished numbers and care-fraught hearts, huddled over a fire, grown selfish and grovelling through suffering. Without the aid of servants, it was necessary to discharge all household duties; hands unused to such labour must knead the bread, or in the absence of flour, the statesmen or perfumed courtier must undertake the butcher's office. Poor and rich were now equal, or rather the poor were the superior, since they entered on such tasks with alacrity and experience; while ignorance, inaptitude, and habits of repose, rendered them fatiguing to the luxurious, galling to the proud, disgustful to all whose minds, bent on intellectual improvement, held it their dearest privilege to be exempt from attending to mere animal wants.

But in every change goodness and affection can find field for exertion and display. Among some these changes produced a devotion and sacrifice of self at once graceful and heroic. It was a sight for the lovers of the human race to enjoy; to behold, as in ancient times, the patriarchal modes in which the variety of kindred and friendship fulfilled their duteous and kindly offices. Youths, nobles of the land, performed for the sake of mother or sister, the services of menials with amiable cheerfulness. They went to the river to break the ice, and draw water: they assembled on foraging expeditions, or axe in hand felled the trees for fuel. The females received them on their return with the simple and affectionate welcome known before only to the lowly cottage – a clean hearth and bright fire; the supper ready cooked by beloved hands; gratitude for the provision for tomorrow's meal: strange enjoyments for the high-born English, yet they were now their sole, hard earned, and dearly prized luxuries.

None was more conspicuous for this graceful submission to circumstances, noble humility, and ingenious fancy to adorn such acts with romantic colouring, than our own Clara. She saw my despondency, and the aching cares of Idris. Her perpetual study was to relieve us from labour and to spread ease and even elegance over our altered mode of life. We still had some attendants spared by disease, and warmly attached to us. But Clara was jealous of their services; she would be sole handmaid of Idris, sole minister to the wants of her little cousins; nothing gave her so much pleasure as our employing her in this way; she went beyond our desires, earnest, diligent, and unwearied –

Abra was ready ere we called her name,
And though we called another, Abra came.

It was my task each day to visit the various families assembled in our town, and when the weather permitted, I was glad to prolong my ride, and to muse in solitude over every changeful appearance of our destiny, endeavouring to gather lessons for the future from the experience of the past. The impatience with which, while in society, the ills that afflicted my species inspired me, were softened by loneliness, when individual suffering was merged in the general calamity, strange to say, less afflicting to contemplate. Thus often, pushing my way with difficulty through the narrow snow-blocked town, I crossed the bridge and passed through Eton. No youthful congregation of gallant-hearted boys thronged the portal of the college; sad silence pervaded the busy school-room and noisy playground. I extended my ride towards Salt Hill, on every side impeded by the snow. Were those the fertile fields I loved – was that the interchange of gentle upland and cultivated dale, once covered with waving corn, diversified by stately trees, watered by the meandering Thames? One sheet of white covered it, while bitter recollection told me that cold as the winter-clothed earth, were the hearts of the inhabitants. I met troops of horses, herds of cattle, flocks of sheep, wandering at will; here throwing down a hay-rick, and nestling from cold in its heart, which afforded them shelter and food – there having taken possession of a vacant cottage. Once on a frosty day, pushed on by restless unsatisfying reflections, I sought a favourite haunt, a little wood not far distant from Salt Hill. A bubbling spring prattles over stones on one side, and a plantation of a few elms and beeches, hardly deserve, and yet continue the name of wood. This spot had for me peculiar charms. It had been a favourite resort of Adrian; it was secluded; and he often said that in boyhood, his happiest hours were spent here; having escaped the stately bondage of his mother, he sat on the rough hewn steps that led to the spring, now reading a favourite book, now musing, with speculation beyond his years, on the still unravelled skein of morals or metaphysics. A melancholy foreboding assured me that I should never see this place more; so with careful thought, I noted each tree, every winding of the streamlet and irregularity of the soil, that I might better call up its idea in absence. A robin red-breast dropt from the frosty branches of the trees, upon the congealed rivulet; its panting breast and half-closed eyes shewed that it was dying: a hawk appeared in the air; sudden fear seized the little creature; it exerted its last strength, throwing itself on its back, raising its talons in impotent defence against its powerful enemy. I took it up and placed it in my breast. I fed it with a few crumbs from a biscuit; by degrees it revived; its warm fluttering heart beat against me; I cannot tell why I detail this trifling incident – but the scene is still before me; the snow-clad fields seen through the silvered trunks of the beeches – the brook, in days of happiness alive with sparkling waters, now choked by ice – the leafless trees fantastically dressed in hoar frost – the shapes of summer leaves imaged by winter's frozen hand on the hard ground – the dusky sky, drear cold, and unbroken silence – while close in my bosom, my feathered nursling lay warm, and safe, speaking its content with a light chirp – painful reflections thronged, stirring my brain with wild commotion – cold and death-like as the snowy fields was all earth – misery-stricken the life-tide of the inhabitants – why should I oppose the cataract of destruction that swept us away? – why string my nerves and renew my wearied efforts – ah, why? But that my firm courage and cheerful exertions might shelter the dear mate, whom I chose in the spring of my life; though the throbbings of my heart be replete with pain, though my hopes for the future are chill, still while your dear head, my gentlest love, can repose in peace on that heart, and while you derive from its fostering care, comfort, and hope, my struggles shall not cease – I will not call myself altogether vanquished.

One fine February day, when the sun had reassumed some of its genial power, I walked in the forest with my family. It was one of those lovely winter-days which assert the capacity of nature to bestow beauty on barrenness. The leafless trees spread their fibrous branches against the pure sky; their intricate and pervious tracery resembled delicate sea-weed; the deer were turning up the snow in search of the hidden grass; the white was made intensely dazzling by the sun, and trunks of the trees, rendered more conspicuous by the loss of preponderating foliage, gathered around like the labyrinthine columns of a vast temple; it was impossible not to receive pleasure from the sight of these things. Our children, freed from the bondage of winter, bounded before us; pursuing the deer, or rousing the pheasants and partridges from their coverts. Idris leant on my arm; her sadness yielded to the present sense of pleasure. We met other families on the Long Walk, enjoying like ourselves the return of the genial season. At once, I seemed to awake; I cast off the clinging sloth of the past months; earth assumed a new appearance, and my view of the future was suddenly made clear. I exclaimed, "I have now found out the secret!"

"What secret?"

In answer to this question, I described our gloomy winter-life, our sordid cares, our menial labours:

"This northern country," I said, "is no place for our diminished race. When mankind were few, it was not here that they battled with the powerful agents of nature, and were enabled to cover the globe with offspring. We must seek some natural Paradise, some garden of the earth, where our simple wants may be easily supplied, and the enjoyment of a delicious climate compensate for the social pleasures we have lost. If we survive this coming summer, I will not spend the ensuing winter in England; neither I nor any of us."

I spoke without much heed, and the very conclusion of what I said brought with it other thoughts. Should we, any of us, survive the coming summer? I saw the brow of Idris clouded; I again felt, that we were enchained to the car of fate, over whose coursers we had no control. We could no longer say, This we will do, and this we will leave undone. A mightier power than the human was at hand to destroy our plans or to achieve the work we avoided. It were madness to calculate upon another winter. This was our last. The coming summer was the extreme end of our vista; and, when we arrived there, instead of a continuation of the long road, a gulph yawned, into which we must of force be precipitated. The last blessing of humanity was wrested from us; we might no longer hope. Can the madman, as he clanks his chains, hope? Can the wretch, led to the scaffold, who when he lays his head on the block, marks the double shadow of himself and the executioner, whose uplifted arm bears the axe, hope? Can the ship-wrecked mariner, who spent with swimming, hears close behind the splashing waters divided by a shark which pursues him through the Atlantic, hope? Such hope as theirs, we also may entertain!

Old fable tells us, that this gentle spirit sprung from the box of Pandora, else crammed with evils; but these were unseen and null, while all admired the inspiriting loveliness of young Hope; each man's heart became her home; she was enthroned sovereign of our lives, here and here-after; she was deified and worshipped, declared incorruptible and everlasting. But like all other gifts of the Creator to Man, she is mortal; her life has attained its last hour. We have watched over her; nursed her flickering existence; now she has fallen at once from youth to decrepitude, from health to immedicinable disease; even as we spend ourselves in struggles for her recovery, she dies; to all nations the voice goes forth, Hope is dead! We are but mourners in the funeral train, and what immortal essence or perishable creation will refuse to make one in the sad procession that attends to its grave the dead comforter of humanity?

> *Does not the sun call in his light? and day*
> *Like a thin exhalation melt away –*
> *Both wrapping up their beams in clouds to be*
> *Themselves close mourners at this obsequie.*

Volume III

Chapter I

HEAR YOU not the rushing sound of the coming tempest? Do you not behold the clouds open, and destruction lurid and dire pour down on the blasted earth? See you not the thunderbolt fall, and are deafened by the shout of heaven that follows its descent? Feel you not the earth quake and open with agonizing groans, while the air is pregnant with shrieks and wailings – all announcing the last days of man? No! none of these things accompanied our fall! The balmy air of spring, breathed from nature's ambrosial home, invested the lovely earth, which wakened as a young mother about to lead forth in pride her beauteous offspring to meet their sire who had been long absent. The buds decked the trees, the flowers adorned the land: the dark branches, swollen with seasonable juices, expanded into leaves, and the variegated foliage of spring, bending and singing in the breeze, rejoiced in the genial warmth of the unclouded empyrean: the brooks flowed murmuring, the sea was waveless, and the promontories that over-hung it were reflected in the placid waters; birds awoke in the woods, while abundant food for man and beast sprung up from the dark ground. Where was pain and evil? Not in the calm air or weltering ocean; not in the woods or fertile fields, nor among the birds that made the woods resonant with song, nor the animals that in the midst of plenty basked in the sunshine. Our enemy, like the Calamity of Homer, trod our hearts, and no sound was echoed from her steps –

> *With ills the land is rife, with ills the sea,*
> *Diseases haunt our frail humanity,*
> *Through noon, through night, on casual wing they glide,*
> *Silent – a voice the power all-wise denied.*

Once man was a favourite of the Creator, as the royal psalmist sang, "God had made him a little lower than the angels, and had crowned him with glory and honour. God made him to have dominion over the works of his hands, and put all things under his feet." Once it was so; now is man lord of the creation? Look at him – ha! I see plague! She has invested his form, is incarnate in his flesh, has entwined herself with his being, and blinds his heaven-seeking eyes. Lie down, O man, on the flower-strown earth; give up all claim to your inheritance, all you can ever possess of it is the small cell which the dead require. Plague is the companion of spring, of sunshine, and plenty. We no longer struggle with her. We have forgotten what we did when she was not. Of old navies used to stem the giant ocean-waves betwixt Indus and the Pole for slight articles of luxury. Men made perilous journies to possess themselves of earth's splendid trifles, gems and gold. Human labour was wasted – human life set at nought. Now life is all that we covet; that this automaton of flesh should, with joints and springs in order, perform its functions, that this dwelling of the soul should be capable of containing its dweller. Our minds, late spread abroad through countless spheres and endless combinations of thought, now retrenched themselves behind this wall of flesh, eager to preserve its well-being only. We were surely sufficiently degraded.

At first the increase of sickness in spring brought increase of toil to such of us, who, as yet spared to life, bestowed our time and thoughts on our fellow creatures. We nerved ourselves to the task: 'in the midst of despair we performed the tasks of hope.' We went out with the resolution of disputing with our foe. We aided the sick, and comforted the sorrowing; turning from the multitudinous dead to the rare survivors, with an energy of desire that bore the resemblance of power, we bade them – live. Plague sat paramount the while, and laughed us to scorn.

Have any of you, my readers, observed the ruins of an anthill immediately after its destruction? At first it appears entirely deserted of its former inhabitants; in a little time you see an ant struggling through the upturned mould; they reappear by twos and threes, running hither and thither in search of their lost companions. Such were we upon earth, wondering aghast at the effects of pestilence. Our empty habitations remained, but the dwellers were gathered to the shades of the tomb.

As the rules of order and pressure of laws were lost, some began with hesitation and wonder to transgress the accustomed uses of society. Palaces were deserted, and the poor man dared at length, unreproved, intrude into the splendid apartments, whose very furniture and decorations were an unknown world to him. It was found, that, though at first the stop put to all circulation of property, had reduced those before supported by the factitious wants of society to sudden and hideous poverty, yet when the boundaries of private possession were thrown down, the products of human labour at present existing were more, far more, than the thinned generation could possibly consume. To some among the poor this was matter of exultation. We were all equal now; magnificent dwellings, luxurious carpets, and beds of down, were afforded to all. Carriages and horses, gardens, pictures, statues, and princely libraries, there were enough of these even to superfluity; and there was nothing to prevent each from assuming possession of his share. We were all equal now; but near at hand was an equality still more levelling, a state where beauty and strength, and wisdom, would be as vain as riches and birth. The grave yawned beneath us all, and its prospect prevented any of us from enjoying the ease and plenty which in so awful a manner was presented to us.

Still the bloom did not fade on the cheeks of my babes; and Clara sprung up in years and growth, unsullied by disease. We had no reason to think the site of Windsor Castle peculiarly healthy, for many other families had expired beneath its roof; we lived therefore without any particular precaution; but we lived, it seemed, in safety. If Idris became thin and pale, it was anxiety that occasioned the change; an anxiety I could in no way alleviate. She never complained, but sleep and appetite fled from her, a slow fever preyed on her veins, her colour was hectic, and she often wept in secret; gloomy prognostications, care, and agonizing dread, ate up the principle of life within her. I could not fail to perceive this change. I often wished that I had permitted her to take her own course, and engage herself in such labours for the welfare of others as might have distracted her thoughts. But it was too late now. Besides that, with the nearly extinct race of man, all our toils grew near a conclusion, she was too weak; consumption, if so it might be called, or rather the over active life within her, which, as with Adrian, spent the vital oil in the early morning hours, deprived her limbs of strength. At night, when she could leave me unperceived, she wandered through the house, or hung over the couches of her children; and in the day time would sink into a perturbed sleep, while her murmurs and starts betrayed the unquiet dreams that vexed her. As this state of wretchedness became more confirmed, and, in spite of her endeavours at concealment more apparent, I strove, though vainly, to awaken in her courage and hope. I could not wonder at the vehemence of her care; her very soul was tenderness; she trusted indeed that she should not outlive me if I became the prey of the vast calamity, and this thought sometimes relieved her. We had for many years trod the highway of life hand in hand, and still thus linked, we might step within the shades of death; but her children, her lovely, playful, animated children – beings sprung from her own dear side – portions of her own being – depositories of our loves – even if we died, it would be comfort to know that they ran man's accustomed course. But it would not be so; young and blooming as they were, they would die, and from the hopes of maturity, from the proud name of attained manhood, they were cut off forever. Often with maternal affection she had figured their merits and talents exerted on life's wide stage. Alas for these latter days! The world had grown old, and all its inmates partook of the decrepitude. Why talk of infancy, manhood, and old age? We all stood equal sharers of the last throes of time-worn nature. Arrived at the same point of the world's age – there was no difference in us; the name of parent and child had lost their meaning; young boys and girls were level now with men. This was all true; but it was not less agonizing to take the admonition home.

Where could we turn, and not find a desolation pregnant with the dire lesson of example? The fields had been left uncultivated, weeds and gaudy flowers sprung up – or where a few wheat-fields shewed signs of the living hopes of the husbandman, the work had been left halfway, the ploughman had died beside the plough; the horses had deserted the furrow, and no seedsman had approached the dead; the cattle unattended wandered over the fields and through the lanes; the tame inhabitants of the poultry yard, baulked of their daily food, had become wild – young lambs were dropt in flower-gardens, and the cow stalled in the hall of pleasure. Sickly and few, the country people neither went out to sow nor reap; but sauntered about the meadows, or lay under the hedges, when the inclement sky did not drive them to take shelter under the nearest roof. Many of those who remained, secluded themselves; some had laid up stores which should prevent the necessity of leaving their homes; – some deserted wife and child, and imagined that they secured their safety in utter solitude. Such had been Ryland's plan, and he was discovered dead and half-devoured by insects, in a house many miles from any other, with piles of food laid up in useless superfluity. Others made long journeys to unite themselves to those they loved, and arrived to find them dead.

London did not contain above a thousand inhabitants; and this number was continually diminishing. Most of them were country people, come up for the sake of change; the Londoners had sought the country. The busy eastern part of the town was silent, or at most you saw only where, half from cupidity, half from curiosity, the warehouses had been more ransacked than pillaged: bales of rich India goods, shawls of price, jewels, and spices, unpacked, strewed the floors. In some places the possessor had to the last kept watch on his store, and died before the barred gates. The massy portals of the churches swung creaking on their hinges; and some few lay dead on the pavement. The wretched female, loveless victim of vulgar brutality, had wandered to the toilet of high-born beauty, and, arraying herself in the garb of splendour, had died before the mirror which reflected to herself alone her altered appearance. Women whose delicate feet had seldom touched the earth in their luxury, had fled in fright and horror from their homes, till, losing themselves in the squalid streets of the metropolis, they had died on the threshold of poverty. The heart sickened at the variety of misery presented; and, when I saw a specimen of this gloomy change, my soul ached with the fear of what might befall my beloved Idris and my babes. Were they, surviving Adrian and myself, to find themselves protectorless in the world? As yet the mind alone had suffered – could I forever put off the time, when the delicate frame and shrinking nerves of my child of prosperity, the nursling of rank and wealth, who was my companion, should be invaded by famine, hardship, and disease? Better die at once – better plunge a poinard in her bosom, still untouched by drear adversity, and then again sheathe it in my own! But, no; in times of misery we must fight against our destinies, and strive not to be overcome by them. I would not yield, but to the last gasp resolutely defended my dear ones against sorrow and pain; and if I were vanquished at last, it should not be ingloriously. I stood in the gap, resisting the enemy – the impalpable, invisible foe, who had so long besieged us – as yet he had made no breach: it must be my care that he should not, secretly undermining, burst up within the very threshold of the temple of love, at whose altar I daily sacrificed. The hunger of Death was now stung more sharply by the diminution of his food: or was it that before, the survivors being many, the dead were less eagerly counted? Now each life was a gem, each human breathing form of far, O! far more worth than subtlest imagery of sculptured stone; and the daily, nay, hourly decrease visible in our numbers, visited the heart with sickening misery. This summer extinguished our hopes, the vessel of society was wrecked, and the shattered raft, which carried the few survivors over the sea of misery, was riven and tempest tost. Man existed by twos and threes; man, the individual who might sleep, and wake, and perform the animal functions; but man, in himself weak, yet more powerful in congregated numbers than wind or ocean; man, the queller of the elements, the lord of created nature, the peer of demi-gods, existed no longer.

Farewell to the patriotic scene, to the love of liberty and well earned meed of virtuous aspiration! – farewell to crowded senate, vocal with the councils of the wise, whose laws were keener than the sword blade tempered at Damascus! – farewell to kingly pomp and warlike pageantry; the crowns are in the dust, and the wearers are in their graves! – farewell to the desire of rule, and the hope of victory; to high vaulting ambition, to the appetite for praise, and the craving for the suffrage of their fellows! The nations are no longer! No senate sits in council for the dead; no scion of a time honoured dynasty pants to rule over the inhabitants of a charnel house; the general's hand is cold, and the soldier has his untimely grave dug in his native fields, unhonoured, though in youth. The market-place is empty, the candidate for popular favour finds none whom he can represent. To chambers of painted state farewell! – To midnight revelry, and the panting emulation of beauty, to costly dress and birth-day shew, to title and the gilded coronet, farewell!

Farewell to the giant powers of man – to knowledge that could pilot the deep-drawing bark through the opposing waters of shoreless ocean – to science that directed the silken balloon through the pathless air – to the power that could put a barrier to mighty waters, and set in motion wheels, and beams, and vast machinery, that could divide rocks of granite or marble, and make the mountains plain!

Farewell to the arts – to eloquence, which is to the human mind as the winds to the sea, stirring, and then allaying it; – farewell to poetry and deep philosophy, for man's imagination is cold, and his enquiring mind can no longer expatiate on the wonders of life, for "there is no work, nor device, nor knowledge, nor wisdom in the grave, whither thou goest!" – to the graceful building, which in its perfect proportion transcended the rude forms of nature, the fretted gothic and massy saracenic pile, to the stupendous arch and glorious dome, the fluted column with its capital, Corinthian, Ionic, or Doric, the peristyle and fair entablature, whose harmony of form is to the eye as musical concord to the ear! – farewell to sculpture, where the pure marble mocks human flesh, and in the plastic expression of the culled excellencies of the human shape, shines forth the god! – farewell to painting, the high wrought sentiment and deep knowledge of the artists's mind in pictured canvas – to paradisaical scenes, where trees are ever vernal, and the ambrosial air rests in perpetual glow: to the stamped form of tempest, and wildest uproar of universal nature encaged in the narrow frame, O farewell! Farewell to music, and the sound of song; to the marriage of instruments, where the concord of soft and harsh unites in sweet harmony, and gives wings to the panting listeners, whereby to climb heaven, and learn the hidden pleasures of the eternals! – Farewell to the well-trod stage; a truer tragedy is enacted on the world's ample scene, that puts to shame mimic grief: to high-bred comedy, and the low buffoon, farewell! – Man may laugh no more. Alas! to enumerate the adornments of humanity, shews, by what we have lost, how supremely great man was. It is all over now. He is solitary; like our first parents expelled from Paradise, he looks back towards the scene he has quitted. The high walls of the tomb, and the flaming sword of plague, lie between it and him. Like to our first parents, the whole earth is before him, a wide desart. Unsupported and weak, let him wander through fields where the unreaped corn stands in barren plenty, through copses planted by his fathers, through towns built for his use. Posterity is no more; fame, and ambition, and love, are words void of meaning; even as the cattle that grazes in the field, do thou, O deserted one, lie down at evening-tide, unknowing of the past, careless of the future, for from such fond ignorance alone canst thou hope for ease!

Joy paints with its own colours every act and thought. The happy do not feel poverty – for delight is as a gold-tissued robe, and crowns them with priceless gems. Enjoyment plays the cook to their homely fare, and mingles intoxication with their simple drink. Joy strews the hard couch with roses, and makes labour ease.

Sorrow doubles the burthen to the bent-down back; plants thorns in the unyielding pillow; mingles gall with water; adds saltness to their bitter bread; cloathing them in rags, and strewing ashes on their bare heads. To our irremediable distress every small and pelting inconvenience came with added force; we had strung our frames to endure the Atlean weight thrown on us; we sank beneath the added feather chance threw on us, "the grasshopper was a burthen." Many of the survivors had been bred in luxury – their servants were gone, their powers of command vanished like unreal shadows: the poor even suffered various privations; and the idea of another winter like the last, brought affright to our minds. Was it not enough that we must die, but toil must be added? – must we prepare our funeral repast with labour, and with unseemly drudgery heap fuel on our deserted hearths – must we with servile hands fabricate the garments, soon to be our shroud?

Not so! We are presently to die, let us then enjoy to its full relish the remnant of our lives. Sordid care, avaunt! menial labours, and pains, slight in themselves, but too gigantic for our exhausted strength, shall make no part of our ephemeral existences. In the beginning of time, when, as now, man lived by families, and not by tribes or nations, they were placed in a genial clime, where earth fed them untilled, and the balmy air enwrapt their reposing limbs with warmth more pleasant than beds of down. The south is the native place of the human race; the land of fruits, more grateful to man than the hard-earned Ceres of the north – of trees, whose boughs are as a palace-roof, of couches of roses, and of the thirst-appeasing grape. We need not there fear cold and hunger.

Look at England! the grass shoots up high in the meadows; but they are dank and cold, unfit bed for us. Corn we have none, and the crude fruits cannot support us. We must seek firing in the bowels of the earth, or the unkind atmosphere will fill us with rheums and aches. The labour of hundreds of thousands alone could make this inclement nook fit habitation for one man. To the south then, to the sun! – where nature is kind, where Jove has showered forth the contents of Amalthea's horn, and earth is garden.

England, late birth-place of excellence and school of the wise, thy children are gone, thy glory faded! Thou, England, wert the triumph of man! Small favour was shewn thee by thy Creator, thou Isle of the North; a ragged canvas naturally, painted by man with alien colours; but the hues he gave are faded, never more to be renewed. So we must leave thee, thou marvel of the world; we must bid farewell to thy clouds, and cold, and scarcity forever! Thy manly hearts are still; thy tale of power and liberty at its close! Bereft of man, O little isle! the ocean waves will buffet thee, and the raven flap his wings over thee; thy soil will be birth-place of weeds, thy sky will canopy barrenness. It was not for the rose of Persia thou wert famous, nor the banana of the east; not for the spicy gales of India, nor the sugar groves of America; not for thy vines nor thy double harvests, nor for thy vernal airs, nor solstitial sun – but for thy children, their unwearied industry and lofty aspiration. They are gone, and thou goest with them the oft trodden path that leads to oblivion –

Farewell, sad Isle, farewell, thy fatal glory
Is summed, cast up, and cancelled in this story.

Chapter II

IN THE AUTUMN of this year 2096, the spirit of emigration crept in among the few survivors, who, congregating from various parts of England, met in London. This spirit existed as a breath, a wish, a far off thought, until communicated to Adrian, who imbibed it with ardour, and instantly engaged himself in plans for its execution. The fear of immediate death vanished with the heats of September. Another winter was before us, and we might elect our mode of passing it to the best advantage. Perhaps in rational philosophy none could be better chosen than this scheme of migration, which would draw us from the immediate scene of our woe, and, leading us through pleasant and picturesque countries, amuse for a time our despair. The idea once broached, all were impatient to put it in execution.

We were still at Windsor; our renewed hopes medicined the anguish we had suffered from the late tragedies. The death of many of our inmates had weaned us from the fond idea, that Windsor Castle was a spot sacred from the plague; but our lease of life was renewed for some months, and even Idris lifted her head, as a lily after a storm, when a last sunbeam tinges its silver cup. Just at this time Adrian came down to us; his eager looks shewed us that he was full of some scheme. He hastened to take me aside, and disclosed to me with rapidity his plan of emigration from England.

To leave England forever! to turn from its polluted fields and groves, and, placing the sea between us, to quit it, as a sailor quits the rock on which he has been wrecked, when the saving ship rides by. Such was his plan.

To leave the country of our fathers, made holy by their graves! – We could not feel even as a voluntary exile of old, who might for pleasure or convenience forsake his native soil; though thousands of miles might divide him, England was still a part of him, as he of her. He heard of the passing events of the day; he knew that, if he returned, and resumed his place in society, the entrance was still open, and it required but the will, to surround himself at once with the associations and habits of boyhood. Not so with us, the remnant. We left none to represent us, none to repeople the desart land, and the name of England died, when we left her,

In vagabond pursuit of dreadful safety.

Yet let us go! England is in her shroud – we may not enchain ourselves to a corpse. Let us go – the world is our country now, and we will choose for our residence its most fertile spot. Shall we, in these desart halls, under this wintry sky, sit with closed eyes and folded hands, expecting death? Let us rather go out to meet it gallantly: or perhaps – for all this pendulous orb, this fair gem in the sky's diadem, is not surely plague-striken – perhaps, in some secluded nook, amidst eternal spring, and waving trees, and purling streams, we may find Life. The world is vast, and England, though her many fields and wide spread woods seem interminable, is but a small part of her. At the close of a day's march over high mountains and through snowy vallies, we may come upon health, and committing our loved ones to its charge, replant the uprooted tree of humanity, and send to late posterity the tale of the ante-pestilential race, the heroes and sages of the lost state of things.

Hope beckons and sorrow urges us, the heart beats high with expectation, and this eager desire of change must be an omen of success. O come! Farewell to the dead! farewell to the tombs of those we loved! – farewell to giant London and the placid Thames, to river and mountain or fair district, birth-place of the wise and good, to Windsor Forest and its antique castle, farewell! themes for story alone are they – we must live elsewhere.

Such were in part the arguments of Adrian, uttered with enthusiasm and unanswerable rapidity. Something more was in his heart, to which he dared not give words. He felt that the end of time was come; he knew that one by one we should dwindle into nothingness. It was not adviseable to wait this sad consummation in our native country; but travelling would give us our object for each day, that would distract our thoughts from the swift-approaching end of things. If we went to Italy, to sacred and eternal Rome, we might with greater patience submit to the decree, which had laid her mighty towers low. We might lose our selfish grief in the sublime aspect of its desolation. All this was in the mind of Adrian; but he thought of my children, and, instead of communicating to me these resources of despair, he called up the image of health and life to be found, where we knew not – when we knew not; but if never to be found, forever and forever to be sought. He won me over to his party, heart and soul.

It devolved on me to disclose our plan to Idris. The images of health and hope which I presented to her, made her with a smile consent. With a smile she agreed to leave her country, from which she had never before been absent, and the spot she had inhabited from infancy; the forest and its mighty trees, the woodland paths and green recesses, where she had played in childhood, and had lived so happily through youth; she would leave them without regret, for she hoped to purchase thus the lives of her children. They were her life; dearer than a spot consecrated to love, dearer than all else the earth contained. The boys heard with childish glee of our removal: Clara asked if we were to go to Athens. "It is possible," I replied; and her countenance became radiant with pleasure. There she would behold the tomb of her parents, and the territory filled with recollections of her father's glory. In silence, but without respite, she had brooded over these scenes. It was the recollection of them that had turned her infant gaiety to seriousness, and had impressed her with high and restless thoughts.

There were many dear friends whom we must not leave behind, humble though they were. There was the spirited and obedient steed which Lord Raymond had given his daughter; there was Alfred's dog and a pet eagle, whose sight was dimmed through age. But this catalogue of favourites to be taken with us, could not be made without grief to think of our heavy losses, and a deep sigh for the many things we must leave behind. The tears rushed into the eyes of Idris, while Alfred and Evelyn brought now a favourite rose tree, now a marble vase beautifully carved, insisting that these must go, and exclaiming on the pity that we could not take the castle and the forest, the deer and the birds, and all accustomed and cherished objects along with us. "Fond and foolish ones," I said, "we have lost forever treasures far more precious than these; and we desert them, to preserve treasures to which in comparison they are nothing. Let us not for a moment forget our object and our hope; and they will form a resistless mound to stop the overflowing of our regret for trifles."

The children were easily distracted, and again returned to their prospect of future amusement. Idris had disappeared. She had gone to hide her weakness; escaping from the castle, she had descended to the little park, and sought solitude, that she might there indulge her tears; I found her clinging round an old oak, pressing its rough trunk with her roseate lips, as her tears fell plenteously, and her sobs and broken exclamations could not be suppressed; with surpassing grief I beheld this loved one of my heart thus lost in sorrow! I drew her towards me; and, as she felt my kisses on her eyelids, as she felt my arms press her, she revived to the knowledge of what remained to her. "You are very kind not to reproach me," she said: "I weep, and a bitter pang of intolerable sorrow tears my heart. And yet I am happy; mothers lament their children, wives lose their husbands, while you and my children are left to me. Yes, I am happy, most happy, that I can weep thus for imaginary sorrows, and that the slight loss of my adored country is not dwindled and annihilated in mightier misery. Take me where you will; where you and my children are, there shall be Windsor, and every country will be England to me. Let these tears flow not for myself, happy and ungrateful as I am, but for the dead world – for our lost country – for all of love, and life, and joy, now choked in the dusty chambers of death."

She spoke quickly, as if to convince herself; she turned her eyes from the trees and forest-paths she loved; she hid her face in my bosom, and we – yes, my masculine firmness dissolved – we wept together consolatory tears, and then calm – nay, almost cheerful, we returned to the castle.

The first cold weather of an English October, made us hasten our preparations. I persuaded Idris to go up to London, where she might better attend to necessary arrangements. I did not tell her, that to spare her the pang of parting from inanimate objects, now the only things left, I had resolved that we should none of us return to Windsor. For the last time we looked on the wide extent of country visible from the terrace, and saw the last rays of the sun tinge the dark masses of wood variegated by autumnal tints; the uncultivated fields and smokeless cottages lay in shadow below; the Thames wound through the wide plain, and the venerable pile of Eton college, stood in dark relief, a prominent object; the cawing of the myriad rooks which inhabited the trees of the little park, as in column or thick wedge they speeded to their nests, disturbed the silence of evening. Nature was the same, as when she was the kind mother of the human race; now, childless and forlorn, her fertility was a mockery; her loveliness a mask for deformity. Why should the breeze gently stir the trees, man felt not its refreshment? Why did dark night adorn herself with stars – man saw them not? Why are there fruits, or flowers, or streams, man is not here to enjoy them?

Idris stood beside me, her dear hand locked in mine. Her face was radiant with a smile. – "The sun is alone," she said, "but we are not. A strange star, my Lionel, ruled our birth; sadly and with dismay we may look upon the annihilation of man; but we remain for each other. Did I ever in the wide world seek other than thee? And since in the wide world thou remainest, why should I complain? Thou and nature are still true to me. Beneath the shades of night, and through the day, whose garish light displays our solitude, thou wilt still be at my side, and even Windsor will not be regretted."

I had chosen night time for our journey to London, that the change and desolation of the country might be the less observable. Our only surviving servant drove us. We past down the steep hill, and entered the dusky avenue of the Long Walk. At times like these, minute circumstances assume giant and majestic proportions; the very swinging open of the white gate that admitted us into the forest, arrested my thoughts as matter of interest; it was an every day act, never to occur again! The setting crescent of the moon glittered through the massy trees to our right, and when we entered the park, we scared a troop of deer, that fled bounding away in the forest shades. Our two boys quietly slept; once, before our road turned from the view, I looked back on the castle. Its windows glistened in the moonshine, and its heavy outline lay in a dark mass against the sky – the trees near us waved a solemn dirge to the midnight breeze. Idris leaned back in the carriage; her two hands pressed mine, her countenance was placid, she seemed to lose the sense of what she now left, in the memory of what she still possessed.

My thoughts were sad and solemn, yet not of unmingled pain. The very excess of our misery carried a relief with it, giving sublimity and elevation to sorrow. I felt that I carried with me those I best loved; I was pleased, after a long separation to rejoin Adrian; never again to part. I felt that I quitted what I loved, not what loved me. The castle walls, and long familiar trees, did not hear the parting sound of our carriage-wheels with regret. And, while I felt Idris to be near, and heard the regular breathing of my children, I could not be unhappy. Clara was greatly moved; with streaming eyes, suppressing her sobs, she leaned from the window, watching the last glimpse of her native Windsor.

Adrian welcomed us on our arrival. He was all animation; you could no longer trace in his look of health, the suffering valetudinarian; from his smile and sprightly tones you could not guess that he was about to lead forth from their native country, the numbered remnant of the English nation, into the tenantless realms of the south, there to die, one by one, till the LAST MAN should remain in a voiceless, empty world.

Adrian was impatient for our departure, and had advanced far in his preparations. His wisdom guided all. His care was the soul, to move the luckless crowd, who relied wholly on him. It was useless to provide many things, for we should find abundant provision in every town. It was Adrian's wish to prevent all labour; to bestow a festive appearance on this funeral train. Our numbers amounted to not quite two thousand persons. These were not all assembled in London, but each day witnessed the arrival of fresh numbers, and those who resided in the neighbouring towns, had received orders to assemble at one place, on the twentieth of November. Carriages and horses were provided for all; captains and under officers chosen, and the whole assemblage wisely organized. All obeyed the Lord Protector of dying England; all looked up to him. His council was chosen, it consisted of about fifty persons. Distinction and station were not the qualifications of their election. We had no station among us, but that which benevolence and prudence gave; no distinction save between the living and the dead. Although we were anxious to leave England before the depth of winter, yet we were detained. Small parties had been dispatched to various parts of England, in search of stragglers; we would not go, until we had assured ourselves that in all human probability we did not leave behind a single human being.

On our arrival in London, we found that the aged Countess of Windsor was residing with her son in the palace of the Protectorate; we repaired to our accustomed abode near Hyde Park. Idris now for the first time for many years saw her mother, anxious to assure herself that the childishness of old age did not mingle with unforgotten pride, to make this high-born dame still so inveterate against me. Age and care had furrowed her cheeks, and bent her form; but her eye was still bright, her manners authoritative and unchanged; she received her daughter coldly, but displayed more feeling as she folded her grand-children in her arms. It is our nature to wish to continue our systems and thoughts to posterity through our own offspring. The Countess had failed in this design with regard to her children; perhaps she hoped to find the next remove in birth more tractable. Once Idris named me casually – a frown, a convulsive gesture of anger, shook her mother, and, with voice trembling with hate, she said – "I am of little worth in this world; the young are impatient to push the old off the scene; but, Idris, if you do not wish to see your mother expire at your feet, never again name that person to me; all else I can bear; and now I am resigned to the destruction of my cherished hopes: but it is too much to require that I should love the instrument that providence gifted with murderous properties for my destruction."

This was a strange speech, now that, on the empty stage, each might play his part without impediment from the other. But the haughty Ex-Queen thought as Octavius Caesar and Mark Antony,

> We could not stall together
> In the whole world.

The period of our departure was fixed for the twenty-fifth of November. The weather was temperate; soft rains fell at night, and by day the wintry sun shone out. Our numbers were to move forward in separate parties, and to go by different routes, all to unite at last at Paris. Adrian and his division, consisting in all of five hundred persons, were to take the direction of Dover and Calais. On the twentieth of November, Adrian and I rode for the last time through the streets of London. They were grass-grown and desert. The open doors of the empty mansions creaked upon their hinges; rank herbage, and deforming dirt, had swiftly accumulated on the steps of the houses; the voiceless steeples of the churches pierced the smokeless air; the churches were open, but no prayer was offered at the altars; mildew and damp had already defaced their ornaments; birds, and tame animals, now homeless, had built nests, and made their lairs in consecrated spots. We passed St. Paul's. London, which had extended so far in suburbs in all direction, had been somewhat deserted in the midst, and much of what had in former days obscured this vast building was removed. Its ponderous mass, blackened stone, and high dome, made it look, not like a temple, but a tomb. Methought above the portico was engraved the Hic jacet of England. We passed on eastwards, engaged in such solemn talk as the times inspired. No human step was heard, nor human form discerned. Troops of dogs, deserted of their masters, passed us; and now and then a horse, unbridled and unsaddled, trotted towards us, and tried to attract the attention of those which we rode, as if to allure them to seek like liberty. An unwieldy ox, who had fed in an abandoned granary, suddenly lowed, and shewed his shapeless form in a narrow door-way; everything was desert; but nothing was in ruin. And this medley of undamaged buildings, and luxurious accommodation, in trim and fresh youth, was contrasted with the lonely silence of the unpeopled streets.

Night closed in, and it began to rain. We were about to return homewards, when a voice, a human voice, strange now to hear, attracted our attention. It was a child singing a merry, lightsome air; there was no other sound. We had traversed London from Hyde Park even to where we now were in the Minories, and had met no person, heard no voice nor footstep. The singing was interrupted by laughing and talking; never was merry ditty so sadly timed, never laughter more akin to tears. The door of the house from which these sounds proceeded was open, the upper rooms were illuminated as for a feast. It was a large magnificent house, in which doubtless some rich merchant had lived. The singing again commenced, and rang through the high-roofed rooms, while we silently ascended the stair-case. Lights now appeared to guide us; and a long suite of splendid rooms illuminated, made us still more wonder. Their only inhabitant, a little girl, was dancing, waltzing, and singing about them, followed by a large Newfoundland dog, who boisterously jumping on her, and interrupting her, made her now scold, now laugh, now throw herself on the carpet to play with him. She was dressed grotesquely, in glittering robes and shawls fit for a woman; she appeared about ten years of age. We stood at the door looking on this strange scene, till the dog perceiving us barked loudly; the child turned and saw us: her face, losing its gaiety, assumed a sullen expression: she slunk back, apparently meditating an escape. I came up to her, and held her hand; she did not resist, but with a stern brow, so strange in childhood, so different from her former hilarity, she stood still, her eyes fixed on the ground. "What do you do here?" I said gently; "Who are you?" – she was silent, but trembled violently. – "My poor child," asked Adrian, "are you alone?" There was a winning softness in his voice, that went to the heart of the little girl; she looked at him, then snatching her hand from me, threw herself into his arms, clinging round his neck, ejaculating – "Save me! save me!" while her unnatural sullenness dissolved in tears.

"I will save you," he replied, "of what are you afraid? you need not fear my friend, he will do you no harm. Are you alone?"

"No, Lion is with me."

"And your father and mother? –"

"I never had any; I am a charity girl. Every body is gone, gone for a great, great many days; but if they come back and find me out, they will beat me so!"

Her unhappy story was told in these few words: an orphan, taken on pretended charity, ill-treated and reviled, her oppressors had died: unknowing of what had passed around her, she found herself alone; she had not dared venture out, but by the continuance of her solitude her courage revived, her childish vivacity caused her to play a thousand freaks, and with her brute companion she passed a long holiday, fearing nothing but the return of the harsh voices and cruel usage of her protectors. She readily consented to go with Adrian.

In the meantime, while we descanted on alien sorrows, and on a solitude which struck our eyes and not our hearts, while we imagined all of change and suffering that had intervened in these once thronged streets, before, tenantless and abandoned, they became mere kennels for dogs, and stables for cattle: while we read the death of the world upon the dark fane, and hugged ourselves in the remembrance that we possessed that which was all the world to us – in the meanwhile –

We had arrived from Windsor early in October, and had now been in London about six weeks. Day by day, during that time, the health of my Idris declined: her heart was broken; neither sleep nor appetite, the chosen servants of health, waited on her wasted form. To watch her children hour by hour, to sit by me, drinking deep the dear persuasion that I remained to her, was all her pastime. Her vivacity, so long assumed, her affectionate display of cheerfulness, her light-hearted tone and springy gait were gone. I could not disguise to myself, nor could she conceal, her life-consuming sorrow. Still change of scene, and reviving hopes might restore her; I feared the plague only, and she was untouched by that.

I had left her this evening, reposing after the fatigues of her preparations. Clara sat beside her, relating a story to the two boys. The eyes of Idris were closed: but Clara perceived a sudden change in the appearance of our eldest darling; his heavy lids veiled his eyes, an unnatural colour burnt in his cheeks, his breath became short. Clara looked at the mother; she slept, yet started at the pause the narrator made – Fear of awakening and alarming her, caused Clara to go on at the eager call of Evelyn, who was unaware of what was passing. Her eyes turned alternately from Alfred to Idris; with trembling accents she continued her tale, till she saw the child about to fall: starting forward she caught him, and her cry roused

Idris. She looked on her son. She saw death stealing across his features; she laid him on a bed, she held drink to his parched lips.

Yet he might be saved. If I were there, he might be saved; perhaps it was not the plague. Without a counsellor, what could she do? stay and behold him die! Why at that moment was I away? "Look to him, Clara," she exclaimed, "I will return immediately."

She inquired among those who, selected as the companions of our journey, had taken up their residence in our house; she heard from them merely that I had gone out with Adrian. She entreated them to seek me: she returned to her child, he was plunged in a frightful state of torpor; again she rushed down stairs; all was dark, desert, and silent; she lost all self-possession; she ran into the street; she called on my name. The pattering rain and howling wind alone replied to her. Wild fear gave wings to her feet; she darted forward to seek me, she knew not where; but, putting all her thoughts, all her energy, all her being in speed only, most misdirected speed, she neither felt, nor feared, nor paused, but ran right on, till her strength suddenly deserted her so suddenly, that she had not thought to save herself. Her knees failed her, and she fell heavily on the pavement. She was stunned for a time; but at length rose, and though sorely hurt, still walked on, shedding a fountain of tears, stumbling at times, going she knew not whither, only now and then with feeble voice she called my name, adding with heart-piercing exclamations, that I was cruel and unkind. Human being there was none to reply; and the inclemency of the night had driven the wandering animals to the habitations they had usurped. Her thin dress was drenched with rain; her wet hair clung round her neck; she tottered through the dark streets; till, striking her foot against an unseen impediment, she again fell; she could not rise; she hardly strove; but, gathering up her limbs, she resigned herself to the fury of the elements, and the bitter grief of her own heart. She breathed an earnest prayer to die speedily, for there was no relief but death. While hopeless of safety for herself, she ceased to lament for her dying child, but shed kindly, bitter tears for the grief I should experience in losing her. While she lay, life almost suspended, she felt a warm, soft hand on her brow, and a gentle female voice asked her, with expressions of tender compassion, if she could not rise? That another human being, sympathetic and kind, should exist near, roused her; half rising, with clasped hands, and fresh springing tears, she entreated her companion to seek for me, to bid me hasten to my dying child, to save him, for the love of heaven, to save him!

The woman raised her; she led her under shelter, she entreated her to return to her home, whither perhaps I had already returned. Idris easily yielded to her persuasions, she leaned on the arm of her friend, she endeavoured to walk on, but irresistible faintness made her pause again and again.

Quickened by the increasing storm, we had hastened our return, our little charge was placed before Adrian on his horse. There was an assemblage of persons under the portico of our house, in whose gestures I instinctively read some heavy change, some new misfortune. With swift alarm, afraid to ask a single question, I leapt from my horse; the spectators saw me, knew me, and in awful silence divided to make way for me. I snatched a light, and rushing up stairs, and hearing a groan, without reflection I threw open the door of the first room that presented itself. It was quite dark; but, as I stept within, a pernicious scent assailed my senses, producing sickening qualms, which made their way to my very heart, while I felt my leg clasped, and a groan repeated by the person that held me. I lowered my lamp, and saw a negro half clad, writhing under the agony of disease, while he held me with a convulsive grasp. With mixed horror and impatience I strove to disengage myself, and fell on the sufferer; he wound his naked festering arms round me, his face was close to mine, and his breath, death-laden, entered my vitals. For a moment I was overcome, my head was bowed by aching nausea; till, reflection returning, I sprung up, threw the wretch from me, and darting up the staircase, entered the chamber usually inhabited by my family. A dim light shewed me Alfred on a couch; Clara trembling, and paler than whitest snow, had raised him on her arm, holding a cup of water to his lips. I saw full well that no spark of life existed in that ruined form, his features were rigid, his eyes glazed, his head had fallen back. I took him from her, I laid him softly down, kissed his cold little mouth, and turned to speak in a vain whisper, when loudest sound of thunderlike cannon could not have reached him in his immaterial abode.

And where was Idris? That she had gone out to seek me, and had not returned, were fearful tidings, while the rain and driving wind clattered against the window, and roared round the house. Added to this, the sickening sensation of disease gained upon me; no time was to be lost, if ever I would see her again. I mounted my horse and rode out to seek her, fancying that I heard her voice in every gust, oppressed by fever and aching pain.

I rode in the dark and rain through the labyrinthine streets of unpeopled London. My child lay dead at home; the seeds of mortal disease had taken root in my bosom; I went to seek Idris, my adored, now wandering alone, while the waters were rushing from heaven like a cataract to bathe her dear head in chill damp, her fair limbs in numbing cold. A female stood on the step of a door, and called to me as I galloped past. It was not Idris; so I rode swiftly on, until a kind of second sight, a reflection back again on my senses of what I had seen but not marked, made me feel sure that another figure, thin, graceful and tall, stood clinging to the foremost person who supported her. In a minute I was beside the suppliant, in a minute I received the sinking Idris in my arms. Lifting her up, I placed her on the horse; she had not strength to support herself; so I mounted behind her, and held her close to my bosom, wrapping my riding-cloak round her, while her companion, whose well known, but changed countenance, (it was Juliet, daughter of the Duke of L – -) could at this moment of horror obtain from me no more than a passing glance of compassion. She took the abandoned rein, and conducted our obedient steed homewards. Dare I avouch it? That was the last moment of my happiness; but I was happy. Idris must die, for her heart was broken: I must die, for I had caught the plague; earth was a scene of desolation; hope was madness; life had married death; they were one; but, thus supporting my fainting love, thus feeling that I must soon die, I revelled in the delight of possessing her once more; again and again I kissed her, and pressed her to my heart.

We arrived at our home. I assisted her to dismount, I carried her up stairs, and gave her into Clara's care, that her wet garments might be changed. Briefly I assured Adrian of her safety, and requested that we might be left to repose. As the miser, who with trembling caution visits his treasure to count it again and again, so I numbered each moment, and grudged every one that was not spent with Idris. I returned swiftly to the chamber where the life of my life reposed; before I entered the room I paused for a few seconds; for a few seconds I tried to examine my state; sickness and shuddering ever and anon came over me; my head was heavy, my chest oppressed, my legs bent under me; but I threw off resolutely the swift growing symptoms of my disorder, and met Idris with placid and even joyous looks. She was lying on a couch; carefully fastening the door to prevent all intrusion; I sat by her, we embraced, and our lips met in a kiss long drawn and breathless – would that moment had been my last!

Maternal feeling now awoke in my poor girl's bosom, and she asked: "And Alfred?"

"Idris," I replied, "we are spared to each other, we are together; do not let any other idea intrude. I am happy; even on this fatal night, I declare myself happy, beyond all name, all thought – what would you more, sweet one?"

Idris understood me: she bowed her head on my shoulder and wept. "Why," she again asked, "do you tremble, Lionel, what shakes you thus?"

"Well may I be shaken," I replied, "happy as I am. Our child is dead, and the present hour is dark and ominous. Well may I tremble! but, I am happy, mine own Idris, most happy."

"I understand thee, my kind love," said Idris, "thus – pale as thou art with sorrow at our loss; trembling and aghast, though wouldest assuage my grief by thy dear assurances. I am not happy," (and the tears flashed and fell from under her down-cast lids), "for we are inmates of a miserable prison, and there is no joy for us; but the true love I bear you will render this and every other loss endurable."

"We have been happy together, at least," I said; "no future misery can deprive us of the past. We have been true to each other for years, ever since my sweet princess-love came through the snow to the lowly cottage of the poverty-striken heir of the ruined Verney. Even now, that eternity is before us, we take hope only from the presence of each other. Idris, do you think, that when we die, we shall be divided?"

"Die! when we die! what mean you? What secret lies hid from me in those dreadful words?"

"Must we not all die, dearest?" I asked with a sad smile.

"Gracious God! are you ill, Lionel, that you speak of death? My only friend, heart of my heart, speak!"

"I do not think," replied I, "that we have any of us long to live; and when the curtain drops on this mortal scene, where, think you, we shall find ourselves?" Idris was calmed by my unembarrassed tone and look; she answered: "You may easily believe that during this long progress of the plague, I have thought much on death, and asked myself, now that all mankind is dead to this life, to what other life they may have been borne. Hour after hour, I have dwelt on these thoughts, and strove to form a rational conclusion concerning the mystery of a future state. What a scare-crow, indeed, would death be, if we were merely to cast aside the shadow in which we now walk, and, stepping forth into the unclouded sunshine of knowledge and love, revived with the same companions, the same affections, and reached the fulfilment of our hopes, leaving our fears with our earthly vesture in the grave. Alas! the same strong feeling which makes me sure that I shall not wholly die, makes me refuse to believe that I shall live wholly as I do now. Yet, Lionel, never, never, can I love any but you; through eternity I must desire your society; and, as I am innocent of harm to others, and as relying and confident as my mortal nature permits, I trust that the Ruler of the world will never tear us asunder."

"Your remarks are like yourself, dear love," replied I, "gentle and good; let us cherish such a belief, and dismiss anxiety from our minds. But, sweet, we are so formed, (and there is no sin, if God made our nature, to yield to what he ordains), we are so formed, that we must love life, and cling to it; we must love the living smile, the sympathetic touch, and thrilling voice, peculiar to our mortal mechanism. Let us not, through security in hereafter, neglect the present. This present moment, short as it is, is a part of eternity, and the dearest part, since it is our own unalienably. Thou, the hope of my futurity, art my present joy. Let me then look on thy dear eyes, and, reading love in them, drink intoxicating pleasure."

Timidly, for my vehemence somewhat terrified her, Idris looked on me. My eyes were bloodshot, starting from my head; every artery beat, methought, audibly, every muscle throbbed, each single nerve felt. Her look of wild affright told me, that I could no longer keep my secret: "So it is, mine own beloved," I said, "the last hour of many happy ones is arrived, nor can we shun any longer the inevitable destiny. I cannot live long – but, again and again, I say, this moment is ours!"

Paler than marble, with white lips and convulsed features, Idris became aware of my situation. My arm, as I sat, encircled her waist. She felt the palm burn with fever, even on the heart it pressed: "One moment," she murmured, scarce audibly, "only one moment." –

She kneeled, and hiding her face in her hands, uttered a brief, but earnest prayer, that she might fulfil her duty, and watch over me to the last. While there was hope, the agony had been unendurable; – all was now concluded; her feelings became solemn and calm. Even as Epicharis, unperturbed and firm, submitted to the instruments of torture, did Idris, suppressing every sigh and sign of grief, enter upon the endurance of torments, of which the rack and the wheel are but faint and metaphysical symbols.

I was changed; the tight-drawn cord that sounded so harshly was loosened, the moment that Idris participated in my knowledge of our real situation. The perturbed and passion-tossed waves of thought subsided, leaving only the heavy swell that kept right on without any outward manifestation of its disturbance, till it should break on the remote shore towards which I rapidly advanced: "It is true that I am sick," I said, "and your society, my Idris is my only medicine; come, and sit beside me."

She made me lie down on the couch, and, drawing a low ottoman near, sat close to my pillow, pressing my burning hands in her cold palms. She yielded to my feverish restlessness, and let me talk, and talked to me, on subjects strange indeed to beings, who thus looked the last, and heard the last, of what they loved alone in the world. We talked of times gone by; of the happy period of our early love; of Raymond, Perdita, and Evadne. We talked of what might arise on this desert earth, if, two or three being saved, it were slowly re-peopled. – We talked of what was beyond the tomb; and, man in his human shape being nearly extinct, we felt with certainty of faith, that other spirits, other minds, other perceptive beings, sightless to us, must people with thought and love this beauteous and imperishable universe.

We talked – I know not how long – but, in the morning I awoke from a painful heavy slumber; the pale cheek of Idris rested on my pillow; the large orbs of her eyes half raised the lids, and shewed the deep blue lights beneath; her lips were unclosed, and the slight murmurs they formed told that, even while asleep, she suffered. "If she were dead," I thought, "what difference? now that form is the temple of a residing deity; those eyes are the windows of her soul; all grace, love, and intelligence are throned on that lovely bosom – were she dead, where would this mind, the dearer half of mine, be? For quickly the fair proportion of this edifice would be more defaced, than are the sand-choked ruins of the desert temples of Palmyra."

Chapter III

IDRIS STIRRED and awoke; alas! she awoke to misery. She saw the signs of disease on my countenance, and wondered how she could permit the long night to pass without her having sought, not cure, that was impossible, but alleviation to my sufferings. She called Adrian; my couch was quickly surrounded by friends and assistants, and such medicines as were judged fitting were administered. It was the peculiar and dreadful distinction of our visitation, that none who had been attacked by the pestilence had recovered. The first symptom of the disease was the death-warrant, which in no single instance had been followed by pardon or reprieve. No gleam of hope therefore cheered my friends.

While fever producing torpor, heavy pains, sitting like lead on my limbs, and making my breast heave, were upon me; I continued insensible to everything but pain, and at last even to that. I awoke on the fourth morning as from a dreamless sleep. An irritating sense of thirst, and, when I strove to speak or move, an entire dereliction of power, was all I felt.

For three days and nights Idris had not moved from my side. She administered to all my wants, and never slept nor rested. She did not hope; and therefore she neither endeavoured to read the physician's countenance, nor to watch for symptoms of recovery. All her thought was to attend on me to the last, and then to lie down and die beside me. On the third night animation was suspended; to the eye and touch of all I was dead. With earnest prayer, almost with force, Adrian tried to draw Idris from me. He exhausted every adjuration, her child's welfare and his own. She shook her head, and wiped a stealing tear from her sunk cheek, but would not yield; she entreated to be allowed to watch me that one night only, with such affliction and meek earnestness, that she gained her point, and sat silent and motionless, except when, stung by intolerable remembrance, she kissed my closed eyes and pallid lips, and pressed my stiffening hands to her beating heart.

At dead of night, when, though it was mid winter, the cock crowed at three o'clock, as herald of the morning change, while hanging over me, and mourning in silent, bitter thought for the loss of all of love towards her that had been enshrined in my heart; her dishevelled hair hung over her face, and the long tresses fell on the bed; she saw one ringlet in motion, and the scattered hair slightly stirred, as by a breath. It is not so, she thought, for he will never breathe more. Several times the same thing occurred, and she only marked it by the same reflection; till the whole ringlet waved back, and she thought she saw my breast heave. Her first emotion was deadly fear, cold dew stood on her brow; my eyes half opened; and, re-assured, she would have exclaimed, "He lives!" but the words were choked by a spasm, and she fell with a groan on the floor.

Adrian was in the chamber. After long watching, he had unwillingly fallen into a sleep. He started up, and beheld his sister senseless on the earth, weltering in a stream of blood that gushed from her mouth. Increasing signs of life in me in some degree explained her state; the surprise, the burst of joy, the revulsion of every sentiment, had been too much for her frame, worn by long months of care, late shattered by every species of woe and toil. She was now in far greater danger than I, the wheels and springs of my life, once again set in motion, acquired elasticity from their short suspension. For a long time, no one believed that I should indeed continue to live; during the reign of the plague upon earth, not one person, attacked by the grim disease, had recovered. My restoration was looked on as a deception; every moment it was expected that the evil symptoms would recur with redoubled violence, until confirmed convalescence, absence of all fever or pain, and increasing strength, brought slow conviction that I had recovered from the plague.

The restoration of Idris was more problematical. When I had been attacked by illness, her cheeks were sunk, her form emaciated; but now, the vessel, which had broken from the effects of extreme agitation, did not entirely heal, but was as a channel that drop by drop drew from her the ruddy stream that vivified her heart. Her hollow eyes and worn countenance had a ghastly appearance; her cheek-bones, her open fair brow, the projection of the mouth, stood fearfully prominent; you might tell each bone in the thin anatomy of her frame. Her hand hung powerless; each joint lay bare, so that the light penetrated through and through. It was strange that life could exist in what was wasted and worn into a very type of death.

To take her from these heart-breaking scenes, to lead her to forget the world's desolation in the variety of objects presented by travelling, and to nurse her failing strength in the mild climate towards which we had resolved to journey, was my last hope for her preservation. The preparations for our departure, which had been suspended during my illness, were renewed. I did not revive to doubtful convalescence; health spent her treasures upon me; as the tree in spring may feel from its wrinkled limbs the fresh green break forth, and the living sap rise and circulate, so did the renewed vigour of my frame, the cheerful current of my blood, the new-born elasticity of my limbs, influence my mind to cheerful endurance and pleasurable thoughts. My body, late the heavy weight that bound me to the tomb, was exuberant with health; mere common exercises were insufficient for my reviving strength; methought I could emulate the speed of the race-horse, discern through the air objects at a blinding distance, hear the operations of nature in her mute abodes; my senses had become so refined and susceptible after my recovery from mortal disease.

Hope, among my other blessings, was not denied to me; and I did fondly trust that my unwearied attentions would restore my adored girl. I was therefore eager to forward our preparations. According to the plan first laid down, we were to have quitted London on the twenty-fifth of November; and, in pursuance of this scheme, two-thirds of our people – thepeople – all that remained of England, had gone forward, and had already been some weeks in Paris. First my illness, and subsequently that of Idris, had detained Adrian with his division, which consisted of three hundred persons, so that we now departed on the first of January, 2098. It was my wish to keep Idris as distant as possible from the hurry and clamour of the crowd, and to hide from her those appearances that would remind her most forcibly of our real situation. We separated ourselves to a great degree from Adrian, who was obliged to give his whole time to public business. The Countess of Windsor travelled with her son. Clara, Evelyn, and a female who acted as our attendant, were the only persons with whom we had contact. We occupied a commodious carriage, our servant officiated as coachman. A party of about twenty persons preceded us at a small distance. They had it in charge to prepare our halting places and our nightly abode. They had been selected for this service out of a great number that offered, on account of the superior sagacity of the man who had been appointed their leader.

Immediately on our departure, I was delighted to find a change in Idris, which I fondly hoped prognosticated the happiest results. All the cheerfulness and gentle gaiety natural to her revived. She was weak, and this alteration was rather displayed in looks and voice than in acts; but it was permanent and real. My recovery from the plague and confirmed health instilled into her a firm belief that I was now secure from this dread enemy. She told me that she was sure she should recover. That she had a presentiment, that the tide of calamity which deluged our unhappy race had now turned. That the remnant would be preserved, and among them the dear objects of her tender affection; and that in some selected spot we should wear out our lives together in pleasant society. "Do not let my state of feebleness deceive you," she said; "I feel that I am better; there is a quick life within me, and a spirit of anticipation that assures me, that I shall continue long to make a part of this world. I shall throw off this degrading weakness of body, which infects even my mind with debility, and I shall enter again on the performance of my duties. I was sorry to leave Windsor: but now I am weaned from this local attachment; I am content to remove to a mild climate, which will complete my recovery. Trust me, dearest, I shall neither leave you, nor my brother, nor these dear children; my firm determination to remain with you to the last, and to continue to contribute to your happiness and welfare, would keep me alive, even if grim death were nearer at hand than he really is."

I was only half re-assured by these expressions; I could not believe that the over-quick flow of her blood was a sign of health, or that her burning cheeks denoted convalescence. But I had no fears of an immediate catastrophe; nay, I persuaded myself that she would ultimately recover. And thus cheerfulness reigned in our little society. Idris conversed with animation on a thousand topics. Her chief desire was to lead our thoughts from melancholy reflections; so she drew charming pictures of a tranquil solitude, of a beauteous retreat, of the simple manners of our little tribe, and of the patriarchal brotherhood of love, which would survive the ruins of the populous nations which had lately existed. We shut out from our thoughts the present, and withdrew our eyes from the dreary landscape we traversed. Winter reigned in all its gloom. The leafless trees lay without motion against the dun sky; the forms of frost, mimicking the foliage of summer, strewed the ground; the paths were overgrown; the unploughed cornfields were patched with grass and weeds; the sheep congregated at the threshold of the cottage, the horned ox thrust his head from the window. The wind was bleak, and frequent sleet or snow-storms, added to the melancholy appearance wintry nature assumed.

We arrived at Rochester, and an accident caused us to be detained there a day. During that time, a circumstance occurred that changed our plans, and which, alas! in its result changed the eternal course of events, turning me from the pleasant new sprung hope I enjoyed, to an obscure and gloomy desert. But I must give some little explanation before I proceed with the final cause of our temporary alteration of plan, and refer again to those times when man walked the earth fearless, before Plague had become Queen of the World.

There resided a family in the neighbourhood of Windsor, of very humble pretensions, but which had been an object of interest to us on account of one of the persons of whom it was composed. The family of the Claytons had known better days; but, after a series of reverses, the father died a bankrupt, and the mother heartbroken, and a confirmed invalid, retired with her five children to a little cottage between Eton and Salt Hill. The eldest of these children, who was thirteen years old, seemed at once from the influence of adversity, to acquire the sagacity and principle belonging to a more mature age. Her mother grew worse and worse in health, but Lucy attended on her, and was as a tender parent to her younger brothers and sisters, and in the meantime shewed herself so good-humoured, social, and benevolent, that she was beloved as well as honoured, in her little neighbourhood.

Lucy was besides extremely pretty; so when she grew to be sixteen, it was to be supposed, notwithstanding her poverty, that she should have admirers. One of these was the son of a country-curate; he was a generous, frank-hearted youth, with an ardent love of knowledge, and no mean acquirements. Though Lucy was untaught, her mother's conversation and manners gave her a taste for refinements superior to her present situation. She loved the youth even without knowing it, except that in any difficulty she naturally turned to him for aid, and awoke with a lighter heart every Sunday, because she knew that she would be met and accompanied by him in her evening walk with her sisters. She had another admirer, one of the head-waiters at the inn at Salt Hill. He also was not without pretensions to urbane superiority, such as he learnt from gentlemen's servants and waiting-maids, who initiating him in all the slang of high life below stairs, rendered his arrogant temper ten times more intrusive. Lucy did not disclaim him – she was incapable of that feeling;

but she was sorry when she saw him approach, and quietly resisted all his endeavours to establish an intimacy. The fellow soon discovered that his rival was preferred to him; and this changed what was at first a chance admiration into a passion, whose main springs were envy, and a base desire to deprive his competitor of the advantage he enjoyed over himself.

Poor Lucy's sad story was but a common one. Her lover's father died; and he was left destitute. He accepted the offer of a gentleman to go to India with him, feeling secure that he should soon acquire an independence, and return to claim the hand of his beloved. He became involved in the war carried on there, was taken prisoner, and years elapsed before tidings of his existence were received in his native land. In the meantime disastrous poverty came on Lucy. Her little cottage, which stood looking from its trellice, covered with woodbine and jessamine, was burnt down; and the whole of their little property was included in the destruction. Whither betake them? By what exertion of industry could Lucy procure them another abode? Her mother nearly bed-rid, could not survive any extreme of famine-struck poverty. At this time her other admirer stept forward, and renewed his offer of marriage. He had saved money, and was going to set up a little inn at Datchet. There was nothing alluring to Lucy in this offer, except the home it secured to her mother; and she felt more sure of this, since she was struck by the apparent generosity which occasioned the present offer. She accepted it; thus sacrificing herself for the comfort and welfare of her parent.

It was some years after her marriage that we became acquainted with her. The accident of a storm caused us to take refuge in the inn, where we witnessed the brutal and quarrelsome behaviour of her husband, and her patient endurance. Her lot was not a fortunate one. Her first lover had returned with the hope of making her his own, and met her by accident, for the first time, as the mistress of his country inn, and the wife of another. He withdrew despairingly to foreign parts; nothing went well with him; at last he enlisted, and came back again wounded and sick, and yet Lucy was debarred from nursing him. Her husband's brutal disposition was aggravated by his yielding to the many temptations held out by his situation, and the consequent disarrangement of his affairs. Fortunately she had no children; but her heart was bound up in her brothers and sisters, and these his avarice and ill temper soon drove from the house; they were dispersed about the country, earning their livelihood with toil and care. He even shewed an inclination to get rid of her mother – but Lucy was firm here – she had sacrificed herself for her; she lived for her – she would not part with her – if the mother went, she would also go beg bread for her, die with her, but never desert her. The presence of Lucy was too necessary in keeping up the order of the house, and in preventing the whole establishment from going to wreck, for him to permit her to leave him. He yielded the point; but in all accesses of anger, or in his drunken fits, he recurred to the old topic, and stung poor Lucy's heart by opprobrious epithets bestowed on her parent.

A passion however, if it be wholly pure, entire, and reciprocal, brings with it its own solace. Lucy was truly, and from the depth of heart, devoted to her mother; the sole end she proposed to herself in life, was the comfort and preservation of this parent. Though she grieved for the result, yet she did not repent of her marriage, even when her lover returned to bestow competence on her. Three years had intervened, and how, in their pennyless state, could her mother have existed during this time? This excellent woman was worthy of her child's devotion. A perfect confidence and friendship existed between them; besides, she was by no means illiterate; and Lucy, whose mind had been in some degree cultivated by her former lover, now found in her the only person who could understand and appreciate her. Thus, though suffering, she was by no means desolate, and when, during fine summer days, she led her mother into the flowery and shady lanes near their abode, a gleam of unmixed joy enlightened her countenance; she saw that her parent was happy, and she knew that this happiness was of her sole creating.

Meanwhile her husband's affairs grew more and more involved; ruin was near at hand, and she was about to lose the fruit of all her labours, when pestilence came to change the aspect of the world. Her husband reaped benefit from the universal misery; but, as the disaster increased, the spirit of lawlessness seized him; he deserted his home to revel in the luxuries promised him in London, and found there a grave. Her former lover had been one of the first victims of the disease. But Lucy continued to live for and in her mother. Her courage only failed when she dreaded peril for her parent, or feared that death might prevent her from performing those duties to which she was unalterably devoted.

When we had quitted Windsor for London, as the previous step to our final emigration, we visited Lucy, and arranged with her the plan of her own and her mother's removal. Lucy was sorry at the necessity which forced her to quit her native lanes and village, and to drag an infirm parent from her comforts at home, to the homeless waste of depopulate earth; but she was too well disciplined by adversity, and of too sweet a temper, to indulge in repinings at what was inevitable.

Subsequent circumstances, my illness and that of Idris, drove her from our remembrance; and we called her to mind at last, only to conclude that she made one of the few who came from Windsor to join the emigrants, and that she was already in Paris. When we arrived at Rochester therefore, we were surprised to receive, by a man just come from Slough, a letter from this exemplary sufferer. His account was, that, journeying from his home, and passing through Datchet, he was surprised to see smoke issue from the chimney of the inn, and supposing that he should find comrades for his journey assembled there, he knocked and was admitted. There was no one in the house but Lucy, and her mother; the latter had been deprived of the use of her limbs by an attack of rheumatism, and so, one by one, all the remaining inhabitants of the country set forward, leaving them alone. Lucy intreated the man to stay with her; in a week or two her mother would be better, and they would then set out; but they must perish, if they were left thus helpless and forlorn. The man said, that his wife and children were already among the emigrants, and it was therefore, according to his notion, impossible for him to remain. Lucy, as a last resource, gave him a letter for Idris, to be delivered to her wherever he should meet us. This commission at least he fulfilled, and Idris received with emotion the following letter:

Honoured Lady,

I am sure that you will remember and pity me, and I dare hope that you will assist me; what other hope have I? Pardon my manner of writing, I am so bewildered. A month ago my dear mother was deprived of the use of her limbs. She is already better, and in another month would I am sure be able to travel, in the way you were so kind as to say you would arrange for us. But now everybody is gone – everybody – as they went away, each said, that perhaps my mother would be better, before we were quite deserted. But three days ago I went to Samuel Woods, who, on account of his new-born child, remained to the last; and there being a large family of them, I thought I could persuade them to wait a little longer for us; but I found the house deserted. I have not seen a soul since, till this good man came. – What will become of us? My mother does not know our state; she is so ill, that I have hidden it from her.

Will you not send someone to us? I am sure we must perish miserably as we are. If I were to try to move my mother now, she would die on the road; and if, when she gets better, I were able, I cannot guess how, to find out the roads, and get on so many many miles to the sea, you would all be in France, and the great ocean would be between us, which is so terrible even to sailors. What would it be to me, a woman, who never saw it? We should be imprisoned by it in this country, all, all alone, with no help; better die where we are. I can hardly write – I cannot stop my tears – it is not for myself; I could put my trust in God; and let the worst come, I think I could bear it, if I were alone. But my mother, my sick, my dear, dear mother, who never, since I was born, spoke a harsh word to me, who has been patient in many sufferings; pity her, dear Lady, she must die a miserable death if you do not pity her. People speak carelessly of her, because she is old and infirm, as if we must not all, if we are spared, become so; and then, when the young are old themselves, they will think that they ought to be taken care of. It is very silly of me to write in this way to you; but, when I hear her trying not to groan, and see her look smiling on me to comfort me, when I know she is in pain; and when I think that she does not know the worst, but she soon must; and then she will not complain; but I shall sit guessing at all that she is dwelling upon, of famine and misery – I feel as if my heart must break, and I do not know what I say or do; my mother – mother for whom I have borne much, God preserve you from this fate! Preserve her, Lady, and He will bless you; and I, poor miserable creature as I am, will thank you and pray for you while I live.

Your unhappy and dutiful servant,
Dec. 30th, 2097. Lucy Martin.

This letter deeply affected Idris, and she instantly proposed, that we should return to Datchet, to assist Lucy and her mother. I said that I would without delay set out for that place, but entreated her to join her brother, and there await my return with the children. But Idris was in high spirits, and full of hope. She declared that she could not consent even to a temporary separation from me, but that there was no need of this, the motion of the carriage did her good, and the distance was too trifling to be considered. We could dispatch messengers to Adrian, to inform him of our deviation from the original plan. She spoke with vivacity, and drew a picture after her own dear heart, of the pleasure we should bestow upon Lucy, and declared, if I went, she must accompany me, and that she should very much dislike to entrust the charge of rescuing them to others, who might fulfil it with coldness or inhumanity. Lucy's life had been one act of devotion and virtue; let her now reap the small reward of finding her excellence appreciated, and her necessity assisted, by those whom she respected and honoured.

These, and many other arguments, were urged with gentle pertinacity, and the ardour of a wish to do all the good in her power, by her whose simple expression of a desire and slightest request had ever been a law with me. I, of course, consented, the moment that I saw that she had set her heart upon this step. We sent half our attendant troop on to Adrian; and with the other half our carriage took a retrograde course back to Windsor.

I wonder now how I could be so blind and senseless, as thus to risk the safety of Idris; for, if I had eyes, surely I could see the sure, though deceitful, advance of death in her burning cheek and increasing weakness. But she said she was better; and I believed her. Extinction could not be near a being, whose vivacity and intelligence hourly increased, and whose frame was endowed with an intense, and I fondly thought, a strong and permanent spirit of life. Who, after a great disaster, has not looked back with wonder at his inconceivable obtuseness of understanding, that could not perceive the many minute threads with which fate weaves the inextricable net of our destinies, until he is inmeshed completely in it?

The cross roads which we now entered upon, were even in a worse state than the long neglected high-ways; and the inconvenience seemed to menace the perishing frame of Idris with destruction. Passing through Dartford, we arrived at Hampton on the second day. Even in this short interval my beloved companion grew sensibly worse in health, though her spirits were still light, and she cheered my growing anxiety with gay sallies; sometimes the thought pierced my brain – Is she dying? – as I saw her fair fleshless hand rest on mine, or observed the feebleness with which she performed the accustomed acts of life. I drove away the idea, as if it had been suggested by insanity; but it occurred again and again, only to be dispelled by the continued liveliness of her manner.

About mid-day, after quitting Hampton, our carriage broke down: the shock caused Idris to faint, but on her reviving no other ill consequence ensued; our party of attendants had as usual gone on before us, and our coachman went in search of another vehicle, our former one being rendered by this accident unfit for service. The only place near us was a poor village, in which he found a kind of caravan, able to hold four people, but it was clumsy and ill hung; besides this he found a very excellent cabriolet: our plan was soon arranged; I would drive Idris in the latter; while the children were conveyed by the servant in the former. But these arrangements cost time; we had agreed to proceed that night to Windsor, and thither our purveyors had gone: we should find considerable difficulty in getting accommodation, before we reached this place; after all, the distance was only ten miles; my horse was a good one; I would go forward at a good pace with Idris, leaving the children to follow at a rate more consonant to the uses of their cumberous machine.

Evening closed in quickly, far more quickly than I was prepared to expect. At the going down of the sun it began to snow heavily. I attempted in vain to defend my beloved companion from the storm; the wind drove the snow in our faces; and it lay so high on the ground, that we made but small way; while the night was so dark, that but for the white covering on the ground we should not have been able to see a yard before us. We had left our accompanying caravan far behind us; and now I perceived that the storm had made me unconsciously deviate from my intended route. I had gone some miles out of my way. My knowledge of the country enabled me to regain the right road; but, instead of going, as at first agreed upon, by a cross road through Stanwell to Datchet, I was obliged to take the way of Egham and Bishopgate. It was certain therefore that I should not be rejoined by the other vehicle, that I should not meet a single fellow-creature till we arrived at Windsor.

The back of our carriage was drawn up, and I hung a pelisse before it, thus to curtain the beloved sufferer from the pelting sleet. She leaned on my shoulder, growing every moment more languid and feeble; at first she replied to my words of cheer with affectionate thanks; but by degrees she sunk into silence; her head lay heavily upon me; I only knew that she lived by her irregular breathing and frequent sighs. For a moment I resolved to stop, and, opposing the back of the cabriolet to the force of the tempest, to expect morning as well as I might. But the wind was bleak and piercing, while the occasional shudderings of my poor Idris, and the intense cold I felt myself, demonstrated that this would be a dangerous experiment. At length methought she slept – fatal sleep, induced by frost: at this moment I saw the heavy outline of a cottage traced on the dark horizon close to us: "Dearest love," I said, "support yourself but one moment, and we shall have shelter; let us stop here, that I may open the door of this blessed dwelling."

As I spoke, my heart was transported, and my senses swam with excessive delight and thankfulness; I placed the head of Idris against the carriage, and, leaping out, scrambled through the snow to the cottage, whose door was open. I had apparatus about me for procuring light, and that shewed me a comfortable room, with a pile of wood in one corner, and no appearance of disorder, except that, the door having been left partly open, the snow, drifting in, had blocked up the threshold. I returned to the carriage, and the sudden change from light to darkness at first blinded me. When I recovered my sight – eternal God of this lawless world! O supreme Death! I will not disturb thy silent reign, or mar my tale with fruitless exclamations of horror – I saw Idris, who had fallen from the seat to the bottom of the carriage; her head, its long hair pendent, with one arm, hung over the side. – Struck by a spasm of horror, I lifted her up; her heart was pulseless, her faded lips unfanned by the slightest breath.

I carried her into the cottage; I placed her on the bed. Lighting a fire, I chafed her stiffening limbs; for two long hours I sought to restore departed life; and, when hope was as dead as my beloved, I closed with trembling hands her glazed eyes. I did not doubt what I should now do. In the confusion attendant on my illness, the task of interring our darling Alfred had devolved on his grandmother, the Ex-Queen, and she, true to her ruling passion, had caused him to be carried to Windsor, and buried in the family vault, in St. George's Chapel. I must proceed to Windsor, to calm the anxiety of Clara, who would wait anxiously for us – yet I would fain spare her the heart-breaking spectacle of Idris, brought in by me lifeless from the journey. So first I would place my beloved beside her child in the vault, and then seek the poor children who would be expecting me.

I lighted the lamps of my carriage; I wrapt her in furs, and placed her along the seat; then taking the reins, made the horses go forward. We proceeded through the snow, which lay in masses impeding the way, while the descending flakes, driving against me with redoubled fury, blinded me. The pain occasioned by the angry elements, and the cold iron of the shafts of frost which buffetted me, and entered my aching flesh, were a relief to me; blunting my mental suffering. The horses staggered on, and the reins hung loosely in my hands. I often thought I would lay my head close to the sweet, cold face of my lost angel, and thus resign myself to conquering torpor. Yet I must not leave her a prey to the fowls of the air; but, in pursuance of my determination place her in the tomb of her forefathers, where a merciful God might permit me to rest also.

The road we passed through Egham was familiar to me; but the wind and snow caused the horses to drag their load slowly and heavily. Suddenly the wind veered from south-west to west, and then again to north-west. As Sampson with tug and strain stirred from their bases the columns that supported the Philistine temple, so did the gale shake the dense vapours propped on the horizon, while the massy dome of clouds fell to the south, disclosing through the scattered web the clear empyrean, and the little stars, which were set at an immeasurable distance in the crystalline fields, showered their small rays on the glittering snow. Even the horses were cheered, and moved on with renovated strength. We entered the forest at Bishopgate, and at the end of the Long Walk I saw the Castle, 'the proud Keep of Windsor, rising in the majesty of proportion, girt with the double belt of its kindred and coeval towers.' I looked with reverence on a structure, ancient almost as the rock on which it stood, abode of kings, theme of admiration for the wise. With greater reverence and, tearful affection I beheld it as the asylum of the long lease of love I had enjoyed there with the perishable, unmatchable treasure of dust, which now lay cold beside me. Now indeed, I could have yielded to all the softness of my nature, and wept; and, womanlike, have uttered bitter plaints; while the familiar trees, the herds of living deer, the sward oft prest by her fairy-feet, one by one with sad association presented themselves. The white gate at the end of the Long Walk was wide open, and I rode up the empty town through the first gate of the feudal tower; and now St. George's Chapel, with its blackened fretted sides, was right before me. I halted at its door, which was open; I entered, and placed my lighted lamp on the altar; then I returned, and with tender caution I bore Idris up the aisle into the chancel, and laid her softly down on the carpet which covered the step leading to the communion table. The banners of the knights of the garter, and their half drawn swords, were hung in vain emblazonry above the stalls. The banner of her family hung there, still surmounted by its regal crown. Farewell to the glory and heraldry of England! – I turned from such vanity with a slight feeling of wonder, at how mankind could have ever been interested in such things. I bent over the lifeless corpse of my beloved; and, while looking on her uncovered face, the features already contracted by the rigidity of death, I felt as if all the visible universe had grown as soulless, inane, and comfortless as the clay-cold image beneath me. I felt for a moment the intolerable sense of struggle with, and detestation for, the laws which govern the world; till the calm still visible on the face of my dead love recalled me to a more soothing tone of mind, and I proceeded to fulfil the last office that could now be paid her. For her I could not lament, so much I envied her enjoyment of 'the sad immunities of the grave.'

The vault had been lately opened to place our Alfred therein. The ceremony customary in these latter days had been cursorily performed, and the pavement of the chapel, which was its entrance, having been removed, had not been replaced. I descended the steps, and walked through the long passage to the large vault which contained the kindred dust of my Idris. I distinguished the small coffin of my babe. With hasty, trembling hands I constructed a bier beside it, spreading it with the furs and Indian shawls, which had wrapt Idris in her journey thither. I lighted the glimmering lamp, which flickered in this damp abode of the dead; then I bore my lost one to her last bed, decently composing her limbs, and covering them with a mantle, veiling all except her face, which remained lovely and placid. She appeared to rest like one over-wearied, her beauteous eyes steeped in sweet slumber. Yet, so it was not – she was dead! How intensely I then longed to lie down beside her, to gaze till death should gather me to the same repose.

But death does not come at the bidding of the miserable. I had lately recovered from mortal illness, and my blood had never flowed with such an even current, nor had my limbs ever been so instinct with quick life, as now. I felt that my death must be voluntary. Yet what more natural than famine, as I watched in this chamber of mortality, placed in a world of the dead, beside the lost hope of my life? Meanwhile as I looked on her, the features, which bore a sisterly resemblance to Adrian, brought my thoughts back again to the living, to this dear friend, to Clara, and to Evelyn, who were probably now in Windsor, waiting anxiously for our arrival.

Methought I heard a noise, a step in the far chapel, which was re-echoed by its vaulted roof, and borne to me through the hollow passages. Had Clara seen my carriage pass up the town, and did she seek me here? I must save her at least from the horrible scene the vault presented. I sprung up the steps, and then saw a female figure, bent with age, and clad in long mourning robes, advance through the dusky chapel, supported by a slender cane, yet tottering even with this support. She heard me, and looked up; the lamp I held illuminated my figure, and the moon-beams, struggling through the painted glass, fell upon her face, wrinkled and gaunt, yet with a piercing eye and commanding brow – I recognized the Countess of Windsor. With a hollow voice she asked, "Where is the princess?"

I pointed to the torn up pavement: she walked to the spot, and looked down into the palpable darkness; for the vault was too distant for the rays of the small lamp I had left there to be discernible.

"Your light," she said. I gave it her; and she regarded the now visible, but precipitous steps, as if calculating her capacity to descend. Instinctively I made a silent offer of my assistance. She motioned me away with a look of scorn, saying in an harsh voice, as she pointed downwards, "There at least I may have her undisturbed."

She walked deliberately down, while I, overcome, miserable beyond words, or tears, or groans, threw myself on the pavement near – the stiffening form of Idris was before me, the death-struck countenance hushed in eternal repose beneath. That was to me the end of all! The day before, I had figured to my self various adventures, and communion with my friends in after time – now I had leapt the interval, and reached the utmost edge and bourne of life. Thus wrapt in gloom, enclosed, walled up, vaulted over by the omnipotent present, I was startled by the sound of feet on the steps of the tomb, and I remembered her whom I had utterly forgotten, my angry visitant; her tall form slowly rose upwards from the vault, a living statue, instinct with hate, and human, passionate strife: she seemed to me as having reached the pavement of the aisle; she stood motionless, seeking with her eyes alone, some desired object – till, perceiving me close to her, she placed her wrinkled hand on my arm, exclaiming with tremulous accents, "Lionel Verney, my son!" This name, applied at such a moment by my angel's mother, instilled into me more respect than I had ever before felt for this disdainful lady. I bowed my head, and kissed her shrivelled hand, and, remarking that she trembled violently, supported her to the end of the chancel, where she sat on the steps that led to the regal stall. She suffered herself to be led, and still holding my hand, she leaned her head back against the stall, while the moon beams, tinged with various colours by the painted glass, fell on her glistening eyes; aware of her weakness, again calling to mind her long cherished dignity, she dashed the tears away; yet they fell fast, as she said, for excuse, "She is so beautiful and placid, even in death. No harsh feeling ever clouded her serene brow; how did I treat her? wounding her gentle heart with savage coldness; I had no compassion on her in past years, does she forgive me now? Little, little does it boot to talk of repentance and forgiveness to the dead, had I during her life once consulted her gentle wishes, and curbed my rugged nature to do her pleasure, I should not feel thus."

Idris and her mother were unlike in person. The dark hair, deep-set black eyes, and prominent features of the Ex-Queen were in entire contrast to the golden tresses, the full blue orbs, and the soft lines and contour of her daughter's countenance. Yet, in latter days, illness had taken from my poor girl the full outline of her face, and reduced it to the inflexible shape of the bone beneath. In the form of her brow, in her oval chin, there was to be found a resemblance to her mother; nay in some moods, their gestures were not unlike; nor, having lived so long together, was this wonderful.

There is a magic power in resemblance. When one we love dies, we hope to see them in another state, and half expect that the agency of mind will inform its new garb in imitation of its decayed earthly vesture. But these are ideas of the mind only. We know that the instrument is shivered, the sensible image lies in miserable fragments, dissolved to dusty nothingness; a look, a gesture, or a fashioning of the limbs similar to the dead in a living person, touches a thrilling chord, whose sacred harmony is felt in the heart's dearest recess. Strangely moved, prostrate before this spectral image, and enslaved by the force of blood manifested in likeness of look and movement, I remained trembling in the presence of the harsh, proud, and till now unloved mother of Idris.

Poor, mistaken woman! in her tenderest mood before, she had cherished the idea, that a word, a look of reconciliation from her, would be received with joy, and repay long years of severity. Now that the time was gone for the exercise of such power, she fell at once upon the thorny truth of things, and felt that neither smile nor caress could penetrate to the unconscious state, or influence the happiness of her who lay in the vault beneath. This conviction, together with the remembrance of soft replies to bitter speeches, of gentle looks repaying angry glances; the perception of the falsehood, paltryness and futility of her cherished dreams of birth and power; the overpowering knowledge, that love and life were the true emperors of our mortal state; all, as a tide, rose, and filled her soul with stormy and bewildering confusion. It fell to my lot, to come as the influential power, to allay the fierce tossing of these tumultuous waves. I spoke to her; I led her to reflect how happy Idris had really been, and how her virtues and numerous excellencies had found scope and estimation in her past career. I praised her, the idol of my heart's dear worship, the admired type of feminine perfection. With ardent and overflowing eloquence, I relieved my heart from its burthen, and awoke to the sense of a new pleasure in life, as I poured forth the funeral eulogy. Then I referred to Adrian, her loved brother, and to her surviving child. I declared, which I had before almost forgotten, what my duties were with regard to these valued portions of herself, and bade the melancholy repentant mother reflect, how she could best expiate unkindness towards the dead, by redoubled love of the survivors. Consoling her, my own sorrows were assuaged; my sincerity won her entire conviction.

She turned to me. The hard, inflexible, persecuting woman, turned with a mild expression of face, and said, "If our beloved angel sees us now, it will delight her to find that I do you even tardy justice. You were worthy of her; and from my heart I am glad that you won her away from me. Pardon, my son, the many wrongs I have done you; forget my bitter words and unkind treatment – take me, and govern me as you will."

I seized this docile moment to propose our departure from the church.

"First," she said, "let us replace the pavement above the vault."

We drew near to it; "Shall we look on her again?" I asked.

"I cannot," she replied, "and, I pray you, neither do you. We need not torture ourselves by gazing on the soulless body, while her living spirit is buried quick in our hearts, and her surpassing loveliness is so deeply carved there, that sleeping or waking she must ever be present to us."

For a few moments, we bent in solemn silence over the open vault. I consecrated my future life, to the embalming of her dear memory; I vowed to serve her brother and her child till death. The convulsive sob of my companion made me break off my internal orisons. I next dragged the stones over the entrance of the tomb, and closed the gulph that contained the life of my life. Then, supporting my decrepid fellow-mourner, we slowly left the chapel. I felt, as I stepped into the open air, as if I had quitted an happy nest of repose, for a dreary wilderness, a tortuous path, a bitter, joyless, hopeless pilgrimage.

Chapter IV

OUR ESCORT had been directed to prepare our abode for the night at the inn, opposite the ascent to the Castle. We could not again visit the halls and familiar chambers of our home, on a mere visit. We had already left forever the glades of Windsor, and all of coppice, flowery hedgerow, and murmuring stream, which gave shape and intensity to the love of our country, and the almost superstitious attachment with which we regarded native England. It had been our intention to have called at Lucy's dwelling in Datchet, and to have re-assured her with promises of aid and protection before we repaired to our quarters for the night. Now, as the Countess of Windsor and I turned down the steep hill that led from the Castle, we saw the children, who had just stopped in their caravan, at the inn-door. They had passed through Datchet without halting. I dreaded to meet them, and to be the bearer of my tragic story, so while they were still occupied in the hurry of arrival, I suddenly left them, and through the snow and clear moon-light air, hastened along the well known road to Datchet.

Well known indeed it was. Each cottage stood on its accustomed site, each tree wore its familiar appearance. Habit had graven uneraseably on my memory, every turn and change of object on the road. At a short distance beyond the Little Park, was an elm half blown down by a storm, some ten years ago; and still, with leafless snow-laden branches, it stretched across the pathway, which wound through a meadow, beside a shallow brook, whose brawling was silenced by frost – that stile, that white gate, that hollow oak tree, which doubtless once belonged to the forest, and which now shewed in the moonlight its gaping rent; to whose fanciful appearance, tricked out by the dusk into a resemblance of the human form, the children had given the name of Falstaff; – all these objects were as well known to me as the cold hearth of my deserted home, and every moss-grown wall and plot of orchard ground, alike as twin lambs are to each other in a stranger's eye, yet to my accustomed gaze bore differences, distinction, and a name. England remained, though England was dead – it was the ghost of merry England that I beheld, under those greenwood shade passing generations had sported in security and ease. To this painful recognition of familiar places, was added a feeling experienced by all, understood by none – a feeling as if in some state, less visionary than a dream, in some past real existence, I had seen all I saw, with precisely the same feelings as I now beheld them – as if all my sensations were a duplex mirror of a former revelation. To get rid of this oppressive sense I strove to imagine change in this tranquil spot – this augmented my mood, by causing me to bestow more attention on the objects which occasioned me pain.

I reached Datchet and Lucy's humble abode – once noisy with Saturday night revellers, or trim and neat on Sunday morning it had borne testimony to the labours and orderly habits of the housewife. The snow lay high about the door, as if it had remained unclosed for many days.

"What scene of death hath Roscius now to act?" I muttered to myself as I looked at the dark casements. At first I thought I saw a light in one of them, but it proved to be merely the refraction of the moon-beams, while the only sound was the crackling branches as the breeze whirred the snow flakes from them – the moon sailed high and unclouded in the interminable ether, while the shadow of the cottage lay black on the garden behind. I entered this by the open wicket, and anxiously examined each window. At length I detected a ray of light struggling through a closed shutter in one of the upper rooms – it was a novel feeling, alas! to look at any house and say there dwells its usual inmate – the door of the house was merely on the latch: so I entered and ascended the moon-lit staircase. The door of the inhabited room was ajar: looking in, I saw Lucy sitting as at work at the table on which the light stood; the implements of needlework were about her, but her hand had fallen on her lap, and her eyes, fixed on the ground, shewed by their vacancy that her thoughts wandered.

Traces of care and watching had diminished her former attractions – but her simple dress and cap, her desponding attitude, and the single candle that cast its light upon her, gave for a moment a picturesque grouping to the whole. A fearful reality recalled me from the thought – a figure lay stretched on the bed covered by a sheet – her mother was dead, and Lucy, apart from all the world, deserted and alone, watched beside the corpse during the weary night. I entered the room, and my unexpected appearance at first drew a scream from the lone survivor of a dead nation; but she recognised me, and recovered herself, with the quick exercise of self-control habitual to her. "Did you not expect me?" I asked, in that low voice which the presence of the dead makes us as it were instinctively assume.

"You are very good," replied she, "to have come yourself; I can never thank you sufficiently; but it is too late."

"Too late," cried I, "what do you mean? It is not too late to take you from this deserted place, and conduct you to –"

My own loss, which I had forgotten as I spoke, now made me turn away, while choking grief impeded my speech. I threw open the window, and looked on the cold, waning, ghastly, misshaped circle on high, and the chill white earth beneath – did the spirit of sweet Idris sail along the moon-frozen crystal air? – No, no, a more genial atmosphere, a lovelier habitation was surely hers!

I indulged in this meditation for a moment, and then again addressed the mourner, who stood leaning against the bed with that expression of resigned despair, of complete misery, and a patient sufferance of it, which is far more touching than any of the insane ravings or wild gesticulation of untamed sorrow. I desired to draw her from this spot; but she opposed my wish. That class of persons whose imagination and sensibility have never been taken out of the narrow circle immediately in view, if they possess these qualities to any extent, are apt to pour their influence into the very realities which appear to destroy them, and to cling to these with double tenacity from not being able to comprehend anything beyond. Thus Lucy, in desert England, in a dead world, wished to fulfil the usual ceremonies of the dead, such as were customary to the English country people, when death was a rare visitant, and gave us time to receive his dreaded usurpation with pomp and circumstance – going forth in procession to deliver the keys of the tomb into his conquering hand. She had already, alone as she was, accomplished some of these, and the work on which I found her employed, was her mother's shroud. My heart sickened at such detail of woe, which a female can endure, but which is more painful to the masculine spirit than deadliest struggle, or throes of unutterable but transient agony.

This must not be, I told her; and then, as further inducement, I communicated to her my recent loss, and gave her the idea that she must come with me to take charge of the orphan children, whom the death of Idris had deprived of a mother's care. Lucy never resisted the call of a duty, so she yielded, and closing the casements and doors with care, she accompanied me back to Windsor. As we went she communicated to me the occasion of her mother's death. Either by some mischance she had got sight of Lucy's letter to Idris, or she had overheard her conversation with the countryman who bore it; however it might be, she obtained a knowledge of the appalling situation of herself and her daughter, her aged frame could not sustain the anxiety and horror this discovery instilled – she concealed her knowledge from Lucy, but brooded over it through sleepless nights, till fever and delirium, swift forerunners of death, disclosed the secret. Her life, which had long been hovering on its extinction, now yielded at once to the united effects of misery and sickness, and that same morning she had died.

After the tumultuous emotions of the day, I was glad to find on my arrival at the inn that my companions had retired to rest. I gave Lucy in charge to the Countess's attendant, and then sought repose from my various struggles and impatient regrets. For a few moments the events of the day floated in disastrous pageant through my brain, till sleep bathed it in forgetfulness; when morning dawned and I awoke, it seemed as if my slumber had endured for years.

My companions had not shared my oblivion. Clara's swollen eyes shewed that she has passed the night in weeping. The Countess looked haggard and wan. Her firm spirit had not found relief in tears, and she suffered the more from all the painful retrospect and agonizing regret that now occupied her. We departed from Windsor, as soon as the burial rites had been performed for Lucy's mother, and, urged on by an impatient desire to change the scene, went forward towards Dover with speed, our escort having gone before to provide horses; finding them either in the warm stables they instinctively sought during the cold weather, or standing shivering in the bleak fields ready to surrender their liberty in exchange for offered corn.

During our ride the Countess recounted to me the extraordinary circumstances which had brought her so strangely to my side in the chancel of St. George's chapel. When last she had taken leave of Idris, as she looked anxiously on her faded person and pallid countenance, she had suddenly been visited by a conviction that she saw her for the last time. It was hard to part with her while under the dominion of this sentiment, and for the last time she endeavoured to persuade her daughter to commit herself to her nursing, permitting me to join Adrian. Idris mildly refused, and thus they separated. The idea that they should never again meet grew on the Countess's mind, and haunted her perpetually; a thousand times she had resolved to turn back and join us, and was again and again restrained by the pride and anger of which she was the slave. Proud of heart as she was, she bathed her pillow with nightly tears, and through the day was subdued by nervous agitation and expectation of the dreaded event, which she was wholly incapable of curbing. She confessed that at this period her hatred of me knew no bounds, since she considered me as the sole obstacle to the fulfilment of her dearest wish, that of attending upon her daughter in her last moments. She desired to express her fears to her son, and to seek consolation from his sympathy with, or courage from his rejection of, her auguries.

On the first day of her arrival at Dover she walked with him on the sea beach, and with the timidity characteristic of passionate and exaggerated feeling was by degrees bringing the conversation to the desired point, when she could communicate her fears to him, when the messenger who bore my letter announcing our temporary return to Windsor, came riding down to them. He gave some oral account of how he had left us, and added, that notwithstanding the cheerfulness and good courage of Lady Idris, he was afraid that she would hardly reach Windsor alive. "True," said the Countess, "your fears are just, she is about to expire!"

As she spoke, her eyes were fixed on a tomblike hollow of the cliff, and she saw, she averred the same to me with solemnity, Idris pacing slowly towards this cave. She was turned from her, her head was bent down, her white dress was such as she was accustomed to wear, except that a thin crape-like veil covered her golden tresses, and concealed her as a dim transparent mist. She looked dejected, as docilely yielding to a commanding power; she submissively entered, and was lost in the dark recess.

"Were I subject to visionary moods," said the venerable lady, as she continued her narrative, "I might doubt my eyes, and condemn my credulity; but reality is the world I live in, and what I saw I doubt not had existence beyond myself. From that moment I could not rest; it was worth my existence to see her once again before she died; I knew that I should not accomplish this, yet I must endeavour. I immediately departed for Windsor; and, though I was assured that we travelled speedily, it seemed to me that our progress was snail-like, and that delays were created solely for my annoyance. Still I accused you, and heaped on your head the fiery ashes of my burning impatience. It was no disappointment, though an agonizing pang, when you pointed to her last abode; and words would ill express the abhorrence I that moment felt towards you, the triumphant impediment to my dearest wishes. I saw her, and anger, and hate, and injustice died at her bier, giving place at their departure to a remorse (Great God, that I should feel it!) which must last while memory and feeling endure."

To medicine such remorse, to prevent awakening love and new-born mildness from producing the same bitter fruit that hate and harshness had done, I devoted all my endeavours to soothe the venerable penitent. Our party was a melancholy one; each was possessed by regret for what was remediless; for the absence of his mother shadowed even the infant gaiety of Evelyn. Added to this was the prospect of the uncertain future. Before the final accomplishment of any great voluntary change the mind vacillates, now soothing itself by fervent expectation, now recoiling from obstacles which seem never to have presented themselves before with so frightful an aspect. An involuntary tremor ran through me when I thought that in another day we might have crossed the watery barrier, and have set forward on that hopeless, interminable, sad wandering, which but a short time before I regarded as the only relief to sorrow that our situation afforded.

Our approach to Dover was announced by the loud roarings of the wintry sea. They were borne miles inland by the sound-laden blast, and by their unaccustomed uproar, imparted a feeling of insecurity and peril to our stable abode. At first we hardly permitted ourselves to think that any unusual eruption of nature caused this tremendous war of air and water, but rather fancied that we merely listened to what we had heard a thousand times before, when we had watched the flocks of fleece-crowned waves, driven by the winds, come to lament and die on the barren sands and pointed rocks. But we found upon advancing farther, that Dover was overflowed – many of the houses were overthrown by the surges which filled the streets, and with hideous brawlings sometimes retreated leaving the pavement of the town bare, till again hurried forward by the influx of ocean, they returned with thunder-sound to their usurped station.

Hardly less disturbed than the tempestuous world of waters was the assembly of human beings, that from the cliff fearfully watched its ravings. On the morning of the arrival of the emigrants under the conduct of Adrian, the sea had been serene and glassy, the slight ripples refracted the sunbeams, which shed their radiance through the clear blue frosty air. This placid appearance of nature was hailed as a good augury for the voyage, and the chief immediately repaired to the harbour to examine two steamboats which were moored there. On the following midnight, when all were at rest, a frightful storm of wind and clattering rain and hail first disturbed them, and the voice of one shrieking in the streets, that the sleepers must awake or they would be drowned; and when they rushed out, half clothed, to discover the meaning of this alarm, they found that the tide, rising above every mark, was rushing into the town. They ascended the cliff, but the darkness permitted only the white crest of waves to be seen, while the roaring wind mingled its howlings in dire accord with the wild surges. The awful hour of night, the utter inexperience of many who had never seen the sea before, the wailing of women and cries of children added to the horror of the tumult. All the following day the same scene continued. When the tide ebbed, the town was left dry; but on its flow, it rose even higher than on the preceding night. The vast ships that lay rotting in the roads were whirled from their anchorage, and driven and jammed against the cliff, the vessels in the harbour were flung on land like sea-weed, and there battered to pieces by the breakers. The waves dashed against the cliff, which if in any place it had been before loosened, now gave way, and the affrighted crowd saw vast fragments of the near earth fall with crash and roar into the deep. This sight operated differently on different persons. The greater part thought it a judgment of God, to prevent or punish our emigration from our native land. Many were doubly eager to quit a nook of ground now become their prison, which appeared unable to resist the inroads of ocean's giant waves.

When we arrived at Dover, after a fatiguing day's journey, we all required rest and sleep; but the scene acting around us soon drove away such ideas. We were drawn, along with the greater part of our companions, to the edge of the cliff, there to listen to and make a thousand conjectures. A fog narrowed our horizon to about a quarter of a mile, and the misty veil, cold and dense, enveloped sky and sea in equal obscurity. What added to our inquietude was the circumstance that two-thirds of our original number were now waiting for us in Paris, and clinging, as we now did most painfully, to any addition to our melancholy remnant, this division, with the tameless impassable ocean between, struck us with affright. At length, after loitering for several hours on the cliff, we retired to Dover Castle, whose roof sheltered all who breathed the English air, and sought the sleep necessary to restore strength and courage to our worn frames and languid spirits.

Early in the morning Adrian brought me the welcome intelligence that the wind had changed: it had been south-west; it was now north-east. The sky was stripped bare of clouds by the increasing gale, while the tide at its ebb seceded entirely from the town. The change of wind rather increased the fury of the sea, but it altered its late dusky hue to a bright green; and in spite of its unmitigated clamour, its more cheerful appearance instilled hope and pleasure. All day we watched the ranging of the mountainous waves, and towards sunset a desire to decypher the promise for the morrow at its setting, made us all gather with one accord on the edge of the cliff. When the mighty luminary approached within a few degrees of the tempest-tossed horizon, suddenly, a wonder! three other suns, alike burning and brilliant, rushed from various quarters of the heavens towards the great orb; they whirled round it. The glare of light was intense to our dazzled eyes; the sun itself seemed to join in the dance, while the sea burned like a furnace, like all Vesuvius a-light, with flowing lava beneath. The horses broke loose from their stalls in terror – a herd of cattle, panic struck, raced down to the brink of the cliff, and blinded by light, plunged down with frightful yells in the waves below. The time occupied by the apparition of these meteors was comparatively short; suddenly the three mock suns united in one, and plunged into the sea. A few seconds afterwards, a deafening watery sound came up with awful peal from the spot where they had disappeared.

Meanwhile the sun, disencumbered from his strange satellites, paced with its accustomed majesty towards its western home. When – we dared not trust our eyes late dazzled, but it seemed that – the sea rose to meet it – it mounted higher and higher, till the fiery globe was obscured, and the wall of water still ascended the horizon; it appeared as if suddenly the motion of earth was revealed to us – as if no longer we were ruled by ancient laws, but were turned adrift in an unknown region of space. Many cried aloud, that these were no meteors, but globes of burning matter, which had set fire to the earth, and caused the vast cauldron at our feet to bubble up with its measureless waves; the day of judgment was come they averred, and a few moments would transport us before the awful countenance of the omnipotent judge; while those less given to visionary terrors, declared that two conflicting gales had occasioned the last phaenomenon. In support of this opinion they pointed out the fact that the east wind died away, while the rushing of the coming west mingled its wild howl with the roar of the advancing waters. Would the cliff resist this new battery? Was not the giant wave far higher than the precipice? Would not our little island be deluged by its approach? The crowd of spectators fled. They were dispersed over the fields, stopping now and then, and looking back in terror. A sublime sense of awe calmed the swift pulsations of my heart – I awaited the approach of the destruction menaced, with that solemn resignation which an unavoidable necessity instils. The ocean every moment assumed a more terrific aspect, while the twilight was dimmed by the rack which the west wind spread over the sky. By slow degrees however, as the wave advanced, it took a more mild appearance; some under current of air, or obstruction in the bed of the waters, checked its progress, and it sank gradually; while the surface of the sea became uniformly higher as it dissolved into it. This change took from us the fear of an immediate catastrophe, although we were still anxious as to the final result. We continued during the whole night to watch the fury of the sea and the pace of the driving clouds, through whose openings the rare stars rushed impetuously; the thunder of conflicting elements deprived us of all power to sleep.

This endured ceaselessly for three days and nights. The stoutest hearts quailed before the savage enmity of nature; provisions began to fail us, though every day foraging parties were dispersed to the nearer towns. In vain we schooled ourselves into the belief, that there was nothing out of the common order of nature in the strife we witnessed; our disasterous and overwhelming destiny turned the best of us to cowards. Death had hunted us through the course of many months, even to the narrow strip of time on which we now stood; narrow indeed, and buffeted by storms, was our footway overhanging the great sea of calamity –

> As an unsheltered northern shore
> Is shaken by the wintry wave –
> And frequent storms for evermore,
> (While from the west the loud winds rave,
> Or from the east, or mountains hoar)
> The struck and tott'ring sand-bank lave.

It required more than human energy to bear up against the menaces of destruction that everywhere surrounded us.

After the lapse of three days, the gale died away, the sea-gull sailed upon the calm bosom of the windless atmosphere, and the last yellow leaf on the topmost branch of the oak hung without motion. The sea no longer broke with fury; but a swell setting in steadily for shore, with long sweep and sullen burst replaced the roar of the breakers. Yet we derived hope from the change, and we did not doubt that after the interval of a few days the sea would resume its tranquillity. The sunset of the fourth day favoured this idea; it was clear and golden. As we gazed on the purple sea, radiant beneath, we were attracted by a novel spectacle; a dark speck – as it neared, visibly a boat – rode on the top of the waves, every now and then lost in the steep vallies between. We marked its course with eager questionings; and, when we saw that it evidently made for shore, we descended to the only practicable landing place, and hoisted a signal to direct them. By the help of glasses we distinguished her crew; it consisted of nine men, Englishmen, belonging in truth to the two divisions of our people, who had preceded us, and had been for several weeks at Paris. As countryman was wont to meet countryman in distant lands, did we greet our visitors on their landing, with outstretched hands and gladsome welcome. They were slow to reciprocate our gratulations. They looked angry and resentful; not less than the chafed sea which they had traversed with imminent peril, though apparently more displeased with each other than with us. It was strange to see these human beings, who appeared to be given forth by the earth like rare and inestimable plants, full of towering passion, and the spirit of angry contest. Their first demand was to be conducted to the Lord Protector of England, so they called Adrian, though he had long discarded the empty title, as a bitter mockery of the shadow to which the Protectorship was now reduced. They were speedily led to Dover Castle, from whose keep Adrian had watched the movements of the boat. He received them with the interest and wonder so strange a visitation created. In the confusion occasioned by their angry demands for precedence, it was long before we could discover the secret meaning of this strange scene. By degrees, from the furious declamations of one, the fierce interruptions of another, and the bitter scoffs of a third, we found that they were deputies from our colony at Paris, from three parties there formed, who, each with angry rivalry, tried to attain a superiority over the other two. These deputies had been dispatched by them to Adrian, who had been selected arbiter; and they had journied from Paris to Calais, through the vacant towns and desolate country, indulging the while violent hatred against each other; and now they pleaded their several causes with unmitigated party-spirit.

By examining the deputies apart, and after much investigation, we learnt the true state of things at Paris. Since parliament had elected him Ryland's deputy, all the surviving English had submitted to Adrian. He was our captain to lead us from our native soil to unknown lands, our lawgiver and our preserver. On the first arrangement of our scheme of emigration, no continued separation of our members was contemplated, and the command of the whole body in gradual ascent of power had its apex in the Earl of Windsor. But unforeseen circumstances changed our plans for us, and occasioned the greater part of our numbers to be divided for the space of nearly two months, from the supreme chief. They had gone over in two distinct bodies; and on their arrival at Paris dissension arose between them.

They had found Paris a desert. When first the plague had appeared, the return of travellers and merchants, and communications by letter, informed us regularly of the ravages made by disease on the continent. But with the increased mortality this intercourse declined and ceased. Even in England itself communication from one part of the island to the other became slow and rare. No vessel stemmed the flood that divided Calais from Dover; or if some melancholy voyager, wishing to assure himself of the life or death of his relatives, put from the French shore to return among us, often the greedy ocean swallowed his little craft, or after a day or two he was infected by the disorder, and died before he could tell the tale of the desolation of France. We were therefore to a great degree ignorant of the state of things on the continent, and were not without some vague hope of finding numerous companions in its wide track. But the same causes that had so fearfully diminished the English nation had had even greater scope for mischief in the sister land. France was a blank; during the long line of road from Calais to Paris not one human being was found. In Paris there were a few, perhaps a hundred, who, resigned to their coming fate, flitted about the streets of the capital and assembled to converse of past times, with that vivacity and even gaiety that seldom deserts the individuals of this nation.

The English took uncontested possession of Paris. Its high houses and narrow streets were lifeless. A few pale figures were to be distinguished at the accustomed resort at the Tuileries; they wondered wherefore the islanders should approach their ill-fated city – for in the excess of wretchedness, the sufferers always imagine, that their part of the calamity is the bitterest, as, when enduring intense pain, we would exchange the particular torture we writhe under, for any other which should visit a different part of the frame. They listened to the account the emigrants gave of their motives for leaving their native land, with a shrug almost of disdain – "Return," they said, "return to your island, whose sea breezes, and division from the continent gives some promise of health; if Pestilence among you has slain its hundreds, with us it has slain its thousands. Are you not even now more numerous than we are? – A year ago you would have found only the sick burying the dead; now we are happier; for the pang of struggle has passed away, and the few you find here are patiently waiting the final blow. But you, who are not content to die, breathe no longer the air of France, or soon you will only be a part of her soil."

Thus, by menaces of the sword, they would have driven back those who had escaped from fire. But the peril left behind was deemed imminent by my countrymen; that before them doubtful and distant; and soon other feelings arose to obliterate fear, or to replace it by passions, that ought to have had no place among a brotherhood of unhappy survivors of the expiring world.

The more numerous division of emigrants, which arrived first at Paris, assumed a superiority of rank and power; the second party asserted their independence. A third was formed by a sectarian, a self-erected prophet, who, while he attributed all power and rule to God, strove to get the real command of his comrades into his own hands. This third division consisted of fewest individuals, but their purpose was more one, their obedience to their leader more entire, their fortitude and courage more unyielding and active.

During the whole progress of the plague, the teachers of religion were in possession of great power; a power of good, if rightly directed, or of incalculable mischief, if fanaticism or intolerance guided their efforts. In the present instance, a worse feeling than either of these actuated the leader. He was an impostor in the most determined sense of the term. A man who had in early life lost, through the indulgence of vicious propensities, all sense of rectitude or self-esteem; and who, when ambition was awakened in him, gave himself up to its influence unbridled by any scruple. His father had been a methodist preacher, an enthusiastic man with simple intentions; but whose pernicious doctrines of election and special grace had contributed to destroy all conscientious feeling in his son. During the progress of the pestilence he had entered upon various schemes, by which to acquire adherents and power. Adrian had discovered and defeated these attempts; but Adrian was absent; the wolf assumed the shepherd's garb, and the flock admitted the deception: he had formed a party during the few weeks he had been in Paris, who zealously propagated the creed of his divine mission, and believed that safety and salvation were to be afforded only to those who put their trust in him.

When once the spirit of dissension had arisen, the most frivolous causes gave it activity. The first party, on arriving at Paris, had taken possession of the Tuileries; chance and friendly feeling had induced the second to lodge near to them. A contest arose concerning the distribution of the pillage; the chiefs of the first division demanded that the whole should be placed at their disposal; with this assumption the opposite party refused to comply. When next the latter went to forage, the gates of Paris were shut on them. After overcoming this difficulty, they marched in a body to the Tuileries. They found that their enemies had been already expelled thence by the Elect, as the fanatical party designated themselves, who refused to admit any into the palace who did not first abjure obedience to all except God, and his delegate on earth, their chief. Such was the beginning of the strife, which at length proceeded so far, that the three divisions, armed, met in the Place Vendome, each resolved to subdue by force the resistance of its adversaries. They assembled, their muskets were loaded, and even pointed at the breasts of their so called enemies. One word had been sufficient; and there the last of mankind would have burthened their souls with the crime of murder, and dipt their hands in each other's blood. A sense of shame, a recollection that not only their cause, but the existence of the whole human race was at stake, entered the breast of the leader of the more numerous party. He was aware, that if the ranks were thinned, no other recruits could fill them up; that each man was as a priceless gem in a kingly crown, which if destroyed, the earth's deep entrails could yield no paragon. He was a young man, and had been hurried on by presumption, and the notion of his high rank and superiority to all other pretenders; now he repented his work, he felt that all the blood about to be shed would be on his head; with sudden impulse therefore he spurred his horse between the bands, and, having fixed a white handkerchief on the point of his uplifted sword, thus demanded parley; the opposite leaders obeyed the signal. He spoke with warmth; he reminded them of the oath all the chiefs had taken to submit to the Lord Protector; he declared their present meeting to be an act of treason and mutiny; he allowed that he had been hurried away by passion, but that a cooler moment had arrived; and he proposed that each party should send deputies to the Earl of Windsor, inviting his interference and offering submission to his decision. His offer was accepted so far, that each leader consented to command a retreat, and moreover agreed, that after the approbation of their several parties had been consulted, they should meet that night on some neutral spot to ratify the truce. At the meeting of the chiefs, this plan was finally concluded upon. The leader of the fanatics indeed refused to admit the arbitration of Adrian; he sent ambassadors, rather than deputies, to assert his claim, not plead his cause.

The truce was to continue until the first of February, when the bands were again to assemble on the Place Vendome; it was of the utmost consequence therefore that Adrian should arrive in Paris by that day, since an hair might turn the scale, and peace, scared away by intestine broils, might only return to watch by the silent dead. It was now the twenty-eighth of January; every vessel stationed near Dover had been beaten to pieces and destroyed by the furious storms I have commemorated. Our journey however would admit of no delay. That very night, Adrian, and I, and twelve others, either friends or attendants, put off from the English shore, in the boat that had brought over the deputies. We all took our turn at the oar; and the immediate occasion of our departure affording us abundant matter for conjecture and discourse, prevented the feeling that we left our native country, depopulate England, for the last time, to enter deeply into the minds of the greater part of our number. It was a serene starlight night, and the dark line of the English coast continued for some time visible at intervals, as we rose on the broad back of the waves. I exerted myself with my long oar to give swift impulse to our skiff; and, while the waters splashed with melancholy sound against its sides, I looked with sad affection on this last glimpse of sea-girt England, and strained my eyes not too soon to lose sight of the castellated cliff, which rose to protect the land of heroism and beauty from the inroads of ocean, that, turbulent as I had lately seen it, required such cyclopean walls for its repulsion. A solitary sea-gull winged its flight over our heads, to seek its nest in a cleft of the precipice. Yes, thou shalt revisit the land of thy birth, I thought, as I looked invidiously on the airy voyager; but we shall, never more! Tomb of Idris, farewell! Grave, in which my heart lies sepultured, farewell forever!

We were twelve hours at sea, and the heavy swell obliged us to exert all our strength. At length, by mere dint of rowing, we reached the French coast. The stars faded, and the grey morning cast a dim veil over the silver horns of the waning moon – the sun rose broad and red from the sea, as we walked over the sands to Calais. Our first care was to procure horses, and although wearied by our night of watching and toil, some of our party immediately went in quest of these in the wide fields of the unenclosed and now barren plain round Calais. We divided ourselves, like seamen, into watches, and some reposed, while others prepared the morning's repast. Our foragers returned at noon with only six horses – on these, Adrian and I, and four others, proceeded on our journey towards the great city, which its inhabitants had fondly named the capital of the civilized world. Our horses had become, through their long holiday, almost wild, and we crossed the plain round Calais with impetuous speed. From the height near Boulogne, I turned again to look on England; nature had cast a misty pall over her, her cliff was hidden – there was spread the watery barrier that divided us, never again to be crossed; she lay on the ocean plain,

In the great pool a swan's nest.

Ruined the nest, alas! the swans of Albion had passed away forever – an uninhabited rock in the wide Pacific, which had remained since the creation uninhabited, unnamed, unmarked, would be of as much account in the world's future history, as desert England.

Our journey was impeded by a thousand obstacles. As our horses grew tired, we had to seek for others; and hours were wasted, while we exhausted our artifices to allure some of these enfranchised slaves of man to resume the yoke; or as we went from stable to stable through the towns, hoping to find some who had not forgotten the shelter of their native stalls. Our ill success in procuring them, obliged us continually to leave someone of our companions behind; and on the first of February, Adrian and I entered Paris, wholly unaccompanied. The serene morning had dawned when we arrived at Saint Denis, and the sun was high, when the clamour of voices, and the clash, as we feared, of weapons, guided us to where our countrymen had assembled on the Place Vendome. We passed a knot of Frenchmen, who were talking earnestly of the madness of the insular invaders, and then coming by a sudden turn upon the Place, we saw the sun glitter on drawn swords and fixed bayonets, while yells and clamours rent the air. It was a scene of unaccustomed confusion in these days of depopulation Roused by fancied wrongs, and insulting scoffs, the opposite parties had rushed to attack each other; while the elect, drawn up apart, seemed to wait an opportunity to fall with better advantage on their foes, when they should have mutually weakened each other. A merciful power interposed, and no blood was shed; for, while the insane mob were in the very act of attack, the females, wives, mothers and daughters, rushed between; they seized the bridles; they embraced the knees of the horsemen, and hung on the necks, or enweaponed arms of their enraged relatives; the shrill female scream was mingled with the manly shout, and formed the wild clamour that welcomed us on our arrival.

Our voices could not be heard in the tumult; Adrian however was eminent for the white charger he rode; spurring him, he dashed into the midst of the throng: he was recognized, and a loud cry raised for England and the Protector. The late adversaries, warmed to affection at the sight of him, joined in heedless confusion, and surrounded him; the women kissed his hands, and the edges of his garments; nay, his horse received tribute of their embraces;

some wept their welcome; he appeared an angel of peace descended among them; and the only danger was, that his mortal nature would be demonstrated, by his suffocation from the kindness of his friends. His voice was at length heard, and obeyed; the crowd fell back; the chiefs alone rallied round him. I had seen Lord Raymond ride through his lines; his look of victory, and majestic mien obtained the respect and obedience of all: such was not the appearance or influence of Adrian. His slight figure, his fervent look, his gesture, more of deprecation than rule, were proofs that love, unmingled with fear, gave him dominion over the hearts of a multitude, who knew that he never flinched from danger, nor was actuated by other motives than care for the general welfare. No distinction was now visible between the two parties, late ready to shed each other's blood, for, though neither would submit to the other, they both yielded ready obedience to the Earl of Windsor.

One party however remained, cut off from the rest, which did not sympathize in the joy exhibited on Adrian's arrival, or imbibe the spirit of peace, which fell like dew upon the softened hearts of their countrymen. At the head of this assembly was a ponderous, dark-looking man, whose malign eye surveyed with gloating delight the stern looks of his followers. They had hitherto been inactive, but now, perceiving themselves to be forgotten in the universal jubilee, they advanced with threatening gestures: our friends had, as it were in wanton contention, attacked each other; they wanted but to be told that their cause was one, for it to become so: their mutual anger had been a fire of straw, compared to the slow-burning hatred they both entertained for these seceders, who seized a portion of the world to come, there to entrench and incastellate themselves, and to issue with fearful sally, and appalling denunciations, on the mere common children of the earth. The first advance of the little army of the elect reawakened their rage; they grasped their arms, and waited but their leader's signal to commence the attack, when the clear tones of Adrian's voice were heard, commanding them to fall back; with confused murmur and hurried retreat, as the wave ebbs clamorously from the sands it lately covered, our friends obeyed. Adrian rode singly into the space between the opposing bands; he approached the hostile leader, as requesting him to imitate his example, but his look was not obeyed, and the chief advanced, followed by his whole troop. There were many women among them, who seemed more eager and resolute than their male companions. They pressed round their leader, as if to shield him, while they loudly bestowed on him every sacred denomination and epithet of worship. Adrian met them half way; they halted: "What," he said, "do you seek? Do you require anyhting of us that we refuse to give, and that you are forced to acquire by arms and warfare?"

His questions were answered by a general cry, in which the words election, sin, and red right arm of God, could alone be heard.

Adrian looked expressly at their leader, saying, "Can you not silence your followers? Mine, you perceive, obey me."

The fellow answered by a scowl; and then, perhaps fearful that his people should become auditors of the debate he expected to ensue, he commanded them to fall back, and advanced by himself. "What, I again ask," said Adrian, "do you require of us?"

"Repentance," replied the man, whose sinister brow gathered clouds as he spoke. "Obedience to the will of the Most High, made manifest to these his Elected People. Do we not all die through your sins, O generation of unbelief, and have we not a right to demand of you repentance and obedience?"

"And if we refuse them, what then?" his opponent inquired mildly.

"Beware," cried the man, "God hears you, and will smite your stony heart in his wrath; his poisoned arrows fly, his dogs of death are unleashed! We will not perish unrevenged – and mighty will our avenger be, when he descends in visible majesty, and scatters destruction among you."

"My good fellow," said Adrian, with quiet scorn, "I wish that you were ignorant only, and I think it would be no difficult task to prove to you, that you speak of what you do not understand. On the present occasion however, it is enough for me to know that you seek nothing of us; and, heaven is our witness, we seek nothing of you. I should be sorry to embitter by strife the few days that we any of us may have here to live; when there," he pointed downwards, "we shall not be able to contend, while here we need not. Go home, or stay; pray to your God in your own mode; your friends may do the like. My orisons consist in peace and good will, in resignation and hope. Farewell!"

He bowed slightly to the angry disputant who was about to reply; and, turning his horse down Rue Saint Honore, called on his friends to follow him. He rode slowly, to give time to all to join him at the Barrier, and then issued his orders that those who yielded obedience to him, should rendezvous at Versailles. In the meantime he remained within the walls of Paris, until he had secured the safe retreat of all. In about a fortnight the remainder of the emigrants arrived from England, and they all repaired to Versailles; apartments were prepared for the family of the Protector in the Grand Trianon, and there, after the excitement of these events, we reposed amidst the luxuries of the departed Bourbons.

Chapter V

AFTER THE REPOSE of a few days, we held a council, to decide on our future movements. Our first plan had been to quit our wintry native latitude, and seek for our diminished numbers the luxuries and delights of a southern climate. We had not fixed on any precise spot as the termination of our wanderings; but a vague picture of perpetual spring, fragrant groves, and sparkling streams, floated in our imagination to entice us on. A variety of causes had detained us in England, and we had now arrived at the middle of February; if we pursued our original project, we should find ourselves in a worse situation than before, having exchanged our temperate climate for the intolerable heats of a summer in Egypt or Persia. We were therefore obliged to modify our plan, as the season continued to be inclement; and it was determined that we should await the arrival of spring in our present abode, and so order our future movements as to pass the hot months in the icy vallies of Switzerland, deferring our southern progress until the ensuing autumn, if such a season was ever again to be beheld by us.

The castle and town of Versailles afforded our numbers ample accommodation, and foraging parties took it by turns to supply our wants. There was a strange and appalling motley in the situation of these the last of the race. At first I likened it to a colony, which borne over the far seas, struck root for the first time in a new country. But where was the bustle and industry characteristic of such an assemblage; the rudely constructed dwelling, which was to suffice till a more commodious mansion could be built; the marking out of fields; the attempt at cultivation; the eager curiosity to discover unknown animals and herbs; the excursions for the sake of exploring the country? Our habitations were palaces our food was ready stored in granaries – there was no need of labour, no inquisitiveness, no restless desire to get on. If we had been assured that we should secure the lives of our present numbers, there would have been more vivacity and hope in our councils. We should have discussed as to the period when the existing produce for man's sustenance would no longer suffice for us, and what mode of life we should then adopt. We should have considered more carefully our future plans, and debated concerning the spot where we should in future dwell. But summer and the plague were near, and we dared not look forward. Every heart sickened at the thought of amusement; if the younger part of our community were ever impelled, by youthful and untamed hilarity, to enter on any dance or song, to cheer the melancholy time, they would suddenly break off, checked by a mournful look or agonizing sigh from any one among them, who was prevented by sorrows and losses from mingling in the festivity. If laughter echoed under our roof, yet the heart was vacant of joy; and, when ever it chanced that I witnessed such attempts at pastime, they increased instead of diminishing my sense of woe. In the midst of the pleasure-hunting throng, I would close my eyes, and see before me the obscure cavern, where was garnered the mortality of Idris, and the dead lay around, mouldering in hushed repose. When I again became aware of the present hour, softest melody of Lydian flute, or harmonious maze of graceful dance, was but as the demoniac chorus in the Wolf's Glen, and the caperings of the reptiles that surrounded the magic circle.

My dearest interval of peace occurred, when, released from the obligation of associating with the crowd, I could repose in the dear home where my children lived. Children I say, for the tenderest emotions of paternity bound me to Clara. She was now fourteen; sorrow, and deep insight into the scenes around her, calmed the restless spirit of girlhood; while the remembrance of her father whom she idolized, and respect for me and Adrian, implanted an high sense of duty in her young heart. Though serious she was not sad; the eager desire that makes us all, when young, plume our wings, and stretch our necks, that we may more swiftly alight tiptoe on the height of maturity, was subdued in her by early experience. All that she could spare of overflowing love from her parents' memory, and attention to her living relatives, was spent upon religion. This was the hidden law of her heart, which she concealed with childish reserve, and cherished the more because it was secret. What faith so entire, what charity so pure, what hope so fervent, as that of early youth? and she, all love, all tenderness and trust, who from infancy had been tossed on the wide sea of passion and misfortune, saw the finger of apparent divinity in all, and her best hope was to make herself acceptable to the power she worshipped. Evelyn was only five years old; his joyous heart was incapable of sorrow, and he enlivened our house with the innocent mirth incident to his years.

The aged Countess of Windsor had fallen from her dream of power, rank and grandeur; she had been suddenly seized with the conviction, that love was the only good of life, virtue the only ennobling distinction and enriching wealth. Such a lesson had been taught her by the dead lips of her neglected daughter; and she devoted herself, with all the fiery violence of her character, to the obtaining the affection of the remnants of her family. In early years the heart of Adrian had been chilled towards her; and, though he observed a due respect, her coldness, mixed with the recollection of disappointment and madness, caused him to feel even pain in her society. She saw this, and yet determined to win his love; the obstacle served the rather to excite her ambition. As Henry, Emperor of Germany, lay in the snow before Pope Leo's gate for three winter days and nights, so did she in humility wait before the icy barriers of his closed heart, till he, the servant of love, and prince of tender courtesy, opened it wide for her admittance, bestowing, with fervency and gratitude, the tribute of filial affection she merited. Her understanding, courage, and presence of mind, became powerful auxiliaries to him in the difficult task of ruling the tumultuous crowd, which were subjected to his control, in truth by a single hair.

The principal circumstances that disturbed our tranquillity during this interval, originated in the vicinity of the impostor-prophet and his followers. They continued to reside at Paris; but missionaries from among them often visited Versailles – and such was the power of assertions, however false, yet vehemently iterated, over the ready credulity of the ignorant and fearful, that they seldom failed in drawing over to their party some from among our numbers. An instance of this nature coming immediately under our notice, we were led to consider the miserable state in which we should leave our countrymen, when we should, at the approach of summer, move on towards Switzerland, and leave a deluded crew behind us in the hands of their miscreant leader. The sense of the smallness of our numbers, and expectation of decrease, pressed upon us; and, while it would be a subject of congratulation to ourselves to add one to our party, it would be doubly gratifying to rescue from the pernicious influence of superstition and unrelenting tyranny, the victims that now, though voluntarily enchained, groaned beneath it. If we had considered the preacher as sincere in a belief of his own denunciations, or only moderately actuated by kind feeling in the exercise of his assumed powers, we should have immediately addressed ourselves to him, and endeavoured with our best arguments to soften and humanize his views. But he was instigated by ambition, he desired to rule over these last stragglers from the fold of death; his projects went so far, as to cause him to calculate that, if, from these crushed remains, a few survived, so that a new race should spring up, he, by holding tight the reins of belief, might be remembered by the post-pestilential race as a patriarch, a prophet, nay a deity; such as of old among the post-diluvians were Jupiter the conqueror, Serapis the lawgiver, and Vishnou the preserver. These ideas made him inflexible in his rule, and violent in his hate of any who presumed to share with him his usurped empire.

It is a strange fact, but incontestible, that the philanthropist, who ardent in his desire to do good, who patient, reasonable and gentle, yet disdains to use other argument than truth, has less influence over men's minds, than he who, grasping and selfish, refuses not to adopt any means, nor awaken any passion, nor diffuse any falsehood, for the advancement of his cause. If this from time immemorial has been the case, the contrast was infinitely greater, now that the one could bring harrowing fears and transcendent hopes into play; while the other had few hopes to hold forth, nor could influence the imagination to diminish the fears which he himself was the first to entertain. The preacher had persuaded his followers, that their escape from the plague, the salvation of their children, and the rise of a new race of men from their seed, depended on their faith in, and their submission to him. They greedily imbibed this belief; and their over-weening credulity even rendered them eager to make converts to the same faith.

How to seduce any individuals from such an alliance of fraud, was a frequent subject of Adrian's meditations and discourse. He formed many plans for the purpose; but his own troop kept him in full occupation to ensure their fidelity and safety; beside which the preacher was as cautious and prudent, as he was cruel. His victims lived under the strictest rules and laws, which either entirely imprisoned them within the Tuileries, or let them out in such numbers, and under such leaders, as precluded the possibility of controversy. There was one among them however whom I resolved to save; she had been known to us in happier days; Idris had loved her; and her excellent nature made it peculiarly lamentable that she should be sacrificed by this merciless cannibal of souls.

This man had between two and three hundred persons enlisted under his banners. More than half of them were women; there were about fifty children of all ages; and not more than eighty men. They were mostly drawn from that which, when such distinctions existed, was denominated the lower rank of society. The exceptions consisted of a few high-born females, who, panic-struck, and tamed by sorrow, had joined him. Among these was one, young, lovely, and enthusiastic, whose very goodness made her a more easy victim. I have mentioned her before: Juliet, the youngest daughter, and now sole relic of the ducal house of L—. There are some beings, whom fate seems to select on whom to pour, in unmeasured portion, the vials of her wrath, and whom she bathes even to the lips in misery. Such a one was the ill-starred Juliet. She had lost her indulgent parents, her brothers and sisters, companions of her youth; in one fell swoop they had been carried off from her. Yet she had again dared to call herself happy; united to her admirer, to him who possessed and filled her whole heart, she yielded to the lethean powers of love, and knew and felt only his life and presence. At the very time when with keen delight she welcomed the tokens of maternity, this sole prop of her life failed, her husband died of the plague. For a time she had been lulled in insanity; the birth of her child restored her to the cruel reality of things, but gave her at the same time an object for whom to preserve at once life and reason. Every friend and relative had died off, and she was reduced to solitude and penury; deep melancholy and angry impatience distorted her judgment, so that she could not persuade herself to disclose her distress to us. When she heard of the plan of universal emigration, she resolved to remain behind with her child, and alone in wide England to live or die, as fate might decree, beside the grave of her beloved. She had hidden herself in one of the many empty habitations of London; it was she who rescued my Idris on the fatal twentieth of November, though my immediate danger, and the subsequent illness of Idris, caused us to forget our hapless friend. This circumstance had however brought her again in contact with her fellow-creatures; a slight illness of her infant, proved to her that she was still bound to humanity by an indestructible tie; to preserve this little creature's life became the object of her being, and she joined the first division of migrants who went over to Paris.

She became an easy prey to the methodist; her sensibility and acute fears rendered her accessible to every impulse; her love for her child made her eager to cling to the merest straw held out to save him. Her mind, once unstrung, and now tuned by roughest inharmonious hands, made her credulous: beautiful as fabled goddess, with voice of unrivalled sweetness, burning with new lighted enthusiasm, she became a stedfast proselyte, and powerful auxiliary to the leader of the elect. I had remarked her in the crowd, on the day we met on the Place Vendome; and, recollecting suddenly her providential rescue of my lost one, on the night of the twentieth of November, I reproached myself for my neglect and ingratitude, and felt impelled to leave no means that I could adopt untried, to recall her to her better self, and rescue her from the fangs of the hypocrite destroyer.

I will not, at this period of my story, record the artifices I used to penetrate the asylum of the Tuileries, or give what would be a tedious account of my stratagems, disappointments, and perseverance. I at last succeeded in entering these walls, and roamed its halls and corridors in eager hope to find my selected convert. In the evening I contrived to mingle unobserved with the congregation, which assembled in the chapel to listen to the crafty and eloquent harangue of their prophet. I saw Juliet near him. Her dark eyes, fearfully impressed with the restless glare of madness, were fixed on him; she held her infant, not yet a year old, in her arms; and care of it alone could distract her attention from the words to which she eagerly listened. After the sermon was over, the congregation dispersed; all quitted the chapel except she whom

I sought; her babe had fallen asleep; so she placed it on a cushion, and sat on the floor beside, watching its tranquil slumber.

I presented myself to her; for a moment natural feeling produced a sentiment of gladness, which disappeared again, when with ardent and affectionate exhortation I besought her to accompany me in flight from this den of superstition and misery. In a moment she relapsed into the delirium of fanaticism, and, but that her gentle nature forbade, would have loaded me with execrations. She conjured me, she commanded me to leave her – "Beware, O beware," she cried, "fly while yet your escape is practicable. Now you are safe; but strange sounds and inspirations come on me at times, and if the Eternal should in awful whisper reveal to me his will, that to save my child you must be sacrificed, I would call in the satellites of him you call the tyrant; they would tear you limb from limb; nor would I hallow the death of him whom Idris loved, by a single tear."

She spoke hurriedly, with tuneless voice, and wild look; her child awoke, and, frightened, began to cry; each sob went to the ill-fated mother's heart, and she mingled the epithets of endearment she addressed to her infant, with angry commands that I should leave her. Had I had the means, I would have risked all, have torn her by force from the murderer's den, and trusted to the healing balm of reason and affection. But I had no choice, no power even of longer struggle; steps were heard along the gallery, and the voice of the preacher drew near. Juliet, straining her child in a close embrace, fled by another passage. Even then I would have followed her; but my foe and his satellites entered; I was surrounded, and taken prisoner.

I remembered the menace of the unhappy Juliet, and expected the full tempest of the man's vengeance, and the awakened wrath of his followers, to fall instantly upon me. I was questioned. My answers were simple and sincere. "His own mouth condemns him," exclaimed the impostor; "he confesses that his intention was to seduce from the way of salvation our well-beloved sister in God; away with him to the dungeon; tomorrow he dies the death; we are manifestly called upon to make an example, tremendous and appalling, to scare the children of sin from our asylum of the saved."

My heart revolted from his hypocritical jargon: but it was unworthy of me to combat in words with the ruffian; and my answer was cool; while, far from being possessed with fear, methought, even at the worst, a man true to himself, courageous and determined, could fight his way, even from the boards of the scaffold, through the herd of these misguided maniacs. "Remember," I said, "who I am; and be well assured that I shall not die unavenged. Your legal magistrate, the Lord Protector, knew of my design, and is aware that I am here; the cry of blood will reach him, and you and your miserable victims will long lament the tragedy you are about to act."

My antagonist did not deign to reply, even by a look; – "You know your duty," he said to his comrades, "obey."

In a moment I was thrown on the earth, bound, blindfolded, and hurried away – liberty of limb and sight was only restored to me, when, surrounded by dungeon-walls, dark and impervious, I found myself a prisoner and alone.

Such was the result of my attempt to gain over the proselyte of this man of crime; I could not conceive that he would dare put me to death. – Yet I was in his hands; the path of his ambition had ever been dark and cruel; his power was founded upon fear; the one word which might cause me to die, unheard, unseen, in the obscurity of my dungeon, might be easier to speak than the deed of mercy to act. He would not risk probably a public execution; but a private assassination would at once terrify any of my companions from attempting a like feat, at the same time that a cautious line of conduct might enable him to avoid the enquiries and the vengeance of Adrian.

Two months ago, in a vault more obscure than the one I now inhabited, I had revolved the design of quietly laying me down to die; now I shuddered at the approach of fate. My imagination was busied in shaping forth the kind of death he would inflict. Would he allow me to wear out life with famine; or was the food administered to me to be medicined with death? Would he steal on me in my sleep; or should I contend to the last with my murderers, knowing, even while I struggled, that I must be overcome? I lived upon an earth whose diminished population a child's arithmetic might number; I had lived through long months with death stalking close at my side, while at intervals the shadow of his skeleton-shape darkened my path. I had believed that I despised the grim phantom, and laughed his power to scorn.

Any other fate I should have met with courage, nay, have gone out gallantly to encounter. But to be murdered thus at the midnight hour by cold-blooded assassins, no friendly hand to close my eyes, or receive my parting blessing – to die in combat, hate and execration – ah, why, my angel love, didst thou restore me to life, when already I had stepped within the portals of the tomb, now that so soon again I was to be flung back a mangled corpse!

Hours passed – centuries. Could I give words to the many thoughts which occupied me in endless succession during this interval, I should fill volumes. The air was dank, the dungeon-floor mildewed and icy cold; hunger came upon me too, and no sound reached me from without. Tomorrow the ruffian had declared that I should die. When would tomorrow come? Was it not already here?

My door was about to be opened. I heard the key turn, and the bars and bolts slowly removed. The opening of intervening passages permitted sounds from the interior of the palace to reach me; and I heard the clock strike one. They come to murder me, I thought; this hour does not befit a public execution. I drew myself up against the wall opposite the entrance; I collected my forces, I rallied my courage, I would not fall a tame prey. Slowly the door receded on its hinges – I was ready to spring forward to seize and grapple with the intruder, till the sight of who it was changed at once the temper of my mind. It was Juliet herself; pale and trembling she stood, a lamp in her hand, on the threshold of the dungeon, looking at me with wistful countenance. But in a moment she re-assumed her self-possession; and her languid eyes recovered their brilliancy. She said, "I am come to save you, Verney."

"And yourself also," I cried: "dearest friend, can we indeed be saved?"

"Not a word," she replied, "follow me!"

I obeyed instantly. We threaded with light steps many corridors, ascended several flights of stairs, and passed through long galleries; at the end of one she unlocked a low portal; a rush of wind extinguished our lamp; but, in lieu of it, we had the blessed moon-beams and the open face of heaven. Then first Juliet spoke: "You are safe," she said, "God bless you! – farewell!"

I seized her reluctant hand – "Dear friend," I cried, "misguided victim, do you not intend to escape with me? Have you not risked all in facilitating my flight? and do you think, that I will permit you to return, and suffer alone the effects of that miscreant's rage? Never!"

"Do not fear for me," replied the lovely girl mournfully, "and do not imagine that without the consent of our chief you could be without these walls. It is he that has saved you; he assigned to me the part of leading you hither, because I am best acquainted with your motives for coming here, and can best appreciate his mercy in permitting you to depart."

"And are you," I cried, "the dupe of this man? He dreads me alive as an enemy, and dead he fears my avengers. By favouring this clandestine escape he preserves a shew of consistency to his followers; but mercy is far from his heart. Do you forget his artifices, his cruelty, and fraud? As I am free, so are you. Come, Juliet, the mother of our lost Idris will welcome you, the noble Adrian will rejoice to receive you; you will find peace and love, and better hopes than fanaticism can afford. Come, and fear not; long before day we shall be at Versailles; close the door on this abode of crime – come, sweet Juliet, from hypocrisy and guilt to the society of the affectionate and good."

I spoke hurriedly, but with fervour: and while with gentle violence I drew her from the portal, some thought, some recollection of past scenes of youth and happiness, made her listen and yield to me; suddenly she broke away with a piercing shriek: "My child, my child! he has my child; my darling girl is my hostage."

She darted from me into the passage; the gate closed between us – she was left in the fangs of this man of crime, a prisoner, still to inhale the pestilential atmosphere which adhered to his demoniac nature; the unimpeded breeze played on my cheek, the moon shone graciously upon me, my path was free. Glad to have escaped, yet melancholy in my very joy, I retrod my steps to Versailles.

Chapter VI

EVENTFUL winter passed; winter, the respite of our ills. By degrees the sun, which with slant beams had before yielded the more extended reign to night, lengthened his diurnal journey, and mounted his highest throne, at once the fosterer of earth's new beauty, and her lover. We who, like flies that congregate upon a dry rock at the ebbing of the tide, had played wantonly with time, allowing our passions, our hopes, and our mad desires to rule us, now heard the approaching roar of the ocean of destruction, and would have fled to some sheltered crevice, before the first wave broke over us. We resolved without delay, to commence our journey to Switzerland; we became eager to leave France. Under the icy vaults of the glaciers, beneath the shadow of the pines, the swinging of whose mighty branches was arrested by a load of snow; beside the streams whose intense cold proclaimed their origin to be from the slow-melting piles of congelated waters, amidst frequent storms which might purify the air, we should find health, if in truth health were not herself diseased.

We began our preparations at first with alacrity. We did not now bid adieu to our native country, to the graves of those we loved, to the flowers, and streams, and trees, which had lived beside us from infancy. Small sorrow would be ours on leaving Paris. A scene of shame, when we remembered our late contentions, and thought that we left behind a flock of miserable, deluded victims, bending under the tyranny of a selfish impostor. Small pangs should we feel in leaving the gardens, woods, and halls of the palaces of the Bourbons at Versailles, which we feared would soon be tainted by the dead, when we looked forward to vallies lovelier than any garden, to mighty forests and halls, built not for mortal majesty, but palaces of nature's own, with the Alp of marmoreal whiteness for their walls, the sky for their roof.

Yet our spirits flagged, as the day drew near which we had fixed for our departure. Dire visions and evil auguries, if such things were, thickened around us, so that in vain might men say –

These are their reasons, they are natural,

we felt them to be ominous, and dreaded the future event enchained to them. That the night owl should screech before the noon-day sun, that the hard-winged bat should wheel around the bed of beauty, that muttering thunder should in early spring startle the cloudless air, that sudden and exterminating blight should fall on the tree and shrub, were unaccustomed, but physical events, less horrible than the mental creations of almighty fear. Some had sight of funeral processions, and faces all begrimed with tears, which flitted through the long avenues of the gardens, and drew aside the curtains of the sleepers at dead of night. Some heard wailing and cries in the air; a mournful chaunt would stream through the dark atmosphere, as if spirits above sang the requiem of the human race. What was there in all this, but that fear created other senses within our frames, making us see, hear, and feel what was not? What was this, but the action of diseased imaginations and childish credulity? So might it be; but what was most real, was the existence of these very fears; the staring looks of horror, the faces pale even to ghastliness, the voices struck dumb with harrowing dread, of those among us who saw and heard these things. Of this number was Adrian, who knew the delusion, yet could not cast off the clinging terror. Even ignorant infancy appeared with timorous shrieks and convulsions to acknowledge the presence of unseen powers. We must go: in change of scene, in occupation, and such security as we still hoped to find, we should discover a cure for these gathering horrors.

On mustering our company, we found them to consist of fourteen hundred souls, men, women, and children. Until now therefore, we were undiminished in numbers, except by the desertion of those who had attached themselves to the impostor-prophet, and remained behind in Paris. About fifty French joined us. Our order of march was easily arranged; the ill success which had attended our division, determined Adrian to keep all in one body. I, with a hundred men, went forward first as purveyor, taking the road of the Cote d'Or, through Auxerre, Dijon, Dole, over the Jura to Geneva. I was to make arrangements, at every ten miles, for the accommodation of such numbers as I found the town or village would receive, leaving behind a messenger with a written order, signifying how many were to be quartered there. The remainder of our tribe was then divided into bands of fifty each, every division containing eighteen men, and the remainder, consisting of women and children. Each of these was headed by an officer, who carried the roll of names, by which they were each day to be mustered. If the numbers were divided at night, in the morning those in the van waited for those in the rear. At each of the large towns before mentioned, we were all to assemble; and a conclave of the principal officers would hold council for the general weal. I went first, as I said; Adrian last. His mother, with Clara and Evelyn under her protection, remained also with him. Thus our order being determined, I departed. My plan was to go at first no further than Fontainebleau, where in a few days I should be joined by Adrian, before I took flight again further eastward.

My friend accompanied me a few miles from Versailles. He was sad; and, in a tone of unaccustomed despondency, uttered a prayer for our speedy arrival among the Alps, accompanied with an expression of vain regret that we were not already there. "In that case," I observed, "we can quicken our march; why adhere to a plan whose dilatory proceeding you already disapprove?"

"Nay," replied he, "it is too late now. A month ago, and we were masters of ourselves; now –" he turned his face from me; though gathering twilight had already veiled its expression, he turned it yet more away, as he added – "a man died of the plague last night!"

He spoke in a smothered voice, then suddenly clasping his hands, he exclaimed, "Swiftly, most swiftly advances the last hour for us all; as the stars vanish before the sun, so will his near approach destroy us. I have done my best; with grasping hands and impotent strength, I have hung on the wheel of the chariot of plague; but she drags me along with it, while, like Juggernaut, she proceeds crushing out the being of all who strew the high road of life. Would that it were over – would that her procession achieved, we had all entered the tomb together!"

Tears streamed from his eyes. "Again and again," he continued, "will the tragedy be acted; again I must hear the groans of the dying, the wailing of the survivors; again witness the pangs, which, consummating all, envelope an eternity in their evanescent existence. Why am I reserved for this? Why the tainted wether of the flock, am I not struck to earth among the first? It is hard, very hard, for one of woman born to endure all that I endure!"

Hitherto, with an undaunted spirit, and an high feeling of duty and worth, Adrian had fulfilled his self-imposed task. I had contemplated him with reverence, and a fruitless desire of imitation. I now offered a few words of encouragement and sympathy. He hid his face in his hands, and while he strove to calm himself, he ejaculated, "For a few months, yet for a few months more, let not, O God, my heart fail, or my courage be bowed down; let not sights of intolerable misery madden this half-crazed brain, or cause this frail heart to beat against its prison-bound, so that it burst. I have believed it to be my destiny to guide and rule the last of the race of man, till death extinguish my government; and to this destiny I submit.

"Pardon me, Verney, I pain you, but I will no longer complain. Now I am myself again, or rather I am better than myself. You have known how from my childhood aspiring thoughts and high desires have warred with inherent disease and overstrained sensitiveness, till the latter became victors. You know how I placed this wasted feeble hand on the abandoned helm of human government. I have been visited at times by intervals of fluctuation; yet, until now, I have felt as if a superior and indefatigable spirit had taken up its abode within me or rather incorporated itself with my weaker being. The holy visitant has for a time slept, perhaps to show me how powerless I am without its inspiration. Yet, stay for a while, O Power of goodness and strength; disdain not yet this rent shrine of fleshly mortality, O immortal Capability! While one fellow creature remains to whom aid can be afforded, stay by and prop your shattered, falling engine!"

His vehemence, and voice broken by irrepressible sighs, sunk to my heart; his eyes gleamed in the gloom of night like two earthly stars; and, his form dilating, his countenance beaming, truly it almost seemed as if at his eloquent appeal a more than mortal spirit entered his frame, exalting him above humanity. He turned quickly towards me, and held out his hand. "Farewell, Verney," he cried, "brother of my love, farewell; no other weak expression must cross these lips, I am alive again: to our tasks, to our combats with our unvanquishable foe, for to the last I will struggle against her."

He grasped my hand, and bent a look on me, more fervent and animated than any smile; then turning his horse's head, he touched the animal with the spur, and was out of sight in a moment.

A man last night had died of the plague. The quiver was not emptied, nor the bow unstrung. We stood as marks, while Parthian Pestilence aimed and shot, insatiated by conquest, unobstructed by the heaps of slain. A sickness of the soul, contagious even to my physical mechanism, came over me. My knees knocked together, my teeth chattered, the current of my blood, clotted by sudden cold, painfully forced its way from my heavy heart. I did not fear for myself, but it was misery to think that we could not even save this remnant. That those I loved might in a few days be as clay-cold as Idris in her antique tomb; nor could strength of body or energy of mind ward off the blow. A sense of degradation came over me. Did God create man, merely in the end to become dead earth in the midst of healthful vegetating nature? Was he of no more account to his Maker, than a field of corn blighted in the ear? Were our proud dreams thus to fade? Our name was written 'a little lower than the angels;' and, behold, we were no better than ephemera. We had called ourselves the 'paragon of animals,' and, lo! we were a 'quint-essence of dust.' We repined that the pyramids had outlasted the embalmed body of their builder. Alas! the mere shepherd's hut of straw we passed on the road, contained in its structure the principle of greater longevity than the whole race of man. How reconcile this sad change to our past aspirations, to our apparent powers!

Sudden an internal voice, articulate and clear, seemed to say: Thus from eternity, it was decreed: the steeds that bear Time onwards had this hour and this fulfilment enchained to them, since the void brought forth its burthen. Would you read backwards the unchangeable laws of Necessity?

Mother of the world! Servant of the Omnipotent! eternal, changeless Necessity! who with busy fingers sittest ever weaving the indissoluble chain of events! – I will not murmur at thy acts. If my human mind cannot acknowledge that all that is, is right; yet since what is, must be, I will sit amidst the ruins and smile. Truly we were not born to enjoy, but to submit, and to hope.

Will not the reader tire, if I should minutely describe our long-drawn journey from Paris to Geneva? If, day by day, I should record, in the form of a journal, the thronging miseries of our lot, could my hand write, or language afford words to express, the variety of our woe; the hustling and crowding of one deplorable event upon another? Patience, oh reader! whoever thou art, wherever thou dwellest, whether of race spiritual, or, sprung from some surviving pair, thy nature will be human, thy habitation the earth; thou wilt here read of the acts of the extinct race, and wilt ask wonderingly, if they, who suffered what thou findest recorded, were of frail flesh and soft organization like thyself. Most true, they were – weep therefore; for surely, solitary being, thou wilt be of gentle disposition; shed compassionate tears; but the while lend thy attention to the tale, and learn the deeds and sufferings of thy predecessors.

Yet the last events that marked our progress through France were so full of strange horror and gloomy misery, that I dare not pause too long in the narration. If I were to dissect each incident, every small fragment of a second would contain an harrowing tale, whose minutest word would curdle the blood in thy young veins. It is right that I should erect for thy instruction this monument of the foregone race; but not that I should drag thee through the wards of an hospital, nor the secret chambers of the charnel-house. This tale, therefore, shall be rapidly unfolded. Images of destruction, pictures of despair, the procession of the last triumph of death, shall be drawn before thee, swift as the rack driven by the north wind along the blotted splendour of the sky.

Weed-grown fields, desolate towns, the wild approach of riderless horses had now become habitual to my eyes; nay, sights far worse, of the unburied dead, and human forms which were strewed on the road side, and on the steps of once frequented habitations, where,

Through the flesh that wastes away
Beneath the parching sun, the whitening bones
Start forth, and moulder in the sable dust.

Sights like these had become – ah, woe the while! so familiar, that we had ceased to shudder, or spur our stung horses to sudden speed, as we passed them. France in its best days, at least that part of France through which we travelled, had been a cultivated desert, and the absence of enclosures, of cottages, and even of peasantry, was saddening to a traveller from sunny Italy, or busy England. Yet the towns were frequent and lively, and the cordial politeness and ready smile of the wooden-shoed peasant restored good humour to the splenetic. Now, the old woman sat no more at the door with her distaff – the lank beggar no longer asked charity in courtier-like phrase; nor on holidays did the peasantry thread with slow grace the mazes of the dance. Silence, melancholy bride of death, went in procession with him from town to town through the spacious region.

We arrived at Fontainebleau, and speedily prepared for the reception of our friends. On mustering our numbers for the night, three were found missing. When I enquired for them, the man to whom I spoke, uttered the word "plague," and fell at my feet in convulsions; he also was infected. There were hard faces around me; for among my troop were sailors who had crossed the line times unnumbered, soldiers who, in Russia and far America, had suffered famine, cold and danger, and men still sterner-featured, once nightly depredators in our over-grown metropolis; men bred from their cradle to see the whole machine of society at work for their destruction. I looked round, and saw upon the faces of all horror and despair written in glaring characters.

We passed four days at Fontainebleau. Several sickened and died, and in the meantime neither Adrian nor any of our friends appeared. My own troop was in commotion; to reach Switzerland, to plunge into rivers of snow, and to dwell in caves of ice, became the mad desire of all. Yet we had promised to wait for the Earl; and he came not. My people demanded to be led forward – rebellion, if so we might call what was the mere casting away of straw-formed shackles, appeared manifestly among them. They would away on the word without a leader. The only chance of safety, the only hope of preservation from every form of indescribable suffering, was our keeping together. I told them this; while the most determined among them answered with sullenness, that they could take care of themselves, and replied to my entreaties with scoffs and menaces.

At length, on the fifth day, a messenger arrived from Adrian, bearing letters, which directed us to proceed to Auxerre, and there await his arrival, which would only be deferred for a few days. Such was the tenor of his public letters. Those privately delivered to me, detailed at length the difficulties of his situation, and left the arrangement of my future plans to my own discretion. His account of the state of affairs at Versailles was brief, but the oral communications of his messenger filled up his omissions, and shewed me that perils of the most frightful nature were gathering around him. At first the re-awakening of the plague had been concealed; but the number of deaths increasing, the secret was divulged, and the destruction already achieved, was exaggerated by the fears of the survivors. Some emissaries of the enemy of mankind, the accursed Impostors, were among them instilling their doctrine that safety and life could only be ensured by submission to their chief; and they succeeded so well, that soon, instead of desiring to proceed to Switzerland, the major part of the multitude, weak-minded women, and dastardly men, desired to return to Paris, and, by ranging themselves under the banners of the so called prophet, and by a cowardly worship of the principle of evil, to purchase respite, as they hoped, from impending death. The discord and tumult induced by these conflicting fears and passions, detained Adrian. It required all his ardour in pursuit of an object, and his patience under difficulties, to calm and animate such a number of his followers, as might counterbalance the panic of the rest, and lead them back to the means from which alone safety could be derived. He had hoped immediately to follow me; but, being defeated in this intention, he sent his messenger urging me to secure my own troop at such a distance from Versailles, as to prevent the contagion of rebellion from reaching them; promising, at the same time, to join me the moment a favourable occasion should occur, by means of which he could withdraw the main body of the emigrants from the evil influence at present exercised over them.

I was thrown into a most painful state of uncertainty by these communications. My first impulse was that we should all return to Versailles, there to assist in extricating our chief from his perils. I accordingly assembled my troop, and proposed to them this retrograde movement, instead of the continuation of our journey to Auxerre. With one voice they refused to comply. The notion circulated among them was, that the ravages of the plague alone detained the Protector; they opposed his order to my request; they came to a resolve to proceed without me, should I refuse to accompany them. Argument and adjuration were lost on these dastards. The continual diminution of their own numbers, effected by pestilence, added a sting to their dislike of delay; and my opposition only served to bring their resolution to a crisis. That same evening they departed towards Auxerre. Oaths, as from soldiers to their general, had been taken by them: these they broke. I also had engaged myself not to desert them; it appeared to me inhuman to ground any infraction of my word on theirs. The same spirit that caused them to rebel against me, would impel them to desert each other; and the most dreadful sufferings would be the consequence of their journey in their present unordered and chiefless array. These feelings for a time were paramount; and, in obedience to them, I accompanied the rest towards Auxerre. We arrived the same night at Villeneuve-la-Guiard, a town at the distance of four posts from Fontainebleau. When my companions had retired to rest, and I was left alone to revolve and ruminate upon the intelligence I received of Adrian's situation, another view of the subject presented itself to me. What was I doing, and what was the object of my present movements? Apparently I was to lead this troop of selfish and lawless men towards Switzerland, leaving behind my family and my selected friend, which, subject as they were hourly to the death that threatened to all, I might never see again. Was it not my first duty to assist the Protector, setting an example of attachment and duty? At a crisis, such as the one I had reached, it is very difficult to balance nicely opposing interests, and that towards which our inclinations lead us, obstinately assumes the appearance of selfishness, even when we meditate a sacrifice. We are easily led at such times to make a compromise of the question; and this was my present resource. I resolved that very night to ride to Versailles; if I found affairs less desperate than I now deemed them, I would return without delay to my troop; I had a vague idea that my arrival at that town, would occasion some sensation more or less strong, of which we might profit, for the purpose of leading forward the vacillating multitude – at least no time was to be lost – I visited the stables, I saddled my favourite horse, and vaulting on his back, without giving myself time for further reflection or hesitation, quitted Villeneuve-la-Guiard on my return to Versailles.

I was glad to escape from my rebellious troop, and to lose sight for a time, of the strife of evil with good, where the former forever remained triumphant. I was stung almost to madness by my uncertainty concerning the fate of Adrian, and grew reckless of any event, except what might lose or preserve my unequalled friend. With an heavy heart, that sought relief in the rapidity of my course, I rode through the night to Versailles. I spurred my horse, who addressed his free limbs to speed, and tossed his gallant head in pride. The constellations reeled swiftly by, swiftly each tree and stone and landmark fled past my onward career. I bared my head to the rushing wind, which bathed my brow in delightful coolness. As I lost sight of Villeneuve-la-Guiard, I forgot the sad drama of human misery; methought it was happiness enough to live, sensitive the while of the beauty of the verdure-clad earth, the star-bespangled sky, and the tameless wind that lent animation to the whole. My horse grew tired – and I, forgetful of his fatigue, still as he lagged, cheered him with my voice, and urged him with the spur. He was a gallant animal, and I did not wish to exchange him for any chance beast I might light on, leaving him never to be refound. All night we went forward; in the morning he became sensible that we approached Versailles, to reach which as his home, he mustered his flagging strength. The distance we had come was not less than fifty miles, yet he shot down the long Boulevards swift as an arrow; poor fellow, as I dismounted at the gate of the castle, he sunk on his knees, his eyes were covered with a film, he fell on his side, a few gasps inflated his noble chest, and he died. I saw him expire with an anguish, unaccountable even to myself, the spasm was as the wrenching of some limb in agonizing torture, but it was brief as it was intolerable. I forgot him, as I swiftly darted through the open portal, and up the majestic stairs of this castle of victories – heard Adrian's voice – O fool! O woman nurtured, effeminate and contemptible being – I heard his voice, and answered it with convulsive shrieks; I rushed into the Hall of Hercules, where he stood surrounded by a crowd, whose eyes, turned in wonder on me, reminded me that on the stage of the world, a man must repress such girlish extacies. I would have given worlds to have embraced him; I dared not – Half in exhaustion, half voluntarily, I threw myself at my length on the ground – dare I disclose the truth to the gentle offspring of solitude? I did so, that I might kiss the dear and sacred earth he trod.

I found everything in a state of tumult. An emissary of the leader of the elect, had been so worked up by his chief, and by his own fanatical creed, as to make an attempt on the life of the Protector and preserver of lost mankind. His hand was arrested while in the act of poignarding the Earl; this circumstance had caused the clamour I heard on my arrival at the castle, and the confused assembly of persons that I found assembled in the Salle d'Hercule. Although superstition and demoniac fury had crept among the emigrants, yet several adhered with fidelity to their noble chieftain; and many, whose faith and love had been unhinged by fear, felt all their latent affection rekindled by this detestable attempt. A phalanx of faithful breasts closed round him; the wretch, who, although a prisoner and in bonds, vaunted his design, and madly claimed the crown of martyrdom, would have been torn to pieces, had not his intended victim interposed. Adrian, springing forward, shielded him with his own person, and commanded with energy the submission of his infuriate friends – at this moment I had entered.

Discipline and peace were at length restored in the castle; and then Adrian went from house to house, from troop to troop, to soothe the disturbed minds of his followers, and recall them to their ancient obedience. But the fear of immediate death was still rife amongst these survivors of a world's destruction; the horror occasioned by the attempted assassination, past away; each eye turned towards Paris. Men love a prop so well, that they will lean on a pointed poisoned spear; and such was he, the impostor, who, with fear of hell for his scourge, most ravenous wolf, played the driver to a credulous flock.

It was a moment of suspense, that shook even the resolution of the unyielding friend of man. Adrian for one moment was about to give in, to cease the struggle, and quit, with a few adherents, the deluded crowd, leaving them a miserable prey to their passions, and to the worse tyrant who excited them. But again, after a brief fluctuation of purpose, he resumed his courage and resolves, sustained by the singleness of his purpose, and the untried spirit of benevolence which animated him. At this moment, as an omen of excellent import, his wretched enemy pulled destruction on his head, destroying with his own hands the dominion he had erected.

His grand hold upon the minds of men, took its rise from the doctrine inculcated by him, that those who believed in, and followed him, were the remnant to be saved, while all the rest of mankind were marked out for death. Now, at the time of the Flood, the omnipotent repented him that he had created man, and as then with water, now with the arrows of pestilence, was about to annihilate all, except those who obeyed his decrees, promulgated by the ipse dixit prophet. It is impossible to say on what foundations this man built his hopes of being able to carry on such an imposture. It is likely that he was fully aware of the lie which murderous nature might give to his assertions, and believed it to be the cast of a die, whether he should in future ages be reverenced as an inspired delegate from heaven, or be recognized as an impostor by the present dying generation. At any rate he resolved to keep up the drama to the last act. When, on the first approach of summer, the fatal disease again made its ravages among the followers of Adrian, the impostor exultingly proclaimed the exemption of his own congregation from the universal calamity. He was believed; his followers, hitherto shut up in Paris, now came to Versailles. Mingling with the coward band there assembled, they reviled their admirable leader, and asserted their own superiority and exemption. At length the plague, slow-footed, but sure in her noiseless advance, destroyed the illusion, invading the congregation of the elect, and showering promiscuous death among them. Their leader endeavoured to conceal this event; he had a few followers, who, admitted into the arcana of his wickedness, could help him in the execution of his nefarious designs. Those who sickened were immediately and quietly withdrawn, the cord and a midnight-grave disposed of them forever; while some plausible excuse was given for their absence. At last a female, whose maternal vigilance subdued even the effects of the narcotics administered to her, became a witness of their murderous designs on her only child. Mad with horror, she would have burst among her deluded fellow-victims, and, wildly shrieking, have awaked the dull ear of night with the history of the fiend-like crime; when the Impostor, in his last act of rage and desperation, plunged a poignard in her bosom. Thus wounded to death, her garments dripping with her own life-blood, bearing her strangled infant in her arms, beautiful and young as she was, Juliet, (for it was she) denounced to the host of deceived believers, the wickedness of their leader. He saw the aghast looks of her auditors, changing from horror to fury – the names of those already sacrificed were echoed by their relatives, now assured of their loss. The wretch with that energy of purpose, which had borne him thus far in his guilty career, saw his danger, and resolved to evade the worst forms of it – he rushed on one of the foremost, seized a pistol from his girdle, and his loud laugh of derision mingled with the report of the weapon with which he destroyed himself.

They left his miserable remains even where they lay; they placed the corpse of poor Juliet and her babe upon a bier, and all, with hearts subdued to saddest regret, in long procession walked towards Versailles. They met troops of those who had quitted the kindly protection of Adrian, and were journeying to join the fanatics. The tale of horror was recounted – all turned back; and thus at last, accompanied by the undiminished numbers of surviving humanity, and preceded by the mournful emblem of their recovered reason, they appeared before Adrian, and again and forever vowed obedience to his commands, and fidelity to his cause.

Chapter VII

THESE EVENTS occupied so much time, that June had numbered more than half its days, before we again commenced our long-protracted journey. The day after my return to Versailles, six men, from among those I had left at Villeneuve-la-Guiard, arrived, with intelligence, that the rest of the troop had already proceeded towards Switzerland. We went forward in the same track.

It is strange, after an interval of time, to look back on a period, which, though short in itself, appeared, when in actual progress, to be drawn out interminably. By the end of July we entered Dijon; by the end of July those hours, days, and weeks had mingled with the ocean of forgotten time, which in their passage teemed with fatal events and agonizing sorrow. By the end of July, little more than a month had gone by, if man's life were measured by the rising and setting of the sun: but, alas! in that interval ardent youth had become grey-haired; furrows deep and uneraseable were trenched in the blooming cheek of the young mother; the elastic limbs of early manhood, paralyzed as by the burthen of years, assumed the decrepitude of age. Nights passed, during whose fatal darkness the sun grew old before it rose; and burning days, to cool whose baleful heat the balmy eve, lingering far in eastern climes, came lagging and ineffectual; days, in which the dial, radiant in its noon-day station, moved not its shadow the space of a little hour, until a whole life of sorrow had brought the sufferer to an untimely grave.

We departed from Versailles fifteen hundred souls. We set out on the eighteenth of June. We made a long procession, in which was contained every dear relationship, or tie of love, that existed in human society. Fathers and husbands, with guardian care, gathered their dear relatives around them; wives and mothers looked for support to the manly form beside them, and then with tender anxiety bent their eyes on the infant troop around. They were sad, but not hopeless. Each thought that someone would be saved; each, with that pertinacious optimism, which to the last characterized our human nature, trusted that their beloved family would be the one preserved.

We passed through France, and found it empty of inhabitants. Someone or two natives survived in the larger towns, which they roamed through like ghosts; we received therefore small increase to our numbers, and such decrease through death, that at last it became easier to count the scanty list of survivors. As we never deserted any of the sick, until their death permitted us to commit their remains to the shelter of a grave, our journey was long, while every day a frightful gap was made in our troop – they died by tens, by fifties, by hundreds. No mercy was shewn by death; we ceased to expect it, and every day welcomed the sun with the feeling that we might never see it rise again.

The nervous terrors and fearful visions which had scared us during the spring, continued to visit our coward troop during this sad journey. Every evening brought its fresh creation of spectres; a ghost was depicted by every blighted tree; and appalling shapes were manufactured from each shaggy bush. By degrees these common marvels palled on us, and then other wonders were called into being. Once it was confidently asserted, that the sun rose an hour later than its seasonable time; again it was discovered that he grew paler and paler; that shadows took an uncommon appearance. It was impossible to have imagined, during the usual calm routine of life men had before experienced, the terrible effects produced by these extravagant delusions: in truth, of such little worth are our senses, when unsupported by concurring testimony, that it was with the utmost difficulty I kept myself free from the belief in supernatural events, to which the major part of our people readily gave credit. Being one sane amidst a crowd of the mad, I hardly dared assert to my own mind, that the vast luminary had undergone no change – that the shadows of night were unthickened by innumerable shapes of awe and terror; or that the wind, as it sung in the trees, or whistled round an empty building, was not pregnant with sounds of wailing and despair. Sometimes realities took ghostly shapes; and it was impossible for one's blood not to curdle at the perception of an evident mixture of what we knew to be true, with the visionary semblance of all that we feared.

Once, at the dusk of the evening, we saw a figure all in white, apparently of more than human stature, flourishing about the road, now throwing up its arms, now leaping to an astonishing height in the air, then turning round several times successively, then raising itself to its full height and gesticulating violently. Our troop, on the alert to discover and believe in the supernatural, made a halt at some distance from this shape; and, as it became darker, there was something appalling even to the incredulous, in the lonely spectre, whose gambols, if they hardly accorded with spiritual dignity, were beyond human powers. Now it leapt right up in the air, now sheer over a high hedge, and was again the moment after in the road before us. By the time I came up, the fright experienced by the spectators of this ghostly exhibition, began to manifest itself in the flight of some, and the close huddling together of the rest. Our goblin now perceived us; he approached, and, as we drew reverentially back, made a low bow. The sight was irresistibly ludicrous even to our hapless band, and his politeness was hailed by a shout of laughter; – then, again springing up, as a last effort, it sunk to the ground, and became almost invisible through the dusky night. This circumstance again spread silence and fear through the troop; the more courageous at length advanced, and, raising the dying wretch, discovered the tragic explanation of this wild scene. It was an opera-dancer, and had been one of the troop which deserted from Villeneuve-la-Guiard: falling sick, he had been deserted by his companions; in an access of delirium he had fancied himself on the stage, and, poor fellow, his dying sense eagerly accepted the last human applause that could ever be bestowed on his grace and agility.

At another time we were haunted for several days by an apparition, to which our people gave the appellation of the Black Spectre. We never saw it except at evening, when his coal black steed, his mourning dress, and plume of black feathers, had a majestic and awe-striking appearance; his face, one said, who had seen it for a moment, was ashy pale; he had lingered far behind the rest of his troop, and suddenly at a turn in the road, saw the Black Spectre coming towards him; he hid himself in fear, and the horse and his rider slowly past, while the moonbeams fell on the face of the latter, displaying its unearthly hue. Sometimes at dead of night, as we watched the sick, we heard one galloping through the town; it was the Black Spectre come in token of inevitable death. He grew giant tall to vulgar eyes; an icy atmosphere, they said, surrounded him; when he was heard, all animals shuddered, and the dying knew that their last hour was come. It was Death himself, they declared, come visibly to seize on subject earth, and quell at once our decreasing numbers, sole rebels to his law. One day at noon, we saw a dark mass on the road before us, and, coming up, beheld the Black Spectre fallen from his horse, lying in the agonies of disease upon the ground. He did not survive many hours; and his last words disclosed the secret of his mysterious conduct. He was a French noble of distinction, who, from the effects of plague, had been left alone in his district; during many months, he had wandered from town to town, from province to province, seeking some survivor for a companion, and abhorring the loneliness to which he was condemned. When he discovered our troop, fear of contagion conquered his love of society. He dared not join us, yet he could not resolve to lose sight of us, sole human beings who besides himself existed in wide and fertile France; so he accompanied us in the spectral guise I have described, till pestilence gathered him to a larger congregation, even that of Dead Mankind.

It had been well, if such vain terrors could have distracted our thoughts from more tangible evils. But these were too dreadful and too many not to force themselves into every thought, every moment, of our lives. We were obliged to halt at different periods for days together, till another and yet another was consigned as a clod to the vast clod which had been once our living mother. Thus we continued travelling during the hottest season; and it was not till the first of August, that we, the emigrants – reader, there were just eighty of us in number – entered the gates of Dijon.

We had expected this moment with eagerness, for now we had accomplished the worst part of our drear journey, and Switzerland was near at hand. Yet how could we congratulate ourselves on any event thus imperfectly fulfilled? Were these miserable beings, who, worn and wretched, passed in sorrowful procession, the sole remnants of the race of man, which, like a flood, had once spread over and possessed the whole earth? It had come down clear and unimpeded from its primal mountain source in Ararat, and grew from a puny streamlet to a vast perennial river, generation after generation flowing on ceaselessly. The same, but diversified, it grew, and swept onwards towards the absorbing ocean, whose dim shores we now reached. It had been the mere plaything of nature, when first it crept out of uncreative void into light; but thought brought forth power and knowledge; and, clad with these, the race of man assumed dignity and authority. It was then no longer the mere gardener of earth, or the shepherd of her flocks; 'it carried with it an imposing and majestic aspect; it had a pedigree and illustrious ancestors; it had its gallery of portraits, its monumental inscriptions, its records and titles.'

This was all over, now that the ocean of death had sucked in the slackening tide, and its source was dried up. We first had bidden adieu to the state of things which having existed many thousand years, seemed eternal; such a state of government, obedience, traffic, and domestic intercourse, as had moulded our hearts and capacities, as far back as memory could reach. Then to patriotic zeal, to the arts, to reputation, to enduring fame, to the name of country, we had bidden farewell. We saw depart all hope of retrieving our ancient state – all expectation, except the feeble one of saving our individual lives from the wreck of the past. To preserve these we had quitted England – England, no more; for without her children, what name could that barren island claim? With tenacious grasp we clung to such rule and order as could best save us; trusting that, if a little colony could be preserved, that would suffice at some remoter period to restore the lost community of mankind.

But the game is up! We must all die; nor leave survivor nor heir to the wide inheritance of earth. We must all die! The species of man must perish; his frame of exquisite workmanship; the wondrous mechanism of his senses; the noble proportion of his godlike limbs; his mind, the throned king of these; must perish. Will the earth still keep her place among the planets; will she still journey with unmarked regularity round the sun; will the seasons change, the trees adorn themselves with leaves, and flowers shed their fragrance, in solitude? Will the mountains remain unmoved, and streams still keep a downward course towards the vast abyss; will the tides rise and fall, and the winds fan universal nature; will beasts pasture, birds fly, and fishes swim, when man, the lord, possessor, perceiver, and recorder of all these things, has passed away, as though he had never been? O, what mockery is this! Surely death is not death, and humanity is not extinct; but merely passed into other shapes, unsubjected to our perceptions. Death is a vast portal, an high road to life: let us hasten to pass; let us exist no more in this living death, but die that we may live!

We had longed with inexpressible earnestness to reach Dijon, since we had fixed on it, as a kind of station in our progress. But now we entered it with a torpor more painful than acute suffering. We had come slowly but irrevocably to the opinion, that our utmost efforts would not preserve one human being alive. We took our hands therefore away from the long grasped rudder; and the frail vessel on which we floated, seemed, the government over her suspended, to rush, prow foremost, into the dark abyss of the billows. A gush of grief, a wanton profusion of tears, and vain laments, and overflowing tenderness, and passionate but fruitless clinging to the priceless few that remained, was followed by languor and recklessness.

During this disastrous journey we lost all those, not of our own family, to whom we had particularly attached ourselves among the survivors. It were not well to fill these pages with a mere catalogue of losses; yet I cannot refrain from this last mention of those principally dear to us. The little girl whom Adrian had rescued from utter desertion, during our ride through London on the twentieth of November, died at Auxerre. The poor child had attached herself greatly to us; and the suddenness of her death added to our sorrow. In the morning we had seen her apparently in health – in the evening, Lucy, before we retired to rest, visited our quarters to say that she was dead. Poor Lucy herself only survived, till we arrived at Dijon. She had devoted herself throughout to the nursing the sick, and attending the friendless. Her excessive exertions brought on a slow fever, which ended in the dread disease whose approach soon released her from her sufferings. She had throughout been endeared to us by her good qualities, by her ready and cheerful execution of every duty, and mild acquiescence in every turn of adversity. When we consigned her to the tomb, we seemed at the same time to bid a final adieu to those peculiarly feminine virtues conspicuous in her; uneducated and unpretending as she was, she was distinguished for patience, forbearance, and sweetness. These, with all their train of qualities peculiarly English, would never again be revived for us. This type of all that was most worthy of admiration in her class among my countrywomen, was placed under the sod of desert France; and it was as a second separation from our country to have lost sight of her forever.

The Countess of Windsor died during our abode at Dijon. One morning I was informed that she wished to see me. Her message made me remember, that several days had elapsed since I had last seen her. Such a circumstance had often occurred during our journey, when I remained behind to watch to their close the last moments of someone of our hapless comrades, and the rest of the troop past on before me. But there was something in the manner of her messenger, that made me suspect that all was not right. A caprice of the imagination caused me to conjecture that some ill had occurred to Clara or Evelyn, rather than to this aged lady. Our fears, forever on the stretch, demanded a nourishment of horror; and it seemed too natural an occurrence, too like past times, for the old to die before the young. I found the venerable mother of my Idris lying on a couch, her tall emaciated figure stretched out; her face fallen away, from which the nose stood out in sharp profile, and her large dark eyes, hollow and deep, gleamed with such light as may edge a thunder cloud at sun-set. All was shrivelled and dried up, except these lights; her voice too was fearfully changed, as she spoke to me at intervals. "I am afraid," said she, "that it is selfish in me to have asked you to visit the old woman again, before she dies: yet perhaps it would have been a greater shock to hear suddenly that I was dead, than to see me first thus."

I clasped her shrivelled hand: "Are you indeed so ill?" I asked.

"Do you not perceive death in my face," replied she, "it is strange; I ought to have expected this, and yet I confess it has taken me unaware. I never clung to life, or enjoyed it, till these last months, while among those I senselessly deserted: and it is hard to be snatched immediately away. I am glad, however, that I am not a victim of the plague; probably I should have died at this hour, though the world had continued as it was in my youth."

She spoke with difficulty, and I perceived that she regretted the necessity of death, even more than she cared to confess. Yet she had not to complain of an undue shortening of existence; her faded person shewed that life had naturally spent itself. We had been alone at first; now Clara entered; the Countess turned to her with a smile, and took the hand of this lovely child; her roseate palm and snowy fingers, contrasted with relaxed fibres and yellow hue of those of her aged friend; she bent to kiss her, touching her withered mouth with the warm, full lips of youth. "Verney," said the Countess, "I need not recommend this dear girl to you, for your own sake you will preserve her. Were the world as it was, I should have a thousand sage precautions to impress, that one so sensitive, good, and beauteous, might escape the dangers that used to lurk for the destruction of the fair and excellent. This is all nothing now.

"I commit you, my kind nurse, to your uncle's care; to yours I entrust the dearest relic of my better self. Be to Adrian, sweet one, what you have been to me – enliven his sadness with your sprightly sallies; sooth his anguish by your sober and inspired converse, when he is dying; nurse him as you have done me."

Clara burst into tears; "Kind girl," said the Countess, "do not weep for me. Many dear friends are left to you."

"And yet," cried Clara, "you talk of their dying also. This is indeed cruel – how could I live, if they were gone? If it were possible for my beloved protector to die before me, I could not nurse him; I could only die too."

The venerable lady survived this scene only twenty-four hours. She was the last tie binding us to the ancient state of things. It was impossible to look on her, and not call to mind in their wonted guise, events and persons, as alien to our present situation as the disputes of Themistocles and Aristides, or the wars of the two roses in our native land. The crown of England had pressed her brow; the memory of my father and his misfortunes, the vain struggles of the late king, the images of Raymond, Evadne, and Perdita, who had lived in the world's prime, were brought vividly before us. We consigned her to the oblivious tomb with reluctance; and when I turned from her grave, Janus veiled his retrospective face; that which gazed on future generations had long lost its faculty.

After remaining a week at Dijon, until thirty of our number deserted the vacant ranks of life, we continued our way towards Geneva. At noon on the second day we arrived at the foot of Jura. We halted here during the heat of the day. Here fifty human beings – fifty, the only human beings that survived of the food-teeming earth, assembled to read in the looks of each other ghastly plague, or wasting sorrow, desperation, or worse, carelessness of future or present evil. Here we assembled at the foot of this mighty wall of mountain, under a spreading walnut tree; a brawling stream refreshed the green sward by its sprinkling; and the busy grasshopper chirped among the thyme. We clustered together a group of wretched sufferers. A mother cradled in her enfeebled arms the child, last of many, whose glazed eye was about to close forever. Here beauty, late glowing in youthful lustre and consciousness, now wan and neglected, knelt fanning with uncertain motion the beloved, who lay striving to paint his features, distorted by illness, with a thankful smile. There an hard-featured, weather-worn veteran, having prepared his meal, sat, his head dropped on his breast, the useless knife falling from his grasp, his limbs utterly relaxed, as thought of wife and child, and dearest relative, all lost, passed across his recollection. There sat a man who for forty years had basked in fortune's tranquil sunshine; he held the hand of his last hope, his beloved daughter, who had just attained womanhood; and he gazed on her with anxious eyes, while she tried to rally her fainting spirit to comfort him. Here a servant, faithful to the last, though dying, waited on one, who, though still erect with health, gazed with gasping fear on the variety of woe around.

Adrian stood leaning against a tree; he held a book in his hand, but his eye wandered from the pages, and sought mine; they mingled a sympathetic glance; his looks confessed that his thoughts had quitted the inanimate print, for pages more pregnant with meaning, more absorbing, spread out before him. By the margin of the stream, apart from all, in a tranquil nook, where the purling brook kissed the green sward gently, Clara and Evelyn were at play, sometimes beating the water with large boughs, sometimes watching the summer-flies that sported upon it. Evelyn now chased a butterfly – now gathered a flower for his cousin; and his laughing cherub-face and clear brow told of the light heart that beat in his bosom. Clara, though she endeavoured to give herself up to his amusement, often forgot him, as she turned to observe Adrian and me. She was now fourteen, and retained her childish appearance, though in height a woman; she acted the part of the tenderest mother to my little orphan boy; to see her playing with him, or attending silently and submissively on our wants, you thought only of her admirable docility and patience; but, in her soft eyes, and the veined curtains that veiled them, in the clearness of her marmoreal brow, and the tender expression of her lips, there was an intelligence and beauty that at once excited admiration and love.

When the sun had sunk towards the precipitate west, and the evening shadows grew long, we prepared to ascend the mountain. The attention that we were obliged to pay to the sick, made our progress slow. The winding road, though steep, presented a confined view of rocky fields and hills, each hiding the other, till our farther ascent disclosed them in succession. We were seldom shaded from the declining sun, whose slant beams were instinct with exhausting heat. There are times when minor difficulties grow gigantic – times, when as the Hebrew poet expressively terms it, "the grasshopper is a burthen;" so was it with our ill fated party this evening. Adrian, usually the first to rally his spirits, and dash foremost into fatigue and hardship, with relaxed limbs and declined head, the reins hanging loosely in his grasp, left the choice of the path to the instinct of his horse, now and then painfully rousing himself, when the steepness of the ascent required that he should keep his seat with better care. Fear and horror encompassed me. Did his languid air attest that he also was struck with contagion? How long, when I look on this matchless specimen of mortality, may I perceive that his thought answers mine? how long will those limbs obey the kindly spirit within? how long will light and life dwell in the eyes of this my sole remaining friend? Thus pacing slowly, each hill surmounted, only presented another to be ascended; each jutting corner only discovered another, sister to the last, endlessly. Sometimes the pressure of sickness in one among us, caused the whole cavalcade to halt; the call for water, the eagerly expressed wish to repose; the cry of pain, and suppressed sob of the mourner – such were the sorrowful attendants of our passage of the Jura.

Adrian had gone first. I saw him, while I was detained by the loosening of a girth, struggling with the upward path, seemingly more difficult than any we had yet passed. He reached the top, and the dark outline of his figure stood in relief against the sky. He seemed to behold something unexpected and wonderful; for, pausing, his head stretched out, his arms for a moment extended, he seemed to give an All Hail! to some new vision. Urged by curiosity, I hurried to join him. After battling for many tedious minutes with the precipice, the same scene presented itself to me, which had wrapt him in extatic wonder.

Nature, or nature's favourite, this lovely earth, presented her most unrivalled beauties in resplendent and sudden exhibition. Below, far, far below, even as it were in the yawning abyss of the ponderous globe, lay the placid and azure expanse of lake Leman; vine-covered hills hedged it in, and behind dark mountains in cone-like shape, or irregular cyclopean wall, served for further defence. But beyond, and high above all, as if the spirits of the air had suddenly unveiled their bright abodes, placed in scaleless altitude in the stainless sky, heaven-kissing, companions of the unattainable ether, were the glorious Alps, clothed in dazzling robes of light by the setting sun. And, as if the world's wonders were never to be exhausted, their vast immensities, their jagged crags, and roseate painting, appeared again in the lake below, dipping their proud heights beneath the unruffled waves – palaces for the Naiads of the placid waters. Towns and villages lay scattered at the foot of Jura, which, with dark ravine, and black promontories, stretched its roots into the watery expanse beneath. Carried away by wonder, I forgot the death of man, and the living and beloved friend near me. When I turned, I saw tears streaming from his eyes; his thin hands pressed one against the other, his animated countenance beaming with admiration; "Why," cried he, at last, "Why, oh heart, whisperest thou of grief to me? Drink in the beauty of that scene, and possess delight beyond what a fabled paradise could afford."

By degrees, our whole party surmounting the steep, joined us, not one among them, but gave visible tokens of admiration, surpassing any before experienced. One cried, "God reveals his heaven to us; we may die blessed." Another and another, with broken exclamations, and extravagant phrases, endeavoured to express the intoxicating effect of this wonder of nature. So we remained awhile, lightened of the pressing burthen of fate, forgetful of death, into whose night we were about to plunge; no longer reflecting that our eyes now and forever were and would be the only ones which might perceive the divine magnificence of this terrestrial exhibition. An enthusiastic transport, akin to happiness, burst, like a sudden ray from the sun, on our darkened life. Precious attribute of woe-worn humanity! that can snatch extatic emotion, even from under the very share and harrow, that ruthlessly ploughs up and lays waste every hope.

This evening was marked by another event. Passing through Ferney in our way to Geneva, unaccustomed sounds of music arose from the rural church which stood embosomed in trees, surrounded by smokeless, vacant cottages. The peal of an organ with rich swell awoke the mute air, lingering along, and mingling with the intense beauty that clothed the rocks and woods, and waves around. Music – the language of the immortals, disclosed to us as testimony of their existence – music, "silver key of the fountain of tears," child of love, soother of grief, inspirer of heroism and radiant thoughts, O music, in this our desolation, we had forgotten thee! Nor pipe at eve cheered us, nor harmony of voice, nor linked thrill of string; thou camest upon us now, like the revealing of other forms of being; and transported as we had been by the loveliness of nature, fancying that we beheld the abode of spirits, now we might well imagine that we heard their melodious communings. We paused in such awe as would seize on a pale votarist, visiting some holy shrine at midnight; if she beheld animated and smiling, the image which she worshipped. We all stood mute; many knelt. In a few minutes however, we were recalled to human wonder and sympathy by a familiar strain. The air was Haydn's "New-Created World," and, old and drooping as humanity had become, the world yet fresh as at creation's day, might still be worthily celebrated by such an hymn of praise. Adrian and I entered the church; the nave was empty, though the smoke of incense rose from the altar, bringing with it the recollection of vast congregations, in once thronged cathedrals; we went into the loft. A blind old man sat at the bellows; his whole soul was ear; and as he sat in the attitude of attentive listening, a bright glow of pleasure was diffused over his countenance; for, though his lack-lustre eye could not reflect the beam, yet his parted lips, and every line of his face and venerable brow spoke delight. A young woman sat at the keys, perhaps twenty years of age. Her auburn hair hung on her neck, and her fair brow shone in its own beauty; but her drooping eyes let fall fast-flowing tears, while the constraint she exercised to suppress her sobs, and still her trembling, flushed her else pale cheek; she was thin; languor, and alas! sickness, bent her form. We stood looking at the pair, forgetting what we heard in the absorbing sight; till, the last chord struck, the peal died away in lessening reverberations. The mighty voice, inorganic we might call it, for we could in no way associate it with mechanism of pipe or key, stilled its sonorous tone, and the girl, turning to lend her assistance to her aged companion, at length perceived us.

It was her father; and she, since childhood, had been the guide of his darkened steps. They were Germans from Saxony, and, emigrating thither but a few years before, had formed new ties with the surrounding villagers. About the time that the pestilence had broken out, a young German student had joined them. Their simple history was easily divined. He, a noble, loved the fair daughter of the poor musician, and followed them in their flight from the persecutions of his friends; but soon the mighty leveller came with unblunted scythe to mow, together with the grass, the tall flowers of the field. The youth was an early victim. She preserved herself for her father's sake. His blindness permitted her to continue a delusion, at first the child of accident – and now solitary beings, sole survivors in the land, he remained unacquainted with the change, nor was aware that when he listened to his child's music, the mute mountains, senseless lake, and unconscious trees, were, himself excepted, her sole auditors.

The very day that we arrived she had been attacked by symptomatic illness. She was paralyzed with horror at the idea of leaving her aged, sightless father alone on the empty earth; but she had not courage to disclose the truth, and the very excess of her desperation animated her to surpassing exertions. At the accustomed vesper hour, she led him to the chapel; and, though trembling and weeping on his account, she played, without fault in time, or error in note, the hymn written to celebrate the creation of the adorned earth, soon to be her tomb.

We came to her like visitors from heaven itself; her high-wrought courage; her hardly sustained firmness, fled with the appearance of relief. With a shriek she rushed towards us, embraced the knees of Adrian, and uttering but the words, "O save my father!" with sobs and hysterical cries, opened the long-shut floodgates of her woe.

Poor girl! – she and her father now lie side by side, beneath the high walnut-tree where her lover reposes, and which in her dying moments she had pointed out to us. Her father, at length aware of his daughter's danger, unable to see the changes of her dear countenance, obstinately held her hand, till it was chilled and stiffened by death. Nor did he then move or speak, till, twelve hours after, kindly death took him to his breakless repose. They rest beneath the sod, the tree their monument; – the hallowed spot is distinct in my memory, paled in by craggy Jura, and the far, immeasurable Alps; the spire of the church they frequented still points from out the embosoming trees; and though her hand be cold, still methinks the sounds of divine music which they loved wander about, solacing their gentle ghosts.

Chapter VIII

WE HAD NOW reached Switzerland, so long the final mark and aim of our exertions. We had looked, I know not wherefore, with hope and pleasing expectation on her congregation of hills and snowy crags, and opened our bosoms with renewed spirits to the icy Biz, which even at Midsummer used to come from the northern glacier laden with cold. Yet how could we nourish expectation of relief? Like our native England, and the vast extent of fertile France, this mountain-embowered land was desolate of its inhabitants. Nor bleak mountain-top, nor snow-nourished rivulet; not the ice-laden Biz, nor thunder, the tamer of contagion, had preserved them – why therefore should we claim exemption?

Who was there indeed to save? What troop had we brought fit to stand at bay, and combat with the conqueror? We were a failing remnant, tamed to mere submission to the coming blow. A train half dead, through fear of death – a hopeless, unresisting, almost reckless crew, which, in the tossed bark of life, had given up all pilotage, and resigned themselves to the destructive force of ungoverned winds. Like a few furrows of unreaped corn, which, left standing on a wide field after the rest is gathered to the garner, are swiftly borne down by the winter storm. Like a few straggling swallows, which, remaining after their fellows had, on the first unkind breath of passing autumn, migrated to genial climes, were struck to earth by the first frost of November. Like a stray sheep that wanders over the sleet-beaten hill-side, while the flock is in the pen, and dies before morning-dawn. Like a cloud, like one of many that were spread in impenetrable woof over the sky, which, when the shepherd north has driven its companions "to drink Antipodean noon," fades and dissolves in the clear ether – Such were we!

We left the fair margin of the beauteous lake of Geneva, and entered the Alpine ravines; tracing to its source the brawling Arve, through the rock-bound valley of Servox, beside the mighty waterfalls, and under the shadow of the inaccessible mountains, we travelled on; while the luxuriant walnut-tree gave place to the dark pine, whose musical branches swung in the wind, and whose upright forms had braved a thousand storms – till the verdant sod, the flowery dell, and shrubbery hill were exchanged for the sky-piercing, untrodden, seedless rock, "the bones of the world, waiting to be clothed with everything necessary to give life and beauty." Strange that we should seek shelter here! Surely, if, in those countries where earth was wont, like a tender mother, to nourish her children, we had found her a destroyer, we need not seek it here, where stricken by keen penury she seems to shudder through her stony veins. Nor were we mistaken in our conjecture. We vainly sought the vast and ever moving glaciers of Chamounix, rifts of pendant ice, seas of congelated waters, the leafless groves of tempest-battered pines, dells, mere paths for the loud avalanche, and hill-tops, the resort of thunder-storms. Pestilence reigned paramount even here. By the time that day and night, like twin sisters of equal growth, shared equally their dominion over the hours, one by one, beneath the ice-caves, beside the waters springing from the thawed snows of a thousand winters, another and yet another of the remnant of the race of Man, closed their eyes forever to the light.

Yet we were not quite wrong in seeking a scene like this, whereon to close the drama. Nature, true to the last, consoled us in the very heart of misery. Sublime grandeur of outward objects soothed our hapless hearts, and were in harmony with our desolation. Many sorrows have befallen man during his chequered course; and many a woe-stricken mourner has found himself sole survivor among many. Our misery took its majestic shape and colouring from the vast ruin, that accompanied and made one with it. Thus on lovely earth, many a dark ravine contains a brawling stream, shadowed by romantic rocks, threaded by mossy paths – but all, except this, wanted the mighty back-ground, the towering Alps, whose snowy capes, or bared ridges, lifted us from our dull mortal abode, to the palaces of Nature's own.

This solemn harmony of event and situation regulated our feelings, and gave as it were fitting costume to our last act. Majestic gloom and tragic pomp attended the decease of wretched humanity. The funeral procession of monarchs of old, was transcended by our splendid shews. Near the sources of the Arveiron we performed the rites for, four only excepted, the last of the species. Adrian and I, leaving Clara and Evelyn wrapt in peaceful unobserving slumber, carried the body to this desolate spot, and placed it in those caves of ice beneath the glacier, which rive and split with the slightest sound, and bring destruction on those within the clefts – no bird or beast of prey could here profane the frozen form. So, with hushed steps and in silence, we placed the dead on a bier of ice, and then, departing, stood on the rocky platform beside the river springs. All hushed as we had been, the very striking of the air with our persons had sufficed to disturb the repose of this thawless region; and we had hardly left the cavern, before vast blocks of ice, detaching themselves from the roof, fell, and covered the human image we had deposited within. We had chosen a fair moonlight night, but our journey thither had been long, and the crescent sank behind the western heights by the time we had accomplished our purpose. The snowy mountains and blue glaciers shone in their own light. The rugged and abrupt ravine, which formed one side of Mont Anvert, was opposite to us, the glacier at our side; at our feet Arveiron, white and foaming, dashed over the pointed rocks that jutted into it, and, with whirring spray and ceaseless roar, disturbed the stilly night. Yellow lightnings played around the vast dome of Mont Blanc, silent as the snow-clad rock they illuminated; all was bare, wild, and sublime, while the singing of the pines in melodious murmurings added a gentle interest to the rough magnificence. Now the riving and fall of icy rocks clave the air; now the thunder of the avalanche burst on our ears. In countries whose features are of less magnitude, nature betrays her living powers in the foliage of the trees, in the growth of herbage, in the soft purling of meandering streams; here, endowed with giant attributes, the torrent, the thunder-storm, and the flow of massive waters, display her activity. Such the church-yard, such the requiem, such the eternal congregation, that waited on our companion's funeral!

Nor was it the human form alone which we had placed in this eternal sepulchre, whose obsequies we now celebrated. With this last victim Plague vanished from the earth. Death had never wanted weapons wherewith to destroy life, and we, few and weak as we had become, were still exposed to every other shaft with which his full quiver teemed. But pestilence was absent from among them. For seven years it had had full sway upon earth; she had trod every nook of our spacious globe; she had mingled with the atmosphere, which as a cloak enwraps all our fellow-creatures – the inhabitants of native Europe – the luxurious Asiatic – the swarthy African and free American had been vanquished and destroyed by her. Her barbarous tyranny came to its close here in the rocky vale of Chamounix.

Still recurring scenes of misery and pain, the fruits of this distemper, made no more a part of our lives – the word plague no longer rung in our ears – the aspect of plague incarnate in the human countenance no longer appeared before our eyes. From this moment I saw plague no more. She abdicated her throne, and despoiled herself of her imperial sceptre among the ice rocks that surrounded us. She left solitude and silence co-heirs of her kingdom.

My present feelings are so mingled with the past, that I cannot say whether the knowledge of this change visited us, as we stood on this sterile spot. It seems to me that it did; that a cloud seemed to pass from over us, that a weight was taken from the air; that henceforth we breathed more freely, and raised our heads with some portion of former liberty. Yet we did not hope. We were impressed by the sentiment, that our race was run, but that plague would not be our destroyer. The coming time was as a mighty river, down which a charmed boat is driven, whose mortal steersman knows, that the obvious peril is not the one he needs fear, yet that danger is nigh; and who floats awe-struck under beetling precipices, through the dark and turbid waters – seeing in the distance yet stranger and ruder shapes, towards which he is irresistibly impelled. What would become of us? O for some Delphic oracle, or Pythian maid, to utter the secrets of futurity! O for some Oedipus to solve the riddle of the cruel Sphynx! Such Oedipus was I to be – not divining a word's juggle, but whose agonizing pangs, and sorrow-tainted life were to be the engines, wherewith to lay bare the secrets of destiny, and reveal the meaning of the enigma, whose explanation closed the history of the human race.

Dim fancies, akin to these, haunted our minds, and instilled feelings not unallied to pleasure, as we stood beside this silent tomb of nature, reared by these lifeless mountains, above her living veins, choking her vital principle. "Thus are we left," said Adrian, "two melancholy blasted trees, where once a forest waved. We are left to mourn, and pine, and die. Yet even now we have our duties, which we must string ourselves to fulfil: the duty of bestowing pleasure where we can, and by force of love, irradiating with rainbow hues the tempest of grief. Nor will I repine if in this extremity we preserve what we now possess. Something tells me, Verney, that we need no longer dread our cruel enemy, and I cling with delight to the oracular voice. Though strange, it will be sweet to mark the growth of your little boy, and the development of Clara's young heart. In the midst of a desert world, we are everything to them; and, if we live, it must be our task to make this new mode of life happy to them. At present this is easy, for their childish ideas do not wander into futurity, and the stinging craving for sympathy, and all of love of which our nature is susceptible, is not yet awake within them: we cannot guess what will happen then, when nature asserts her indefeasible and sacred powers; but, long before that time, we may all be cold, as he who lies in yonder tomb of ice. We need only provide for the present, and endeavour to fill with pleasant images the inexperienced fancy of your lovely niece. The scenes which now surround us, vast and sublime as they are, are not such as can best contribute to this work. Nature is here like our fortunes, grand, but too destructive, bare, and rude, to be able to afford delight to her young imagination. Let us descend to the sunny plains of Italy. Winter will soon be here, to clothe this wilderness in double desolation; but we will cross the bleak hill-tops, and lead her to scenes of fertility and beauty, where her path will be adorned with flowers, and the cheery atmosphere inspire pleasure and hope."

In pursuance of this plan we quitted Chamounix on the following day. We had no cause to hasten our steps; no event was transacted beyond our actual sphere to enchain our resolves, so we yielded to every idle whim, and deemed our time well spent, when we could behold the passage of the hours without dismay. We loitered along the lovely Vale of Servox; passed long hours on the bridge, which, crossing the ravine of Arve, commands a prospect of its pine-clothed depths, and the snowy mountains that wall it in. We rambled through romantic Switzerland; till, fear of coming winter leading us forward, the first days of October found us in the valley of La Maurienne, which leads to Cenis. I cannot explain the reluctance we felt at leaving this land of mountains; perhaps it was, that we regarded the Alps as boundaries between our former and our future state of existence, and so clung fondly to what of old we had loved. Perhaps, because we had now so few impulses urging to a choice between two modes of action, we were pleased to preserve the existence of one, and preferred the prospect of what we were to do, to the recollection of what had been done. We felt that for this year danger was past; and we believed that, for some months, we were secured to each other. There was a thrilling, agonizing delight in the thought – it filled the eyes with misty tears, it tore the heart with tumultuous heavings; frailer than the "snow fall in the river," were we each and all – but we strove to give life and individuality to the meteoric course of our several existences, and to feel that no moment escaped us unenjoyed. Thus tottering on the dizzy brink, we were happy. Yes! as we sat beneath the toppling rocks, beside the waterfalls, near

– Forests, ancient as the hills,

And folding sunny spots of greenery, where the chamois grazed, and the timid squirrel laid up its hoard – descanting on the charms of nature, drinking in the while her unalienable beauties – we were, in an empty world, happy.

Yet, O days of joy – days, when eye spoke to eye, and voices, sweeter than the music of the swinging branches of the pines, or rivulet's gentle murmur, answered mine – yet, O days replete with beatitude, days of loved society – days unutterably dear to me forlorn – pass, O pass before me, making me in your memory forget what I am. Behold, how my streaming eyes blot this senseless paper – behold, how my features are convulsed by agonizing throes, at your mere recollection, now that, alone, my tears flow, my lips quiver, my cries fill the air, unseen, unmarked, unheard! Yet, O yet, days of delight! let me dwell on your long-drawn hours!

As the cold increased upon us, we passed the Alps, and descended into Italy. At the uprising of morn, we sat at our repast, and cheated our regrets by gay sallies or learned disquisitions. The live-long day we sauntered on, still keeping in view the end of our journey, but careless of the hour of its completion. As the evening star shone out, and the orange sunset, far in the west, marked the position of the dear land we had forever left, talk, thought enchaining, made the hours fly – O that we had lived thus forever and forever! Of what consequence was it to our four hearts, that they alone were the fountains of life in the wide world? As far as mere individual sentiment was concerned, we had rather be left thus united together, than if, each alone in a populous desert of unknown men, we had wandered truly companionless till life's last term. In this manner, we endeavoured to console each other; in this manner, true philosophy taught us to reason.

It was the delight of Adrian and myself to wait on Clara, naming her the little queen of the world, ourselves her humblest servitors. When we arrived at a town, our first care was to select for her its most choice abode; to make sure that no harrowing relic remained of its former inhabitants; to seek food for her, and minister to her wants with assiduous tenderness. Clara entered into our scheme with childish gaiety. Her chief business was to attend on Evelyn; but it was her sport to array herself in splendid robes, adorn herself with sunny gems, and ape a princely state. Her religion, deep and pure, did not teach her to refuse to blunt thus the keen sting of regret; her youthful vivacity made her enter, heart and soul, into these strange masquerades.

We had resolved to pass the ensuing winter at Milan, which, as being a large and luxurious city, would afford us choice of homes. We had descended the Alps, and left far behind their vast forests and mighty crags. We entered smiling Italy. Mingled grass and corn grew in her plains, the unpruned vines threw their luxuriant branches around the elms. The grapes, overripe, had fallen on the ground, or hung purple, or burnished green, among the red and yellow leaves. The ears of standing corn winnowed to emptiness by the spendthrift winds; the fallen foliage of the trees, the weed-grown brooks, the dusky olive, now spotted with its blackened fruit; the chestnuts, to which the squirrel only was harvest-man; all plenty, and yet, alas! all poverty, painted in wondrous hues and fantastic groupings this land of beauty. In the towns, in the voiceless towns, we visited the churches, adorned by pictures, master-pieces of art, or galleries of statues – while in this genial clime the animals, in new found liberty, rambled through the gorgeous palaces, and hardly feared our forgotten aspect. The dove-coloured oxen turned their full eyes on us, and paced slowly by; a startling throng of silly sheep, with pattering feet, would start up in some chamber, formerly dedicated to the repose of beauty, and rush, huddling past us, down the marble staircase into the street, and again in at the first open door, taking unrebuked possession of hallowed sanctuary, or kingly council-chamber. We no longer started at these occurrences, nor at worse exhibition of change – when the palace had become a mere tomb, pregnant with fetid stench, strewn with the dead; and we could perceive how pestilence and fear had played strange antics, chasing the luxurious dame to the dank fields and bare cottage; gathering, among carpets of Indian woof, and beds of silk, the rough peasant, or the deformed half-human shape of the wretched beggar.

We arrived at Milan, and stationed ourselves in the Vice-Roy's palace. Here we made laws for ourselves, dividing our day, and fixing distinct occupations for each hour. In the morning we rode in the adjoining country, or wandered through the palaces, in search of pictures or antiquities. In the evening we assembled to read or to converse. There were few books that we dared read; few, that did not cruelly deface the painting we bestowed on our solitude, by recalling combinations and emotions never more to be experienced by us. Metaphysical disquisition; fiction, which wandering from all reality, lost itself in self-created errors; poets of times so far gone by, that to read of them was as to read of Atlantis and Utopia; or such as referred to nature only, and the workings of one particular mind; but most of all, talk, varied and ever new, beguiled our hours.

While we paused thus in our onward career towards death, time held on its accustomed course. Still and forever did the earth roll on, enthroned in her atmospheric car, speeded by the force of the invisible coursers of never-erring necessity. And now, this dew-drop in the sky, this ball, ponderous with mountains, lucent with waves, passing from the short tyranny of watery Pisces and the frigid Ram, entered the radiant demesne of Taurus and the Twins. There, fanned by vernal airs, the Spirit of Beauty sprung from her cold repose; and, with winnowing wings and soft pacing feet, set a girdle of verdure around the earth, sporting among the violets, hiding within the springing foliage of the trees, tripping lightly down the radiant streams into the sunny deep. 'For lo! winter is past, the rain is over and gone; the flowers appear on the earth, the time of the singing of birds is come, and the voice of the turtle is heard in our land; the fig tree putteth forth her green figs, and the vines, with the tender grape, give a good smell.' Thus was it in the time of the ancient regal poet; thus was it now.

Yet how could we miserable hail the approach of this delightful season? We hoped indeed that death did not now as heretofore walk in its shadow; yet, left as we were alone to each other, we looked in each other's faces with enquiring eyes, not daring altogether to trust to our presentiments, and endeavouring to divine which would be the hapless survivor to the other three. We were to pass the summer at the lake of Como, and thither we removed as soon as spring grew to her maturity, and the snow disappeared from the hill tops. Ten miles from Como, under the steep heights of the eastern mountains, by the margin of the lake, was a villa called the Pliniana, from its being built on the site of a fountain, whose periodical ebb and flow is described by the younger Pliny in his letters. The house had nearly fallen into ruin, till in the year 2090, an English nobleman had bought it, and fitted it up with every luxury. Two large halls, hung with splendid tapestry, and paved with marble, opened on each side of a court, of whose two other sides one overlooked the deep dark lake, and the other was bounded by a mountain, from whose stony side gushed, with roar and splash, the celebrated fountain. Above, underwood of myrtle and tufts of odorous plants crowned the rock, while the star-pointing giant cypresses reared themselves in the blue air, and the recesses of the hills were adorned with the luxuriant growth of chestnut-trees. Here we fixed our summer residence. We had a lovely skiff, in which we sailed, now stemming the midmost waves, now coasting the over-hanging and craggy banks, thick sown with evergreens, which dipped their shining leaves in the waters, and were mirrored in many a little bay and creek of waters of translucent darkness. Here orange plants bloomed, here birds poured forth melodious hymns; and here, during spring, the cold snake emerged from the clefts, and basked on the sunny terraces of rock.

Were we not happy in this paradisiacal retreat? If some kind spirit had whispered forgetfulness to us, methinks we should have been happy here, where the precipitous mountains, nearly pathless, shut from our view the far fields of desolate earth, and with small exertion of the imagination, we might fancy that the cities were still resonant with popular hum, and the peasant still guided his plough through the furrow, and that we, the world's free denizens, enjoyed a voluntary exile, and not a remediless cutting off from our extinct species.

Not one among us enjoyed the beauty of this scenery so much as Clara. Before we quitted Milan, a change had taken place in her habits and manners. She lost her gaiety, she laid aside her sports, and assumed an almost vestal plainness of attire. She shunned us, retiring with Evelyn to some distant chamber or silent nook; nor did she enter into his pastimes with the same zest as she was wont, but would sit and watch him with sadly tender smiles, and eyes bright with tears, yet without a word of complaint. She approached us timidly, avoided our caresses, nor shook off her embarrassment till some serious discussion or lofty theme called her for awhile out of herself. Her beauty grew as a rose, which, opening to the summer wind, discloses leaf after leaf till the sense aches with its excess of loveliness. A slight and variable colour tinged her cheeks, and her motions seemed attuned by some hidden harmony of surpassing sweetness. We redoubled our tenderness and earnest attentions. She received them with grateful smiles, that fled swift as sunny beam from a glittering wave on an April day.

Our only acknowledged point of sympathy with her, appeared to be Evelyn. This dear little fellow was a comforter and delight to us beyond all words. His buoyant spirit, and his innocent ignorance of our vast calamity, were balm to us, whose thoughts and feelings were over-wrought and spun out in the immensity of speculative sorrow. To cherish, to caress, to amuse him was the common task of all. Clara, who felt towards him in some degree like a young mother, gratefully acknowledged our kindness towards him. To me, O! to me, who saw the clear brows and soft eyes of the beloved of my heart, my lost and ever dear Idris, re-born in his gentle face, to me he was dear even to pain; if I pressed him to my heart, methought I clasped a real and living part of her, who had lain there through long years of youthful happiness.

It was the custom of Adrian and myself to go out each day in our skiff to forage in the adjacent country. In these expeditions we were seldom accompanied by Clara or her little charge, but our return was an hour of hilarity. Evelyn ransacked our stores with childish eagerness, and we always brought some new found gift for our fair companion. Then too we made discoveries of lovely scenes or gay palaces, whither in the evening we all proceeded. Our sailing expeditions were most divine, and with a fair wind or transverse course we cut the liquid waves; and, if talk failed under the pressure of thought, I had my clarionet with me, which awoke the echoes, and gave the change to our careful minds. Clara at such times often returned to her former habits of free converse and gay sally; and though our four hearts alone beat in the world, those four hearts were happy.

One day, on our return from the town of Como, with a laden boat, we expected as usual to be met at the port by Clara and Evelyn, and we were somewhat surprised to see the beach vacant. I, as my nature prompted, would not prognosticate evil, but explained it away as a mere casual incident. Not so Adrian. He was seized with sudden trembling and apprehension, and he called to me with vehemence to steer quickly for land, and, when near, leapt from the boat, half falling into the water; and, scrambling up the steep bank, hastened along the narrow strip of garden, the only level space between the lake and the mountain. I followed without delay; the garden and inner court were empty, so was the house, whose every room we visited. Adrian called loudly upon Clara's name, and was about to rush up the near mountain-path, when the door of a summer-house at the end of the garden slowly opened, and Clara appeared, not advancing towards us, but leaning against a column of the building with blanched cheeks, in a posture of utter despondency. Adrian sprang towards her with a cry of joy, and folded her delightedly in his arms. She withdrew from his embrace, and, without a word, again entered the summer-house. Her quivering lips, her despairing heart refused to afford her voice to express our misfortune. Poor little Evelyn had, while playing with her, been seized with sudden fever, and now lay torpid and speechless on a little couch in the summer-house.

For a whole fortnight we unceasingly watched beside the poor child, as his life declined under the ravages of a virulent typhus. His little form and tiny lineaments encaged the embryo of the world-spanning mind of man. Man's nature, brimful of passions and affections, would have had an home in that little heart, whose swift pulsations hurried towards their close. His small hand's fine mechanism, now flaccid and unbent, would in the growth of sinew and muscle, have achieved works of beauty or of strength. His tender rosy feet would have trod in firm manhood the bowers and glades of earth – these reflections were now of little use: he lay, thought and strength suspended, waiting unresisting the final blow.

We watched at his bedside, and when the access of fever was on him, we neither spoke nor looked at each other, marking only his obstructed breath and the mortal glow that tinged his sunken cheek, the heavy death that weighed on his eyelids. It is a trite evasion to say, that words could not express our long drawn agony; yet how can words image sensations, whose tormenting keenness throw us back, as it were, on the deep roots and hidden foundations of our nature, which shake our being with earth-quake-throe, so that we leave to confide in accustomed feelings which like mother-earth support us, and cling to some vain imagination or deceitful hope, which will soon be buried in the ruins occasioned by the final shock. I have called that period a fortnight, which we passed watching the changes of the sweet child's malady – and such it might have been – at night, we wondered to find another day gone, while each particular hour seemed endless. Day and night were exchanged for one another uncounted; we slept hardly at all, nor did we even quit his room, except when a pang of grief seized us, and we retired from each other for a short period to conceal our sobs and tears. We endeavoured in vain to abstract Clara from this deplorable scene. She sat, hour after hour, looking at him, now softly arranging his pillow, and, while he had power to swallow, administered his drink. At length the moment of his death came: the blood paused in its flow – his eyes opened, and then closed again: without convulsion or sigh, the frail tenement was left vacant of its spiritual inhabitant.

I have heard that the sight of the dead has confirmed materialists in their belief. I ever felt otherwise. Was that my child – that moveless decaying inanimation? My child was enraptured by my caresses; his dear voice cloathed with meaning articulations his thoughts, otherwise inaccessible; his smile was a ray of the soul, and the same soul sat upon its throne in his eyes. I turn from this mockery of what he was. Take, O earth, thy debt! freely and forever I consign to thee the garb thou didst afford. But thou, sweet child, amiable and beloved boy, either thy spirit has sought a fitter dwelling, or, shrined in my heart, thou livest while it lives.

We placed his remains under a cypress, the upright mountain being scooped out to receive them. And then Clara said, "If you wish me to live, take me from hence. There is something in this scene of transcendent beauty, in these trees, and hills and waves, that forever whisper to me, leave thy cumbrous flesh, and make a part of us. I earnestly entreat you to take me away."

So on the fifteenth of August we bade adieu to our villa, and the embowering shades of this abode of beauty; to calm bay and noisy waterfall; to Evelyn's little grave we bade farewell! and then, with heavy hearts, we departed on our pilgrimage towards Rome.

Chapter IX

NOW – SOFT AWHILE – have I arrived so near the end? Yes! it is all over now – a step or two over those new made graves, and the wearisome way is done. Can I accomplish my task? Can I streak my paper with words capacious of the grand conclusion? Arise, black Melancholy! quit thy Cimmerian solitude! Bring with thee murky fogs from hell, which may drink up the day; bring blight and pestiferous exhalations, which, entering the hollow caverns and breathing places of earth, may fill her stony veins with corruption, so that not only herbage may no longer flourish, the trees may rot, and the rivers run with gall – but the everlasting mountains be decomposed, and the mighty deep putrify, and the genial atmosphere which clips the globe, lose all powers of generation and sustenance. Do this, sad visaged power, while I write, while eyes read these pages.

And who will read them? Beware, tender offspring of the re-born world – beware, fair being, with human heart, yet untamed by care, and human brow, yet unploughed by time – beware, lest the cheerful current of thy blood be checked, thy golden locks turn grey, thy sweet dimpling smiles be changed to fixed, harsh wrinkles! Let not day look on these lines, lest garish day waste, turn pale, and die. Seek a cypress grove, whose moaning boughs will be harmony befitting; seek some cave, deep embowered in earth's dark entrails, where no light will penetrate, save that which struggles, red and flickering, through a single fissure, staining thy page with grimmest livery of death.

There is a painful confusion in my brain, which refuses to delineate distinctly succeeding events. Sometimes the irradiation of my friend's gentle smile comes before me; and methinks its light spans and fills eternity – then, again, I feel the gasping throes –

We quitted Como, and in compliance with Adrian's earnest desire, we took Venice in our way to Rome. There was something to the English peculiarly attractive in the idea of this wave-encircled, island-enthroned city. Adrian had never seen it. We went down the Po and the Brenta in a boat; and, the days proving intolerably hot, we rested in the bordering palaces during the day, travelling through the night, when darkness made the bordering banks indistinct, and our solitude less remarkable; when the wandering moon lit the waves that divided before our prow, and the night-wind filled our sails, and the murmuring stream, waving trees, and swelling canvass, accorded in harmonious strain. Clara, long overcome by excessive grief, had to a great degree cast aside her timid, cold reserve, and received our attentions with grateful tenderness. While Adrian with poetic fervour discoursed of the glorious nations of the dead, of the beauteous earth and the fate of man, she crept near him, drinking in his speech with silent pleasure. We banished from our talk, and as much as possible from our thoughts, the knowledge of our desolation. And it would be incredible to an inhabitant of cities, to one among a busy throng, to what extent we succeeded. It was as a man confined in a dungeon, whose small and grated rift at first renders the doubtful light more sensibly obscure, till, the visual orb having drunk in the beam, and adapted itself to its scantiness, he finds that clear noon inhabits his cell. So we, a simple triad on empty earth, were multiplied to each other, till we became all in all. We stood like trees, whose roots are loosened by the wind, which support one another, leaning and clinging with increased fervour while the wintry storms howl. Thus we floated down the widening stream of the Po, sleeping when the cicale sang, awake with the stars. We entered the narrower banks of the Brenta, and arrived at the shore of the Laguna at sunrise on the sixth of September. The bright orb slowly rose from behind its cupolas and towers, and shed its penetrating light upon the glassy waters. Wrecks of gondolas, and some few uninjured ones, were strewed on the beach at Fusina. We embarked in one of these for the widowed daughter of ocean, who, abandoned and fallen, sat forlorn on her propping isles, looking towards the far mountains of Greece. We rowed lightly over the Laguna, and entered Canale Grande. The tide ebbed sullenly from out the broken portals and violated halls of Venice: sea weed and sea monsters were left on the blackened marble, while the salt ooze defaced the matchless works of art that adorned their walls, and the sea gull flew out from the shattered window. In the midst of this appalling ruin of the monuments of man's power, nature asserted her ascendancy, and shone more beauteous from the contrast. The radiant waters hardly trembled, while the rippling waves made many sided mirrors to the sun; the blue immensity, seen beyond Lido, stretched far, unspecked by boat, so tranquil, so lovely, that it seemed to invite us to quit the land strewn with ruins, and to seek refuge from sorrow and fear on its placid extent.

We saw the ruins of this hapless city from the height of the tower of San Marco, immediately under us, and turned with sickening hearts to the sea, which, though it be a grave, rears no monument, discloses no ruin. Evening had come apace. The sun set in calm majesty behind the misty summits of the Apennines, and its golden and roseate hues painted the mountains of the opposite shore. "That land," said Adrian, "tinged with the last glories of the day, is Greece." Greece! The sound had a responsive chord in the bosom of Clara. She vehemently reminded us that we had promised to take her once again to Greece, to the tomb of her parents. Why go to Rome? what should we do at Rome? We might take one of the many vessels to be found here, embark in it, and steer right for Albania.

I objected the dangers of ocean, and the distance of the mountains we saw, from Athens; a distance which, from the savage uncultivation of the country, was almost impassable. Adrian, who was delighted with Clara's proposal, obviated these objections. The season was favourable; the north-west that blew would take us transversely across the gulph; and then we might find, in some abandoned port, a light Greek caique, adapted for such navigation, and run down the coast of the Morea, and, passing over the Isthmus of Corinth, without much land-travelling or fatigue, find ourselves at Athens. This appeared to me wild talk; but the sea, glowing with a thousand purple hues, looked so brilliant and safe; my beloved companions were so earnest, so determined, that, when Adrian said, "Well, though it is not exactly what you wish, yet consent, to please me" – I could no longer refuse. That evening we selected a vessel, whose size just seemed fitted for our enterprize; we bent the sails and put the rigging in order, and reposing that night in one of the city's thousand palaces, agreed to embark at sunrise the following morning.

> When winds that move not its calm surface, sweep
> The azure sea, I love the land no more;
> The smiles of the serene and tranquil deep
> Tempt my unquiet mind –

Thus said Adrian, quoting a translation of Moschus's poem, as in the clear morning light, we rowed over the Laguna, past Lido, into the open sea – I would have added in continuation,

> But when the roar
> Of ocean's gray abyss resounds, and foam
> Gathers upon the sea, and vast waves burst –

But my friends declared that such verses were evil augury; so in cheerful mood we left the shallow waters, and, when out at sea, unfurled our sails to catch the favourable breeze. The laughing morning air filled them, while sun-light bathed earth, sky and ocean – the placid waves divided to receive our keel, and playfully kissed the dark sides of our little skiff, murmuring a welcome; as land receded, still the blue expanse, most waveless, twin sister to the azure empyrean, afforded smooth conduct to our bark. As the air and waters were tranquil and balmy, so were our minds steeped in quiet. In comparison with the unstained deep, funereal earth appeared a grave, its high rocks and stately mountains were but monuments, its trees the plumes of a herse, the brooks and rivers brackish with tears for departed man. Farewell to desolate towns – to fields with their savage intermixture of corn and weeds – to ever multiplying relics of our lost species. Ocean, we commit ourselves to thee – even as the patriarch of old floated above the drowned world, let us be saved, as thus we betake ourselves to thy perennial flood.

Adrian sat at the helm; I attended to the rigging, the breeze right aft filled our swelling canvas, and we ran before it over the untroubled deep. The wind died away at noon; its idle breath just permitted us to hold our course. As lazy, fair-weather sailors, careless of the coming hour, we talked gaily of our coasting voyage, of our arrival at Athens. We would make our home of one of the Cyclades, and there in myrtle-groves, amidst perpetual spring, fanned by the wholesome sea-breezes – we would live long years in beatific union – Was there such a thing as death in the world? –

The sun passed its zenith, and lingered down the stainless floor of heaven. Lying in the boat, my face turned up to the sky, I thought I saw on its blue white, marbled streaks, so slight, so immaterial, that now I said – They are there – and now, It is a mere imagination. A sudden fear stung me while I gazed; and, starting up, and running to the prow – as I stood, my hair was gently lifted on my brow – a dark line of ripples appeared to the east, gaining rapidly on us – my breathless remark to Adrian, was followed by the flapping of the canvas, as the adverse wind struck it, and our boat lurched – swift as speech, the web of the storm thickened over head, the sun went down red, the dark sea was strewed with foam, and our skiff rose and fell in its increasing furrows.

Behold us now in our frail tenement, hemmed in by hungry, roaring waves, buffeted by winds. In the inky east two vast clouds, sailing contrary ways, met; the lightning leapt forth, and the hoarse thunder muttered. Again in the south, the clouds replied, and the forked stream of fire running along the black sky, shewed us the appalling piles of clouds, now met and obliterated by the heaving waves. Great God! And we alone – we three – alone – alone – sole dwellers on the sea and on the earth, we three must perish! The vast universe, its myriad worlds, and the plains of boundless earth which we had left – the extent of shoreless sea around – contracted to my view – they and all that they contained, shrunk up to one point, even to our tossing bark, freighted with glorious humanity.

A convulsion of despair crossed the love-beaming face of Adrian, while with set teeth he murmured, "Yet they shall be saved!" Clara, visited by an human pang, pale and trembling, crept near him – he looked on her with an encouraging smile – "Do you fear, sweet girl? O, do not fear, we shall soon be on shore!"

The darkness prevented me from seeing the changes of her countenance; but her voice was clear and sweet, as she replied, "Why should I fear? neither sea nor storm can harm us, if mighty destiny or the ruler of destiny does not permit. And then the stinging fear of surviving either of you, is not here – one death will clasp us undivided."

Meanwhile we took in all our sails, save a gib; and, as soon as we might without danger, changed our course, running with the wind for the Italian shore. Dark night mixed everything; we hardly discerned the white crests of the murderous surges, except when lightning made brief noon, and drank the darkness, shewing us our danger, and restoring us to double night. We were all silent, except when Adrian, as steersman, made an encouraging observation. Our little shell obeyed the rudder miraculously well, and ran along on the top of the waves, as if she had been an offspring of the sea, and the angry mother sheltered her endangered child.

I sat at the prow, watching our course; when suddenly I heard the waters break with redoubled fury. We were certainly near the shore – at the same time I cried, "About there!" and a broad lightning filling the concave, shewed us for one moment the level beach a-head, disclosing even the sands, and stunted, ooze-sprinkled beds of reeds, that grew at high water mark. Again it was dark, and we drew in our breath with such content as one may, who, while fragments of volcano-hurled rock darken the air, sees a vast mass ploughing the ground immediately at his feet. What to do we knew not – the breakers here, there, everywhere, encompassed us – they roared, and dashed, and flung their hated spray in our faces. With considerable difficulty and danger we succeeded at length in altering our course, and stretched out from shore. I urged my companions to prepare for the wreck of our little skiff, and to bind themselves to some oar or spar which might suffice to float them. I was myself an excellent swimmer – the very sight of the sea was wont to raise in me such sensations, as a huntsman experiences, when he hears a pack of hounds in full cry; I loved to feel the waves wrap me and strive to overpower me; while I, lord of myself, moved this way or that, in spite of their angry buffetings. Adrian also could swim – but the weakness of his frame prevented him from feeling pleasure in the exercise, or acquiring any great expertness. But what power could the strongest swimmer oppose to the overpowering violence of ocean in its fury? My efforts to prepare my companions were rendered nearly futile – for the roaring breakers prevented our hearing one another speak, and the waves, that broke continually over our boat, obliged me to exert all my strength in lading the water out, as fast as it came in. The while darkness, palpable and rayless, hemmed us round, dissipated only by the lightning; sometimes we beheld thunderbolts, fiery red, fall into the sea, and at intervals vast spouts stooped from the clouds, churning the wild ocean, which rose to meet them; while the fierce gale bore the rack onwards, and they were lost in the chaotic mingling of sky and sea. Our gunwales had been torn away, our single sail had been rent to ribbands, and borne down the stream of the wind. We had cut away our mast, and lightened the boat of all she contained – Clara attempted to assist me in heaving the water from the hold, and, as she turned her eyes to look on the lightning, I could discern by that momentary gleam, that resignation had conquered every fear. We have a power given us in any worst extremity, which props the else feeble mind of man, and enables us to endure the most savage tortures with a stillness of soul which in hours of happiness we could not have imagined. A calm, more dreadful in truth than the tempest, allayed the wild beatings of my heart – a calm like that of the gamester, the suicide, and the murderer, when the last die is on the point of being cast – while the poisoned cup is at the lips – as the death-blow is about to be given.

Hours passed thus – hours which might write old age on the face of beardless youth, and grizzle the silky hair of infancy – hours, while the chaotic uproar continued, while each dread gust transcended in fury the one before, and our skiff hung on the breaking wave, and then rushed into the valley below, and trembled and spun between the watery precipices that seemed most to meet above her. For a moment the gale paused, and ocean sank to comparative silence – it was a breathless interval; the wind which, as a practised leaper, had gathered itself up before it sprung, now with terrific roar rushed over the sea, and the waves struck our stern. Adrian exclaimed that the rudder was gone; – "We are lost," cried Clara, "Save yourselves – O save yourselves!" The lightning shewed me the poor girl half buried in the water at the bottom of the boat; as she was sinking in it Adrian caught her up, and sustained her in his arms. We were without a rudder – we rushed prow foremost into the vast billows piled up a-head – they broke over and filled the tiny skiff; one scream I heard – one cry that we were gone, I uttered; I found myself in the waters; darkness was around. When the light of the tempest flashed, I saw the keel of our upset boat close to me – I clung to this, grasping it with clenched hand and nails, while I endeavoured during each flash to discover any appearance of my companions. I thought I saw Adrian at no great distance from me, clinging to an oar; I sprung from my hold, and with energy beyond my human strength, I dashed aside the waters as I strove to lay hold of him. As that hope failed, instinctive love of life animated me, and feelings of contention, as if a hostile will combated with mine. I breasted the surges, and flung them from me, as I would the opposing front and sharpened claws of a lion about to enfang my bosom. When I had been beaten down by one wave, I rose on another, while I felt bitter pride curl my lip.

Ever since the storm had carried us near the shore, we had never attained any great distance from it. With every flash I saw the bordering coast; yet the progress I made was small, while each wave, as it receded, carried me back into ocean's far abysses. At one moment I felt my foot touch the sand, and then again I was in deep water; my arms began to lose their power of motion; my breath failed me under the influence of the strangling waters – a thousand wild and delirious thoughts crossed me: as well as I can now recall them, my chief feeling was, how sweet it would be to lay my head on the quiet earth, where the surges would no longer strike my weakened frame, nor the sound of waters ring in my ears – to attain this repose, not to save my life, I made a last effort – the shelving shore suddenly presented a footing for me. I rose, and was again thrown down by the breakers – a point of rock to which I was enabled to cling, gave me a moment's respite; and then, taking advantage of the ebbing of the waves, I ran forwards – gained the dry sands, and fell senseless on the oozy reeds that sprinkled them.

I must have lain long deprived of life; for when first, with a sickening feeling, I unclosed my eyes, the light of morning met them. Great change had taken place meanwhile: grey dawn dappled the flying clouds, which sped onwards, leaving visible at intervals vast lakes of pure ether. A fountain of light arose in an increasing stream from the east, behind the waves of the Adriatic, changing the grey to a roseate hue, and then flooding sky and sea with aerial gold.

A kind of stupor followed my fainting; my senses were alive, but memory was extinct. The blessed respite was short – a snake lurked near me to sting me into life – on the first retrospective emotion I would have started up, but my limbs refused to obey me; my knees trembled, the muscles had lost all power. I still believed that I might find one of my beloved companions cast like me, half alive, on the beach; and I strove in every way to restore my frame to the use of its animal functions. I wrung the brine from my hair; and the rays of the risen sun soon visited me with genial warmth. With the restoration of my bodily powers, my mind became in some degree aware of the universe of misery, henceforth to be its dwelling. I ran to the water's edge, calling on the beloved names. Ocean drank in, and absorbed my feeble voice, replying with pitiless roar. I climbed a near tree: the level sands bounded by a pine forest, and the sea clipped round by the horizon, was all that I could discern. In vain I extended my researches along the beach; the mast we had thrown overboard, with tangled cordage, and remnants of a sail, was the sole relic land received of our wreck. Sometimes I stood still, and wrung my hands. I accused earth and sky – the universal machine and the Almighty power that misdirected it. Again I threw myself on the sands, and then the sighing wind, mimicking a human cry, roused me to bitter, fallacious hope. Assuredly if any little bark or smallest canoe had been near, I should have sought the savage plains of ocean, found the dear remains of my lost ones, and clinging round them, have shared their grave.

The day passed thus; each moment contained eternity; although when hour after hour had gone by, I wondered at the quick flight of time. Yet even now I had not drunk the bitter potion to the dregs; I was not yet persuaded of my loss; I did not yet feel in every pulsation, in every nerve, in every thought, that I remained alone of my race – that I was the LAST MAN.

The day had clouded over, and a drizzling rain set in at sunset. Even the eternal skies weep, I thought; is there any shame then, that mortal man should spend himself in tears? I remembered the ancient fables, in which human beings are described as dissolving away through weeping into ever-gushing fountains. Ah! that so it were; and then my destiny would be in some sort akin to the watery death of Adrian and Clara. Oh! grief is fantastic; it weaves a web on which to trace the history of its woe from every form and change around; it incorporates itself with all living nature; it finds sustenance in every object; as light, it fills all things, and, like light, it gives its own colours to all.

I had wandered in my search to some distance from the spot on which I had been cast, and came to one of those watch-towers, which at stated distances line the Italian shore. I was glad of shelter, glad to find a work of human hands, after I had gazed so long on nature's drear barrenness; so I entered, and ascended the rough winding staircase into the guard-room. So far was fate kind, that no harrowing vestige remained of its former inhabitants; a few planks laid across two iron tressels, and strewed with the dried leaves of Indian corn, was the bed presented to me; and an open chest, containing some half mouldered biscuit, awakened an appetite, which perhaps existed before, but of which, until now, I was not aware. Thirst also, violent and parching, the result of the sea-water I had drank, and of the exhaustion of my frame, tormented me. Kind nature had gifted the supply of these wants with pleasurable sensations, so that I – even I! – was refreshed and calmed, as I ate of this sorry fare, and drank a little of the sour wine which half filled a flask left in this abandoned dwelling. Then I stretched myself on the bed, not to be disdained by the victim of shipwreck. The earthy smell of the dried leaves was balm to my sense after the hateful odour of sea-weed. I forgot my state of loneliness. I neither looked backward nor forward; my senses were hushed to repose; I fell asleep and dreamed of all dear inland scenes, of hay-makers, of the shepherd's whistle to his dog, when he demanded his help to drive the flock to fold; of sights and sounds peculiar to my boyhood's mountain life, which I had long forgotten.

I awoke in a painful agony – for I fancied that ocean, breaking its bounds, carried away the fixed continent and deep rooted mountains, together with the streams I loved, the woods, and the flocks – it raged around, with that continued and dreadful roar which had accompanied the last wreck of surviving humanity. As my waking sense returned, the bare walls of the guard room closed round me, and the rain pattered against the single window. How dreadful it is, to emerge from the oblivion of slumber, and to receive as a good morrow the mute wailing of one's own hapless heart – to return from the land of deceptive dreams, to the heavy knowledge of unchanged disaster! – Thus was it with me, now, and forever! The sting of other griefs might be blunted by time; and even mine yielded sometimes during the day, to the pleasure inspired by the imagination or the senses; but I never look first upon the morning-light but with my fingers pressed tight on my bursting heart, and my soul deluged with the interminable flood of hopeless misery. Now I awoke for the first time in the dead world – I awoke alone – and the dull dirge of the sea, heard even amidst the rain, recalled me to the reflection of the wretch I had become. The sound came like a reproach, a scoff – like the sting of remorse in the soul – I gasped the veins and muscles of my throat swelled, suffocating me. I put my fingers to my ears, I buried my head in the leaves of my couch, I would have dived to the centre to lose hearing of that hideous moan.

But another task must be mine – again I visited the detested beach – again I vainly looked far and wide – again I raised my unanswered cry, lifting up the only voice that could ever again force the mute air to syllable the human thought.

What a pitiable, forlorn, disconsolate being I was! My very aspect and garb told the tale of my despair. My hair was matted and wild – my limbs soiled with salt ooze; while at sea, I had thrown off those of my garments that encumbered me, and the rain drenched the thin summer-clothing I had retained – my feet were bare, and the stunted reeds and broken shells made them bleed – the while, I hurried to and fro, now looking earnestly on some distant rock which, islanded in the sands, bore for a moment a deceptive appearance – now with flashing eyes reproaching the murderous ocean for its unutterable cruelty.

For a moment I compared myself to that monarch of the waste – Robinson Crusoe. We had been both thrown companionless – he on the shore of a desolate island: I on that of a desolate world. I was rich in the so called goods of life. If I turned my steps from the near barren scene, and entered any of the earth's million cities, I should find their wealth stored up for my accommodation – clothes, food, books, and a choice of dwelling beyond the command of the princes of former times – every climate was subject to my selection, while he was obliged to toil in the acquirement of every necessary, and was the inhabitant of a tropical island, against whose heats and storms he could obtain small shelter. – Viewing the question thus, who would not have preferred the Sybarite enjoyments I could command, the philosophic leisure, and ample intellectual resources, to his life of labour and peril? Yet he was far happier than I: for he could hope, nor hope in vain – the destined vessel at last arrived, to bear him to countrymen and kindred, where the events of his solitude became a fire-side tale. To none could I ever relate the story of my adversity; no hope had I. He knew that, beyond the ocean which begirt his lonely island, thousands lived whom the sun enlightened when it shone also on him: beneath the meridian sun and visiting moon, I alone bore human features; I alone could give articulation to thought; and, when I slept, both day and night were unbeheld of any. He had fled from his fellows, and was transported with terror at the print of a human foot. I would have knelt down and worshipped the same. The wild and cruel Caribbee, the merciless Cannibal – or worse than these, the uncouth, brute, and remorseless veteran in the vices of civilization, would have been to me a beloved companion, a treasure dearly prized – his nature would be kin to mine; his form cast in the same mould; human blood would flow in his veins; a human sympathy must link us forever. It cannot be that I shall never behold a fellow being more! – never! – never! – not in the course of years! – Shall I wake, and speak to none, pass the interminable hours, my soul, islanded in the world, a solitary point, surrounded by vacuum? Will day follow day endlessly thus? – No! no! a God rules the world – providence has not exchanged its golden sceptre for an aspic's sting. Away! let me fly from the ocean-grave, let me depart from this barren nook, paled in, as it is, from access by its own desolateness; let me tread once again the paved towns; step over the threshold of man's dwellings, and most certainly I shall find this thought a horrible vision – a maddening, but evanescent dream.

I entered Ravenna, (the town nearest to the spot whereon I had been cast), before the second sun had set on the empty world; I saw many living creatures; oxen, and horses, and dogs, but there was no man among them; I entered a cottage, it was vacant; I ascended the marble stairs of a palace, the bats and the owls were nestled in the tapestry; I stepped softly, not to awaken the sleeping town: I rebuked a dog, that by yelping disturbed the sacred stillness; I would not believe that all was as it seemed – The world was not dead, but I was mad; I was deprived of sight, hearing, and sense of touch; I was labouring under the force of a spell, which permitted me to behold all sights of earth, except its human inhabitants; they were pursuing their ordinary labours. Every house had its inmate; but I could not perceive them. If I could have deluded myself into a belief of this kind, I should have been far more satisfied. But my brain, tenacious of its reason, refused to lend itself to such imaginations – and though I endeavoured to play the antic to myself, I knew that I, the offspring of man, during long years one among many – now remained sole survivor of my species.

The sun sank behind the western hills; I had fasted since the preceding evening, but, though faint and weary, I loathed food, nor ceased, while yet a ray of light remained, to pace the lonely streets. Night came on, and sent every living creature but me to the bosom of its mate. It was my solace, to blunt my mental agony by personal hardship – of the thousand beds around, I would not seek the luxury of one; I lay down on the pavement – a cold marble step served me for a pillow – midnight came; and then, though not before, did my wearied lids shut out the sight of the twinkling stars, and their reflex on the pavement near. Thus I passed the second night of my desolation.

Chapter X

I AWOKE in the morning, just as the higher windows of the lofty houses received the first beams of the rising sun. The birds were chirping, perched on the windows sills and deserted thresholds of the doors. I awoke, and my first thought was, Adrian and Clara are dead. I no longer shall be hailed by their good-morrow – or pass the long day in their society. I shall never see them more. The ocean has robbed me of them – stolen their hearts of love from their breasts, and given over to corruption what was dearer to me than light, or life, or hope.

I was an untaught shepherd-boy, when Adrian deigned to confer on me his friendship. The best years of my life had been passed with him. All I had possessed of this world's goods, of happiness, knowledge, or virtue – I owed to him. He had, in his person, his intellect, and rare qualities, given a glory to my life, which without him it had never known. Beyond all other beings he had taught me, that goodness, pure and single, can be an attribute of man. It was a sight for angels to congregate to behold, to view him lead, govern, and solace, the last days of the human race.

My lovely Clara also was lost to me – she who last of the daughters of man, exhibited all those feminine and maiden virtues, which poets, painters, and sculptors, have in their various languages strove to express. Yet, as far as she was concerned, could I lament that she was removed in early youth from the certain advent of misery? Pure she was of soul, and all her intents were holy. But her heart was the throne of love, and the sensibility her lovely countenance expressed, was the prophet of many woes, not the less deep and drear, because she would have forever concealed them.

These two wondrously endowed beings had been spared from the universal wreck, to be my companions during the last year of solitude. I had felt, while they were with me, all their worth. I was conscious that every other sentiment, regret, or passion had by degrees merged into a yearning, clinging affection for them. I had not forgotten the sweet partner of my youth, mother of my children, my adored Idris; but I saw at least a part of her spirit alive again in her brother; and after, that by Evelyn's death I had lost what most dearly recalled her to me; I enshrined her memory in Adrian's form, and endeavoured to confound the two dear ideas. I sound the depths of my heart, and try in vain to draw thence the expressions that can typify my love for these remnants of my race. If regret and sorrow came athwart me, as well it might in our solitary and uncertain state, the clear tones of Adrian's voice, and his fervent look, dissipated the gloom; or I was cheered unaware by the mild content and sweet resignation Clara's cloudless brow and deep blue eyes expressed. They were all to me – the suns of my benighted soul – repose in my weariness – slumber in my sleepless woe. Ill, most ill, with disjointed words, bare and weak, have I expressed the feeling with which I clung to them. I would have wound myself like ivy inextricably round them, so that the same blow might destroy us. I would have entered and been a part of them – so that

If the dull substance of my flesh were thought,

even now I had accompanied them to their new and incommunicable abode.

Never shall I see them more. I am bereft of their dear converse – bereft of sight of them. I am a tree rent by lightning; never will the bark close over the bared fibres – never will their quivering life, torn by the winds, receive the opiate of a moment's balm. I am alone in the world – but that expression as yet was less pregnant with misery, than that Adrian and Clara are dead.

The tide of thought and feeling rolls on forever the same, though the banks and shapes around, which govern its course, and the reflection in the wave, vary. Thus the sentiment of immediate loss in some sort decayed, while that of utter, irremediable loneliness grew on me with time. Three days I wandered through Ravenna – now thinking only of the beloved beings who slept in the oozy caves of ocean – now looking forward on the dread blank before me; shuddering to make an onward step – writhing at each change that marked the progress of the hours.

For three days I wandered to and fro in this melancholy town. I passed whole hours in going from house to house, listening whether I could detect some lurking sign of human existence. Sometimes I rang at a bell; it tinkled through the vaulted rooms, and silence succeeded to the sound. I called myself hopeless, yet still I hoped; and still disappointment ushered in the hours, intruding the cold, sharp steel which first pierced me, into the aching festering wound. I fed like a wild beast, which seizes its food only when stung by intolerable hunger. I did not change my garb, or seek the shelter of a roof, during all those days. Burning heats, nervous irritation, a ceaseless, but confused flow of thought, sleepless nights, and days instinct with a frenzy of agitation, possessed me during that time.

As the fever of my blood increased, a desire of wandering came upon me. I remember, that the sun had set on the fifth day after my wreck, when, without purpose or aim, I quitted the town of Ravenna. I must have been very ill. Had I been possessed by more or less of delirium, that night had surely been my last; for, as I continued to walk on the banks of the Mantone, whose upward course I followed, I looked wistfully on the stream, acknowledging to myself that its pellucid waves could medicine my woes forever, and was unable to account to myself for my tardiness in seeking their shelter from the poisoned arrows of thought, that were piercing me through and through. I walked a considerable part of the night, and excessive weariness at length conquered my repugnance to the availing myself of the deserted habitations of my species. The waning moon, which had just risen, shewed me a cottage, whose neat entrance and trim garden reminded me of my own England. I lifted up the latch of the door and entered. A kitchen first presented itself, where, guided by the moon beams, I found materials for striking a light. Within this was a bed room; the couch was furnished with sheets of snowy whiteness; the wood piled on the hearth, and an array as for a meal, might almost have deceived me into the dear belief that I had here found what I had so long sought – one survivor, a companion for my loneliness, a solace to my despair. I steeled myself against the delusion; the room itself was vacant: it was only prudent, I repeated to myself, to examine the rest of the house. I fancied that I was proof against the expectation; yet my heart beat audibly, as I laid my hand on the lock of each door, and it sunk again, when I perceived in each the same vacancy. Dark and silent they were as vaults; so I returned to the first chamber, wondering what sightless host had spread the materials for my repast, and my repose. I drew a chair to the table, and examined what the viands were of which I was to partake. In truth it was a death feast! The bread was blue and mouldy; the cheese lay a heap of dust. I did not dare examine the other dishes; a troop of ants passed in a double line across the table cloth; every utensil was covered with dust, with cobwebs, and myriads of dead flies: these were objects each and all betokening the fallaciousness of my expectations. Tears rushed into my eyes; surely this was a wanton display of the power of the destroyer. What had I done, that each sensitive nerve was thus to be anatomized? Yet why complain more now than ever? This vacant cottage revealed no new sorrow – the world was empty; mankind was dead – I knew it well – why quarrel therefore with an acknowledged and stale truth? Yet, as I said, I had hoped in the very heart of despair, so that every new impression of the hard-cut reality on my soul brought with it a fresh pang, telling me the yet unstudied lesson, that neither change of place nor time could bring alleviation to my misery, but that, as I now was, I must continue, day after day, month after month, year after year, while I lived. I hardly dared conjecture what space of time that expression implied. It is true, I was no longer in the first blush of manhood; neither had I declined far in the vale of years – men have accounted mine the prime of life: I had just entered my thirty-seventh year; every limb was as well knit, every articulation as true, as when I had acted the shepherd on the hills of Cumberland; and with these advantages I was to commence the train of solitary life. Such were the reflections that ushered in my slumber on that night.

The shelter, however, and less disturbed repose which I enjoyed, restored me the following morning to a greater portion of health and strength, than I had experienced since my fatal shipwreck. Among the stores I had discovered on searching the cottage the preceding night, was a quantity of dried grapes; these refreshed me in the morning, as I left my lodging and proceeded towards a town which I discerned at no great distance. As far as I could divine, it must have been Forli. I entered with pleasure its wide and grassy streets. All, it is true, pictured the excess of desolation; yet I loved to find myself in those spots which had been the abode of my fellow creatures. I delighted to traverse street after street, to look up at the tall houses, and repeat to myself, once they contained beings similar to myself – I was not always the wretch I am now. The wide square of Forli, the arcade around it, its light and pleasant aspect cheered me. I was pleased with the idea, that, if the earth should be again peopled, we, the lost race, would, in the relics left behind, present no contemptible exhibition of our powers to the new comers.

I entered one of the palaces, and opened the door of a magnificent saloon. I started – I looked again with renewed wonder. What wild-looking, unkempt, half-naked savage was that before me? The surprise was momentary.

I perceived that it was I myself whom I beheld in a large mirror at the end of the hall. No wonder that the lover of the princely Idris should fail to recognize himself in the miserable object there portrayed. My tattered dress was that in which I had crawled half alive from the tempestuous sea. My long and tangled hair hung in elf locks on my brow – my dark eyes, now hollow and wild, gleamed from under them – my cheeks were discoloured by the jaundice, which (the effect of misery and neglect) suffused my skin, and were half hid by a beard of many days' growth.

Yet why should I not remain thus, I thought; the world is dead, and this squalid attire is a fitter mourning garb than the foppery of a black suit. And thus, methinks, I should have remained, had not hope, without which I do not believe man could exist, whispered to me, that, in such a plight, I should be an object of fear and aversion to the being, preserved I knew not where, but I fondly trusted, at length, to be found by me. Will my readers scorn the vanity, that made me attire myself with some care, for the sake of this visionary being? Or will they forgive the freaks of a half crazed imagination? I can easily forgive myself – for hope, however vague, was so dear to me, and a sentiment of pleasure of so rare occurrence, that I yielded readily to any idea, that cherished the one, or promised any recurrence of the former to my sorrowing heart. After such occupation, I visited every street, alley, and nook of Forli. These Italian towns presented an appearance of still greater desolation, than those of England or France. Plague had appeared here earlier – it had finished its course, and achieved its work much sooner than with us. Probably the last summer had found no human being alive, in all the track included between the shores of Calabria and the northern Alps. My search was utterly vain, yet I did not despond. Reason methought was on my side; and the chances were by no means contemptible, that there should exist in some part of Italy a survivor like myself – of a wasted, depopulate land. As therefore I rambled through the empty town, I formed my plan for future operations. I would continue to journey on towards Rome. After I should have satisfied myself, by a narrow search, that I left behind no human being in the towns through which I passed, I would write up in a conspicuous part of each, with white paint, in three languages, that 'Verney, the last of the race of Englishmen, had taken up his abode in Rome.'

In pursuance of this scheme, I entered a painter's shop, and procured myself the paint. It is strange that so trivial an occupation should have consoled, and even enlivened me. But grief renders one childish, despair fantastic. To this simple inscription, I merely added the adjuration, "Friend, come! I wait for thee! – Deh, vieni! ti aspetto!" On the following morning, with something like hope for my companion, I quitted Forli on my way to Rome. Until now, agonizing retrospect, and dreary prospects for the future, had stung me when awake, and cradled me to my repose. Many times I had delivered myself up to the tyranny of anguish – many times I resolved a speedy end to my woes; and death by my own hands was a remedy, whose practicability was even cheering to me. What could I fear in the other world? If there were an hell, and I were doomed to it, I should come an adept to the sufferance of its tortures – the act were easy, the speedy and certain end of my deplorable tragedy. But now these thoughts faded before the new born expectation. I went on my way, not as before, feeling each hour, each minute, to be an age instinct with incalculable pain.

As I wandered along the plain, at the foot of the Appennines – through their vallies, and over their bleak summits, my path led me through a country which had been trodden by heroes, visited and admired by thousands. They had, as a tide, receded, leaving me blank and bare in the midst. But why complain? Did I not hope? – so I schooled myself, even after the enlivening spirit had really deserted me, and thus I was obliged to call up all the fortitude I could command, and that was not much, to prevent a recurrence of that chaotic and intolerable despair, that had succeeded to the miserable shipwreck, that had consummated every fear, and dashed to annihilation every joy.

I rose each day with the morning sun, and left my desolate inn. As my feet strayed through the unpeopled country, my thoughts rambled through the universe, and I was least miserable when I could, absorbed in reverie, forget the passage of the hours. Each evening, in spite of weariness, I detested to enter any dwelling, there to take up my nightly abode – I have sat, hour after hour, at the door of the cottage I had selected, unable to lift the latch, and meet face to face blank desertion within. Many nights, though autumnal mists were spread around, I passed under an ilex – many times I have supped on arbutus berries and chestnuts, making a fire, gypsy-like, on the ground – because wild natural scenery reminded me less acutely of my hopeless state of loneliness. I counted the days, and bore with me a peeled willow-wand, on which, as well as I could remember, I had notched the days that had elapsed since my wreck, and each night I added another unit to the melancholy sum.

I had toiled up a hill which led to Spoleto. Around was spread a plain, encircled by the chestnut-covered Appennines. A dark ravine was on one side, spanned by an aqueduct, whose tall arches were rooted in the dell below, and attested that man had once deigned to bestow labour and thought here, to adorn and civilize nature. Savage, ungrateful nature, which in wild sport defaced his remains, protruding her easily renewed, and fragile growth of wild flowers and parasite plants around his eternal edifices. I sat on a fragment of rock, and looked round.

The sun had bathed in gold the western atmosphere, and in the east the clouds caught the radiance, and budded into transient loveliness. It set on a world that contained me alone for its inhabitant. I took out my wand – I counted the marks. Twenty-five were already traced – twenty-five days had already elapsed, since human voice had gladdened my ears, or human countenance met my gaze. Twenty-five long, weary days, succeeded by dark and lonesome nights, had mingled with foregone years, and had become a part of the past – the never to be recalled – a real, undeniable portion of my life – twenty-five long, long days.

Why this was not a month! – Why talk of days – or weeks – or months – I must grasp years in my imagination, if I would truly picture the future to myself – three, five, ten, twenty, fifty anniversaries of that fatal epoch might elapse – every year containing twelve months, each of more numerous calculation in a diary, than the twenty-five days gone by – Can it be? Will it be? – We had been used to look forward to death tremulously – wherefore, but because its place was obscure? But more terrible, and far more obscure, was the unveiled course of my lone futurity. I broke my wand; I threw it from me. I needed no recorder of the inch and barley-corn growth of my life, while my unquiet thoughts created other divisions, than those ruled over by the planets – and, in looking back on the age that had elapsed since I had been alone, I disdained to give the name of days and hours to the throes of agony which had in truth portioned it out.

I hid my face in my hands. The twitter of the young birds going to rest, and their rustling among the trees, disturbed the still evening-air – the crickets chirped – the aziolo cooed at intervals. My thoughts had been of death – these sounds spoke to me of life. I lifted up my eyes – a bat wheeled round – the sun had sunk behind the jagged line of mountains, and the paly, crescent moon was visible, silver white, amidst the orange sunset, and accompanied by one bright star, prolonged thus the twilight. A herd of cattle passed along in the dell below, untended, towards their watering place – the grass was rustled by a gentle breeze, and the olive-woods, mellowed into soft masses by the moonlight, contrasted their sea-green with the dark chestnut foliage. Yes, this is the earth; there is no change – no ruin – no rent made in her verdurous expanse; she continues to wheel round and round, with alternate night and day, through the sky, though man is not her adorner or inhabitant. Why could I not forget myself like one of those animals, and no longer suffer the wild tumult of misery that I endure? Yet, ah! what a deadly breach yawns between their state and mine! Have not they companions? Have not they each their mate – their cherished young, their home, which, though unexpressed to us, is, I doubt not, endeared and enriched, even in their eyes, by the society which kind nature has created for them? It is I only that am alone – I, on this little hill top, gazing on plain and mountain recess – on sky, and its starry population, listening to every sound of earth, and air, and murmuring wave – I only cannot express to any companion my many thoughts, nor lay my throbbing head on any loved bosom, nor drink from meeting eyes an intoxicating dew, that transcends the fabulous nectar of the gods. Shall I not then complain? Shall I not curse the murderous engine which has mowed down the children of men, my brethren? Shall I not bestow a malediction on every other of nature's offspring, which dares live and enjoy, while I live and suffer?

Ah, no! I will discipline my sorrowing heart to sympathy in your joys; I will be happy, because ye are so. Live on, ye innocents, nature's selected darlings; I am not much unlike to you. Nerves, pulse, brain, joint, and flesh, of such am I composed, and ye are organized by the same laws. I have something beyond this, but I will call it a defect, not an endowment, if it leads me to misery, while ye are happy. Just then, there emerged from a near copse two goats and a little kid, by the mother's side; they began to browze the herbage of the hill. I approached near to them, without their perceiving me; I gathered a handful of fresh grass, and held it out; the little one nestled close to its mother, while she timidly withdrew. The male stepped forward, fixing his eyes on me: I drew near, still holding out my lure, while he, depressing his head, rushed at me with his horns. I was a very fool; I knew it, yet I yielded to my rage. I snatched up a huge fragment of rock; it would have crushed my rash foe. I poized it – aimed it – then my heart failed me. I hurled it wide of the mark; it rolled clattering among the bushes into dell. My little visitants, all aghast, galloped back into the covert of the wood; while I, my very heart bleeding and torn, rushed down the hill, and by the violence of bodily exertion, sought to escape from my miserable self.

No, no, I will not live among the wild scenes of nature, the enemy of all that lives. I will seek the towns – Rome, the capital of the world, the crown of man's achievements. Among its storied streets, hallowed ruins, and stupendous remains of human exertion, I shall not, as here, find everything forgetful of man; trampling on his memory, defacing his works, proclaiming from hill to hill, and vale to vale – by the torrents freed from the boundaries which he imposed – by the vegetation liberated from the laws which he enforced – by his habitation abandoned to mildew and weeds, that his power is lost, his race annihilated forever.

I hailed the Tiber, for that was as it were an unalienable possession of humanity. I hailed the wild Campagna, for every rood had been trod by man; and its savage uncultivation, of no recent date, only proclaimed more distinctly his power, since he had given an honourable name and sacred title to what else would have been a worthless, barren track. I entered Eternal Rome by the Porta del Popolo, and saluted with awe its time-honoured space. The wide square, the churches near, the long extent of the Corso, the near eminence of Trinita de' Monti appeared like fairy work, they were so silent, so peaceful, and so very fair. It was evening; and the population of animals which still existed in this mighty city, had gone to rest; there was no sound, save the murmur of its many fountains, whose soft monotony was harmony to my soul. The knowledge that I was in Rome, soothed me; that wondrous city, hardly more illustrious for its heroes and sages, than for the power it exercised over the imaginations of men. I went to rest that night; the eternal burning of my heart quenched – my senses tranquil.

The next morning I eagerly began my rambles in search of oblivion. I ascended the many terraces of the garden of the Colonna Palace, under whose roof I had been sleeping; and passing out from it at its summit, I found myself on Monte Cavallo. The fountain sparkled in the sun; the obelisk above pierced the clear dark-blue air. The statues on each side, the works, as they are inscribed, of Phidias and Praxiteles, stood in undiminished grandeur, representing Castor and Pollux, who with majestic power tamed the rearing animal at their side. If those illustrious artists had in truth chiselled these forms, how many passing generations had their giant proportions outlived! and now they were viewed by the last of the species they were sculptured to represent and deify. I had shrunk into insignificance in my own eyes, as I considered the multitudinous beings these stone demigods had outlived, but this after-thought restored me to dignity in my own conception. The sight of the poetry eternized in these statues, took the sting from the thought, arraying it only in poetic ideality.

I repeated to myself – I am in Rome! I behold, and as it were, familiarly converse with the wonder of the world, sovereign mistress of the imagination, majestic and eternal survivor of millions of generations of extinct men. I endeavoured to quiet the sorrows of my aching heart, by even now taking an interest in what in my youth I had ardently longed to see. Every part of Rome is replete with relics of ancient times. The meanest streets are strewed with truncated columns, broken capitals – Corinthian and Ionic, and sparkling fragments of granite or porphyry. The walls of the most penurious dwellings enclose a fluted pillar or ponderous stone, which once made part of the palace of the Caesars; and the voice of dead time, in still vibrations, is breathed from these dumb things, animated and glorified as they were by man.

I embraced the vast columns of the temple of Jupiter Stator, which survives in the open space that was the Forum, and leaning my burning cheek against its cold durability, I tried to lose the sense of present misery and present desertion, by recalling to the haunted cell of my brain vivid memories of times gone by. I rejoiced at my success, as I figured Camillus, the Gracchi, Cato, and last the heroes of Tacitus, which shine meteors of surpassing brightness during the murky night of the empire; – as the verses of Horace and Virgil, or the glowing periods of Cicero thronged into the opened gates of my mind, I felt myself exalted by long forgotten enthusiasm. I was delighted to know that I beheld the scene which they beheld – the scene which their wives and mothers, and crowds of the unnamed witnessed, while at the same time they honoured, applauded, or wept for these matchless specimens of humanity. At length, then, I had found a consolation. I had not vainly sought the storied precincts of Rome – I had discovered a medicine for my many and vital wounds.

I sat at the foot of these vast columns. The Coliseum, whose naked ruin is robed by nature in a verdurous and glowing veil, lay in the sunlight on my right. Not far off, to the left, was the Tower of the Capitol. Triumphal arches, the falling walls of many temples, strewed the ground at my feet. I strove, I resolved, to force myself to see the Plebeian multitude and lofty Patrician forms congregated around; and, as the Diorama of ages passed across my subdued fancy, they were replaced by the modern Roman; the Pope, in his white stole, distributing benedictions to the kneeling worshippers; the friar in his cowl; the dark-eyed girl, veiled by her mezzera; the noisy, sun-burnt rustic, leading his herd of buffaloes and oxen to the Campo Vaccino. The romance with which, dipping our pencils in the rainbow hues of sky and transcendent nature, we to a degree gratuitously endow the Italians, replaced the solemn grandeur of antiquity. I remembered the dark monk, and floating figures of "The Italian," and how my boyish blood had thrilled at the description. I called to mind Corinna ascending the Capitol to be crowned, and, passing from the heroine to the author, reflected how the Enchantress Spirit of Rome held sovereign sway over the minds of the imaginative, until it rested on me – sole remaining spectator of its wonders.

I was long wrapt by such ideas; but the soul wearies of a pauseless flight; and, stooping from its wheeling circuits round and round this spot, suddenly it fell ten thousand fathom deep, into the abyss of the present – into self-knowledge – into tenfold sadness. I roused myself – I cast off my waking dreams; and I, who just now could almost hear the shouts of the Roman throng, and was hustled by countless multitudes, now beheld the desart ruins of Rome sleeping under its own blue sky; the shadows lay tranquilly on the ground; sheep were grazing untended on the Palatine, and a buffalo stalked down the Sacred Way that led to the Capitol. I was alone in the Forum; alone in Rome; alone in the world. Would not one living man – one companion in my weary solitude, be worth all the glory and remembered power of this time-honoured city? Double sorrow – sadness, bred in Cimmerian caves, robed my soul in a mourning garb. The generations I had conjured up to my fancy, contrasted more strongly with the end of all – the single point in which, as a pyramid, the mighty fabric of society had ended, while I, on the giddy height, saw vacant space around me.

From such vague laments I turned to the contemplation of the minutiae of my situation. So far, I had not succeeded in the sole object of my desires, the finding a companion for my desolation. Yet I did not despair. It is true that my inscriptions were set up for the most part, in insignificant towns and villages; yet, even without these memorials, it was possible that the person, who like me should find himself alone in a depopulate land, should, like me, come to Rome. The more slender my expectation was, the more I chose to build on it, and to accommodate my actions to this vague possibility.

It became necessary therefore, that for a time I should domesticate myself at Rome. It became necessary, that I should look my disaster in the face – not playing the school-boy's part of obedience without submission; enduring life, and yet rebelling against the laws by which I lived.

Yet how could I resign myself? Without love, without sympathy, without communion with any, how could I meet the morning sun, and with it trace its oft repeated journey to the evening shades? Why did I continue to live – why not throw off the weary weight of time, and with my own hand, let out the fluttering prisoner from my agonized breast? – It was not cowardice that withheld me; for the true fortitude was to endure; and death had a soothing sound accompanying it, that would easily entice me to enter its demesne. But this I would not do. I had, from the moment I had reasoned on the subject, instituted myself the subject to fate, and the servant of necessity, the visible laws of the invisible God – I believed that my obedience was the result of sound reasoning, pure feeling, and an exalted sense of the true excellence and nobility of my nature. Could I have seen in this empty earth, in the seasons and their change, the hand of a blind power only, most willingly would I have placed my head on the sod, and closed my eyes on its loveliness forever. But fate had administered life to me, when the plague had already seized on its prey – she had dragged me by the hair from out the strangling waves – By such miracles she had bought me for her own; I admitted her authority, and bowed to her decrees. If, after mature consideration, such was my resolve, it was doubly necessary that I should not lose the end of life, the improvement of my faculties, and poison its flow by repinings without end. Yet how cease to repine, since there was no hand near to extract the barbed spear that had entered my heart of hearts? I stretched out my hand, and it touched none whose sensations were responsive to mine. I was girded, walled in, vaulted over, by seven-fold barriers of loneliness. Occupation alone, if I could deliver myself up to it, would be capable of affording an opiate to my sleepless sense of woe. Having determined to make Rome my abode, at least for some months, I made arrangements for my accommodation – I selected my home. The Colonna Palace was well adapted for my purpose. Its grandeur – its treasure of paintings, its magnificent halls were objects soothing and even exhilarating.

I found the granaries of Rome well stored with grain, and particularly with Indian corn; this product requiring less art in its preparation for food, I selected as my principal support. I now found the hardships and lawlessness of my youth turn to account. A man cannot throw off the habits of sixteen years. Since that age, it is true, I had lived luxuriously, or at least surrounded by all the conveniences civilization afforded. But before that time, I had been "as uncouth a savage, as the wolf-bred founder of old Rome" – and now, in Rome itself, robber and shepherd propensities, similar to those of its founder, were of advantage to its sole inhabitant. I spent the morning riding and shooting in the Campagna – I passed long hours in the various galleries – I gazed at each statue, and lost myself in a reverie before many a fair Madonna or beauteous nymph. I haunted the Vatican, and stood surrounded by marble forms of divine beauty. Each stone deity was possessed by sacred gladness, and the eternal fruition of love. They looked on me with unsympathizing complacency, and often in wild accents I reproached them for their supreme indifference – for they were human shapes, the human form divine was manifest in each fairest limb and lineament. The perfect moulding brought with it the idea of colour and motion; often, half in bitter mockery, half in self-delusion, I clasped their icy proportions, and, coming between Cupid and his Psyche's lips, pressed the unconceiving marble.

I endeavoured to read. I visited the libraries of Rome. I selected a volume, and, choosing some sequestered, shady nook, on the banks of the Tiber, or opposite the fair temple in the Borghese Gardens, or under the old pyramid of Cestius, I endeavoured to conceal me from myself, and immerse myself in the subject traced on the pages before me. As if in the same soil you plant nightshade and a myrtle tree, they will each appropriate the mould, moisture, and air administered, for the fostering their several properties – so did my grief find sustenance, and power of existence, and growth, in what else had been divine manna, to feed radiant meditation. Ah! while I streak this paper with the tale of what my so named occupations were – while I shape the skeleton of my days – my hand trembles – my heart pants, and my brain refuses to lend expression, or phrase, or idea, by which to image forth the veil of unutterable woe that clothed these bare realities. O, worn and beating heart, may I dissect thy fibres, and tell how in each unmitigable misery, sadness dire, repinings, and despair, existed? May I record my many ravings – the wild curses I hurled at torturing nature – and how I have passed days shut out from light and food – from all except the burning hell alive in my own bosom?

I was presented, meantime, with one other occupation, the one best fitted to discipline my melancholy thoughts, which strayed backwards, over many a ruin, and through many a flowery glade, even to the mountain recess, from which in early youth I had first emerged.

During one of my rambles through the habitations of Rome, I found writing materials on a table in an author's study. Parts of a manuscript lay scattered about. It contained a learned disquisition on the Italian language; one page an unfinished dedication to posterity, for whose profit the writer had sifted and selected the niceties of this harmonious language – to whose everlasting benefit he bequeathed his labours.

I also will write a book, I cried – for whom to read? – to whom dedicated? And then with silly flourish (what so capricious and childish as despair?) I wrote:

> *Dedication to the illustrious dead. Shadows, arise, and*
> *read your fall! Behold the history of the last man.*

Yet, will not this world be re-peopled, and the children of a saved pair of lovers, in some to me unknown and unattainable seclusion, wandering to these prodigious relics of the ante-pestilential race, seek to learn how beings so wondrous in their achievements, with imaginations infinite, and powers godlike, had departed from their home to an unknown country?

I will write and leave in this most ancient city, this 'world's sole monument,' a record of these things. I will leave a monument of the existence of Verney, the Last Man. At first I thought only to speak of plague, of death, and last, of desertion; but I lingered fondly on my early years, and recorded with sacred zeal the virtues of my companions. They have been with me during the fulfilment of my task. I have brought it to an end – I lift my eyes from my paper – again they are lost to me. Again I feel that I am alone.

A year has passed since I have been thus occupied. The seasons have made their wonted round, and decked this eternal city in a changeful robe of surpassing beauty. A year has passed; and I no longer guess at my state or my prospects – loneliness is my familiar, sorrow my inseparable companion. I have endeavoured to brave the storm – I have endeavoured to school myself to fortitude – I have sought to imbue myself with the lessons of wisdom. It will not do. My hair has become nearly grey – my voice, unused now to utter sound, comes strangely on my ears. My person, with its human powers and features, seem to me a monstrous excrescence of nature. How express in human language a woe human being until this hour never knew! How give intelligible expression to a pang none but I could ever understand! – No one has entered Rome. None will ever come. I smile bitterly at the delusion I have so long nourished, and still more, when I reflect that I have exchanged it for another as delusive, as false, but to which I now cling with the same fond trust.

Winter has come again; and the gardens of Rome have lost their leaves – the sharp air comes over the Campagna, and has driven its brute inhabitants to take up their abode in the many dwellings of the deserted city – frost has suspended the gushing fountains – and Trevi has stilled her eternal music. I had made a rough calculation, aided by the stars, by which I endeavoured to ascertain the first day of the new year. In the old out-worn age, the Sovereign Pontiff was used to go in solemn pomp, and mark the renewal of the year by driving a nail in the gate of the temple of Janus. On that day I ascended St. Peter's, and carved on its topmost stone the aera 2100, last year of the world!

My only companion was a dog, a shaggy fellow, half water and half shepherd's dog, whom I found tending sheep in the Campagna. His master was dead, but nevertheless he continued fulfilling his duties in expectation of his return. If a sheep strayed from the rest, he forced it to return to the flock, and sedulously kept off every intruder. Riding in the Campagna I had come upon his sheep-walk, and for some time observed his repetition of lessons learned from man, now useless, though unforgotten. His delight was excessive when he saw me. He sprung up to my knees; he capered round and round, wagging his tail, with the short, quick bark of pleasure: he left his fold to follow me, and from that day has never neglected to watch by and attend on me, shewing boisterous gratitude whenever I caressed or talked to him. His pattering steps and mine alone were heard, when we entered the magnificent extent of nave and aisle of St. Peter's. We ascended the myriad steps together, when on the summit I achieved my design, and in rough figures noted the date of the last year. I then turned to gaze on the country, and to take leave of Rome. I had long determined to quit it, and I now formed the plan I would adopt for my future career, after I had left this magnificent abode.

A solitary being is by instinct a wanderer, and that I would become. A hope of amelioration always attends on change of place, which would even lighten the burthen of my life. I had been a fool to remain in Rome all this time: Rome noted for Malaria, the famous caterer for death. But it was still possible, that, could I visit the whole extent of earth, I should find in some part of the wide extent a survivor. Methought the sea-side was the most probable retreat to be chosen by such a one. If left alone in an inland district, still they could not continue in the spot where their last hopes had been extinguished; they would journey on, like me, in search of a partner for their solitude, till the watery barrier stopped their further progress.

To that water – cause of my woes, perhaps now to be their cure, I would betake myself. Farewell, Italy! – farewell, thou ornament of the world, matchless Rome, the retreat of the solitary one during long months! – to civilized life – to the settled home and succession of monotonous days, farewell! Peril will now be mine; and I hail her as a friend – death will perpetually cross my path, and I will meet him as a benefactor; hardship, inclement weather, and dangerous tempests will be my sworn mates. Ye spirits of storm, receive me! ye powers of destruction, open wide your arms, and clasp me forever! if a kinder power have not decreed another end, so that after long endurance I may reap my reward, and again feel my heart beat near the heart of another like to me.

Tiber, the road which is spread by nature's own hand, threading her continent, was at my feet, and many a boat was tethered to the banks. I would with a few books, provisions, and my dog, embark in one of these and float down the current of the stream into the sea; and then, keeping near land, I would coast the beauteous shores and sunny promontories of the blue Mediterranean, pass Naples, along Calabria, and would dare the twin perils of Scylla and Charybdis; then, with fearless aim, (for what had I to lose?) skim ocean's surface towards Malta and the further Cyclades. I would avoid Constantinople, the sight of whose well-known towers and inlets belonged to another state of existence from my present one; I would coast Asia Minor, and Syria, and, passing the seven-mouthed Nile, steer northward again, till losing sight of forgotten Carthage and deserted Lybia, I should reach the pillars of Hercules. And then – no matter where – the oozy caves, and soundless depths of ocean may be my dwelling, before I accomplish this long-drawn voyage, or the arrow of disease find my heart as I float singly on the weltering Mediterranean; or, in some place I touch at, I may find what I seek – a companion; or if this may not be – to endless time, decrepid and grey headed – youth already in the grave with those I love – the lone wanderer will still unfurl his sail, and clasp the tiller – and, still obeying the breezes of heaven, forever round another and another promontory, anchoring in another and another bay, still ploughing seedless ocean, leaving behind the verdant land of native Europe, adown the tawny shore of Africa, having weathered the fierce seas of the Cape, I may moor my worn skiff in a creek, shaded by spicy groves of the odorous islands of the far Indian ocean.

These are wild dreams. Yet since, now a week ago, they came on me, as I stood on the height of St. Peter's, they have ruled my imagination. I have chosen my boat, and laid in my scant stores. I have selected a few books; the principal are Homer and Shakespeare – But the libraries of the world are thrown open to me – and in any port I can renew my stock. I form no expectation of alteration for the better; but the monotonous present is intolerable to me. Neither hope nor joy are my pilots – restless despair and fierce desire of change lead me on. I long to grapple with danger, to be excited by fear, to have some task, however slight or voluntary, for each day's fulfilment. I shall witness all the variety of appearance, that the elements can assume – I shall read fair augury in the rainbow – menace in the cloud – some lesson or record dear to my heart in everything. Thus around the shores of deserted earth, while the sun is high, and the moon waxes or wanes, angels, the spirits of the dead, and the ever-open eye of the Supreme, will behold the tiny bark, freighted with Verney – the LAST MAN.

If you enjoyed this, you might also like...
Frankenstein, see page 11
'The Mourner', see page 264

Roger Dodsworth
The Reanimated Englishman

IT MAY BE REMEMBERED, that on the fourth of July last, a paragraph appeared in the papers importing that Dr. Hotham, of Northumberland, returning from Italy, over Mount St. Gothard, a score or two of years ago, had dug out from under an avalanche, in the neighbourhood of the mountain, a human being whose animation had been suspended by the action of the frost. Upon the application of the usual remedies, the patient was resuscitated, and discovered himself to be Mr. Dodsworth, the son of the antiquary Dodsworth, who perished in the reign of Charles I. He was thirty-seven years of age at the time of his inhumation, which had taken place as he was returning from Italy, in 1654. It was added that as soon as he was sufficiently recovered he would return to England, under the protection of his preserver.

We have since heard no more of him, and various plans for public benefit, which have started in philanthropic minds on reading the statement, have already returned to their pristine nothingness. The antiquarian society had eaten their way to several votes for medals, and had already begun, in idea, to consider what prices it could afford to offer for Mr. Dodsworth's old clothes, and to conjecture what treasures in the way of pamphlet, old song, or autographic letter his pockets might contain. Poems from all quarters, of all kinds, elegiac, congratulatory, burlesque and allegoric, were half written. Mr. Godwin had suspended for the sake of such authentic information the history of the Commonwealth he had just begun. It is hard not only that the world should be baulked of these destined gifts from the talents of the country, but also that it should be promised and then deprived of a new subject of romantic wonder and scientific interest. A novel idea is worth much in the commonplace routine of life, but a new fact, an astonishment, a miracle, a palpable wandering from the course of things into apparent impossibilities, is a circumstance to which the imagination must cling with delight, and we say again that it is hard, very hard, that Mr. Dodsworth refuses to appear, and that the believers in his resuscitation are forced to undergo the sarcasms and triumphant arguments of those sceptics who always keep on the safe side of the hedge.

Now we do not believe that any contradiction or impossibility is attached to the adventures of this youthful antique. Animation (I believe physiologists agree) can as easily be suspended for a hundred or two years, as for as many seconds. A body hermetically sealed up by the frost, is of necessity preserved in its pristine entireness. That which is totally secluded from the action of external agency, can neither have any thing added to nor taken away from it: no decay can take place, for something can never become nothing; under the influence of that state of being which we call death, change but not annihilation removes from our sight the corporeal atoma; the earth receives sustenance from them, the air is fed by them, each clement takes its own, thus seizing forcible repayment of what it had lent. But the elements that hovered round Mr. Dodsworth's icy shroud had no power to overcome the obstacle it presented. No zephyr could gather a hair from his head, nor could the influence of dewy night or genial morn penetrate his more than adamantine panoply.

The story of the Seven Sleepers rests on a miraculous interposition – they slept. Mr. Dodsworth did not sleep; his breast never heaved, his pulses were stopped; death had his finger pressed on his lips which no breath might pass. He has removed it now, the grim shadow is vanquished, and stands wondering. His victim has cast from him the frosty spell, and arises as perfect a man as he had lain down a hundred and fifty years before. We have eagerly desired to be furnished with some particulars of his first conversations, and the mode in which he has learnt to adapt himself to his new scene of life. But since facts are denied to us, let us be permitted to indulge in conjecture. What his first words were may be guessed from the expressions used by people exposed to shorter accidents of the like nature.

But as his powers return, the plot thickens. His dress had already excited Doctor Hotham's astonishment – the peaked beard – the love locks – the frill, which, until it was thawed, stood stiff under the mingled influence of starch and frost; his dress fashioned like that of one of Vandyke's portraits, or (a more familiar similitude) Mr. Sapio's costume in Winter's Opera of the Oracle, his pointed shoes – all spoke of other times. The curiosity of his preserver was keenly awake, that of Mr. Dodsworth was about to be roused. But to be enabled to conjecture with any degree of likelihood the tenor of his first inquiries, we must endeavour to make out what part he played in his former life. He lived at the most interesting period of English History – he was lost to the world when Oliver Cromwell had arrived at the summit of his ambition, and in the eyes of all Europe the commonwealth of England appeared so established as to endure forever. Charles I was dead; Charles II was an outcast, a beggar, bankrupt even in hope. Mr. Dodsworth's father, the antiquary, received a salary from the republican general, Lord Fairfax, who was himself a great lover of antiquities, and died the very year that his son went to his long, but not unending sleep, a curious coincidence this, for it would seem that our frost-preserved friend was returning to England on his father's death, to claim probably his inheritance – how short lived are human views! Where now is Mr. Dodsworth's patrimony? Where his co-heirs, executors, and fellow legatees? His protracted absence has, we should suppose, given the present possessors to his estate – the world's chronology is an hundred and seventy years older since he seceded from the busy scene, hands after hands have tilled his acres, and then become clods beneath them; we may be permitted to doubt whether one single particle of their surface is individually the same as those which were to have been his – the youthful soil would of itself reject the antique clay of its claimant.

Mr. Dodsworth, if we may judge from the circumstance of his being abroad, was no zealous commonwealth's man, yet his having chosen Italy as the country in which to make his tour and his projected return to England on his father's death, renders it probable that he was no violent loyalist. One of those men he seems to be (or to have been) who did not follow Cato's advice as recorded in the Pharsalia; a party, if to be of no party admits of such a term, which Dante recommends us utterly to despise, and which not unseldom falls between the two stools, a seat on either of which is so carefully avoided. Still Mr. Dodsworth could hardly fail to feel anxious for the latest news from his native country at so critical a period; his absence might have put his own property in jeopardy; we may imagine therefore that after his limbs had felt the cheerful return of circulation, and after he had refreshed himself with such of earth's products as from all analogy he never could have hoped to live to eat, after he had been told from what peril he had been rescued, and said a prayer thereon which even appeared enormously long to Dr. Hotham – we may imagine, we say, that his first question would be: "if any news had arrived lately from England?"

"I had letters yesterday," Dr. Hotham may well be supposed to reply.

"Indeed," cries Mr. Dodsworth, "and pray, sir, has any change for better or worse occurred in that poor distracted country?"

Dr. Hotham suspects a Radical, and coldly replies: "Why, sir, it would be difficult to say in what its distraction consists. People talk of starving manufacturers, bankruptcies, and the fall of the Joint Stock Companies – excrescences these, excrescences which will attach themselves to a state of full health. England, in fact, was never in a more prosperous condition."

Mr. Dodsworth now more than suspects the Republican, and, with what we have supposed to be his accustomed caution, sinks for awhile his loyalty, and in a moderate tone asks "Do our governors look with careless eyes upon the symptoms of over-health?"

"Our governors," answers his preserver, "if you mean our ministry, are only too alive to temporary embarrassment." (We beg Doctor Hotham's pardon if we wrong him in making him a high Tory; such a quality appertains to our pure anticipated cognition of a Doctor, and such is the only cognizance that we have of this gentleman.) "It were to be wished that they showed themselves more firm – the king, God bless him!"

"Sir!" exclaims Mr. Dodsworth.

Doctor Hotham continues, not aware of the excessive astonishment exhibited by his patient: "The king, God bless him, spares immense sums from his privy purse for the relief of his subjects, and his example has been imitated by all the aristocracy and wealth of England."

"The King!" ejaculates Mr. Dodsworth.

"Yes, sir," emphatically rejoins his preserver; "the king, and I am happy to say that the prejudices that so unhappily and unwarrantably possessed the English people with regard to his Majesty are now, with a few" (with added severity) "and I may say contemptible exceptions, exchanged for dutiful love and such reverence as his talents, virtues, and paternal care deserve."

"Dear sir, you delight me," replies Mr. Dodsworth, while his loyalty late a tiny bud suddenly expands into full flower; "yet I hardly understand; the change is so sudden; and the man – Charles Stuart, King Charles, I may now call him, his murder is I trust execrated as it deserves?"

Dr. Hotham put his hand on the pulse of his patient – he feared an access of delirium from such a wandering from the subject. The pulse was calm, and Mr. Dodsworth continued: "That unfortunate martyr looking down from heaven is, I trust, appeased by the reverence paid to his name and the prayers dedicated to his memory. No sentiment, I think I may venture to assert, is so general in England as the compassion and love in which the memory of that hapless monarch is held?"

"And his son, who now reigns? –"

"Surely, sir, you forget; no son; that of course is impossible. No descendant of his fills the English throne, now worthily occupied by the house of Hanover. The despicable race of the Stuarts, long outcast and wandering, is now extinct, and the last days of the last Pretender to the crown of that family justified in the eyes of the world the sentence which ejected it from the kingdom forever."

Such must have been Mr. Dodsworth's first lesson in politics. Soon, to the wonder of the preserver and preserved, the real state of the case must have been revealed; for a time, the strange and tremendous circumstance of his long trance may have threatened the wits of Mr. Dodsworth with a total overthrow. He had, as he crossed Mount Saint Gothard, mourned a father – now every human being he had ever seen is 'lapped in lead,' is dust, each voice he had ever heard is mute. The very sound of the English tongue is changed, as his experience in conversation with Dr. Hotham assures him. Empires, religions, races of men, have probably sprung up or faded; his own patrimony (the thought is idle, yet, without it, how can he live?)

is sunk into the thirsty gulf that gapes ever greedy to swallow the past; his learning, his acquirements, are probably obsolete; with a bitter smile he thinks to himself, I must take to my father's profession, and turn antiquary. The familiar objects, thoughts, and habits of my boyhood, are now antiquities. He wonders where the hundred and sixty folio volumes of MS. that his father had compiled, and which, as a lad, he had regarded with religious reverence, now are – where – ah, where? His favourite play-mate, the friend of his later years, his destined and lovely bride, tears long frozen are uncongealed, and flow down his young old cheeks.

But we do not wish to be pathetic; surely since the days of the patriarchs, no fair lady had her death mourned by her lover so many years after it had taken place. Necessity, tyrant of the world, in some degree reconciles Mr. Dodsworth to his fate. At first he is persuaded that the later generation of man is much deteriorated from his contemporaries; they are neither so tall, so handsome, nor so intelligent. Then by degrees he begins to doubt his first impression. The ideas that had taken possession of his brain before his accident, and which had been frozen up for so many years, begin to thaw and dissolve away, making room for others. He dresses himself in the modern style, and does not object much to anything except the neck-cloth and hard-boarded hat. He admires the texture of his shoes and stockings, and looks with admiration on a small Genevese watch, which he often consults, as if he were not yet assured that time had made progress in its accustomed manner, and as if he should find on its dial plate ocular demonstration that he had exchanged his thirty-seventh year for his two hundredth and upwards, and had left a.d. 1654 far behind to find himself suddenly a beholder of the ways of men in this enlightened nineteenth century. His curiosity is insatiable; when he reads, his eyes cannot purvey fast enough to his mind, and every now and then he lights upon some inexplicable passage, some discovery and knowledge familiar to us, but undreamed of in his days, that throws him into wonder and interminable reverie. Indeed, he may be supposed to pass much of his time in that state, now and then interrupting himself with a royalist song against old Noll and the Roundheads, breaking off suddenly, and looking round fearfully to see who were his auditors, and on beholding the modern appearance of his friend the Doctor, sighing to think that it is no longer of import to any, whether he sing a cavalier catch or a puritanic psalm.

It were an endless task to develop all the philosophic ideas to which Mr. Dodsworth's resuscitation naturally gives birth. We should like much to converse with this gentleman, and still more to observe the progress of his mind, and the change of his ideas in his very novel situation. If he be a sprightly youth, fond of the shows of the world, careless of the higher human pursuits, he may proceed summarily to cast into the shade all trace of his former life, and endeavour to merge himself at once into the stream of humanity now flowing. It would be curious enough to observe the mistakes he would make, and the medley of manners which would thus be produced. He may think to enter into active life, become whig or tory as his inclinations lead, and get a seat in the, even to him, once called chapel of St. Stephens. He may content himself with turning contemplative philosopher, and find sufficient food for his mind in tracing the march of the human intellect, the changes which have been wrought in the dispositions, desires, and powers of mankind. Will he be an advocate for perfectibility or deterioration? He must admire our manufactures, the progress of science, the diffusion of knowledge, and the fresh spirit of enterprise characteristic of our countrymen. Will he find any individuals to be compared to the glorious spirits of his day? Moderate in his views as we have supposed him to be, he will probably fall at once into the temporising tone of mind now so much in vogue. He will be pleased to find a calm in politics; he will greatly admire the ministry who have succeeded in conciliating almost all parties – to find peace where he left feud. The same character which he bore a couple of hundred years ago, will influence him now; he will still be the moderate, peaceful, unenthusiastic Mr. Dodsworth that he was in 1647.

For notwithstanding education and circumstances may suffice to direct and form the rough material of the mind, it cannot create, nor give intellect, noble aspiration, and energetic constancy where dullness, wavering of purpose, and grovelling desires, are stamped by nature. Entertaining this belief we have (to forget Mr. Dodsworth for awhile) often made conjectures how such and such heroes of antiquity would act, if they were reborn in these times: and then awakened fancy has gone on to imagine that some of them are reborn; that according to the theory explained by Virgil in his sixth Aeneid, every thousand years the dead return to life, and their souls endued with the same sensibilities and capacities as before, are turned naked of knowledge into this world, again to dress their skeleton powers in such habiliments as situation, education, and experience will furnish. Pythagoras, we are told, remembered many transmigrations of this sort, as having occurred to himself, though for a philosopher he made very little use of his anterior memories. It would prove an instructive school for kings and statesmen, and in fact for all human beings, called on as they are, to play their part on the stage of the world, could they remember what they had been.

Thus we might obtain a glimpse of heaven and of hell, as, the secret of our former identity confined to our own bosoms, we winced or exulted in the blame or praise bestowed on our former selves. While the love of glory and posthumous reputation is as natural to man as his attachment to life itself, he must be, under such a state of things, tremblingly alive to the historic records of his honour or shame. The mild spirit of Fox would have been soothed by the recollection that he had played a worthy part as Marcus Antoninus – the former experiences of Alcibiades or even of the emasculated Steeny of James I. might have caused Sheridan to have refused to tread over again the same path of dazzling but fleeting brilliancy. The soul of our modern Corinna would have been purified and exalted by a consciousness that once it had given life to the form of Sappho. If at the present moment the witch, memory, were in a freak, to cause all the present generation to recollect that some ten centuries back they had been somebody else, would not several of our free thinking martyrs wonder to find that they had suffered as Christians under Domitian, while the judge as he passed sentence would suddenly become aware, that formerly he had condemned the saints of the early church to the torture, for not renouncing the religion he now upheld – nothing but benevolent actions and real goodness would come pure out of the ordeal.

While it would be whimsical to perceive how some great men in parish affairs would strut under the consciousness that their hands had once held a sceptre, an honest artizan or pilfering domestic would find that he was little altered by being transformed into an idle noble or director of a joint stock company; in every way we may suppose that the humble would be exalted, and the noble and the proud would feel their stars and honours dwindle into baubles and child's play when they called to mind the lowly stations they had once occupied. If philosophical novels were in fashion, we conceive an excellent one might be written on the development of the same mind in various stations, in different periods of the world's history.

But to return to Mr. Dodsworth, and indeed with a few more words to bid him farewell. We entreat him no longer to bury himself in obscurity; or, if he modestly decline publicity, we beg him to make himself known personally to us. We have a thousand inquiries to make, doubts to clear up, facts to ascertain. If any fear that old habits and strangeness of appearance will make him ridiculous to those accustomed to associate with modern exquisites, we beg to assure him that we are not given to ridicule mere outward shows, and that worth and intrinsic excellence will always claim our respect.

This we say, if Mr. Dodsworth is alive. Perhaps he is again no more. Perhaps he opened his eyes only to shut them again more obstinately; perhaps his ancient clay could not thrive on the harvests of these latter days. After a little wonder; a little shuddering to find himself the dead alive – finding no affinity between himself and the present state of things – he has bidden once more an eternal farewell to the sun. Followed to his grave by his preserver and the wondering villagers, he may sleep the true death-sleep in the same valley where he so long reposed. Doctor Hotham may have erected a simple tablet over his twice-buried remains, inscribed:

To the Memory of R. Dodsworth,
An Englishman,
Born April 1, 1617; Died July 16, 1618; Aged 187

An inscription which, if it were preserved during any terrible convulsion that caused the world to begin its life again, would occasion many learned disquisitions and ingenious theories concerning a race which authentic records showed to have secured the privilege of attaining so vast an age.

If you enjoyed this, you might also like...
'The Mortal Immortal', see page 254
'The Invisible Girl', see page 287

Biographies

Mary Shelley

Mary Shelley (1797–1851) was born in London, England. Encouraged to write at a young age by her father, William Godwin, who was a journalist, philosopher and novelist, Shelley became an essayist, biographer, short story writer and novelist. Her mother was the radical feminist writer Mary Wollstonecraft, who died shortly after giving birth to Shelley, undoubtedly having a deep impact on her. Shelley is most famous for her horror novel *Frankenstein: or The Modern Prometheus*, a seminal work in the history of SF and horror fiction. She was also married to the poet Percy Bysshe Shelley, eloping with him when she was only 17 years old. Suffering the loss of three children and widowed early on in her life, it is no surprise that even her most horror-filled works are also deeply humane, and concerned with love and loss.

Fiona Sampson

Foreword: Mary Shelley Horror Stories

Fiona Sampson is the author of a critically acclaimed biography, *In Search of Mary Shelley*. She has been published in more than thirty languages and received an MBE for services to literature, as well as a number of national and international awards for her poetry. She is a Fellow of the Royal Society of Literature.

Further contributions by:

Johann August Apel

Johann August Apel (1771–1816) was a German writer and jurist who inspired others with his popular creative works. Born in Leipzig, Germany, Apel collaborated with Fiedrich Laun to create *Gespensterbuch*, an anthology in which they collected and rewrote German ghost stories and folktales. Some of Apel's tales were translated into French by Jean-Baptiste Benoît Eyriès in the French ghost collection *Fantasmagoriana*, which was ready by the group at the Villa Diodati. One of these stories, 'The Family Portraits', may be alluded to by Shelley in her introduction to the 1831 edition of *Frankenstein*.

Lord Byron

Known formally as Lord Byron, George Gordon Byron (1788–1824) was an English nobleman, poet, peer, politician, and leading figure in the Romantic movement. Regarded as one of the greatest British poets, his lengthy narrative poems 'Don Juan' and 'Childe Harold's Pilgrimage', as well as his short lyric poem 'She Walks in Beauty,' are still widely read and influential today. While travelling extensively around Europe, he frequently visited his friend and fellow poet, Percy Bysshe Shelley, whenever he was in Italy. His contribution to the ghost writing competition at the Villa Diodati was a barely-started story featuring a vampire.

Samuel Taylor Coleridge

Samuel Taylor Coleridge (1772–1834) was an English poet, literary critic, philosopher, and theologian who was a founder of the Romantic Movement in England and a member of the Lake Poets. Among his most popular works are the two poems 'The Rime of the Ancient

Mariner' and 'Kubla Khan'. Regarded by many as the greatest living writer on the demonic, Coleridge suffered from crippling anxiety and depression throughout his adult life. However, his creative work coined many familiar words and phrases of today, including 'suspension of disbelief.' As a close friend of Mary Shelley, 'The Rime of the Ancient Mariner' is directly mentioned twice in *Frankenstein*, and some of the poem's descriptions are echoed throughout the novel. His poem 'Christabel' was said to have been read during the infamous gathering at the Villa Diodati.

Friedrich Laun

Friedrich August Schulze (1770–1849) was a German novelist who wrote under the pen name Friedrich Laun. Born in Dresden, Germany, his first novel, *Der Mann, auf Freiersfüssen*, was well received. He collaborated with Johann August Apel on a book of ghost stories called *Gespensterbuch*, some of which were included in the French collection *Fantasmagoria*, which inspired both Shelley's *Frankenstein* and Polidori's *The Vampyre*.

Karl August Musäus

A popular German author, Johann Karl August Musäus (1735–87) was one of the first collectors of German folk stories. His collection of German fairy tales retold as satires, *Volksmärchen der Deutschen* ('Folktales of the Germans'), was celebrated by the public. His story 'Stumme Liebe' (literally translated as 'Dumb Love') was included in the French anthology *Fantasmagoriana*, and was titled 'The Specrre-Barber' by Utterson in her English translation.

John Polidori

One of the first to write about the popular subject of vampires in English, John Polidori (1795–1821) was born in London, England and is deeply associated with both the Romantic and Gothic movements in literature. He was greatly influenced by the work of Lord Byron, for whom he worked as a personal physician. Polidori was with Byron, Percy Bysshe Shelley, and Mary Shelley on the night the group of writers gathered to write and share ghost stories, and where he got the idea for *The Vampyre*, a work that would go on to inspire Bram Stoker's own iconic story Dracula.

Sarah Elizabeth Utterson

Most famously known for her anthology *Tales of the Dead*, Sarah Elizabeth Utterson (1781–1851) was also a contributor to the influential collection. Translated from a French collection of ghost stories titled *Fantasmagoriana*, Utterson selected the stories she felt to be most chilling, as well as adding her own story, 'The Storm.' Some parts of *Frankenstein* are very similar to those found in *Fantasmagoriana* and suggest a direct influence on Mary Shelley's writing.

Sources

The Birth of Frankenstein

Frankenstein
Originally Published by Lackington, Hughes, Harding, Mavor & Jones,
London, 1818. The text in this anthology is from
the 1831 revised edition.

A Fragment by Lord Byron
Originally Published in *Mazeppa*, John Murray, London, 1819

The Vampyre by John Polidori
Originally Published in *New Monthly Magazine*, 1819
(falsely attributed to Lord Byron).

Christabel by Samuel Taylor Coleridge
Originally Published in *Christabel; Kubla Khan*: A Vision;
The Pains of Sleep, John Murray Press, 1816

Tales of the Dead (Various authors, translated by Sarah Elizabeth Utterson)
Originally Published by White, Cochrane and Co, London, 1813

The Family Portraits by Johann August Apel
Originally Published in *Cicaden*, 1810. This English
translation is from *Tales of the Dead*, 1813.

The Fated Hour by Friedrich Laun
Originally Published in *Das Gespensterbuch* vol. 2, by Johann August Apel
and Friedrich Laun, c. 1811/12. This English translation is
from *Tales of the Dead*, 1813.

The Death's Head by Friedrich Laun
Originally Published in *Das Gespensterbuch* vol. 2, by Johann August Apel
and Friedrich Laun, c. 1811/12. This English translation
is from *Tales of the Dead*, 1813.

The Spectre-Barber by Johann Karl August Musäus
Originally Published in *Volksmärchen der Deutschen*, 1786. This
English translation is from *Tales of the Dead*, 1813.

Eerie Supernatural

On Ghosts
Originally Published in *London Magazine*, March 1824

Transformation
Originally Published in *The Keepsake* for 1831, 1830

The Mortal Immortal
Originally Published in *The Keepsake* for 1834, 1833

Gothic Tales

The Mourner
Originally Published in *The Keepsake* for 1830, 1829

A Dirge
Originally Published in *The Keepsake* for 1831, 1830

The Dream
Originally Published in 1831

The Invisible Girl
Originally Published in *The Keepsake* for 1833, Nov/Dec

The Pilgrims
Originally Published in 1838

The Heir of Mondolfo
Originally Published in *Appleton's Journal*, January 1877 (

The Horrors of Isolati

The Last Man (Volume II, chapter IV–Th
Originally Published by Henry Colburn, London, 1826, and

Roger Dodsworth
Originally Published in *Yesterday and To-day*, Cyr

FLAME TREE PUBLISHING
Epic, Dark, Thrilling & Gothic

New & Classic Writing

Flame Tree's Gothic Fantasy books offer a carefully curated series of new titles, each with combinations of original and classic writing:

Chilling Horror • Chilling Ghost • Science Fiction
Murder Mayhem • Crime & Mystery • Swords & Steam
Dystopia Utopia • Supernatural Horror • Lost Worlds
Time Travel • Heroic Fantasy • Pirates & Ghosts • Agents & Spies
Endless Apocalypse • Alien Invasion • Robots & AI • Lost Souls
Haunted House • Cosy Crime • American Gothic • Urban Crime
Epic Fantasy • Detective Mysteries • Detective Thrillers • A Dying Planet
Footsteps in the Dark • Bodies in the Library • Strange Lands
Lovecraft Mythos • Terrifying Ghosts • Black Sci-Fi • Chilling Crime

Also, new companion titles offer rich collections of classic fiction, myths and tales in the gothic fantasy tradition:

Charles Dickens Supernatural • George Orwell Visions of Dystopia
H.G. Wells • Lovecraft • Sherlock Holmes • Edgar Allan Poe • Bram Stoker Horror
Mary Shelley Horror • M.R. James Ghost Stories • The Divine Comedy
Hans Christian Andersen Fairy Tales • Brothers Grimm Fairy Tales
Alice's Adventures in Wonderland • King Arthur & The Knights of the Round Table
The Wonderful Wizard of Oz • The Age of Queen Victoria • Ramayana
One Thousand and One Arabian Nights • Persian Myths & Tales • African Myths & Tales
Celtic Myths & Tales • Greek Myths & Tales • Norse Myths & Tales • Chinese Myths & Tales
Japanese Myths & Tales • Native American Myths & Tales • Irish Fairy Tales
Heroes & Heroines Myths & Tales • Gods & Monsters Myths & Tales
Witches, Wizards, Seers & Healers Myths & Tales

Available from all good bookstores, worldwide, and online at
flametreepublishing.com

See our new fiction imprint
FLAME TREE PRESS | FICTION WITHOUT FRONTIERS
New and original writing in Horror, Crime, SF and Fantasy

And join our monthly newsletter with offers and more stories:
FLAME TREE FICTION NEWSLETTER
flametreepress.com

GOTHIC FANTASY

For our books, calendars, blog
and latest special offers please see:
flametreepublishing.com

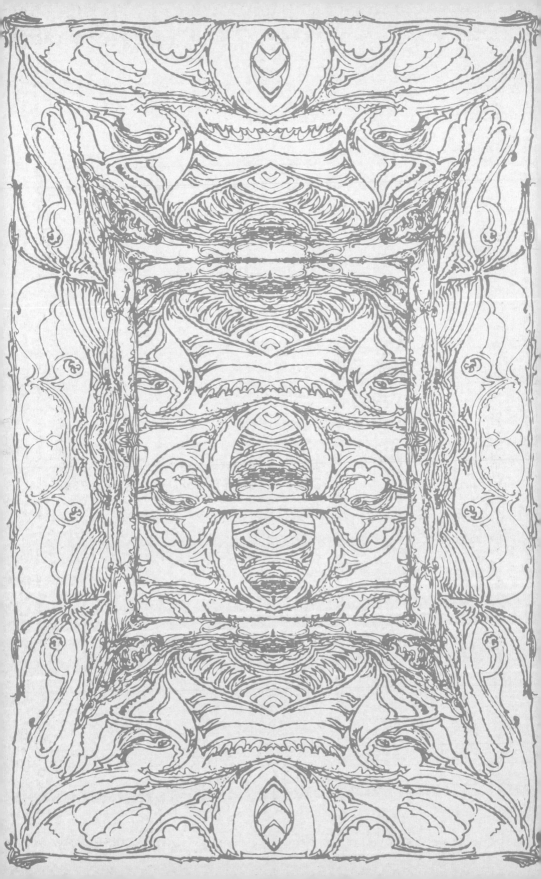